THE CHRISTMAS WIFE

L. STEELE

THE BILLIONAIRE'S CHRISTMAS BRIDE

L. STEELE

1

"I am just a girl standing in front of a salad, asking it to be a doughnut."
-From Amelie's diary

Amelie

"Aww, they clearly like each other," the radio show host exclaims.

"They hated each other, couldn't stop trading insults—" the male announcer interrupts her.

"Only it was all build-up, OMG..." the first announcer cuts in. "The feels, the emotions.. They wanted to stab each other, but turned out, it was a different kind of stabby that they had for each other."

"Is that what they're calling it these days, Ivy?" The man snickers, "Good thing this is a late-night chat show."

"I can always count on you to keep me in line, Wolfgang," Ivy quips.

"Call me Wolf," the male announcer drawls.

"Right, well," Ivy clears her throat. " For everyone listening on this blustery night in the lead up to Christmas..." She pauses to take a breath, "The question I'd like to pose is, is it rude to interrupt someone mid-sentence by uh! distracting them? Email us, text us, call in and tell us after the break. This is Smile FM..."

I snort aloud, then switch off the radio tuned into the local radio station. The talk show hosts seem to be living in la-la land, or is it the Christmas spirit that's affecting them? More likely, it's the chemistry, between them, which not even the airwaves could disguise. Must be nice, to have that kind of sizzling attraction, huh?

The kind that makes you want to slap the man, punch him in the nuts, maybe; right before you jump on him, wrap your legs around him, and—

That...had been the kind of no-holds-barred romance I'd hoped for when I had met my ex. He'd done everything right, hadn't attempted to kiss me until our third date. In short, he'd been a gentleman...of the double-crossing kind.

Bastard had dumped me after three weeks.

He'd seen my name connected to all the notoriety that had followed my friend Victoria and her now-husband Saint's wedding... His mother hadn't been happy about it, and as he'd rushed to inform me, he couldn't go against his mama's word... So, I'd been dropped.

On the other hand, my fledgling pastry business had taken off.

Everyone wanted the desserts that had been featured prominently in the publicity accompanying the marriage... I had more orders than I could fulfill. I had worked around the clock in the lead up to Christmas. I'd fulfilled my last booking this morning and handed over the reins of the company to my assistant—yep, I made enough money in the last month to finally hire the intern who had worked with me since I'd started the business.

I can trust her to keep the business going, while I take some time off over Christmas and New Year's. A few days of no work, no waking up in the early hours to bake... Not unless I want to do it for pleasure; and damn, if I am not going to bake the hell out of some new recipes that I want to try out.

I am going to use the next week to unwind, to reconnect with the girl I'd once been—carefree, happy, with hope in her eyes and a spring in her step—before business worries had taken over my life. I hunch my shoulders. At twenty-five, I am not that old... Except for the fact that I've never met a man with whom I've managed to hold a relationship down for more than uh—three months.

Well, to hell with that.

I am going to make the most of what I have. To start, I'll rejuvenate over the festive season, then bounce back into London all bright-eyed and ready to take the New Year by storm. Yeah! I turn off the highway, down the narrow road that leads me deeper into the countryside. My sturdy Volkswagen eats up the miles, until I get to a turn-off. I glance at the GPS… Yup, this is the road. Well, what the hell? I turn down the unpaved path. I'd wanted solitude. Guess I am getting it, one way or the other. I drive another mile, turn another corner…and drive up to massive gates.

I roll down my window, pull up the security app I'd installed on my phone, then reach out and wave my phone over the keypad in the wall.

The gates swing open. Awesome, and on the first try!

I continue down the driveway to a single-story bungalow, with a porch running around it, then park the car. I switch off the engine and listen. There… I can hear it… The silence. I can't stop the smile that lifts my cheeks. Most people don't like to be alone… Me? I thrive on it. As long as I can bake during the day, then curl up with my book-boyfriend in the evenings, with a glass of my favorite bubbly—champagne only, I'm strict like that—and surrounded by bubbles in a bathtub… Oh yeah, that would be a bonus. I push the door open, then walk around to retrieve my two suitcases. Don't judge. I like to have the comforts of home with me when I travel. So, what if I am only a few hours away from home? I need my favorite set of PJs, my bath bombs, my wine…and this. I walk around to the front of the car, open the door to the passenger side, and retrieve my most prized possession, the tools of my trade—my pastry chef bag, without which, I never go anywhere.

Sliding the strap of my baking toolkit across my chest, my handbag over one shoulder, I begin to drag one of the suitcases…which promptly gets stuck in the muddy ground. I haul at it, there's a cracking sound, then the valise dips to one side. Shit, did I break it already? To be fair, it had been a surprisingly cheap buy from the charity shop. I should have known better than to buy it, even though it had been marked down by about 70%. I wipe the sweat from my forehead. I straighten, take a step back, and instantly lose my footing. I hit the ground on my butt.

Bloody hell, this is all going tits over arse. A whistling sound emerges from the trees.

Goosebumps flare on my skin. Shit, is there someone…or something out there? It's all well and good to want to be alone… But in the coun-tryside? I hadn't considered how…spooky it could all be. A low humming sounds in the distance. Is that a bird? A plane? Crap, there is no Superman around here to rescue me. I am on my own. *Better get your arse in gear, woman.* I jump up to my feet. Best get indoors, turn on some lights, then I can come back for my luggage.

A breeze blows and I hunch my shoulders. *Damn it, how can I be warm and cold at the same time?*

I take another step, trip over some rocks. *Hell, I need lights, and fast. Okay, hold on, I've got this.*

I grab my phone from my handbag, switch on the flashlight. A beam of light illuminates the way. I walk toward the patio, take the steps up to the front door, shove my hand into my handbag and scrounge around for the key. Where is it? Where the hell is it? There! I pull out the key and insert it into the lock. The door unlocks. Woo!

I push against the door, walk into a spacious living room. Switching off the light, I drop the phone into my handbag. Then I take stock.

There's an unlit fireplace in the center, a settee beyond that, facing the door, complete with a rug in front of it. To my right are big French windows, to my left is a bookcase, with floor to ceiling shelves, filled with books. Yay, that's another point for this place. Next to it is a small table with liquor bottles.

I walk to it, place my handbag on the bar counter, next to a wall clock that's turned face down. I turn it face up; realize it's stopped. Huh? Guess it ran out of batteries. I replace it on the counter, turn around. That's when I hear the low sound of whistling again. I gulp. Guess I hadn't imagined it then?

It's a whistling, and of the human variety. This is not from an animal or a bird. The hell? I glance around the comfortable space. Everything looks undisturbed, though how would I know? I hear the sound of something sloshing from the direction of the back door... What the—? Did the intruder decide to take a bath?

Is there a hot tub of some kind on the patio at the back?

I take a step forward, then stop. I need a weapon. I am not going out there alone. Shit, why had I thought it was a good idea to come here on my own, remind me again? I hadn't been running away, I hadn't... Yeah, right. I'd needed to take myself away from all of those shiny, happy, faces celebrating bloody Christmas, which honestly, I do love... I do... Just not this year. This year, I need to catch a break... And hell, if I haven't caught something, alright. A burglar, more like it. I unclasp my satchel of baking tools, reach in and remove a—spatula? The humming sound increases in pitch, then a full-blown song reaches me. The hell? I squeeze my fingers around my weapon... Don't laugh;

a spatula can do plenty of damage when it connects with someone's balls.

I lower my chef's satchel to the ground, then unbutton my coat and shrug it off. I stalk toward the door at the far end.

The sounds of water splashing reaches me through the patio door. Huh? Maybe there is a hot tub out there...

Then a male voice breaks into a rendition of *Nothing Else Matters* by Metallica. What the—? There's someone out there, all right, and the singing's not bad, actually. My thief, has a thing for classic rock, and can carry a tune. I hum the lyrics in sync with him... *The hell?* I pause, draw in another breath. *Now or never. Do it, Amelie. Go for it. Whoever it is, he has no right to be here. Shit, should I have called the cops?*

The singing stops abruptly. *What the—? Did he hear me approaching?*

I half angle my body, turn to leave; the door to the patio flies open.

I pivot around, raise my weapon, and find I am confronted with a wall of muscle. Naked chest, water running in rivulets down those sculpted abs that narrow into a concave belly which points to his thick, long—

"My face is up here," he drawls.

Heat flushes my cheeks; I jerk my gaze up. Grey eyes clash with mine—stormy clouds that boil in a sky which hints at oncoming snow. Sleet. Hail. An uncompromising will to get his way, no matter what. A shiver runs down my spine and moisture pools between my legs.

The skin between his eyebrows crinkles and his nostrils flare. *No way.* He can't smell my arousal, can he?

That mean upper lip thins further. His pouty lower lip juts out above a chin that wears days' old growth of beard. Thick dark hair covers his jaw. *How would it feel to have him draw those rough whiskers across my inner thighs? Right before he dips his head, darts out his tongue, and licks my innermost secret place.* Goosebumps dot my skin. *Shit, what's wrong with me? Why did my mind go there? You know why... Because this handsome piece of 100% male goodness is, quite simply, the most wickedly delicious piece of dessert I've ever laid my eyes on.* My throat dries. Also, I happen to know him.

"You?" my voice comes out breathless.

"What are you doing here?" he snaps at the same time.

"What are *you* doing here?" I retort. "And in a hot tub, on the patio of this house, no less?"

"I am not in the habit of answering queries posited by women who look like they've been dragged in from a storm."

"What?" My jaw drops. I am gaping, and it's not only because the words complete the image of the man I've loathed from the moment I first saw him at the wedding of one of my best friends. "Dr. f'ing Weston," I snarl.

"That's Doc Kincaid to you." He yawns.

Of course, his surname would have to have the word kink in it in some form. "And are you?" I scowl.

"What?"

"A real doctor?"

He raises his hand, stabs the air with a cigar I only now realize he holds between his fingers. "Do you want to find out?" He looks me up and down, waggles his eyebrows. "I could give you a thorough examination." His gaze settles on my breasts, slides down to my core. "Make sure everything is in working order." He snickers.

Heat fizzes low in my belly. Hell, with that kind of hotness, this man could clearly get my cake batter to rise in seconds... *Wait, did I just think that?*

I make a gagging noise in my throat, "Does that line actually work?"

"You'd be surprised." His lips curl.

Oh, that smirk. My stomach seems to bottom out... Or maybe that's because I haven't eaten since breakfast.

He draws on his cigar, cheeks hollowing for an instant, before he puffs out smoke. Cherries, cloves...cinnamon. Yum. My mouth waters, "How would it be to bake a cigar dessert?"

"What?" He frowns.

Shit, did I just say that aloud?

"Nothing," I mumble, "and you haven't answered my question."

His voice lowers to a hush, "I'll answer yours if you answer mine." Another shiver ladders up my spine. How *did he manage to make that seem like an innuendo?*

"Is everything a trade to you?"

"You should try it." He smiles, a full-blown grin that highlights the laughter lines that stretch from the corners of his eyes. I mean, could this guy be any more perfect? I allow my gaze to take in the breadth of his shoulders, that gorgeous neck, the swell of those hard biceps, the smattering of hair on those forearms—*No, do not look lower; don't do it*—to the splint that he sports around middle finger of his right hand.

"What happened to you?" I scowl.

"This?" He raises his middle finger to show me the bird by default, "I fractured my middle finger in a car accident."

"How convenient," I scoff. "You can announce your jerk-face nature without speaking a word."

He chuckles, "You always this nice to injured men?"

"You always go around flashing women?"

"You enjoyed the view." He raises that goddam cigar again to his mouth, wraps those beautiful lips around the smoke stick.

And I'd love to get my mouth around his fat, juicy cigar too.

No, no. Enough with the terrible metaphors. But, hello, can you blame me? I am only a woman standing in front of a man—a naked, gorgeous-as-hell, stud muffin of a male who pulls the cigar from his mouth, and blows out a cloud of fragrant smoke from between pursed lips.

Moisture melts my core. My toes curl.

Jesus, there should be a law against him using his mouth like that. Of course, I could find other uses for that mouth of his too... *No, no no. Why are you insisting on going back down that route?*

"Nothing I haven't seen," I toss my head.

"Unlikely." He lowers his right hand—the one with the splint and the default flip-me-off-bird to his crotch.

What the—? Don't look there, bitch— Don't bloody watch him grasp himself and squeeze.

I gulp, the sound audible in the small space. And damn him, but I can't take my gaze off of that gorgeous part of his anatomy.

He moves his arm to his side, "I rest my case."

Hell, but a certain part of him is far from being in resting position. Gulp. *Did I just word play on his dick play?* Clearly, his proximity is rubbing off if all I can think of are these poor jokes.

"By the way," his tone is conversational, "you planning on defending yourself with that?" He jerks his chin.

I tighten my grasp around the spatula and raise it. "This has been known to strike fear in the heart of burglars and those who've tried to break in on me before," I snap.

"You were burgled?" His jaw hardens.

"None of your business."

"Answer the bloody question." He takes a step forward. I scoot back. My leg brushes something warm and furry, which moves.

"Whoa!" I struggle to find my balance then, for the second time in ten minutes, the world tilts, and I find myself falling... Falling.

The spatula slips from my grasp. I squeeze my eyes shut, waiting for my butt to connect with the hard ground, only I'm yanked upright. Heat envelops me and my breasts flatten against something unyielding. I don't need to open my eyelids to know it's his chest, the one with the cut planes, the eight-pack abs. I slap my palm against that wall of muscles which coil, move, and writhe under my fingertips. I gulp and my legs threaten to give way under me, but his hold around my shoulders tightens. I spot the smoldering smoke stick of his on the ground.

"Your…cigar," I stutter.

"You noticed," he quips.

I grimace, then nod my head toward the floor. "I meant that one."

"Forget that." His breath feathers over my hair and liquid lust shoots through my veins. The scent of pine and cloves mixes with that edgy darkness that is purely Weston. Speaking of—something hard stabs into my waist—the aforementioned "cigar." A groan boils up my throat. Not fair—this crazy attraction to someone I've barely met a couple of times. Why does he have to smell so delicious? Bet if I licked his chest, he'd taste more decadent than the chocolate mud pie cake recipe I've been wanting to bake. I'll lick the frosting off his cupcake any time. *Nooooo.* Not again. Enough with comparing his unmentionables with my favorite stuffed goodies. OMG, how would it feel to have him stuff his goodies in my cannoli? *Wait, did that even make sense?*

His voice dips, "You haven't answered my question."

"What?" I blink.

"Someone broke in on you?" He enunciates his words at a slow pace as if I am slow of mind… Which, I admit, at the moment, I seem to be. His larger-than-life charisma has turned my brain cells to mush. "Tell me," he coaxes. Is he using the same tone he'd use with the puppy to make him obey? Well, hell, if it isn't working on me as well.

"Y…yes." My stomach clenches. "But I fought off the thief…." I force out the words.

His muscles coil; tension radiates off of his body. "You confronted the man?" he snaps.

"Yeah," I hunch my shoulders, "It happened a week ago… No biggie." I swallow as my heart begins to race. It hadn't been pleasant, that almost encounter. I had been alone in the kitchen of my bakery at 4 am… Hell, it had been horrible, actually. The guy had thrown a fright into me and I had thrown this spatula at him. "I chased him off. Yay.

See? I'm fine, still alive." And bloody shaken, but I'm not going to tell him that.

His grip tightens, "Did he hurt you?" His jaw tics.

I stare up into his tight features. You'd think Mr. Jerkass here is all concerned about my safety.

"Did he?" his voice snaps through the noise in my head.

"N…no," I shake my head.

"No, what?"

No, I will not give in to this insane chemistry between us. I didn't come all this way to run slap-bang into a man who is, surely, far worse than the one who recently broke my heart. "No, he didn't do any harm. He ran off before I could use the spatula on him." I tip up my chin. "Though I can't promise the same to you."

He chuckles, "I love a good fight, don't you?"

Jackass.

A whine sounds behind me.

I shoot a sideways glance to spot a puppy plant his behind on the ground…exactly the kind of position I'd have been in, if 'Mr. Overbearing Brute' here hadn't grabbed me first. Oh, so that's what I'd brushed against earlier and almost fallen over.

"Max," Weston talks to the dog, "you hungry, buddy?"

The puppy whines again.

"I'll be right there, little fella." His voice takes on a cajoling tone, and damn him, but my ovaries seem to spasm. *The hell is he doing to me?* Before this, I've never thought about kids… Hell, I've barely managed to embark on a halfway decent career, and I've never thought of myself as someone who'd want a family. But Weston, with his smoldering glare, his hard face, his harder—um—body, and that coaxing manner with which he talks to Max… I can see him with a child tucked under one arm, and me under his other… Heck, I can see me under him, period. My mouth waters. My panties dampen further. *Get your mind out of the gutter, you slut.*

"Isn't he Sinclair and Summer's pet?" I frown. My friend Summer had married Sinclair Sterling, one of the seven billionaire co-owners of 7A investments. The media had labelled them the Seven and, Dr Douche here is one of them.

"Summer and Sinclair are away on an extended honeymoon," Weston grunts.

"Aww. So you decided to puppy-sit?" A warm glowing ball lights up inside of me.

He glowers, "Don't gush any sweet icky stuff now — uh, what's your name again?"

Poof — that warm feeling I mentioned? Forget about it. The hell is wrong with this man? "You know my name all right, you ass." I stab my finger in his chest, "So why are you pretending otherwise?"

"Me?" He blinks, "Do I?" He tilts his head, pretending to think, "Is it Lily?"

A slow burn starts up my spine.

"No... No." He cracks his neck, "It will come to me, it will... It's Malia, right?"

Anger laces the edges of my vision. I draw in a breath, then another. *Stay calm, he can only get so much more obnoxious, right?*

"Wait, let me try, one more time..." He pats his temple with the palm of his injured hand. "It's...something French, isn't it? Like... Valerie, Malory, maybe? No, I have it." He snaps his fingers, "It's Celine. I got that right, didn't I?" He chuckles.

I clench my fists, then raise my hand toward his face.

He catches my wrist. "Tsk, tsk," he clicks his tongue. "What a temper you have, little one."

"Don't 'little one' me... You... You wanker."

"Finally," his eyes gleam, "here kitty, kitty, show me your claws."

"I'll do better than that," I hiss, "I'll show you how it is to see the sun at night time."

I bring up my knee, aim for his groin.

2

Weston

What the hell? I know what she intends to do, a second before she moves. I step aside and her knee grazes the outside of my thigh. I release her shoulders only to grab the nape of her neck. "Stop that," I scold her, "or you'll hurt yourself."

"The only one who's gonna be hurt here, buster, is you." She swings out with her fist.

As if this tiny thing could do anything to injure me? Oh wait, I'd done that on my own, when someone had run my car off the road a few days ago.

I angle my body, but I'm not fast enough. Her fist grazes my side; a burn of heat trickles down my spine. She didn't hurt me. Instead, my body is responding to her in a manner that leaves no doubt of the fact that certain parts of me would very much prefer to be in more intimate contact with her.

"Stop," I growl.

She makes a noise deep in her throat, "You uncouth, obnoxious, horrible, man." She swings with her other hand, the shot too wide to do any harm. But it causes her to lose her balance, and she topples over, crashing into me.

Softness, curves, the weight of her breasts, even through the layers she is wearing, is a thing of beauty against my chest. I release her nape, only to wrap my hand about her shoulders and haul her close.

"Let me go," she chokes.

"No." I say all casual-like, hoping she'll take the bait. Whaddya know? The little thing hits out with her fist again, this time catching me on the wrist of my injured hand. Pain flashes up my arm and sparks of brightness dot my vision. Shit, she hadn't been kidding about her threat.

I grit out the words through clenched teeth, "Stop it before I do something I regret."

"Ha," she scoffs. "I am not scared of bullies like you."

I draw in a deep breath. "Don't threaten me."

"Don't underestimate me." She raises her fists.

Ooh, I am so scared. I stifle the chuckle that crowds my throat. Max whines again, I glare at him from over her shoulder. He wags his tail, mouth open, tongue lolling. Of course, I could get my staff in the hospital to behave with that look, but it has little effect on the little rascal. I frown at Max. He pants back, then turns and runs off in the direction of the kitchen. That buys me, maybe, a minute before he'll be back. Best make full use of it. I train my glare on the handful of woman who glowers up at me. She barely comes to chest level… And that hair? Is she actually sporting streaks of purple? And there is so much of it… Her hair, I mean. It flows like spun gold around her shoulders, catching the light that filters in from the patio behind her.

"Hey," she snaps her fingers, "what are you staring at?"

"Your hair." I reach out with my bandaged hand to touch the shining strands. I bring it up to my nose and sniff it.

She stiffens. "What are you doing?"

"What's that smell?"

"What?" She tips up her perky little nose, sniffs the air.

"That." I grasp a handful of her hair, bury my nose in it, and draw in a deep breath. "Vanilla, sugar, apples…butter." The mix of scents go straight to my head. "Why the hell do you smell of dessert?" I frown.

"Ah, maybe because I'm a pastry chef?" She scowls. "What the hell do you think you're doing anyway?"

"Speaking of." I let the hair slide out from between my fingers-…*Why do I miss its softness already?* "I'm not letting you stay here. You do realize that?"

"What?" She blinks. "What did you say?"

"I was here first."

"Excuse me?"

The light in her blue eyes intensifies and little creases appear on her forehead. Oh, this is going to be good. "Here, at the cabin." I smirk. "I am staying here until New Year's."

"*I'm* staying here until New Year's," she says through clenched teeth.

"Nope," I emphasize the word with a popping sound, and practically see the smoke pour out of her tiny ears. Beautiful, shell shaped ears, that I'd like to curl my tongue around, suck on those pretty earlobes before easing it into that hole. My groin hardens. Hell… there are other parts of her which I'd like to push into as well… Lick her up, suck on the melting flesh between her thighs, nip on her lower lips, before I thrust my tongue inside her soaking channel and bring her to the edge.

"I am too." She props her hands on her hips, her curvy, deliciously rounded hips, which is one of the first things I'd noticed about her too. She's so different from the women I normally encounter… Hell, she's not my type at all. Soft, sassy, perfectly shaped for my hands. My fingers tingle. *I will not touch her, will not.* I tilt my head. "From where I am, you are…on your way out."

"What?" She blinks. "I am standing right here."

"That can be easily changed."

I take a step forward, and honestly, I'd totally expected her to retreat. To shuffle back, maybe even turn and run out of the house… I should have known better, after how she'd threatened me with that spatula earlier, for she doesn't move. She stands her ground, so my feet bump hers. I lean into her; she tips her chin up.

I lower my face toward hers, closer, closer. "You can't win this, Buttercup."

"Buttercup?" She scrunches up her forehead. "Why the hell are you calling me after the Princess Bride?"

"It was after a Powerpuff Girl, actually," I chuckle.

"Powerpuff?" She grimaces.

I nod, "You're small, annoying, and too headstrong for your own good."

"How do you even know about those cartoons?"

"I may have watched them with my little niece."

"Awww." Her gaze widens; her eyes go all sparkly as fuck. *Ah, hell!*

My neck heats. "Don't make it out to be anything more than what it is," I grunt.

"Which is?"

"That I babysit on occasion," I mutter.

"You also babysit?" Her features take on the expression I have seen on the faces of the women who have fallen for some of my friends. Specifically, Jace, Sinner and that mofo Saint. All of them ended up married, and shackled, and buying townhouses, and planning extended honeymoons, and baby showers... *Argh!* A shiver of trepidation runs up my spine. *Shit, no, no, no, I am not going there.* These kinds of entanglements, and all the bloody relationship fuck-ups that come with it? Not for me. So not my tumbler of whiskey—you didn't think I'd say cup of tea, now, would you?

Besides, what the hell am I doing, sharing that piece of information about myself? She'd gotten past my guard, obviously. It's the only reason I'd let that slip. More to the point, why the hell are we still talking, here in the house I co-own?

The hair on my nape prickles.

"How the hell did you get here?" I frown.

"I drove, of course." She sniffs, "What about you?"

"I was driven here by my chauffeur," I grumble.

"That's why there's no car parked outside." She nods. "How do you plan to get around for the time you are here?"

"I don't."

"Guess you can't drive with that finger, huh?"

"I can bloody drive, if I want." I scowl, "I choose not to; besides, every time I want to head out, I'll message my driver."

She opens and shuts her mouth, "Let me get this right. Every time you want to go out, you'll message your chauffeur who'll come in from where? London?"

I glare at her, "Don't be daft. He's staying in the nearest town. It takes him, maybe, 45 minutes to get here."

"To take you back into the village, and return."

"Umm, yeah." I raise my shoulders, "That's why he's called a driver. He drives me around," I snicker.

"I could do that."

"What?"

"Drive you around."

"Why should I want that?"

"Since we are going to be sharing this house—"

"Nope, we're not. I own this place with the rest of the Seven."

"Saint offered it to me for the duration of the holidays." She scowls, "Pretty sure he loaned the space to me first."

"I am one of the Seven. I take precedence," I declare.

She gapes at me and… Damn… Every time she opens her mouth, I want to shut her up with my tongue, or other parts of me that would very happily nestle into that warmth. Why the fuck does she turn me on, when she's the type of complication I can do without?

"Out," I snarl.

"What the hell is wrong with you?" She sniffs, "Why can't we work this out like adults?"

"Like adults, huh?" I smirk. "Trust me, the kind of things I want to do with you right now would definitely be classified as 'adult.'"

She reddens. "Can't you speak a sentence without coming across all lecherous?"

"I haven't even started," I smirk, "and PS, it's you who can't take a hint. Do you want me to spell it out for you?"

"You're a jerk, you know that?"

I yawn. "Get out of the house or I'll throw you out bodily."

"You wouldn't."

"Try me."

She raises her fist and I move. I grab her around the waist, haul her over my shoulder.

She yelps, "Let go of me, you oaf."

"You sure about that, Buttercup?"

"Stop calling me that."

"Not gonna oblige you. Next?"

She makes a huffing sound and the warmth of her breath sears my back. She wriggles her body, tries to scramble off. I place my arm across the back of her thighs.

She brings her fists down on my back, rains blows. How cute. As if that's gonna make a difference. From where I am, it's more like a massage. Don't tell her that, though. I stalk forward, and Max chooses that time to dart out.

Blame it on the fact I was distracted by her wriggling arse positioned so close to my face. Or the fact that I was having too much fun. Or that a part of me was bloody angry with that turd Saint, for having put me in this situation.

Clearly, he'd double booked me and this little puff pastry of a woman… whatever the fuck he'd been thinking, he is mistaken. I have no interest in her; none whatsoever... especially when she's proving to be such a distraction that I barely manage to sidestep Max.

My bare feet slip from under me. The world tilts.

The woman across my shoulder shrieks. I tighten my grip on her, as the ceiling recedes further. I manage to find my balance, lurch back a couple of steps, through the door. I must have spilled something earlier. My legs slip out from under me a second time.

I arc back through the air...and still holding her, hit the hot tub and tumble into the water.

"Woman," I growl, "you're going to rupture my eardrums."

"I'll do more than that, you...you horrible man. You...you Fruit Salad."

I blink, "Did you compare me to a dessert?"

"I'm not done you...you Carrot Cake." She rears up so quickly, I loosen my grip. She pulls away, and over...smashes straight into my injured finger. Bright lights flash behind my eyes... Jesus F... She hadn't been kidding when she'd said she'd show me the sun in the night time... Hold on. What the hell am I thinking? My brain seems to freeze, then pain ratchets up my spine, through my skull... A growl rips from me, "The hell are you doing?"

"You started this." She lurches up to her feet, stands over me, with my torso in between her legs.

Her wet blouse stretches across her chest, highlighting every gorgeous curve of that magnificent bust.

My cock twitches; my mouth dries. I can only stare at the nipples that salute me, the water that drips down the fabric outlining her flat stomach, the indentation of her bellybutton, down to the valley between her thighs, where her jeans have ridden up to kiss the cleft between her lower lips. What I wouldn't give to be able to place my lips there... I swallow. My dick lengthens.

Shit, bet if she looks down, she'll see exactly which parts of me are excited by this little rough play... Which it isn't... Foreplay, that is. It is an accident, that's all.

"Why the hell couldn't you watch where you were going?" She glowers.

"Me...?" I scowl. "I am as steady on my feet as I am with my fingers... Speaking of," I raise my throbbing hand, and glare at the offending digit, "You probably fractured it again, thanks to your clumsiness."

"It was already broken, you idiot."

"Heard about multiple fractures?" I growl. "And don't call me an idiot."

"Oh, pfft. I'll call you anything I want, you reprobate."

"Mind your tongue, Buttercup."

"Oh, stuff it." She swings one leg over. "And for the record, I'm the one who's staying, not you."

"Oh, no, you're not." I grab for her leg. She squeaks, evades me and jumps up and out of the tub. There's a howl… "Max." I turn to find her squatting down. She rubs the puppy's head. "Oooh, little fellow, did I hurt you? I didn't, did I?" Max whines again.

"Oh, I'm sorry, I'm sorry," she coos, makes kissing noises at the mutt, who whines. No wonder he's making the most of having her attention.

She plops onto her butt, cross-legged, pulls the puppy into her lap. The dog, lifts his head, licks her face, her mouth. Hmm. He whines again, she strokes him, and lifts him to her chest. The little bugger cuddles against her breasts. *What the —?* I glower. *How does he get to do that and not me? Wait, hold on? Am I seriously jealous of a canine?* I shake my head.

"Enough of this nonsense," my voice rings around the space.

The puppy shivers, snuggles his body tighter against her chest.

"Put him aside," I scowl.

She peers up at me, "Shh."

"What?"

"You're scaring the baby," she admonishes me.

"Baby?" I growl.

Max moans… No, really. That dog has definitely been taking acting classes, for he bleats out another piteous little whine that has her cuddling him, rocking him side to side. "There, there, little fella. Did Daddy's heavy voice make your heart go pitter-patter?" She lifts him up, and the dog plays along. He licks her lips…right on the mouth.

"Hey!" I growl.

I push up to standing in the hot tub, water flowing from me like I turned on the shower. The water splashes out onto the dog and the woman, who bows her head to shield him. "Stop that, you're making him wet." She huffs.

"Oh, yeah?" I scowl down at her bent head, the way she croons to the pet, hair flowing in a blonde waterfall about her shoulders, her dripping clothes that outline the curve of her shoulder…and that… The sight of the perfectly turned swell of a what should not be a seductive part of anyone's body… But on Buttercup… It's a bloody turn on. The blood rushes to my groin and my head spins. Must be the fact that I hit my hand. That's why I am feeling lightheaded. No other reason. It's why I step up and out of the sunken hot tub, to loom over her.

More water pours over her, drenching both woman and dog. He yelps, cowers into her further.

"What are you doing?" She tries to protect him with her body. "You're an insensitive dog parent."

"I'm not a parent, this is not a child, and you…are completely insane."

She peers up at me, from under her spiky eyelashes. Her gaze runs up my thighs, my crotch, getting an eyeful of my rather spectacular appendage—yeah, I'm well hung, deal with it—up my impressive eight pack—it is eight, I know, I've seen myself in the mirror—to my mouth. She gulps; her cheeks turn a fiery red. "You… you…" She swallows, "Why are you flashing the little mite?" She props her palm over Max's eyes. "You could have stunted his growth, with that exhibition," she huffs. "I mean just because you are … Uh, massive… You don't need to go around shocking little doggies with your penchant for running around naked."

And that's when something inside of me snaps. My vision tunnels and the blood thunders at my temples—anger…and frustration…and jealousy… Yeah, bloody hell, I am living with rage that she's giving all of her attention to that…that… Usurper… I am going to teach her a lesson about ignoring me—one she won't forget in a hurry. I bend over, grab the nape of her neck with my unhurt hand, and haul her up to her feet, with just enough force for her gaze to widen.

"What did you say?'

"Th…that you're scaring him."

"After that."

"That you're running around naked."

"Before that."

She blinks rapidly, the dog wriggles in her hold. "M…max," she stutters.

I click my tongue, "Not the word that you are looking for."

"M…massive?" she wheezes.

"You noticed, huh?"

"Kinda....h...hard not to..." she swallows, tips up her chin, "considering..."

"Considering." I drop my head, thrust my face into hers. "Considering?" I lower my voice. "Complete the sentence, Buttercup."

She gulps, "Considering you've been waving that in my face since —"

I lower my head, close my mouth over hers.

3

———————

Amelie

Finally, finally, finally he's kissing me… He's… Oh! Warmth, heat, the taste of him pours through my veins, fills my senses. Hot, lush, complex and fiery, notes of ginger, cardamom, bitter orange and sumptuous creamy champagne. Oh, my…he tastes like my very personal favorite dessert… If I had to bottle this taste, make it into a dessert, it would be called… Kinky Banana Split? No, Kinky Pavlova, maybe… Kinky Almond and Chocolate cookies with pomegranate seeds and a splash of brandy… Oh, my, my. I'd totally dive into that concoction headfirst; after I'd scooped up the cream from the dark surface, licked it up, and my fingers... Then rub the mixture all over that delicious torso, down to his impressive bon-bons and — Wait, did I just call his balls bon-bons? Does that make his very impressive dick a…rhubarb and chocolate cock pop?

A giggle boils up my throat. Above me, he freezes, leans back until his mouth is poised just above mine. "What's so funny?" he rasps.

"N…nothing." I'd lick his shaft like a penis cake — I choke.

"Are you laughing at me?"

"N…no," I gasp.

"What are you thinking?" He frowns down at me. An expression of genuine frustration on his face. My stomach flutters. Jesus, if that isn't the hottest thing I have seen… This alpha male, all flummoxed… Not to mention, still wet and naked, and holding my nape like I am a kitten.

Max whines in my arms. I glance down. "I think he's cold; I need to get him inside the house."

"He can wait."

"You'd allow a baby to freeze?" I scowl.

"He's a dog…"

"A pet."

"A mutt."

"A child." I frown.

"Fine."

"Fine what?"

"We'll take him to the other room, but first, 'fess up."

"What?" I blink rapidly.

"What made you chuckle earlier?"

"Nothing."

"It's something." He glares at me and a shiver runs down my spine.

"Maybe," I finally say.

"So, you were lying to me?"

"No," I stutter.

"I hate liars."

"Trust me, you don't want to hear this," I mumble.

"Trust me," he lowers his thick brows, "I do."

"You won't like it."

"Let me decide that."

Like hell, I will. I snicker to myself. *If you think I am going to tell you my X-rated thoughts, you have another think coming.*

"Fine," I grumble just as Max whines again, "Can I set him down first?"

He peers into my face, then nods.

"Let go of me," I demand.

"No."

I stare, "You serious?"

"Always."

Tell me about it. This grumpy-pants a-hole needs to be shown how to laugh a little more, in life.

"Fine," I mutter, then bend down. He bends with me, not taking his palm off of the nape of my neck. *Don't look at his crotch, don't.* I stare at his turgid cock that springs from a nest of dark hair as I lower myself, place the puppy on the ground. Max shoots off toward the kitchen.

He hauls me up. "Tell me now," he threatens, his voice hard.

"But… I need to go with him and—"

He glowers at me, and that familiar melting sensation crawls in my gut.

"P…penis-shaped cake," I blurt out.

"What?" His glare intensifies.

"It…it's a thing…" I assure him. "There's this town in Portugal where penis-shaped cakes are gifted to women as fertility charms." Not that I need any such help with this man. Just being this close to him is enough for me to get pregnant… *Eeeugh! What am I thinking?* I pull back, but his large hand on my nape tightens.

"And you know this, how?"

"It…it's ah, based on research I came across."

"Research, huh?" He bends his knees, so his face is more at eye-level with mine. "Why do I have this sneaking suspicion that is not true?"

"It is…" I lie, casting about in my head for something…anything to tell him. "Uh, I am writing a book."

"A book?"

"A cook…cookbook…for desserts that are aphrodisiacs…"

"And this… Uh, cock cake—" He frowns.

"A chocolate cock pop," I correct him.

"Chocolate cock pop…is an aphrodisiac, hmm?" His lips twitch.

"Don't mock it till you try it," I mumble.

"Hmm." He tilts his head, "You have a point there." He applies pressure on my neck—not enough to hurt, just sufficient for my knees to tremble.

"Wh…what are you doing?"

"What do you think?"

He peels back his lips and his teeth flash against his tanned skin. He eases me down and I drop to my knees.

Hell, he handles my body like I am made of room-temperature butter… Would he lick me like I am a toffee-topped crumpet too? That large rough tongue of his would lave my flesh, dig into the nooks and crannies of my sensitive core, strum on my pussy lips, nibble on my cream and sugar… *No.. No… No.* "No," I shake my head.

"Don't mock it till you try it," he growls.

I'm eye level with that part of him that has taunted me since I walked into this house. No, even before that... Since I first saw him, across a crowded room at my friend Summer's wedding, when he'd prowled toward the bar, leaned against the barrier, stance wide, reached for a tumbler for whiskey and I'd seen the tendons of his throat stretch as he'd swallowed it down.

"Open," he growls.

I tip up my chin. "You're no dessert," I huff.

"No, I'm better."

He releases me, only to grab his dick and—what the—? I stare. I can't help it. I mean, I shouldn't. I should look away, spring to my feet and follow Max into the kitchen, then keep going until I reach my car and get out of here. I could do it, too. He's not holding me back. I should get away from him; away from this insane start to what was supposed to have been a quiet time, of reflection, and experimentation, of coming up with ideas for new desserts that I could use to differentiate my business from the rest... Which is exactly what I have been doing since I walked in here.

Hold on a second... Is being with him sparking off brainwaves of the culinary, and face it, the lustful kind? And hell, if the two don't go together. Desserts and orgasms, puddings and sex, cupcakes and clit stimulators...

Whoa. Hold on. Back up there. That idea I'd pulled out of my arse earlier, of writing a book about desserts that are stimulants... Well, it's not a bad idea at all... In fact, it could inspire an entire range of recipes...that I could use for my occasions-themed menu—valentines, anniversaries, birthdays, weddings... Hmm. I chew on my lower lip, watch as he squeezes himself from root to swollen head of his fat dick. My mouth waters and my belly clenches... Hell, what am I thinking? I'm not seriously considering...

He squeezes his cock, so it stands straight out, staring at me in the face, with precum oozing from the slit, and hell... I'm only a woman kneeling in front of a beautiful dick, wanting to lick it.

"Do it," he insists. "Open up, Buttercup."

"Did you just rhyme your words with my so-called pet name—?"

He shoves his dick in between my lips... He's not tender or gentle, by any means... He takes it like it's his right, to have his shaft in my mouth, filling me, bumping up over my tongue. "Swallow," he growls.

What the hell? How dare he think he can command me and I'll obey? How can he take me for granted...? Because I haven't left yet, have followed his directions so far, allowed him to maneuver me into this place of supplication, where I peer up at him, watch the sweat bead his forehead,

"Now." He glares at me, and heat flares in my belly; a shudder runs down my spine and my thighs spasm, I resist the urge to squeeze them together. I will not show him that his dominance is turning me on, that his complete arrogance in assuming I'll do what he asks is…a bloody turnoff.

"Amelie." His voice lowers to a hush.

So, he remembers my name, huh?

His jaw tics, "Take me down your throat."

And his tone brooks no argument. I tip my chin up, open my mouth further—wide enough for his cock to slip in, ease down my gullet. I cough and tears squeeze out of my eyes. I swallow and a groan rips out of him. His massive thighs on either side of my face ripple as if unseen currents grip him, the same ones that writhe down my legs, to my toes. My fingers tingle and my scalp itches. I raise my hands, grip the outside of each of his legs.

"Fuck," he rasps, "you have no idea what you're doing to me."

Oh, trust me, I do. Question is, why the hell am I still here?

"You want to leave?" His voice cuts through my mind. *Huh?* Has he been reading my thoughts? "Do you, Buttercup?" he asks.

Is it the fact that his nickname is growing on me—because it belonged to my childhood heroine…the one I'd wanted to be when I grew up? Or because the strain in his tone is evident? Because he doesn't touch me anywhere… Well, except for the most intimate part of him in one of my orifices. I swipe my tongue up the bottom of his cock over the throbbing vein, to the rim of his swollen head. I circle it, and another growl rips out of him. The heat pours off of him, and down on me. The strength of his dominance seems to grow, coiling around me, pinning me in place. Moisture pools between my thighs. Hell, what is he doing to me? What am I going to do to ensure that he doesn't take me for granted again? That he doesn't simply put me down as another of the women who've succumbed to his charms… Okay, so I am as guilty, but hell, if I am going to walk away from this encounter without making an impression. Yeah, did I mention I am bloody competitive by nature? It's been my downfall… The reason I'm here, about to spend Christmas on my own… I should take him up on the out he's extended to me and scram… I should.

"You scared you won't be able to finish what you started?"

He snickers. The bastard snickers—with his dick in my mouth. *Sheesh, men!* They can be so naïve. So full of their own ego, they can't see the truth when it stares them in the face. That I am going to make him regret every little insult he's thrown my way since I walked in there.

"You make up your mind yet, Buttercup? Either get out so I can complete this on my own or—"

I cup his balls and squeeze.

His big body freezes. I bring up my other palm, begin to knead that gorgeous well-hung part of him. His dick thickens and the muscles under his belly coil, ripple like there's some kind of internal struggle that holds his guts hostage.

"Are you sure, you want to do this?" His voice is so low, so harsh, a tremor courses through my veins and my toes curl. I lean in just a millimeter more, enough for his shaft to slip further down my throat. A growl rips out of him, "Last chance, Amelie." His voice is strained.

I peer up into his features. His jaw tics; a vein pops at his temple. The pulse between my legs beats in tandem. I lean back on my haunches, so his shaft slides out to the edge of my mouth. Then wrap my lips around his head, squeeze his balls at the same time.

"Jesus, fuck," he swears.

A thrill runs down my spine.

I knead his balls and the muscles in his stomach jump.

"You've done it now." He digs the fingers of his uninjured hand into my hair, and tugs. Pinpricks of pleasure race across my scalp. "I am going to fuck your face."

4

Weston

The hell am I doing? I'd meant to haul her to her feet and throw her out of the house, so I could get on with the quiet time I'd hoped to have over the holidays. Instead, I can't stop myself from tugging down on her hair. She flinches, raises her head, and the sight of those pink lips wrapped around my cock — bloody fuck — lust spirals through my veins hot and hard. Fuck. "I am going to do this my way, Buttercup. You understand that, hmm?"

She stares up at me, pupils blown, the green of her irises a slim circle around the black. Bloody hell, she's aroused, and so hot. I ease her head forward, and my dick disappears inside her mouth. My vision narrows and my scalp tightens, "Bloody fuck, I can't stop." I tighten my fingers in her hair; she winces. Lust spirals down my spine. The thought of bringing her to the edge, of hurting her just enough to give her the kind of pain which will heighten her pleasure…hell. My breathing grows ragged and my chest heaves. "Nod if you understand," I snarl.

Her eyebrows knit and her tiny hands massage my balls.

Pinpricks of heat race up my back. "Amelie," I warn her.

Her gaze widens and her movements become more frantic.

She leans into me until her elbows are positioned on my thighs, her head tipped up, her entire body tiny enough to fit exactly between my legs. She releases me, only to whisper her fingers up the back of my butt, into the crease between my arse cheeks…and that's when I snap. I drag her back a few inches…enough for her to pull back her hand. She draws in a breath, her cheeks hollow, and fuck, if I don't feel the suction all the way to my head. This woman, where did she learn to blow me like this? If I give her free rein, she'll suck my brains through my dick. A chuckle flicks up my throat, and anger…a slow burn of an emotion that's very much like jealousy. *What the—?* Am I jealous of whoever she was with before me? I've never had a problem with that before. All of my partners have been seasoned, experienced enough… Jaded and cynical. Happy to fuck and walk away… And her… I am going to fuck her, all right… And then what? I'll have to let her go. My guts twist. Why the hell is that an issue? This entire encounter has had the touch of surreal to it from the moment I'd opened the door of the hot tub area and seen this pixie of a woman.

Fuck her mouth, show her I'll take no quarter, make sure she understands that all of those dreams she carries around in her head—babies and puppies and all things nice? That's *not* what she's going to get from me. What she can expect is a man who knows what he wants, who goes after it and claims it…who takes no prisoners, as I am about to show her. "I need to see you nod your assent," I reiterate.

She pauses…a beat, another, then she jerks her chin.

Thank fuck. I haul her forward and my dick slides down her throat. Hot, moist, so fucking good that I almost come on the spot. I bring my other hand to the base of my cock, squeeze it to stop myself. Then I begin to use her mouth. I pull her back and forward, and again. Each time, my cock slips in between her gorgeous lips. Once more and her teeth graze the skin of my shaft. Ripples of pleasure flood my skin, my balls harden, my groin tightens, and I can't remember the last time I came this close, this quickly. I haul her close; this time her lips fasten around the girth of my cock, and when I pull her back, she curls her tongue around my swollen head. Goosebumps pop on my skin, my thigh muscles bunch, and the tension in my belly grows, becomes enormous. *Fuck.* "I am going to come."

She stares up, holds my gaze.

"You're going to take all of me, you understand?"

She nods.

"Every single last drop."

She brings her hand back up to cup my balls again and I explode.

Hot gusts of cum pour out of me, and she swallows, not breaking eye contact, and damn her, but it's the hottest, most erotic thing I have seen ever. Liquid spills down her chin, onto her top, but she doesn't pause. She continues to suck on me, swallowing until I swear there's nothing left in me to come. I step back; my cock drops from her lips with a wet plop. The hair on the back of my nape rises. I haul her to her feet, peer into her features. "You're something else, you know that?"

She opens her mouth, and damn her, but I don't want to hear her speak. No explanations. No need to dissect what just happened. So I do the only thing I can, considering the circumstances. I drop my head, place my lips over hers.

Mistake... Mistake... All of my senses jangle. A shudder of electricity screams up my spine and my dick instantly perks up... *The fuck?* I just came. It's a record, even for me. *Why the hell is she having this effect on me?* I pull back, but she rises on tip toe, throws her arms around me... Or as much of me as she can reach which, considering she comes to chest level, means she winds herself about my upper arms. She tilts her head, follows me. She parts her lips, swings her leg about my thigh. Only when my palm cups her butt, do I realize I've hoisted her up. She locks her ankles around my waist, licks my mouth. Heat flushes my cheeks; blood thunders at my temples. A growl rips from me, and I tighten my hold under her butt.

The scent of her, that sweet pastry essence, fills my senses, goes to my head. I can't stop myself; I kiss her back. Then yank her close enough for her breasts to flatten against my chest; for me to feel the hard buds of her nipples bite into my flesh.

A moan whines from her. She loops her fingers around my neck, digs her fingers into my hair and strains in my hold. Her melting core cocoons my hardness. My dick nestles against the crotch of her jeans, which I am happy to report is soaked right through. She wriggles around, trying to get closer. A chuckle rips from me. So impatient, this little thing is. I drag a hand up her spine, to lock my palm about her nape. She stills; a sigh trembles from her lips.

Hmm, she likes a firm hand, huh? Happy to oblige. I swipe my tongue over her teeth, down the seam of her lower lip. She groans; her body trembles. She pushes her core into my cock, which happily nestles into her. Fuck. This willing, quivering mass of woman is too enticing, too seductive...too much everything. If I continue to kiss her, I'll have to take her, and one time won't be enough. I'll have to fuck whatever it is between us out of my system, which could take…days… Hell, weeks… Probably all of the time that I'd allowed myself here… And how is that going to work out, hmm?

I lessen the intensity of the kiss. She whines, coils herself into me, as if she wants to crawl under my skin… Fuck, if she hasn't already, in some way. *Which is not too bad, hmm? What the — what am I thinking?* I don't want a woman in my life. Not now. Not when I'm trying to heal myself. I need to rest up, ensure my mind and body are rested and ready to go. It is my career at stake, if I don't mend. As a surgeon, the operations I perform demand that my faculties be more than a 100% when I perform procedures. It's the one thing that makes my life worthwhile — being able to save others. Perhaps because when I am in surgery, I am in control. It is in my hands to take charge, to see the operation through, ensure I do my best, snatch people back from the jaws of death and restore them back to their lives.

Something I could only hope for during the time I had been kidnapped and held hostage. Is that why I like to play God? Or as close to it as it gets, when I hold someone's heart in my palms…like she held my balls in hers. Her touch, her kisses, the flow of her hair about her shoulders, the pulse of her blood at the base of her neck, at her chest, between her thighs… Why do I want to acquaint myself with every goddam nook and crevasse of her body? I tear my mouth from hers.

Her chin wobbles, she blinks, and a whine spills from her lips. "Weston," she mumbles.

My name from her mouth, her tongue drawing out the vowels, her every part reaching, aching, wanting me… Fuck… I can't do this. Can't allow myself to feel whatever it is that connects us. I am not ready for this… Will never be ready for whatever it is that she wants from me — the kind of commitment not spoken, but voiced with her actions, her reactions to me, since she had entered.

"Weston?" She peers up at me, "Hey…" She cups my cheek, and her touch sinks into my blood. My pulse rate ratchets up and my cock — that needy part of me — instantly stands to attention. Fucking fuck, I gotta get out of here. Max chooses that moment to come tearing back into the space. Thank fuck. He parks his little body next to my leg, then paws at my ankle.

"The puppy," I say, "he needs to be fed."

She swallows; the brightness dulls in her eyes. My heart stutters. It fucking stutters at that. Why the hell is she affecting me like this? I can't let her get to me. Not now. Not ever.

"So you know, I am not sorry."

"Huh?" Her eyebrows knit, "What are you talking about—?" Her gaze widens as I grip her under her armpits and hold her away from my body. The cold instantly infiltrates my chest. Fuck… Now I am getting melodramatic, or perhaps, I've simply been standing around without clothes for too long.

"Don't you dare, Wes—"

I release her.

She plops into the hot tub and water splashes over the sides.

"You asshole," she splutters. "How dare you?"

"Oh, I dare, alright. In fact, I'm just getting started. I am taking over the house for the holidays. You'll have to find yourself other accommodations."

"Weston— You motherfucker," her screech follows me. "Come back right now, or else…"

I pause, glance at her over my shoulder, "Or else?"

"Or else…you'll never find out about the proposal I have in mind for you."

5

———————

Amelie

"Proposal, huh?" He arches an eyebrow.

"Yeah." I nod. *What the hell am I doing? And after I'd blown him… Willingly, I might add… What the hell was that all about?*

Not that I have anything against giving a blowjob, but honestly, it's not something I've done before with a man I don't know well… And that is the problem. With Weston, there had been this instant reaction to him, from the time I'd first seen him. I'd wanted to slap that smirk off his face, then hit him in the dick, right before I pulled him close and smooched the hell out of him. Shit, this…push-pull reaction I am having to him is insane. From the time he'd walked through the patio door, he'd been mean to me. He'd been pushing my buttons, all right, trying to get a reaction out of me. And you know what? I am not going to let him win this David and Goliath game we have going on here. I'd been promised I could have this space over the holidays and I intend to make sure I do.

If it means sharing with this a-hole of a man… This hot and sexy, ripped, 100% macho maleness of a billionaire, doctor… Gulp. Then so be it. I am not going to let him crowd me into corner, or overpower me with his status…. Okay, so maybe I am a little overwhelmed by his uh, larger than life assets…but come on, who wouldn't be? And that kiss at the end? When I'd flung myself at him…because, well, I am a slut…

Fine, fine, so berate me, but I swear, there had been something about the power I'd been able to wield over him, when I had taken him in my mouth, and his body had responded to mine.

Whatever his issues with me... Physically, the signals he's been broadcasting are clear—he wants me. And let me tell you, there's something very satisfying in that, in knowing that this powerful man is helpless in the face of whatever it is that our bodies are communicating with each other. And face it...sharing a space with him would be no...hardship... Except for that horrible attitude of his, of course. I'm willing to give him a chance though... Who wouldn't? Not when he'd kissed me back... He had. He had pulled me to him, closed that big sexy mouth of his over mine and kissed the hell out of me... Enough for my knees to go weak, for my pussy to clench, and my panties to dampen all over again, like I'd just run into the Thames. Okay, so maybe not the last comparison, considering the Thames is grimy as hell, but you get what I mean, huh?

"I... I am not leaving," I say.

"Yes, you are," he reiterates.

"Nope."

"Yes."

He leans a hip against the door, and damn him, couldn't he have, at least, put on some clothes? I mean, this entire encounter? He's been butt-naked, and it's a mighty fine butt, and massively corded thighs, and that eight pack...and... Hell, not going down that path right now.

"You'll want me to stay, I promise you."

"Huh?" He folds his arms over his chest. Those biceps bulge, his shoulders fill the doorway, and it's not because its narrow. The entrance, I mean.

"I'll be your housekeeper—cook your food, clean..." I wave a hand in the air, "Considering you're laid up with that...uh, injury, you'll need someone to take care of your needs."

"Needs, huh?"

Shit, I hadn't meant to word it that way, but whatever, at least he's listening to me.

"You bet." I swing one leg up over the lip of the hot tub, then scramble up and straighten. "You hadn't thought about how you were going to manage over the holidays without being able to use your hand."

"Hmm." He raises his injured palm, then scratches at his jaw. "You offering to help?"

"Do you want me to help?"

"You want to keep house for me?" He smirks.

I frown. Asshole, of course he'd twist my words around to suit his needs.

"I'd cook and clean the house..." I mutter, " You'd have to pick up after yourself. I am not picking up your dirty laundry."

"What else?"

"What do you mean?" I frown.

"What else can you do for me?" he drawls.

"I could...uh, drive you around, like I already said."

"And?" His lips curl and his eyes gleam.

Oh, no, no, he's not getting at that. "Whatever it is you're thinking, you can forget about it," I huff.

"How do you know what I am thinking?"

"A man like you has only one thing on your mind."

"As opposed to a woman like you?"

"I'm not the one walking around naked."

"Does it bother you?"

"Of course, it bothers me." I swipe my hair over my shoulders. "How would it feel if I were to walk around without clothes?"

"Are you offering?" He smirks.

I throw up my hands, "Oh, forget I said anything. Clearly, this entire discussion is going nowhere... Meanwhile—" A whine sounds from beyond him, "Don't keep Max waiting. Feed the poor thing, will you?"

He scowls, "Don't tell me what to do."

"Oh, my God." I plant my hands on my hips, grimace when that dislodges more water from my clothes. "You're bloody impossible."

"And you're staying out here."

He walks inside, slams the door behind him. *The hell?* I race forward, try the door. It's locked. Of course, it is. I bang on it. "Weston, you asshole, let me in."

No answer, not that I expected one... But how dare he simply...lock me out? I kick at the door. Pain shoots up my leg. I groan, then glance around the patio. There are heaters out here around the hot tub, so I'm not cold. The wind blows, and I shiver... Okay, scratch that. I won't freeze, but damn, if I am standing around here waiting for that bastard to come back and get me.

I stalk past the tub, jump down onto the grass. I walk around the side. Ha, he's going to keep me out the house, is he? Not if I can help it.

I break into a sprint, jog up the field surrounding the house, around to the front. Reaching the door, I find it...closed. *Bugger.* I try the door handle, and it's locked. I throw up my fists, ready to punch my way through...? As if that would help... Think... Think... What can I do...? I walk down the steps, get back into the car...search for my phone. Shit. My handbag—I left it inside the bloody house, along with my chef's satchel. *Argh!*

I slam my palm on the steering wheel, and the horn blares. Hell. I press down on the horn a little longer. I'd left the keys in the ignition... So, at least, I am mobile, but without my phone and my wallet... Hell, even if I went out into the village... which is a 45-minute drive away, I couldn't do much. Damn it, I can't even call anyone for help.

Ugh! I grip the steering wheel, take a deep breath, then another. *Don't lose it. You can think it through.* He isn't going to leave me out... Nah! He wouldn't...would he? Damn it. It would be just like that reprobate who has chocolate tarts for brains to do something exactly so...assholish. *Argh!* Anger ladders up my spine. I swipe my wet hair out of my eyes... Great. Here I am, soaking wet, with no dry clothes in sight... Uhm, no, I do have my suitcase where I left it outside. There's a distinct boom, then drops of water drizzle down. Shit. That doesn't help. No way am I going to get soaked all over again. I snatch up the keys, step out of the car and lock it. Then run over to my suitcase... I drag it up the steps to the front entryway, and place it against the wall.

Then retrace my path down the steps, then around to the back porch.

The wind blows. I shiver and step closer to the warmth emanating from the tub. Hmm. Should I? I glance around for the controls, spot a switch. When I throw it, the bubbles begin to churn in the tub. I dip my hand, and yep, the water's warm. I turn the dial further toward the red. With the rain smattering outside and the floor patio heaters going full force... Well, it is not too bad. But that doesn't get me inside the cabin. I hear scratching at the door—Max trying to get out again.

Okay, I'm not going to stand around here, as if waiting for him... I am going to... I grab the hem of my blouse, pull it off. I hear Weston talking to Max, then the sound of the door being unlocked. I strip out of my jeans. The door begins to open. I race toward the tub, jump inside, unhooking my bra at the same time.

6

———————

Weston

What the—? What the hell is she up to now?

I walk out of the door and onto the patio in time to watch her sink into the hot tub. There's a flash of pink, then she holds up her bra... something slinky and made of scraps of nylon. My jaw drops and my belly hardens. She can't be doing what I think she is. She can't be undressed...and turning the tables on me...can she?

I'd fed the mutt...then proceeded to take a cold shower...before pulling out clothes. When I could delay no longer, I'd walked out. Okay, also because I was curious. The last thing I'd expected was for her to reverse engineer the scene I'd played out for her earlier.

I stalk forward and my foot brushes something wet. I glance down to find her abandoned blouse...then her jeans... I follow a trail of clothes strewn across the patio that leads me to stand over her.

"What are you up to?"

"What do you think?" She tosses her bra at me and I catch it. Damn her, but I want to smell it. Would it have her scent...of sugar and spices and everything nice? *Argh!* I really have to stop reading to Birdie, my niece. Now I am thinking in nursery rhymes? Or is it simply her nearness going to my head?

She scoops up some of the hot water, pours it over her shoulders.

The bubbles cover her up to the swell of her breasts, but she's naked below it... Is she? Did she take off her panties? I glance around, can't see the abandoned lingerie...so she must have it on... Would the cloth be transparent enough for me to see through it to that melting center of her, that I desperately want to get my hands on? My cock throbs and blood thunders at my temples. "Get out of there."

"No."

"If you don't step out..."

"What? You'll step in?"

Oh, I'm tempted to, but considering I spent the last few hours in there already, I'll pass. Doesn't mean I am going to let her get away with this little tease-filled antic, either.

I toss her bra aside then reach over to grab her shoulder. She twists her body and water splashes onto my shirt. "Oops." She giggles in a voice that seems to imply she's not sorry at all.

"Why you little—" I scowl, then straighten. "Stand up," I snarl.

"Make me."

"You don't want me coming in there. Trust me."

"Oh?" She tilts her head, "We'll see, shall we?" She slaps the water; more of it splashes onto me. *What the—?* I fold my arms over my chest, lower my voice to a hush, "Up." I growl.

She swallows.

"Do it."

"You sure?" she asks.

"I won't repeat myself."

"Fine." She juts out her chin.

"Fine?" I frown. Why is she agreeing so readily? She's up to no good, for sure, she— She rises to her feet. Water pours from her slim frame down the jut of her hips, in between her legs...and fuck, I was wrong. She doesn't have her panties on.

The water slides down her flat stomach, down to the triangle between her legs. And I can only watch as a drop clings to her pussy lips, begging me to go closer, closer. My knees bump into the side of the hot water tub. I blink.

"My face is up here," she drawls.

I can't stop the chuckle that rumbles up my throat. "Very good." I tilt my head. "Clearly, you've been paying attention to our conversation, and PS," I make air quotes with my fingers, "you ain't got nothin' that I haven't seen already."

She blinks, then gapes at me, "I was wrong about you."

"Oh?"

"You're not just an asshole, but a bloody, egoistical brute with no manners."

A grin threatens to split my face. I swallow it with a cough. "I'll give you one thing though; you got my attention."

"Hallelujah." She raises her arms skyward and tilts her head back. Her tits jiggle with the action. My cock instantly springs to attention. Fuck. It's not like I haven't seen better-looking women — certainly, those with bigger tits, slimmer waists...curvier hips... But the complete package of the woman who stands knee-deep in bubbles, with her hair sticking to her forehead...the flushed cheeks, the pink lips... Yeah, the ones between her legs as well... All of it comes together in an amalgamation that is uniquely her... Something I want to get to know better... To own and to understand, to pull apart and piece together until she makes more sense... Until I get her out of my system, that's all. Perhaps that's reason to keep her around a little longer?

I jerk my chin, "Come on."

"Huh?" She frowns.

"Out of there. Chop, chop." I clap my hand. "You've got a lot of work to do."

Turning, I head for the doorway leading back to the house.

"Wait," she calls out.

I reach the door, step inside.

"Does this mean you accept my proposition?"

"It means," I turn to glance at her, "you'd better get inside before I change my mind."

She stares back, spine straight, shoulders hitched back. She props a hand on her hip, breasts thrust up, nipples pebbled — Hell, if she isn't as aroused as I am feeling. This is going to be interesting. I start to close the door. She springs into action, clambers over the side of the tub. "Wait," she screeches.

My lips twitch as I try to keep the smile off of my face. "You have one minute to get your arse in here," I drawl.

"Bastard," she huffs.

I yawn, "You're getting repetitive, Buttercup."

"Aargh." She makes a sound deep in her throat, "I hate that ridiculous name."

"Prefer Blossom? Or Bubbles, maybe?"

"No," she scoffs, "all three of the Powerpuff girls are dumb."

"Hey," I lower my chin, "you did not just say that."

"Yes, I did." She grabs her blouse, pulls it on and it falls to mid-thigh.

My gaze, of course, goes there, to the curved flesh that jiggles as she moves. The women I've dated before have been emaciated, by comparison. None of them had that lustrous skin that I itch to mark, the delicate turn of ankles that invites me to run my tongue up the hollow, scooping the water droplets that are sure to be nestled there, up her calf and her inner leg, to that object of my obsession—her beautiful gorgeous core. *Fuck*.

"Just for that, your first punishment is watching the cartoon characters on loop."

"Punishment?" She grabs her boots and her socks; one of her shoes slips from her hold and hits the ground. "Crummy apple crumble," she swears,

"Did you use a dessert as a swear word?" I chuckle.

She rescues her footwear. "You could help, instead of ogling my body," she grumbles.

"Oh, if I were ogling, you'd know it, sweet thing."

She straightens, her cheeks rosier than they had been a few moments ago, "You're a chauvinist."

"You're a submissive."

She stiffens, "How dare you say that?"

"You want to be taken without being given a choice. Somewhere deep inside, you want to be dominated. At your core, you prefer to have all options taken from you, so you can relax into your true self."

She scoffs, "The hell you mean?"

"Right now, as we speak, you want me to bend you over the nearest chair, then part your legs, strum your clit, finger your pussy and make you come, right before I sink my hard, throbbing…aching…length into your melting center."

She draws in a breath, stares at me. Even through the darkness, her blue irises shine… The light in my darkness, the silvery fucking lining to my black cloud of a bloody life... And I am waxing poetic, all right, and all because this woman here has crawled under my skin. I want to grab her and pull her close and kiss her… Right after I turn her over my lap and spank all that impudence out of her. Speaking of... "Okay, I'm shutting the door." I let the barrier swing.

"W-a-i-t!" She scampers forward, then slips through the crack between the door and the frame. The door snicks shut. Silence, a beat, then another. This close, the scent of her—that vanilla and apples essence of her, laced with that sugary-tart sweetness that lingers on my tongue like a memory of that smell…when you go to the mall and you walk past the candy shop and smell the sugar? That smell intensifies. My mouth waters as my cock lengthens. I curl my fingers at my sides.

"Go on," I jerk my chin, temporarily capable of little more than monosyllabic words and spastic movements.

She scowls, "So you can stare at my arse?"

"If you'd rather ogle my butt instead…" I shrug, which has the added benefit of relieving some of the tension I'm feeling.

She snatches up her satchel, wears it across her chest, then bends to pick up her coat. Her toolkit jostles forward and smacks the back of her head. "Ow." She straightens, and her coat slips down to trail on the floor. "Shit," she swears aloud, "I am a mess."

"And I'd love to mess up my bed with you in it," I cough.

"What did you say?" she sputters as she scoops up her coat again.

"Just that you are pretty in your disarray."

She stares. "Somehow, I don't believe you."

"Somehow, I don't think I care."

"Is this some kind of NLP technique?" She frowns.

"No idea what you are talking about." I turn away.

"This entire mirroring my words thing you have happening."

"The only mirroring I want to do is of the 69 kind," I snicker.

"That's it," she snarls, "I've changed my mind."

"Hmm."

"I thought we could find a way to get through the holiday season, but clearly, if I spend any time with you, it's going to drive me insane."

"Goes both ways, sugar," I retort. The patter of paws on the wooden floor announces the arrival of Max. He jumps up, places his paws on my legs, as if he hasn't seen me in years, instead of minutes ago when I'd fed him. "Hey Buddy, whatcha doin', hmm?" I scratch at his head behind his ears and he makes a low, rumbling sound in his throat. He attempts to jump up again, but this time I oblige. I snatch him up, cuddle him, turn to watch her watching me.

I tilt my head, "What?"

"Every time I think you're a horrible monster, Max saves the day."

"Should I be thankful?" I smirk, digging my fingertips into Max's skin. He makes a deep groaning sound.

"Did he just...?" She blinks.

"Max is every bit as expressive as you," I snicker.

"Thanks." She tosses her head, "Doesn't get you off the hook. I'm still leaving." She marches past me, snatches up her handbag from where she'd placed it on the bar counter.

She heads for the door, then pauses, to rifle around in her purse.

Wait for it.

Wait for it.

Wait for —

"You asshole." She turns on me.

"Alphahole." I correct her.

"You took my phone."

I lower Max to the floor and he darts off toward the kitchen. I follow him, shut the door that leads from the living room, then lean against it.

"You did, didn't you?" she grumbles.

"If you mean that piece of shit technology that went out of date..."

"Hey, don't insult Hedwig."

"Hedwig?"

"My phone, you idiot."

"Who gives a phone a name? Wait, you named your phone after the owl in Harry Potter?"

"Wow." She swallows, "You placed that?"

She stares at me, her gaze taking on that familiar googly-eyed look.

I hold my hands out in front of me. "Don't go reading anything into it. And for the record, owl post wouldn't work, in real life," I mutter.

"What do you mean?"

"It's a scientifically-proven fact that owls can't stay in flight while carrying packages."

"Just because it isn't supported by science, doesn't mean it doesn't work."

"What do you mean?" I frown.

"Magic, remember?"

"Which is what you believe in, of course? Stars and unicorns and all that girlie shit."

Her face heats, "You could do with believing in a little of that yourself."

"When you're kidnapped and starved for days, and tortured to within an inch of your life, you lose faith in all that stupid stuff very quickly," I snap.

Her features scrunch up, "I'm so sorry for what happened to you and the Seven."

"I'm not. If it weren't for that incident, I'd still be naive—"

"Like me, you mean?"

"You said it." I let my lips curl.

She frowns, "Why am I debating this with you?" She holds out her hand, "Give Hedwig back to me."

"Sorry, I can't."

"What do you mean?"

"I can't remember where I put it." I grimace.

"What?"

"If you find it, you can keep it." I raise my shoulders.

"He belonged to me in the first place."

"He..." I shake my head, "It...the phone's mine now."

"No, it's not."

"Alas, poor Hedwig, he's going to have to spend Christmas without you, I'm afraid."

Her features contort, and I am sure she's going to stamp her foot and rage, and have a full-on tantrum. This should be interesting. I head to the armchair by the fireplace, drop into it, then pick up my novel.

"The hell are you doing?" she squawks.

"Reading."

She makes a snarling sound at the back of her throat. I hear the thump of her toolkit satchel hitting the floor, then a softer crash—that's her handbag—followed by the soft sound of her wet clothes hitting the wooden floor. Good. Footsteps approach; the next second she grabs the book from my hand.

"Hey, you only had to ask."

"I did, for my phone. Remember?"

"I mean the book." I lean back in the chair, fold one leg over the other.

She peruses the cover of the book, then blinks. "Harry Potter? You're reading Harry Potter?"

She glances at me, with...stars in her eyes, once more.

Oh, no, no, damn it. "Why do you think I recognized your reference, which I can tell you, is way too obvious. You need to up your game, Buttercup."

Her features tighten.

Bloody fuck, I shouldn't have insulted her...but what the hell? I need to live up to my reputation as someone who doesn't give a damn about anyone else... Besides, that strange gooey expression of hers... It scares the shit out of me. Har, har. Ask me to perform a complicated bypass, I am there. Ask me to try to figure out why I have this strange push-pull reaction to her, and hell, if it doesn't flummox me. Time to set this right and lay down the rules. We'll see then, how she copes. Fuck that hint of hopefulness I've spotted on her face throughout the evening. It is time to show her what I am actually made of.

"Don't let the fact that I am reading the Potter fool you."

"God forbid," she mutters.

"It's only so I can keep up with my older niece."

"How many nieces do you have?"

"Two...and I am not answering any more questions."

"Like I care."

"I think you do, actually. And I have to warn you right now."

"What?"

"Don't fall in love with me, Buttercup. You'll only have your heart broken."

7

Amelie

My jaw drops. Again. The arrogance of the man. "I wouldn't fall for you, if you were the last man on earth.

"I'll hold you to that."

"What is that supposed to mean?" My heart begins to race.

"You know," he replies, his tone hard.

Sweat beads my palms, and it's not because the inside of the room is warmer than it was before... When had he lit the fireplace? Probably when I was outside. The light from the flames flickers over his face, throwing his features into relief, deepening the shadows under his cheekbones, hollowing out the spaces under his eyes. His dark hair appears almost blue, and those grey eyes seem almost colorless. Deep and fathomless. What would I find if I looked into those depths? A soul that would take, a male who'd possess, who'd pleasure me in the way no one else ever has. A dominant man who'd push aside all of my doubts and teach me how it is to be claimed. A shiver runs down my spine. *Is that what I want? Is that why I haven't left?* Hell, it could be just the two of us in this house—a faint scratching comes from the direction of the kitchen—and the puppy. Not another living soul for miles around; no business demands on either of us. He'd come to heal and I had come to find…something… That spark inside of me that had vanished…and which I had been hoping to recapture. That leap of faith that had pushed me to start my own business… That makes me take a step forward…close the distance between us.

He watches me as I move closer. He lowers his feet to the floor, parts his thighs. I step in between them. He tips his chin up. It feels… different this way. Me looking down on him. The angle intensifies that brooding edge that coils under the surface. I want to find out what makes him tick. Why he blows hot and cold; why he'd decided to spend the holidays alone…when he could have been with any woman… Instead, he's gotten me. I frown.

He shakes his head.

I scowl.

"You have no idea what you're letting yourself in for," he mutters, half to himself.

"And you do?"

"I've been around the block many more times than you."

"You sure?"

"Have you?" he shoots back.

"Maybe not as much as you," I concede, "but I've had my share of boyfriends."

"How many?"

"What's it to you?" I snap.

"If we're going to get through our time together, then there are some ground rules you need to follow."

"*You?*" I scowl.

He tilts his head.

"You meant *we* need to follow, surely?" I elaborate.

He stares at me with those almost-colorless eyes and another shiver of electricity runs up my spine. *Shit, he doesn't even need to speak to me and I know what he means. Is it because I am that tuned into him?* More likely, I know exactly the kind of obnoxious, merciless man he is. My toes curl. *Why the hell does that turn me on?* It shouldn't be so appealing. I shouldn't be this attracted to him… It's precisely the fact that he wouldn't care about my needs, that he'd simply take what he wants from me, that I find…refreshing. There would be no pretensions with this man. It would be all give… At least, there would be no surprises, huh? So, I won't be disappointed. Is that how low my expectations have fallen?

"You shouldn't overanalyze everything," he remarks.

"You shouldn't take everyone around you for granted."

"Now you're doing that NLP shit..." he points out.

I half laugh, "You going to explain exactly what this is about?"

"This?" He looks perplexed.

I point to the space between us, "This."

"Ah." He steeples his fingers together. "It's simple. I am willing to let you stay here for the holiday season."

I frown.

"But?"

"Did I say a 'but'?"

"There's always a 'but' with people like you."

"People like me?"

"Overindulgent, spoilt, rich pricks who think they own the world."

"That's because I do."

I snort; I can't help it. "Why am I not surprised that you said that?"

He raises his shoulders, "It's a fact."

"Whatever," I mutter.

"What was that?"

"I said, 'What-fucking-ever,'" I say, with more aggression that I am feeling.

"Hmm, you have spirit. That's good."

"Oh, stop talking in riddles."

"That's Saint," he chuckles.

"What?"

"Doesn't matter." He draws in a breath, then straightens his shoulders, "Enough beating around the bush. It's six days to Christmas. We spend it together. You do everything I ask of you in that time."

"What does that mean?" I stare.

"Exactly what it sounds like. Nothing hidden."

"Does it mean...uh...?"

"What?"

"You know."

"No, I don't." He smirks.

Oh, spit it out already, why the hell am I being coy? "Sexual favors," I burst out.

"Only if you want it to," he replies.

I blink. "You mean..."

He nods.

"So, if I decided I didn't want to blow you again..."

"You'd be missing out," he rolls his shoulders, "but your call."

"You sure?"

"Would I lie?"

"Wouldn't you?"

He grins. "I love this little sparring thing we have going on..."

I purse my lips together, "It's not 'little' anything."

"That's true," he chuckles.

"Oh, my God!" I throw up my hands. "We get on each other's nerves. That's all it is."

"Hmm," he scratches his jaw, "you may be right there. We'll have to tone it down though, when we're seen in public."

"Public?"

He nods, "I have to go to visit my family sometime before Christmas and you'll come along, of course."

I stare at him. Has he gone mad? Why is he jumping around topics like that? "Wh...what do you mean?"

"You'll come with me, as my date, to visit with my family in the lead up to Christmas." He speaks slower this time, as if I didn't understand him the first time around. I still don't.

"No, I won't."

"Yes, you will."

I blink. He's so bloody confident, it borders on delusional. *I hadn't mistakenly agreed to this earlier, had I? No, of course not.* "Why the hell would I do that?" I scoff.

"Because you wanted a place to spend the holiday season, and this is the only space available."

"No, it isn't." I shuffle my feet.

"Ever tried finding a place to stay over the holiday season? It's either sold out, or so expensive, it would be out of your price range.

"How do you know what my price range is?"

"Whatever it is, I can afford it." He smirks.

My jaw drops. Again. Shit, I've been doing a lot of that since I got here... But this...this...wanker... He's got his head up his arse. No doubt, he thinks the sun shines out of it too. I snicker.

He frowns. "Also, you can't do that while you are here," he drawls.

"What?"

"Think impertinent thoughts."

I blink, then laugh, "Man, you're something else, you know?"

"As you are going to find out."

I open and shut my mouth, I mean... Why am I standing here arguing with him? I should just march out of here, figure out alternate arrangements across the new year.

"Giving up so soon?" he drawls.

"What do you mean?"

"Guess you know that you can't last the next six days without falling for my charms."

"What charms?" I look him and down, "You're a douchebag, is all."

"Exactly what you find so attractive, hmm?"

"You have no idea what I like, or not."

"Oh, trust me," He sits forward in the chair, "I have a very good idea what you...want.... Question is," he lowers his voice to that hushed tone that sinks into my skin. My blood heats; moisture laces my core. *How the hell does he draw that reaction from me without trying too hard?*

"Do you, Buttercup?"

I swallow, "I have no idea what you're talking about."

"We'll have to work on that too."

"What?"

"This entire self-denial thing you have going on... It's cute..." he tilts his head, "but it can get wearying after a while, for both of us."

I stare, trying to keep pace with his thoughts.

"It is?"

He nods, "And we don't want that."

My head spins; my skin heats further. *Why the hell is it so warm inside?*

"I... I think I need to go."

I turn to leave, reach the door, when he calls out.

"A million pounds."

I pause, then turn, "Excuse me?"

He's standing in front of the chair. "You heard me." He props his palms on his hips. "I know how much in debt you are."

"My business is doing well." My heart begins to race; sweat dampens my palms. *Dammit, why the hell does this guy make me nervous?* "In fact, that's why I am here, to recuperate from the stress —"

"No doubt, caused by the college loans you carry. Not to mention, the ones you took out to finance your fledgling little business."

Argh, did he just call my thriving enterprise 'little,' which it is, but what the hell gives him the right to come across all condescending like that? "And you know all this...how?"

"Do you deny it?" he asks.

Do it. Don't give him the satisfaction of finding out how right he is. I open my mouth, shut it again. Damn it, but I can't tell a white lie. Not even to save my arse. Which might be more literal than I realize. A giggle bubbles up.

He frowns. "If you did make a success of your business—"

I open my mouth to protest.

He holds up his hand to stop me, "—which is dependent on your business acumen as much as on your ability to be a cook—"

"I'm a pastry chef, you knob."

"Cook." He closes the distance between us, "Even then, you'll be paying off your loans for the next twenty years."

My pulse rate ratchets up. *Shit,* those numbers... Not that I wasn't aware of them. I prefer not to think about it, that's all. I mean, sure, I could look on the negative and the fact that I'll be paying off the loans forever... But I've been confident I could turn the corner at some point. What's the other option? Not take risks, work a nine-to-five... Nothing wrong with that. It's not for me, that's all.

"So?" I sniff.

"So, you'll work back-breaking, long hours, behind a stove—"

"An oven, you prick."

"If you keep alluding to that part of me, I'll have to assume you've been thinking of it."

"No, I haven't."

He grins. *Bastard.* My cheeks heat. So, fine, I've been thinking about that particular attribute of his nonstop since I sucked on him, like my own private lollypop. *Gah!* So? Hey, it was a bloody good blowjob too, thank you very much.

"As I was saying," he drums his fingers on his chest, "you'll waste away your best years, working non-stop, trying to pay off the loans. Before you know it, you'll be forty and single, not having had the time to find a man—"

"I don't need one," I snarl.

He laughs, "Meanwhile, the debt is going to stop you from expanding your business further... And that, you do want, hmm?"

I scowl. He's got me there. I have plans. I want to grow my business to set up a store front... Then a chain, not only in England, but abroad.

And while I'm sure I won't let debt stop me, not with the help of expert advice on how to structure my business holdings... Still, nothing like cash in hand to inspire confidence, especially from future creditors.

"One million, huh?"

His eyes gleam.

I frown. Damn it, have I walked into a trap? I shouldn't have shown interest in his offer, but I'm human, okay? I mean... No, I won't sell my principles for money... But this is an awful lot of money. Not something to sneer at, get me? Besides, what principles is he really trying to pay me to betray? It's not like he's offering to pay me for sex. I chew on my lower lip; his gaze drops there. The tendons of his throat move as he swallows. Huh? He's affected by me as well? I mean, I know he wants me... That entire blowjob thing between us... It had confirmed he wants to get in my pants... But this... His hooded eyelids, the way he watches me with single-minded focus... My scalp tingles. A bead of sweat trickles down my spine.

I clear my throat.

He jerks his chin up, "Per day."

"What the—?" I gape. "You didn't... Why would you—?" I rake my fingers through my hair. "This entire thing is bizarre."

"It's a little out of your comfort zone, I understand." He shoves his hand in the pocket of his jeans, "But opportunities like this don't come often."

"You're telling me," I laugh. The sound comes out weak. Shit, I sound uncertain. And I am not. Not about my answer... Just his intention. "Why?" I frown. "Why are you so keen on ensuring that I stay?"

"You said it." He tilts his head, "I am not much use with this—" He holds up his finger in the splint. "Until you pointed it out, I hadn't realized it." He nods.

Nice one. Blame it on me that he'd come up with this insane idea, huh.?

"You could get a housekeeper...or something."

"Not over the holiday season. Besides, why would I look for a stranger when I want you?"

"Umm, because you don't know me well either?"

His gaze drops to my mouth.

"That...that was a one off." I redden. "It doesn't mean you know me as a person."

He raises his shoulders, "You're a friend of Summer and Victoria's, women who are trusted by the Seven."

"Right," I draw in a breath.

"So?" He tilts his head.

"So?" I shuffle my weight from foot to foot. *What do I say?* I twist my fingers together. "One million for every day makes it…"

"Six million pounds." He nods.

"S… six?" I squeak.

"It'll set you up for any kind of expansion you want to finance for your business."

I narrow my gaze. How could he have intuited my plans? "How do you know that?"

"You're ambitious, I get it." He stares back, "Not that much of a stretch, to know that you'd be planning to grow your enterprise.

"Right." I scowl at him. "I guess that makes sense. I mean, you weren't stalking me or anything, before I came here to find out this information, were you? Although, it does beg the question, how did you know about my debt?"

He chuckles, "Don't flatter yourself, babe. We check into anyone who enters our orbit. Can't be too careful, you know?"

"Hmm." I fold my arms around my waist. "It's what Sinclair and then Saint did before they proposed to my friends," I say, referring to the now-husbands of Summer and Victoria, respectively.

His lips quirk, "You think that's what this is about? My sneaky way of trying to form some kind of fake marriage proposal with you?"

Hmm, when he puts it like that, it sounds pretty far-fetched, but still, "You did ask me to accompany you to see your family."

"Just a way to get them off my back," he grumbles. "You're going to be hanging about here. I may as well as put your time to good use."

"Jeez, you have a foolproof way of charming women," I mutter.

"Right?" His smile broadens and his features light up. He is taking the piss, isn't he? I mean, no one could mistake his attitude to be anything but self-satisfying, egoistical, narcissistic —*gah*— I'm running out of adjectives.

"Well then, you'd best get your luggage in…"

"Hold on, hold on." I blow out a breath, "Nothing's settled."

"Of course, it is."

Gah! I almost cross my eyes at the sheer lunacy of this situation. Six days with an egomaniac, who is going to make every moment a living hell. Would it be worth the money? Six million freakin' quid! *Ohmigod!* That's what's at stake here. How many zeros are there in that number anyway? I pout, "You sure…uh…this isn't another way to—"

"Get in your knickers?" He raises an eyebrow, scans my features. "Face it, Buttercup. If I wanted," his voice lowers to that seductive hush, "I could take you now, and you wouldn't say 'no.'" His lips curl in that hotter-than-bubbling-custard-sauce smirk. *OMG, how could I compare him to one of the food dishes that I am famous for?*

He closes the remaining distance between us and that scent of his—pine and cloves and an edgy depth that coils around me—pins me in place. I can't move, can't think, can only watch as he looks down on me from his superior height.

"N…no," I stutter.

He pauses inches in front of me, "Did I ask a question?" His lips twitch. What a stupid idea this was. Damn…but six million. Six freakin' million pounds. Hell, I'd do anything for that. Even put up with his alphaholeness for a limited period of time. I mean, this is only for a short period of time, right? It has an end, after all, this time with him.

"Fine," I mutter and my stomach flip-flops. *Shit, what am I getting myself into?*

"The arrangement is dependent on one thing."

Knew it. I scowl, "Now what?"

"You can't sleep with me during our time together."

I blink. "So, you'll pay me a million pounds a day, to be your glorified housekeeper, and sex is not part of the bargain?" I pause. "And if I sleep with you?"

"Then the deal is off."

Huh? I peruse his features. Is he for real? Is this…weird-ass bargain as good as it sounds?

"So…" I try to give voice to my thoughts, "Everything but sex?"

"Not gonna repeat myself." His lips quirk.

What's the catch, huh? What is it?

I stare at him; a low smoldering burn begins to curl in my belly, "So…" I gulp. "Wh…what's not off limits, then?" *Why is my voice shaking?*

"You sure you want to know?"

No.

No.

"Yes." I clear my throat, "I need to know before I sign on the dotted line, right?"

"Hmm." His eyes gleam. He bends his knees, thrusts his face into mine, "What's not off limits includes, but is not limited to, squeezing, fondling, strumming, stuffing, kneading, massaging, pinching, spanking, hurting you, tying you up, making you scream, cry, beg, plead, howl—"

"Stop," I gasp.

He nods. "That's another thing you need to learn—to not tell me to stop when you don't mean it."

"Of course, I do."

His lips curl. He swoops out his hand to cup my pussy through the blouse that covers me to mid-thigh.

I squeak, grab at his wrist. He digs the heel of his palm into my core, and the strength of his touch, presses up through the soft fabric of my blouse into my clit. Sparks of heat, of lust, and streaks of emptiness slam into my gut. I shudder, "Oh, my God."

He rotates his palm in circles. Pinpricks of need swirl up my spine, my thighs spasm, my toes curl, my scalp tingles, and damn him, but he's barely touched me. How could my body betray me like this? Is this what I want?

He releases me, retracts his palm, and I jerk my pelvis forward. *What the hell?*

He tilts his head, brings his palm to his nose and sniffs, "That's what I thought. You are so aroused, if I had continued my ministrations, you'd have come."

"Not," I sniff.

"Fine then. " He smirks, straightens, turns to leave.

"Stop," I burst out.

He keeps going. *Asshole.*

"Don't," I call out, then bite on the inside of my cheek. "Please," I mumble.

"What was that?" he asks.

"Please," I half snarl, "don't go."

He pauses, then shoots me a glance over his shoulders "Admit it first."

"What?"

"That you want me."

I swallow.

He glares at me.

All of my nerve endings pop; a delicious edge of anticipation crackles up my legs, my back. I nod.

"Say it." He lowers his chin, "Tell me you wanted me to caress your pussy, shove my fingers into your cunt, make you wet, drag the moisture around your slit, and bring you to the edge."

My breathing grows shallow and my chest heaves.

"Well?"

"Yes," I sputter. "Yes." Jesus, now I sound like I am about to orgasm and he isn't even touching me. And everything he'd said… It was filthy, and erotic, and no holds barred…and I want it. *Gah!* Maybe that last breakup had gone to my head? On the flip side, I haven't thought about my ex since I got here, huh? Perhaps that's what I need—a firm hand to keep me under control, a jerk-ass to occupy my thoughts and keep them off of my past, and his dick… Admit it. Since seeing that gorgeous cock… All you can think of is how it would feel inside of you—pulling, stretching, filling, bumping up against your innermost walls, driving you higher, higher. My knees seem to buckle. I push my heels into the floor to steady myself.

"You're right," I manage to force out the words. "What you said turned me on."

"That's a start." He draws himself up to his full height, walks back toward me. "Believe me, it's good for you to speak what's on your mind."

"Oh?"

"You have no idea what it does to keep your innermost desires bottled up inside."

"Is that your prognosis?" I mumble.

"That's my advice, as your doctor." His eyes gleam. "Don't hide your needs. Bring them out. Live them, revel in them. It's good for your mind, and of course, your heart." He leans forward places his palm over the skin above my left breast, "Let go of your inhibitions. Put yourself in my hands for this interval of time. I promise, I'll take care of you, Princess Buttercup."

I stare at him. He meets my gaze, unblinking. His features are composed, even sincere. And my soufflé rises every time I make it. Not.

I shuffle my feet. "Well…" I blink rapidly. *It seems too good to be true. Is there a catch? There has to be a catch. An egomaniac like this wouldn't suggest this unless there was something in it to trip me up. But the money, OMG, what I couldn't do with it.*

"You'll stick to your part of the bargain?" I scowl.

His eyes gleam. He holds out his hand, "You have my word."

I glance down at his palm, then back at his face, "Hmm."

"Go on," he cajoles, "I promise, I'll keep my end of the agreement."

"Will you?"

"Try me." His lips curl. Bastard. He's challenging me. Bet he thinks I'll turn tail and run out screaming about now. Which I should, but I won't. Because... Yeah I'm stubborn that way. I haven't come this far by backing down at the first sign of trouble, and no dominant, macho, sexy as fuck, obnoxious prat is going to deprive me of my much-needed holiday, not to mention the opportunity to get a head start on my career...my life. My bloody future beckons. All I have to do is embrace it.

"Fine." I place my hand in his.

His wide palm engulfs mine, warmth from his skin sizzles up my arm. Electricity zings up my spine. *Whoa. The hell was that?* I try to pull back my hand, he holds on.

"You good, Princess?"

No.

No.

"Of course," I stutter. "Why would you think otherwise?"

He surveys my features, "You seem pale."

My guts twist. *Bloody hell, this is happening. This is really, really happening.* My stomach flips and my heart thumps in my chest. *Damn... What the hell am I doing?*

"You not going to faint or anything, are you?" he asks.

I stiffen; my head instantly clears. "Of course not," I huff.

He nods, "Also...you're welcome."

I blink. *No, no, don't react. Don't say anything to this obnoxious bonehead.* He pauses a few inches from me. Sweat breaks out on my forehand. "For what?" I force out the words, knowing I shouldn't, but wanting to know what twisted notion his very clever mind has thought up.

"For accepting my invitation to the most exclusive private New Year's Eve party in London."

I open my mouth to refuse, but he shakes his head, "Think before you say anything. Trust me, you want to be there. The kind of contacts you'll make there will give you a lead over your nearest competitor."

I firm my lips together, mind racing.

"The list of guests is a who's who of the well-connected from around the world. It's perfect to build contacts, invaluable for a fledgling business like yours."

I peer into his face. Is he making fun of me? Trying to undermine my efforts as a business person? But his features take on a sincere expression. Hmph. Not that I am buying it, but he has a point. It won't hurt to be there. Invitations to those kinds of events…are like gold dust. Of course, I could work hard…but being at the right place, at the right time… Well, that's when things get interesting.

"I…guess…that makes sense," I venture.

He nods. "If we last until then." He smirks.

"Is that a challenge?"

"No, it's a fact. Do you think you can get through our time together without walking out in a huff?

8

-----

5 mins later

Weston

"OMG, you're such an ass."

She marches out of the house, slamming the door behind her. The crash reverberates through the living room. Max whines and runs to the exit. He scratches at the door, then barks and jumps up onto it.

"Hey buddy." I amble toward the puppy and scoop him up. He stares up at me with soulful eyes; a small whine catches in his throat.

"What?" I growl. "Why are you making those moony faces at me?"

What the—? Am I talking in some kind of puppy lingo with him? I mean, seriously. I scowl at him. "Don't go thinking you can soften my heart or anything." I frown.

He blinks at me.

I angle my head.

He tips up his head and licks my face, my mouth…

"Hey—" I arch my neck, but am no match for the little guy's persistent slobbering. A chuckle rumbles up my throat. Who'd have thought I'd be giving in to a mutt, of all things?

"You want me to go get her, huh?"

He licks his chops, and I swear, he jerks his little head.

"What the — ?" I frown, "You can't understand me, can you?"

He pops his head on my shoulder, gazes at me with those soulful brown eyes, pleading, asking… Something hot stabs at my chest. *That… is probably my ego having a cardiac. The fuck am I thinking? And I am supposed to be a heart surgeon. Duh.* If anyone knows the ins and outs of that particular organ, it's me, and here I am, imagining all kinds of ridiculous things. Blame it on the pup. Blame it on that sassy, little Buttercup, who had taken one look at the bedroom…and the queen-sized bed in there, and had thrown up her hands in disgust. She'd marched right out — still holding onto her handbag and that infernal satchel-like bag over her back, and banged the door shut.

"It's not my fault. You know that, right?" I address the puppy. "She should have asked if there was a second bedroom. Hell, she could have asked to inspect the premises before agreeing." I frown. "Why hadn't she?" I muse. "Why had she agreed so easily to the arrangement? I mean, sure, six mil is a lot… " I glower at the little dog, who stares back, unblinking. Had I wanted her to turn it down? Show me that she was different from the other women I'd dated so far? And what? I'd expected her to throw it in my face and walk out? I raise my shoulders.

Well, my conscience is clear, at least. I am more than compensating her for her time... Which begs the question, "What the hell had I been thinking when I'd asked her to stay? And accompany me for the Christmas visit to my family…?" I ask the mutt. It had seemed like a brilliant idea — two birds, one stone, and all that. And the little fact that we'd have to share the bed? Hell, I hadn't thought of it until she'd walked into the room, but it's going to make things entertaining, for sure, huh?

The puppy yawns.

"Thanks." My lips twist. "You sure know how to handle me, little bugger, huh?"

He licks my mouth again.

I wince. "Okay, not sure how I feel about that."

He whines again, wriggles in my hold. I put him down and he runs to the exit. I follow him, shove open the door, and he races down the steps to the parked car. He leaps on the door. She opens it, careful not to hurt him… He jumps inside. Through the darkness, I make out the two of them in the front seat.

I watch for a second longer. Is she wearing her coat? I don't think she took it with her. So that means she is wearing that skimpy blouse… in the biting cold. At least, she had her boots back on.

I march inside, shrug into my coat, grab hers, then stalk to the car. I reach the passenger side, try the handle. it's unlocked. *The hell?* I slip inside, drop the coat on the space between the seats, "You forgot this." I glare at her.

She pales, holds the puppy closer.

Max snuggles into her breasts, and stares at me.

His expression implies he's got something I don't. I scowl at him and he pants, tongue lolling. *Is the damn mutt laughing at me? And now I'm jealous of a bloody puppy? The hell? Do I still have my balls?*

I glare at her profile. "Why didn't you lock the bloody door?" my voice booms out in the space.

Max whines.

She frowns. "Do you have a thing for scaring helpless puppies?"

"Not as much as for ensuring that sassy women don't get themselves kidnapped."

"Who's going to kidnap me here?" She waves a hand in the air.

"Things are not as safe as they seem."

She huffs, "You're acting too dramatic."

"No, that's you."

She strokes Max's head and addresses him, "What are you doing here?"

"If you're going to stay in the car, you may as well turn on the heater."

"It's my car—"

"No mistaking that." I glance around the cramped space. My knees are almost doubled up in front of me. I lean down, grab the lever to push the seat back.

"What are you doing—?"

The grip comes off in my hand. I stare at it.

"Yeah… I was going to warn you…" Her voice trails off.

"Does this thing even start up?" I reach for the car keys, but she grabs them first.

"Stop insulting KITT."

I stare. "You named your car after—"

"Knight Rider." She nods, then brightens. "You know about the series?"

"This isn't anything like that KITT," I growl.

"Shh," she pats the dash, "you'll upset her."

"Of course, your car had to be female." A headache begins to drum behind my eyes.

"Why not? KITT isn't the prerogative for a male name."

"What-fucking-ever." I massage my temples.

"You're a sore loser."

"The only thing getting sore here are my knees."

"I know you're getting along in your years...but maybe you need to get that looked at."

I scowl.

Her lips kick up and her entire face brightens. Damn, when she smiles, her features resemble those of an angel... *No. What?* Hello, bloody Christmas spirit must be getting to me.

"I'm not old."

"You're older than me."

"You're what, twenty-five?" I snicker.

"If you wanted to know my age, you only had to ask."

"Like I bloody care?"

She purses her lips, "Don't swear in front of the baby."

That's when something inside of me snaps. *Of all the annoying, getting-on-my-nerves, blonde-haired bombshells in the world... This...tiny, pint-sized, sassy-as-fuck, with the sexiest tits-that-I-want-to-suck-on-like-cotton-candy woman walks into my house... Yeah, my place... Mine. Hold on. The fuck am I calling mine? Her? The cabin ... Yeah, that's what I'm referring to. That's all it is. It's not about her... Not at all. Naw. Hold on... Did I compare her breasts to a treat...? Cotton candy? What the fuck?* I reach forward, grab her shoulder.

She squeaks.

Max growls in his throat.

I shoot him a dirty look. Fucker changed camps, deserted me so easily... Wait until he comes looking for treats. *Guess who wears the pants around here, you mutt!*

Max whines.

"Hey," she hunches her shoulders over the puppy, "back off, you big bully."

"Not happening." I firm my grip on her. She winces but doesn't back down. *Hmm.* This woman has a backbone, all right. I am going to take so much pleasure in breaking her down. "Get out of the car," I growl.

"No." She firms her lips.

"You have until I count to five."

"Whatever." She continues to pat the puppy's head.

"Four." I set my jaw.

"Count faster." She rubs behind Max's ears and the mutt makes a contented sound. *Hell. How dare she ignore me...for a...a dog?* She is fucking with my head, all right.

"Three." I lower my chin.

"Guess he knows his numbers, huh?" she sing-songs to the puppy.

My pulse begins to race.

"Two." I move in closer.

"I am soo scared," she simpers

Adrenaline spikes my blood. My pulse thuds at my temples, behind my eyelids, even in my fucking balls. "Don't say I didn't warn you," I lower my voice to a hush. She pales, a visible shudder running up her spine. *Good.*

"One." I apply just enough pressure so she turns to me.

"What are you doin—?" Her gaze widens.

I yank her toward me, puppy and all, lower my lips to her taunting mouth.

9

———————

"I could give up chocolate, but I am not a quitter."
-From Amelie's diary

Amelie

Warmth, heat, the hardness of his chest digging into my breasts... But his lips...his lips... They're soft and coaxing...and completely not what I expected. Not after how he'd grasped my shoulder... Certainly not, after how he'd kissed me that first time...all demanding and dominating... Oh, he's still ruthless, hellbent on taking from me... But with his mouth, he seduces me. He nibbles on my lower lip and I part them. He swipes his tongue across the seam of my mouth, and a moan trembles up my throat. He releases my shoulder, only to cup my cheek. His warm breath mixes with mine and I draw of his in greedy gulps. I want to bottle that essence of his, roll around in it, absorb in it, bathe in it, let it tease my core, slink up my channel... *Argh!* Everything in me wants him to lick me down there with as much finesse as he's demonstrating with his very able mouth. "Wes," I hear myself plead with him... *Did I say that aloud or was I simply thinking it in my mind?* He tilts his head, easing his tongue over mine. A ripple of pleasure darts up my spine. All thoughts drain from my head. I move in closer, strain against his chest. Bring my arms around his—a whine cuts through the air.

I pull away, but he holds me in place. "Ignore him."

"But..."

"The pooch will survive."

"He's getting restless," I insist. "Did you take him out earlier?""

"Open the door and let him out."

"No." I stare at him. "Out here?"

"It's a gated property," he replies.

I turn down my lips and he glares at me. A frisson of something—nervousness, fear, something I can't quite identify—quivers in my stomach. I lick my lips and his gaze drops there. Those colorless eyes seem to turn into mirrors—cold, hard. He could cut me, and hurt me, rip me apart, and I'd enjoy it all. I gulp, the sound audible. He jerks his chin up, then draws in a breath. "Fuck," he growls, "you owe me."

"What—?

He reaches across me and I shudder, then almost cry out when he straightens. He cuddles the puppy against his chest, "Stay," he growls.

Is he talking to me? Before I can respond, he's shoved open the door, and stalked toward the house. What the hell is he up to?

He pushes open the door, squats down to lower the puppy to the floor, then pats him. Even now, when he's angry with me, he can't resist making sure the puppy is comfortable, huh? The man may disagree, but it's clear to me that he has a soft spot for the pet... Which, surely, shows that he isn't all that alphaholish as he makes himself out to be, huh?

He rises to his feet.

Which doesn't mean I am going to stay out here and wait for him to come back. And what? Finish what he started? The way he'd kissed me earlier... Softly, gently, revealing that part of him I'd sensed under those layers of brutishness... If he did it again, I know I'd give in to him... And hell, if I am going to let that happen. At the very least, I am not going to give in to him that easily.

He turns.

I shove open my car door and race out.

"Hey," his voice follows me.

I pick up speed.

"Stop. Where are you going?"

Good question. If I'd wanted to get away, all I'd have had to do was turn the keys, start the car, and drive away; I'd have had to wait while the gates opened, but I'd have managed to leave. Which I hadn't.

And it's not like I can leave the property, considering I have no way of opening the gates now.

So, what is this? A dash for freedom, to show him that I don't mean to obey him? Do I want him to chase me? Either way, I'm not going to give in so easily.

"Amelie," his voice whips through the still night… My name from his lips…? Ohmigod! A thrill runs down my spine. Moisture laces my core. I increase my pace.

If he wants me, he has to come and get me.

I pound down the driveway.

"Princess." He's so close. Adrenaline laces my blood; a giggle catches in my throat. *What the hell am I doing? What's wrong with me? Am I toying with him? With myself? Doesn't matter.* This is one race I plan to win. I plan to… Something—someone—his big arms catch me around my waist. I scream as the ground comes up to meet me. The next second, I am hauled up and around, and against that firm chest. Heat from his body surrounds me, envelops me; my thighs clench; my scalp tingles. A burst of excitement ignites in my veins. "Let me go," I squeak.

"No."

He drops my coat—he'd picked it up from the car?—and yanks me up to my toes, thrusts his face into mine, "Where the hell do you think you are going?"

"Somewhere… Anywhere… To get away from you."

"What if I don't let you leave?"

"Do you want me to stay?" I jut my chin, daring him. *Say it, do it. Just one word… Anything to show you're as affected with this…chemistry between us.*

He looks me up and down, "I don't care either way."

Jerk. My insides twist; anger sputters up my spine. He releases me so suddenly, that I stumble. Then right myself. *Goddamn him.*

I stand there and watch that snickerdoodle of a man bend to pick my coat.

He straightens and his shoulders once more block my line of sight. I take in how his waist tapers down to meet his powerful thighs. My mouth waters. My fingers itch. I want to reach out and trace the cut abs outlined by his shirt.

His lips kick up. Heat flushes my cheeks. Of course he is well aware of the effect of his nearness on me.

He tilts his head, "Have you decided?"

I peer up into his face, rake my gaze across his strong features, that mean upper lip, his broad jaw. My nipples pucker and my toes curl. What would happen if I stayed? And if I leave? Will I always wonder how it would have been to spend a few days with him?

"Amelie?" His voice is impatient.

"I.... I...am not sure," I stutter.

He peruses my features. "Turn around," he orders.

I do. I sense him close the distance between us, then he drops the coat over my shoulders. I shove my hands through the sleeves, and he pivots me to face him. I stare at that broad chest that's going to haunt my dreams for a long time. *Hell.*

He places his knuckles under my chin, applies pressure so I have to tilt my head up. I meet his gaze.

"You can leave now," his voice is harsh, "or you can come into the warmth."

"Come into the parlor, said the spider to the fly," I mumble.

"Oh, you're no fly, Buttercup." He grunts, "More of an annoying, pesky mosquito."

"And you're what…an octopus?"

"I can certainly wrap my arms and legs around you in a similar fashion." He chuckles. "To keep you warm, of course."

"Of course." I draw in a breath, "Fine, I'll stay."

"Good."

"On one condition."

"You don't make the rules, babe." His voice is soft, almost playful. His eyes take on that flinty look I'm coming to anticipate, and hate. My toes curl.

"But I'll let you have your say," he adds, "this time."

"You…you'll sleep on the couch," I state.

"No."

"Fine, I'll sleep on the couch." I tip up my chin.

"You think I'd let you do that?"

"Why not?" I scowl.

"A deal is a deal." His grin widens, "Six days—same house, *same bed.* You'll cook and clean and do everything I ask of you. Every day you complete, I deposit one million pounds in your account."

I gulp. OMG, I'm going to do this. I am. I can't turn this down. I tried. I went so far as trying to run away, but who am I kidding?

I can never turn down a challenge; and I admit, a tiny part of me is curious about whether I can actually resist him. I have to, of course. Otherwise, I'll lose any measure of self-confidence I have in myself.

I pull back; his hands drop away. I tug the coat closed, then turn and walk around him toward the house. I reach the porch steps, then turn around, "Coming?"

He scowls. My insides knot. Guess he's not happy I took the lead. Too bad. I don't care that he's pissed-off. That seems to be his perpetual state of mind. But why does he have to be so hot when he glowers at me? I reach the door, then turn again. "Would you bring in my remaining luggage, while you're at it?" I suppress a giggle as I walk into the cabin.

10

Weston

"What the fuck do you have in them, stones?" I'd hauled her bag over the threshold of the house, and into the bedroom.

"Did you pack for a month?" I glower.

"I believe in traveling with everything I need."

"Clearly," I mutter.

Grabbing a bottle of beer from the kitchen, I return and prop myself on the bed.

"What are you doing?" She drags her second suitcase into the bedroom.

"What does it look like?"

She dumps the bag in the middle of the floor of the room, "Why don't you drink in the living room?"

"My house."

"It's not yours," she huffs. "You co-own it with the Seven."

"Semantics," I grumble. "It's more mine than yours, at any rate."

She opens her mouth.

I shake my head. "What made you decide to become a pastry chef?"

She blinks. "Why do you want to know?"

Good question. Why the hell do I care? Except I am intrigued… Fine, I want to understand what makes this bundle of energy tick.

"I don't care either way," I take a healthy swig of the beer, "but it's the kind of conversation you women seem to love."

She opens and shuts her mouth, then straightens, "So this is your idea of being polite?"

"Nope," I finish off the beer, place the bottle on the sideboard, "but this is." I yank my shirt over my head, toss it aside.

"What are you doing?" she squeaks.

"What do you think?" I rise to my feet, drop my pants, along with my boxers.

Her indrawn breath fills the space. I don't stop the grin that tugs at my lips. Buttercup can deny it all she wants, but the attraction between us is alive and kicking. It's making this entire exercise a hell of a lot more interesting. It's definitely the reason I'm allowing her to stay. If nothing else, to see how far I can go before I stop resisting her. I get back into bed, pull the covers up to my waist, then switch off the lamp on my side, leaving the room in darkness.

Silence for a beat, then another.

"How is this polite?" her voice cracks. She clears her throat, "Seriously, can you enlighten me here?"

"I'm sleeping on my side of the bed, aren't I?"

"Gah." She makes a sound deep in her throat.

A chuckle rumbles up my throat. I swallow it. "You're welcome."

I hear her moving around, then, "Why is this clock not working?"

I glance up to find her holding the digital timepiece in her hands. She turns it over, fiddles with the little compartment at the back, "Huh, it has no batteries." She turns to me, "Did you do that?" She frowns.

My heartbeat begins to race. "I don't know what you're talking about." I sink back into my pillow, close my eyes.

"The clock in the living room, too, had been dismantled."

What the hell does she want to know? Why can't she leave it alone already?

"Do you have something against clocks or something? Maybe you don't like the idea of time running out?" She chuckles.

I turn my back on her.

I hear her open the drawers, "Okay I found the batteries. I am going to—"

"Put it back." I snap.

"What?"

"Put the bloody clock back where you found it."

There's a pause.

"If you don't do it, I swear I'll come there and make you do it."

She huffs. There's a click as she places the timepiece back on the table.

"I've returned the batteries to the drawer," she mutters. "So don't get your dander up about it."

The breath I'd not been aware of holding rushes out.

Shit, the hell is wrong with me? Why the hell am I getting worked up over this little thing? It is a clock—a functioning clock. Doesn't mean anything. *Why the hell can't I bear the thought of it counting down the time as I sleep?*

The numbers mounting, the hands moving, the tick-tock-tick-tock of the countdown as he'd watched me closely, peered into my face, searched for a reaction, anything to show I was afraid, that I'd give in and break, ask for help. Ask it, do it. My heart thunders in my chest. Close your eyes. Count down the time.

Twelve o'clock.

Eleven o'clock—

I hear the sound of something connecting with that massive suitcase. Then a howl, "Bloody hell!"

I switch on the light. "What are you doing?"

She sits on the ground, nursing one booted foot. "Taking out my frustration, you oaf." Her hair flows about her shoulders. Her cheeks are pink. From anger? From embarrassment at seeing me naked? Considering she's already had her mouth on my dick… Well, isn't that cute.

"There are better ways of dealing with it." I lower my gaze to her heaving breasts.

"Aargh, stop that." She yanks off one boot, then the other. "Turn away."

"Why?"

"I want to undress, you… you neanderthal."

I laugh, "Running out of insults?"

"Oh, I have plenty where that came from." She pulls off her other boot, then rises to her feet. "Some privacy please?"

"Not happening." I lean back against the headboard, fold an arm behind my neck. Her gaze darts to my biceps; she swallows. I scratch my chest and her breasts heave. A glimmer of sweat gleams over her upper lip. "Is it too hot in here for you?" I grin.

She huffs, then undoes the button of her coat and pushes it off her shoulder. She glances around, then walks to the closet and pulls it open.

She surveys the contents, then hangs it up. "You didn't bring too many clothes, did you?" she grumbles.

"Worried about me?" I smirk.

She throws up her hands, then steps back and slams the closet doors shut, "It's pointless making any conversation with you."

"You were the one who declined to answer my question."

"Whatever." She pulls off her jeans, giving me a flash of pink underwear. My groin instantly tightens. *Fuck.* She is more modestly dressed than women wearing skimpy bikinis on the beach... So why does she seem so much more alluring, so attractive...? So fucking gorgeous, as she folds her jeans then places them on the chair near the bed. She lifts a corner of the cover, then slips inside. She stays on the far end... Right at the end. "Any further and you'll slip off."

"I'll manage."

"I won't bite."

"Ha," she snorts, "famous last words."

"Unless you want me to?"

She stills. Tension pours off of her to fill the space between us on the bed. I switch off the light, then fold my arms over my chest. "If you stay that stiff, I'll have to tickle you."

"Wh...what?" she squeaks.

"Not good for your muscles to be so bunched up. You'll have a headache when you wake up."

"Like you care?"

"A deal is a deal, Buttercup."

"I wish you wouldn't call me that."

"I wish you'd relax a little."

If anything, she tenses further. I turn away from her, close my eyes. The stress that rolls off of her slams into my back. My shoulders bunch, My muscles coil, ready to spring... *Fuck.* I turn back to her, scoot over.

Her gaze widens, "What are you — ?"

"Hush." I pull her to me, so her back is pressed into my chest, then I spoon her.

She makes a noise of alarm.

I tighten my arm around her waist. "Raise your head."

"What?"

"Do it, woman," I snap.

She does as I ask. *Fuck, finally.* I slip my arm under her neck, throw my leg over hers.

She doesn't say a word. Nothing. Her entire body goes stiff... As hard as my dick, which instantly lengthens. It nestles against the curve of her hip. Well, someone's happy, at least. I tuck her head under my chin.

"Weston," she whispers.

I sigh, "Now what?"

"What is it with you and clocks? Do you have a phobia or something?"

Or something. Not that I am going to tell her about it. I'd already given away enough with that half-arsed fit I'd thrown. Shit, do I have my balls about me or what?

"Weston—"

"Goodnight, Princess."

She huffs, but stay's silent.

Thank fuck.

I close my eyes, count back the time on the hands of a clock. Restart the stopwatch.

Twelve o' clock.

Eleven o'clock.

Her shoulder muscles relax.

Ten o'clock.

Nine o'clock.

Her breathing grows more uniform.

Eight o'clock.

Seven o'clock.

She wriggles her butt. The blood rushes to my groin.

Six o'clock.

She thrusts her feet in between my legs. The coldness from her toes shivers over my skin. I swear aloud, "Did you dip your feet in ice?"

"Sorry," she mutters.

Five o'clock.

Four o' clock.

She pushes her body into mine. My cock lengthens, stabs into the valley between her butt cheeks.

Three o'clock.

She rubs her cheek against the pillow. Then digs her toes into my calf. "The hell are you doing?" I grouse.

"Can't sleep," she mumbles.

I turn her over to face me. *Mistake.* The moonlight floods in from the

open window, highlighting her baby blues. Her hair clings to her forehead; her nose turns up above those gorgeous pink lips. My heart stutters. It fucking stutters. The fuck? "What is it?" I grumble.

"I forgot the chocolate."

"Chocolate?"

"And I need fresh eggs, cinnamon, butter —"

"You've lost me."

"To make breakfast."

I shudder and mime throwing up in my mouth. "Who has chocolate
for breakfast?"

She laughs. "Chocolate pancakes, dummy." Then she adds, "What do
you like to eat in the morning?"

"Anything but chocolate." I grumble.

"Wh-a-a-t?" Her eyes go all round, "You don't like chocolate?"

"Why settle for chocolate, when," I drag my gaze down her body,
"there are other things that make for a tastier breakfast."

She gapes, "Do you only think of sex?"

"Do you only think of desserts?"

"What else is there?" her voice cracks.

I scan her pink-tinged features. "Are you blushing?"

"Of course, not." Her face grows fiery.

"What are you thinking?"

"Nothing."

Oh, it was something all right. "Go on, you can tell me."

She shakes her head.

I glare at her, lower my voice to a hush, "Say it."

She trembles. "I… I was thinking how much I'd like for you to eat
me out."

Amelie

What the hell am I doing? Why did I blurt that out? I'd honestly not realized
that it was what I had in mind, until he'd commanded me to speak…
And hell, when he assumes that voice, that hushed tone which whips
through my mind, I can't stop myself. I have to obey him. *But did I have to
tell him the truth? Couldn't I have deflected?*

His nostrils flare and his grip on my waist tightens. "Say that again," he rasps.

"I… I…" My throat closes. How can I repeat what had come out in a moment of utter lunacy?

"Complete your sentence," his hot breath sears my lips. My panties instantly dampen. My thighs clench and I can't stop the small whine that spills from my mouth.

"Ask…and you shall receive." His lips curl. An answering quiver thrums at my center. *OMFG! I can't even… This man… How can I refuse him anything? Why the hell had I agreed to stay…? Is that why I hadn't wanted to leave?* I blink; all thoughts empty from my mind.

"Please," I breathe out. "Eat me."

Even before the words are out of my mouth, he's flipped me on my back, "With pleasure, Alice." He smirks from above me.

"A…are you my white rabbit?"

"You'll have to let me know."

I blink, then heat sears my cheeks. Is he alluding to my favorite vibrator? "That's not what I—" My breath hitches as he slides down my body.

His hard chest presses down on my breasts, my belly, then his head is between my thighs. He shoulders apart my legs, places one of my hands on his ear, then the other on the other side. "Hold on." His eyes glitter.

"What the—"?" I gasp, then tighten my fingers around his ears, for he's buried his face in my pussy.

He nuzzles my flesh.

I whimper.

He blows on my throbbing core, and hell, but I almost come right then.

"Not yet, Buttercup." I sense his lips curve against my center.

"Don't…don't stop," I gasp.

"Hmm," he makes an appreciative sound deep in his throat.

All of my nerve endings seem to explode.

"Which dessert should I sample first, you think?"

"Wait," I gasp.

He peers up at me.

"The arrangement."

"What of it?"

"You said no sex."

"So?"

"Does this count as sex?"

"I thought we already covered this, Buttercup."

"As long as you don't…uh…you don't—"

"Sink my dick into your pussy?"

My cheeks flush, "Yeah, no penetration, in the traditional fashion, equals no sex, right?"

"Sure, if that's how you want to see it."

"I…"

He drags his fingers up my pussy lips.

I huff.

"So?" He smirks.

"Yes…" I force out the word.

He stares back.

"Yes, that's the definition, for the…uh, the arrangement." I clarify, "As long as you don't uh, penetrate my puss—eee" The word comes out on a whine for he's replaced his finger with his mouth. OMG. OMG. A moan trembles from my lips.

"My, my, Buttercup," he mutters against my core, " is this how greedy you are when you bake?"

What the—? I blink. Why is he still talking? Didn't his mom teach him not to talk when his mouth is full? Why can't he—?

He raises his head. Cool air envelops the heated, melting triangle between my legs, right before he slaps my pussy. Right on it, across my swollen core, which erupts in a miasma of sparks, that travels out from the contact, up my spine, and explodes behind my eyes. The room tilts. *Ohmigod.* Sweat beads my brow. The pain fades, leaving behind an ache that swallows me up from the center. "What was that for?" I shudder.

"Answer the question, doll."

"Wh…which one?"

"Should I taste you here?" He dips his head, slips his tongue inside my backhole.

My entire body snaps to attention. All of my pores pop. My chest rises and falls.

"Or here?" He drags his wicked tongue up my slit.

I moan.

"Maybe I should be as greedy as you and not wait?" He fixes that instrument of torture-pleasure, aka his mouth, around my throbbing bud, and I shoot upfrom the bed.

"Wes!" I howl.

He releases my pussy. "You still haven't answered the question," he rumbles.

"Wh…what?"

"Last chance, babe."

He leans back, and I thrust up with my pelvis, trying to recapture that earlier feeling, honing in on his tongue.

"Well?" he asks. "You need to ask for what you want, darlin'."

Maybe it's that endearment that makes me crack my eyes open. "All of it," I gasp. "Please lick me, suck on me, thrust your tongue inside my —" I huff, for he's done just that.

He twists his tongue inside of me and goosebumps flare on my skin. He slides his big arms under my legs, pushes up my knees on either side of my body, then he swipes his tongue in and out of me, and again. He slurps his way down to my backhole and up to my cunt again and again. I cry out, but he doesn't stop. He slips his tongue in between my pussy lips, samples me like I am the tastiest puff pastry. He bites down on my clit and I scream, dig my fingers into the space behind his ears and yank.

A growl rumbles up his chest and the vibrations swell my core, pour over me like the sound waves from a fucking dinner gong— *Wait, why am I thinking with this bizarre metaphor?* Except, hell, if I am not ready, I'm going to…

"Come," he growls into my hot, melting core, and I explode.

My climax crashes over me, shoves me up…up…up. Maybe I black out. I force myself to open my eyelids, look down to where he's still between my legs, my knees splayed out. "Wow," I breathe.

He doesn't smile back. He stares at me. His gaze unwavering.

"What?" I croak.

"You ready, yet?"

"Huh?"

He drops his mouth, nuzzles my pussy.

I moan, "I can't."

"I haven't even started, babe."

"No…no."

He licks my lower lips and pleasure radiates out from my core.

"Oh, my God."

"Hold on," he says.

"What?"

He rises up, grabs my wrists and holds them over my head. He wraps my fingers around the wooden bars of the headboard. "Stay," he commands.

I stare at him. *As if I could move.*

One side of his lips kicks up; he presses a firm kiss to my lips, then slides down to position his face over my pussy. He grabs my knees, pries them further apart so I am splayed wide for him. I should blush or feel shy, for heaven's sake. Those are my most intimate parts, served up to him for display; but all I can think is, *please... please... please.*

"Lick or suck?" he asks.

"Anything, either... Both," I gasp out.

He glares at me.

I shiver... "Anything you want."

"Right answer."

He drops his head and thrust his tongue back inside my melting channel.

"Oh, my God," I whine. "More, please, don't stop...don't..." I push myself up and into his face, not caring what he thinks of me. Any restraint holding me back is gone. Poof. All he has to do is touch me and I'll do anything for him. Damn it, I should have known that... But I'm not sleeping with him.. Yet. I mean, technically this doesn't count. Like the blowjob... Anything other than full penetration... Yep, that's it; anything else is fine. It is. "Fuck me with your mouth, please," I plead.

He laughs, "One fuck-me-with-your-mouth, coming up." He releases my knees, only to grip my arsecheeks. He squeezes down and I whine. He pries them apart. *What the—?* He hauls me up, slips his tongue down and inside my arsehole. *Oh, my f'ing god.* It's like nothing I have experienced before. No one...has touched me there, and this man? He slides his tongue into that forbidden part of me... As if, as if... We are lovers. No, fuckbuddies... Not... Anything-but-fucking-buddies, that's what we are. A giggle wells up, turns into a scream, when he begins to fuck my backhole with his tongue. He thrusts in and out, in and out, brings his hand up to grind his heel against my clit, and that tightness inside of me snaps out, expands... "Wes..." I moan. "Weston..."

He doesn't answer. He can't, because his mouth is full of me.

"Wes. Wes. Wes," I chant. *Aloud, or in my mind?* No matter, if food is a religious experience for me, then his tongue-fucking me has to count as a close second. The orgasm screeches up my legs, up my spine.

He slides his tongue out, replaces it with his finger, another, then shoves his tongue inside my pussy.

"Weston," I scream.

He releases my other knee and grabs my breast, squeezes my nipple so hard, stars burst behind my eyes.

"Oh, my God, I am going to…going to…"

He slips his thumb inside my mouth, at the same time that he crooks his fingers inside my backhole, then tears his mouth from my pussy and growls, "Come."

11

Weston

Her body bucks, her spine curves, she opens her mouth, but no sound emerges. Her eyes roll back in her head as she shatters. I tilt my head, lick up the cum from between her pussy lips. *So fucking sweet. Is she made of the sugar that she likes to bake with?* Her climax seems to go on and on. Her shoulders jerk, her head thrown back, and the arch of her throat beckons.

I crawl up her body, fit my mouth to hers. I slide my fingers inside her pussy, she moans, and I swallow it up. I swipe my tongue over hers, tasting our joined-up essences. I drag my other hand up the curve of her waist. She shivers. I cup her cheek, lean back and peer into her features, "Look at me."

Her eyelids flutter. Those blue eyes peek up at me, pupils blown, still high on the orgasm. Something hot stabs at my chest. I flip over on the bed, pulling her with me. I coil her over my chest. Another spasm runs up her spine. I tug her closer, wrap her up in my arms.

Fuck, fuck, fuck, what am I doing? I hadn't meant for it to get this... intense, this complicated. *Keep things light, stay away from all entanglements,* has always been my motto. And I've succeeded so far, haven't I? I had asked her to stay...because I'd thought it would be entertaining. Okay so that's not the full truth. The last time I'd spoken to my mother, she'd asked me if I'd met anyone yet. It is the one thing—the only thing—she wants from me. For me, I guess. It had been a flash of instinct that had had me stipulating she come along to the Christmas dinner. My family... They'd pulled me out of the depression I had fallen into after the 'incident' when I had been kidnapped along with the rest of the Seven. They'd reassured me, never allowing me to falter.

The incident had turned everything upside down. The only people who had seemed to get me after that were the rest of the Seven, and not only because they were, each of them, mean motherfuckers, as unfeeling as me... It was the shared experience of the days that had changed our lives, scarred each of us in similar, yet unique, ways.

Still, my parents had been encouraging, supportive, taken me to therapy, tolerated my outbursts at them as I'd struggled to come to terms with what had happened. They had been stellar in their roles and duties toward me. It's not their fault I've turned out to be an asshole. Blame that on me... Maybe it's the way I was born.

So, it had been a spur of the moment decision that she accompany me to see my family for Christmas. *The hell had I been thinking?*

This pint-sized woman with the sassy attitude, honeyed mouth, and a cunt that tastes like all the forbidden delights she specializes in baking —has clearly addled my thought processes.

I drag my fingers down the waterfall of her golden hair. Softer than cookie dough— *What the fuck? I do not think in food metaphors.* Her proximity is definitely affecting me. I stay still, watch her eyeballs move behind her now-closed eyelids. She snuggles into me; her breathing deepens. I stay still until her body twitches. She's definitely out cold. Apparently, I tired her out. Too bad I can't say the same about me. My muscles coil and bunch, my mind racing. I need to figure out what the hell to do with her. My proposal stands, but the boundaries are blurring... Hell, I am still here, holding her, caressing her, watching her as she sleeps. The fuck is up with that? I ease her down onto the bed. She doesn't stir. Good.

I slide out of bed, pull the duvet over her. Turning, I crash into her suitcase, which plops over. I glance over to find she's still sleeping. I shake my head. What I wouldn't give to be able to switch off like that, huh? Since the incident... I've never slept for more than three, maybe four hours a night. Useful when you're at medical school and need to study before exams… A bitch at any other time. I pull on my jeans, a sweatshirt over my long-sleeved T, socks and boots.

Grabbing my phone from the side table, I walk through the living room, Max stirs from his rug near the fireplace, lifting his head. I go over, pat him on his flank. He licks my hand, then burrows into the special cushion I'd ordered for him. Hey, don't go all gooey-eyed. It was simply to ensure he'd be comfortable enough to not want to share my bed, okay?

I slip out onto the back porch. Early dawn lights up the horizon as I head toward the shed at the back of the property. I open the door and walk in, then head for the work bench. I switch on the desk lamp, and when my phone buzzes, I slide it out of my pocket, swipe the screen.

"Hey, motherfucker," Damian's image fills the space.

"Same to you, dickwad," I mutter.

"What's gotten into you?" He peers into the screen as if he's there in real life with me.

"What's gotten into you?" I growl. Now I'm doing the fucking NLP mirroring shit Buttercup had talked about. *Why the hell am I thinking about her, huh? Didn't I come here to get away from her? Huh? Had she actually pushed me out of my own space?* I scratch my jaw. Now, that would be the first.

"Uh-oh." Damian clicks his tongue, "I've seen that look before."

"What bloody look?" I frown.

"The one that says you're about to fall."

"Fall?"

"For her."

"Who?"

"The woman who's there in the country manor—"

"Cabin," I correct him.

"Whatever." He grins, "Admit it. You're attracted to her.'

"What shit are you talking about?" I grumble.

"You denying you hooked up with a woman in a difficult-to-reach place?"

"It's four hours away from London."

"My point exactly," he smirks.

"You city fox."

"So are you," he replies, "which is why, when Saint mentioned that you were going to be there, and not alone…"

"Hold on." I rub my temple, "Saint told you I was going to be here with a woman?'

"Aren't you?"

"That's not the point." I tilt my head, "How did he know that I was here…ah!" I stiffen. "That cunt," I growl. "He fucking played me, didn't he?"

"Hold on, I'm adding Arpad to the call," Damian says.

"What? No," I protest.

Too late. The screen blinks, then Arpad appears in another window. "Hey, bitches, you're chin-wagging like old ladies, I see."

"Hey, fuckface," I growl, "why aren't you in a boat in the middle of somewhere with no reception?"

"I have my own satellite, dickwad."

"Of course, you do." I rake my fingers through my hair. "Why are you guys calling me, anyway?"

"Checking in, ol' chap." Damian chuckles, "Making sure you're still alive after that face-off."

What face-off?

"You and Amelie…?" Damian prompts.

"What is it with you guys?" I crack my jaw from side to side, "Can't you give a man space?"

"Space?" Arpad cackles, "Did he just say what I think he did?"

"Aww, cho chweet," Damian makes kissing sounds.

Arpad cracks up laughing.

My face reddens. "That's it; I'm hanging up now."

"Hold on." Damian pretends to wipe the tears from his face, "You haven't told us what you intend to do with her?"

"What's it to you?" I growl, "And don't talk about her."

"So, it's like that, huh?" Arpad snickers. "You seeing what I'm seeing, Rockstar?" he asks Damian.

Damian stares at me, then shakes his head, "My, my, the doctor who had his arse splashed all over the internet for making a sex tape has met his match, huh?"

"It's a damn fine arse," I grumble, "and if you don't have a sex tape to your credit, you technically are persona non grata in the online world."

"But does she know about it?" Damian asks.

My neck heats and my heart begins to thud. "Why would it matter to her?"

"It would matter if you didn't tell her," Arpad points out, "Hold on, I'm adding the Father to our chinwag, so he doesn't feel left out."

"What the fuck?" I growl as Edward's face appears in another window on the screen.

"Hey Doc, how's it going?" Edward asks.

"It was going all fine and dandy until you lot decided to intrude."

"Sorry to cut in on your alone time with your lady—"

"Not my lady," I grumble.

Damian snickers.

Arpad chortles.

"What the fuck are you jokers laughing at?"

"You, arsehole, and how you've been played."

I scowl, "Fucking Saint."

Damian nods.

"He double-booked me with her. Wait until I get my hands on the dickwad; I'm going to throttle his neck.

"Victoria won't like you getting your hands on her husband."

"Man," I rub the back of my neck, "not that I begrudge them their happiness, not after everything they've been through... But he could have *not* intruded in my life," I grouse.

"Jace, then Sinner, and Saint," Damian drawls. "You'd think it was catching…all that happiness."

"Bull-fucking-shit." I sink into my chair, tip it back. "I'm not falling for whatever madness possessed those knobs to get hitched."

"Just make sure you give me enough notice," Edward pipes in.

"Notice?" I crack my neck, "The hell you going on about Father?"

"If you plan on getting hitched—"

The two front legs of the chair land on the ground with a thump, "Hitched? What the fuck are you talking about?"

"Your last-minute plan that you don't know about yet." Edward stabs a finger at me, "If you're planning on doing it, I need a little notice. I have a life too, you know. I can't always drop everything and put in an appearance to marry you guys, you know—?

"Wait, what?" I run a finger under the collar of my shirt. "You lost me there."

"A million?" Arpad asks Damian.

"Money is beginning to lose its appeal," Damian grumbles.

"You wankers," I growl, "the fuck are you all betting on?"

"We need to up the odds," Arpad replies, as if he didn't hear me. What a tosser.

I grip my phone with such force that my fingers hurt. "Shut the fuck up, you bitches."

"It's happening, all right. You see how he's losing his shit, huh?" Arpad continues.

"What do you suggest?" Damian talks over me, "Wanna play with something a little more personal?"

"What do you have in mind?" Arpad rubs his jaw. "Property? Shares…" He snaps his fingers, "I have it."

"What you thinking of, dipshit?" Damian drawls.

"If he gets married, accept the gift I send you."

"Ooh, thanks darling, for thinking of me," Damian deadpans.

Arpad grimaces, "Cut that shit out. You won't be laughing when you see what is it."

"A woman?" He waggles his eyebrows, "A hot honey, no doubt. Why would I refuse it, huh?"

"You on then?" Arpad asks.

"And if he doesn't?" Damian jerks his chin at me.

"I'm here, you bitches."

"Oh, he will." Arpad smirks, "I present to you exhibit A… Also known as, the man who has no idea that he's counting his last few days of freedom."

"Newsflash, you toffs, I ain't planning on giving up my bachelor status anytime soon, and PS," I growl, "you can't go around placing bets involving the lives of others."

Damian's gaze widens, "Since when has Mr. Obnoxious here, developed a conscience?"

"Since he's the one about whom such bets are being placed?" Edward offers.

"Since he decided to shack up with her?" Arpad replies.

"I am not shacking up with her, you reprobates," I snarl.

"The two of you…in a cabin…in the middle of nowhere…" Arpad waggles his eyebrows.

"It's four hours from London," I remind them again.

"Wait until it snows," Edward chimes in… "I am not marrying you in a remote ceremony."

"For the final time," I jump up from my chair so fast, it crashes back,

"I'm not getting married. She just happens to be here, and I'm putting the time with her to good use."

"No doubt," Damian says with a straight face. "If that's the story you're going with."

"I am taking her home to meet my family."

Silence, then Damian addresses Arpad, "Shit, can I take back that bet I agreed to?"

"Too late, old sport." Arpad chuckles, "Told ya, he won't last the holidays, but wow." He scowls at me, "You've only been with her since yesterday. Isn't that a little too soon...?"

"What are you talking about?" Clearly I am being slow on the uptake here. "And how do all of you know about her—?" Realization dawns. "That fucker—Saint." Anger sweeps my blood, "He let you all in on his dumbass plan?" I roll my shoulders, "Don't you have anything better to do than trade gossip?"

"Aw, he's no longer any more fun," Arpad shakes his head.

"Wankers gone for a toss." Damian grins, "Does that make him a tossing wanker or a wanking tosser?"

"Guys, go easy on him." Edward grins, "He's one dropkick away from having his heart broken."

I raise my phone and bring it down, intent on smashing it, then stop myself. Fuck, if I don't need the bloody device right now. Not that I can't replace it, but if what the Father said is true and snow is on its way... Then hell, all the money in the world couldn't deliver me an alternative mode of communication. Maybe I should have insisted on having the helicopter parked on the helipad in the field. Damn, missed opportunity.

"For the last time, there's nothing between us," I growl. *Why the fuck am I even explaining it to these douchebags, huh?* Maybe it's because they are the closest I have to non-blood family; though right now, I'm not sure if they are my friends or my enemies.

"You don't have to convince us," Arpad nods.

"Right, I don't care about your personal uh—relations. Of course, I care about your state of mind, which at the moment, seems rather frayed at the edges," Edward points out.

"As I was saying," I draw in a breath, "she happens to be here; so am I. We've come to an agreement, and that includes taking her home to get my mother off my back."

"Right, you keep fooling yourself, ol' sport." Damian grins. "Not that

I'm not rooting for you. I mean, I want you to get through the holiday season without getting hitched." He scratches his chin, "Although, if you did get married, I'd still win, in a matter of speaking, so—"

"Fuck you, motherfuckers." I hang up. *What the fuck was that all about?*

The hair on the back of my neck rises and I hear a sound behind me. All of my senses go on alert; I pivot, fists raised.

12

Amelie

"It's me; it's only me," I squeak.

His chest heaves, his color pale. He glares at me as if he's seen a ghost.

"Weston?" I prompt.

His gaze fixes on my face. His jaw tics. The tendons of his throat move. The skin across his knuckles stretches tight. If his control had been less than perfect, I have no doubt, I'd be on the ground, with his fist buried in my face. Hell, I wouldn't mind other parts of him buried inside of me, given what had transpired between us earlier. It's clear that we are as compatible as cheese and biscuits. *WTF?* Enough with the cheesy comparisons... *Noooo, now I am punning on my own poor jokes? Gah!*

"Wes?" I take a step forward; he watches me. I raise a hand; his gaze stays on mine. I reach up on tip toe and cup his cheek. "You okay?"

He blinks, lowers his fists.

A breath I hadn't realized I was holding whooshes out. At the same time, he draws his in.

"Wes?" I step close enough for my boots to kiss his. His gaze intensifies. Those colorless eyes seem to mirror every emotion, every confusion, every screwed-up, mixed-up thought that I feel inside.

"Everything okay?" I ask.

"Why wouldn't it be?" He steps back from me and the heat of his big body recedes.

A hollow feeling coils low in my belly. *What had I been expecting?* That after the way he'd made me orgasm earlier, he'd...be more tender toward me? Maybe throw me down and decide to forget about our 'arrangement' and make love to me? *Hell, I want him to fuck me... There, I've said it out loud. Well, not really out loud, thank God.* I'd settle for him having me any which way—frontways, sideways, bent over, with my arse up in the air for him... My cheeks heat. *Jesus H, something about this man brings out the filthy girl hidden inside of me.* The one who wanted to hold onto more than his ears as I rode him off into the sunset. Huh? That picture... It's hot... And all wrong.

"What are you doing here?" He frowns.

"I, uh, woke up and you were gone—"

He looks me up and down, "Is that a... What are you wearing?"

I glance down at my pullover. "What?"

"Is that a reindeer with glitter on his nose?"

"Oh, you mean my Christmas jumper?"

His features take on an expression best described as loathing.

"Let me guess." I push a finger into my cheek, "You hate Christmas-themed sweaters."

He grunts, "And reindeer, and Christmas carols, and mulled wine..."

"What?" I stare at him. "You're joking."

"Nope." He rolls his shoulders, "Can do without that shit, and anything to do with the festive season."

"But it's the silly season." I stare at him, horrified. I mean, Mr. Grumpy McDick here is surely just trying his best to scare me off. "It's not working."

"Huh?"

"This entire, alphaholish, man-about-town, who sacrifices baby goats to the devil and screams at little kids—"

"And kicks kittens," he adds, "don't forget that."

"That's what I mean," I slap my palms on my hips. "You'd never do that."

"Because you've seen me tolerate Max?"

"More than tolerate." I scowl, "Why are you so intent on putting yourself down?"

"Why are you so intent on believing I am something I am not?"

"And what are you? Billionaire—"

"Gazillionaire."

"Doctor."

"Surgeon," he corrects me.

"Someone who's hiding away from the world because he has some deep-rooted hurt."

He laughs—a fake, hard noise that prickles over my skin. My stomach clenches. *Shit,* this is not the man who had pulled me on top of him and stroked my hair until I'd fallen asleep. This is not the generous lover, who'd dived into my pussy and eaten it out like it was creme brûlée.

"What happened?" I frown. "Why are you like a chef with a hangover."

"Maybe because I don't like the look of your face this morning?"

My heart cracks a little; it fucking splinters. *Asshole, jerk, clod.* I glare at him, "Oh, you seemed to like me well enough last night."

"I was proving a point."

"What?" My heart begins to race and sweat beads my palms. It can't be... He can't be this...arrogant and mean, this ready to hurt me... Not after how he'd kissed me and touched me like I belonged to him. *Does he do this to every woman he' takes to bed? Does he make them all feel that special?* Maybe, whichever female he's with for the moment is made to feel like the center of his universe. "What point?" I insist, "Tell me."

"That you won't get through the holiday period without sleeping with me. That all I have to do is look at you and you'll open your legs for me. That you're so needy, you'll do anything for a touch, a kiss, little bit of attention, to make you feel special—you—"

My hand connects with his cheek before the thought has time to form in my brain. Pain shoots up my arm and my palm stings. I lower my arm, my breath coming in pants like I've run a mile to get here... When I'd walked over to the shed in search of him, and overheard the last of the conversation... I don't mean anything to him. Fine. I'm a transaction. That's all right too. But this... Insulting me just out of spite... No, this is unacceptable.

I step back, "The deal's off, you horrible man. All the money in the world isn't worth putting up with the lies that pour out of your mouth."

He tilts his head as the outline of my fingerprints blooms on his cheek. "Leave then," he drawls.

"You think I can't?"

"Do it. See if I stop you." His features close; those colorless eyes seem to grow darker. *Is he hurt? Why should he be hurt? He provoked me. What did he expect?* That I'd simply take it…because…of this attraction to him…that I'd hope would deepen into something else? Ha! How stupid could I be. Or maybe, he thought I'd stay because of the money. Think again, asshole.

I pivot to walk away, and that's when the world seems to explode. I slap my hands to my ears as a clanging sound overpowers the space. *What the hell? What is that?* All of my brain cells seem to knock together at once. I turn… "What's happening—?" That's when I notice the wall… No walls, plural, of clocks. Every single available space across the walls of the room is chockablock with clocks. Old clocks, antiques, made of steel, of wood, newer models made of glass and chrome… And every single one of them is mechanical. Their alarms clang out in different tones to indicate it's nine in the morning. I blink…turn around in a circle, taking in the sheer variety of time-keeping devices. "Wow." I turn to face him as the last of the sound dies away. "Holy shit," I breathe. "What is this…place?"

"It's mine," he says simply.

"But the cabin… I mean, that palatial house which you guys refer to as the cabin." I mutter, "It belongs to Saint?"

"It belongs to all of the Seven."

"Oh."

"The last person who had access to it was Saint. When I injured my finger, I told them I needed to borrow it for the duration of the season."

"Right, so he sent me here…"

"Knowing I was here already."

"Why would he do that?"

"To fuck with me?" His lips twist.

"But this place…" I glance around the walls again, "This is yours?"

"I built it in the backyard."

"You constructed it by yourself?"

"I employed an architect. And a builder."

"Of course." I walk up to a clock on my left. In the center is a horse, hind legs reared up in the air, its white mane caught as if in mid-jump. "And these clocks?"

"I collect them."

"Are they valuable…?"

"What do you think?"

I hear the humor in his voice, turn around to find him seated at the desk pushed up against the wall. I walk over, lean over his shoulder to find him looking through a magnifying glass at the guts of a clock.

"You repair them?"

He picks up what seems to be forceps, and which seem too delicate for his thick fingers to hold, and begins to tinker with the parts of the clock.

"You're an uh, horologist?"

"I like to repair clocks. It's a way to unwind."

I snicker, "Ha, you can be funny sometimes."

"Yeah, that's me—a hoot," he says in a voice that signifies something to the contrary.

I stare at his bent head. His dark hair falls to about his shoulders, and is mussed on top. Has he been running his fingers through them? The locks had been surprisingly silky to touch yesterday when I'd held onto those ears and… I shift my weight from foot to foot.

"But you disabled the clocks in the cabin."

"They came with the house. I hadn't acquired them."

"So, because you found—" I wave my hand in the air, "all these, and fixed them, you're fine with them?"

"I put them together; I know what they are made of. I can trust them to be accurate."

"Unlike the ones back there."

"Yep."

"So, you are fine surrounded by these…" I turn a circle, "time pieces on the wall, just not the ones you didn't acquire yourself."

"Sounds about right."

"You know how weird you sound?"

He shoots me a glance, "Says the woman who calls her phone Hedwig, and who uses the names of desserts as swearwords."

"So, what's wrong with that?" I frown.

He snickers, "My point exactly." He focusses on his work.

I shuffle my feet, wind a strand of hair through my fingers.

"I haven't forgiven you yet," I mutter.

"You can leave at any time."

But I don't want to, and therein lies the problem. What the hell is keeping me here? Him? This chemistry between us that I have to explore? What happens if I do explore it further? Will I survive the time we spend together?

And what if I did walk away?

Would I forever wonder how it could have been between us? What if he was…

the one? Ha, me and my romantic notions. But this is Christmas; I'm allowed to indulge myself, right?

I lean around him and stare at the contents of the clock's insides on the table.

He continues tinkering away…or whatever it is he's doing there.

The pieces of the machinery seem to be disjointed, yet they come together to form a certain symmetry, to dance together and make music. Like us.

If he were to only give us a chance. Do I want to give him a chance? "Weston, you're not a douche, you know."

He grunts.

I resist the urge to roll my eyes. "Why do you have to be this macho?"

"Why are you still here?" he growls.

"Because I cooked bloody breakfast and came here to call you. Then, you had to go and pull that…"

He straightens, "What?"

"That…" I wave a hand in the air. "That…obnoxious McFuck act of yours."

He swivels around to face me, "What was that? What did you call me?"

"Obnoxious?"

"After that."

"Mc…McFuck?"

"What does it mean?"

I raise my shoulders, "Dunno, it just, uh, seemed appropriate."

He chuckles, "You're a funny one, Buttercup."

I groan, "I am not sure I like that name yet."

"I am not sure I like you either." He looks me up and down, his tone serious, "But hell, if I don't want you to stay."

"Is that an apology?"

"For what?" He glares.

"For being horrible to me."

"Was I?"

I huff, "Fine. Whatever. And," I tuck my elbows into my sides, "I'm sorry too."

"For what."

I jerk my chin toward the reddened skin of his cheek.

"I deserved it," he replies.

I open and shut my mouth, "You...you did?"

"You should know though, that it turns me on when you get physical with me."

I squeeze my eyes shut. *Do not lose it; do not.* I draw in a breath, "I'll ignore that."

Turning, I stalk to the door.

"Where are you going?"

"I made breakfast." I pause, then turn to scowl at him, "Aren't you coming?"

Fifteen minutes later he pushes back the plate with a sigh. I'd made chocolate pancakes for me, regular ones for him. Why had I bothered...? Good question. Perhaps because, as much as I hate him, I hate seeing him starve. Food is sacred. It's how we nourish not just our bodies, but our souls, and if there is a soul that needs some sustenance... It is this alphahole's. A slurping sound fills the space. I glance sideways as Max licks the bottom of his bowl. He raises his head, then patters over to push his nose into my lap. "Hey boy, you still hungry?"

"Don't feed him more," Weston warns.

I frown, "I wasn't going to."

"Yes, you were too." He grins, "When you twitch your nose, it means you're thinking something sappy in your head."

"Am not." I set my jaw.

"Yep, you were." He chuckles, "And PS, you're welcome."

I frown up at him, "For what?"

"For the compliment I'm about to give you."

I shake my head. Jeez, this man... I mean, he can't be real. He can't be this incorrigible, can he? He stares at me; I meet his gaze.

His lips curl, and of course, my heart does that little flip-flop it always does when he goes all bad boy on me. "Fine. I give in." I huff, "What compliment?"

"You're not a bad cook." He smirks.

I open and close my mouth. "That was a delicious breakfast," I half-snarl.

"My, but you like your own cooking, huh?"

My lips turn down, "You can tell, huh?"

His brow furrows. "What's that supposed to mean?"

"I know I'm not svelte and long-limbed, like some of the women you date."

He frowns, then looks me up and down, "Firstly, let's get something straight. You look incredible."

Wait, was that a compliment? It was a compliment. Wasn't it?

"And secondly," his eyes gleam, "have you been keeping tabs on me?"

"Of course not." I huff.

"You've been keeping tabs," he concludes, looking way too self-satisfied.

"Hardly."

"It's okay, you can admit it." He smirks, "It's only natural to want to follow what I have been up to. Some of us have the kind of irresistible charisma that attracts attention."

Oh, that compliment thing I said earlier, forget it.

"You're so full of yourself," I scoff. "Seriously, how can someone say what you do and keep a straight face?"

He stares at me.

I fidget in my seat opposite him. "And yeah, maybe I tracked your exploits in the media, a little." I admit.

He arches an eyebrow.

I throw up my hands. "Oh, all right, so I did read up about you."

His grin widens.

"I was curious how you looked in your scrubs, okay?" My cheeks flush.

He blinks, "In my scrubs?"

I nod, "I have a thing for men in uniform."

His grey eyes grow stormy, "I could wear them for you, if you ask nicely."

I gulp, chafe my thighs together to relieve that gnawing emptiness that's been building since I woke up this morning. Then he had to go and spoil it all with his rudeness.

His features tighten. "I'm sorry," he offers.

I stare. "For which part?" I ask. "For being horrible to me from the moment I walked in here or is it for a specific insult?"

He tips back his chair until it rests on the back legs, "On second thought..." He scratches his chin, "What can I say? That's me. It's not my fault."

"No?" I frown.

"It's the way I was born."

"That's your excuse, huh?"

"At least, I don't lie. My life is an open book." He winces as he says it.

"What?" I ask.

"Maybe too open, on occasion."

"What do you mean?"

He rolls his shoulders, a dead giveaway that he's uncomfortable. Less than 48 hours with him, and I'm interpreting his actions. What is that about anyway?

"Tell me."

He folds his arms over his chest, "For the record, I like your curves."

Heat sears my cheeks. "You're kidding me."

He shakes his head, "I like that you have a healthy appetite. There's something sexy about a woman who enjoys cooking and eating."

"Thank you, and it's baking."

"You cooked breakfast," he points out.

"Yeah." I shift in my seat. Hell, I'm terrible with taking compliments. "And you are deflecting."

He barks out a laugh, "You caught me there."

"What is it?" I ask, genuinely curious. What could make this confident, dominant man, this uncomfortable?

"I may have a…uh, sex video to my name."

"Sex video." I blink.

"My ex—" He raises his shoulders, "She got hissy when I dumped her. Took it out by leaking a video."

"Oh," I swallow. My guts twist and something bubbles up my throat —something hot and angry and twisted. Something like jealous. *Holy shit, why the hell do I care who he slept with? Except, I do, for some reason.* Not like I have a claim on him or anything, but hell, for some reason, I've been trying to not think of the women in his past. I mean, if I don't acknowledge them, then they don't exist, right?

"A sex video, huh?" I clear my throat, "Is it uh—explicit?"

He glares at me.

Right. "Of course, it is," I mutter. Something hot presses down at my temples. *Shit, okay. This isn't good. What does it matter to me what he did?* He's paying me. It's the only reason I'm here, right? Not. I stare back at him, and therein lies the issue. I've been falling for this obnoxious, alphahole from the time I'd first laid eyes on him. A ripple of something claws down my spine. *Don't fall in love with him; don't.* He'd warned me about that already. Apparently, he knows me better than I know myself. I push away from the table so fast that Max yelps. "Sorry, buddy," I mutter, then walk past the table.

"Where are you going?" he asks

"None of your concern."

"You haven't finished your breakfast."

"So?"

"So, you'll need your strength."

"Oh, to hell with you. Don't pretend to care about me when you clearly don't, and—" He swoops out his arm, snags my wrist.

"Let go," I say through clenched teeth.

He doesn't answer. Instead, he tugs on me, with just enough force that I am pulled toward him. He turns his chair, then lifts me up by my waist and props me on his lap.

"What are you doing?" I mumble. My cheeks heat. Not that his lap isn't comfortable, and hell, if the entire maneuver wasn't hot. I mean, he'd handled my body like I'm made of candy floss. Do I taste as sweet to him? "Let me go." I dig my elbow into his chest.

He huffs, "Stop wriggling." There's a hint of a smile in his voice.

"And if I don't?" I twist around to face him. The curve of my waist bumps against the hard length of him in his pants. "Oh."

He grins. "See what you do to me?"

"Did you say that to *Ms. Sex Video* woman?"

His features shudder. *Damn it, why did I have to go there?*

"Sorry, none of my business."

"I didn't." His tone is clipped, "I never told her that. Nor did I ever seat her in my lap like this or…" he leans around me, grabs my plate and pulls it over, "…feed her breakfast." He scoops up some of my chocolate pancake, then holds the fork up to my lips.

"Open," his voice is husky.

A shiver runs down my spine. He's only giving me food, so why does it have to feel this…erotic?

"I'll eat it if you do," I whisper.

"Hmm." He glances from me to the piece of food on the fork, then back at me. "I have a better idea."

He brings the fork to his mouth, closes his lips around the chocolate crepe. He chews, swallows, then leans in and places his lips on mine. I gasp, and he darts his tongue inside my mouth. The taste of chocolate, of dark edginess and hot sex...the unique flavor that is Weston-fucking-Kincaid fills my mouth, coats my tongue, overwhelms my senses. My head spins. My toes curl. He pulls away and I lean forward. I hear a sound of protest. Hell, is that me?

I crack open my eyelids—when had I shut them?—to find he's scooping up another forkful of the breakfast that I will always associate with him. *Gah!* I did not think that, did not allow myself to indulge in such utter sentimental crap.

"Did you like that?" I whisper.

"Let's say that I may have underestimated the merits of dessert for breakfast."

"Are we talking about the same thing?" I frown.

"I was talking about your chocolate pancake," he snickers, "which you should eat." He raises the fork, "You need your nourishment."

I part my lips and he slides the food into my mouth.

I chew then lick my lips.

His gaze drops to my mouth, "My, my, what beautiful lips you have, little Red." His eyes gleam.

"All the better to kiss you with," I murmur.

His gaze intensifies. The heat from his body seems to deepen. A bead of sweat slides down my spine.

He picks up another forkful of the crepe, holds it up. "Finish it," his voice lowers to a hush, and I'm instantly wet. My nerve endings pop; my brain cells seem to melt all at once.

I close my mouth around the fork, wipe the tines clean, chew, then swallow.

"What a gorgeous throat you have, little Red," his voice is hard. As is the evidence of his arousal that stabs into the valley between my butt cheeks.

"All the better to take you in my mouth," the words tumble from my lips. *What am I doing?* Indulging this man's love for nursery rhymes and children's fairy tales is one thing, but taking it to the extent where the story of Little Red Riding Hood comes to mean something else completely? Not to mention, what was that thing with the rabbit? Had he actually compared himself to my favorite vibrator?

He scoops up the last morsel of food from the plate, holds it up to my lips. "You have a choice," he says.

"I do?" *Do I even want to know?*

He nods, "You can have your last bite before, or after."
"After?" I gulp, "After what?"
"After Christmas shopping."

13

Weston

I watch as she peruses the range of baking produce on the shelf in the only grocery store in the nearest village.

A woman walks behind me, "Excuse me," she says stiffly. I move aside. Hell, the aisles of this place are so narrow I have to flatten my back against the shelf to ensure I am not blocking the route. And the ride in the car over here? Why the hell had I agreed to that torture? Probably because, by the time I'd realized that the only means of transportation available to get to the village was in her dinky car—a bloody Volkswagen—it was too late. When was the last time I'd been a passenger in anything other than my chauffeur driven car...? I don't even remember.

So why had I done it now?

Why had I told her that I'd take her out shopping?

When what I'd wanted to do was eat her out right there on the dining table...for breakfast; and if I had my way, for lunch and dinner too. One taste of her sweet cunt had not been enough. The blood rushes to my groin.

Is that why I'd brought her here...? Because I'd wanted to get away from the cabin and the intimate atmosphere that seemed to be building between us. I lean a hip against the shelf. My shoulder brushes the stocked cans; one falls off of the top shelf, bumps me on the head. I throw my arm out, catch the can before it hits the ground, even as stars flash behind my eyes.

The fuck? From the time I'd met her I seem to be getting rather well acquainted with heavenly bodies, especially hers… Jesus, what's wrong with me? Next, I'll be spouting poetry, comparing her to a summer's day… No, not Shakespeare now. I'd loved poetry in school, had not hidden my love for the Bard, even acted in school plays. Then the incident had taken place. I'd been enroute home from a rehearsal for a play. And that had changed my proclivity to take part in extracurricular activities. Other than hanging out with the Seven… Not that we'd spoken much. We'd preferred to take our frustrations out on each other… You could say we'd spent a lot of that post-incident time beating each other up. It had been our own personal coping mechanism.

I wonder, have I channeled my love for the spoken word into the nursery rhymes I recite with my nieces? Is that why the fairy tales I read to them have etched themselves into my subconscious mind?

It had been hot though… That entire series of events at the breakfast table… I'd wanted to take her right then. Tempt her into spreading her legs open for me, so I could bury myself inside her sweet cunt. Would she have resisted me? Was the money so important to her that she'd continue to deny herself the release that came from only the most intimate act, of my cock enveloped within her wet channel? Is that why I can't stop myself from tempting her to cross the line? Is that why I'd set such an impossible-to-uphold term to the agreement?

Does she really think she is going to get through the next six days without giving in to me? And if I want her to fail, why hadn't I moved in when I had her ready and willing this morning? Fuck. I drag my fingers through my hair. She is not the only one getting in too deep. The difference is, I know how to turn the tide so it won't drown me. Hopefully.

I stare at the can—it's chocolate. Figures. The one thing in the world I hate more than the thought of losing her. *Hold on… Hold on… I meant losing to her. Yep, that's what it is. Bloody fuck.* I rub at the rapidly forming bump on my head. Did the run-in with the can knock my brains out of whack too?

I prowl up the aisle to where she stands in front of a display of frozen treats.

"How much longer will you take?" I growl

She squeaks, then shoots me a sideways glance. "You startled me," she mutters, then turns her attention back to the display. I follow her gaze to the Sticky Toffee Pudding she's salivating over. I reach for it, but she grabs my arm. "What are you doing?" she scolds.

"You want this?"

"Of course, not."

"Why do you deny yourself?"

"I'm going to be baking enough, as it is. If I also buy these goodies, I'll turn into a Christmas butter ball," she mutters.

"Don't you mean buttercup ball?" I chuckle.

She shoots me a sideways glance. "Knew I could count on you," she snarls, then turns and pushes her loaded shopping cart forward.

"Hold on."

She doesn't stop. No matter. I catch up with her, drop the tin of chocolate onto the heap of shopping. "You sure you have enough there?"

She frowns. "You mind your own business."

"But you are my business."

"Whatever." She speeds up, turns the corner and crashes her cart into a man. Some of the items fall out.

"Oh, I'm sorry." She bends at the same time that the man she'd run into says, "Excuse me." The stranger grabs a can of chocolate—motherfucker, it's the same can I'd placed there earlier. I scowl. He snatches up a few of the other items, then straightens at the same time as her. Their heads bump. Something explodes inside of my chest. My vision narrows. I stalk forward.

He places the items in her shopping cart. "I'm Hunter," he holds out his hand.

"I'm Amelie." She raises her arm, and I plant myself between them.

"And she was just leaving." I thrust my hand in his, squeeze the motherfucker's palm.

The expression on his face doesn't change; he doesn't flinch. I scowl at him.

He glances from me to Amelie. "Uh, a pleasure to meet you," he says.

"Can't say the same," I grunt.

Amelie huffs, "Don't mind him." She grumbles, "He was born with a lemon in his mouth."

I frown, "What does that mean?"

"It means that you have a terrible attitude and you are the most impolite person I know."

"Good," I mutter. "You done here?"

Hunter chuckles, "How long you guys been together?"

"We're not—" Amelie starts.

"Long enough." I thrust out my chin at Hunter. "What kind of a bloody name is that anyway?"

His expression hardens, then he barks out a laugh. "You're refreshingly candid."

"That's not all I'll be if you don't get out of my face," I shoot back.

He holds up his hands, "Not intruding on your patch, buddy." He glances around me, "Bye Amelie."

"Bye," she choruses back.

The man squeezes past me; my shoulder bumps his. He shoots me a narrowed gaze over his shoulder.

I glare back at him.

He frowns.

I glower.

His shoulders tense, then he jerks his chin.

Good, he got the message.

He pivots, walks away.

"What the hell was that?" Amelie huffs.

"None of your bloody business."

"Why are you so angry?"

"Why were you talking to him?" I snap.

She gapes, "What do you mean? He helped me pick up the groceries. What did you expect me to do? Ignore him?"

"Yes."

She shakes her head, "You've lost it." She pushes the cart forward, muttering, "Of all the crazy, asinine things you could do, this one takes the cake."

I stare after her. *The hell is wrong with me?* So maybe I did overreact, but hell, when he'd bumped into her, all I could think was, mine. *She's mine...* For the next few days, at least.

She struggles with the shopping cart, and I stalk forward, grab at it. "Gimme that."

"Fine." She raises her hands. "For being such a crazy-ass jealous man—"

"I'm not jealous."

She rolls her eyes, then snorts, "No, I forget that's your CRGPF."

I frown. "Excuse me?"

"Your chronic resting grumpy pants face," she clarifies.

Only when I'm around you. She does something to me. Yeah, she confuses me... I blow out a breath. Jesus, now I am going all googly-eyed over some chick who'd dropped in on my life and turned it upside down. *You can't let her get to you; no way.*

I jerk my chin.

She frowns.

I glare at her.

She pales, then juts out her chin and walks forward and out of the shop. I join the queue. When it's my turn, the woman at the checkout counter opens her mouth.

"Don't—" I growl.

"But, Sir—"

Bloody fuck, is the entire population of this village out to get me? I pull out my wallet, then separate a large stack of bills...and prop them on the counter. "Keep the change."

Her gaze widens, then she proceeds to check out the items.

Thank fuck. So, this is how it is to shop for yourself? What a nightmare. I pull out my phone, depress the buttons on the keypad. When my driver comes on the line I tell him, "I need a few things delivered to the cabin." I give him the list.

Arms full of shopping bags—I had to leave the shopping cart behind at the store—I step out and stalk toward the Volkswagen. Of course, she's nowhere to be seen. *Where the fuck is she?*

I place the bags next to the car, look around. A familiar figure in tight jeans, coat buttoned to show off those curves, catches my eye. She's talking to the man from the store—Hunter. *What the fuck!* My feet eat up the distance between us.

She reaches up, pats him on the shoulder, and a hot sensation stabs in my chest. I lengthen my strides, reach them. "Get away from her."

Hunter looks between us and frowns. "I didn't mean any harm."

"Of course, you didn't," she interjects.

I glare at her.

She pales.

"Go to the car."

She frowns.

"Now."

"But," she pouts, "I was only..."

I bend my knees, thrust my face into hers. "Do it," I command.

She opens her mouth, then seems to change her mind. Turning, she stalks off.

Thank fuck.

Can't let her out of my sight; got to keep her safe from anything untoward, and that includes strange men sniffing about her.

Hunter glances after her, "Everything okay?" He frowns.

"Shut the fuck up." I growl at him.

He turns to me, "You're Weston?"

I stiffen.

"Dr Weston Kincaid, I presume?"

"How the fuck do you know my name?"

"I'm a friend of Damian's."

"Hmph," I glare at him. "And you know him, how?"

"Our fathers are good friends."

"What are you doing here?"

"The same thing as you, I assume."

I frown.

He chuckles, "I am home for the holidays. I am also the MP for the area."

"Right." I roll my shoulders, "That why you were here? Campaigning?"

"Among other things." He smiles, "Anything you need." He holds out his hand, I ignore it.

"Stay away from her."

"You got it." He keeps his hand extended, "Take it, you never know when you might need help."

I ignore his hand while I stare at his face and something clicks, "You're Hunter Whittington?"

He tilts his head.

"You're standing for the upcoming elections."

A genuine smile splits his face, "Whew." He mock mops his brow. "My PR isn't that bad then."

I jerk my chin. So, he's a well-known politician, albeit one who's being tipped to be the next Prime Minister. *We'll see.*

I turn to leave.

"Make sure you stock up for the next few days."

"Why's that?" I ask.

"The weather," he says. "There's a cold spell coming on."

14

Amelie

"Cold spell, is that what they're calling it? More like, the Beast from the East," I grumble.

The wind whistles through the gaps in the shutters. I shiver, pull the shawl around my shoulders tighter. I'm sprawled out on a cushion, near the fireplace. Sir Grumpy Dickface here, had hauled in wood from the woodshed... Yep, this place has a freakin' designated space where the wood blocks are stocked. All chopped by minions before the onset of winter. To my surprise, Alphahole here, had hauled enough wood in on his own—broken finger notwithstanding—and without protest. Okay, so maybe that's unfair.

He'd helped me with my luggage, hadn't balked about carrying the bags of groceries to the car and then to the house... He'd even ridden, without complaint, in the cramped passenger seat. Unlike the journey through the grocery shop, which had been interesting. In fact, I'd been half-expecting that he'd have called his own driver to ferry us to the village, but he hadn't. Huh?

I shoot a sideways glance at the stony-faced man reading Harry Potter, Max at his feet. His hair is tousled—a perpetual just-rolled-out-of-bed look, which suits him too bloody well. He'd changed into a Henley and jeans, with soft moccasins on his feet, when we'd gotten home. Dinner had been…without incident… Actually, he hadn't said a word. And that had been…a relief…or not. Maybe I prefer his alpha-holish behavior…to this lack of communication which…seems uncharacteristic.

I clear my throat, then glance toward him. His head is bent over the book. He raises his cigar to take a puff. The scent of cloves and pinewood deepens.

I'd wanted to buy a Christmas Tree but I hadn't raised it with him… Well, given how he'd blown his fuse at my talking with Hunter… It had been cute, actually, that fit of jealousy he'd exhibited. Not that he'd admit to it. He had nothing to be jealous of, of course, but it had been refreshing to see him show some semblance of human emotion, after that rather brutish start to our relationship. Relationship? Are we in a relationship? Nah.

He blows out another puff of cigar smoke, that almost-Christmassy scent deepening. My mouth waters and I rise to my feet. "Do you have another?"

"What?" He replies without looking up. Huh?

I pause in front of him. His eyes stay glued to the page.

So, Mr. Potter is worthy of a lot of attention, but darn it, this once, I wish he'd prioritize me over the adventures of the boy wizard.

He raises the damned cigar to his lips and this time I snatch it from him.

He frowns.

I raise my shoulders, "I asked."

He watches as I lift the smoke stick, purse my mouth around the end wet from his. A shiver runs down my spine. It seems intimate to do this. I draw on the cigar, choke a little. A slight burn races down my throat. I blow out the smoke. My head spins. "Whoa," I giggle, "This is good."

"Don't inhale," he cautions me.

"I know how to smoke a cigar."

"How to puff a cigar," he corrects me.

"That's what I said." I scowl down at the smoke stick, then raise it to my lips, I take a long drag. The smoke swirls down my throat, fills my lungs. I blow it out without coughing. A buzz works its way down my limbs. My fingers tingle; my toes curl. "Hmm." I stare at the cigar, "Why is it that smoking a cigar kissed by you is almost as good as kissing you?"

"You sure about that?" His voice is tinged with humor.

I glance up, "Oh, what?"

"You want to test out that theory?"

I blink, then heat sears my cheeks. "Damn." I drag my fingers through my hair. "I didn't just say that aloud, did I?"

"You sure did." He sets the book aside on the side table, then leans back in his chair. The firelight glows off of his beautiful face, highlighting the shadows under his cheekbones. The dark blonde strands of his days-old beard glint. He resembles a pirate, an old-world marauder, someone who'd swoop in and take and ravish. A melting sensation flares to life between my legs. Oh, hell… This man, he's bloody potent.

His eyelids grow hooded; he watches me as I take a final puff from the cigar. The smoke lingers between us, framing those gleaming colorless eyes that survey me with more than a modicum of interest, and questions. Damn, he has so many questions in his eyes. As do I.

"Why did you tell me about the sex tape?" I blurt out.

The expression on his face doesn't change. He doesn't speak immediately. The silence grows, a beat, another. At his feet Max sighs. He springs up to his feet, looks at me, then at Weston, before pattering away toward the kitchen.

I glance back at Weston to find he's staring at my face.

"What?" I tilt my head. "Shouldn't I have asked that?"

He shakes his head, "Truth is, I am not sure why I mentioned it."

He rolls his shoulders, then settles deeper into the chair, "It felt like it was best to be upfront with you, considering—"

"Considering?" I prompt.

"You're coming home to meet my family, and if it did come up in conversation, I didn't want you to be surprised."

"Your family knows about it?"

He stares back.

"My mother is aware, yes..."

"Oh." I swallow, "And your father?"

"He died when I was sixteen."

Right.

"Heart attack."

My throat closes. Why is he sharing his past with me? What does it mean? *Nothing.* It means nothing at all. We're having a conversation, that's all it is. "Is that why you became a heart-surgeon?"

"Among other things." His features close.

Right. That sharing part? Guess I spoke too soon.

"My parents are retired and in Spain." I shuffle my feet. "I'd visit them more often, but they are happy in each other's company. They had me late, you see. I don't think they were prepared for how a child would turn their lives upside down. I mean, they never shirked their duties. Just... I think they were happy when I left home."

He scowls, "You miss them?"

"Sometimes." I raise my shoulders.

"You don't want to spend Christmas with them?"

"They uh, don't care either way, and this year... Well, I wanted some downtime, know what I mean?" I peer up into his face.

"You're spending Christmas with my family, so you won't be alone," he declares.

I frown. Am I that transparent that he'd guessed that I didn't particularly want to be alone through Christmas?

"Careful," I warn him, "or I'll begin to think that you are being nice to me."

"And what? Is it Christmas?" He smirks.

I stare, "You made a joke? Wow!" I clutch my chest, "It's a Christmas miracle."

"Don't get your hopes up." He firms his lips, "My family isn't the easiest to get along with."

"What family is?" I pull my hair over my shoulder.

"Now who's being nice?" He chuckles.

"Not me." I tip up my chin.

"Liar." His gaze grows intense.

I swallow, glance away. Shit, this is...getting... Uh, more emotional than I'd expected. "Your family," I prompt. "What did they say when they found out about your, uh, escapades?" *No, I don't want to talk about his sex tape, but damn if I don't want to know more about him.*

He frowns, then rolls his shoulders, "They were...disappointed."

"No!" I blink. "You Mr. Billionaire, money bags, surgeon of all he surveys."

"Yeah," he blows out a breath. "Impressing the world is so much easier than impressing your own blood."

"Tell me about it." I glance around for an ashtray to drop the cigar in, then spot it on the side table.

I lean toward it, when he reaches for the stub, "Don't."

"Don't what?"

"Don't snub it out." He takes the stub from my fingers, lays it to rest on the ashtray. "If you do, the cigar oils flow out and burn, and it causes an unpleasant smell."

"So cigars are another of your passions huh?"

"It's a thing that unites us Seven."

"All of you smoke? I mean," I make air quotes, "puff?"

"I like to occasionally indulge."

"Is it bad for you?"

"You mean because I am a surgeon?"

I nod.

"Most things that you have a weakness for are bad for you." He looks me up and down.

"And you?" I meet his gaze, "What about you?"

"I am the worst, of course."

I take a step forward. He widens his stance, and I step in the 'V' between his legs. *What am I doing? Why can't I stay away from him? As long as I don't sleep with him, it's fine, right?* The arrangement still stands.

"The papers?" I lower my chin. "From your lawyers, I mean. When will they arrive?"

"I'll have them for you by tomorrow."

His phone vibrates from the side table, "In fact, that must be it."

He makes no move no reach for it.

"So…" I swallow.

"So?" He runs a finger up the side of my arm. Goosebumps flare in the wake of his touch. A slow burn begins to hum, creeping, swirling up toward my heart. It would be so easy to lose myself in his presence, to forget the outside world exists. Just him and me, locked away in this cabin and—the lights blink off just then. "Oh." I glance up toward the bulbs set in the rustic settings in the ceiling.

"The wind must have gotten to the power supply."

Right. I glance down to find him watching me from under hooded eyes. If he'd been handsome before, lit by the firelight and nothing else, he's devastating now. My throat dries, my belly twists, and moisture laces the secret area between my legs.

"Weston." I whisper, "I—"

Barking sounds from outside.

15

———————

Weston

"Did you hear that?" I stiffen.

She freezes and her gaze widens. "Was that—?"

"Max." I'm already moving. I grab her by the waist, lift her and set her aside.

She squeaks. I jump to my feet, race toward the back door. I grab the handle and the door swings open. "I swear I shut it."

Footsteps sound behind me. I turn. "Stay inside," I stab my finger at her.

"Like hell, I am." She pauses, chest heaving. Her beautiful tits rise and fall. I glance at them and my belly hardens. *Shit, not the time to get distracted.*

"Get back in," I growl.

"No way." She folds her arms over her chest.

More barking, this time farther away. "Fuck." I pivot, race down the steps. She follows. "Stay behind me," I growl at her over my shoulder.

Amelie juts out her chin, then nods. *Thank Fuck.* If she'd tried to disobey me, I'd have bodily hauled her inside and tied her up. I shake my head, dislodging the image. Hell, if she doesn't bring out the caveman in me. I turn, then bolt across the back garden. The light from the patio streams out. I race toward the shed, the direction from which

I'd heard the barking. It's silent now. *Fuck, fuck, fuck.* My heart begins to race and my pulse rate ratchets up. I slow down as I near the shed. I hear movement behind me, then she pulls abreast. "Is there someone in the shed?" she whispers.

I train my gaze on the darkened shed. The hair on the back of my neck prickles. The knot in my stomach grows. I reach the side of the shed, press myself against the wall. Amelie follows my lead. I turn, place a finger to my lips. She swallows. I hold up my hand. *Don't move,* I mouth the words.

She bites the inside of her cheek, then nods. I point to myself then at the door of the shed; she jerks her chin. I turn back toward the door. *Shit, wish I had some kind of weapon.* I bite back a laugh as I think of her spatula. I bunch my left fist at my side. Of course, the finger on my right hand is hurt, so I won't be much use if there is, indeed, someone inside. A whine sounds from inside the shed so I move toward it. *Wait, wait.* There's no other sound inside. If there's someone in there… Well, I'll have to deal with it. I slip in through the crack between the door and the frame. There's a shuffling sound, then a low bark. "Max." I feel my way across the wall, hit the switch. The lights blaze in the space. I glance around, draw in a breath.

"Oh, my God," Amelie breathes next to me.

"I told you to stay outside," I remind her.

She ignores me, takes a step forward. "Wes… Your… your clocks."

My stomach knots and a hardness winds itself around my chest. "Fuck, bloody, fuck." Almost every clock in the place has been smashed. I move forward and my loafers crunch on the glass. Shit, should have changed into my boots before I rushed out, but fuck that. I stalk forward to my table. A shuffling sounds from underneath it. I pull back the chair and a growl rips out of me.

"What happened? Where's Max?" Amelia rushes forward. I plant my body in between her and the dog, but she's already there. "Oh, no," she cries out, "Max."

I sink down to my haunches, reach for Max. He whines, shrinks away. *Fuck.* "Something—more likely, someone—scared him."

The poor pup is shaking. My gut tightens and my pulse pounds behind my eyes. "I am not going to let him get away with this," I swear.

"Who? Who could do this?" Amelie's voice is low.

"I don't know, but you can bet your ass, I am going to find out." I lean forward, lay my hand on the side of Max's head, "Shh, it's okay, little guy. I'm here now. We'll take care of you, hmm?"

Max whines, folds further into himself.

"Fuck," I swear aloud and he flinches.

"You're frightening him."

"Don't be silly," I growl.

Amelie squats down next to me, loses her balance and grabs at my thigh to right herself. Pinpricks of heat vibrate out from her touch. I glance at her hand, which seems too delicate, too fragile against the broadness of my leg. She leans forward, on her knees, holds out her hand. "You okay, baby?" she croons.

Max blinks up at her, then whines. *Is he playing it up for her? No, he's hurt, but why the hell did he back away from me? And why is he shuffling forward toward her?* She caresses the side of his face, rubs her palm over his flank. He whimpers, then crawls toward her. She lifts him up, carefully, and cradles him. "You poor thing, are you hurt? Don't worry, we'll take care of you now." She turns to me, "We need to take him to the vet."

I place my hand in front of the mutt's mouth. He blinks, then licks my fingers. "Let's go." I rise to my feet. She follows, cuddling the dog close to her chest. His little body trembles. *Why the hell didn't he want to come to me?* I frown, looking from the dog to the tiny woman who rocks him, making soothing noises in her throat. A strange feeling coils in my chest. Jealousy? A little… That the dog preferred her over me… Not that I blame him. Given a choice I'd have laid my head on her breast… and done more than just cuddle, of course. *Enough, motherfucker.* Best get them both out of the shed, at least. I step over the glass. "Watch out," I caution her. She glances down at the glass, places a foot between the shards. "You're in your socks?" I swear.

"Yeah… I didn't have time to get my shoes."

More glass shards crunch under her feet. I growl, "Fuck that." I turn and sweep up both woman and dog into my arms. She squeaks, "Put… me down." Max continues to shake.

"Not a chance"

"But you're hurt."

"And you'll be hurting on parts other than the soles of your feet if you don't shut up."

"Oh," she draws in a breath. "I can walk," she mumbles.

"You're not wearing shoes." I stalk forward. "How could you be stupid enough to come out without your shoes?"

"Excuse me for caring enough about little Max," she huffs.

"You should have stayed inside, like I told you to."

"Why the hell are you angry now?" She frowns.

"You don't want to know." I stalk toward the cabin. "It's enough that I have to take care of the mutt, add you to the mix and—"

"You don't have to take care of me."

"Right," I mutter. "Tell that to the thief who decided to break in."

"Not my fault that the lock to the cabin was weak."

"There's a security system for both the cabin and the shed… And one that runs around the perimeter of the property that—"

"The cabin," we both say in unison.

I jerk my gaze down to hers.

Her face whitens. "You don't think he went to the—"

"Only one way to find out."

I tighten my arms around her, "You should stay here while I go check out the cabin."

The lights flicker then go out.

"Oh, no," Amelie squeaks. "Do you think the intruder had anything to do with this?"

I frown, not wanting to answer her.

She draws in a sharp breath, coils in closer to my chest. Hmm… this is not too bad, huh?

"Are we safe here?" She gulps, "Maybe you should call your driver and we should leave here?"

What, and miss this opportunity to find out how much more she can take before I break her? No fucking way.

"Relax." I infuse a tone of reassurance into my voice. "It's probably the incoming storm."

"You… you sure?" She peers up at me.

"Positive." I glance down at her upturned face. The starlight brings out the silver in her blue eyes, turns the blonde hair about her shoulders to spun gold. *Spun gold?* What the fuck? Clearly, I've been reading too many fairytales to my younger niece. Jesus, do I still have my balls or what?

"Oh, look." She raises her chin.

I glance up as the first flakes of snow hit my nose. "That's all we need," I grumble. "Fucking snow."

"It's beautiful, isn't it?" Her voice is dreamy.

I glance down to find her sticking out her tongue to catch a flake.

"It's polluted water," I warn her.

She scowls, "No one can accuse you of being a romantic."

"No one can accuse you of being practical."

"If I were, I never would have left home at eighteen to go to culinary school, against my parents' wishes."

"Where did you study?"

"At Le Cordon Bleu, Paris."

"Funny, I can't see you at a snooty French course like that."

She frowns up at me. "You're right," she replies, "I hated it. The course taught me a lot, gave me the basics, but... I couldn't wait to get out of there and into the real world."

"You don't like rules, huh?"

"I like to be free."

"Do you?" I allow my lips to twist.

"Of course." She scowls, "Why do you ask?"

"I think you'd like to be tied down. In fact, I am positive you'd love to test your limits; to find out how much you could take before you break down and beg for your release."

She gulps; her pupils dilate.

"You... You're wrong." She whispers.

"Are you sure?"

16

Amelie

"Of course, I am." I squeeze my thighs together. Damn it, stop imagining the scene he's laid out.

He doesn't know me or my needs or my likes. He has no idea how close he came to hitting on a certain forbidden dream I've harbored... One that I won't give in to, no matter that it is being laid out by the meanest, sexiest toad-in-the-hole ever. And that would be an insult to toad-in-the-hole's everywhere. I blow out a breath. I totally have to stop with these weird food-related metaphors that I seem to come up with when I am around him.

"How do you know if you haven't tried it?" He lowers his voice and studies me, "Have you tried it?"

I bite down on my lower lip. *Damn it, why can't I lie to him? Say it; do it* . "Uh... Not really," I venture.

His eyes gleam, "I think you might be surprised."

"The only surprise would be if there isn't an intruder in the cabin," I mutter.

He walks up the patio, past the now-silent hot tub. He stops at the entrance. "I need to go in and check the place first," he grumbles.

"I'm coming with you."

"It's safer here."

"It's colder." The snowflakes intensify, more of the white, powdery stuff sticking to my lips. I lick them off. His nostrils flare. Did that turn him on? Why is he so attuned to me? Is that why he'd laid out that stupid condition that I can't sleep with him if I want the money? Maybe it was to give me a way out of having sex with him... Except damn it, now I want to shag him. OMG!

Do I want the money so badly that I'll do everything but allow him to fuck me? Okay, don't answer that. It isn't fair, putting this big ol' hunk of chocolate slab on one side and my future on the other. *Would you give up his spotted dick for the chance at realizing your dreams?* Not that his dick is spotted…but it has a certain rhyme to it, know what I mean?

He bends as if to lower me to the floor.

"No, no, please no." I pout, "Don't do this. Don't leave me out here alone." Max whines to punctuate my words. *Good boy.*

He glares at me. His shoulders seem to swell. The full force of his dominance seems to weigh down on my shoulders.

I gulp, "We…Weston?" *Crap, why is my voice trembling?*

"You owe me, Buttercup." His voice is low, hushed.

"Can… can we go in?" I shiver.

He frowns, then jerks his gaze away and in front. Whew. The breath shudders out of me. I glance forward as he steps inside the house. He walks into the living room. It's silent, the space lit by the flames from the fire.

He glances around the space, his muscles tensed. I look up at the jut of his jaw. The hair covering his face seems thicker. Jeez. Do his whiskers multiply by the hour or something? Isn't that a sign of virility? At this rate, he's gonna have a Santa Claus beard by the time it's Christmas Day. And he can take me across his knee anytime. I snicker, and he looks down at me, catching me off guard. Heat sears my cheeks.

"What were you thinking?" he growls.

"N…nothing."

"Don't try that. I know exactly when your thoughts turn X-rated."

"Huh?"

Max grumbles in his throat.

"I think you can put us down now," I manage to say.

He stares at me a second longer, then stalks over to the cushion in front of the fire. He lowers me down to it. Max wriggles in my hold. I place him on the floor and he stretches, yawns, then patters off toward the kitchen.

"Well, he seems okay." I clear my throat, the adrenaline fades away and my limbs tremble.

"Hmm."

"Should we take him to the vet?"

Weston straightens. "Let's watch him tonight, and if he shows any signs of trauma tomorrow, we can take him then. I think he just had a fright."

"That's a plan." I yawn so hard, my jaw cracks. My eyelids seem heavy all of a sudden. "Sorry," I mumble. "It hit me all at once, I think."

He peels off the socks from my feet. His fingers brush my ankle. I shiver. He runs his fingers up the heels of one foot, then the other. Goosebumps pop on my skin. "What are you doing?" I say, breathless.

"Making sure you didn't cut yourself."

"I'm not hurt," I insist. I tug on my foot and he releases me.

"You should take off your loafers." I say.

"Excuse me?"

I glance down at his feet, "Uh, you're dragging in the snow from outside, not to mention the glass pieces from the shed."

He frowns, then retraces his steps to the door, toes off his shoes. I stare at his beautiful feet... beautiful naked large feet. My throat closes. My belly flutters.

I had no idea I had a foot fetish, until I met Dr Grumpy Pants Kincaid. Hell I had no idea I had a fetish for other male parts either... Not *all* male parts... Only *his* male parts. My belly flutters. My throat closes. Bloody hell. Clearly, I am obsessed.

"Why don't you wait here?" His voice cuts through my thoughts.

I tip my head up to meet his gaze, and warmth laces my cheeks.

"You okay?" He frowns.

No, of course not.

"Of course I am." I fold my hands in my lap.

He looks at me intently until I nod, then straightens. "I'll check the cabin and lockup, to ensure we're safe. Then we can go to bed." He grabs a log and heads toward the bedroom.

My eyes widen, but before I can worry too much, that dumb voice inside of my head chimes in. *We. Gah!* He used the *'We'* word. I stare up in his direction. *Doesn't signify anything, bitch.* Wait, does he mean go to bed to sleep or go to bed for something else? And omigosh, isn't that all cozy? So domestic. Would it be like this if we were together...? Maybe married, with kids... *What the f—?*

"Bedroom's clear," he says as he stalks toward the other end of the house.

I shake my head, push myself up to my feet. Clearly, I am delusional, or the Christmas season is affecting me, or the way he'd swept me up in his arms like I didn't weigh anything at all, and proceeded to carry me in here had made a huge impact on me. No one had ever done that before. No one. *Shit.* I am this…close to doing something stupid. *Gah!* Like giving up the money and giving in to him. *No, no, no.* I need advice. Need to talk with someone.

I march to the bedroom, which is illuminated by the moonlight coming in from the window, then reach for my handbag; my fingers brush my phone. Huh?

So he decided to return it to me? When had he put it back? Why would he do that? Is this his way of making up for the douche he's been thus far? My head spins. Talk about being complex. The alphahole is certainly the most complicated man I've ever met; and the most intriguing... Don't forget gorgeous. Why does he have to be this difficult though? It sure makes this entire relationship hard work... And unique... No wonder I can't stop thinking of him. And no... Our relationship is strictly professional. *Yea, keep telling yourself that, bitch.* Regardless, I am going to take every break I get... Like this phone. He returned it; now I can use it.

I grab the phone, glance around.

Where can I speak without him hearing me? I walk into the ensuite bathroom, lock the door behind me. *Shit, it's dark.* I switch on the light on my phone, walk over to the bath candle at the head of the tub. I grab it, rummage around in the drawers under the sink, until I find a lighter. I light the candle, place it on the counter next to the sink.

Then, for good measure, I crawl into the bathtub.

I swipe the phone screen, notice a text message. It's from Julia, one of my oldest friends. She'd left high school, gone to Australia for her gap year and stayed on as a nanny for a family there. Last I heard, she'd planned to stay on for another year. I peruse her text:

Hey Amelie, change of plans. I'm returning to London. Should be there just after Christmas. Can I stay with you until I find a place of my own?

. . .

Oh, yay!

It's going to be awesome to have her back, especially considering Summer is on her honeymoon. Victoria is still in that early stars and sunshine phase in her relationship with Saint. Karma... Well, she seems to have forgotten about us, since discovering her hottie on her extended Sicilian sojourn—a hottie she is still hiding from us. So that leaves me and Isla—the only other single woman in our clique, and Julia, when she returns.

I text her back:

Awesome news.

Can't wait to see you! Of course you can stay with me. Come over when you land.

I press send, then call Isla. She picks up on the third ring.

"Hey," her voice is breathless.

"Did I disturb you?" I keep my voice low.

"Nope. Just me and my Hitachi getting all cuddly." She snickers. "If I were to fall pregnant now, I'd give birth to batteries."

"What the—?" I snort, then swallow down the wrong way and start coughing. "That was such a bad joke, it was good." I clear my throat. "At least someone's having fun." I bite down on my lower lip.

The silence stretches, then, "Amelie?"

"Yeah."

"You okay?"

"Of course."

"Why are you whispering?"

"Because I don't want to be heard?"

"Aren't you at the cabin?"

"Yep."

"So why the secrecy thing?"

"What secrecy thing?"

"You're still whispering, babe."

"Right."

"Amelie?" she asks, worry in her voice. "Everything okay there?"

"There was a break-in at the cabin."

"What?" I hear the sheets rustle, then the click of a lamp, "Are you okay? What happened."

The line buzzes and I glance at the screen. She's asking for access to video mode. I decline.

"What the hell?" She demands. "Why aren't you on video?"

"Uh, because, I'm hiding in the bath tub."

"What the—?" Her voice sharpens, "Why are you hiding? Did the intruder hurt you—"

"I'm fine," I mumble.

Why'd I have to go and blurt that out to her? Maybe I needed someone to empathize with me, huh? Not that Weston hadn't. He had taken care of me, even if it was grudgingly… Still, I needed to hear a familiar voice, someone unthreatening with whom I don't need to pretend.

"Then why are you still whispering?" Her voice sharpens, "Is the intruder still there?"

"No, no. I think Wes scared him off."

"Weston?"

"Yeah."

"He's there with you?"

I draw in a breath. "I walked in on him, completely naked, as he was wrapping up his hot tub session."

Silence, then she chuckles, "You found him naked?"

"Yeah."

"In the hot tub?"

"He'd just been in…yeah, and he didn't have a stitch of clothing on and he had a cigar."

"Hot damn." She laughs, "Talk about phallic symbols, hmm?"

That's true. He'd been all but sending me subconscious signals… Okay, seeing his massive dick upfront? Not that subtle…but you have to give the man full marks for making an impression.

"That's not all," I add.

"You mean there's something to top off that picture?" She chuckles.

I frown, "Wipe that image from your mind, please."

Silence again. "Did you just ask me to refrain from imagining the hot doctor naked?"

"Yeah." *Shit, I know how that sounds…* But I really don't want her going there... Nowhere near that very male, very gorgeous naked ass...or dick, of said doctor...because...well I am...

"Are you jealous?"

Of course, I am. "No, no, nothing like that..." I bite my lips.

"It's fine; I understand." I can hear the grin in her voice.

"Nothing to understand."

"You're holed up with him over the festive season, huh? Planning a hot and dirty week, eh?"

"No, no," I hasten to clarify, "nothing like that."

"Oh?" Her voice is credulous.

"No, seriously, uh... He wants me to meet his family over Christmas."

The silence stretches this time. A beat, another.

"Family? Christmas?" Her voice sounds strangled. "Isn't that uh, premature?"

"It's part of the deal."

"The deal...? What deal? Amelie, what the hell is happening there?"

The phone vibrates again; I glance at the screen. She's asking for access to my video again. I huff out a breath, then agree.

Isla's face fills the screen. Her eyes are wide, concern writ across her features.

"Finally," she huffs. "The hell have you gotten yourself into?"

"Me?" I frown, "Why are you yelling at me, when it's that alphahole's fault that I am here in this bath tub?"

"Where is the doctor?"

"He's shutting down the house for the night."

She raises an eyebrow.

"What?"

She makes the motion of zipping her lips, "Nothing."

I scowl, "Out with it, bitch."

"It sounds like you two are playing house up there."

"Yeah, and Max is our child," I say, only half-joking.

"Sinclair and Summer's puppy?"

"Yeah, Weston's dog-sitting."

"He can't be that much of an asshole if he's dog sitting."

"He knows how to fool people, huh?" I mutter.

She peers up at me through the screen. "The deal," she prompts. "What's that all about?"

"He's paying me a million pounds a day for my time."

"A million?" she splutters. "You sure?"

"Yeah, we shook on it."

"Hmph." She purses her lips, "He's filthy rich. No doubt, he can afford it." Her forehead furrows, "And what does he want from you in return?"

"Uh, I'm going to have to housekeep for him, until we leave here."

She bursts out laughing. "You? Housekeeping?" Isla has been to my place.

"Shut up," I say, before giggling along with her.

She snickers, "So, what does that mean? *Housekeeping.*" She emphasizes the word, as if it has a hidden meaning.

My cheeks heat. "Well, uh..." I shift my body. *Why can't I get comfortable?* "It means I have to do everything he wants."

"Ooh," she perks up, "you mean kinky games?"

"Sort of..." I look up at the ceiling before continuing, "except, I'm not supposed to sleep with him."

"Excuse me?"

I hurry to explain. "As long as I don't have sex with him, I get the money."

She blinks rapidly. "That..." she frowns, "that makes no sense."

"Right?" *Glad I'm not the only one who thinks so.*

"I mean, shagging him would be almost as good as getting the money in your account."

I squeeze the bridge of my nose, "This entire thing is gonna go tits-up on me."

"So, he'll come through with the money. You're confident of that, right?"

"Right."

"And all you have to do is get through the next few days... Break bread with his fam..."

"Yeah," I nod.

"So, what's the problem?"

I stare at her.

"Oh." She tilts her head, "OHHHHH."

I turn down my lips, "Now you see?"

"You want to ride him horizontally?"

"Don't be crude." I laugh.

"You want to fuck him, get it on with him, shag him until you can't walk straight, until you're enveloped in a sex haze...?"

"Gee thanks," I mutter. "Thanks for laying it all out there."

"So, do it." She raises her shoulders.

"What?"

"You want him; take him. He won't say no. Shag him; live out your wildest dreams with the dirty doctor."

"And then?"

"Then go back to your life."

"My indebted-to-hell life," I complain.

"That does suck..." she taps a finger to her forehead, "unless."

"Uh-oh!" *Do I want to hear this?*

"You, change the terms of the deal."

"You think I could?"

"Sure. Revise it to include money *and* sex."

"Ah...But..."

"What?"

"Doesn't that make me a slut...in his eyes?"

"Aren't you already one?"

"N...no." I mean... "Maybe."

"Is it him or yourself you're worried about?"

"I don't understand."

"You want to keep your conscience clean—keep your skirts clean, so to speak. Do what he wants, on his terms, take the money, and run."

"Yeah."

"Think you can keep it that simple?"

"I..." I hang my head, "I'm not sure."

"So, call off the deal. Forget about the money. Go for the man."

"But... but, I need the cash."

"Then do as he says."

"I don't want to." I pout.

She throws up her hands, "Gah, you're making my head hurt."

"Tell me about it." I press my fingers to the bridge of my nose.

"So..." she scans my features, "What are you going to do?"

"I don't know."

There's a knock on the door. "Amelie?" Weston's voice reaches me. "You okay in there?"

"Shit, I gotta go."

"Let me know what you decide."

"Thanks, Iz."

"Bye, babe."

Weston bangs on the door again and raises his voice, "Amelie? Is everything okay?"

"Yes, coming." I walk over to the commode and flush it. Then check my appearance in the mirror over the sink. My hair is all over the place, skin flushed, no makeup, lips wiped bare. Ugh. And is that…? I lean in closer. Yep, there's dog hair on my sweater. "Damn it." I take off my sweater, glance around, then toss it into the laundry basket. My blouse is crumpled, but it'll have to do.

"Amelie?" Weston sounds pissed. "You coming out or do I need to come in there?"

"Hold onto your britches," I yell back, slide my phone into my pocket, then turn toward the mirror. I mean, it's not even a question anymore, is it? No sex. That's fine. I can still stick to that plan, but it would be nice to have a bit more fun with him at least, no? I grab the bottom of my blouse and whip it off.

"Amelie." Weston juggles the knob, "I'm coming in."

"Wait!" I toss aside the blouse and scamper for the door.

17

Weston

She opens the door, and I stare. Her tits... Her beautiful...gorgeous breasts, ensconced in her bra salute me. I glare at her chest, then at her face.

"Just," she swallows, "getting ready for bed."

I frown down at her. She walks forward. I don't move.

"Uh, excuse me?" She squeezes through the space between me and the door jamb.

She saunters over to the bed, walks past her suitcases propped up against the wall, to her side of the bed. She unzips her jeans, shoves them down, bends to take them off. Her heart shaped butt juts out. I clench the fingers of my right hand, wince when my injured finger protests. "Fuck," I growl.

"You, okay?" She tilts her head, shoots me a glance from her bent over stance.

I glare at her and she pales. Then straightens and kicks her jeans to the side.

I take a step forward.

She scrambles over to the bed, "Uh, I think I'll go to sleep." She slides in between the sheets, pulls the comforter up to her chin. She turns over on her side.

I'd lit candles on the side tables, and their light flickers across her delicate shoulder blades. Her creamy skin is perfectly smooth, perfectly soft, perfect to be marked by my fingerprints. I take a step toward her, then clench my fist at my side. *What the fuck? Is she playing with me?* And I'd started this goddamn game. What a bloody mistake. *Why the hell had I put the money between us? Why hadn't I flipped the agreement the other way? Asked her to sleep with me in exchange for the money? Fuck.* I reach the bed, stand over her.

Her shoulders quiver. So, she's aware I am here? Hmm.

Her fingers clench at the covering that flows over her shoulder. I reach for the fabric, tug. She shudders, then releases her grip on it. I draw the sheet down the curve of her waist, down the jut of her beautiful arse, until it pools about her ankles.

The swell of her butt catches the candlelight—gorgeous, beautiful, curved at just the right circumference, it'd fit so right into my palms.

My fingertips twitch. I sink to my knees by the bed, press a kiss to that point where her waist meets the swell of her hips.

She shudders. "Weston," she whispers.

"Shh." I nibble my way to the swell of the enticing flesh to the valley between her butt cheeks.

"Oh, my God." Her entire body quivers.

I am not a religious person—well, not unless you count the time I'd been kidnapped and had prayed to every power that might be to help me... And now, faced with the sheer gorgeousness, the beauty that is this woman unclothed— Yeah, I send up a prayer of thanks to that power that I am here. Is this why the cops had found me, still and lifeless, ready to give up? I had been hanging on by a thread, reaching for something in the distance, not within reach...a belief that I'd get through it. Can I get through these days with her? When, with every moment, she is sinking into my blood, wrapping herself up around my heart... *Heart? What? Fuck that.* I am not ready for that kind of entanglement.

Nothing and no one will undermine the lifestyle I've worked so hard to build. I'll never let another in... I fuck them and leave them. That's what I am good at. I'll never allow myself to lose control. Never put myself in a position where I am vulnerable.

I slip my tongue into the space between her arsecheeks. Her entire body jerks. "Wes," she moans, and my groin hardens.

"Do you want me, Princess?"

"Ah," she gulps, "I… You know I do."

I squeeze her arse, part the cheeks then nudge my tongue into her backhole.

"Jesus, Wes," she groans. "What are you…doing?"

"What do you think?"

"Why do you always answer my question with a question?"

"Because it's my prerogative to ask and yours to submit."

She huffs, "Where is that written?"

"In Doc Kincaid's manual of '100 ways to torture — I mean — pleasure a woman,'" I chuckle.

She stills, "Bet you have it written down too." She grumbles, "Methodical and detailed grumpy pants that you are."

"You think you know me, huh?" I nibble my way down to the apex between her legs, slip my tongue in to the sweet hollow of her pussy.

"OMG," she hisses, tries to pull her legs up.

I grip her thigh. "Don't move," I growl.

"But," she whines, "this is not fair."

"Good." Time she felt a little bit of the agony she's been putting me through. I lick the entrance to her channel and her entire body bucks. I slide my hand around to cup her pussy, slide my tongue in and out of her wet, melting core.

She groans, throws out her hand to clutch at a pillow.

I bring my other hand up to squeeze her breast and she cries out, "Why are you doing this?"

"Because… I can?" I murmur against her center. "Because you won't stop me?"

"Does this… Uh, count as — ?"

"Breaking the arrangement?"

She nods.

"No," I slurp the moisture that trickles from her center, "but all you have to do is say the word and I'll put you out of your misery."

"Fuck," she hisses.

"Yeah, exactly." I allow my lips to curve into a smile, then press little kisses to the back of her thigh. I suck on the soft skin, and the taste of her goes to my head. I bite down on the tender flesh and she moans.

"Please, please, please," she pants.

"You know I can't." I smirk. "But say the word, and I can take you —" I drag my tongue up her thigh, retrace my way to her backhole, "here."

"Oh," she gasps. "I… I...am not sure about that."

I raise my head, slip a finger back inside her puckered hole. "You mean this?"

She groans, "I… I think I hate you."

I twist my finger inside her, then slide two fingers inside her pussy.

Her body jerks, goosebumps pop on her skin, a quiver works its way up her legs, her thighs, she clenches her butt around my intrusion, and her pussy clamps down on my finger.

"Oh, my God, Weston, I am going to—"

I pull my finger out from her butthole, from her channel, then rise to my feet.

She stills, "What the fuck?"

She turns on her back, then springs up.

"What are you doing?"

I yawn, "I'm tired."

She gapes, tracks my progress around the bed to my side. I grab my sweatshirt and peel it off, along with the vest I have on underneath. I reach for my pants.

She squeaks, "You're undressing?"

"It happens." I smirk, "I have been known to do so when I want to get into bed."

I shove down my pants and boxers. I kick them aside and straighten. I turn to face her. Her gaze widens as she takes in my full-frontal nudity, rakes her gaze down my stomach to where my dick stands to attention. *I'm aroused—of course, I am. And that's too fucking bad. I don't intend to do anything about it. Guess I am going to suffer along with her… Uh, who am I punishing here? Her or me? Both of us. Right, whose idea had this entire fucked-up arrangement been?*

I climb between the covers, then fold my hands behind my head.

Next to me, she stays perfectly still, muscles vibrating with tension. The nervous energy vibrates off of her, reaches out to me. My shoulders bunch. I close my eyes, begin to count down.

Twelve o'clock.

Eleven o'clock.

Ten o'clock.

She shifts position.

Nine o'clock.

Eight o'clock.

She turns over on her side, facing away from me.

Seven o'clock.

She mutters under her breath.

Six o —

She sighs aloud.

That's it. "What's wrong?" I snap.

Silence from her.

I close my eyes again.

Six o —

She jerks on the cover, pulls it off of me.

"What the fuck?" I turn to her, "What's wrong?"

"I'm…c…cold." Her teeth chatter.

I frown. The temperature had dropped and the heating hasn't come on yet.

She shivers again.

I turn, scoot over, then drag her to me.

She squeaks, "What are you doing?"

"Making the fuck sure that I can get some shut-eye."

I tuck her head under my chin, lock my arm around her waist, and pull her close enough for my dick to nestle between her arsecheeks.

She wriggles her hips, "You're… Uh, you're hard."

"Deal the fuck with it," I growl.

"But, I can't—"

I close my palm over her mouth, "Sleep, Princess."

She draws in a breath, another, then licks my palm. My cock instantly lengthens. "Don't do that, not unless you want to be brought to the edge of climax again…and left unfulfilled."

"You won't," her voice is muffled against my hand.

"Try me." I snuggle her closer, throw my leg over her thigh. She stills, muscles wound up. I close my eyes, start my countdown.

Six o-clock.

Five o'clock.

Her chest rises and falls.

Four o'clock.

Her breathing deepens.

Three o'clock.

Her shoulder muscles loosen; her body twitches.

Two o'clock.

I lower my palm to cup her breast. Not intentionally, of course. It's a logical resting place. Besides, the shape is a perfect fit for my palm. Sleep overcomes me.

Something cold nudges my face, a wet tongue licks my mouth, "Seriously, Buttercup, we need to talk about your morning breath." I crack open my eyelids. Max gazes soulfully at me. I am on my back; Max rides my chest. He flicks out his tongue, I turn my head to the side, then stiffen. The bed is empty. *Where the hell is she?*

I set Max aside, swing my legs over the side, and head out of the room. A crash reaches me from the kitchen, then a scream. *The fuck?* "Princess?" I race toward the commotion.

18

Amelie

"Aw… Hell… Butterfingers." I glance down at the mixing bowl I had overturned. I'd woken up early, determined to try a new recipe for chocolate banana muffins…and managed to drop the bowl.

No wonder he calls me Buttercup. But I admit, I prefer Princess. There's a thud of footsteps, the sound of barking. I glance up as Weston barrels through the door and into the room, Max on his heels.

"What's wrong?" He stalks into the room, "I heard you—"

His shoulders block out the rest of the room. The planes of his chest are hard. I rake my gaze down his concave stomach, to where his cock juts out between those powerful legs and those gorgeous feet that he's currently about to place in a puddle of chocolate sauce.

"Watch out—"

His feet slip on the gooey streak on the floor and his big body tilts back. Shit, I leap forward, reach for him… I mean, what the hell am I trying to do? It's not like I could stop him from falling, and hello, he isn't wearing any clothes, so I couldn't exactly grab onto anything, except…Well… You know. A-n-d nope, I don't want to risk hurting that part of him. I stumble aside.

Too late, I realize I am about to step on a banana peel. Yes, really, a banana peel. Can my life get any more cartoonish? I twist my body, lose my balance anyway, and pitch forward. "Oh, no, no, no," I wail, throw up my hands, squeeze my eyes shut and connect nose first with a hard barrier. Shock waves ricochet through my head, down my spine. The breath whooshes out of me. "Ugh!" I flail around, and my arms are caught and twisted behind me.

"The hell is wrong with you?"

His voice rumbles below my ear and that's when I realize I am sprawled over his body. His very naked body. My cheek is smooshed against that delectable chest, my breasts flattened against that eight pack, my pelvis positioned right over that hard, gorgeous part of him that stabs into the cleft between my pussy lips.

Max dances around us, barking near my ear. "Max, stop," I pant, then try to pull back from the annoying man I am currently draped over.

He scissors his legs around mine, "Stop struggling."

I tip my chin-up, "What are you trying to do?" I scowl.

The light shining through the window brings out the gold flecks in his eyes. Huh? So his eyes aren't completely grey? Imagine that.

"I heard you scream." He glowers up at me, "I was convinced there was an intruder in here."

"No, it's just me," I huff. Gosh, he's grumpy first thing in the morning, huh? Is it because he hasn't had his way with me yet? Would stabbing his dick inside of me put him in a better mood? My thighs clench. My nipples tighten.

He tilts his head, his lips taking on that curl that I hate… And love. *Oh, my God, stop acting like a sex-crazed slut—but hello, can you blame me?* That mussed up hair, that broad chest, over which I am sprawled. That warmth of his that rises up from his big body, to coil around me, sink into my blood, and travel straight to that emptiness in my center. *Gah, stop that.*

I push back; his grasp tightens. That hard length of his pushes up and into my very eager center. I gulp. *Okay, don't panic; don't.* Pretend it's normal. Just a conversation, that's all this is. I tip up my chin. "I, uh, had a little accident," I mutter.

"I can see that." He pushes back my hair that's come lose from its bun on top of my head, then rubs at a spot on my cheek. He brings it to his mouth, sucks on his digit. "Chocolate." He grimaces, "Of course, it's chocolate."

"Is there any other kind of ingredient worth waking up early for?"

"There are other reasons worth losing sleep over," he smirks.

I scoff, push at his chest, "Let me go."

"No."

Max shoves his face between us, aims his tongue at Weston's mouth. Wes groans, turns his face the other way.

Max barks, wags his tail, turns to me instead. I crane my head away, "Chocolate isn't good for you, Max," I scold.

Max pants, then shoves his nose into my throat. "Ooh, it's cold." I giggle. He licks my throat, then proceeds to place his paw on my breast.

"Hey," Weston releases my arm, grabs Max by the scruff of his neck and places him aside. Max barks. The moment Wes lets him go, he jumps forward toward me, shoves his nose down my blouse.

I laugh, "Max, no, that tickles."

"Bloody hell," Weston swears. He releases both of my arms, then grabs Max. I roll away from him. Weston jumps to his feet, stalks across the kitchen and places Max in the hallway. He points a finger at the puppy. "Chocolate on the floor, buddy. I don't want you getting into that." Max groans.

I swear, that dog can speak.

The mutt blinks up at Weston who shakes his head. "Nice try little fella, but you can't come in here right now." He closes the door.

I spring up to my feet, and slip again, on the gooey dough this time, slide forward, tilt back, grab hold of a chair which tips over. *Gah!* The world tilts again; I squeak, throw out a hand, which is grasped. I am pulled upright.

"Steady." There's amusement in his voice.

"Thank you." I tug on my palm, but his grip tightens around my wrist. He tugs, I careen forward, and he grabs me and swings me up. I wind my legs around his waist.

"Hello, there." He waggles his eyebrows.

"What are you doing?" My voice is breathless. Bloody hell. His dark, edgy, masculine scent entwines with the chocolate-banana notes of the muffin mixture. My mouth waters and it's not for the muffins. My head spins and I dig my fingers into his shoulders.

He walks to the other side of the table, then plops me on it. He keeps his fingers on my hips. "That's better."

"For…for what?" I clear my throat.

"For breakfast, of course." He grins, then steps back. He leans around me, grabs the chocolate sauce we bought.

I frown, "I was going to use that to cook."

"I have a better idea." He holds it upside down, squirts. I glance down to find it dripping into the valley between my breasts.

"Wh…what are you doing?" I gulp.

His lips curl, he drops his head, and licks the sauce from the top of my cleavage toward the hollow of my throat.

"Oh," I stutter.

He sucks on the delicate skin at the base of my neck and I feel the tug all the way down to my core. My pussy spasms and my thighs clench. "W…Weston," I plead.

He pauses, "Do you want me to stop?" He leans back, "Should I leave?" He takes a step back.

I throw out a hand and grab his hip, "Wait."

He tilts his head, "What do you want?"

I want you inside me; I want you to fuck me right here. I blink, "I… I want to complete the recipe I set out to cook."

He frowns, "You want to make breakfast?"

"Y...yeah," I nod, "it's a new recipe I'm trying out for —"

He scratches his chest and my gaze drops to those cut abs. Not that I hadn't noticed them before... I mean, I'd managed to look away though, so he wouldn't catch me staring, but now that he's drawing attention to it, well… I can't help but stare. "For a doctor you sure have a great physique."

"For a chef, you sure haven't figured out the obvious."

I frown. "What do you mean?"

"You were making… What was it you were going to create?"

"Muffins." I frown, "Banana chocolate muffins."

"The oven," he jerks his chin over my shoulder, "the electricity's not back."

"Oh!"

"And the refrigerator isn't working either," he adds. "Or didn't you notice?"

"I... I didn't," I confess, and I had opened the refrigerator to pull out the ingredients I needed. Hell! I drag my fingers through my hair. "How can I be such a ditz?"

"Maybe your mind was otherwise occupied?" He chuckles.

"How do you mean?"

"Want me to spell it out?" He takes a step forward.

I shake my head, "No, no, it's fine. You're right, I was, uh, thinking of other things."

"Oh?" He smirks, "Did it involve me in anyway?"

"Ah, your family actually. When, uh, when do we set off to see them?"

"In four days."

"Four days." I gulp, glance around the room. Four days, during which I still have to resist him. *How the hell am I going to get through this?*

"What should I do about breakfast?" I pout.

"I have an idea." His grin widens, "Why don't I make my special instead?"

Twenty minutes, later I sit across the table from him. He'd, thankfully, changed into sweats and a long sleeved T-shirt, which damn, it only set off his broad shoulders even more. I mean, the only thing to beat the sight of this man unclothed is him sitting across the table, with Max at his feet. I'd cleaned up the kitchen by the time Weston had returned with the little guy in tow. I'd topped off Max's bowl, which he'd wolfed down in minutes, before taking up his position by the table.

Now, he watches as Weston pours the cereal into the bowls. He tops his off with milk, offers it to me. I refuse. Yeah, for a chef, I don't like milk. Not in my tea, nor in anything else.

"This?" I mutter, "This is your idea of cooking?"

"Hey, don't mock it until you've tried it."

He uses his uninjured hand to dip his spoon into his bowl, and begins to eat.

"It's not chocolate," I whine.

"Precisely." He scoops up more of the stuff.

I frown, "How the hell am I going to get through the days without cooking?"

"You could clean."

"Yeah, well." I shuffle in my seat. I absolutely hate household chores. Yeah, a tiny detail I'd left out. I know.

I glance down at my bowl, begin to scoop up the mixture. I eye it, then force some of it into my mouth. The flavors explode on my tongue. I crunch down, swallow it, reach for more.

"Not bad, huh?"

I raise a shoulder, "It's all right." I eat some more. "I couldn't use firewood to fire up the oven, could I?"

He stares across the table, "Probably not."

"Can I call someone to come and take a look?"

"I already called for service, but they won't come until the storm blows over."

I frown, glance out the window. Snow comes down in heavy flakes. It does look bad, and if people are being careful before venturing out... "Maybe the roads will be blocked and we won't be able to get there?"

"The storm's supposed to blow itself out in 48 hours."

Right.

"Maybe the roads will be too slippery?"

"I've asked my driver to come by to take us there."

"Your driver?"

"He's on standby in the village."

Of course. My shoulders droop. And I'd been hoping to put the time to good use by trying out new recipes, huh?

"Perhaps," he rolls his neck, "I could take a look at the generator."

"You would do that?" I cry.

"Hmm." He looks me up and down, "How badly do you want it?"

I frown, "What is that supposed to mean?"

He leans forward, "I mean, how far would you go to get the generator working, I wonder?"

I swallow, wriggle around in my seat, "How far do you want me to go?"

"I want you to beg."

"Excuse me?"

"Beg me to do it."

"No," I scowl.

"Fine then." He pushes back from the table, pivots to leave.

I frown, watch him as he prowls toward the door. I train my gaze back on the man, or rather on that fine piece of ass of his, those power thighs that undulate as he puts more distance between me... And the muffins I so very much want to bake. Is there not one thing in your life that you can complete? Not a relationship? Just about hold onto a business that if you don't comply with his wishes... You'll lose the money to ensure that it survives. Ugh, why do I always find myself stuck between a rock and a hard place? And no, I am not talking about certain parts of his anatomy that would give granite a run for its money.

He steps out of the kitchen and I call out, "Wait." I spring up and my chair careens back. "I beg you," I call out, "please fix the generator."

He shoots me a look over his shoulder, "Get on your knees, and ask like you mean it"

"Wh…what?"

"You heard me."

I scowl. *If he thinks I am getting down on the floor—I confess, I didn't do a great job of cleaning up earlier and there are crumbs everywhere. Ugh! Note to self: make sure to be more detailed in all parts of your life, so it doesn't come to bite you in the arse—or in the pussy—* My thighs tremble.

"Do it," he tilts his head, "or our deal is off."

"Fine, fine, whatever," I huff, then swing my leg onto the table.

19

Weston

"What are you up to?" I frown as she scrambles up onto the table, on her knees.

She looks at me with wide eyes, "What? I'm doing what you ordered me to do."

I growl.

"You didn't specify where." She flutters her eyelashes at me.

I scowl. Of course, I didn't, but then, I hadn't expected her to kneel on the table either. This woman... Every time I think I have her pegged, she throws me a surprise. *Goddam it.* I pause at the door. Max whines, and I bend down to pat him. He pushes his nose into my hand, then drops back on his hind legs.

"Stay there." I growl, then straighten, and shut the door in his face.

"Why...why did you do that?" she squeaks, her tone so close to panting that a chuckle grips my throat. I swallow it down, then turn and crack my knuckles. "Why do you think?" I growl.

She gulps. Fear and excitement wafts off of her. Fuck! My dick thickens. She watches me as I prowl toward her, closer, closer. I pause in front of her; her spine straightens.

I roll my neck; she winces.

I glare at her and color fades from her face. "What...what are you going to do?" she whispers, all wide eyed, and my groin tightens.

I put my finger to my lips.

She swallows. Her eyebrows knit as I circle around the table to stand behind her.

"You misinterpreted what I said," I chide.

"What?"

"I told you to kneel."

"I'm kneeling."

True. I scratch my chin, "Sassy and impertinent. You don't know how to follow orders, huh?"

"I'm not one of your patients," she scoffs.

"No, our relationship could never be that...professional." I place my palms on either side of her body, bend toward her, forcing her upper body forward until she puts her palms on the table.

She shivers. Does she feel the heat from my body? Does she realize how much I want her right now?

"Weston," her breath hitches, "what are you doing?"

I palm her butt. The silence stretches a beat, another.

She shudders. "You... Are you..." She arches her back, and I flatten my palm onto the center.

"Am I?" I prompt her.

"Are you going to punish me?" her voice cracks.

"Should I?" My lips curl. I apply pressure and she curves her spine, juts out her arse.

I release her, step back. Hmm, perfect. I raise my left hand, "Beg for it." I take aim.

"For what?" She turns to glance at me over her shoulder, her gaze wide, lips parted.

Blood rushes to my groin. Hell, I haven't started, and already, I am so close to losing control. One glance at her upturned nose, that sweet mouth, and all my promises to myself go out of the window.

"Eyes forward," I growl.

She gulps, then obliges, turns her face to look ahead. *Thank fuck.* Any more sass from her, and I swear I'd have turned her over my knee... And that would have been too easy...for her...for me... Yeah, this is more arousing—the anticipation, the build-up, the sweet ache as she waits...waits.

"Say it," I snap.

"Please," the words tumble from her lips, "slap me, spank me, treat me like I'm your…"

"My — ?"

"Your property, your uh — Christmas present."

"That the best you can do, Princess?"

"Like you're Santa and I'm a naughty child." She swallows.

"And have you been a bad girl?" I lower my voice to a hush, "Tell me, Princess."

"Yes," she breathes, "I have been terrible. I disobeyed you. I willfully misinterpreted your directive, I — "

My palm connects with her butt.

"Ow," she howls, "What are you — ?"

I raise my hand, bring it down on her arse with enough force that her entire body jolts.

"Ah!" she cries out.

Crack, crack, crack. I slap her on alternate arse cheeks.

"Argh." She throws her head back, her shoulders shudder, she squirms, and tries to pull away.

I grip her hip. "Stay," I command.

A ripple shivers up her spine. She tenses, clenches her thighs together.

"Or you can go."

She draws in a breath.

So do I.

Will she go? Will she take this opportunity I am giving her to get away?

"Nothing standing in your way, Princess," I remind her. "You can leave right now. Walk away, and I won't stop you."

"The money," her voice is low, but I hear her. Of course, it comes down to that.

"I'll pay you for the two nights you spent here."

"You…you would?" She half turns, then changes her mind and positions her head to stare forward. "You'd do that?"

"Of course," I mutter. "I'm a jerk, not a cheat."

"And I'm not leaving."

"Say that again."

She gulps, the sound loud in the silence of the room.

"I… I want to stay."

"You want to see this through?"

She nods.

"Why?"

"You're not the only one who wants to fulfill your side of the bargain."

"Good." I slap her arse.

"Hey," she snarls, "I told you I wasn't leaving."

"And I am not letting up."

She lowers her chin, "And when you're done, you'll take a look at the generator?"

"You bet."

"Fine," she tosses her head, "have at it —"

I step back, walk around her to drop into my seat, and resume eating.

"What are you doing?"

I crunch down more cereal.

"I'm talking to you," she scowls.

"I'm not."

She stares at me as I shovel more of the disgusting stuff into my mouth. Cold breakfasts have never been my thing. And since when have I wanted to taste chocolate-laced savories in the morning, huh? Come to think of it, when had I begun to stop hating chocolate? Bloody hell, this woman is changing me and she isn't even trying.

I push back, stand, "I'll check out the generator now."

I turn to leave and there's a sound behind me. I hold up my hand. "What do you think you're doing?" I ask without turning around.

"Uh, I'm going to finish my cereal?"

"No."

"What?"

I pivot to glare at her over my shoulder, "You stay right there, Princess."

"Bu...but," she blinks rapidly, "you're leaving."

"And I haven't given you permission to move."

She gapes, "So you want me to stay right here, on the table, on all fours?"

"You can get naked if you want," I chuckle, "or not. Up to you."

"You're a prick," she mumbles, "a sadistic, jerk-face, wanker."

"And you're going to obey me," I inform her.

She glowers at me, "I hate you."

"And I love that wrinkle you get between your eyebrows when

you're angry." I blink. *Did I just say that? I didn't say that. And the worst thing? It's the truth.* I frown at her.

She stares back.

"Stay." I stab a finger in her direction, because well, I need to reinforce my rich prick status. Then turn and leave.

I make a detour to collect my phone from the bedroom, then step out, past the silent hot tub. At some point in the night the snow had turned to rain. Now as I stalk across the lawns they glisten from the overnight storms.

When I reach the shed at the back, I hesitate, draw in a breath, and walk in. The glass from the broken clocks glitters on the floor. I stare at it, my life's work—a fortune in antique clocks that I'd bought and fixed myself. I walk to the nearest one, pick it up. Its face is cracked, but the mechanism works. I could piece it together once more. I glance around the space… Hell, I am going to reassemble every single one of these pieces. That's not the problem, though. I stalk forward, toward the table at the far end. Fact is, someone was here… They intruded on my privacy… Which I don't give a fuck about… But her… She was here. So was Max. They'd frightened the dog and it could have easily been her. They could have hurt her… My belly knots. Fuck, if I am going to let that happen again. And it's only because I am responsible for her, until Christmas… Perhaps until the New Year, if I have my way. I cannot put her at risk again. Whoever targeted me, won't hesitate to come for her either.

I have to find a way to protect her…for as long as she is here… And later? I cannot allow them to get to her.

I pull out my phone. My first call is to the company that manages the services to the cabin and the shed.

I give them the go-ahead to switch on the electricity to the kitchen, and only to the kitchen. With the fancy bucks we pay to the private supplier, anything is possible. As for the water supply? I ask them to ensure there's only enough for two days—nothing like water running out to test the mettle of a person, huh? As for the power cut? I orchestrated that too. Just a test, a way to exert complete control over the situation, and on her. Only I hadn't counted on a goddam intruder, violating my personal space. If something had happened to her—! My shoulders bunch. Goddam it, I have to find out who was behind the break-in.

Then I dial Damian's number.

"What?" he grumbles.

"Did I disturb you?" I ask.

"Yes." He yawns. "You woke me up, you knob."

"Good." I roll my shoulders, "We have a problem."

"Not we," he mutters, "you." He yawns again, so loudly, I hear the sound of his jaw cracking over the phone. "Don't pull me into your personal shitstorm, motherfucker," he warns.

"The shed was broken into last night."

There's silence, then, "What do you mean 'broken into'?"

"Exactly that." I begin to pace. "Someone got in, then got to my collection of clocks."

There's a pause. "Didn't know you still collect and repair them."

"I never stopped."

I also don't talk about this affliction of mine with the Seven.

"I had Karina check on the security for both the cabin and the shed, so whoever managed to break in—"

"Was no ordinary burglar," he completes my thought.

I stay quiet and the silence extends.

"The Mafia." I blow out a breath. "They were behind this," I growl. "I should have known that they wouldn't stop coming after those close to us."

"And is she?" Damian asks.

"What?"

"Is she close to you?"

"We are sharing the same cabin," I snap.

"That's not what I meant."

"That's all you're getting," I retort.

Damian doesn't respond.

"If the Mafia thinks this is going to scare us off, they are wrong." I snarl.

"We won't stop until we find out who among the Mafia was behind our kidnapping," Damian agrees.

"If they're breaking in and entering now, they must be getting desperate," I mutter.

"We must be getting close to a breakthrough." Damian grunts, "Have you heard anything from Saint or Sinner about the latest on the investigations?"

"Not since they found their lady loves," I gripe. "Not that I begrudge them their happiness, but clearly, it's time we take things into our own hands."

"The New Year's eve party," Damian replies. "We'll all be there."

"Everyone except Baron." I say, referring to one of the Seven who prefers to stay clear of us and conduct his business remotely.

"Except fucking Baron," Damian agrees. "The rest of us will be there. We are bound to get an update then."

"Right." I pinch the bridge of my nose, "Meanwhile, I need to up the security here at the cabin."

"You going to ask Karina for help, again?" Damian asks.

"Why wouldn't I?"

"You know how upset Arpad's going to be about that?" he replies.

"Whatever is between her and Arpad is not my problem," I bite out. "Her investigative and security services are the best in the business and—"

"You can't trust anyone else when it concerns the safety of those you care about?"

"Right," I nod.

He chuckles.

I frown, then straighten. "I mean, no," I growl. "I mean, yes, I can't trust anyone else with securing the space and no, I don't care about her."

"Man, you're delusional," he scoffs.

"What is that supposed to mean, you piece of shit?"

He laughs, "When you get repetitive in your insults, I know you're not thinking straight."

"Fuck that." I frown, "Are you helping me or not?"

"Do I have a choice?" he replies.

"Nope," I bark, then move the phone to my right hand. "I'm stuck here with this bloody broken finger, with my woman…"

"Did you say *your* woman?"

"A slip of the tongue." I grunt, "I'm here with her and Max, and it's my responsibility to keep them both safe."

"That's all this is about, huh?"

"Of course, what else would it be?"

"You tell me." I hear the grin in his voice.

"Once you're done indulging your asinine sense of humor—maybe you could sober enough to hear me out?"

"Aren't you forgetting to say something?" he drawls.

I stay silent.

"A word beginning with 'p'?" he prompts.

"Piss off." I oblige him.

He chuckles, "Good to know you have some game left in you yet."

"That was me being polite, you tosser," I growl. "If you don't help me out, I'm going to release the video I have of you making out with your harem."

"Harem?" his voice is cautious.

"You don't think that what takes place in Vegas actually stays in Vegas."

"You recorded me?" his tone is flat

"Don't pretend you didn't do the same." It was a trip the two of us had taken, a few years ago. The rest of the Seven hadn't been available that year over the Christmas break and I had flown into LA to join Damian. We'd taken his private jet to Las Vegas… And the rest, well… as they say, it's recorded for posteriority. His, not mine.

"What do you take me for?" Damian laughs, "Of course, I have a stockpile of pics and videos on each of the Seven, including you." His voice is pleasant. "Perhaps I should upload the video of you…" his voice trails off.

"Yeah," I quip, "I jerked off to you and your three women, which face it, is nowhere as interesting as what I have on you. Not that it doesn't make you look good… I mean, they were all over you, and your face can only be seen in one frame." Which would be more than enough for him to capture the headlines of the media that day. "It's slow over Christmas, and you have a big single coming out. No doubt, it would ensure that happy families everywhere would want to look you up to find out what the fuss is all about." Not. It would effectively cost him his reputation… Oh, he'd recover from it all right, but not before the Christmas single tanked… Probably.

"Whose idea was it to release a Christmas song anyway, huh?" I snicker. "Isn't that what reality show winners and washed-up rock stars go for… Oh, wait." I laugh, "That's what you are, someone who's yesterdays' news."

"Fuck off," he growls.

"With pleasure, after you've promised to help me."

"After that incredible selling job, how can I refuse?"

"Aww," I coo, "did I hurt your itty-bitty wittle feewings, Mr. Rock Star?"

"Sometimes I am not sure why the Seven of us keep in touch," he grumbles. "It's not like there's much love lost between us."

"Maybe it's something deeper," I muse, "a shared moment—a few days in time that changed the course of our future."

"There is that." He sighs, "I could, of course, release your video anyway and see how it plays with your little girlfriend, huh?"

"Not my girlfriend, and PS, I told her about the sex tape already, so—"

"You told her?" He coughs. "Isn't that unusual for you?"

"What?" I frown, "Just making sure she understood that she can't underestimate my sex god status." I brush an imaginary speck from my sweater, as if he can see me.

"You being upfront with a woman?" I sense him shake his head. "So, it's that serious, huh?"

"Of course, not."

"Just for that, I'll do this for you."

"For what?" I crack my neck.

"To see you fall. Fuck, it must be something in the air..." He continues, "It started with Sinner, then Saint, and now you."

I move the phone away from my ear, and stare at it before switching to speakerphone, "I have no idea what you're talking about." I frown.

"Of course, not." His voice is calm, "You have no idea, do you?"

I grit my teeth, "You're getting on my balls, Savage." I growl, "One click and your video gets uploaded."

"No, you won't do it," he retorts.

"Wanna test me?"

There's silence, then he sighs, "The fuck do you want from me?"

"Listen," I speak into the phone.

20

———————

"There is no we in chocolate."
-From Amelie's diary

Amelie

The overhead light flickers and comes on. I blink. Guess the alphahole kept his word. He managed to fix the power supply to the kitchen, which means I can bake. Yay. I bite down on the inside of my cheek, glance around the space. Why does everything seem so bright? The place is bigger than I realized. The candles I had lit earlier appear weak. Too bad the attraction I feel for him shows no similar signs of waning. Dark or light, morning or night... It's a constant source of irritation that gnaws at my gut, forces me to act out of character. Like now. Why am I still on my hands and knees, on the bloody kitchen table, waiting for him?

I had said that I would obey him, but surely, this is out of bounds, even for someone like him. I mean, leaving me stationed here like I am his...possession? Am I his? Do I belong to him...? What hold does he have on me that I'd rushed to do his bidding? What would have happened if I'd gone against his decree? Hello... What am I thinking? Decree, huh? I snort. Like he is the master of all he surveys and I am his... *Don't think it; don't think it. Slave!*

Noooo, I can't allow myself to think that.

I can't allow him to have this hold on me.

But the money...the bloody millions that he holds over me? Well, he said he'd deposit the money for the nights I've already spent here...and Weston wouldn't go back on his word. Well neither would I, and I am still here, right? I'm not leaving.

I am simply, a woman standing in front of the most dominant, hot-as-fuck, alpha male she's ever met, wanting to ask him to fuck her.

There you have it—the story of my life. That ol' perception-reality thingummy... The one I can't hide from when I face the mirror.

Guess there had been more comfort in the gloom of the morning light. Everything had seemed so much more intimate. Now—I glance down at myself—I see myself through his eyes. A stupid woman, who'd allowed this obnoxious, mean-ass to manipulate me... To use his money to seduce me, to coerce me to do his bidding. *Where's your pride, Amelie? Where's that strength of character, that streak of obstinacy, that blind confidence in yourself that had you taking risks...and loans...and putting everything you have into this venture? Turning your passion into a livelihood?* My bloody foot. What a pipe dream. I'd sailed along blissfully in my little boat, even though I was fighting against the current... Until Weston bloody Kincaid had unleashed a storm that threatened to engulf my teacup. *He can dip his teabag in my hot water anytime.* I giggle, then shake my head. That's it. I am losing it, completely.

I straighten, scramble back, then off the table. My knees creak and my thighs spasm. Jesus, am I out of shape or what? I stalk over to the shelves by the oven, lean down and rummage around. There! I snatch up another large bowl—not a mixing bowl, but it could work. Thank God, we bought enough flour and chocolate and bananas to last me another round. I grab my provisions, measure out the flour on the old-fashioned scale. Seriously, it has weights and everything, I snort again. Lifestyles of the rich and famous, huh? They have all the time in the world... No, they have servants; that's what it is.

I pour the flour into the mixing bowl, break the eggs, then begin to beat it together. When it's smooth enough, I reach for the ripe bananas, peel the remaining three and drop them in. I mix them in too, then pour in the milk.

I hum to myself, shimmy my hips, taste some of the concoction. Yum.

Footsteps sound behind me, "What are you doing, Princess?"

His voice is all casual, nothing threatening about it, and that makes it worse. I straighten, reach for the pack of chocolate chips.

"You're only making it worse by not answering."

His voice is right behind and above me. I yelp, lose my grip on the packet and the entire thing tips in. "Gah!" I place the half-empty pack to the side, then whirl on him, "Look what you made me do."

"I give you one thing to do." He holds a finger right in front of my face, "One, and you disobey."

"You were gone a long time."

"Less than half an hour."

I throw up my hands, "Exactly. How long did you think I'd stay in that ridiculous position for you?"

He bends his knees, then peers into my face, "Until I gave you permission to move."

I toss my hair back from my face, "I couldn't wait, I wanted to get back to the baking."

"Is that right?" His voice lowers to a hush and my nerve endings spark, "So eager to make your crumpets—"

"Muffins." I correct him.

"Same thing." He shrugs.

"It's not." I gape at him, "Why do you constantly try to get on my nerves?"

"Because I can?" He looks me up and down and my belly quivers. He raises his gaze to my face, "Because you are mine for the next four days—mine to command, to order about, to play with as I see fit."

"I'm not your...fuck toy."

His eyes gleam, "Don't bet on it."

I purse my lips, then tilt my chin-up, "You're beginning to annoy me. You're illogical as hell, full of yourself, totally obnoxious, and cannot decide what you want."

"Oh?" He peels back his lips and his teeth shine against his tanned skin.

"If it wasn't for your...your...broken finger...I'd..."

"You'd..."

"Teach you a lesson."

"Go on," he drawls, "try me."

"Don't say I didn't warn you," I mumble.

"I'm soooo afraid." He holds up his hands, as if to ward off an attack. "Princess Buttercup and her idle threats. Has no one warned you not to play with the big bad wolf?"

"Your references are all mixed up," I snarl.

"And that disgusting mixture in that bowl... Is that the best you can do for breakfast?"

That's it, I am letting him have it. He can say anything about me, but my cooking? No fucking way. I am bloody good at what I do, and no one, definitely not a neanderthal, alpha billionaire can take that away from me. I make a noise deep in my throat.

His features brighten, "Ooh, did I hurt your feelings? Does the princess want to be saved from herself, yet?"

"Newsflash, alphahole." I shove my hand behind me, search for the mixing bowl. "This Princess can save herself."

My fingers brush the smooth surface, I snatch the vessel, fling its contents at him.

21

Weston

"Oops." Her lips quiver and her chin wobbles. She drops her gaze to my chest.

I glance down to find splotches of the brown gooey mixture sticking to my pullover. "That item of clothing costs £7000," my voice is calm. No hint of the anger that bubbles up inside... Along with something else—frustration. 48 hours... I've tried to teach her to obey. I've ordered her to obey me, told her to follow my directions. I've walked naked in front of her, slept with my body coiled around hers. I've raced toward her when I thought she was in danger... Been on the phone making sure I could find a way to protect her... And what does she do? She greets me with this...this goop? A low growl rumbles up my chest.

She blinks, "Did you just...did you?"

"What?"

"You, ah, sounded like Max when he's frustrated."

I glower, "Did you compare me to a bloody mutt?"

A snort spills from her throat.

The fuck? "Are you laughing at me?"

"Me?" She bites down on her lower lip. Her cheeks redden. She lowers the bowl—her hand trembles... Is it from my proximity or from the weight of the vessel? Maybe it's fear of how I'll react. Good. The blasted container dips. I grab hold of it.

"Ah, thanks," her voice is strangled.

"Don't thank me." I reach past her, lower the bowl to the counter.

"Wait," she bursts out.

"What?" I frown.

She angles her body, scoops up some of the mixture. She glances from it to me, "It, uh, has chocolate."

"So?"

"I missed a spot."

"Excuse me?" I glare at her.

She bites her lips and her eyes gleam.

"Don't you fucking dare, Princess, I—"

She tosses the stuff at my face. It hits my cheek, and some of it drips down my chin, onto my chest.

"There," she angles her head to the side, "much better."

"That's it," I growl, "you're going to pay for that."

She squeaks, tries to duck around me. I plant my injured hand on the other side of her, caging her in.

"Apologize," I growl.

"No."

"Say you're sorry."

She sticks out her tongue, "You can go and dunk your swollen head in that stupid hot tub."

"I have a better idea." I reach for the mixture in the bowl, scoop up a palmful.

"No, no, no." She angles her body, takes in what I am doing. "You won't," she breathes.

"Oh, you bet I will." I smash the gooey stuff in her face.

She screams, wriggles around. I thrust my hips into her, to hold her in place, then rub the mix into her face, down her neck, across her chest… over the fabric of her blouse that encloses her breasts, and draw circles around her erect nipples. The blood rushes to my groin. My dick lengthens, nestles happily into the valley between her legs.

"Wes… Weston," she gulps.

"Shh!"

I glare at those peaked delights. I reach behind her to gather more of the goop and trail it over one breast, then the other. The mixture dribbles down from each mound. "Beautiful." I lower my head, close my mouth around one.

"Ah," a moan leaves her mouth. "Wes… Please."

I glare up at her. "Stay still," I command. "Don't say a word."

She purses her lips, draws down her eyebrows. She opens her mouth.

I click my tongue. "Don't," I growl, "Nothing; nada."

"But—"

"Another word and I'll stuff this mix in your mouth, and I promise you, that would be a waste, cause I plan to use every drop of your muffin mix to draw out your pleasure."

She swallows, then presses her lips together.

"Excellent."

She stares at me.

"Should I reward you for that little bit of compliance, hmm?"

She nods.

"All right then." I reach behind her, snatch up some of the mix. I hold my fingers to her lips, "Open."

"But—"

I plop my fingers inside her mouth. She bites down with her teeth and I feel the tug all the way to the tip of my dick. My cock thickens, pushes up into her.

Her gaze widens.

"Feel that, Buttercup?"

I bring my other hand to massage her breast, then press my hips forward with enough pressure that her pelvis cradles every throbbing inch of my very aroused shaft.

She swallows, and the suction on my fingers, sends a shudder of heat racing down my spine.

"Fuck." My breathing grows shallow. I ease my finger out from between her lips, and bring it to my own. I lick my glistening fingertips.

She moans, "Jesus." She gulps.

"Nothing to do with the man above," I mutter, "but if I don't have you right now, the one between my legs is going to hate me for a long time."

She chuckles. "You're so corny." She grins up at me, her features alight, with so much mischief, so much life, that fuck, my cock thickens even more.

I frown. "Silence," I snap.

She winces, then pouts.

Fucking adorable. I shake my head. The fuck am I doing, thinking about her in those cutesy adjectives? And cutesy—? What the fuck? How did that even get in my vocabulary. I frown down at her and she stares back.

"I'm corny, hmm?" I reach behind her, grab the bowl with both hands, then upturn it over her head.

She gasps.

The mixture flows down her face, her neck, her chest, down to where our bodies are joined. "That's better." I place it down behind her, then straighten. I step back, rub the mix down her front, across her stomach, to the valley between her thighs.

Her breath hitches.

I pat the mix into the apex of her thighs, onto her jeans.

"Ah," she trembles. I sink down to my knees, then thrust my face into her sweet, core. I bite down on the fabric that covers the crotch of her jeans and her entire body bucks. She grabs at my hair and tugs. The pain rams straight down my spine, to my cock. I grip her thighs, pry them apart, then dig my teeth into the now-damp cloth that stretches across her pussy.

She screams. "Oh, my God, ohmigod…oh…my…"

I rise to my feet, bringing her up with me, and hoist her onto the counter and straight onto the bowl I'd placed behind her, which tips sending more of the gooey mess to pool around her. She shivers, tips her chin up.

"I need to be inside of you."

She nods. She opens and closes her mouth, her gaze pleading with me. But she doesn't speak. About time. "You worried about our arrangement?"

She jerks her chin.

"So maybe I should…" I step back.

She scissors her legs around my waist.

"Don't want me to go, huh?" I study her face. "Want me to fuck you?"

She frowns back.

"Where?"

She purses her lips.

"In your mouth?"

She shakes her head.

"Your pussy?"

She nods.

"I have a better idea." I lean in until our breaths mingle, "How about I take your arse?"

She swallows; her pupils dilate.

"You want that, huh?"

She bites down on her lower lip and her little teeth worry the tender skin.

I rub my thumb over the swollen skin and she gulps. "Maybe I'll save that for later, huh?"

Her shoulders rise and fall.

"Maybe I shove my fingers in your arse, while I tear into your pussy with my dick, while I stick my tongue down your throat?"

She nods, then shakes her head, then throws her hands up.

I know the feeling. "Decisions, decisions." I chuckle.

She digs her thighs into my hips, uses it to leverage herself up, then smashes her lips to mine.

22

***

Amelie

I press my mouth to his, fold my arms about his shoulders, and proceed to climb him, like he's a massive tree… Or hell, like he's Santa fucking Claus, come to grant me all of my wishes. Is it Christmas yet? Gah! Almost…though it sure seems like all of my dreams have come true. This man… He drives me mad, he makes me want to slap him and kiss him. Love him and hate him… Throw myself at his feet and beg him to put an end to this growing, yearning, emptiness inside. I cling to his big frame, bite down on that full, pouty lower lip of his that's hypnotized me since the first time I saw him. I slip my tongue inside his mouth, suck on him, pour all of myself into that kiss. My head spins, my pussy clenches, and my nipples hurt. I lose my hold and begin to slip down, the muffin mixture sloshing and giving with each contact of my clothes against his. Shit, I scramble to hold on, and he places his broad palm against the seat of my butt.

Heat instantly flushes up my spine. I shudder.

He wraps his other palm around the back of my neck, and holds me there.

I release his lips, lean back—well, put as much distance between us as his firm grip allows, which is about uh—an inch…maybe a little more. Our noses bump; his long eyelashes graze my forehead. Hell, how can a man have such feminine lashes?

"So greedy," he mutters, "so damn sexy. Such a tiny package, but so much potency packed into those curves."

Shut up and fuck me already, is what I want to say. Instead, I hold his gaze, look deeply into those grey eyes, past the colorless, mirror-like surface, to that darkness that pools inside, the flecks of gold that intersperse their depths. Contradictions, such complexity he holds within himself.

"You can trust me." I whisper.

He blinks and his features open with the surprise.

"I won't hurt you," I add.

Where is this coming from? If anything, he's the one who can break me. His dominance could crush me, his strength could render me powerless, as his lips tease me, taunt me, his fingers dig into the curve of my hips, and his dick throbs against my aching center... "Please," I mumble. *What do I want from him? Why is it that this push-pull between us makes it so difficult to bare myself to him?* I cup his cheek, "Take me. Use me. Fill me up with your cum, bury yourself inside of me, and fuck your past out of me."

Wait, did that even make sense...? "I mean—"

"Shh..." He rubs his nose against mine, the gesture tender and gentle and so unlike any other emotion he's shown toward me. A pressure builds behind my eyes. Shit. A little bit of affection, and I'm ready to bawl my eyes out.

He rakes his gaze down my features, then he brushes his lips across mine, once, twice. He lowers me back onto the countertop. "You on birth control?"

I blink.

"Are you?" He frowns.

I nod. "Yes," I clear my throat, "I'm just coming off a relationship so..."

He glares at me and I feel the blood drain to my core. How the hell does my body recognize his intentions before my mind has fully digested what he wants from me?

The sound of a zipper being lowered reaches me. Air hits my swollen center. "Up," he growls.

I wind my arms about his shoulder, raise my butt. He shoves down at my jeans which move an inch, then get stuck around my hips. "Umm."

He shakes his head and I stop talking. He glances around, notices my chef's satchel on the table. He hauls me up by the waist, turns and takes a step, then plants me on the table. I'm not light, I have curves — Hey, don't begrudge me my chocolate — and of course, he's a power-house of muscles, but the way he maneuvers my body... Well... My knees turn to jelly. Bloody hell, this guy is machismo personified, and I am putty in his hands. And now — he whips out a pair of kitchen scis-sors. Then steps back, holds up my leg and proceeds to cut the fabric up one side.

What the —?

He does the same for the fabric on my other leg and it falls away, then cuts my blouse at each shoulder.

"Weston — "

He shakes his head.

"You can trust me," his lips quirk as he repeats my words back at me.

Can I though?

I frown.

He locks his gaze with mine, then raises the scissors. He glances down, then I feel the give of my bra straps. My breasts spring free. His nostrils flare. He bends, licks a nipple, before sucking on it.

Goosebumps flare on my skin.

"So fucking sweet, you're one melting mass of chocolate, Buttercup."

Jeez, he makes me sound like a dessert...which is flattering, I suppose.

He pulls back, I hear the snap of the blades cutting through the fabric of my blouse. The garment falls off. Air hits my skin, goosebumps pop along my forearms, and my nipples harden.

He straightens, places the tip of the scissors to the center of my chest, without cutting the skin. I shiver. He drags the blade up over the mound of one breasts, circles the nipple, which instantly pebbles further. Down to my belly button. I swallow. He glances down and his breathing grows labored, "Fuck me," he growls. "I can't hold out any longer."

He tosses the scissors aside, reaches for his zipper and lowers it. His cock springs forward — big, throbbing. I've seen it before...but some-how, he seems bigger. More aroused. The swollen tip is almost purple with need, and drops of precum bead the slit. Saliva pools in my mouth; my chest rises and falls.

I reach for him, but he grabs my wrist. "If you touch me, I won't last," he growls.

I frown, implore him with my eyes.

His gaze intensifies, then his lips quirk. "Later," he promises. "For now, I am going to take your cunt." He swoops down, grabs my thighs under my knees, pulls my legs up and apart so they're at my ears and I fall back to my elbows. He glares down directly at my sex.

OMFG! My head spins. I am open and displayed for him, my arousal so strong I can smell myself. Is that gross? His nostrils flare… Uh, guess he can scent me too?

"Look at yourself." His grip tightens, "You're so wet, so ready. You want me, Princess?"

Gah, is that even a question? "I…" I open my mouth and his lips curl.

Trick question, huh? I pout again, thrust my pelvis up and against his hold.

His smile widens. "Hold yourself open for me," he commands.

I blink. He can't be serious.

"Do it," he snaps.

I don't even realize I've rushed to obey him until I feel my fingers brush my cunt. Damn him, is there anything this man can't get me to do? I pry open my pussy lips, and his gaze intensifies. "Fuck me," he mutters, "I am going to drink from you."

Yes. Yes.

"Scoop up your cum and offer it to me."

Wh-a-a-t? My vision narrows. Black spots dot my line of sight. My heart begins to pound so hard, I am sure it's going to break out of my chest.

"Now."

His hard voice whips through my head, erasing every other thought. I am a vessel, an empty canvas which he'll paint with his cum. No, what? *Don't think. Don't react. Do what he asks.* I slip one finger, then a second into my channel. My chest heaves. His throat moves as he swallows. He's as affected by this connection… This, whatever it is that he's doing to me, is arousing him just as much. I curl my fingers inside of myself and a moan rises up. It's nowhere close to what I need, but the way he watches me... How he follows my movements with his heavy-lidded gaze…is as erotic as looking on while he fucks me… Okay, I lie… Not the same… But it is hot nevertheless. Know what I mean? I hold up my glistening fingers, and he closes his mouth around my digits, drags his tongue over the skin. My sex clenches and more moisture pools in my core.

"How the hell do you taste so sweet?" He licks his lips, "Of chocolate and the most tempting honey."

"You hate chocolate," I mutter.

"That's true." He tilts his head, "But, it tastes different on you."

"It does?"

He nods. "It tastes like sin when I lick it off your lips."

"Oh." My belly quivers. That was almost poetic. *Gah!* Who'd have thought the brute could actually string words together until they sound erotic.

"In fact," he peers into my features, "I am convinced you have desserts for all three meals." He stares at me, "You do, don't you?"

"What do you think?"

"I bet you sneak that black gold in between, too." He lowers his gaze back to the triangle between my thighs, "Makes me wonder if you taste as incredible there as you did the last time..."

Why don't you try it for yourself; why don't you—? I gasp as he does just that—drops his head, licks me from arsehole to cunt, and again. He stabs his tongue inside my channel, and begins to drink from me. He slurps on me, licks my swollen nub, lavishes attention on it, then bites on it. Goosebumps flare on my skin; I arch my back off the table, push myself up and into his face. More, more. My fingers tingle. I itch to take my hands off my pussy, to grab hold of his hair and tug him to me, to force him to fuck me with his tongue until I come.

"Don't you dare."

I blink, to find him leaning above me.

"I'm not done yet."

What's he talking about? I'm done, more than done. I'm on the verge of exploding like a pie that's been left too long in the oven. Ugh, these comparisons are terrible, and my brain cells have turned to mush.

"Eyes on me," he commands.

I watch him as he lowers his chin, his unshaven whisker-edged visage, and rubs it up my pussy.

"Ah!" My entire body bucks. I writhe under his touch, thrash my head from side to side, "Oh, my God, oh, my God." He does it again and I see stars. The climax rushes up from my toes, screams up my spine, and threatens to explode. I can't stop, I can't.

The next second he straightens over me, positions his dick at my entrance. "Condom," he growls, then reaches into the back pocket of his pants, pulls out a wrapper.

Does he walk around with one all the time? Was he that confident that he was going to fuck me…? When the agreement was for us to do everything but? Will this change things between us? What will become of the money? Could I allow him to pay me after this…? Wouldn't that reduce everything between us to something it wasn't? What is it anyway, what—?

"Stop."

He frowns down into my face.

I draw in a breath. Am I that transparent? Or is he that perceptive? Does he have a sixth sense that he can focus on simultaneously wrapping his dick and reading my expression? What the hell am I thinking? Why am I tying myself up in such knots? I glance around… What the hell am I doing here, with him, holding my pussy open to him like a sex-crazed pervert? I withdraw my fingers from my cunt, open my mouth to speak. He leans in and presses his lips to mine. He swipes his tongue inside my mouth, across my teeth, draws from me, shares my breath so absolutely. I stutter.

He pulls back, peers into my face, "Do you want me to stop?"

Do I?

"Once I take you, there's no going back."

Uhhh?

"If you want to leave, I won't stop you."

Won't he?

"But if you stay…" he glares at me, "if you stay, you're mine."

23

Weston

"Mine to protect. Mine to possess and break. Mine to fuck so hard you won't walk straight for days, and when you do, you'll sense my cock in your deepest most intimate of places. I plan to not stop, not until we've fucked whatever is between us into the open, until my skin fuses with yours and I have invaded your secrets, gleaned your fears, and infused your innermost thoughts with my presence."

Her pupils dilate, and her face pales.

This is it then; she's going to refuse me. I've bared myself to her, told her what I am thinking about and she'll decide it's not for her. She's going to turn away from me, tell me she doesn't want me or my money. She's going to— She reaches out her hand, tugs at the condom I hold. She rips open the wrapper, then reaches down between us. She eases the condom over the swollen head of my cock, struggles with it. The condom slides over the rim and she smooths it down. I glance up to find her forehead furrowed in concentration. That line between her eyebrows crinkles. I lean down and press my lips to it. She positions my shaft at the entrance to her pussy.

"I want you," I mutter against her forehead. I press my lips to her eyelids, one after the other, to the tip of her nose, then press my mouth to hers, " I want to kiss you until your mouth can't ask for more." I nip on her chin. "Every part of you tastes of a different dessert."

She giggles and the sound is so light, so beautiful. My throat closes. I pull back enough to take in her features, watch her gaze widen as I kick my hips forward and impale her. Her mouth parts, a soundless scream that only I can hear. I wait for her pussy to adjust to my girth, for her channel to grip my dick, flow, melt, tug on my shaft. The tension builds at the base of my spine. Shit, I've never been so close to coming, so quickly before. The taste of her swirls on my tongue; the scent of her envelops my senses. I grip the backs of her thighs, drag my hand up one, then the other, urge her legs over my shoulders. "Hold on."

She nods, locks her ankles around my neck. I press my elbows to the table on either side of her head, then push in further. Her entire body seems to thrum; her eyelids flicker. She brings a hand up to my face. I turn my head and kiss her palm, then grip her wrist and twist her hand over her head. Her gaze widens and her breathing grows ragged. Fuck, if my little show of dominance didn't turn her on even more. I bring her other hand up, shackle both of her wrists with my uninjured hand.

I pull back, then thrust into her with enough force that the entire table jostles. Something—one of the plates, or both—crashes to the floor. I begin to fuck her in earnest. Pull back, push forward, back, forward again. With every plunge, her body moves up the table. I wrap my fingers around her neck, lean some of my weight on her to hold her in place. Her pupils dilate further, the blue so light, the color of her eyes seems to mirror mine. I see my reflection in them, sense the climax building inside of her. I squeeze my fingers around her neck, and she gasps. Her chest heaves. She digs her heels into my back, tugs her hands in my grasp. I pull back, all the way back to the edge of her channel, then tilt my hips and impale her with such force that her eyelids flutter, she throws her head back, arches her spine, and the trembling shudders up her body, her chest. "Come." I loosen my grasp and she shatters. Her pussy clamps around my dick and moisture bathes my shaft. Her orgasm seems to go on and on, and when her shoulders slump, sweat beads her forehead, her upper lip. I bend down, lick it off. She stirs.

"Eyes on me," I demand.

She cracks her eyelids open, locks her gaze with mine, and I begin to move again, thrust into her, angle my hips and sink deep inside of her. Bury myself in her sweet melting cunt again and again. She reaches up, locks her lips with mine, her eyes still on mine. Something hot stabs at my chest, my balls draw up, the tension in my groin snaps and I come inside her.

Her eyelids flutter; her body twitches. I pull back, just enough for our breaths to mingle, then stay there and watch as her muscles uncoil, one by one. I watch her as her breathing deepens. A flush creeps up her cheeks. When I pull out of her, she stirs. "Don't move," I whisper. Her lips curve. I pull off the condom, tie it up, then leave it on the table. I'll have to come back for it later.

I scoop her up in my arms, kick the door to the kitchen closed behind me, and carry her to the ensuite in the bedroom. I lower her to the floor near the tub, take in her curves. "You're gorgeous." I lean in to kiss her, before placing her in the shower stall.

"Your splint," she murmurs, "you'll get it wet."

"It's waterproof." I reassure her.

She wraps her arms around me, presses her nose into the skin bared by the 'V' of my shirt collar. "You smell like chocolate." She giggles.

I lower my chin and kiss her head, "And you smell of me."

"Mmm." She nuzzles against me and my heart begins to race. A tightness coils in my chest. Shit... This... Tenderness... This whatever connection is there between us... It is the beginning of the end. If I continue down this path, it leads to a slippery slope. One I have no intention of traversing. Not for a long time. If ever.

I pry her arms from round me, and step back.

She frowns.

"Gonna look in on Max," I say. "Why don't you shower first, huh?"

She peers up into my face, then nods.

I pivot, shrug out of my sodden pullover and pants and dump the clothes in the laundry basket on the way out.

Once in the kitchen, I dispose of the used condom, along with the remnants of her clothes. I clean up any chocolate within reach of his short, little legs, then top off the food and water bowls for Max, who scrabbles in and attacks the food like he's been starving. Speaking of, I need more of her. Fuck, this is ridiculous. I drag my fingers through my hair.

I've been away from her for a few minutes, and already, I miss her.

That sensation when I was inside her...? Fuck. It was...different, yet familiar. Like coming home. Home? What the fuck? I shake my head. So, the sex had been intense—more intense than any experience I've ever had before—it means we're compatible in bed. So, I'll fuck her, give her pleasure, make her orgasm more than she has ever before. I'll ensure her time with me is the single most incredible experience of her life, that it spoils her for any man after.

The band around my chest tightens. Of course, there'll be men after me... She isn't mine...except for the length of this time that I've bargained from her. For the days that are left, I can make good on my promise. I can protect her, take care of her every need, treat her like the princess she is. And when we are done... I'll walk away without a second thought.

I clench my fist at my side. Why the hell does it matter to me what she does after that, huh? I'll use her for my needs, then leave. It's what I do best. No commitments. Nothing holding me back. It will be a great break. I glance down at my hand with the splint... And the sex will, surely, only help the healing, huh? My heart hammers in my chest. So why the fuck am I standing here in the middle of the kitchen, still naked?

I straighten, march toward the door, when a scream sounds from the direction of the bedroom. I race forward.

24

Amelie

I stare at the spider that crawls across the floor. My skin feels too tight, my stomach twists in knots.

Shit, I can face grown chefs having a tantrum, or irate clients. Hell, I'd even face an alphahole who wanted to force me to submit. But the creepy, crawly, eight-legged species…? Gross. I could do without them. My pulse races, my heart hammers, and adrenaline fills my blood. I glance around, then spot the towel and snatch it up. I hold it out in front of me, sidle toward the exit, when footsteps sound and Weston's massive figure fills the doorway.

"What's wrong?" His chest heaves, his gaze alert. He has the fingers of his uninjured hand curled into a fist. Huh?

"The hell?" He stalks inside.

I glance down and scream again.

He flinches, "Jesus, woman, why are you having a breakdown?" He pauses mid-step.

"That…" I point my towel at the floor in front of him.

He glances down, then lowers his foot…missing the spider by an inch. A breath whooshes out of me.

"It's… it's…" I gulp.

"A spider?"

"Eek." I sidle back from both of them… "Please, can you get rid of it?"

He glances down at the bug, which scuttles toward me.

I scream, then dance around it in a wide circle that places me directly in front of Weston. "I hate those things," I whine.

"All that sass and spirit… I thought you were a spitfire, then along came a spider and frightened little Miss Muffet away."

I blink a little. "Did you just compare me to another nursery rhyme?"

"Can't seem to make up my mind about you, huh?" His warm palms descend on my hips. He lifts me up—like literally snatches me up from the floor—and plants me at his side.

My belly and other parts of me flutter. Shucks, every time I try to hate him…he disarms me…shows a part of him that unnerves me.

He grabs a tissue, scoops up the insect then heads for the doorway.

"Wh…where are you going?"

"To get Miss Muffet's spider outside."

"Oh." My cheeks heat. "Won't you be, ah…?" I look his gorgeous, unclothed figure up and down, and all thoughts leave my mind. OMFG, he's…hot. I mean, I knew he was and yep, he's had his cock and tongue and fingers inside of me… But when he flaunts his eight pack and those powerful thighs and the—uh!—all of him in full-frontal, then… Well… Uh, what am I trying to say? I blink.

"I'm beginning to think you prefer the sight of my dick to my face."

I jerk my chin up, "Nothing like that… I mean," I wave my palm in front of me, "yeah, I do… I mean, I like both… I mean…"

His chuckles at my blathering response. "Get in the shower," he orders. "I'll be back."

I shiver. He turns and stalks off, and I admit, I watch that tight, glorious arse of his until he's out of sight. Hell, I'm in a sex haze. And I admit, it's almost as good as the endorphins brought on by a chocolate binge… Okay, better… Surely, it must be the most pleasurable way of losing calories. At this rate, by New Year's, hopefully, I'll have lost some weight. I snort… Likely story. I only have to look at desserts for the pounds to kiss my thighs… Not that he'd complained…

I turn and survey my figure in the mirror—flushed face, reddened patches on my neck and chest... My breasts seem almost too big for my narrow waist and my hips.

But hey, at least, I look like I sample my desserts. I mean, imagine if

I were reed-thin. And a dessert chef? I toss my head. That would send out the wrong signal, completely. I love my curves, okay… Normally… When I'm not having sudden bouts of self-doubt. Doesn't everyone have them?

I hear him talking to Max in the kitchen.

Shit, better get into the shower as alphahole had commanded. I head in that direction, then stop. *The hell am I doing?* Because he'd ordered me to… Would I give in and do what he'd asked? So, we had an arrangement… But won't that be null and void, considering we've slept together? I blow out a breath…

Well, then… Guess I'd better kiss the money goodbye, huh? My guts twist. Okay, so it means I am back where I started—debts to pay off, a business to run… Correction—a business I have nurtured with sweat and passion… and chocolate. I chuckle. A business which I've enjoyed building up. So what, if sometimes, when I'm bone-weary tired, I've wished I had someone by my side to share the load?

I am good at what I do. I don't need some bloody man to help shoulder the burden. Certainly, not a mean-as-hell, epitome of masculinity whose bearded chin is a potent weapon that can rub me to orgasm like Alladin's lamp. I snort out a half-laugh. Those stupid fairy tales and nursery rhymes that he often speaks in… It's getting to me. It's as bad as my pudding fetish.

I hear his footstep thudding down the hallway, and head for the bathtub instead. It's a small act of defiance, but hey, it's the best I can do. I reach over, plug the drain, then flip on the taps.

I am about to step in, then pause. I race to the sink, rummage around in the cabinet underneath… Aha! Bath bombs, and chocolate-flavored, at that… OMG… Yes! Half running back to the tub, I drop them in.

"What are you—?"

I hear his voice taper off as I climb into the tub and stretch out.

The hair on my forearms rises and I tip up my chin to find him watching me through hooded eyes.

I cup my breasts and squeeze; his nostrils flare.

I drag my palms down my waist, to the space between my thighs.

He shakes his head.

I pause, "What?"

"Who does your pussy belong to?"

I swallow.

"Tell me, Princess." He lowers his voice to a hush. My nerve endings pop. "Say it," he insists. "Who owns your sweet cunt?"

"You," I swallow, "you do."

"Damn right." His lips curl and he jerks his chin.

I lean back in the tub.

"Spread your legs," he commands.

I am instantly wet, and it's not from the bath water, I assure you. Hell, he could ask me to eat strawberries instead of chocolate and I would… No… Not that. Anything but that. Honestly, I don't have anything against those fruits, but nothing comes between me and my chocolate, except… I peer up at him from under my eyelashes, "Why is it that only you get to tell me what to do?"

"Because, I can," he growls. "Because you promised to do everything I asked of you," he adds.

"And what about the fact that we already slept together?" I ask. "Doesn't that mean the agreement is void?"

"Fuck the agreement. I propose something new."

"You… you do?"

He nods.

"I'll pay you what I promised, as long as you let me fuck you."

25

Weston

Shut up, shut up. What the fuck are you saying? Why did you have to take everything that happened between the two of you and make it into something twisted?

Because I can? I tense my shoulders.

Because that last time I'd taken her, the way I had kissed her had been…different. *It had meant something… Don't ask me what… I have to figure that shit out, but holy fuck, that had gone beyond fucking…* It's the kind of experience you don't forget, which is why I am back here, watching as her gaze narrows. As she tightens her lips, as the color fades from her cheeks. As she swallows, then folds her arms around herself. "Excuse me?" Her voice is low but firm, "What did you say?"

"You heard me." I fold my arms over my chest, mirroring her… Because she's right, that NLP shit works… Why the hell am I echoing her words? I widen my stance, glance down at her, "I'll pay for the remaining time I bought from you, as long as I can —"

"Fuck me?"

I tilt my head. "I am not going to repeat myself."

She swallows, "So, this is it?" She hunches into herself, "That's all this is to you? A transaction?"

"I told you from the beginning, that's all it was." I lower my chin.

"Wrong place, wrong time… Although, perhaps it was the right occasion for you, huh?" I drag my gaze down her body, pausing at her breasts, then at the gorgeous flesh between her legs. My dick throbs and my balls harden. Of course, I still want her. That hasn't changed. I'll have to do my best to get her out my system; there is no other way out. "Well?" I roll my shoulders, "What do you say?"

"Why are you doing this?" She stares. "Why are you suddenly conforming to your alphahole persona?"

"This is who I am." I raise my shoulders. "Deal with it."

"I don't believe it." The water rises up to over her breasts. "What happened in the last few seconds that you went from…?"

"Dominant?"

"With a heart…to an unfeeling brute who reduces everything to a transaction."

"If you thought everything that happened between us was anything but, you're wrong."

"I'm not." She brings up her knees, covering the sight of both her pussy and her breasts.

My fingertips tingle. *Lean over, pry those long thighs apart. Get in there with her, bury your face against her sweet cunt and bring her to orgasm. Make her forget everything that you said since you walked back in here.* I lock my thighs, dig my feet into the floor.

"What's different between how it was to what it is now?" I frown. "I was going to pay you. I am still paying you… Only now there's sex — the penetrative kind — thrown in for good measure." I shrug, like it means nothing to me.

She doesn't react. *Shit, that's not a good sign.* I'm not that blind; I know exactly how I affect her when I curl my lips and command her.

"Well?" I tap my toes, "You in or out?"

She swallows. "Don't do this," she whispers. "Don't reduce what we had into something it's not."

"You're the one who's making it out to be something different." I glare down at her. "Take it or leave it."

She pushes her forehead into her knees. "I… I can't do it."

My heart begins to thump. Sweat beads my forehead. *Shit, don't make her choose, you wanker. The hell are you doing pushing her away? You had it all… for a few seconds. You could have handled this differently, shown her exactly how much you care. You could have, for once in your fucked-up life, done the right thing.* Instead… I'd decided to go all billionaire alphahole on her… Because…

face it, that's what I am. That's how I intend to stay, and no sassy, curvy, chocolate-scented, gorgeous woman like her is going to reveal the feelings that churn under the surface.

"Fine, then." I turn and stalk to the door, then pause. "I'll pay you for the two days you spent with me, and we leave tomorrow."

I pivot, move forward.

Wait for it. Wait for it.

"Hey," she calls out. "What did you mean? Where are we going?"

I turn, glance over my shoulder, "To meet my family of course."

"It's not yet Christmas." She rises to her feet and the water flows from her shoulders down her waist, to splash onto the almost-filled bath tub. Her blonde hair curls over her forehead, sticks to her shoulders. The scent of…chocolate—of course, what else—laced with something honeyed and spicy swirls through the air.

"It's almost Christmas." I raise a shoulder.

"It's not the same," she scowls.

"It is now," I curl my lips, "because I say so."

She swallows, "And if I say no?"

"Are you saying no?" I glare at her.

She pales, opens her mouth.

I shake my head.

She purses her lips shut.

"Well?" I snap.

"No," she replies.

"What?" I growl.

"No, I'm not saying no." She winces, "I mean, yes, I'll come with you to meet your family. But that New Year's Eve thing? You can forget that."

I glower at her.

She juts out her chin, snaps back her shoulders, and doesn't blink.

Bloody hell, that sass of hers is back, thank fuck. Damn, if I don't hate it when her spirit is cowed.

"Fine."

"Fine." She tosses her head.

I turn.

She calls out again, "But the roads, the storm…"

I can't stop the grin that splits my face.

I wipe it off of my face, turn, "What storm?"

"Uh, the one that caused the roads to close and the electricity—"

The overhead lights come on and she blinks. The brightness pours over us, envelops us, cuts the space between us as if it's a barrier. How strange. Apparently, this time, the darkness had been kinder.

"Oh, and Princess?"

She angles her head.

"Shut off the tap, will you?"

26

"Life is uncertain; eat dessert first."
-From Amelie's diary

Amelie

I stare through the window from the backseat of the luxurious SUV. We'd left early this morning, heading toward the outskirts of Durham, where Weston's family home is.

Max whines from the back. I turn around and pat his head. Weston has his faults, but he hasn't stinted when it comes to Max. The car has a specially fitted pet booster seat in the rear, complete with a tether attached to his harness to keep him safe. Max licks my hand, then turns to glance out of the window. I swear, the puppy is more human than many of the two-legged variety of animals I've met... Present company included, of course. I shoot a sideways glance at the man in the seat next to me. His hair brushes against his collar, his beard seemingly fuller than what it was a few hours ago... Is he sprouting hair by the minute? Does it mean when he drags those whiskers across my pussy it will feel more intense than before? Ha, not possible. Whoever had said that once you go beard, you don't go back, was bloody right.

He raises his hand and drags his fingers through that hair on his chin. I gulp, then squeeze my thighs together. *Come on, you can't be turned on by that simple act.* I wriggle around in my seat. *Get a life, woman. He misled you, remember? Made you think there was a storm outside that kept you marooned in the cabin, without electricity, when there was nothing of the kind taking place.*

"What else did you lie to me about?" I mumble.

After that break-up in the bathroom... Could it be qualified as a break-up when we were never really together? Sure, in the carnal sense, I mean, but there was never any relationship between us, was there...?

Well, after the end of that relationship that never was and which shall never again be referred to by me, I'd stood there dumbstruck and naked and in the bath tub. The water had spilt over the sides and I had scrambled to shut off the tap. Of course, the alphahole had had the last say there, as well. Damn, but I hate the man. Hate his superiority complex, hate how, without even trying, he'd managed to turn my life upside down.

"What do you mean?" his voice rumbles over me. His presence thrums in that enclosed space. His larger-than-life persona pushes down on my shoulders, keeps me pinned to my side of the back seat.

"The storm," I mutter, "you lied to me."

"Not my fault you didn't check the weather."

"My phone didn't have a signal..." I bite the inside of my cheek. I could have tried harder. I could have checked online when I'd called Isla from the bathtub. Bloody bath tub; I hate bath tubs.

I'd clambered over the side of the tub, almost slipped and fallen, dried myself off, wrapped a towel around myself.

For the rest of the day we'd ignored each other. I'd made grilled sandwiches for lunch and we'd eaten them separately. I'd spent the rest of the day avoiding him... Cleaning the house... Or at least, trying to. Dinner had been soup and a pasta dish, the ingredients available, thanks to our trip to the supermarket. We'd eaten together at the dining table in the kitchen. He'd offered to help load up the dishwasher. I'd refused. And he'd headed outdoors with Max. I was reading in the living room, when he'd come in. He'd ignored me, headed off to the bedroom.

By the time I'd gone to bed, jerkface was under the covers...on his side of the bed, the white sheets pulled up to his waist, his sculpted chest all angles and planes, his biceps bulging from where he'd folded his arm behind his neck.

I'd almost crawled into bed right then, and cuddled up next to him... Not. Thankfully, I'd managed to retrieve my clothes from my bag, marched back into the bathroom to change. Dressed in pajamas and socks, I'd slipped between the sheets, after building a virtual fort between us with pillows and cushions. I'd fallen asleep almost at once... At least the sex had worn me out... Fringe benefits. I snort aloud.

"Care to share your thoughts?" he drawls. That voice... Dark and edgy and with an hint of mystery that had entranced me from the beginning, ripples down my spine. My nipples harden and my toes curl. I clutch my handbag to my chest. Hopefully, it will hide exactly how turned on I am. *Gah!* This is so not fair.

I rub at my temples, shake my head. "It's nothing," I respond.

"It's something." I sense him turn to me and tip my head so my heavy hair falls over my face. Anything to hide from him.

"Nothing of consequence," I insist.

"Whatever is in that bag, seems to be of consequence though."

I blink, shift the bag into a more comfortable position. "It's—"

"Don't say nothing," he growls.

"Cookies."

"Huh?" His forehead furrows.

"I baked cookies," I explain.

"Cookies?" He seems taken aback, "You made cookies?"

"We are going to see your family. I am a baker..." I raise my shoulders.

"That's why you were up early this morning?"

I nod. I'd remembered to charge my phone, and set an alarm, and woken up a few minutes before it had gone off. Guess those years of getting up before dawn and heading off to get my baking done for the day had come in handy. I'd switched off the alarm, crawled out of bed and out from under the weight of his arm.

He'd shoved aside the pillows at some point in the night and had pulled my body against his, and spooned me... No wonder I had slept well. I had turned and seen his features relaxed in sleep. His beard had seemed thicker, his pecs closer to a work of art, and that beautiful throat...that gorgeous throat... I'd moved in to inhale his scent at the base of his neck, where it would be the most potent. He'd stirred. I'd frozen. His muscles had relaxed and I'd scrambled off the bed. Lucky escape...

Was it, though? If he'd woken up then, would he have...taken me over his lap and spanked me? My sex clenches. I squeeze my thighs shut. Dip into my bag and pull out the tin—I'd emptied out the contents and repurposed it. I pop the lid and the scent of vanilla and chocolate, and the touch of cinnamon I'd sprinkled on at the end, fills the space.

He reaches for one; I slap the lid on his fingers.

"Ow." He pulls back, shakes out his hand, "Do you want to break a finger in my good hand?"

"Did I succeed?" I bare my teeth.

"It'll take more than a batch of your cookies to bring me down," he retorts.

"Don't bet on it," I scoff.

"Hmm," he glares at the tin, then at my face, "my mother doesn't expect gifts."

"It's Christmas."

"My presence is gift enough."

My jaw drops, "Do you seriously believe that?"

"It's what she insists, every time."

"Of course, she'd say that. She's your mom, after all. Doesn't mean you shouldn't get them anything. Besides..." I peer up at him.

"Besides...?" he prompts.

"Besides, after spending time with you, I can vouch that your presence is less a gift and more of an unwelcome surprise." I snicker.

"Har har." He scowls. "Feeling cheeky this morning, are we?"

"Feeling grumpy, as always, I see?" I shake my head, "You could collapse soufflé, just by your proximity."

He stares at me. "What-fucking-ever."

"That so eloquent. Impressive go-to-word for Mr A-holasaurus." I snort.

"Woman, your metaphors are—"

"Stupid?"

"Creative." He nods, "I'll give you this round."

"Ooh." I hold up my fist.

He glares at me.

"Fist bump. Come on, come on," I coax him.

"Nope." He holds up his right hand, with the upright middle finger, "Injured, remember?"

"Aww." I deflate like the bloody soufflé I'd mentioned, and crap, now I'm hungry.

"Coming back to the topic at hand," he continues. "You could have bought my mother something on the way. We could have stopped at one of the stores in town."

"I believe in the personal touch," I retort. "Unlike you."

"Oh, trust me, when it comes to you, my touch is as personal as it gets." He smirks.

I draw in a breath. Patience, patience. Don't react. *He's being this… overt to get a rise out of you. Don't stoop to his level… Can I be at eye-level with his crotch-candy though?… Eeeeagh, I did not think that.*

I lower my chin, hiding behind my thick fall of hair. "Has your family always lived in Durham?"

He sighs loudly, then leans back.

Whew! Dodged that one. After how he'd pulled that cheap stunt of lying about the storm, I should seriously have been angrier… But for some reason…I'm not. Maybe I'm flattered that he lied to ensure I'd comply with his plan. But…what else did he lie about? I chew on my lower lip.

"My mother moved there after my siblings and I left home. I grew up in London," he explains. "After the incident…" he pauses.

I hold my breath. *Is he going to tell me about himself? Is he going to share a little more of what goes on behind those colorless eyes of his?* Weston doesn't come across as closed off… But his demeanor…that hard outlook of his hides so many secrets. I turn to him, "The kidnapping you mean?"

He nods, then rotates his neck from side to side, "I was one of the lucky ones. My parents rallied around me. Even my asshole of an older brother became protective for a period of time. And my younger sister? Well… She sensed something was amiss. She'd crawl into bed every night and comfort me while I sobbed myself to sleep."

"You…cried every night?"

"I was twelve." His lips twist. "The incident forced me grow up fast… But at night, when I couldn't hide from myself anymore, the demons would come out to play. I don't think I have slept properly since … Until…" He trails off, then turns to me, a strange look on his face.

My throat dries. "Until?" I prompt.

"Until that first night in the cabin, when I spooned you in bed."

My cheeks flush. I turn, crack open the window, and the outside air rushes in. "Why are you telling me this now?"

"No reason," his voice is emotionless.

I turn to find he's staring ahead.

"Not long now," he says in that same colorless tone.

Right, guess that's me being put in my place, huh?

"Did they hurt you?"

"Who?"

I frown, "The…men who kidnapped you with the rest of the Seven."

"Are you really interested in finding out about it?"

I open my mouth, then shut it. "Guess not." I turn away once more, ball my fingers into fists, "I'm trying to be polite, that's all."

"Don't be."

I swallow, "We're going to see your family. We should, at least, put on a veneer of politeness."

"My mother would prefer it if we were to speak our minds; she can spot something fake from a mile off."

I turn on him, "And you think we can get away with…" I point between us, "this?"

His lips stretch in a smile that is not one at all, "Why do you think I asked you and not someone else?"

"I don't understand."

He turns, trains the full force of those grey-silver eyes on me, "There's enough chemistry between us to pull this off."

I open my mouth.

He raises his hand, "Don't deny it. We may not be able to stand each other, but you know what they say?"

"What?"

"There's a thin line between hate and a connection."

What a condescending jerk.

"From where I am, it's a 100% loathing," I force out the words.

"Good."

"Eh?"

"It'll seem realistic, after all. Nothing like make-up sex to cement a relationship, huh?"

27

———————

Weston

Make-up sex? What the fuck am I talking about? Clearly this entire idea—which I'd pulled out of my arse, by the way—is a bad one.

The SUV crawls up the driveway of the Victorian house on the outskirts of Durham where my mother lives. The ivy covers most of the west wing, the leaves a burned red this time of the year.

The vehicle stops in front of the steps leading up to the house.

Before my driver can come around, she's pushed open the door and is hopping out. She opens the passenger door, hauls Max into her arms.

"I have his leash." I frown.

"I'm going to carry the little fella."

Right.

She hauls him closer to her face, "Hey baby, missed me, boy?"

Max licks her nose, her chin.

She laughs.

I scowl.

How dare another male intrude on my territory?

I growl deep in my throat.

Both Max and Amelie turn to me.

"Did you just growl?"

"So?" I glare at her.

She bites her lips, "Uh, you don't have to be jealous of Max." She tips her nose up.

"Me?" I laugh, "Woman, you are delusional."

"Now who's lying?" she scoffs.

"You seriously need to stop being obsessed with me."

She gapes at me, "You know what? This conversation is pointless." She straightens and stalks around the car, heading for the stairs. The dress she's wearing flies up and exposes a flash of her creamy thigh. She takes the steps, and I notice the dark line running up the back of her stockings. My dick twitches, my groin hardens, and this is so, not the fucking time. I don't want to walk into my family's home sporting a hard on.

I adjust myself, then duck out of the car.

Peter — Sinclair's chauffeur who's working with me since Sinclair is away, and because my finger's still bloody busted — walks around to pop open the lid of the trunk.

I turn and stalk her as she walks up the steps to the front door.

"She keeps you on your toes, huh?" Peter asks.

I tilt my head.

"The two of you remind me of how it was with Mr. Sterling and Ms. Summer before they got together."

"You're mistaken." I scowl, "There's nothing like that."

He places both of Amelie's suitcases, and a considerably smaller suit-case —i.e. mine—on the ground; he slaps the trunk shut.

I frown down at Amelie's pink frothy wardrobe on wheels. "You'd think she were packing for a month instead of two nights."

He chuckles, then reaches for the suitcase, but I shake my head, "I'll carry her load."

He peers up at me, "You do that, Sir."

I frown, open my mouth to ask what he means, but he's already walked off, with the rest of the luggage.

What-fucking-ever. My brain cells are, clearly, not functioning at full force, which is why I'd read between the lines. He didn't mean anything by that… He didn't. Did he?

I shake my head and follow Peter up the steps to where she stands, at an angle to the door.

I dump the bag, pause next to her, "Couldn't you have packed more sensibly?"

She turns to me, an expression of almost comical consternation on her face, "No. I need it all. I mean, you weren't helpful at all, gave me no pointers on what to wear, or what to expect, so I had to make sure I had all of my emergency clothes on hand."

"And that?" I point to the chef's toolkit that she has slung over her other shoulder.

She tucks it under her arm. "I don't go anywhere without this."

"Right." I drag my fingers through my hair, "Look, maybe this wasn't a good idea after all, I mean—"

The door opens. "Weston," my sister's voice calls out.

Next to me, Amelie stiffens. She swallows, clutches at her handbag. The skin stretches white across her knuckles. I should revel in her nervousness, in how out of her depth she seems. I mean, isn't that the point of this entire charade, to show her who is more superior in this relationship? *Is there a relationship between us? And who, exactly, is out of their depth? Her? Or me?*

I grip her shoulder. She peers up at me, and I hold her gaze before saying softly, "It will be fine." *What will be fine? Why the hell am I trying to put her at ease?*

She parts her lips, and fuck it, I can't resist. I lower my head and brush my mouth over hers. She draws in a breath and I deepen the kiss. Swipe my tongue inside to tangle with hers, draw of that chocolate and honey taste of hers. My head spins.

I break the kiss, survey her face. Flushed cheeks, dazed eyes. She blinks, sways. Good, that should take her mind off of the upcoming ordeal—I mean, the family stuff. Not that I don't want to spend time with them, but so many people all at once, can be a little overwhelming, especially since my family doesn't take shit from me.

There's a commotion behind me, then, "Unca Wes." Arms wrap around my legs. I glance down at my niece.

"Present… Christmas." The little imp smiles up at me. Well, one of us has our priorities right, at least.

"Phoenix," my sister calls out to her daughter, "let Uncle Wes and his friend inside the house, at least, and it's impolite to ask him what he's got for you. Speaking of," she turns to me, "I didn't realize you were bringing a guest." She looks between us.

Amelie's body goes even more rigid; she turns to me, "You didn't tell them?" Her gaze narrows on me and color flushes her cheeks.

Oh, this is going to be so much fun. That thing about keeping her off kilter? I intend to deliver on that.

"I like to be spontaneous," I allow my lips to curve.

Amelie makes a sound deep into her throat.

I train my gaze on my sister, "Kirsten this is Amelie. Amelie…this is my younger sister, Kirsten."

"Amelie," Kirsten's eyes bob between us. She shuffles her feet in that manner which is a dead giveaway that she's dying to quiz me… Not that I am going to allow that.

Max barks from his vantage point against Amelie's breasts. I seriously needed to have a man-to-man with that pooch.

Phoenix tugs on my hand. "Moosic…" she chants, "mooooosic."

"Hey, honey." I release my hold on Amelie, then bend to swing Phoenix up in my arms.

The little girl giggles, "Mooooosic."

"Music?" I turn to Kirsten for help.

"Yea, music," Kirsten sighs. "She's driving us mad with her music blocks."

"Moooosic bo-k-ssss," Phoenix warbles. "Unca Wezz."

I chuck her under her chin and she giggles. "Play…play… Unca Wezz."

Right.

I glance toward Amelie, who smiles at the little girl. "Hey, baby doll," she coos, "What's your name?"

Phoenix blinks at Amelie, then holds out her arms.

"Oh." Amelie looks at Phoenix, then at me.

I reach over, fasten Max's leash to his collar. "Told ya so," I whisper into her ear.

She scowls, lowers Max to the floor, and her handbag slides down her arm.

"Let me get that." I grab the bag before it hits the floor.

Then I straighten and hand Phoenix over to her. Amelie cuddles Phoenix, and her other bag—the chef's toolkit—bumps her back. I reach for it; Amelie frowns.

"You can trust me," I snicker.

She raises one eyebrow, "Can I?"

"Of course, Sweetheart." I raise one eyebrow.

She opens her mouth, to protest, no doubt. I lean down, press another kiss to her lips, and slide the bag off of her shoulder in the same move.

I step back, swinging her chef's satchel over my other shoulder.

"Smooth," Kirsten laughs.

"Doggy," Phoenix pants.

Max woofs, wags his tail, pawing at Amelie as he tries to get to the little girl.

"Wait…." Amelie protests. Phoenix pats her cheek. Amelie glances down at her and her face breaks into a smile. "Hey pumpkin, what's your name?"

"Phe," she grins, jumping a little in Amelie's arms.

Amelie props her on her hip, "Hey, Phe." Amelie's smile widens, "Whatcha wearing on your head."

Phoenix touches the unicorn shaped hairband, "Pepper."

"Good name." She leans in closer, "What about your friend behind you?"

Phoenix gazes at her wide-eyed, "You…can see him?" She gulps.

"Yep, I can. What's his name?"

"Jack." Phoenix bobs her head, "Jack. Jack."

"Jack?" I turn to Kirsten.

Kirsten nods. "He's imaginary," she says in a low voice.

"Ah." I glance back at the woman, who bends her glossy blonde head toward the dark blonde-haired kid. Something hot stabs at my chest.

"You want one of your own, huh?" Kirsten nudges me.

"What?" I turn to her, "Of course, not."

Kirsten tilts her head, "Hmm." She looks me up and down. Seeing…what? The bags over my shoulders, the dog straining at the leash, the other end of which I hold onto with my uninjured hand…

I scowl at her, "You have a weird look on your face."

"I am not the one who's changed." She grins, then reaches up to pat my cheek. "Finally," she titters, "I can't tell you how I was looking forward to this day."

"You are not making any sense," I grumble.

"It's normal—so much happening in so little time," she waggles her head, "but when it's right, it's right, you know?"

"No," I glower.

The fuck is wrong with my sister? Had I grown another head on my way here?

"Hey," a new voice mumbles. I glance up as my eleven year old niece ambles into the room.

"Skye." I hold out my fist. "Whassup?"

She walks over, ignores me, then frowns at Amelie, "Who're you?"

"Skye!" Kirsten exclaims. "You apologize right now to Amelie, you hear me?"

Skye rolls her eyes, then sighs, "Yeah, fine, whatever. Sorry... Amelie. Pleased to meet you, Amelie. Hey, Uncle Wes." She tosses her head. "There," she jerks her chin in Kirsten's direction. "Happy now?" She turns on her heel and flounces off.

"Whoa." I blink. "What happened there?"

"Sorry." Kirsten turns red. "She's already turning into a teenager. I shudder to think how she's going to be in a few years' time."

She crosses over to Amelie, "Let's get you inside." She holds out her arms to Phoenix, who jumps back into Kirsten's arms.

"Mommy!" Phoenix throws her arms around Kirsten's neck, then strains in her grasp to peer at Max, "Doggy, doggy, play...play."

Kirsten lowers the little girl to the ground, "Come on, let's go in." She hitches her arm through Amelie's, "Was the trip okay?"

The three of them walk in.

I stare after them, then down at Max, who whines, and strains at his leash. Amelie's bag slides down to the crook of my arm. How the hell did I get stuck with this? Brilliant surgeon? Check. Obnoxious billionaire? You bet. Carrying my girlfriend's luggage into my family home? Wh-a-t? Time for a reality check. Why the fuck did I think this was a good idea? Who suggested this? Oh, wait, that was me.

Peter walks out. He glances down at the pink suitcase then at me,

"Keep this the fuck to yourself," I mutter. "Not a word to the rest of the Seven."

He chuckles, then schools his expression into one of indifference. "Of course, Sir, you can trust my discretion."

What-fucking-ever. I stalk forward, my progress somewhat impeded by the blasted tank on wheels that I pull along.

"Oh, Sir?"

I turn.

"The pink brings out the blonde in your beard."

Peter walks off.

Blonde hairs in my beard? I don't have blonde hairs in my beard. The only blonde hair my beard has been close to...is her pussy hair. Those luscious lower lips of hers that had indicated that she was a natural blonde, and fuck me, if that hadn't been a turn-on. My dick twitches in agreement. I pause. Nope, not going there. The last thing I need is walking in with a chub the size of England in my pants. I shake my head, and follow Max into the house. Of course, the bloody pooch has to lead the way.

He barks, tugs on his leash, which slips from my hand, He darts forward.

"Max." I quicken my pace.

Footsteps approach down the curved stairwell.

"Weston," a woman's voice calls out.

I pause, turn toward the woman who walks down the steps, the first love of my life, the one woman who has my complete irrevocable devotion.

I smile up at her.

Her features light up, "You came."

28

Amelie

I hear the sound of barking, the patter of nails on the wooden floor. I turn as Max races toward me, his leash dragging behind. "Hey, you." I bend down to pet the little guy, who jumps up and licks my face as if he hadn't done the same thing not five minutes ago. "Down, boy," I laugh.

Phoenix squats down to rub the puppy's back, "Doggy," she squeals. "Love doggy." She holds out her arms to Max, who jumps on her; the two collapse on the floor in a flurry of arms and legs and doggy barks and little girl exclamations of delight. My smile widens so big that my cheeks hurt. Damn, I love this. What are little girls made of? Sugar and spice and puppy dog tails. Ha! Why should only little boys have the right to dogs, huh? Talk about my own spin on the ol' nursery rhyme.

The hair on the back of my neck prickles. I glance up to find Weston walking forward to greet a woman approaching him. She's wearing a beautiful peacock-green colored dress that flows to below her knee.

He bends and kisses her cheek, "Mother."

I straighten, holding onto Max's leash. So, this is his Mum? Guess alphaholes have parents too… I mean, of course they do; it's just difficult to imagine Weston as a small boy…vulnerable and innocent.

She reaches up to touch his face, "Why do you look different?"

He frowns down at her, "It's the beard, perhaps?"

She tilts her head, the gesture so similar to Weston's, my throat closes. There's no doubt about the blood relationship between the two.

"That's not it." She steps back, takes him in, "It's not the handbag you're carrying either." She giggles.

He shuffles his feet. I blink. I mean, I've never seen him this uncomfortable before. I stifle the giggle that rises up. Trust a mom to put her son in his place huh?

He straightens and turns to me.

I stiffen. Not that I am doing anything wrong, but I bet it seems like I was staring at him, which I wasn't. Okay, I was. I clutch Max's leash. He whines, pulls toward Weston. "Shh, Max," I whisper to him, "Not now."

Weston turns to me; he jerks his chin.

I shake my head.

He glares at me.

I pale.

He holds out his hand.

I sigh. Okay, hell, I'd been hoping to put off this meeting with his family… Not that they are my in-laws or anything, but authority figures of any kind? I run a mile. And not because my own Ma was a strict disciplinarian — okay, maybe it is that. It doesn't take a shrink to tell me my issues with not wanting to conform have to do with my home and the convent school I was educated in. Yeah, the nuns wouldn't be happy with how I've turned out. I purse my lips.

"Amelie," Weston's tone lowers to a hush. To anyone else, I'll bet it sounds normal, but damn, if I don't recognize the demand in it. Shit, I'd left home because I wanted to be independent, I thought… Until I met him, and the kind of disciplining Weston has in mind… Hell, if I don't respond to it from that place deep inside that had resisted being told what to do. My head spins. Is that why I want his kind of dominance? Because I had hankered for it… A structure that imposes boundaries within which I can be myself... Had I held onto the illusion of control until I met a man who I trusted enough to hand it over to? Is that man Weston? I gulp.

Weston frowns, "You okay?" I hear his voice across the short distance.

Max whines, brushes against my leg. I bend, scratch his ear, then straighten. Best to treat this like breaking an egg. Just aim for the center, tap it against the side of the bowl, do your best… Either way it's going to break, you just want to be around to catch the yolk. Me and my stupid metaphors. I walk forward, Max straining at the leash.

When I reach them, I pause. "I'm Amelie." I hold out my hand, "Pleased to meet you."

Weston's mother smiles. The lines etched around her eyes deepen. "What a pretty name."

She takes my hand between both of hers.

"That's very kind of you to say so," I reply, schooling my features into a neutral expression, "and thank you for having me."

Max yelps, she glances at him, and her face breaks into a broad grin. Her features brighten and those grey eyes sparkle. The resemblance between her and Weston becomes more pronounced. Strange, huh? Considering Mr Grumpy-grump's face rarely wears an expression that's not borderline angry.

"And who's this?"

"Max," I reply.

She releases my hand, bends down to pat the puppy. He wags his tail, jumps up at her.

"Is he yours?"

"Uh, he belongs to my friend Summer and her husband."

"Ah, the Sinclairs." She straightens, "Is that how the two of you met?"

"Yes," I say.

"No," Weston declares.

We stare at each other, for a beat, another. I scowl at him. This is what happens when you don't get your stories right. And jerkalope here, didn't want to talk about it before-hand.

I tuck my elbows into my side, open my eyes wide, stare at the alphahole. *He got us into this one, he can dig us out of it. This should be good.*

His mother chuckles, "Which is it, then?"

"I saw her shopping for groceries at my local supermarket. She was talking to herself as she decided which brand of chocolate to buy for baking, and that was it."

"Oh," I blink. *Damn, but he sounds so sincere. I almost believe it myself.*

"Ah." His mother nods. "Chocolate and sex—the unbeatable combination."

"Wha—?" I gape at her.

"Mother," Weston admonishes.

She laughs, "It's not like you were conceived through immaculate conception." She chuckles and looks at me, "I hope I didn't shock you."

"No...Yes." I chew the inside of my cheek, "I mean, it's not shocking, except it came from you, so..."

"Ah," she grins, "you mean from a woman in her fifties. We're supposed to know our place, take care of our grandkids, and leave the running of the world to our husbands and sons."

I hunch my shoulders. Shit, what is the right response here, "No, I think it's women, and especially those in the prime of their life, who have brought up children to face the world, and who have stood by their men, supported them while following their own passions, who wield the power."

She tilts her head, then laughs. "Good save." She chuckles, "Call me Rosie." She pulls me in for a hug.

I take it. "Rosie." I nod.

Phew! Guess I passed that test... Whatever that was.

She releases me, and steps back, "You can take him off the leash, dear."

I stare at her.

"Weston, I mean." Her eyes twinkle.

"Ah," I open and shut my mouth.

"Just messing with you," she chuckles, then glances at Max.

Right. Is that where Weston gets his warped sense of humor, not to mention his dominance?

I unhook the leash from Max's collar. Max bounds off, toward the living space at the far end of the hallway, following the sound of Phoenix's laughter.

I twist the leash around my palm, wondering what to do with it. Weston places his hand on mine; I look up. One side of his lips kicks up. Is that supposed to be reassuring? The warmth from his touch sinks into my blood. I draw in a breath and my heartbeat slows. How strange. This man... Who I am not sure how to react to... Who I am sure I hate... Who I have definite feelings for... When did his presence become so reassuring?

He twines his fingers with mine and the leash slips from my grasp. He catches it, glances around. A maid wearing a uniform materializes. Huh? Of course, they'd have staff. They are rich and the house... Well, it seems the kind that has been in their family for generations. "Master Weston?" The older woman smiles.

"Mary, how are you?" He hands the leash over to her.

"I'm very good, Sir." Her smile widens. "The luggage has been sent to your suite already," she adds.

"Excellent," he grins at her.

Wow. That's two smiles in as many minutes. Seems the alphahole can lose the obnoxiousness on occasion... Just not with me.

"How is Veronica?" he asks Mary.

"Grown up and at university. She has her own life now."

"You miss her, huh?"

Mary raises her shoulders, "Always. But I'm also glad to have her out of my hair." She chuckles.

She turns to Rosie, "Dinner is served Ma'am."

Rosie touches my arm, "Shall we?"

29

———————

Weston

"You're not sleeping on the couch." I growl at her.

Dinner had been mercifully quiet. Kirsten had taken Phe and Skye up to get them ready for bed. Max had mercifully tagged along, not wanting to part from the girls.

Which means we are alone, in my room, and I intend to take full advantage of that.

"Excuse me?" She frowns up at me.

"You heard me," I drawl. "Get your sweet tush into bed." I jerk my thumb over my shoulder, pointing at the massive four-poster that occupies the center of the room.

"We are not together; this is all a farce." She glowers, "Have you forgotten that you wanted me to come here to put on a front with your family? I have done that, and now I want some privacy."

"No." I fold my arms over chest.

She gapes, "What…what do you mean?"

"Exactly that." I glance down my nose at her, "We need to keep up the pretense."

"In here?" She glances around the spacious suite that takes up the entire top floor of the house. It also comes equipped with its own kitchen, a fact I had pointed out to her earlier. Why was that? Why does it matter to me that she feels at home in this space? I shake my head, narrow my gaze on the woman who scowls up at me.

"No-one's going to come in here," she insists.

"You don't know that. One slip-up, and this entire charade will amount to nothing."

"That's all this is—a farce." She juts out a hip, props her hand on it, "So why the hell can't you allow me to sleep on my own?"

"Because…" *You're mine,* is what I want to say, but fuck that. I have no claim to her. I can't call her mine. I don't want to have any relationship with her, do I? So why the hell am I being this unreasonable? I crack my neck, draw in a breath, "As long as you are here, under my roof, you do as I say."

"It's not your roof," she growls.

"It belongs to my family," I retort.

"I don't care."

"You should, because in one second you are going to be breaking a record, one that you'll remember for the rest of your life."

She balks, "Wh…what do you mean?"

"Just try to walk out of that door, and I'll have you on your back and make you orgasm so fast, and so many times, that you'll forget all about the world outside this bedroom."

Her chest heaves, her face pales, she swallows hard, and clenches her fists by her sides, "You wouldn't dare."

"You know better than to challenge me, Princess."

"I'm not your princess."

"You're right," I look her up and down, "you're the woman I am paying to keep me company."

She falters, then pulls her shoulders back, "You forget that we no longer have an arrangement."

"So why are you here?"

She bites the inside of her cheek, "Because…"

"Because?"

"Uh, I didn't want you to let your family down."

"Bull-fucking-shit," my words crackle through the space.

She winces. "Keep your voice down," she hisses at me. "You may not care about your family hearing us, but I do."

"The walls of this suite are thick enough for you to scream all night long and no one would notice."

She swallows, twists her fingers together, "You're lying."

"Want to try it out, hmm?" I take a step toward her; she skitters back.

I tilt my head.

She holds my gaze.

I widen my stance.

She tips her chin, "You…you don't scare me."

"So you keep saying."

"We are here with your family; your sister and nieces are sleeping on the floor below. You won't try anything with them so close."

"You think I'll stop because of that?"

"I saw you with them, Weston." She narrows her gaze, "You respect your mother, you love your nieces, you'd do anything to protect your sister… You're not half as much of an unfeeling man as you make yourself out to be."

"You're right about that."

"I… I am?"

I nod, "I'm much worse." I lunge forward.

She screams, pivots, then makes a run for the door.

I swoop down toward her, grab her across the waist and throw her over my shoulder.

"Let me go, you oaf," she yells.

I stalk toward the bed.

She wriggles, brings her fists down on my back. The jolt travels down to my cock, which is already erect. Is it wrong that I am getting off on her struggle? On her curvy butt that wriggles so near my face. I tilt my head to nuzzle the side of her hips.

She stills. "Did you…" Her voice cracks, "Did you just do what I think, you did?"

I bring down my hand on her arse.

She howls, "What the fuck?"

"Language, Princess." I smirk, "And don't question me again."

Her body tenses, all of her of muscles coil, and tension rolls off of her in waves. *Wait for it. Wait for it.* She bucks her body, then digs her knee into my chest with enough force that my breath catches. She lowers her head, buries her teeth in my back. Pin pricks of pain race from the contact. My dick throbs and my groin hardens. I change direction and head for the ensuite bath.

"The hell are you doing?" she yells again.

"Not so worried about waking up the family now, huh?" I chuckle.

"You douche, how dare you use your strength against me?"

"Because I like to play dirty?" *Because I am losing my mind, that's why.* The thought of her walking out of here, never looking back… Hell no. My chest tightens. No way, am I letting that happen. And it's not my ego speaking… It's the fear that I'll never see her again. Never scent her gorgeous essence, never hold her curves, bury myself in her sweet cunt; never pit my will against hers. I stumble, then right myself.

The challenge… That's what attracted me to her. It's why I keep taunting her, trying to get a rise out of her, and why I can't let go of her either. What do I want to do with her? I want to get a rise out of her. Revel in her spirit, that fire inside of her that could burn through my past, rejuvenate me, give me a reason to move forward. I want to live fully, to feel for the first time in my life. I want her. Only her. I march into the bathroom, turn on the shower.

"Let go of me," her scream slices through my ear drum.

"Stop that," I growl.

"You stop what you're doing and release me this instant."

"Your wish is my command." I swing her around, plonk her down under the shower. She opens her mouth and the water pelts her face. Her scream is cut off in a series of unintelligible words.

"I can't hear you," I taunt.

She kicks out, I angle away, and she tips over.

I grasp her shoulder and keep her upright.

She swings at me, connects with the arm of my injured hand. Pain explodes behind my eyes.

"Fuck!"

I loosen my grip and she throws herself at me. Her weight connects with my chest. I stagger back, hit the wall of the shower cubicle. She hooks her leg around my waist, hauls herself up, and climbs me like she's a cat and I am her personal scratching post… Fuck. She lowers her head, digs her teeth into my neck, on the side of my injured finger.

"You little hellion!" I grab the back of her neck, tug. She doesn't let go. I apply pressure; she holds on. Pain shoots down my injured arm and my finger hurts. I squeeze down, her shoulders tremble, and her body arches. She gasps and her hold loosens. I pull her back, lower my face to hers, "I am going to teach you a lesson that you'll never forget."

30

Amelie

Water from the shower drums against me. His grey gaze clashes with mine. His features twist into an expression of rage…? Of arousal? His nostrils flare. "I am going to fuck you like you are mine."

Am I his?

Is he mine?

Do I want him to fuck me?

No.

No.

"Yes." I peel back my lips, "Finally."

He crashes his mouth into mine, thrusts his tongue inside, sucks on me, demands that I open myself to him, that I give in to him. *No, no. I can't. Yes, you can. Show him you won't back down, that you're not scared of what he does to you. That you will not turn and hide from the emotions he evokes in you.* I tip up my chin, wind my arms around his neck, dig my thighs into his waist, press my melting center to the hardness that tents his pants.

"Fuck me," his harsh whisper chafes my skin and my nerve endings flare. My brain cells seem to evaporate. Poof, I am smoke. I am one melting, writhing mass of need in his arms.

Take me. Tear into me. Sink into me. Push all thoughts out of my head. I don't want to think, don't want to worry about the future, the past. All that matters is me, here, with him, clinging to him, holding on with every single strand of strength in my body. Him. I want him. Only him. I tear my mouth from his, "Fuck me."

Before the words are out of my mouth, he's flipped positions. My back presses into the wall. The weight of him pins me. His massive body cuts off the water. The blood drums in my ears; my pulse thuds against my neck, my wrists, at my ankles... The beat between my legs grows, louder, needier, angrier. "Now," I huff. "Do it."

His lips twist. He brings his hand up to curl his large fingers around my neck. I gulp. Shit, I'd asked... Demanded that he fuck me. Isn't that, like, against the rules of dominance with this man? Am I not supposed to ask for what I want?

His fingers meet around the diameter of my neck. He presses his thumb into the pulse that skitters at the base of my throat. "Aren't you forgetting something?"

I frown.

He tilts his head.

I lower my chin.

He glares at me and the blood drains from my face, straight to my cunt. My head spins. My throat closes. I flick out my tongue to touch my lips; his gaze drops to my mouth.

He growls and my stomach seems to bottom out. Oh, my God. This man... He's too hot, too much. Too everything.

"Do it," he barks.

I hesitate.

"Or not." He steps back.

I lose my grasp around his waist; my legs begin to slide down. *No, no, no. I want this. I do.* "Please," I gasp.

"Please what?" His fingers tighten around my neck and my airflow slows. I open my mouth, try to breathe. My lungs burn. I thrust my thighs into his, hold on. *Don't let go. He's testing you. Don't give in; not yet.*

"I... I..." I try to form the words, but my brain cells don't comply. "Wes... I..."

"Want me to help you?"

I nod.

"Want me to play with your pretty cunt?" He tilts his hips and his thick length stabs my sensitized core.

I moan. I'm not proud. I tried to resist, tried to hold onto the last shred of my dignity that lies in tatters around me now. "Yes," I beg. "Yes."

"Want me to squeeze your butt," he grips my arse, "before I cram my fingers into your arsehole?" He drags his fingers down the valley between my butt cheeks. His touch sinks through the sodden mess of my clothes, my panties, into that empty part of me inside, that curls in on itself, throbbing with a need that only Doc Grumpyface can fulfill.

"Don't stop," I whine.

"Want me to..." He brings his hand around, and grabs my pussy.

I wordlessly push my core forward, begin to fuck his palm like the out-of-my-head, sex-starved, stupid idiot that I am.

He hauls me up, his right hand around my neck—apparently, his injured finger does nothing to restrain his movements; with his other, he grips my pussy—pins me against the wall, and stares into my face.

My feet don't touch the ground, and I should be scared. This position implies exactly what we are—me at his disposal, at his mercy, his to do with as he pleases. His grasp is firm enough to prop me up, allowing enough air to reach my lungs that I don't suffocate, and yet... The lowered oxygen heightens my reactions, my sensitivity to his every move. I watch him watch me strain against that large hand at my core, and all of my nerve-endings seem to catch fire all at once.

He slides his palm under me so his fingers are flat against my butt. He presses his thumb through my tights and my panties into my swollen nub. Sparks explode behind my eyes. I throw my head back and pant. He rubs circles with his thumb around my clit. My pulse rate ratchets up.

"Look at me," his command whips through my thoughts.

I lower my face, crack my eyes open.

"Who do you belong to?"

"You."

"Who do you come for?"

"You."

"Who will you shatter for?"

"You," I groan, "Only you."

"Shatter for me, my Princess. Right fucking now."

He releases the hold on my neck and my climax explodes up my spine. Spots of white fold in to my line of sight. My pussy clenches; moisture floods between my legs. I hear the sound of someone wailing...

Me? Is that me? My ears pop; my throat closes. A whine pours from me.

"Good, girl." He bends, licks my lips, "I am going to fuck you now."

Wh-a-a-t?

I blink as he lowers me to the floor. My knees give way; he holds me up with his fingers around my neck. My shoulders slump, I should say something… Do something…?

He reaches around to shut off the shower, then grabs the hem of my dress, pulls it over my head, and tosses it aside.

He glances down at the tights, reaches for the waistband with his injured hand. He pauses. I hook my fingers in the waistband of my tights and tug them down along with my panties. The lycra sticks around my thighs. Shit, and I'd worn them in the hope of seeming sophisticated. Go figure! I try to peel them off, but the damn thing resists. Shit! I yank it down further, manage to twist it around my knees. Another tug and I shove it down to my ankles, peel it off. Whew! I straighten, and with a low growling sound he's on me.

He lowers himself to his knees, pushes his face into my pussy and fastens his mouth on my melting core. "OMG." I yell, "Wes, Wes… Wes." I chant his name as he stabs his tongue inside my channel, swipes his tongue up from my backhole to my clit. He bites on my clit and I arch off the wall. OMFG! This man's tongue should be worshipped; also his mouth, and his dick, and his digits… Gah! He slides his finger inside my melting pussy and I shudder. My knees seem to give away. I begin to slide down the wall, dig my fingers into his hair for purchase and tug on it. He growls. My nerve endings spark. *Ooh, I like that.* A lot, actually. I yank at that luxurious hair on his head.

He peers up at me, "You know you'll have to pay for that, huh?"

"Promises, promises." I smack my lips.

His nostrils flare. He rises to his feet, and keeps rising. I mean, he is tall. I know that, but in that enclosed space he is larger than life. A lethal, vital, sex machine of a man. My sex clenches, heat coils low in my belly, emptiness gnaws deep inside. I need him. Want him… Yearn for him to fill me up and put me out of my misery. "Wes," I groan.

"Here baby, right here."

He plants his thigh between my legs.

"I am going to make this so fucking good for you, Princess." He thrusts his fingers…two…three inside my pussy.

I gasp; my knees buckle. One thing I can confirm. Weston-built-like Adonis-Kincaid, always delivers.

He wraps his fingers around my neck, holds me upright, even as he shoves the fingers of his other hand in and out of me. I moan, reach for his shoulders. He doesn't stop; he scissors his fingers inside of me. Goosebumps dot my skin; a trembling begins from the soles of my feet, inches upward. He releases his hold on my neck, then turns me around. *What the—?* I sense his hot breath on the curve of my hip a second before he pries my butt cheeks apart and rims his tongue around my backhole. *Oh, my God.* The trembling pulsates from where he slides his tongue in and out of me. He slips his palm between my hips and the shower wall, then grinds the heel of his hand against my pussy.

"Weston," his name is torn from my lips. I sense his lips curve against my arse... Is that even possible? Then he thrusts his fingers inside my pussy, and I explode. The orgasm sweeps up my thighs, my spine. I slap my palm against the shower wall, hold onto his forearm with my other hand. He continues to lick me, shove his fingers in and out of me, extending the climax, which seems to go on and on. He pulls away his hand, removes his tongue, and just like that, my orgasm fades. No way, he can't command my body with such...finesse, can he? My knees give way, for real this time. His arms come around me. He turns me toward him, pinches my chin, so I look up at him.

"Wow," I gasp, "that was..." I swallow, "It was..."

"Just the beginning."

"Huh?" My head spins. "I... I don't think I can..."

"You can."

He grins down at me, that toe curling, sex clenching, scalp tingling smirk that sends a surge of heat racing up my spine.

"Are you a sex god?" I mumble. *Hell, did I blurt that out?* Must be my sex-addled brain that's speaking. Not my fault. *Gah.*

"That's Dr Sex God to you." He laughs, "And you're welcome, again."

"Huh?" *Do I want to know why? Don't ask him; don't.* "For what?"

"For the third, fourth and fifth orgasm that you are going to experience."

"No." I blink.

"Yes." His lips curl. He reaches behind him, shuts off the shower, then steps back and rakes his gaze down my naked body. I will not cover myself, will not hide what he's already pinched and massaged and teased and licked and sucked and... I press my thighs together.

"Hmm," he smirks.

"You going to take off your clothes, or what?" I mutter.

He unbuttons his shirt, whips it off, then unfastens his belt. My gaze drops to his crotch. *Don't stare; look away, you slut.* He shoves down his pants and his boxers, kicks them aside. He straightens and I gulp. OMFG. I take in his cock that stands to attention against his stomach. It's thick and wide, and longer than I remember it to be. How had I managed to take him down my throat?

I must have made a strangled noise, for he chuckles. "It will fit," he assures me, "I'll make it."

That's what I'm afraid of.

I sidle away and toward the door of the shower cubicle.

"Where do you think you're going?" he drawls.

"Ah, I...uh... I need to pee."

"Will you pee on me?"

"What?" I stare at him, "Are you serious?"

He laughs, "No, but coming to think of it..." He scratches his chin, "Can I pee on you, instead?"

"No," I stutter. "Is that, like, your kink or something?"

He frowns, "Never thought of it before, but," he looks me up and down, "you have to admit, it's an effective way of marking my territory."

My jaw drops, "You're crazy."

He steps forward, plants himself in the doorway, "Crazy is what I feel every time Max insists on occupying your attention."

I frown, then stiffen, "Wow, you're jealous."

He frowns.

"You resent that Max prefers my company to yours."

He folds his arms over his broad chest, "You done?"

I plant my hands on my hips. "Come on," I wheedle, "at least, admit that you don't want Max anywhere near me."

"You're wrong."

"Oh?"

He nods. "I don't want any male—no man or animal of any kind— near you."

I swallow. My heart begins to race. I know he's dominant, and an alpha, and demanding... But this crazy possessive side of him? Wow, it's hot as fuck. We stare at each other. Water drips from the shower onto the ground. I swallow and the hair on the back of my neck rises. *Say something…anything to break the silence.* I lower my arms to my sides, "Do…do you mean that?" I ask.

He tilts his head, drums his fingers on his chest, then straightens, "Want me to show you?"

31

Weston

What the fuck am I playing at? Why are you allowing her to see how much she affects you? Peeing on her? Seriously? Fucking fuck, it's not something that had crossed my mind... Not before her. Is that how much I want to possess her? Is that how much I want to imprint myself on every cell of her body? My vision narrows. The hair on my forearms rises. This crazy-ass need to own her... It's new, it's different, it's real. I bend my knees, peer into her face.

Her pupils are blown; the blue in them has deepened to an almost purple. Her cheeks are flushed, her pulse skitters at the base of her neck. "Do you, Princess?"

"I..." She bites the inside of her cheek, then lowers her chin, "I do."

"I didn't hear you."

She draws in a breath, tips up her chin. She takes a step forward until her toes bump mine. "I want you to show how much you want me, what you'll do to possess me, how much you need to ensure that no one will have me like you do."

"Good." I step away from the entrance of the shower stall, jerk my chin, "After you."

She frowns, then walks past me. I follow her past the bath tub, out the door of the ensuite, into the bedroom. She approaches the foot of the bed.

"Stop," I call out.

She pauses, angles her body.

"Don't turn around."

She trembles, but obeys.

I stalk over to her, wrap the towel I'd snatched on my way out of the bathroom around her shoulders, drag it down her back, over the lush curves of her butt, her strong calves, about those shapely ankles—that I want locked around my neck, fast.

She gasps.

I straighten, then circle around to her front.

Her chest rises and falls.

I lower my gaze to her chest and her shoulders quiver. I pat the towel about her creamy breasts; her nipples pucker. I lower my head, bite down on the pebbled flesh. She moans.

A droplet of water slides down the valley between her breasts. I lick it up, then follow the trail of another down to her belly button. I curl my tongue into the indentation; she groans. Lower my face to her pussy and close my mouth around the delectable flesh. She gasps, and the sound of her pleasure percolates into my cells, filters through my blood, straight to my balls.

I straighten, peer into her face.

"Get on the bed—on your back, legs apart, pussy exposed, hands behind your neck, so you can't touch yourself," I growl.

Her muscles quiver.

"Do it," I snap.

She scrambles up on the bed, turns around, lies flat, spreads her knees, locks her fingers behind her neck.

I smile, "My, aren't you the obedient one today."

She glowers at me and I widen my stance. I draw the towel, now damp with the water from her body, down my chest, my stomach, my thighs. Her gaze follows my every move, her pupils dilated, breasts swollen. I toss aside the towel, lower my gaze to her pussy, to where the evidence of her arousal drips down her inner thigh. My dick throbs; my groin hardens.

I lean over, scoop up her cum, and suck on it.

She whines.

"Want some?"

She nods.

I tilt my head, arch an eyebrow. "Maybe later." I smirk, "If you've been good enough, that is."

She groans, mumbles something under her breath.

"What's that, Princess?"

She stares at me, then presses her lips together.

I laugh, "You're learning fast."

I fist my cock, swipe it from root to tip. She glances at it and her lips part.

"Want a taste of this?"

She pouts, doesn't reply.

"Damn, but you beat me at my own game, huh?"

She scowls.

I chuckle. Then walk around the bed to the side table, pull it open and get a condom.

I slip it on, walk back to the foot of the bed.

"Soft fuck or hard fuck?"

She purses her lips.

"Both?" I tilt my head, "Neither?"

She shakes her head.

"One after the other, maybe?"

She swallows; her chest rises and falls.

"Maybe I should decide, huh?" I tap a finger to my chin. "Perhaps I should surprise you?"

I lean over, grab her by her ankles.

She squeaks.

I pull her forward, until her hips are almost at the edge. I kneel on the bed, draw her legs over my shoulders, position my dick at her entrance.

Her belly quivers, her thighs spasm, and goosebumps flare on her skin. Good, I am not the only one who's not going to be able to walk away from this unaffected. "You ready, Princess?"

She tips her chin up, opens her mouth. I plunge inside her. Her entire body bucks. She flings out her arms, grabs hold of the sheets. I wait, wait for her to adjust to my size. Her eyelids flutter and a bead of sweat trickles down her temple. "Eyes on me," I order.

She looks up, holds my gaze. The pleasure and hunger, and that edge of desperation in them, mirrors the strange confluence of emotions inside of me. I grip her thighs and hold them further apart.

Her breathing grows shallow, but she jerks her head, and I begin to fuck her in earnest. I plunge into her again and again. The bed shudders with each thrust. The headboard slams into the wall, punctuated by her cries, her moans, her gasps, her whines, her wails. Each sound from her beautiful lips sinks into my blood, curls around my heart, hacks away at the walls I have built up against the world.

My God, this woman… She tears me apart. The scent of her, the taste of her, the sweet poison of her cunt...will be my death. I pull back, stay poised at the edge of her channel, move over her, until my face is close to hers. My lips above hers, breathing in her perfume, her essence. The very breath that we share ties us together.

I kick my hips forward, sink into her. "Come," I command, and she arches up and off the bed. I fit my mouth to hers, draw from her scream as she breaks apart under me. I sink in and out of her, drawing out the aftermath of her orgasm, reveling in her complete submission. My chest hurts, my temples throb, my balls draw up and I let myself come inside of her.

I collapse forward on my elbows. A bead of sweat trickles down my chin and plops on her cheek. Her eyeballs move behind her closed eyelids. I pull out of her, tie the condom, then walk over to the waste basket and toss it in. When I return to the bed, I pull the covers over her, slip in between the sheets and pull her to me.

I spoon her, our bodies in sync from throat to chest to hips. I throw my leg over hers and fall asleep.

When I wake up, I am on my own.

I glance at the dent in the pillows, the mussed-up sheets, the scent of sex, of chocolate and cinnamon, is heavy in the air. Her scent. My dick lengthens. Shit, haven't I had enough of her? My fingertips tingle. Why the hell do I want to touch her, pull her to me and hold her, then bury myself inside her again and again? I shake my head. The fuck is wrong with me?

I sit up, swing my legs over the side of the bed. I head for the walk-in closet, step in and pull on a pair of sweat pants. When I step out, I hear a sound from behind the door that leads to the kitchen. I head toward it and the scent of chocolate deepens. I wasn't dreaming then? I step inside, come to a stop.

She stands at the counter, back to me, wearing a shirt—my shirt. It falls to half-way down her thighs, clings to the swell of her butt. The valley between her arsecheeks is a dark shadow that calls to me. I curl my fingers into fists. Fuck, get a grip on your desires, asshole. I take a step forward. She throws her head back, sways those ample hips from side to side, bumps, grinds. I reach down adjust the thickness that tents my crotch. Jesus H Christ, what is she up to now?

She flicks her head from side to side, holds up her spatula—that same infernal spatula she'd threatened me with the first time I saw her at the cabin. I move toward her. She lowers her chin and screeches. What the fuck? I stare as she croons under her breath, then rotates her body in a figure eight. Huh, is that what they call twerking? I grab my very interested dick, pull on it as she moves her butt in the opposite direction. Sweat beads my forehead. Fuck, she only has to twitch that gorgeous arse and this asshole will come running. Fuck.

I stalk to her. She angles her body, lowers her head and sings into the spatula, the lyrics from a famous Christmas anthem—so famous that even I recognize it.

I shake my head. "Are you singing Last Christmas by Wham!?"

She howls out the next set of lyrics in answer.

I wince. As gorgeous as her pussy is, as sassy as her temperament is, as beautifully sharp as her mind is… Her singing voice…? Well, let's just say I sing better, and I've been asked not to sing.

I close the distance between us, place a hand on her shoulder.

She screams, turns, and brings the spatula down on me.

32

Amelie

The spatula connects with his hand... His injured hand. His shoulders bunch and the color fades from his cheeks. To his credit, he doesn't cry out in pain. His big body goes solid; his chest planes seem to expand and grow bigger as he draws in a breath. Then he takes a step back, another, until the backs of his knees connect with one of the stools at the breakfast bar. He sinks down into it, brings his hand up to his chest and cradles it there. Sweat beads his forehead.

"Ow," he mumbles.

"Bloody apple crumble," I wheeze. The spatula slips from my hand, falls to the floor, bounces once. Gooey chocolate sprays across the floor, dots the edges of his sweats.

"Oh. My," I gasp, "Ohmygod." I take a step forward and my foot slides on the chocolate crepe batter. I stumble, then right myself. "Oh, hell," I cry. "I am so sorry. So sorry. I didn't mean it." I leap forward, reach for his hand.

He jerks back.

I freeze.

"I didn't mean it. You surprised me," I blubber, "Did I hurt you? Ohmigod, omigod, of course, I hurt you. Oh my—"

"Stop," he barks out the command.

I stutter, "I'm sorry, I really am."

"You mean you didn't hurt me on purpose?"

I open and close my mouth. "How could you think that?" I cry. "Do you really think I would—?"

One side of his mouth curls.

I purse my lips together. "You horrible man." I step toward him.

He holds up his good hand, "Stop, before you make it worse."

"Oh." A pressure builds behind my eyes. "Is it bad? Did I break it again?"

"It hadn't healed enough for that to happen." He grunts, "No, you hit the finger in the same place it broke the first time around."

"I didn't." I scowl. I hadn't hit his finger, only his palm, I swear. I stare at his finger in the splint, then back up at his face. "You're so adept at working around that, that I forget sometimes you are injured."

"Is that a compliment for my dexterity?" His lips kick up.

"Something like that." I stare at his features. His color's definitely better than it was a minute ago. "Do you want any painkillers?" I shuffle my weight from foot to foot, "Maybe some of the chocolate cookies I baked and brought here?"

"Haven't you given them to Mother?" He frowns.

I glance away, twist my fingers together. "You were right. It was a stupid idea. I should have ordered something from the shops or stopped on the way here to buy something."

"It was a thoughtful gesture," he replies.

I shoot him a sideways glance. Is he, like, pulling my leg?

He meets my gaze, holds up his hand and winces.

"Oh." My chest tightens. "It's hurting, isn't it? Is it bleeding? Sure I can't get you something for the pain?" I step forward. He widens his stance. I slip in between his legs, glance at his injured palm. "Can you, uh, wiggle the other fingers or something?"

He bends the others, shows me the bird by default.

"Guess you're feeling all right, huh?" I slide back, but he moves his thighs in, traps me in place.

"Oh." I gulp.

"Hmm," he tilts his head, "were you serious about your earlier offer?"

Which one?"

"About making the pain better."

I chew the inside of my cheeks, survey his features, which take on an expression of innocence. As if. I'd bet my last chocolate eclair that he has something up his sleeve.

"Depends," I venture.

"On what?"

"On what you want me to do."

"I'll only tell you if you agree to it."

"I can't agree to it unless you tell me what it's about."

"Trust me." His eyes gleam.

Ha, I draw in a breath. "Famous last words," I mumble.

"I heard that." He holds up his uninjured hand. "If you don't want to do it, you don't need to."

"Really?"

He nods, "I swear on chocolate."

Hmm. I frown, "You don't like chocolate."

"But you do."

"You're supposed to swear on something you hold dear." I huff.

"I swear on you."

My mouth drops open. *Oh, my. Did he say that? He didn't. Should I ask him to repeat it? Nah, ignore it.*

"Fine." I swipe my hair over my head, "What is the thing you want of me? What should I do to make the pain better?"

He holds up his injured finger, "Kiss it."

"That's all?"

"That's all."

"Okay." I draw in a breath, lower my head, and press my lips to his finger. I straighten and he tightens the net formed by his thighs, pulls me closer. My core brushes the prominent tent at his crotch, the one I have been trying to ignore.

"I did what you asked," I say, my voice breathless, "let me go."

"That's not the only place it hurts." He sticks out his lower lip.

"No?" I bite the inside of my cheek.

Weston has the kind of pillowy lower lip made for a pout, but honestly, this is the first time he's pulled that one on me.

Apparently, it takes a rap from a spatula to turn him more amicable. Note to self: next time, aim for his hard head. That might knock some sense into him, hmm?

"No." He shakes his head, "What about the finger between my legs."

I stare at him for half a second, then groan. "Eeyuck, your lines are getting worse."

"And you're getting better at easing my pain."

I shake my head, "So, you want a blow job, before breakfast?"

"Definitely before breakfast, and during and after too."

I squeeze my eyes shut, "I'll pretend you didn't say that."

"You promised," he wheedles. "Come on, Princess, just a kiss. Take the frog out of the well; show it the world."

I laugh, "That was almost clever."

"Right?" He smirks; his chest seems to swell with how pleased he is with himself. This man? I don't know if I should slap him or kiss him. Or both, one after the other.

I frown.

He chuckles, "You hurt me; it's up to you to make it better."

He has a point there.

I drop my gaze to his crotch, then to his face.

His gaze narrows.

I bite down on my lower lip, and those grey eyes lighten, a sure hint that he's aroused. I squeeze my thighs together. So am I. He raises his hand, rubs his thumb over my lower lip, until I release it. "You are not allowed to hurt that; only I have the permission to do that."

"Oh." His words coil around my heart and my blood begins to pound in my veins. That possessiveness in him? It kills me every time. I reach forward, palm him through his pants. He groans. His chest planes seem to harden.

I rub at his length, and I swear, his dick thickens.

"Take it out," he murmurs.

I swallow, slide my fingers down his waistband and curl my fingers around his shaft. The muscles of his belly jump. I push down the waistband; the heavy length of him fills my palm. The vein on the underside throbs, the head swollen and angry. Moisture beads the slit.

"Suck me off," he orders.

I bend my head, lick my tongue around the head. The salty, tangy taste of him fills my mouth. I peer up at him. "I want..." I swallow, " Can I...?"

"What is it?"

I reach around him, scoop up some of the chocolate mixture from the table, rub it across the head of his cock.

"Jesus," he breathes.

I hold his gaze, lower my head again and take him inside my mouth.

"Fucking, fuck." He digs his fingers into my hair, tugs. My scalp hurts. Goosebumps ripple down my spine. I lick the chocolate off his dick and the dark taste of cocoa, edged with his cum, the musky taste of Weston, swirls over my tongue. I swallow; he draws in a breath. He loosens the hold of his thighs around me and I sink to my knees. I grip his thigh for support, squeeze the base of his dick, and his entire body seems to grow rock solid.

"Take me down your throat," he growls.

I bob my head forward, and gag. Saliva drips from the edges of my mouth and my lungs burn. Jesus, he's too big. Will I ever get used to his size?

"Breathe through your nose," he directs.

I swallow, and his fingers dig into my scalp. Shockwaves of lust race across my skin. I moan, take in a breath, then another.

"Eyes on me."

I peer up at him, at those colorless eyes that reflect back what I am —his woman, his slave, his to do with as he wants. And what do I want? Him. All of him. His corrupted tastes, his filthy ways, that tenderness he hides deep inside and reveals to his nieces, his family, to Max. I want that. I want to be at the center of his world, command his attention as he demands mine.

I tilt my head and he slips further down my throat. My chest heaves, my breasts ache, and that empty sensation between my legs intensifies.

His features twist. He brings his hand to my face, rubs away the drool from my chin. He cups my cheek, and something like tenderness glitters in those eyes. He tugs on my hair; I pull back. His dick slips out with a pop. He hauls me up to my feet, peers into my face. "What are you doing to me?" he whispers.

"Whatever it is," I lean in close enough for us to share breath, "I feel the same."

His eyebrows knit. He searches my face again. The raw intensity of his gaze sweeps through my mind, pushes away all other thoughts. He bridges the distance between us, then closes his mouth over mine.

33

———————

Weston

It wasn't supposed to be like this. This sweetness. This feeling of absolute surrender from her that punches me in the gut. My heart begins to pound and the blood thuds at my temples. She parts her lips; I deepen the kiss, swipe my tongue inside her mouth, draw from her taste, suck on her lips... And she gives and gives. A hot sensation coils in my chest.

Without taking my mouth from hers, I bend my knees, grip her under her thighs and lift her up. She wraps her legs around my waist. Her soft core cradles my dick, her breasts thrust up and into my chest. I tilt my head, crush my lips to hers. Her scent fills my senses, her taste goes to my head. I stalk forward and into the bedroom. She winds her arms about my shoulders, tilts her chin up. The softness of her mouth, the heat of her pussy, her pebbled nipples that are imprinted into my skin—all of it sinks into my blood. A pressure builds behind my rib cage. I lower her to the bed, but she doesn't let go.

I lean over her, supporting my weight on my elbows. I press her down into the mattress, thrust my tongue down her throat, drink from her, wanting more…more. I reach down, position my throbbing shaft at the entrance of her pussy.

She moans deep in her throat, digs her heels into my back. The condom. I tear my mouth from hers. "Protection," I mutter.

"I'm on birth control." She stares up, blue eyes darkened to an azure, stormy clouds in their depths. "Come inside me," she whispers, "I want you, Weston."

"Like this?"

"Only like this." She pushes her hips up, her melting core opening, giving, needing.

"Fuck." I kick my hips forward, and slide into her, all the way in.

Her body jerks and the breath leaves her in a rush. I hold her gaze and begin to move, thrusting harder with each shove, plunge, thrust, propelling forward again and again. She grips me with her thighs, buries her fingers in my hair and tugs. I look deeply into her eyes, into the horizon I've seen all this time, the one that had seemed so far away when it was always right here. In front of me. Under me. With me... Next to me. "Come with me," I push into her, impale her, bury myself so deeply that my balls slap against her thighs.

She opens her mouth in a wordless scream; her body shudders and moisture fills her channel and bathes my dick, as I come inside of her. I thrust a few more times, as her body trembles in the aftermath of the climax, then reach down, scoop up the liquid that spills from us. I hold it to her lips. She sucks on it, swallows.

"How do we taste?" I ask.

"Of sin and chocolate," her lips quirk, "of cruelty and togetherness; of lust and secrets." Her voice lowers, "A strength to do what it takes."

"Can you take what I am going to do to you?" I wonder aloud.

"What?" She frowns.

I pull out of her.

She lowers her legs. I lean back on my knees, then stand and step away, over to the side of the bed. "Get up," I jerk my chin at her.

Her forehead creases, but she sits up. Her shirt—my shirt—that she wears is pushed up about her waist and her pussy glistens with the evidence of our combined cum. The sleeve slips down one shoulder, baring the reddened skin of her chest. Skin I'd touched, sucked, marked, fondled...lips I'd worshipped, breasts I'd cupped, nipples I'd pinched. I step back, rake my gaze one last time over the concave of her stomach, the curve of her hips, the creamy expanse of her thighs, the delicate nip of her ankle, her toes, her hitched breath as she swings her legs over and straightens.

"You can go now," I tell her.

"Wait," she straightens her shirt, "what do you mean?"

"Leave," I jerk my chin toward the door.

"W...where?" she stutters, "What just happened."

Everything. "Nothing," I growl.

She takes a step forward, "That… What took place between us... It was different. I was sure you felt something for me. I know that you want me."

"So?" I pull the waistband of my sweats up my waist. "I want many women… Doesn't mean I have to keep them around."

"I am not one of them," she snarls.

"Oh?" I look her up and down, "Just because my dick loves you," I smirk, "because I see your face and my dick gets hard, I hear your voice and my dick gets hard, I know you're in the next room and my dick gets hard… Doesn't mean I feel the same."

"You're not making any sense." She twists her fingers together. "I know you're scared. You've never allowed yourself to open up to another—"

"You think I opened up to you?"

"You did." She steps close and our toes bump, her nipples brush up against me; that chocolate and honey of her scent intensifies. My heart begins to pound and my chest hurts. *Shit. Let go of her; get her out of here. Walk away; don't look back. Release her from that stupid-ass arrangement that never was.*

"You'll get your money. All of it," I snap.

She blinks, "Excuse me?"

"The million a day for six days? It's yours."

"You think this was only about money?"

It had to be. "What else could it be about?"

"Did you think, for even one second, that maybe I wanted to be with you?"

"You wanted to be shut up with me in a cabin with no electricity, over Christmas?"

"Why not?"

"You wanted to spend Christmas getting to know my family?"

"It's the first time I've felt at home anywhere." She sets her jaw.

My guts twist. Shit, this isn't easy. Why do I feel like I am tearing out my heart? Why the hell do I care that she seems close to a break down? You've barely met her... You know everything about her. I know nothing of what she wants… She wants you, that's clear. She needs you as much as you are drawn to her. She senses the connection that binds you together…

And that is the fucking problem. I don't want it. I can do without it. I have enough demons of my own to contend with. I don't need this beautiful, gorgeous angel who swept in and threatens to upset my carefully structured life… Which had, by the way, gone down the shitter since she'd flounced into that cabin and turned my life upside down.

"Too bad; they are not yours."

"Too bad for you." She tips up her chin, "I'm yours. You know it and it scares you."

"You think I am scared?" I laugh.

"I think you are petrified. For the first time, you don't have a plan and it terrifies the hell out of you."

"The only thing that terrifies me is that I'll have to hold you while you have a breakdown, and trust me, Princess, that's not on my list of most-wanted things to do right now."

"I don't believe you." She clenches her fists by her side. "All of this is an act."

"That…" I tilt my head in the direction of the bed, "was an act. Guess I'm good, huh? I take credit."

"For what?"

"I won the bet with myself."

"What bet?"

"Making you fall in love with me… Remember what I told you?"

She squeezes her eyes shut, "That you'd break my heart."

"Have I, Princess?"

She stiffens, opens her eyes, stares straight into mine, "Mine is not the only heart that's breaking; and you know what else?"

I tilt my head.

"You care about me. You're in love with me, but you don't want to admit it. By the time you realize it, it will be too late. You'll come begging for forgiveness, and guess what I am going to do then?"

Sweat beads my palm… *Tell her to leave, to take her chocolate scent, her crazy-ass satchel of baking tools, her penchant for swearing in a vocabulary that consists solely of desserts, and walk out of here. Don't look back at her. Don't indulge her questions. Don't ask her what she means by that tirade.* "What?" I growl, "What the fuck would you do then?"

She reaches behind her, grabs the box of cookies she'd baked and empties it over my head, "Is that answer enough for you?"
Turning, she walks out.

34

———————

Amelie

What the hell had happened there? One second, he'd been inside of me, his cock nestled in my pussy, his lips on mine, my legs tangled about him... The next, he'd ordered me to leave.

If there were a classic case of a man who was running scared that would be Weston Fucking Kincaid. Alphahole extraordinaire. Douchebag of the highest order. Bloody fruitcake, who doesn't know his arse from his head... No. I shake my head. Reprobate snackadoodle who has his head stuck so far up his arse, he has no idea how good the pie is. I sniff. Not even when said pie hits him in the face, and splatters its contents over his beautiful mouth, and he licks it off and— *OMG, what am I thinking?*

I stumble down the stairs, almost miss a step, then right myself, slip on the next one, and come to a halt at the landing. My heart races, my pulse pounds, and a pressure boils behind my eyes. *I will not cry; will not.*

There's a patter of paws on the wooden floor. Max comes bounding out of the open doors of the suite adjacent to the landing.

I bend down, gather him up, then sink down to sit on the step. "Hey little fella, did you miss me? Did ya now?" I rub his head, hold him close. A tear runs down my cheek; Max licks it up. He whines, then pushes his nose into the crook of my neck. I hug his little body closely as more tears flow down my face. *Shit, stop it, stop it. Not your fault if he's such an ass, a completely obnoxious man, Mr. Scrooge McFuck... Gah!* Just because one of my favorite authors had released a book about a similar a-hole with that name doesn't mean I have to call him that, huh?

I swallow down the ball of emotion in my throat. I have to get out of here, return to my life... Spend Christmas alone? My heart begins to thud. How could he do this? How? A sob catches in my chest. I glance around, then down at myself. Shit, I am still wearing his shirt—nothing else. I had left everything behind in that alphahole's room. No way, am I going back for it.

Max barks, wriggles in my hold. "Oh, sorry little guy, did I crush you, huh?" I set him down, he darts forward toward the double doors that lead into the suite. Kirsten bends to pat him. Max brushes past her and rushes inside.

She straightens, then takes in my appearance.

I flush, "Umm... Uh, it's not like what it seems."

She tilts her head, "Why don't you come in and tell me about it?"

Twenty minutes later, I curl my legs under me, and take a sip of the fragrant cup of hot chocolate—no, it's never too early in the day for comfort food—that she'd handed me.

Max places his paw on my borrowed PJ's, and stares up at me. "I swear he has a sixth sense, huh?"

"Mum, why was Auntie Amelie crying?" Phoenix asks in a loud whisper.

Kirsten, pats her shoulder, "Because, uh, she had a fight."

"Lover's quarrel, huh?" Skye wanders into the living room, her specs too big for her face. She has a book in her hand.

"Don't you have homework to do?" Kirsten scolds her.

"I've completed my math assignment."

"What about Latin?"

"I hate Latin."

"Does she have to study Latin?" I ask.

"At her school, yes." Kirsten's forehead furrows, then turns to Skye, "Go on, finish it."

"But... M-o-m," she wails, once more seeming her eleven-year-old self.

"I don't need to study Latin to become a vet."

"You want to become a vet?"

She smiles, "I looove animals." She snaps her fingers; Max perks up, jumps off the sofa and races toward her.

"She and animals." Kirsten shakes her head, "I swear, she is a dog whisperer."

"And a cat one, and a hedgehog one," Skye adds.

"Hedgehog?" Kirsten scowls, "Young lady, if I find any more of those creatures in your room...I'll..."

"Relax, Ma, I was only kidding you," she smirks. Her features resemble her uncle's, aka the alphahole, aka the man who'd fucked me so thoroughly a few seconds ago... I blink. That tightness in my chest returns. I lower my chin, hide my face once again in my mug.

Kirsten draws in a breath, "Back to your studies, with you."

"Whatever." She returns to her room, Max at her heels.

"Can I do my homework too?" Phoenix beams up at her Mom.

"Go on then." Kirsten pulls Phe close, kisses her on the cheek. Phoenix turns to leave, then turns and runs to me. I place my mug back on the table, just in time, for she throws her arms around me.

"Oh," I hug the little girl back, "thanks, baby."

She kisses me on the cheek, then turns and races away.

"Kids," Kirsten sinks back in the arm chair, "they can sense when you're unhappy, you know?"

I nod. "They are both beautiful; congratulations."

"Thanks." She beams. "Their father's the disciplinarian; I spoil them I'm afraid."

"When will he be back?"

"Patrick?" Her face takes on a dreamy look, "Tomorrow, or tonight, if he can. He's on a business trip with our oldest brother."

"Really?"

She frowns, "I take it, Weston didn't mention that they work together?"

I shake my head.

"My father started a media company, that Liam now heads up."

"That's your oldest sibling?"

She nods, "Patrick works with him. Weston... Well, after the incident, he changed. He needed to do something more meaningful with his life."

"Is that why he became a heart surgeon?" I ask, "Or was that to protect his own heart?"

She stares at me.

I flush. "Umm, sorry, didn't mean for it to come out that way, it's just..."

She waves her hand, "No offense taken. I was surprised, is all. I never thought about it like that, but you may be onto something." She pauses, as if to commiserate with me. "I know how obnoxious my brother can be."

"That's putting it mildly." I mutter.

"I assume he's told you about the incident?" she asks.

"Some." I reply, my tone cautious. "He mentioned he and six of his friends were kidnapped and held captive for nearly a month when he was twelve, and during that time, each of them was exposed to some horrific punishment meted out to each of them by the kidnappers. It's why he has a trigger when it comes to clocks and time-keeping devices," I swallow, "I guess."

She nods. "After the cops rescued Weston and the other boys from the kidnappers," she leans forward, "he felt like he had been given a new lease on life. He wanted to make sure he made the most of the opportunity. It's one of the reasons he wanted to become a surgeon." She crinkles her forehead, "Then our father died of an heart attack and that strengthened his resolve."

So, I'd been right about the second part, at least. I meet her gaze, "He seems to think it's because it gives him control over life and death."

"Do you believe him?" she scoffs.

"I am not sure what to make of him," I say honestly.

She looks me up and down, "So you guys had a fight this morning?"

"More than that." I heave out a sigh.

To her credit, she hadn't been taken aback when she'd found me standing by the doorway to her suite. She hadn't asked me any questions either. She'd loaned me her clothes, then handed me the cup of hot chocolate. Hell, she hadn't even been surprised that I'd asked her for cocoa, instead of tea… And that, puts her right at the top of my list.

"What happened between you two?" she asks.

"I…" I glance away, "I think we broke up."

"Fights are normal. They're healthy in a relationship—"

"This is more than that." I jump up and begin to pace. "He told me to leave."

"The room?" her tone sharpens.

"His suite, his life… He told me it was over."

"He told you so, in no uncertain terms?"

Had he? I turn to her. "Yes," I reply.

"I don't believe it," she scowls. "I saw the way he looks at you—"

"How?" I fold my arms around my waist. "How does he look at me?"

"Like he wants to eat you up?"

"Yeah." My cheeks heat. "I mean, we don't have any issues in that, uh, department."

"The kind of chemistry between you two? It could boil water at fifty paces."

I laugh, "I thought I was the only one who made cooking analogies."

"I've been spending too much at home with the kids, ensuring dinner's on the table when my husband arrives from work every evening."

"Do you regret it?"

"Not for a second." She leans back in her chair, reaches for her mug of tea. "I had a corporate career as a lawyer. I enjoyed it, but I wanted more. I needed the entire 360 experience—home, kids... I'll go back to practicing part-time when the kids are older."

"And you'll be fine with that?"

"It's all about balance, Amelie." She smiles, "Once they are old enough to leave home, I am sure I'll go back to practicing full time."

"And you don't see it as a compromise?" I head back to the couch, drop into it.

"For whom?" She chuckles, "I have it all, as far as I can see."

And I have nothing. I twist my fingers together in front of me.

Her features twist, "Hell, I didn't mean it that way. The last thing I want to do is hurt your feelings by rubbing in my..." she circles her hand, "...all this, in your face."

"You're not." I lean forward and touch her knee. "Honestly, you aren't. I appreciate your giving me the time to recover, and for the clothes."

"Anytime." She takes my hand in hers, "I like you, Amelie."

I laugh, "You've known me all of two seconds."

"I go by my gut, and unlike my brother, I actually heed what my instincts tell me."

"Too bad that idiot McDick has no such inclinations." I take a deep breath, "Well, I guess I need to head off."

"Where will you go?"

"I need to call my friend Isla, make arrangements to stay with her. I also need my clothes, which are—"

"Stay here."

"What?" I attempt to withdraw my hand, but she doesn't let go. "I mean it," she says. "Stay with me, as my guest. We have the entire floor, and the guest room is free.

I stare at her, "But—"

"We'd love to have you."

"You don't need to say that..."

"I never say anything I don't mean." Her features take on a haughty look, one so familiar, one I've seen on his face. Shit, staying here, surrounded by his family, where their every action would remind me of the man I need to try to forget? No, just no. Not that I don't like Kirsten, but... To be so near him, and yet, not with him? Gah. I'd have to OD on chocolates to get through the ordeal, and that's definitely not something I can afford, not if I hope to get through the festive season with some semblance of a waistline.

"Thank you," I turn my palm over and clasp hers, "but no thank you."

Her lips droop. She peers into my eyes, then lets out a breath, "There's nothing I can do to convince you, huh?"

I shake my head.

"One night." She lowers her chin. "Stay for dinner tonight, meet Liam and Patrick."

I frown, open my mouth to decline, and she drops her gaze to my pajamas. "You owe me."

"You don't play fair, do you?" *Just like him.*

"It's genetic. Our father ingrained the habit of negotiation at the dining table, I'm afraid."

She rises to her feet.

"Where are you going?" I ask.

"To get your things from Weston's suite."

35

Weston

"You seem nervous, ol' chap," Damian drawls at me from the screen of my phone.

"And you seem full of shit, as usual," I mutter, as I pace in front of the fire in the living room of my mother's home. I'd gone for a run, and when I'd returned, Amelie's clothes and bags had gone from the bedroom. Guess she'd left, after all.

I'd sat on the bed in a daze and wondered if I'd done the right thing.

Yeah, I had. Of course, I had. I didn't need her staying and complicating the situation, aka the state of my feelings for her, further. I'd worked out at the gym after that, pushed myself as much as I could, considering I couldn't do weights yet with my broken finger. Then I had showered and changed into formal clothes for the traditional family dinner at home.

I run my finger around the collar of my shirt. Not that I dislike suits… But hell, if I don't feel more comfortable in scrubs. There is a certain freedom that comes from not having to pretend, when all the power and control is at your fingertips as you perform a surgery, knowing the life of a human depends on you. It is the best adrenaline rush—a responsibility I never take lightly, walking on the edge of a thrill that I crave. One slip up and things would never be the same. *Did I slip up with her?* I scowl. Fuck that. I am not second guessing my actions, no way.

"Fake girlfriend, slash fiancée, slash wife-to-be not helping with your problem then?" Damian smirks.

"What problem?" I growl.

"That you can't get it up, of course."

I frown, "Where do you get your asinine ideas from?"

"The same place you come up with your brainwaves of sharing a cabin with a woman you've met only once before." He chuckles.

"About that," I crack my neck, "it's over."

"Oh, yeah?" Damian tilts his head, "Hold on, I'm adding Arpad to the call."

"Don't..." I begin to protest, when Arpad's face appears in a window. "Man, and I thought I was bad at relationships, this has to be a record, even for you," he snickers.

"Fuck off," I growl.

"So, you think it's over, but it's not really over?" Damian pipes in.

"I am not going to explain myself."

"What are friends for, if you can't use our shoulders to cry on... Or not." Arpad's screen shakes and droplets of water splash the surface.

"Where the fuck are you?"

"On my yacht, enjoying everything life has to offer, unlike you."

"Why the fuck do I take your calls?" I grumble.

"Because you have something on your mind, and need to vent, like a girl?" Damian laughs.

"Because you are heart-broken?" Arpad snickers.

"Okay, bye," I hold my finger over the screen.

"Ooh, someone's antsy. Did we hurt your feelings? Are you upset you're not getting married like Saint and Sinner before you?"

"You look grumpy. Not jerking off either, are you?"

I shake my head, "Fuck that, and fuck you two," *and fuck the woman who put me in this situation, where I am not able to string together two words. Fucking fuck!*

I hear the pattering of paws on the floor, then Max jumps up on the sofa and shoves his face in mine. "Hey," I protest, but he licks my mouth, then turns and peers into the screen.

"Hello, ol' boy," Damian chuckles. "You keeping Uncle Weston company while he fucks up his life?"

"A woman *and* a dog?" Arpad chuckles, "Should I fetch your slippers and dressing gown next ol' chap?"

"Jesus, fuck." I am not sure what I'd intended to accomplish through this conversation, but it wasn't being at the mercy of a mutt and two of my 'friends.'

"At least, I saved the Father from the burden of a virtual wedding." I grouse.

"Speaking of," Arpad drawls, "I'm adding Edward to the call."

No, fuck, no. Why do I insist on calling my 'friends,' knowing I'll be put through the wringer each time?

"Someone mention my name?" Edward's face flickers onto the screen.

"I was just leaving," I grumble.

"You want to hear this." Edward gazes at me with those clear eyes of his which have seen so much and which have yet managed to retain a modicum of innocence. Enough for him to sleep with his thoughts at night, at least.

"How do you manage it?" I snap out.

"You mean, hold down a conversion without losing my wits?"

"That too," I grunt. "How do you always seem so upbeat and energetic?"

"Umm…Maybe because he has no worldly attachments?" Damian offers.

I stare at the Father, who jerks his chin, "I realized the only way out of the aftermath of the incident, was to be true to myself at all times," he says.

"What if the only thing that can soothe my mind is the one thing I must never have?" I mutter.

"Are we talking about someone in particular or a metaphor?"

"What do you think?" I mutter.

Silence stretches across the space. Neither of the other two assholes respond with an off-the-cuff remark. Thank fuck for that. Perhaps it had been the Father I had been waiting for. Guess that's why I'd agreed to this call, which was supposed to be about 7A investments and FOK Media—which stood for Full of Kindness by the way—the companies that the seven of us own.

"I think you're fighting your future," Edward's tone is serious.

"I make my own future," I insist.

He quirks his lips, "You believe that, after everything you've been through?"

"It's because of everything I've been through that I believe it."

Edward tilts his head, "You can't control everything around you."

"Is that why you took the easy way out and gave up the real world for the spiritual one?"

Edward pales. Damian stiffens. Arpad's silent disapproval communicates through the screen.

"Fucking hell." I drag my fingers through my hair. "I didn't mean that Father," I mumble.

"You did," Edward's voice is calm. "I'm glad you are able to speak your mind. In such matters, clear, concise communication is the only way forward."

"What do you mean?" I peer into the screen, trying to discern his features. "Tell me, Father."

"Some of that honesty you displayed earlier... That's what you need to bring to your relationship with her."

"Eh?" I shake my head, "You're making absolutely no sense."

"You know I am." Edward's lips quirk, "Hand on heart, ask yourself what it is that you must do in this situation."

"Haven't I been asking myself that all along? Would I be asking you this question if the answer was at all clear to me?"

"You're the business man here, Weston. Your gut knows what it wants; your heart simply has to fall in line."

"You're not shoddy in the business space yourself." I crack my neck. "You've held your own in all of the business decisions we've made thus far."

"Don't change the topic," Edward admonishes. "What is it that your gut says you should do now?"

"What if it's not clear to me for the first time, huh?"

"Wrong answer," Edward snaps. "You're beginning to piss me off."

I blink. Edward angry? It never happens. That he swore at me? I can count on my fingers the number of times he's done that. "I am not sure what to say," I rasp.

"You don't have to say anything, and you do know what you have to do. Your stubborn-ass head is getting in the way. You're trying to think about this along rational lines, when you know what you have to do."

I laugh, "Have you been spending much time with Saint?" I ask. "You're speaking in riddles."

Edward shakes this head, "Stop deflecting; it won't work." He frowns, "You going to follow your gut and your heart on this? Or are you going to spend the rest of your years regretting the one decision you should have made, which would have changed the course of your life, but you didn't because you were too much of a pussy?"

I stare at him. "I can't believe you said that." I shake my head. "You, of all people, should know I don't shy away from hard decisions."

"But this is much more than that." He tilts his head, "It's, perhaps, not your decision to make. Perhaps this time, you have to allow the circumstances to wash over you, and go with the flow?"

I laugh. *As if I would ever do that?* I haven't come this far in life to bow before events, not if I have my way. "I'm not sure what you're implying but—"

The screen pixelates and my voice echoes back at me. *Huh?* Bloody technology, always fails you when you need it the most. The connection restores.

"Hey man." Damian peers back at me from the screen.

Arpad jerks his chin. "Still here for my sins," he grumbles.

"Where's Edward?" I frown.

"Seems he dropped off?" Damian mutters, "Perhaps he's had enough of you acting like a fool, and decided to cut out?"

"Yeah, well, fuck that." *And fuck him.* My heart begins to race. "Not my decision to make, huh? We'll see." I toss my head.

"You coming out to London for the New Year's party?" Damian asks.

"I'll be there."

"Are you bringing her?"

"That's up to her." I frown. The hair on the back of my neck rises and a tingle runs down my spine. "I need to go, guys."

I hang up and turn. My gaze widens. "What are you doing here?"

36

Amelie

I tip up my chin and march into the room. *What the hell am I doing here? Why had I allowed Kirsten to convince me to stay?* He frowns as I walk past him to the bar, and pour myself some sparkling water. Yeah, I need my wits about me. I'm not going to fuck this up, or give the alphahole the time of the day either.

I glance around the beautifully furnished living room. The painting above the fire place is definitely an original, the settee in the room is made of plush leather and strewn with cushions, giving it a homey look. The wooden floor gleams, no doubt, polished every day by minions. I take in the corners of the room, the other walls—no clocks. Of course, not. Is his family aware of Weston's trigger? Had they done away with all time pieces? Of course, they know about his affliction, right?

Footsteps sound behind me as Weston prowls over, "I thought I told you to leave?"

A ripple runs past my nerve endings. *Don't show how nervous you are. Don't let on how much his nearness affects you.*

I turn, glance around him. "Hey, Kirsten," I wave at his sister.

"Come on over, babe, you gotta see what Phe has drawn for you."

"Coming." I march past him, head high, spine straight, my heart booming in my rib cage. He locks his fingers around my wrist.

I squeak.

"Don't ignore me," he growls under his breath. That harsh edge to his voice? Gah! My nerve endings all flare at once.

I stiffen, glance sideways. "Let go of me," I whisper.

"You don't tell me what to do."

"And you don't get to tell me what to do anymore. You told me to leave, remember?"

"And you disobeyed me."

"You're not my keeper, not even my lover. Any right you had over me, you forfeited right then."

"Have I now?" His fingers tighten on my wrist—and he's using his left hand, which is not his dominant hand, but it might as well be. Is any part of this guy less than 100% assertive? *And why am I going all gooey inside?* Hell, he told me to leave, and just before Christmas. What kind of a monster does that? *And why the hell does my body refuse to behave around him?*

"Yes, you did." I raise my gaze, force myself to see this through, "I'm done with you."

He frowns and something flickers in his gaze. "Amelie, I—"

"Aunteee Amelieee." Phe runs across the room and throws herself at me.

I tug my hand, but Weston still doesn't release it. I half bend, rub the little girl's hair. "Hey, baby, watcha have there for me?"

She holds up the craft paper, showing an outline of a princess that she's colored in, complete with tiara. "Who's this?"

"It's you." She smiles widely. "Princess Amelie."

"Awww." My heart stutters. I tug on my hand again, and this time, Weston releases me. I lower myself to a squat as he takes my drink from my hand. I ignore the gesture, accept the drawing from Phe. "It's beautiful."

"So pretty," Phoenix giggles.

"Yes, you are." I pull the little girl close and kiss her cheek loudly.

She bursts out laughing, then pulls away. I rise to my feet, glance at the drawing. "Aww," I sigh, "it really is pretty."

"You're prettier," Weston's deep rumble surrounds me. I shiver. *Hell, this really was a bad idea.*

I begin to walk away.

"Amelie," he calls out.

Don't stop; don't.

"Your drink."

I wave a hand in the air, "You have it."

I walk toward Kirsten, joining her and the girls. Skye has her nose buried in a book, as usual. She glances up at me, then at the drawing. She snorts under her breath, turns back to her reading.

Kirsten grimaces, then mouths 'sorry.'

I laugh. I remember being far worse at her age. Of course, my parents, being the strict disciplinarians they were, didn't help. It's why I had rebelled every inch of the way. Christmas at home had been quiet, my parents not wanting to change their routine much, even for the festive season. Perhaps there is comfort in everyday chores? More likely, they were so content in each other's company, I'd never fit in with them. Always the third wheel, the outsider looking in. Then they'd retired to Spain; and with that, all expectation of my visiting them for Christmas had been dropped—on both our sides. Our communication had dwindled down to the occasional phone calls, then that had stopped too.

Don't get me wrong, they did their best for me, always provided for me, gave me everything I needed... Except a sense of belonging... The kind of warmth I find here. Max runs into the room, heads straight for me and jumps up.

"Hey boy," I lift him into my arms. "Missed me huh?" He licks my face, and I giggle, "Wow, so much affection, and you saw me what, three minutes ago, huh?"

I glance up and meet Weston's gaze. He raises the glass—the one he had taken from me—and brings it to his lips. He drains the water, then lowers the glass and licks his lips.

I swallow. Shit, what craziness is this, that his every glance is filled with undertones? A crazy sexual tension that will never abate between us. Too bad... He is an alphahole who will never change colors.

"Patrick," Kirsten cries out, then moves forward to greet the man who's just walked in. He opens his arms wide as Phe races for him. He catches the little girl, swings her high and she squeals. "Daddy, you're home," Phe cries.

"I told you I'd be." He kisses her on the cheek, lowers her to the floor, then turning, sweeps his wife into a kiss.

"Ugh," Skye makes a gagging sound, then turns back to her book, which she's reading standing up, by the way.

"Hey, sweetheart, a kiss for your old man?" Patrick grins at her.

Skye glances up, sighs, then walks forward and offers her cheek. Patrick hugs her close, and Skye seems to thaw enough to put her arm around him to hug him.

I can't stop the giggle that bounces out of me.

Warmth envelops me, and I don't need to turn round to know that Weston has moved in to stand behind me. "You went against my order."

I snort. "What you going to do about it?" I tip up my chin, "Oh, and I am here because Kirsten asked me to stay. I'll be gone tomorrow, and then we'll never have to meet each other again." I thrust Max at him.

Weston grabs the puppy, mostly because I took him by surprise, no doubt.

Max whines, wriggles around. Weston sets him down and he prances toward the girls.

He straightens, glares at me, "You're still on my turf."

"Whatever." I throw my hands up, pivot and flounce toward the door. Wide shoulders fill the door and a tall man walks in. His features are vaguely familiar. *Huh?*

He glances at me, and his face lights up, "Amelie." He strides toward me.

I blink up, trying to place him. "Hunter?"

"How are you?" He places his hands on my shoulders, then bends to kiss me on each cheek. "This evening just got more exciting," he whispers in my ear.

I chuckle, pat his shoulder, "What are you doing here?"

"Yes, that's what I'd like to know." Weston stalks forward to glare at him. The two men are the same height. Hunter wears a suit that is every bit as well cut as Weston's. His dark hair curls over his collar. He's every bit as handsome as Weston. So why the hell don't I feel the same attraction toward him?

He glances between us, then grins, "I was invited."

"Who the fuck by?" Weston snaps.

"By me."

Another man stalks into the room. I blink. His features, his build, that bored, annoyed perma-dick face... It could be Weston, only it isn't. The creases around his eyes are deeper, his gaze so cold that I shiver. I take a step back and Weston's warmth cocoons me. His big palm rests on my waist and I don't push it off. His touch grounds me in the face of his darker, older sibling walking through the door."

"Liam," Weston drawls, confirming my suspicion.

"Weston," Liam jerks his chin. His gaze rests on me for a second; there's no change in expression on his face, no acknowledgement that he's seen me. And I thought Weston was a jerk? I bite the inside of my cheek. "Hunter's with me," Liam tilt his head. "I am supporting his campaign to run for Prime Minister."

"Thought this was meant to be family only," Weston growls.

Liam barely glances in my direction, "Considering you have your latest piece here, you shouldn't speak, huh?"

I wince. Weston's big body stiffens behind me. Anger thrums from him and he takes a step forward. "Apologize to her," he growls.

I blink. Go figure. Alphahole here, gets all macho and protective when faced with the threat of an enemy. Or perhaps he wants to save face because I'm here as his guest… Except, I'm not.

I turn on him. "I don't need you to fight my battles," I snap, then turn to Liam. "For your information, I am here because Kirsten invited me to stay." I step forward, tip my chin up, "And I don't really care for your impoliteness...and for your apology, even less."

"Liam," a female voice whips through the space.

I look around him and wince. It's Rosie. Of course, it's their mother. That's all I need. What a nightmare. Why did I accept Kirsten's invitation to stay, again?

Phe skips over to me, then slips her hand through mine. I meet her gaze. She tugs on my arm, I bend down, and she whispers, "You're not leaving, are you?"

I draw in a breath, then shake my head. "Not yet," I whisper back.

I straighten as Rosie walks into the room. She glances between her sons, "Everything okay?" There's a warning edge to her voice.

"Yes, Mother," Liam grates out.

She turns to Weston, who hesitates. She tilts her head, and Weston pulls back his shoulders, gives Liam a hard look. "Apologize first," he insists.

I am about to tell him to forget it, when Liam walks over to me. He takes my shoulders then bends to kiss my cheek. "I am sorry about my earlier remark," he says, "I'm afraid Weston tends to get on my nerves. I didn't mean to insult you that way."

He straightens. Weston tugs me closer so I am out of Liam's reach.

Liam looks between us and smirks, then walks around us toward the dining room. *What the hell was that? Apology my foot.* He may have sounded earnest, but that condescending look on his face? Jesus, he is one tough customer.

Rosie turns to Weston, who draws in a breath. He walks over to her, kisses her cheek, "We're good, Mother."

"Good." She pats his cheek. "Let's eat." She walks toward the dining room.

OMG, now that's power, huh? She's got these alphas to heel, and that's a talent she'd have learned early. And how, I mean, seriously, how does she do it? She's the true leader here.

Hunter, Kirsten and Patrick follow. Phe skips forward, with Skye trailing behind.

Weston turns on me and the scowl on his face deepens. He bends his knees, thrusts his face into mine, "I've called the car service. They'll be here after dinner for you. Don't find an excuse to stay back this time, you get me?"

37

Weston

Why the hell is she sitting next to him? I frown across the table as Hunter leans over to say something to Amelie. She giggles, her cheeks rosy. From his company? From the wine? From the warmth in the fireplace, maybe?

I stab my fork into the chestnut and bring it to my mouth. "Why is she talking to him?" I grumble under my breath.

"Because unlike you, she has manners and knows when to be polite, especially at family dinners." Kirsten nudges me with her elbow, "Can't take your eyes off her, huh?"

"Of course, not." I glance down at my plate, "This food is fucking bland."

"Lost your appetite, huh?" She snickers.

I glower, "Don't try to get a rise out of me."

"I thought I was the only one who could," she replies, "until—"

"Until?"

"Her, of course," she chuckles.

I don't need to look up to know she's glanced across at the pesky, curvy woman who I'd invited into my life. Holy fuck, what the hell had I been thinking? "Why is she still here?" I roll my shoulders.

"I can't believe you asked her to leave, and so close to Christmas."

"It's two days to Christmas," I grumble. "Enough time for her to join her family, if she chooses."

"You're a class-A douche," she hisses at me. "Is it because you're in love with her that you're being so terrible to her? Is that why you're going out of your way to insult her, to ensure she'll never look at you again?"

"No, to the first, and as to the second... Well, that's my nature."

"Ha," she snorts. "You can't pull off your mean-ass persona with me, dear brother. You and I are too close for that."

And isn't that the truth. Kirsten is two years younger than me, close enough for us to hang out together. Growing up, I was her protector and she was my shadow, who tagged along with me on all my boyhood adventures. Unlike Liam, who at eight years older than me, was someone I hadn't gotten to know as well. There'd always been a chasm between us, which had only increased after our father had passed on.

I blow out a breath. "I'm not in love with her," I insist again.

"Keep telling yourself lies; that's a specialty of yours, huh?"

"Don't push me on this one," I say through clenched teeth.

Amelie's giggle reaches me. I glance up to find her leaning into Hunter. I clench my hand around my fork, which slips from my fingers and smashes into the plate. The clash rings out and everyone at the table turns to glance at me.

"Sorry, still getting used to using my non-dominant hand for every day stuff," I scowl.

Amelie straightens, glances at me and away. Good. At least, she's heeding the warning.

"Your finger troubling you, much?" my mother asks.

I glance down at my right hand. "The cast comes off next week, then a few more weeks of therapy and I should be back at work by mid-January, at the latest," I reply.

"How did the accident take place?" Liam asks from his position at the foot of the table.

After father passed, Mother assumed the responsibility of running the business, until Liam took over. She still holds veto power on the board and is the head of the family.

"I was forced off the road," I reply.

"Forced off?" Liam frowns.

"No need to concern yourself. I am looking into it, with the Seven."

"The Seven." His lips twitch, "You place too much importance on their friendship."

"At least I have friends, unlike you," I shoot back, then wince. Shit, a few minutes in the company of my family, and hell, if the old insecurities don't come tumbling back.

"I'm focused on my goals, on preserving and growing the family name. I'd do anything for it."

"Including getting married and producing an heir, no doubt?" I scowl.

"If that's what's needed of me, I won't shirk my duties." Liam wipes the edges of his lips with his napkin.

"You're getting married?" Amelie leans forward, her gaze sparkling. "Who's the lucky woman?"

"Someone I haven't met yet," he says coolly.

"So, you don't know her, but you're marrying her?" She frowns.

"Until he does, he doesn't get to take over the family business," Kirsten explains. "Nor, for that matter, can Weston."

"Huh?" Amelie scowls across the table.

I stiffen, nudge Kirsten with my knee. She shuffles away. Fuck! Why do little sisters always have to be such a pain?

"Explain," Amelie insists.

"Until both of my brothers marry, and specifically for Liam, until he produces an heir, they cannot get access to the family business —"

"—Or to their trust funds," my mother completes the sentence. "It's tradition," she elaborates. "Something decreed by my husband's grandfather, and which I hope my sons will honor."

"And Kirsten?" Amelie asks.

"I don't count," she smirks. "Only a woman, after all, and all that."

"And you know your father changed his will to ensure that you inherit your share of the money," Mother retorts.

"I don't get access to the company," she protests.

"Do *you* want access to the company?"

"Guess not," she admits. "Still, it would have been nice if Dad had given me the choice."

"He made sure you'd be taken care of —"

"Not that Kirsten would have lacked for anything, as long as I am here." Patrick folds his arm around her and pulls her close.

Amelie's features grow wistful and she glances from Kirsten to me. I glare at her, she bites down on her lower lip, and damn it, of course, my cock instantly notices.

I hold her gaze. She looks away, raises her glass, "A toast to Kirsten and Patrick." She smiles.

I glance over to my mother, who seems surprised. Then she surprises me, by raising her glass. "A toast." She coughs, rubs at her chest.

"You okay?" I frown.

"Never been better," she smiles, the skin stretching around her mouth. A gleam of sweat glistens on her forehead. She raises her glass in her left hand, her dominant hand, which trembles. All of my senses pop. My visions, tunnels. Even before the glass slips from her fingers, I rise, then rush over to her. I catch her as she sinks into her chair, her breathing ragged, her skin pallid.

"Liam," I snap at my brother, "call an ambulance."

He jumps to his feet so fast, his chair topples over with a crash. He pulls out his phone, walks away as he dials.

I hear the sound of Max barking. Phe begins to cry, then is hushed. More chairs being shoved back, the slap of footsteps on the floor, then Hunter and Patrick crowd me. "Move back," I snap, and they comply.

"Weston," my mother whispers as I lower her to the ground. Sweat beads her upper lip, "Weston." She coughs again.

"Don't talk," I say.

I reach for my mother's wrist to check her pulse and glimpse the steel band attached to her watch—the bloody watch that my father presented to her when they got married; the one she'd put away after the incident, when she'd found out about my trigger. Why the hell is she wearing it? My heart begins to race, the blood thundering at my temples. *I stare at the watch—the hands on the face, the big hand moving fast, so fast, the small hand following pace, the countdown for my life as my kidnapper had hauled me into the small room across the corridor from where I had been imprisoned with the rest, as he'd tied me to the chair, attached the rigged clock to my chest. "Will you survive it this time? Follow the countdown, the ticking of the clock as it edges closer to the end."*

He'd ripped off my blindfold—the light had cast his face in shadow so I hadn't been able to get a good look at him—then left me with only the ticking for company, and I had screamed against the gag, tried to pull free. "If you move, the bomb goes off. If you disturb the clock, it goes off. If you so much as breathe too hard…it goes off. Hell, if you so much as live…it may go off… Will you survive this round?" His voice echoes through my head. I stare at the moving hands of the watch.

"What do you think, Weston?" my kidnapper asks. "Will you live or will you die this round?"

Live or die?

Do I want to die?

What do I have to live for? Why can't someone rescue me and put me out of my misery? If I get out of here, I'll never allow anyone else to control my life...never. Never.

"Weston?"

Never relinquish your power. Never.

"Weston!" Something connects with my cheek. I fall back, glance up into familiar blue eyes. The eyes of an angel. The blue of the ocean, the sky. The only place where I could be safe, where I can soar above it all, away from here, away from these memories, the clocks that tick down to my demise.

"Weston." Those blue eyes blaze at me; silver sparks in their depths. Huh? "You need to help her. Snap out of your shock. Now!" She raises her palm, then slaps me again, and again.

I blink. "Amelie?"

"Thank God," she cries. She pinches my chin, turns my face to where my mother is sprawled on the floor, her hand extended. I press my thumb to her wrist. *There's no pulse.*

"Mother!" I touch her shoulder. "Rosie," I call out her name but she doesn't respond.

Fuck, fuck, fuck. I tilt her head back, lift the tip of her chin and, lean in closer. Her chest doesn't move. I listen over her mouth and nose for breathing sounds, hold my cheek over her nose. Fuck, she's not breathing.

I place the heel of my left hand on the center of her chest, place the heel of the other hand on top of the first hand, interlace my fingers, My injured finger screams in protest — I ignore it. I push down with my arms and hands, using my body weight to compress her chest.

Tick-tock-tick-tock- Push-now-push-now.

My own personal song that has a rhythm that corresponds to the compressions per minute required for the rhythm.

Tick-tock-tick-tock. Push-now-push-now.

Sweat beads my brow; pain sears my arm. I reject it, continue with the momentum.

Tick-tock-tick-tock-push-now-push-now.

I count to 30 compressions, then tilt her head, lift her chin up, pinch her nose. I seal my mouth over hers, blow. Check to make sure that her chest rises. Blow again twice. Then back to chest compressions, count to 30, followed by 2 rescue breaths.

"Weston?"

I focus on my mother's face. *Come on, come on, breathe.*

"Weston, the paramedics are here."

Breathe. Breathe. I continue to push down to the rhythm in my head. *Tick-tock-tick-tock-breathe-now-breathe-now.*

"Weston!" Arms grab my shoulders. I wince; pain radiates from my injured finger; a coldness coils in my gut. I am pulled back. I lower my injured arm to my side, watch as the paramedics take over, blocking out the view of my mother. "It's my fault," I gasp.

"What? No." Amelie's face fills my line of sight. "Weston, it's nobody's fault."

"I froze," I mumble under my breath.

"Weston." Amelie cups my cheek, "Baby, look at me."

"The one time I needed to be in control of my senses, and I lost it. I couldn't move, couldn't breathe… All I could think of was—"

"The incident," she whispers. "Oh, baby, stop torturing yourself."

I raise my gaze to her face, "What's it to you?"

"What?"

"Why are you still here? Didn't I tell you to leave?"

"Weston, man, get a grip on yourself." Hunter touches my shoulder and something inside of me snaps. I rise to my feet, plant my uninjured fist in his face.

He reels back. Fire burns a trail up my arm from the burst skin on my knuckles. "Fuck." That hurt like a bitch, but what-fucking ever. "You keep the fuck away from her, you hear me."

"Man, you have this all wrong." Hunter puts up his hands; blood drips from his cut lip. *Good.*

"Weston," Amelie shoves herself between us, "what's wrong with you?"

"You," I growl. "You're what's wrong." *Fuck you, what the hell are you doing? Making sure you cut all ties with her, huh? You could have accepted her tenderness, her compassion, her softness—that always seems to make you unravel, that makes you weak. She makes me want everything I swore I don't need. Fuck me. And fuck her and,* "Fuck all of you." I stumble back.

She grabs hold of my suit jacket. "Weston, please stop," she sobs.

"Look at you," I snarl, "all empathetic and shit, when really all you want is my money. Admit it."

"No."

"Don't lie, that's why you accepted my deal. Its why you came here, why you're still here. Because you think I'll succumb to your charms? That perhaps I'll settle down and play happy family with you? Well, you can think again. That's not what I want."

"You don't mean it."

"You're right." *Shut the fuck up. you wanker. What the fuck are you saying? Don't do it; don't do it.* "I do want it."

Her chin wobbles, "You do?"

I nod, "Just not with you."

"At least you are being honest." Her features crumple and tears drip from her eyes. She wipes them away, straightens herself, "You may as well admit that you thought up this arrangement, because you wanted to fake a marriage in order to access your trust fund."

As if I need the family money? I am doing fine, more than fine, on my own steam.

I glare at her.

She tips her head back.

I flatten my lips. "Fine," I snap. "That's why I came up with this idea of a fake relationship. I should have known you were all wrong for it."

"Fine." She pulls herself up to her full height, "There's one more thing I need to tell you."

"Oh?"

She nods. "Go fuck yourself."

She brushes past me, walks out of the room, my house, my life… My everything.

My vision tunnels and my heart hammers so fast, I am sure I am having a cardiac as well. *Stop her; stop her.* I step toward her. Liam plants his body in my path.

"Get out of my way," I growl.

"Get ahold of yourself first." Liam grabs my shoulders. I shake him off, raise my fist—the wrong one—the one with my injured finger in a splint. *Fuck.* He swerves; my hand grazes his face. Pain crashes behind my eyes. The next moment something slams into my face, the world tilts, and darkness pulls me under.

38

Weston

"You're a wanker, you ass," Damian frowns down at me.

I tilt my chin up from where I am sprawled out on the examination table.

"Welcome back, Sleeping Beauty," Arpad drawls from the other side.

This scenario is all wrong. As a doctor, I am used to being in there, with the action, inside the OR, where I use my talent, my wits, my instinct, to save lives. Instead, I am sprawled out here…like the loser I am. *Loser, fucking loser.*

I try to sit up, and my entire body protests. I wince. Damian touches my shoulder. "Take it easy, Kincaid," he cautions.

"Fuck off," I mutter. What's wrong with me? I shoved her away. I knew what I was doing, I was aware of it. I had done it while in full possession of my senses. I hadn't been able to stop myself. What should I have said instead? Please stay; don't go. All the shit I threw your way? Those were my issues, not yours. My insecurities, my bloody fallacies about myself. I thought I was invincible, invulnerable, I thought I could control my fate, I thought… I could live without your touch, your kisses, your beautiful cunt…your spirit, your sass, your lips that clung to mine, your heart…your tender heart, your fun-loving attitude, that I admit, sometimes got on my nerves. I mean, can anyone be that chirpy, that happy all the time? What hurts of your own had you been hiding underneath? I'd never bothered to find out… And now, it is too late.

"Too late," I mumble.

"What's that?" Damian lowers his head to my eye level. "The fuck did you say?" he demands.

"It's too fucking late." I drag my fingers through my hair. "I let her go, man."

"Who are you talking about?"

My head whirls; I squeeze my eyes shut to stop it. Run an internal check on my vitals—pain in my right shoulder and my left, my left eye hurts like a bitch, my broken finger is numb and my chest… The band around my chest, that hollow sensation in my abdomen… I straighten, "Mother, how is she? Is she…?" I swallow. *Don't say it; don't think it.* "Is she…?" I swallow down the ball of emotion in my throat. Shit, since when did I become this weak? This unable to take on my share of the burden for my family? This selfish that I am slumped in a corner worrying about myself… My bloody love life, which isn't… It is more than that. Hell. I sit up; my head spins, "Whoa." I slouch down again, "The hell is wrong with me?"

"They had to sedate you."

"What?"

"You had a bit of a breakdown, ol' chap?"

"What?"

"You lost it there," Arpad's somber voice reaches me.

"You're not making any sense, man." I straighten. My shoulder hurts like a bitch—my right shoulder. I glance down at my injured finger; the splint has been replaced by a fresh one.

"Yeah," Damian drawls. "You hit Liam, who decked you. They hauled you into another ambulance, brought you here. You were lucky that you didn't fracture that finger again, though you're going to have to wear that splint for a while longer."

Right!

"And my mother?"

"She's fine," Damian replies.

"She had a—"

"She didn't," He shakes his head.

"What?" I scowl, "She had a cardiac arrest."

"She didn't."

"I don't understand." I scowl.

"She had symptoms resembling a cardiac arrest, but your CPR saved her. But it wasn't a cardiac arrest."

"You are not making any sense."

"She was poisoned."

"What?" I shake my head. "How did that happen?"

"They are trying to find out."

"The food we ate." I rub the back of my neck "The rest of us are fine?"

"Everyone else is, as far as I know," Damian confirms.

"She was targeted," Arpad offers.

"Do they know who did it?" I glance between them. The two men exchange glances.

"What are you thinking?" I growl.

Damian glances down at me, "Who has a vendetta against the Seven?"

"The Mafia," I breathe.

Arpad's features harden; he doesn't comment.

"Fucking asspricks." My stomach churns. Sweat beads my forehead. "They changed our lives… Traumatized us. Hell, I thought I'd gotten over my bloody trigger…but fucking-fuck… I froze when I saw my mother's watch."

"We heard," Damian replies, his tone quiet.

"I couldn't help her." A ball of emotion closes my throat.

"From what we heard, you gave her CPR, which saved her life."

"I didn't do enough." I rake my fingers through my hair.

"Aren't you hearing what we're trying to tell you, asshole? It wasn't your fault."

"Right," I draw in a breath, "I get it." I swing my legs over the side. "I need to go see her,"

Arpad stops me with an arm on my shoulder. "She doesn't want to see you."

"What?"

"No one in your family wants you there."

"Excuse me? Are you joking?"

"Not after how you acted with her…"

"What? You just said my CPR saved her. Why are they pissed at me?"

"Amelie."

"She's not their concern."

"By all accounts, she is now."

"The fuck do you mean?"

"She's in there with them," Arpad adds.

My heart begins to race. *Shit, can I put this right somehow? Have I been given another chance?* If I can get to her and explain my actions... I rise to my feet and the world lurches around me. "Fucking fuck." My legs give way under me and I crash back onto the examination table.

"Man, you're pathetic." Damian glowers down at me. "They don't want to see you. You don't want to go there; it could get ugly."

"They're my family; they'll see me," I insist.

"You sure?"

"I mean, so I was, uh—unreasonable with her."

"You think?"

"Okay, I was an ass. I hurt her—"

"More like broke her heart. What were you thinking? Asking her to leave in front of everyone? A moose would have more sense than you."

"A moose?"

"It's Christmas, and all that," he explains.

"Right." I lurch back up to my feet; my legs seem to hold me this time. I take a step forward, sway. Damian grabs my shoulder. I shake it off, "I can fucking do this on my own."

"Fine, man, whatever." He exchanges a look with Arpad, who shakes his head.

"You bitches have anything to say, you can say it to my face."

"Still crotchety in his old age," Arpad mutters.

"If you cunts can't help me, then you can fuck off," I growl, step toward the exit of the room. By the time I reach the doorway I am panting. I grab the doorframe; sweat beads my forehead. *Shit, the fuck is wrong with me?* My shoulder hurts, but my fractured finger seems to have gone numb, thank fuck. I propel myself forward, make it into the corridor and crash into a nurse. The young woman straightens, shoots me an annoyed glance, then blinks. "Dr Kincaid?"

Thank fuck. She recognizes me from when I'd done my residency in this very hospital. I need all the breaks I can get; so long as I reach her in time.

I glance down at the nurse's badge. "Marcy," I kick my lips up in a smile, "Can you help me?"

She flutters her eyelids and my gag reflex kicks in. *Shit, has to be the drugs I am on. It's no wonder I feel like I am flying. It's also the only reason that I can't tolerate another woman putting the moves on me. Yeah, nothing to do with the fact that a sassy, curvy, pastry chef has entranced me. Sure, keep telling your-self that, fuckhead.* My head spins. I put out my hand to steady myself and Marcy grabs it. *Fuck, this is not right—me touching another woman. The fuck is wrong with you Kincaid?* Eyes on the prize, remember, and right now, I need help in getting to where Amelie…and my mother, and yeah, the entire family is.

I hold onto Marcy's shoulder, "Can you help me?"

39

───────

Amelie

"How dare he do this?" I mumble under my breath. *How dare he tell me that he doesn't want me, doesn't want a future with me? Get over it; get over him.* Every time he's pushed me away, I've returned to him. Like an ant attracted to sugar, like cream on milk, like jelly on the floor—gah, stop. Even my metaphors are beginning to sound pathetic. *Just leave, before he hurts you further. Pulls away at any final shred of self-respect you have left, before he destroys your confidence completely.*

"Did you say something?" Kirsten asks me from her perch on the chair opposite me. We are in the waiting room of the hospital in Durham, where the ambulance had taken Rosie.

I'd seen Liam deck Weston, had seen him crumple to the ground, had lost my shit and run to him, then had ridden with him in the second ambulance to the hospital.

Once the doctors had confirmed that he was going to be okay, I had turned to leave, but Kirsten had stopped me. She'd insisted I stay with them while they waited for the 'all clear' from the surgeon so they could visit with Rosie.

"I think I should leave." I turn to her, "This is a family matter."

"You are family," she insists. "My asshole brother may not see it yet, but he loves you."

"Does he?" I chuckle, but it's completely devoid of humor. "He has a funny way of showing it."

She searches my features; her own soften. She takes my hand in hers, "Sweetheart, I understand how upset you must be with his behavior. I have no words to apologize for god-knows-what-all he's said and done to you. All I can say is, please be patient with him."

"You think I'd be here otherwise?" I swallow. "Only, I'm not sure it's helping."

"Oh, it is, more than you can imagine." She hesitates, "You're the first woman he's brought home. Ever."

"Oh." I swallow, "I… I am…?" My heart begins to beat faster. Does it mean anything? Does it? No.

"That was part of the pretense." I say. "So he could show you all that he intended to settle down. After all, he needs to get married to claim his inheritance, right?"

"Only he doesn't need the money," Kirsten points out. "He's rich enough, not to mention successful enough, in his own right."

"That's true." I admit. "But it doesn't negate that he asked me to pose as his fake girlfriend. Why did he have to boil down the attraction between us to that? Why did he have to turn it into something so...transactional?"

"He can't seem to stop destroying what's dearest to him." Kirsten smiles at me, but it's a sad smile. She holds my hand between her palms.

"Tell me about it," I choke out. "I've tried; I really have. When it comes to him, I seem to have some self-destructive tendencies of my own."

"The chemistry between the two of you..." She fans herself, "Honestly, it's off the charts. I see the way he follows you around with his eyes, like he wants to eat you up."

I redden. "Is it that obvious?"

"You have no idea." Her lips quirk. "It's different, it's special, it's something that's not easy to come by… Maybe once in a lifetime, even."

"You think I don't know that?" I tug on my hand and she releases it. I drag my fingers through my hair. Shit, somewhere during the last few hours, my hair had loosened from the chignon I'd pulled it into. Bet I look a sight, to match how I am feeling inside—beaten, broken, sad… Hell. This isn't why I had left London. This is not what I had bargained for when he'd walked into the cabin naked, swept into my life like a freshly baked baguette which I couldn't keep away from. OMFG, that's it then. That last metaphor... Hell, why does it remind me about certain parts of him which are as beautifully endowed? As thick... As gorgeous to put my mouth on. I rise to my feet.

Kirsten glances up at me. "Where are you going?"

"I... I can't do this." I swallow, "You understand, don't you? If I want to come out of this with even some small part of me intact, I need to go." I turn to leave.

"It's the incident," her voice follows me.

I pause, then turn to her. "So I am told," I say.

"You said he mentioned it to you, but has he told you what they did to him?" she queries.

I shake my head.

"Maybe you should ask him."

"Maybe," I tilt my head, "maybe not." Maybe I've had enough of Weston and his entire family—much as I have come to like them, Kirsten especially, and the kids, and hell, even his mother... She's something—formidable, strong, a true matriarch who holds them together. For good or bad, they are a unit. They fight and hate each other, and when there is a crisis like this, they come together too. They have each other's backs.

Something I've never had. I'm not part of a family; I have my own, but I've never belonged there. Is that why I had wanted to start a company, a business of my own? To create a family, of sorts? Is that what has driven me thus far? Had I sensed that about Weston, and was that one of the reasons I had been attracted to him. That and his gorgeous, beautiful dick, of course, and that caring demeanor of his, which he hides so bloody well. If it had not been for Max, and how he'd taken care of his nieces... Or how he'd been toward his mother, hell, I'd have missed that completely. All in all... It is time to put this behind me, to go home to the future I would build for myself.

I turn, walk toward the exit.

"Amelie," Liam's voice stops me.

I turn to find him striding toward me. "Are you leaving?" He frowns. Those features, so like Weston's, tighten. A lump forms in my throat. Shit, this is not good. Just because he reminds me of the alphahole, who I must try to forget, doesn't mean I need to get all teary.

"Yes," I straighten my spine, "I must go."

"Have you spoken to Weston?" He tilts his head. His dark gaze, so like Weston's yet not, sweeps over my features. No, he's not Weston.

He's colder, darker, unfeeling. Weston has that sly hint of humor in his eyes, that hint of wickedness which tempers that mean edge—not that he couldn't be horrible, but always, always there was that playfulness that peeked out, that sentiment that compelled me to tug on it and unravel the man inside... The one I love. "Bloody hell." I bring my hand to my mouth.

"What's wrong?" he asks.

"Nothing." *Everything.*

A shiver runs down my spine. *What have I done? How could I have fallen in love with that...that grumpy ass?* A hollow sensation permeates my legs. I stumble. He grips my shoulder and rights me. "Are you okay?" he asks.

"No, I am not," I whisper.

Weston's voice slices through the air. "Get away from her."

I stiffen. *Don't turn; don't face him, until you have gotten ahold of yourself.*

He sounds so close to me that I draw in a breath.

The hair on the back of my neck rises, and heat invades my back, a sure indication that he's standing not far from me.

I pull away from Liam, who doesn't let go. The hell? I frown up at him, and his gaze widens. His lips quirk. Huh? Is he toying with Weston? I tilt my head; he subtly shakes his. "About time you decided to make an appearance," he drawls.

"Take your hands off of her," Weston snaps. My nerve endings crackle and I shuffle back, but Liam's hold stops me.

"Or what?" He raises his gaze to meet Weston's. "What are you going to do, little brother?"

"I am going to kill you." Weston's voice is even—no emotion, no sentiment. The hard edge to it ripples over my skin. *Shit, he isn't joking.*

"Let me go," I hiss at Liam, who steps back.

He tilts his head, not breaking eye contact with Weston. "What's got your knickers in a twist, huh?"

"Step aside, Amelie," Weston growls. My heart begins to race. I take in his features, the messed-up hair, those grey eyes, almost colorless, a clear indication that he's in the grip of emotions. When he's like this, he tends to lose control. He doesn't care how much his actions could hurt him, or those around him. He's like a wounded animal, ready to hit out at whoever, whatever seems to be a threat.

"Wes," I whisper.

He raises his fist...his left fist... Shit. If he wounds that...it will take him even longer to heal. What if he wrecks any of the fingers of his intact hand? Already, he's going to be laid up longer than anticipated with his unhealed injury.

"Wes," I grip at his sleeve.

His gaze on Liam, he lowers his chin. "I am going to take you down, motherfucker," he growls.

"Not sure I'd use that adjective considering we are brothers," Liam chuckles.

"How dare you put your hand on her."

"What's it to you? Thought you weren't interested in her."

Weston's features harden.

"None of your business," he snarls. A vein throbs at his forehead. "Come within an inch of her and I'll deck you."

"Oh, I'll do better than that." Liam leans in closer, "In fact, I might make a play for her. After all, you've relinquished your claim on—"

Weston swings.

I gasp.

Liam laughs.

I stand on tip-toe, throw my arms around Weston's shoulders... Or as much of him as I can reach, considering how big he is. "Stop it," I snap. "Now."

He blinks, arm raised. Huh? The alphahole stopped in his tracks? Guess Rosie's not the only one who's able to bring them to heel. Maybe I picked up something from her, after all.

"Wes," I lean into him, push my breasts into his chest, dig my fingers into his uninjured shoulder, "look at me, babe."

His big body shudders; his chest planes seem to go rock hard.

"I should fucking thrash him for laying a finger on you."

"But you won't," I declare.

I peer up, to see his throat move as he swallows. The tendons of his beautiful throat flex; the pulse beats at the base of his neck. I reach up and kiss him there, suck on that space where his scent is most profound. Dark edginess, cool pine, warm cloves... My senses cloud with Weston.

"Wes," I tip my chin up, "kiss me."

He glances down, those colorless eyes filled with an emotion... A hint of something that is so very close to... No, not that. He doesn't feel that for me. Oh, he wants me all right, he lusts for me, needs to possess me and claim me, so no one else can, but love... Ha! The alphahole only loves himself. "Kiss me," I insist. "Do it."

He drops his head, closes his mouth over mine. He swipes his tongue in between my lips and drinks from me. He curves his arm around my shoulders, yanks me to him, crushes me to that beautiful, broad, gorgeous chest of his, and kisses me, and kisses me. My head spins; I swear I see stars. He kisses me until my knees tremble, and I hold onto his sleeves, and then I am kissing him back. I open my mouth wider, grind my pelvis into the hard column that tents his pants and I pour myself into that connection between us, where his mouth takes from me and I offer myself up... Completely, wholly, absolutely. His hand comes up to cup my neck, he tilts his head, softens the kiss, until it's his lips on mine, nibbling on my mouth, brushing over mine, tasting of me, inviting me, enticing me, to slide my tongue inside his mouth, to partake of him, to drink from him, to open myself to accept what he is offering—his past, my life, our future together, what I am, what he is, a shared path, for he is mine. And I am his. His, and only his. I tear my mouth from his, so fast that my teeth catch on his lip.

He winces.

I stare at the drop of blood that blooms on his lower lip.

"I'm sorry," I whisper.

"I'm not." His lips curl.

"I am leaving you." I peer into his eyes.

"No." He frowns.

"Yes," I reply, "let go of me."

"What?" He shakes his head. "I can't."

"You can," I thrust out my chin, " and you will."

"No fucking way," he growls.

"Yes, way." My lips tremble and my voice cracks, "Goodbye, Wes."

He looks into my eyes, really looks, and the color fades from his cheeks. "Princess," he whispers. His fingers curve around the nape of my neck. A shiver runs down my back and my sex clenches. Hell, when he does that... Holds me like I am his, promises with his gaze to fuck me like I am his... When he stares at me like I am the only thing in the world that matters... Then I know...

It's time I get away from him. I hadn't meant to fall in love with him... How could I allow myself to feel so much when I was still the woman he'd paid to bring home to meet his family? I don't mean anything to him. I'd been a challenge... Someone to seduce, to buy with his wealth and use as a fuck-toy to pass the time. Hell. The pressure builds at my temples. I am only making this worse on myself. I need time away, time to process everything that has happened. I needed to get away from here.

"Please," I mumble, "let me have this."

His throat bobs and the skin around his eyes creases. Then he lowers his hand.

I step back, walk around him.

"Princess."

I pause.

"This isn't over."

I turn to him, "Yes, it is. You know it is."

His features twist.

I turn, head for the exit.

40

____

Christmas Day

Weston

I stare into the amber liquid at the bottom of my glass. *Fuck, fucking fuck.* I'd stood back and let her walk away. I hadn't gone after her. I'd held my balls in my hand and allowed her to leave. Am I a man? Can I call myself a male worth his manhood? I hadn't stopped her; I hadn't. *Bloody fuck. Why hadn't I?* For once in my life, I had faltered. I had stood by, and for the second time, let her walk out, and this time, there is no going back. I'd had my chance and I had blown it. I had allowed my emotions to get the better of me.

When she'd stared into my eyes and pleaded with me to allow her to win... I had wanted her to. Not that this is a game, or a war. Okay, so maybe it is a fight between us—this push and pull. This constant thrum of arousal that laces the air, that connects us and makes us want to go head-to-head... Even as I want to yank her to me and kiss her, and suck on those sweet-sugary tits of hers, bury my fingers in her moist pussy, dip my tongue in the crevasse of her belly button, sink to my knees in front of her, thrust my head between her legs and ravish her, please her, make her come.

Hell… Her happiness and her needs, they come first. Her confidence? I never want to shake that. Her sass and fire, her independence? They are a fucking turn on. It's what had challenged me. It's why I had noticed her in the first place. In a world filled with compliance, she had stood out. She had baited me, hated me, pushed me away, and that had only aroused me further.

I'd wanted to...what? Curb her? Tie her to me? I should have known better. A free spirit like Amelie needs to be nurtured, to be allowed to soar as she wants… And I'd be in the background watching, applauding, encouraging, paving her way… Fuck. I shake my head. What am I thinking? What happened to the dominant surgeon who didn't give a fuck about anyone else…except his patients? To be fair, I'd cared for them, but they had been a way to nourish my ego. Fuck. Everything in my life so far has been one long trip to soothe that scared boy inside of me. The one who had never recovered from the incident.

So, I was kidnapped.

I was hurt.

I was…abused. Mentally and emotionally.

Fuck, fuck, fuck. So what? Shit happens; deal with it. How could I have allowed those few days to color my life so completely? Enough to not recognize the only good thing that had come my way. Her.

"Bloody fuck." I drain my glass then hurl it against the wall of the living room. The glass bounces off of the hard surface, hits the floor, bounces again, comes to a rest at my feet. Go figure. *Can't do even one thing properly, can you?* I kick the offending object and it rolls toward the door. A booted foot stops it.

I groan. "Fuck off," I grunt.

"Merry Christmas to you too," Damian's chirpy voice echoes through the drumming in my head.

Fuck.

I turn away, head toward the bar in the corner of the living room. I grab a glass, reach for the bottle, miss it, swoop down on it. *Finally!* I pour myself a healthy measure of Macallan's. *Fuck that.* I fill the snifter to the top. Set the bottle down on the bar counter with a thwack.

"Careful, ol' chap. That whiskey's older than you."

"So's your nagging," I growl.

"Seen yourself in the mirror lately?" Damian continues.

I frown, "Heard yourself lately?"

"No need to, ol' chap." He smirks. "I rest confident in the power of my good looks."

"Jesus," I swear, "Can you hear yourself?" I wince.

"No sweeter sound in the world, right?" He grins.

I stare up at him. "Did you just say that?"

"What?" He frowns.

"Have you any idea how pompous you sound, you prat?"

"So?" He straightens his arm, tugs on the sleeve of the white button-down that shows below his jacket.

"So?" I raise the shoulders, "So it's bloody off-putting."

Damian frowns. "Who are you, and what have you done to my douchebag wanker of a friend?" he mutters.

"I'll let you know when I find the fuck out." I bring the glass to my lips, take a sip, then grimace. Maybe it wasn't a good idea to substitute alcohol for coffee. I hadn't stopped drinking since I'd dragged my sorry ass home, after seeing my mother in the hospital yesterday.

They'd discharged her this morning, thank fuck. The poison, what-ever it was, had vanished from her system. It had left her weak, but she was stable. Thank the bloody gods. I'd lost one parent already; I'm not ready to lose another. I don't want to lose her. "Fuck." I raise the glass, down half of it. Sweat breaks on my brow. My left hand—so far unhurt. Maybe I need to remedy that? Sure, go for it, wipe out the career you've worked so hard to build, huh? Why not, while you're at it, light a flame to everything you've achieved thus far... All of it is nothing, meaningless without her. I slap the glass onto the bar potty it cracks. Huh? The amber liquid bleeds out onto the mahogany counter top.

"You all right?" Damian's voice is concerned.

"Yes. No." I plant my elbows on the bar, in the whiskey which seeps into my sleeves, but whatever. Why the fuck should I care that I smell like a distillery? It's not like she's there to bury her nose in my chest, to rub her cheek into my shoulder, turn her face into my arm pit and coil into me like the feline, sensuous woman she is. "Go away," I moan, then bury my head between my palms. *If I press my hands tightly against my ears, would it block out the sound of her laughter?* I snicker. *Getting delusional now, huh? You've gone mental; admit it.*

"Wes," Damian grips my shoulder, "you've gotta get yourself in hand."

"For what?" I mutter, "I let her leave. Didn't have the balls to go after her either."

"Maybe you aren't ready yet for this relationship."

I stiffen. "The fuck do you mean?"

"She was too good for you, ol' chap."

That she was.

"She's someone who deserves better."

"She deserves the best," I agree.

"And you're all wrong for her."

"Clearly."

"You did the right thing."

Huh? I scowl.

"If you can't make her happy, you should let her go. If she comes back to you—"

"—She won't," I mumble. "She bloody hates me."

"*I* hate you. The world doesn't like you, man, it's normal."

"Thanks," I grumble. "Nice to know I can trust you to have my back."

"Always," I hear the laughter in his voice, turn and shoot him a glance.

His features are schooled into a serious expression, which is seriously weird. Which also means he's trying to rile me.

"The fuck's on your mind?" I growl.

"Me?" He points to himself, "Nothing, man. I'm not the one with a broken heart—"

"I break hearts. I don't get mine broken..." my voice trails off.

He nods. "Sadly, I believe you've crossed over to the dark side."

"What?"

"You remember the thing that had its claws into first Jace, then Sinner, and then Saint?"

"No, I don't." I scowl, and I thought I was delusional?

"I'm afraid you've fallen prey to it as well."

I straighten, lower my chin to my chest, "I have no idea what you're talking about. And it's not because I'm a bit hungover—"

"A bit?" He snorts, "Don't you have to stop drinking before you can be hungover?

I glare at him. "Okay, my head is pounding, and clearly, I've poisoned myself with enough alcohol that I may spontaneously combust at any time—"

"Attaboy." He pats my shoulder, "Tell it like it is. I knew you'd come through."

I shake off his hand, "You're bloody creepy when you go all paternal."

"Me, paternal?" he laughs.

"Stranger things have happened." I roll my shoulders. My stomach copies the motion. "Shit." I wipe the sweat from my upper lip, "I don't think I'm feeling that well."

"Wonder why that is, huh?" Liam stalks in.

"Oh, bloody fuck," I groan. "Thought you'd crawled away under whatever rock you'd been found under."

He shakes his head, "Man, you've gone and done it now."

"What?"

Damian chuckles.

"What?" I ask again.

Liam folds his arms over his chest, "Shit or get off the pot."

"Eloquent, as always." I grimace.

His dark gaze takes in my features, "You look like hell."

"Still better-looking than you."

His forehead crinkles, "Why do I even bother with you, huh?"

"Because you know, at heart, I am the one destined for greatness."

"You've proved that already," he mutters. "You got your way in the end—became a surgeon, saved lives. You make the difference between life and death. You saved mother's life."

He comes forward, grips my shoulder, "Thank you."

Is he for real? "Did you just go all polite as fuck on me?" I scowl.

Liam's features twist, "Guess not even soulless bastards can resist the spirit of Christmas, huh?"

"You mean it, don't you?" I shake my head in disbelief. "You're actually thanking me for the first time ever, that I can remember."

"It is the first time," he confirms. "You can thank your woman for that."

"My woman?"

He nods. "Seeing you fall apart—"

"I didn't fall apart—" I snarl.

"—then give in, for the first time in my living memory, showed me, you have a human side. You're not as obnoxious as you come across."

The headache between my temples intensifies. Should I even bother to make sense of what is happening around here?

Arpad saunters in. "What are you still doing here?" He asks.

"That was my next question," Damian chuckles.

"I don't care either way, by the way," Liam drawls.

I glower. He steps back, then brushes his sleeve, as if to rid himself of all trace of contact. Wanker. Hold on… That's what I was…or had been… Then she'd swept in, and damn, if all those carefully built walls hadn't come collapsing around me like confetti. Did I just think confetti? Does that word even exist in my vocabulary?

Liam turns to leave, then shoots me a look over his shoulder.

"Oh, and Mother said to invite her over when you see her." He stalks off.

"When am I going to see who?" I glower.

"You gonna enlighten him?" Damian smirks.

"Nah, it's inevitable. It's more fun to watch him fight it." Arpad leans his hip against the bar.

Damian glances at me, "Tick-tock, ol' chap."

The blood drains from my face. I stumble, then right myself.

"Fuck." Damian leans forward to grab my shoulder, "I'm sorry, I didn't mean to say it like that. Of all people, I should have remembered about your triggers."

"Fuck that," I growl. "The Mafia; they broke into her bakery."

"When?" Damian straightens.

"She mentioned it to me, when we first met."

"But you weren't connected with her—"

"They'd have seen her at Sinclair's, then at Saint's wedding." I squeeze the bridge of my nose. "If they have been watching us—"

"They may have followed her to the cabin—" Arpad mutters.

"Which was broken into." My heart begins to race. "Fuck. And I let her leave. She's home, alone. If something happens to her…"

"It won't."

"By now, they must realize she means something to me. I brought her to meet my family, after all." Fuck. I'd put her in the path of danger.

"The cops—" Arpad ventures.

"We can't trust them," I growl. "We know they are connected with the Mafia. One leak and—" I don't voice my fears. "Besides, no way am I waiting around here. I need to make sure she is safe."

I stalk past them, toward the door.

"I have to go to her."

"Hold on," Damian calls after me, "You're not planning on driving, are you?"

41

"Yesterday I wanted cookies. Today I am eating cookies. Yay! Follow your dreams."
-From Amelie's diary

Amelie

"I am such a loser," I cry into the phone as I pace my apartment.

"Wait, hold on, back up," Isla calms me. "Start from the beginning."

I balance the phone, with Isla peering out at me from the screen, on the kitchen table, "Kirsten called me a car—okay a limo. It was a freakin' limo service that she ordered to get me from Durham to London. Can you believe it? That's how these rich folks live, and clearly, I am not one of them."

"Who's Kirsten?" Isla asks.

"The alphahole's sister."

"So, we are back to calling him alphahole, huh?"

"Weston fucking a-hole Kincaid," I growl into the phone. "I never want to hear his name again.

"Urm," Isla clears her throat.

"Don't say it—" I warn her.

"I was only going to say that you just mentioned this name."

"That's what I was afraid of." I wrap the strands of my hair around my palm, "I mean, not that I am complaining about the limo, or anything."

"Of course, not."

"Not after I found the liquor bar in the back of the car."

"I assume you did it justice?" she snickers,

"Yeah," I hiccough. "Oops, sorry." I walk to the kitchen, fill a mug with water—because hell, I always drink water from coffee mugs. That's my little rebellious streak, right there. I sip from the mug, and walk over to the window of my studio apartment. The view is nothing like that from the cabin, or from Weston's mother's home. How funny I'd never been to his place. Where does he even live in London? It's official, I am in love with a man whose neuroses I know better than the basic stuff, you know, like his address, his favorite color. That's me, I do everything upside down, like my life. Fuck me now. I hiccough again. "Sorry again," I mumble.

"The bar in the limo?" Isla reminds me. "I assume you drank of all the whiskey?"

"Nope," I say, all smug. "No whiskey for me. Never touching that stuff, from now on."

"O-k-a-y."

"I sucked down all the champagne because I am celebrating."

"You are?"

"Yeap." I walk back to the shelves in the corner of what passes for my kitchen space, and open the door. Scrounge around. There. I retrieve the boxed wine I'd been gifted with, God knows when. Now is the time to open it. I unscrew it, peel back the plastic seal thingy, then look around for a glass, and fuck it! I tilt it to my mouth, draw from it. The cold liquid hits my gullet and I almost gag. Ugh! Is that vinegar or what? "Argh," I gasp.

"What's wrong?"

"Nothing." I place the boxed vinegar-that-had-once-been-wine back on the shelf and eye it. Do I dare drink more of it, or not? Shit, I can't even decide on the small things in life anymore. My mind is well and truly broken, thanks to that, that... "Idiot." I swear down the phone.

"Fucking wanker that he is. A tool. A reprobate. A prick of the first order."

"That, he is," Isla agrees. "So what are you doing back in your apartment?"

"Haven't you heard anything I just told you?" I cry.

"I have, doll, and I think you love that about him."

"Oh." I pull out a chair and sit down with a thump. "That's true, right?"

"So, what made you walk out on him?"

"He was…just insufferable," I snap.

"And?"

"And cock-headed."

"Which is an asset, I assume?"

I hear the smirk in her voice, "Isla, honestly…"

"Admit it, the sex was great."

"Off-the-walls hot," I admit.

"And despite his money, he decided to focus on becoming a doctor."

"True," I admit, reluctantly.

"And he's good with dogs."

"And kids."

"And kids," she agrees. "So?"

"So?"

"What didn't you like about him?"

"Well, I fell in love with him, for one."

"Hmm."

"What?"

"I mean, that was bound to happen. You set yourself up for that, girl-friend, when you agreed to go along with his fake relationship thingy."

"Hello, it was supposed to only be for a few days, and it was contingent on my never sleeping with him."

"That was clever of him, huh?"

"Was it?" I scrunch up my forehead. "You think so?"

"Of course, babe. He used reverse psychology on you. I mean, tell you not to sleep with him and—"

"—and of course, I'd only want to sleep with him." I reach for the wine, swig from it. Grimace. Argh! It's worse than I thought. I set it back with a thump, then jump up and begin to pace.

"And then, he took me home to see his family."

"At Christmas."

"At Christmas." I rake my fingers through my hair. "And he was really cute with his nieces. Hell, the man reads Harry Potter."

She shrieks, "Whaat?"

I wince. "Pipe down," I plead. "You almost burst my eardrum there."

"He reads Harry Potter? How many men do you know who read Harry Potter?"

"He was reading it because he wanted to be able to discuss it with his niece."

"No," she breathes.

"Yes." I hang my head.

"So, he fucks like a god, saves lives like he is God, and reads the kind of books that—"

"—make me want to worship his brain. Yeah," I scowl. When she puts it like that… "I mean, he's not perfect, you know."

"No?"

"He has a beard. I mean, it's unkempt, which is fine if you go in for that sexy just-rolled-out-bed-on-Christmas-morning look."

"Sexy Santa," she snickers.

What I wouldn't give to see him in nothing but a Santa hat.

"Don't call him sexy," I pout.

"But he is," she protests.

"I mean, I can call him sexy, but not you."

She stares at me.

"What?" I frown.

"Nothing." She clears her throat, "What else do you not like about him?"

"He's overbearing, dominant, uh, commands me do stuff, overrides me a lot, hates chocolate—"

"Are you sure?"

"Well, he did eat the chocolate banana muffin batter I made," I offer.

She gives me a perplexed look. "Muffin batter?"

"It's a long story…"

"Okaaay… So, he hates chocolate, but he ate what you made anyway."

"Hmm." And he did say that he was coming around to its taste especially when he licked it off my lips. My cheeks heat. Then he wouldn't let me out of his sight because he wanted to keep me safe. Okay, so I won't tell her that. I bite the inside of my cheek. What else? What else?

"He made his brother apologize to me for being rude."

"Now that's not very gentlemanly is it?" she chuckles.

"Shut up." I wipe my hand across my face. What else? "He did tell me that he wants a future, but not with me."

"You sure? Maybe he was angry or something."

"He was." I hunch my shoulders, "But I can't let that pass, can I? I mean, people speak the truth in the heat of the moment."

"Maybe he wanted to hurt you?"

"And I emptied my box of cookies on his head."

"You did?" She giggles.

"And told him to fuck off."

"Good."

"I should have told him to fuck off more."

"You still can."

"And he doesn't love me."

Isla stares at me, "Did you tell him that you love him?"

"No, of course not."

"Then how can you expect him to reciprocate?"

"Whose side are you on?" I scowl.

"Sweetie, you know I'll always back you up. And I am not saying there is no fault on his side, or that it wasn't wrong of him to have turned your relationship into a barter game of sorts…but—"

"But?"

"It seems there's something between the two of you that's powerful, and if I were in your shoes…"

I tilt my head, "You would…?"

She draws in a breath, "I wouldn't let go of a chance at true happiness that easily. I mean, I'd pursue that guy and sit on him, until he confessed his feelings."

"You would too," I giggle.

"Not that I've been in your shoes."

"Not yet," I smirk.

"Not that I don't want a man or anything…but…"

"But?"

"I'm not in a hurry. The single life's pretty fun too, you know? And as long as I have my book boyfriends…"

"That's what I used to think." I purse my lips, "Then that real life a-hole comes along, and damn, if he doesn't spoil all the book Romeos for me."

"Aww sweetie," she murmurs, "what are you doing there all alone? Why don't you come over to my place?"

I pause.

"I mean, I am only an hour away, if you drive."

"I left my car back at the cabin." Hell, I knew I should have asked the driver to drop me off at the cabin and driven myself here… But yeah, the stupid champagne had gone to my head by then, and I had alternated between giggling and crying. *Why do I always make the wrong decisions, huh?*

"You could call for a taxi?"

The thought of dragging myself out of here and getting dressed and facing her family— Not that I don't like Isla's parents. They're awesome, actually. But to have to put on a face to the world, right now? Nah, no way. I'd rather spend the time baking, and if I happen to eat a lot of what I make? Well, too bad. Life is short, after all. And stressed spelled backwards is desserts, and Mary had a little lamb and the mouse ran up the clock. *Shit, time out. Stop with the nursery rhymes. Stop thinking about anything to do with that asshole, okay?*

"It's fine." I swallow, "I think I'm better off on my own."

"You sure?" She frowns.

"Yeah," I nod. "I'll have a bath and then bake, and I'll feel better then, for sure."

"I don't think you should be on your own now."

"I'll be good." I shake my hair back from my face. "Once I start the baking, I'll lose track of everything."

"But—"

"I'll be fine." I reach for the phone, "I promise."

"You sure?"

I hunch my shoulders, pull my lips up in a smile. "See?" I point at my face, "I'm good."

"Hmm." Isla peers up at me. Someone calls her name and she looks off camera, "I'm coming Mom." She turns back to me, "Gotta go, doll."

"Right."

"Bye."

I blow her a kiss.

She cuts the call. I place the phone down, then glance around the place. Only one way to deal with this. *Fuck the a-hole. Fuck the a-hole. I did fuck him, remember? No, like really fuck him. Gah.* I spring up so fast my chair screeches back on its legs. Oopsie. I bring up my play list on the phone, put it on speaker. Then turn on the oven. What should I bake, huh?

Two hours later, I've pulled the pies out of the oven, left them to cool on the wire mesh. Also, I've chugged down the horrible, almost-vinegary boxed wine, and another bottle of wine. *Gah.* So not a good idea. My stomach rolls and I grab my middle. Argh, maybe a hot bath will help, huh? I march into the bathroom, run the water, toss in a few bath bombs—chocolate, of course. I light the candles, then head back to the kitchen for the wine… Of course, I'm out. Gah! The corner shop should be open and have wine, huh? Should I? Shouldn't I? Fuck that. It's Christmas, after all. I run back to the bathroom, turn off the water, then head over to the shop across the street, pick up one…okay, three bottles of wine, pay the man behind the counter.

"Merry Christmas," he choruses, eyes twinkling.

"And to you." I smile at him, then head back. When I reach home, the door to my apartment is ajar. WTF? My heart begins to race. Is it the same thief who broke into the bakery? Is he back? Gah. I turn to leave. A noise reaches me from the direction of the kitchen. He's in the kitchen. In the kitchen? My pies? No frigging way am I letting him eat them. I made them for myself.

For me. Moi. I deserve that bloody treat after the last few days I've had. I glance around for a weapon. What can I use? I curl my fingers around the bottle of wine, push open the door to my apartment, then creep past the living room. I reach the doorway to the kitchen, pause. His back is to me. His broad shoulders are clad in a black, long-sleeved Henley that clings to the planes of his back which flex, move, ripple with each of his movements. His narrow waist, that tight butt, those powerful thighs outlined in his jeans. He blocks out the sight of the dining table... Where I'd left the pies to cool. His legs are spread apart and the muscles of his triceps flex as he jerks his arm back-forth-back... What the hell? He can't be doing what I think he is. Is he? I take a step forward. He freezes. Shoots me a glance over his shoulder.

"You?" I swallow, "What are you doing?"

42

Weston

"What the hell do you think?" I growl at her, hold her gaze. *Don't let her look down; don't allow her to see what the hell you've gotten into here.* Caught with your dick in a pie...and by the woman you're in love with...? Hold the fuck on there. Firstly, that isn't a metaphor—being caught with my dick in a pie, I mean. And I know what you're thinking, and fuck, but I can promise it wasn't inspired by a certain, uh, notorious movie. I mean, I am past the stage of being pimply-faced and ready to shag everything that moves...because I only want to be inside one woman, her... Or, uh! A pie baked by her. Bloody fuck, this is a shit show.

"I... I am not sure what you're doing here?" She takes a step forward, and every muscle in my body solidifies... Except uh, a particular part of me that's throbbing inside the sweet, moist, center of a certain dessert that was baked by her. I mean, can you blame me? Peter had driven me here, and I'd told him to leave, confident that I was spending the night here. Hey a man can hope, right? It is Christmas, after all. I'd walked in here, and the entire place had smelled festive... and of her—that sweet sugary scent of hers mixed with the scent of apple pie, which happens to be my favorite, and all of it had gone to my head... Or rather, to my groin, and she hadn't been around, so I'd done the next logical thing. I'd reached for the pie she'd baked, buried myself in its center. Not that it's a replacement... Far from it, but needs must and all that. It's what she's reduced me to, a man...standing in front of a woman he loves — *no, no, no, not love, never love, in lust* — *yeah, that's better;* a man in lust, standing in front of his woman with his dick caught in a pie, that she'd baked.

Fuck.

This is all her fucking fault.

I glare at her.

She pales. Her chin wobbles and she bites down on her lower lip, and fuck, if my dick doesn't jump again; inside the goddamn pie I hold with my left hand, in a position that if she came around and saw, it would be very clear what I am up to.

"Don't come closer," I snap. Bloody hell, that's a first — me asking a woman to stay away from me. Not that it matters, of course, because she sidles closer. Bloody woman, can never do what she's told.

"Stop," I growl. "Stay where you are."

She frowns. "My apartment." She huffs, "I can do what I want."

"Wrong."

She blinks. "I rent this flat, you ass."

"Guess who owns the apartment block?"

Her forehead crinkles, then she opens her mouth and shuts it again.

"Well," I smirk, "made the connection yet?"

"You," she swallows, "you own it?"

"Finally." I raise my gaze skywards, "Took you long enough to get that, huh? What's wrong, you eat too much dessert? All that cream gone to your head?" *The fuck?* The connection between my mouth and my brain has well and truly snapped, that I am hurling insults at her... *Shut the fuck up, you wanker.* But fuck, I have to distract her, and what else is a man supposed to do when he's caught with his cock in his hand... Technically, in a warm, soft, juicy, moist confectionary, but you get the picture, huh?

Color sears her cheeks.

"Is that how you got in?"

"I got in because you left the door open." I growl, and my chest tightens, "Do you know how dangerous that is?"

"Did you...did you find out I live here and decide to buy the place?" She frowns.

"Don't flatter yourself," I reply. "It's merely a coincidence, I assure you."

She flattens her lips, "Is it also a coincidence that you're standing like that?" She takes a sideways step; I mirror her movements, in the opposite direction.

"Like what?" I twist my body. Thank fuck for all those gym sessions, not to mention working out with Saint at his horse ranch. My shoulders are wide enough to cover what the rest of my body is up to—I hope?

"Like," she chews the inside of her lip, "like you're holding your...uh.. your..."

"Dick?" I supply. Fuck, yeah. Clearly, she's not going to let go of it, and damned if I am going to be apologetic about being found out. I turn around, allow her to have the full-frontal view. She lowers her gaze to where I hold the plate with the pie in front of my groin...with my dick stuck inside.

She gulps, the sound audible in the silence. Awesome. This is when she tells me to fuck off... Or better still, turns and runs screaming, huh? Instead, she licks her lips. "Why did you stop?" she asks.

"Huh?" I blink, "Excuse me?"

"You heard me." She squeezes her fingers around the bottle of wine, "Why don't you finish what you started?"

"I will, on one condition."

She tilts her head, her gaze locked onto where my dick is sunken into the pie.

"Amelie," I snap.

"What?" She raises her gaze to mine, her pupils blown, her lips parted.

Jesus, I may have just met my match in food kink. Well, figures. She's a baker. I couldn't have picked better.

"Join me," I growl.

"How?" Her forehead crinkles, "How do you mean?"

I glance at the bottle of wine, then back at her.

"No." Her gaze widens.

"Yes."

"No way," she mutters. "I'm not putting that...inside...."

I thrust my hips forward and my cock sinks into the warm, moist, stickiness of the pie. A groan rumbles up my throat.

A whine bleeds from her.

I scowl at her, then at the bottle, "Do it."

"But."

"Now," I snap.

She gulps, pulls the bottle of wine from the brown paper bag. She unscrews it, drops the cap on the floor, then takes a gulp.

"Good girl," I growl.

She draws in a breath, then walks to the table, on the opposite side from me, and places the bottle on it, then hesitates again.

This woman, is she hell bent on killing me? "What is it?" I huff.

She glances toward the doorway, "Uh, I left the door to the apartment ajar when I came in... shouldn't I shut it?"

"Leave it," I order her.

"But—"

My balls ache, my groin hardens, and a snarl rips from me, "I swear, if you don't take off your clothes right now, I'll—"

She unbuttons her coat, tosses it on the chair, then reaches behind to unzip her dress. The material slithers down around her ankles; she steps out of it.

She straightens and the sight of the triangle of pink fabric between her creamy thighs—" Jesus, fuck." The blood drains to my cock, I pull the pie close, and my shaft sinks into the moist center. I stare at the shadow of her flesh outlined against the crotch of her panties, "Take it off," I command. "Don't stop, Amelie."

"Or what?"

I jerk my chin up to her face. Her lips twitch.

"You don't want to tease me."

"Oh?"

I nod, "You have two choices here."

"Do I?"

I allow my mouth to curl, "Either you fuck the bottle and get fucked in the arse by me, or—"

Her chest heaves.

"Or, you fuck the bottle and I fuck you in the cunt, then in the arse."

"Choices, choices," her voice wobbles.

"Take that bloody wine bottle and ride it, Amelie, or I swear, I'll spank you so much you won't be able to sit down for months."

She scoffs, "You exaggerate."

"Do I?" I lower my eyebrows, "Give me a chance to demonstrate just how much I enjoy delivering on my threats." I peel back my lips, "Do it, Amelie. One chance to get my hand on that beautiful curved behind, Princess."

"Jeez," she swipes her hair over her shoulder, "some people have no sense of humor."

"Humor, huh?" I pump my hips forward, impale the bloody apple pie —the hell am I doing? Fucking an inanimate object, when the focus of my obsession is right in front of my eyes.

She shivers, my thigh muscles spasm, and this entire scene is bloody wrong... and so fucking right. "Don't keep me waiting," I grind out.

She swoops down, grabs the wine bottle, brings it to her mouth, then proceeds to close her lips around it, taking it in—as she had my cock, previously. Holy mother of all that's dear to me... That has to be the hottest thing I have ever seen— No, Amelie pulling the bottle out of her mouth, only to lower it between her thighs? That... I swallow. That is bloody erotic. And it shouldn't be. I mean, it is a woman—my woman, turning me on, by easing herself down onto the neck of the bottle. It is not what I expected from her. It's everything I wanted her to do.

My cock lengthens. I grip my fingers around the damned plate of apple pie and follow her movements. In-out-in... She parts her legs, sinks down onto the bottle, the length of which disappears inside her pussy.

My shaft jerks; a pressure coils in my balls.

"Jesus, Princess," I snarl, "you're fucking turning me on."

Her breasts rise and fall, she straightens, lifts her gaze to mine, holds the connection, then impales herself again. She groans and the blue of her irises fades, leaving behind large pupils so black, they seem to take up most of her irises. My throat closes and my heart begins to race. I stare into her eyes, kick my hips forward again. Her movements intensify; so do mine. A bead of sweat trickles down her throat, trails down the shadow between her breasts. My pulse thrums; the blood pumps in my veins. I grip the plate of pie, push into the melting core, again and again. My balls draw up, the pressure in my groin tightens, harder, further, my senses pop, my vision narrows. "Come," I growl.

And she throws her head back, arches her spine, and reveals the slim column of her throat; a shudder grips her body, her thighs clench, a low keening moan spills from her lips, and I can't stop myself. My balls draw up and I come, shooting my load inside the fucking pie. I straighten, slap the plate with the dessert onto the table.

Her legs seem to weaken. She sways, then raises the bottle of wine from between her legs. Her knuckles are white and her hand trembles.

She blinks, then licks her lips. She tips up her chin; I crook my finger at her.

She hesitates.

I jerk my chin. She takes a step forward, and another. She closes the distance, pauses in front of me. Tips the bottle of wine to her lips and drinks from it. Her throat moves as she swallows; a drop of red trickles down her chin. I scoop it up, bring it to my mouth and suck on it.

Her gaze follows my actions; her lips part. She holds out the bottle of wine to me. Is she daring me? Does she think she can match me step for step? Does she? I snatch the bottle from her, raise it to my mouth and chug down a mouthful. The complex notes of wood and cherries, chocolate and honey.

I lower the bottle. "Perfect with pie," I declare.

"Isn't it?" Her lips quirk.

She reaches for the serving spade on the table.

"What are you doing?" I growl.

"What do you think?" She cuts off a slice, brings it to her mouth, "Should I eat it?"

The fuck? I glare at the piece of pie, then at her face.

"You wouldn't."

"Wouldn't I?" She tilts her head.

Woman's enjoying it. The thought of her eating the evidence of my arousal? It's a fucking turn on... Hotter than anything I have experienced before.

"Will you?" I lower my chin.

"You daring me?" She raises the slice, "What would you do if I ate this?"

"What do you want me to do?" I counter.

"I want you to—" She glances at the pie, then at my face, "I want you to let me take the lead in bed."

43

Amelie

His forehead crinkles. He glares at my face, and the skin around his eyes tightens. He's considering it. He's actually thinking about it? A dominant man like him... Would he give in to this? Does he want me to eat this...proof of his desire? Does he think I won't? Am I going to do this? I hold his stare. *Say the word; do it.* A bead of sweat slides down my temple. His gaze darts to it, then back to my eyes.

"Do it," his voice is casual, his stance relaxed. *Huh? Does he think I won't? Is he the only one who can get away with playing games?* He's so sure that I won't surprise him, he raises the bottle of wine, swigs from it, then licks his mouth. "Mmm," he smacks his lips together. "Wine and the honey of your cum," he says. "This has to be my favorite drink ever.

I raise the pie to my mouth.

His gaze intensifies.

Bite off a piece.

He freezes.

I chew on it, swallow, his chest rises and falls.

I bite off another piece, chew on it.

His shoulders bunch. His chest planes seem to harden, and he draws himself up to his full height. "Eat it all," he commands.

His rough voice chafes across my nerve endings. My sex clenches. I squeeze my thighs together, stuff the rest of the piece into my mouth.

He curls his lips. "Swallow," he growls, and moisture pools between my legs. Hell, only Weston fucking Kincaid could make that order sound so filthy, so bloody naughty. I gulp down the food in my mouth.

"Open," his voice is rough, his breathing uneven. I part my lips; he raises the bottle of wine to my mouth. "Drink," his voice lowers to a hush. Hell, why do I get the feeling that he's planning something...a scene that's out of my dirtiest fantasies?

Rolling around in the aftermath of my dessert? Check.

Slurping down wine that tastes of my arousal and his mouth? Double check.

Pulling back with suddenness so the wine spills across my chest? You bet.

"Oops," I murmur, glance down at where the wine blots the cloth of my bra. "I think I am going to have to take it off."

"Hmm." He raises the bottle to his lips, drinks from it. "I have a better idea, Princess."

"You do?" I peer up at him from under my eyelashes.

"I do." He nods. He holds up the bottle; my gaze widens. He tilts it, I open my mouth to protest, but already he's poured the wine on my hair.

"What the—" I splutter, "What are you doing?"

"Worshipping you, of course," his voice is sincere, his tone husky.

I take in his features as the liquid drips down my cheeks, my chin, splashes onto my breasts, clings to the cloth that covers my crotch.

"Weston," his name emerges, breathy from my throat. Damn, if I don't sound aroused and turned on—I glance down to where his erect dick—make that two of us. "Weston?" I swallow. What am I asking of him? What do I want from him? "You...you going to deliver on your promise?"

He smirks, "What do you think?"

"I think," I raise a finger to his cheek, drag it down the luxuriant growth of beard on his chin, "you look like Santa Claus."

He stares, then chuckles, "Have you been a naughty girl, Princess?"

"Oh," I shift my weight from foot to foot, "I tried, Santa. I promise, I wanted to be good...but then...I met this man."

"A man, huh?" He leans forward until his chest grazes my breasts, nipples hard, and surely, outlined by the sodden bra, which, if he'd look down, he'd see. But he isn't, because he's staring into my eyes.

He lowers the now empty bottle to the table with a soft thump. "Pray, tell me more about this...encounter of yours," he breathes. The warmth from his body surrounds me; his big, aching, gorgeous shoulders shut out the rest of the world. He bends his knees, thrusts his face into mine, "Don't make me wait." His voice is low, with an edge of that cruelty that is so Weston, which rolls down my spine.

I shiver. "He..." I clear my throat, "He's the most annoying, most obnoxious, most full-of-himself, egoistical—"

His biceps flex; the next instant he grabs my pussy. A whine bleeds from me, "Ah," I stutter, "He's... he's..."

His mouth curls. "He is...?" he prompts me as he begins to massage my core.

"Hard," I mumble. "So hard."

He grinds the heel of his hand against my clit and goosebumps flare on my skin. I shiver, "And sexy, and dominant, and knows just what to do to arouse me to fever pitch, and when he tells me that he'll let me lead in bed, I know that he—"

He digs his finger into my melting channel through the cloth and I groan.

"You were saying—?" he smirks.

"Was I?" I blink.

"Yep." He nods, "Something about wanting to lead in bed?"

"Yeah," I swallow, "this once."

He fixes his left palm around the nape of my neck, then lifts me up by the hold on my pussy, and plants me on the pie. I squeak, wriggle my hips around, trying to evade the moist filling. He tightens his grip on my pussy. He pushes down with his other hand, and I still.

"Look at me," he growls.

I glance up, trace his features with my gaze—that patrician hooked nose, those clear eyes, the lush dark hair that flows about his shoulders, that pouty lower lip that I want to suck on. I lean up, he holds me in place with his hold on the nape of my neck. His strength is awesome, like really awesome. Why didn't I realize how he could overpower me with minimal resistance?

I reach for his cock, but he clicks his tongue, "So impatient." He snickers.

I scowl. "But I want to touch you."

"Not yet."

"You made a promise."

"And you know what kills me?" He shakes his head, "You actually expect me to keep it too."

"Won't you?" I peer up at him, "Won't you let me take the lead?"

"Nope." He shakes his head.

"But you said—"

"I lied."

Of course, he did. I mean, if he'd allowed me to actually set the pace, I'd have... Thrown myself at him, climbed him, impaled myself on his dick like he'd fucked that pie. The pie... Hell. I wriggle around, and the filling sticks to my behind. "Weston, uh, the filling is getting into all the places it shouldn't," I mumble.

"On the contrary." He grins, "It's filling up exactly the right areas, which I am going to enjoy licking."

"Oh," I gulp; my core clenches. Jesus, is he going to enact the picture he painted right now in my mind?

"Oh, yes." He mocks my strangled exclamation. "And that's only the beginning... Once you are clean, I plan to fill you up with my dick in your pussy, my fingers in your arsehole, and my tongue in your mouth. I am going to make sure every hole in your body bears my imprint. Then I am going to fuck you so hard, you won't know where you begin and where I end, you'll lose sight of what day it is, what time—" he swallows, "what time—" His voice roughens, "What time—"

"What time of day it is," I supply, "whether I am indoors or not, what the weather is like outside, what—"

He releases my pussy, only to plant his big body between my legs, forcing my thighs to widen.

"What ingredients I use in an apple pie—" What the hell am I warbling on about?

He thrusts his dick inside of me, filling me, stretching me, packing me to the brim, with such confidence that I gasp.

"Wes, I... I..."

"Complete the sentence." He glares at my features, "Do it."

"I..." I swallow, "I...want..."

"What?" He brings his free hand to my breast, squeezes it. Sensations radiate outward from the contact. My pussy clenches around his dick and his grin widens. "You were saying?" he prompts, "Something about the apple pie—"

"Fuck the apple pie," I mutter.

"Did that already." He chuckles.

"Sheesh," I grumble, "are you for real?"

"Does this feel real?" He pinches my nipple and I yelp. He bends his head, sucks on it, and I feel the pull deep down in my womb. Everything he does seems to awaken parts of me that had hitherto been happy to exist without communicating with me.

"Weston," I gasp, "you're forgetting something."

He releases my breast, glares up at me, "I am?" He blinks, then his forehead smooths, "I am."

He turns his head, fastens his mouth around my other breast. He sucks on my nipple, curls his tongue around the pebbled bud, bites down with his sharp teeth, and I yell, dig my fingers in his hair and tug.

He grunts and his dick lengthens further inside of me—is that even possible? He continues to lave my nipple, sucking on it, dragging his teeth around the tender flesh, then opens his mouth wider, taking in as much of my breast as he can fit. Heat, lust, pleasure, pain... All of it... None of it... A confluence of emotions whirls inside, tugging at my lower belly, arrowing to my cunt, which clamps tighter around his engorged flesh. Of course, he is pleasuring me, but ultimately, he is the beneficiary. How could someone be so...on target all the time in how he plays my body?

"Weston," I pant, "Please, please, please, please—"

He pulls out of me, raises his head, steps away.

"What the hell?" I blink, "You come back here and fuck me, you hear me?"

"Are you telling me what to do?" His lips quirk.

"You bet I am, you pussy tease, you—" I squeak, for he's grabbed my hips and flipped me over. I am on my arms and knees, butt pushed out in his face. The hell? Then a wetness sinks into my pussy, up my slit, across the valley between my arsecheeks.

"No," I shudder, "Weston, no."

He stops, "No?"

"No," I huff. "I mean, yes. Don't stop, whatever it is that you're doing, don't, oh!" He licks my puckered hole and my entire body trembles. It's filthy, and dirty and it's hot. So bloody hot. "Oh, my God," I breathe. "Oh, my, G-o-d." I yelp, for he swipes his tongue down to my cunt, then licks his way back up to my forbidden hole and back, again and again. My knees tremble and my elbows wobble. I sink down to support my face on my arms. "Wes," I gasp, "oh, you're, I'm—" My entire body seems to shudder. "I'm—"

"Don't you dare come," he growls against my sensitive clit, right before he bites on it. I howl, the sound muffled against my arms. My shoulder shudder, I slide my knees apart, thrust out my arse, giving him more access. He can eat me out like the sweetest of desserts, lick me, suck on me, insert his tongue into my pussy and drink of me. A trembling grips my legs, my back. He begins to fuck my backhole in earnest, shoving his tongue inside, curling it in, before he pulls out and bites on my butt. I huff.

"You taste fucking amazing," he mutters, "like apple pie and my cum."

I chuckle. Now that, would be one hell of a dish to put on the menu of my next pop-up delivery special. He grips my thighs, pushes them further apart. I crack open my eyes, stare down from across the length of my body, to between my legs, to where he swirls his tongue up my inner thigh, licking off the crumbs, then the other side. He meets my gaze, licks his lips, then declares, "I am going in for seconds."

44

Weston

"I am going to fuck you with my tongue." I take in her flushed face, her parted lips, her heaving breasts, "You ready, Princess?"

She blinks. "Do I have a choice?" she moans.

"Nope." I smile in anticipation, smack my lips together. Her breathing grows shallow, she licks her lower lip mirroring my desire, and my cock throbs, reminding me I needed to get on with the program. I'd promised to clean her up, before filling her up again, and I'm a man of my word—when it suits me, of course. I smirk, thrust my face into her pussy and close my mouth around her cunt. She moans, her thighs tremble, and liquid heat streams from her wet channel. I slurp it up, shove my tongue inside her cunt, mirror how I want to fuck her with my shaft—in-out-in— until her entire body shudders, and again.

She groans. "Weston, please..." she whines.

Yeah, I know the feeling. I reach down to grab my cock, pump it once, scoop up some of the pre-cum from the weeping head, then slide my fingers inside her backhole.

"Oh," she wheezes, then pounds her tiny fist into the table, "I'm coming, I'm—"

I tear my mouth from her pussy, grasp her waist and haul her off of the table and onto her feet in front of me. Her legs seem to give way. I hold her up, kick her legs apart, then scoop up her cum and ease it into her backhole.

"Wes..." she moans, "I haven't... I mean... I can't..."

"You can," I growl.

I add a second finger inside of her, and she groans, "It's too much...It's —"

"Not enough." I pull out my fingers, scoop up some of the mushed-up apple and smear it into her puckered hole.

"Oh." She grips the edge of the table, lowers her chin to her chest.

"Relax," I command, then press my palm into the center of her spine. I apply pressure and she bends over, placing her cheek on the table.

"Beautiful." I praise her.

She pushes her hair behind her ear. "Be gentle," she whispers.

"Is that what you want?" I stare at her, "Is that what you truly want, Princess?"

She swallows, then squeezes her eyes shut.

"Tell me," I repeat. "You wanted to take the lead. This is me giving you the choice to direct the proceedings. Do you want it tender or do you want me to take you like you are mine?"

She nods.

"Which one?" I ask.

"Both," she replies. "I want you to take me like I am yours, and I want to take it like you are mine." She cracks her eyelids open. "Please," she whispers.

My heart begins to race, my chest tightens, and something hot twists my heart. *Fuck.* Emotions, feelings, a strange melting sensation that steals up my spine, encircles my ribcage, bears down on my shoulders. I bend over her, until my chest is flush with her back, "You fucking destroy me, you know that?" I press my lips to hers and kiss her. I wrap my fingers around the nape of her neck, tilt my head, ease my tongue inside her mouth, and open myself up to her.

She draws in a breath — my breath, then parts her lips, sucks on my tongue and kisses me back. That melting sensation? It extends to my stomach, my belly, my extremities.

I ease my dick inside her puckered hole.

She groans. I swallow the small sound, bring my hand around to strum her cunt. Good thing it's only my middle finger which is broken. Leaves me plenty of others to play with her clit, slide my forefinger into her pussy, and begin to finger fuck her. She parts her legs, opens her mouth wider. I kiss her in earnest, dance my tongue over hers, allow her to drink from me as I thrust my hips and notch my dick further inside of her. A whine wells up her throat. I drink of it, wind my fingers about her neck, and apply pressure.

Her pulse races at the base of her throat and her chest rises and falls. I slide my thumb inside her pussy, scissor my fingers in her channel. She groans, clenches around my dick, and I fucking see stars. Sweat beads my upper lip, slides down my temple. I dig my heels into the floor, flex my thighs, wait...wait for her to adjust to my size, tear my mouth from hers and kiss her nose, her cheek, her eyelashes, which flutter. "You're perfect, Princess," I whisper, "gorgeous, beautiful, inside and out."

She shudders, opens her mouth, then closes it again. I kiss her on her lips, on her chin, nibble my way up to her earlobe and suck on it.

A moan wheezes from her.

I ease my tongue inside her ear and she trembles. Drag my tongue about the shell of her ear and her entire body bucks. I bite down on her earlobe and she cries out. Her inner muscles give and I slip inside, filling her to the hilt.

A groan erupts from me... Or maybe that was her.

"Jesus." I press my cheek to hers, "You're so tight, so hot...so much everything." My pulse begin to race. "I want you." I mumble half to myself, "I've never needed anything as much as I need you. I have to fuck you, make you mine as completely as I am yours."

She draws in a breath. "Why," she asks, "why do you want me?"

"Because I love you." I snap my eyes open, "Of course, whatever is said in coitus...stays in coitus." I mutter, "I mean, anything said in the heat of passion is —"

"The naked truth?" She stares at me from under hooded eyes. "Will you get out of your own way for bloody once and accept what it is you feel for me?" she snaps.

I glare back at her, but she doesn't back down, "Admit it, alphahole, you fucking love me."

"Love to fuck you," I agree.

"You ache for me." Her lips quirk.

"For the rapier-sharp edge of your mind that I love to challenge."

"You can't live without me," her voice is smug.

I scowl. "Adore your pussy." I rotate my fingers inside of her, and color smears her cheeks. "And your arse, which belongs to me, by the way," I inform her, even as I pull out, then thrust inside her with enough impact that her entire body jolts up the table.

"Stop deflecting," she pants.

"Stop talking," I retort.

"Thought you loved my sassy comebacks," she mutters.

"Love your sassy arse." I propel my hips forward, begin to fuck her in earnest.

Her eyes roll back in her head. "Fuck," she groans, "it hurts."

I frown, begin to pull out, "Maybe I should have waited... Should have prepared you better. I could—"

She lowers her chin, trains those blue eyes on me. "Don't you dare," she growls. "You bloody well finish what you fucking started."

Thank fuck. My dick lengthens. I grit my teeth, stay poised at her entrance.

"Another thing I crush on..." I force the words out through gritted teeth, "Who'd have thought your potty mouth would turn me so on?"

"Thought it was all of me? The entire package?" She flutters her eyelashes at me. "Come on, give credit where it's due, Doc. Give me the satisfaction of hearing it from the horse's mouth."

"You calling me a horse?" I arch an eyebrow, then thrust forward and inside of her.

"Oh." She squeezes her eyes shut. "That..." she gulps, "that feels so fucking good."

She bites down on her lower lip, and fuck her, but I can't resist her when she does that. I lower my head, lick her mouth. "Look at me," I order.

She cracks open her eyelids, and those shining baby blues of her stare into my soul.

"Stay with me," I whisper, then propel my hips forward. My balls slap against the underside of her butt, and I sink into her. Her spine arches and her gaze grows frantic. A ripple speeds up her body. Oh, she's close, so close. I tear my mouth from hers. "Come," I growl, and her pussy clenches around my fingers.

Moisture slides out from between her thighs as she shudders. Her eyelids flutter and I click my tongue, "Open your eyes, darlin.'"

She tips her chin up, and I hold her gaze, as I thrust forward. My balls draw up, my cock lengthens, the tension in my groin explodes out, and I come inside of her.

I slump forward, hold my weight up on my elbows, then lower my lips to hers.

"Wow," she whispers against my mouth. "That was something."

"Yeah," I kiss her, "it was."

I pull out of her and she winces. I pull her up, then scoop her into my arms.

"You okay?"

She gazes up at me, her cheeks flushed, her hair stuck to her forehead, her eyes glazed.

"Princess?" I ask again. "Talk to me."

"Hmm." She snuggles into my chest. "Do I have to?" she mumbles, then yawns so loudly her jaws crack.

"I wore you out, huh?" I stalk out of the kitchen.

"Where are you...going?" She yawns again.

"Where's the shower?" I ask.

"Mmmm... That way." She jerks her chin to the side.

I walk down the hallway, reach the bathroom door and shoulder it open.

"I don't think I can stay awake." Her eyelids flutter.

"Just as long as you're awake when I fuck you again."

Okay, maybe not. I prop her up in the shower, turn on the water, soap her up, and wash every inch of her delectable body. She falls asleep in my arms halfway through. That doesn't stop me from slipping my throbbing dick inside of her and taking her. Or again later... When I've dried her and myself off and pulled the covers over her naked body—after I've made sure to close and lock the door to her apartment and ensured all of the windows are safely shut—I slip in beside her, curl my body around hers and try to fall asleep.

Only I can't, because I have a raging hard-on. Her proximity does that to me—turns me on, twists me inside out until I am sure I am one big, seething mass of need. I pull her leg up and over my hip, then guide myself inside of her soft pussy. A sense of peace, of rightness, steals over me. Fuck, this is what I've been missing all along—this melding sensation as I sink into her melting channel, and finish myself off in a few strokes, as I orgasm inside of her and she stirs. I curve my arm around her waist, pull her close and fall asleep with my dick nestled within her warmth.

Twelve o'clock.

Eleven o'clock.

Ten o'clock.

The goddam timer—an old fashioned clock fitted to run backwards—as my kidnapper had informed me, never stops counting down.

Every hour it helpfully rings out the time, so even though I am blindfolded, I have no choice but to follow along in my head.

Nine o'clock

Eight o'clock

Seven o'clock

Every hour brings me closer to the time when my kidnapper is going to come through the door.

Six o'clock

Five o'clock

Four o'clock

Twelve hours, that's how long he'd said he'd be away.

Three o' clock

Two o'clock

One o'clock

The timer passes the twelve-hour mark, and stops. The silence stretches. A beat, another.

My heart begins to race and sweat pools in my armpits. I tug my wrists against my bindings, and pain shoots up my arms. I draw in a breath and the acrid taste of fear fills my mouth. Something is wrong.

Why hasn't the bomb gone off as he'd said it would? Why hasn't my kidnapper returned for that matter? My throat closes, my hands and feet grow cold.

Today, I won't survive the beating. Today, something is different. Today is the day when he finishes it. When he doesn't stop electrocuting me until...my heart gives out.

My heart pounds in my chest, my pulse races, and my stomach coils in knots. The pressure builds at my temples. What's he going to do to me when he gets here?

My head spins and coldness grips my arms and legs... I won't last the day. I have to get through today. Need to focus, focus. Stay still; count down again.

Twelve o'clock.

Eleven o'clock.

Ten o'clock.

My heart beat slows and my pulse steadies. How strange. My biggest nemesis is also the only way I can calm my mind. Stay still, in the moment. You can't give up. Not yet. The door creaks open. I jolt upright. The change in the air indicates he's in the room. Footsteps approach as the door snicks shut. The hair at the back of my neck rises. Fuck. He's here, he's going to hit me...any moment.

The floorboard creaks to my right, to the left, behind me. He circles me, comes closer.

"What should I do with you?" he mutters. "Leave you in your filth or put you out of your misery?"

Let me go, I try to say, the words muffled by my gag. Let me the fuck go, you asshole.

"Weston. Weston," he says. "When will you realize that resistance is futile?"

I yank my wrists against my bindings, strain the muscles of my legs. The ropes around my ankles dig into my skin. The ticking of the clock around my chest fills my ears...my mind. It grows louder, ricocheting inside of my head. The fuck is he up to? Why the hell is he not untying me?

He pats my head; I jerk away. The time-bomb around my chest beeps.

"Oops," he laughs, "sorry." He chuckles, "Forgot for a second there that you had to be absolutely still." He shuffles his feet, "Remember what I said about your being let go in twelve hours?"

I nod.

"Guess what? Today is your lucky day."

I stiffen.

"Today is the day I leave you here, with an hour to countdown. When it hits one o'clock... Boom!" He claps his hands together.

My shoulders bunch and the blood pumps in my ears. My heart hammers so loud, I am sure I am going to be sick. Let me out of here. Let me out.

"Sorry, my boy. Some things are best left up to fate, you understand?"

No. What the fuck is he talking about? I lean forward, shake my head. No, don't leave me here, don't.

His footsteps recede.

Stop. Don't go.

"Oh, I forgot to tell you." His voice reaches me from the direction of the doorway.

"If you're lucky, the bomb may not go off."

Bloody piece of shit, he's fucking toying with me. It won't go off. It won't. The door shuts behind him, leaving me with the ticking of the bloody clock. Tick-tock. Tick-tock.

Three o'clock.

Two 'o clock.

So close. An hour to countdown. An hour to my death. Or not? Any moment now. Any moment.

"Weston?" A man's voice calls out, "Weston, you in there?"

The door slams open and I jerk up.

"What the fuck?"

Stay back, don't come close. The bomb—it's going to detonate, it's going to—

"Weston?"

I tug on my bindings, but they don't give. Fuck this, if I'm going to die, I'm not taking another innocent life down with me. The ticking of the bomb seems to get louder... Or is that hammering in my chest? Sweat slithers down my spine. I tug my feet, strain at my restraints. The chair lurches forward. Tick-tock-tick-tock. The timebomb stops. Then—

"Weston?"

I snap my eyes open.

"Wes?" Her worried gaze holds mine. Her blonde hair is tangled about her shoulders. I rake my gaze down to her bare breasts, to her belly, to where her thighs grip my waist.

"Wes?" She reaches down to touch my face.

I pull away. "Don't," I clear my throat.

"You going to tell me about what happened when you were kidnapped?" she prods. "Is that what your nightmare was about?"

"What's it to you?" I grind my teeth together so hard that pain shoots up my jaw.

"You have to ask me that, after everything we've been through? After you told me that you love me?"

"About that..." I frown, "I didn't—"

"Shut up," she snaps.

"The fuck?" I growl, "You dare tell me to shut up?"

"Oh, I dare more." She smirks. "I dare to fuck you while you are tied up."

"Tied up?" I frown, then pull at my arms, which are bound above me. I glance up, tug at one leg, then the other. "You bound me to the bed?"

"Close." She smiles, "I bound you to the bed spread-eagled."

45

Amelie

What the hell am I doing? I reach down between us, massage his erect shaft. His chest planes lock and his shoulder muscles ripple. "You think you're going to get away with this?" he growls.

My heart begins to race. My throat closes. The taste of fear coats my tongue and I swallow it down.

"Correction." I allow my lips to curl, "I know I am going to get away with this." I swipe my fingers up his dick to where the swollen head throbs. I squeeze and his hips buck. I drag my thumb across the slit and his body jolts.

"Amelie," he warns.

"Weston," I echo his tone.

I slide my other hand down to cup his balls.

His throat moves as he swallows. "You really, really don't want to do this." His voice lowers to that hush as he speaks, to that edge of meanness which chafes at my nerve endings, that ripples down my belly, then coils in between my legs. Moisture laces my core. His gaze intensifies and his nostrils flare. Hell, as usual, he's so tuned into me, he can sense my arousal.

I squeeze his balls; he grunts. I slide back, lower my head, close my mouth around his shaft. His thigh muscles spasm and his entire body seems to go still. I hold his gaze, bob my head, take him in until his length bumps the back of my throat.

"Fuck." His jaw tics; his shoulder muscles bunch. "You don't know what you are doing," he snarls.

I rise up, so his dick plops out with a wet sound, "On the contrary." I lick the angry head of his cock, "I have a very good idea what I am doing to you."

I swirl my tongue around the rim of the angry throbbing head; he growls.

I drag my teeth across the sensitive skin; his body bucks.

"Oh." I blink. This is fun. It seems I can elicit a response with the smallest action.

I slide my tongue down the length of his shaft; sweat beads his forehead.

"Are you hot?" I ask.

"The fuck do you think?" he snarls.

I giggle. I can't help it, honestly. To see this virile, dominant alpha-hole laid low by a touch... Mmm. It's sweet revenge. I weigh his balls in my hand, then drag my finger down between his butt-cheeks to tease his backhole.

He grunts, "Fucking fuck." A vein throbs at his temple, his biceps bulge and the veins of his forearms ripple.

Holy shit, he's not going to break free, is he?

He yanks at his bindings which tighten, but hold—Whoa, guess the knock-off Ferragamo scarves are of good quality, after all.

His thigh muscles tense as he pulls on the bindings that circle his ankles. The bed frame creaks, but he stays tied.

The breath rushes out of me. *Gah, that was close.* I lower my face to his groin, begin to give him head. I take him down my throat—gag—*breathe through your nose, breathe through your nose*—I pull back, glance up to find his gaze fixed on me. A vein throbs at his temple; color highlights his cheeks. Wow. He seems aroused and angry—but definitely turned on.

"That all you got, babe?" His lips twist, "Giving up so easily, hmm?"

I frown. Typical of him to turn this into a competition, huh?

I prop my elbows on his hips, swirl my tongue around his cock. "You taste," I frown, "you taste like dark chocolate with a dash of sea salt."

He groans, "Jesus, woman, only you could compare my dick to a dessert."

"It's good," I offer, "I mean, you could do with a trim — "

"The fuck are you talking about?" he scowls.

"I mean the hair on your chin, you dummy." I chuckle, "What did you think?"

"I think when I get loose, I am going to turn you over my knee and spank you."

"Hmm." I dip my head, take him in, swipe my tongue up his cock, then pull back. His balls harden and his shaft lengthens, "Oh," I blink, "that's interesting." I massage that engorged part of him.

"The fuck?" he snarls. "What the hell do you think you're doing?"

"Having my cake and eating it too." I chuckle. My, but I am full of terrible sayings, but hey, if the shoe fits. I raise my shoulders, open my mouth, and take him down my throat again.

"Fuck." His swearing fills the air above me. His cock jumps. Heat seems to leap off of his chest and slam into my shoulders, pinning me in place. I gasp, rise up and position myself above his erect shaft.

He growls low in his throat, the sound a rumble that hints at an inner conflict. He peels back his lips and his teeth glint against his skin. His shoulder muscles seem to broaden, his big body tenses, waiting, waiting...for me to make my move. *Holy shit... This is true power.* Holding the most responsive part of him in my hand...before I sink down and impale myself on his very erect, very hard cock.

"Ah." I throw my head back, breathe in as I adjust to his size. He'd fucked me earlier, but damn, if his every penetration doesn't feel like the first time.

"Ride me," he growls. "Fuck my dick and make yourself come."

His words sink into my blood. I rise up, slam myself down onto his dick. The entire bed creaks. I clench my insides around his shaft, and he groans.

"Amelie," his voice is strained.

I lower my gaze to his face, hold onto his hips for leverage, then I begin to ride him. I raise and lower myself again and again. I don't break the connection between our eyes. His grey eyes reflect back the heat, the tension, the absolute and complete need to own him that grips me. His heart, his soul, his every emotion. I clench my pussy, squeeze my thighs together. "Weston." Only when I hear my voice do I realize I've breathed his name aloud.

"Don't stop," he replies. "Don't you dare stop, until you come."

I swallow, brace myself, then lift up and sink back down at the same moment that he thrusts upward and into me. His cock fills me, stretches me. His gaze burns into me, and I can all but taste his intensity as his big body stiffens, as his shaft jerks inside of me. He pistons his hips upward—fucking me, cramming into me, setting off pin pricks of heat that radiate out from my core, up my spine. The trembling crashes over me, and I gasp, and strain for release. Close, so close.

"Come," he growls, and I shatter. My climax smashes into me. White noise fills my ears, my mind. When I come to, I'm on my back and he's braced over me.

"How?" I frown, "You got free."

"You didn't think your scarves were strong enough to hold me, did you?"

"So, all this time—?"

He nods, "I pretended to be tied down."

I scowl, "You allowed me to take the lead?"

"This once." He dips his head, kisses me. "Don't expect it to happen again."

"Yeah, yeah," I mutter, "Of course, the Big Bad Alpha Claus isn't going to allow this helpless woman to get away with anything."

"Helpless, my ass!" he scoffs. "You're dangerous, is what you are."

"Why, you flatter me." I flutter my eyelashes.

"And you..." He peers into my face, his features intense, "You..." He swallows, "I love you."

"Oh." A fierce something flares in my chest. Heat sears my cheeks. *Holy shit, am I blushing? No, I am not. Of course, not.*

"Aren't you forgetting something?" he growls.

"Am I?" I tilt my head, "Max is not here, so we don't have to take him for a walk. I showered last night, so I guess I can skip today, and it's Christmas today. Of course, Merry Christmas, Mr. Alpha Claus."

"Merry-fucking-Christmas," he rumbles, "but that's not what I mean."

"No?" I chew the inside of my cheek; my heart flutters in my chest like I'm just about to eat a freshly-baked chocolate croissant. Yum. Only one thing gives me more pleasure. "Umm." I screw up my face, "Let me think... Let me think... Am I forgetting something?" I raise my shoulders, "Nope."

He runs his fingers up my side, "Is that right?"

I giggle. "That's right."

He digs his fingers into my ribcage, and I snort. "Please... Don't—" I gasp.

"My, my, how ticklish you are, little Red."

"All the better to laugh with you, Mr. Claus." I chuckle, then scream, as he tickles my armpits. The laugher wells up my throat. I wriggle around, try to avoid him, but he leans his weight on me.

I howl.

He laughs louder. He holds me captive under him, proceeds to tickle me until I lose my breath. "Stop... No more..." I pant, "Please."

He pauses and his chest heaves. He glares at me, takes in my features. "You're the most beautiful present I have ever received for Christmas," he whispers.

My heart literally melts in my chest. Okay, not literally, but I mean, come on... That was bloody unexpected. I cup his cheek, urge his face closer, "I am still waiting for my gift."

"Oh?"

I nod, "Tell me what happened when you were kidnapped."

He blinks, then his features shutter.

Hell, me and my big mouth. Why did I have to go spoil that perfect moment? He pulls back, shoves off the bed and glances around the room.

I sit up, "Weston, I'm sorry."

He spots his pants and steps into them. Shit, he's leaving... After all that? He loves me. He'd made love to me. Hell, he'd taken my ass... And damn him... It had taken courage to allow him to do that... I'd enjoyed it...but honestly, it had been a leap of faith to trust him with that... And now...what? He decides to up and leave? And why the hell am I apologizing?

He heads for the door. I jump up on my knees; the bloody sheet is wound around me... How the hell did that happen? "Weston stop right there."

He reaches the exit.

"Stop," I yell. "You can't just leave."

He pauses, then turns to glare at me with that look of superior disdain that I hate.

"Don't tell me what to do," he growls.

Argh! I throw up my hands, "You and your stupid dick-headed ideas."

"Didn't see you complaining earlier when I had you pinned on said dickhead," he snaps back.

"Don't change the topic."

He opens his mouth to speak.

I hold up my hand, "What did I say, to get you all hot under the collar, huh?" I scowl. "What's wrong with my asking you about the incident that clearly impacted you so much you're having nightmares to this day?"

He draws himself up to his full height, which only draws my attention to the width of those beautiful shoulders, those eight—no ten-pack abs—ten pack? I mean, who has a ten pack? Is that even a thing? Apparently, yes, I have the evidence right here in front of me.

He widens his stance, "You can't see it, can you?"

"What?"

"You're so involved in your emotions, your need to find out all my secrets. You have no idea how much it hurts to bring it up, do you?"

"If we are..." I pause. *Say it. Should I say it? Whatever.* I have nothing to lose, except my future... Yeah, fine, if I can't say what's on my mind with him, then this, whatever is between us, is worth nothing. I draw in a breath, "If we are going to have a future, then I need to know about this."

"That's where you are wrong."

My heart begins to race.

Don't say it. Don't say it.

"I said I loved you," he rolls his shoulders, "doesn't mean we have anything keeping us together."

Turning, he leaves.

46

Weston

Nice one. Get right to the heart of it, twist her guts and deliver her a sucker punch. *You're a piece of work, you know that?* Fuck! I stalk out of the apartment block. My bare feet hit the sidewalk. Huh? I'd forgotten to put on my shoes, apparently. I drop my shoes on the concrete, reach for the socks. And, of course, I've forgotten them. I shove my feet into my shoes—take a step forward, the backs of the shoes bite into my heels. Great, I'm sure to get blisters. Good. I deserve that...and more, much more for what I just did. What the fuck happened there? She asked me a simple question and I freaked. Not that I hadn't discussed the goddamn incident with the Seven in the years since—and with the shrink my mother had insisted I see. I'd hated it then...but they'd taken no shit from me. Good for them. I thought I'd dealt with the aftermath of what had happened...but apparently, not.

First, I'd frozen when my mother had collapsed...

Then the realization that I love her—fuck! I stumble, then right myself. I love her.

I've fallen for her.

When had she snuck up under my skin, coiled her scent around my heart, wormed her way into my every waking thought? Somewhere between her walking in on me naked at the cabin and apple-pie gate, I'd opened myself up to her in a way I had never done before. Her sass, her ability to hold her own against me, the way she fights to hold onto every inch of her dignity, that need inside of her to be dominated in bed, even as she blazes forward, trying to build her business.

She is a smart cookie, my woman. Takes no shit from anyone, and that includes me. It's one of the things I love—the fact that I can be myself with her, secure in the knowledge that she'll give back as good as she gets. Fuck. I drag my fingers through my hair... I left her and haven't stopped thinking about her. How can I already miss her? Her laughter, the way she wrinkles up her nose when she's thinking, how she talks in her sleep... How her features scrunch up before she climaxes, how she draws herself up to her full height, tips up her chin and assumes that haughty ice-princess persona when she is pissed off with me.

How her features had crumpled when I'd told there was nothing keeping us together. I squeeze the bridge of my nose. Why the hell had I said that? Bloody ego of mine. No way, could I stand to share my weakness with her, huh? Would it have been so fucking terrible to tell her what had happened during the time I had been held hostage as a boy? Why the fuck is it so difficult to talk about it still, huh? All the bloody therapy in the world had clearly not helped. Maybe there is a part inside of me that's broken and nothing can fix it—except her. She could have, had I given her a chance. But I'd opted to lash out at her—at the one person who is more important to me than life itself. Fuck. I rake my fingers through my hair, move forward. My foot connects with something on the ground. There's a dull thud. I look down to find coins spilled on the ground, and next to it a steel can is overturned.

"Sorry." I bend, scoop up the money and drop it back into the container.

"Got a cigarette?" a voice asks.

I glance up at the homeless man seated behind the receptacle. He has a Santa hat perched on his head. Had she actually nicknamed me Alpha Claus? I smirk. Talk about being kinky. But hell, if my North Pole hadn't been a snug fit in her stocking. I shake my head. The hell am I thinking?

"Oy," he waves his hand in front of my face, "got a smoke?"

I blink, shake my head, "Huh? Nope, sorry."

"Spare some change instead?" He peruses my features, "You okay there, man?"

"Sure," I mutter, shove my fingers in my pants pocket, come up empty. Search the other pocket and pull out my phone. Huh. "Guess I forgot my wallet." I glance back at her apartment block—okay, technically my block. But fuck, if I am going back there, not after that scene. Best to give her time to cool off, and then what? Beg her forgiveness? Fuck that. If she can't accept me the way I am...then too fucking bad. Her loss. *And yours.* A fine curvy, gorgeous, love-of-my-life-sized loss. "Fuck," I swear aloud.

"You need a drink," Homeless man drawls.

'Yeah."

"Or maybe two," he offers.

I roll my shoulders, "Sounds about right." *Why not?* Liquor seems to be the way forward. Days and weeks and months of pouring myself into liquid amnesia. At least, I am old enough to cope that way... Hadn't had that luxury in my teenage years when my brain had turned to mush after the incident. It wasn't until I had found my calling as a surgeon, that I'd found a goal in life, a way to ground myself and keep moving forward. Until her—she is what makes it all worthwhile. Someone I can take care of, protect, share my fears, my deepest desires... Someone with whom I can build a future. "Bloody fuck," I growl. *Why the hell can't I stop thinking about her?* This is not good at all. "Not good."

"Women, huh?" Homeless man folds his legs under himself to sit cross-legged. I stare at his bare feet. There's something wrong with this picture. I frown. "Your shoes," I say, "what happened to them?"

"Got stolen." He raises his shoulders, "Shit happens." He scratches his jaw—which is cleanshaven? That's what it is. I glance down at his feet again. His toenails are clean and cut short, so I hadn't been mistaken. This guy is finicky about his grooming.

"Take mine." I reach for my shoe, tug it off and offer it to him.

He eyes it warily, then takes it from me and slips it on. "Imagine that; it fits." He chuckles.

I slip off the other one; he shoves his other foot into it.

The shoes do look good on him, actually. I tilt my head, stare up into his features. His eyes are clear...a glitter of intelligence in their depths.

"What happened to you?" he asks.

I frown, "What do you mean?"

He points at my middle finger in its splint.

"That?" I crack my neck, "Someone ran me off the road."

"The world's a dangerous place." He nods. "Gotta take care of what's yours."

I nod. "You're onto something there."

"Thanks for the shoes." He shakes his head and the bells at the end of his Santa hat jingle. "Merry Christmas."

"Sure. Whatfuckingever, man."

I rise to my feet. A man jostles my shoulder as he passes.

"The fuck?" I turn to watch him hurry into her apartment block. I frown. Clearly, this isn't my day. I turn to leave.

"You've got to see what's in front of your eyes," Homeless Guy calls after me.

I pause.

"When we two parted
In silence and tears,
Half broken-hearted
To sever for years, " his voice fills the space.

I turn on him.

He holds my gaze.

"Pale grew thy cheek and cold,
Colder thy kiss;
Truly that hour foretold
Sorrow to this, " he recites.

"What the fuck was that about?" I growl.

"Byron." He blinks.

My heartbeat ratchets up, "Who the fuck are you talking about?"

"Lord Byron, the poet," he replies. "Who did you think it was?"

I shake my head. Of course, it was the poet. This fucker has no connection to the Byron that the Seven had identified as the head of the Mafia... The ones responsible for kidnapping us and changing our fucking lives. Does he?

"Don't delay." He turns to stare up at the apartment block.

I follow his gaze to the window on the first floor, her apartment. A man's shoulders fill the space.

"The fuck?" I straighten, stare at the window. *There's no one there.* I didn't imagine that. I didn't.

Had she replaced me that quickly? I'd barely left and she'd found someone else to take my place? Someone else to bring her to orgasm, to hold her when she shatters, someone else to gaze into those baby blues of hers and declare his love for her as he holds her in his arms? "How dare she?" I stalk forward, retrace my steps to the apartment block.

47

Amelie

What the hell had happened? One second, he'd been tickling me and we'd been laughing together. The next, he'd rolled off me, off my bed, headed out of the apartment—and what the hell was that whole thing about not having a future together? Did he mean it? That that... Dumbass fruitcake. That... Mother-trifle... Argh! I can't even get my insults together.

I stand in the middle of the kitchen surveying the remnants of the apple pie—now crumbled all over the dining table. I fold my arms around my waist, over the shirt I'd slipped on, his shirt... Because Mr Alpha dickhead had marched out leaving it behind. I glance out the window. He had to be cold with that bare chest of his exposed to the elements. No doubt, every woman who passed him would ogle him. No doubt, he'd indulge them too and preen.

I curl my fingers into fists and my fingernails dig into my palms. The hell is wrong with me? Why do I already miss him? Do I want to see him again? Why the hell do I want to spend time with a man who is an obnoxious, full-of-himself prat of the highest order. I lean forward, scoop up a crumb of the apple pie. I suck on my finger and the familiar taste of sweet and savory fills my mouth, interspersed with that edgy, darkness that is him. I stare at my wet finger—

That's what it is. He is the contrast to my forced self-confidence. I mean, I can try to pretend to the world that I have it all under control. I can live by the "fake it 'til I make it" motto, which I had embraced as my own so long ago— Except, I could never fool him.

He'd cut through all that sassiness, all that bravado I present to the world, and known me. He'd seen me for what I am. A woman who wants to be taken, to be possessed, to be taken care of. With him... I trust him to take control. Only with him can I find the strength to surrender completely; and he...? He'd known what I needed even before I had. He'd seen me for the eclair I am. All hard on the outside, but drop me in water and I'll dissolve and impart my sweetness to my surroundings—no wait, that metaphor is all wrong—I mean, hard on the outside, soft on the inside... Well, partially... There is more to me than that. I am more like a sticky toffee pudding—mess with me and I'll screw you up bad... Hell, what am I thinking?

Fact is, there's something between us—something hot and vital and real, something that attracts us to each other even as the contrasts highlight how different we are. I hate him. I love him. I can't live without him. I stiffen. Damn, why the hell did I have to go and fall for the wrong man? At least, he'd confessed he loves me—right before he'd walked out on me. Why the hell can't he let me in on his secrets? Can't he see I want to understand him? That I want to spend my life with him? And he wants it too; he does. Only the alphahole has too much of a bloody ego to see it.

I kick the chair in front of me, which topples over. Pain shoots through my foot. "Ow." I hop around on one foot, then fall against the table, which creaks, put out a hand to right myself, and my fingers brush against the spatula I had used earlier. It hits the kitchen timer, which rolls over. Ah, just what I am looking for.

I snatch up the egg-timer, rotate the dial, and the ticking of the countdown fills the room. I turn toward the oven when the thud of a footstep vibrates behind me. My heart slams into my chest. *Is it him? Is he back?* The dense scent of a man's cologne fills my senses.

I've smelled this scent before; it's someone else. Someone who is in my kitchen, with me. My hackles rise. I grab the spatula on the table, turn as a hand closes over my mouth. I scream but the sound emerges muffled. My heart begins to thud. My throat closes. *Let go of me, let go.* I swipe at his arm with my weapon of choice. His grip over my face tightens. I pull my knee up to kick back at him. He grabs me around my waist.

"Stop struggling or I'll hurt you," he snarls in my ear. His voice is sharp, an edge of desperation heightening his tone. Hell, this man is dangerous. He wouldn't hesitate to follow up on his promise.

I slump in his grasp. He begins to drag me across the kitchen when I hear, "Amelie?" Weston's voice calls out from the direction of the living room, "Where the fuck are you? Who the fuck are you with? Couldn't wait to get me out your hair and invite your lover in, huh?"

His footsteps approach. *OMG, it's him.* I need to get his attention. If I can just manage to get this intruder's hand off of my mouth... I begin to struggle in earnest, hit out with my leg, pull back my elbow, and it connects with his stomach.

He grunts, then begins to drag me toward the cupboard in the corner. No way, no way am I letting him get me in there. I bite down on his hand. He swears but doesn't release me. He yanks on my hair so hard that I see stars. Pain ricochets down my spine and tears of frustration fill my eyes. Dammit, I am not giving in like this. I refuse to be a damsel in distress. Fuck this. I double up my knee then kick back. I connect with his shin, and pain thuds up my leg. The bastard huffs out a breath. His grip loosens. Finally! I wrench my face to the side, then scream.

"Amelie." Weston barges into the room.

The intruder swings around, putting me in in front of him. He swings his arm around my neck, yanks me against him. He's tall and broad; the heat of his body curls over me and my skin crawls. "Let me...go." I cough, swipe at his arm with my spatula. He grabs it, wrenches it from my hold, then throws it at Weston, who steps aside in a move so graceful that I blink. The man can move...and not just in bed. If I get out of this alive, I am going to sit on him, in said bed, and ensure that we not leave that space for weeks.

Weston glances at me, "You okay?" His voice is toneless. His features are hard. Gone is the kinky doctor, the demanding lover, the son who cares for his mother... In its place, is a man far more lethal than the intruder who has me in his grasp.

"Amelie?" Weston snaps, "Answer me."

"Yes." I squeak, then clear my throat. "I am fine."

He turns his gaze to the man who holds me captive.

"What do you want?" he asks. "If it's money, let me get to my wallet
—" He takes a step forward.

The man swoops out his hand, grabs a knife from the rack next to
the cooking range. He presses its edge to my neck and the blood drains
from my face. No, no, no, this can't be happening. My pulse rate
ratchets up, my heart hammering so hard in my chest, I am sure it's
going to jump out. My head spins. No, I will not faint, no way. I bite
down on the inside of my cheek, draw in a breath, then another. The
silence stretches. A beat, another.

The ticking of the countdown clock fills the space. Weston's gaze
darts to the egg timer—his face pales. A nerve throbs at his temple,
beating in tandem with the stupid tick-tock of the timer. Ugh, why did I
have to wind it up? Because I could? Because I thought I was alone.
Because I was being spiteful... Gah! Death by kitchen timer... Nooo,
that's like a terrible B-grade screamer movie. I am not going out this
way, not without a fight. I raise my hand and the intruder presses the
knife deeper. Pinpricks of pain spark out from the cut and I feel a drop
of blood trickling down my throat. The ball of emotion in my chest
seems to expand. I try to swallow, but find my mouth is too dry. Hell, do
something, anything.

I stare at Weston, at the sweat that glistens on his forehead. *Look at
me, look at me,* I urge him in my mind. *Please baby, tear your gaze away from
that stupid egg timer—if we get out of this, I promise I'll throw away every single,
stupid timer in the house... I'll switch to those silent ones, the newer digital ones
even*—I cringe. Okay, so they are not my favorite, but no choice. Needs
must, and all that. The intruder grips my arm, urges me to take a step
forward.

Weston doesn't move—the muscles of his massive shoulders lock
and his chest planes could be hewn out of rock. Everything within him
seems riveted by that horrible timer. *OMFG, what the hell am I going to
do now?*

The intruder nudges me and I move forward, closer...closer to where
Weston stands, rooted to the spot. His jaw tics and the tendons of his
throat bulge. His arms are locked into his sides—frozen in the moment
that he'd spotted the timer.

*How long did I set it for? Ten minutes? Five? Oh God, please let it be for five or
less. Why did I have to touch that stupid thing?* Can I rewind back this morning...to the time in bed, when he had reached for me and tickled me until
I couldn't stop laughing? Had it been just this morning? And why

hadn't I thrown my arms and legs around him, clung to him and not let him leave? We could have still been in bed, all toasty and warm, and fucked each other until we'd collapsed again. Yes, that's what I want when this is over—an entire non-stop marathon of make-up sex. *Weston, darling, please hold on, just a few more minutes, just a—* The intruder shoves me forward, I stumble, slip on some of the remnants of the apple pie that are still on the ground. My legs slide out from under me, and I scream.

There's a blur of action. I sense Weston move—he swoops down, grabs the egg-timer, hurls it toward me.

48

Weston

The egg-timer rings as it sails through the air. It grazes the forehead of the intruder—who's wearing a mask. Of course, he is. Motherfucker! And my aim with my left hand sucks! Jesus, and I call myself a surgeon? When I most need precision, I am fucking hampered by the bloody splint. The asshole sways, then the knife slips from his fingers and crashes to the ground.

Amelie lurches forward. She stumbles and my heart slams into my ribcage. I jump forward, reach her as she collapses. I yank her to my side and behind me.

I raise my hand at the bastard, who's still standing. Why the hell is he still standing? I bury my fist in his face. He howls. I swing my fist at him again, he arches back, and I graze his shoulder. He straightens, then swings at me. I raise my left arm, deflect the blow. He comes at me again. I swear, angle my body to protect her. He lands a punch in my shoulder. At least it's the unhurt arm. I grunt, try to weave away. Behind me, Amelie stiffens and wriggles in my grasp. I turn my face— big mistake, asshole lands one in the side of my head. Sparks flare between my eyes. I growl, shake my head.

Amelie snarls, tugs in my grasp. "Let me go," she whispers.

"No," I growl, pull away as the bastard tries to deck me again.

"Unhand me, you macho ass." She pulls away, but I refuse to release her. She buries her teeth in my bicep. *The fuck?*

I grunt, loosen my hold on her, just as the intruder buries his fist in my other shoulder. A growl rips from me; my entire arm throbs...especially the motherfucking middle finger in a splint—"F-u-u-c-k!" I shake my head, focus my attention on the motherfucker. I curl my fist—my bloody left fist—swing at him, land a hit, then again. He grunts, lumbers backward. I head butt him, and he crashes into the counter behind him.

I raise my arm as Amelie yells, "Take that you bastard." She heaves the spatula at the stranger, catches him in the nose. He howls, presses his palm to his face, pushes away, turns and lurches around the dining table. "You bloody prick, you dare break into my apartment?" She grabs the next available weapon—which happens to be the other pie—the one left to cool on the counter behind her. She throws it at the retreating figure, catches him in the shoulder. He grunts, stumbles, steadies himself at the doorframe—asshole's wearing gloves as well.

"You think I am afraid? Huh? You think you can come in here and invade my space... you... you..."

"Dickhead?" I supply.

"No, that's an insult I reserve for you," she cries.

She glances around, reaches for another knife, throws it at him...misses. The blade embeds in the doorframe.

The intruder runs out of the kitchen. The next second, the door to the apartment slams behind him.

"You fucking prick, you horrible, mangy-faced, skiving, conniving, dodgy cocksucker—" She grabs hold of a whisk, hurls it at the door, picks up the pastry brush and throws it, then reaches for a wooden spoon.

I reach for her, "Amelie."

"Randy, ass-whipped... ignominious—" She throws the spoon in the direction of the door, but it only makes it halfway over before hitting the floor. She stumbles forward, reaches for the cookie cutter. I grab her wrist. She swings at me, her gaze wild, hair flowing about her shoulders.

"Princess, stop," I admonish her. She stabs the rolling pin in my chest, "Ouch." I grunt, press down with my fingers, "He's gone, Buttercup."

"What if he comes back?" she pants.

"He won't," I promise.

"What if he does?" she insists.

I lower her hand, slide the rolling pin from her fingers, "Then, uh, I promise to defend us from him, with —" I raise the rolling pin, "This?" I frown.

She glances at it, then at my face. "That's ridiculous." She giggles.

"It is, huh?" I quirk my lips, then hold up the blasted thing in a defensive gesture, "Well then, am I Westley enough for you?"

"No." She shakes her head, "I prefer you as Weston."

"And I fucking love you, any which way." I peruse her flushed features. "Even armed with deadly kitchen utensils —"

"Baking tools," she corrects me.

"What-fucking-ever." I fling the rolling pin aside, hold out my arms.

She jumps up and into my embrace.

"Fucking hell, Buttercup, you fucking bloody scared me," I say as I scoop her up.

She wraps her legs around my waist. "You stupid oaf, you left me, in the bed, on my own." She hiccoughs.

"Yeah, I am that and more," I agree. "You can call me any bloody insult under the sun and I deserve it all."

"He...he..." She buries her face in my chest, "He held a knife to my throat, oh, my God!" Her entire body shakes, her shoulders treble and my heart, my bloody heart stutters.

"Shh." I brush my cheek against her hair, "Shh, babe, I am here."

"You turned your back on...," she mumbles. "You walked out. How could you do that?" She digs her fingers into my shoulders and I wince.

Fuck, that's how much of a weak motherfucker I have become. I can't even hold up to being mauled by my woman. I reach the table, lower her onto it.

She clings to me. "Don't leave me," she mumbles between gusts of sobbing.

"Don't cry, Princess, please." I hold her close, wrap my arms around her. She doesn't let go, just buries her face in my chest and sobs. I try to pull back, and she only sobs louder.

"Babe," I mutter, "I just want to make sure that you're not hurt."

"You hurt me." She hiccups, "You ass, you broke my heart."

"I am so sorry, Cookie, I truly am."

"Huh?" She leans back in the circle of my arms. "Say that again."

"I am sorry?"

"No after that."

"I truly am?" I frown.

"No, you stupid goof, in between those two phrases."

"What did I say?" I blink.

"A word beginning with C?"

"Cunt?" I smirk.

She slaps my shoulder.

I wince. "Ouch, easy there, darling. I'm afraid he managed to get in a few hits as well."

"You'll survive," she grumbles. "Say it, you idiot, the nickname you just used."

"You mean Caramel?"

"No."

"Candy."

"Noooo," she growls.

"Cherry pie?"

"You are such a tease." She digs her fingers in the shoulder of my hurt arm.

"Hey," I wince, "you're hurting me."

"Good," she huffs, "you deserve it."

"I do," I agree.

She blinks, "Wow, you're actually agreeing that you are a jerkface?"

"Yep."

"And a dickhead?"

"But I am your dickhead, darling Cookie."

"I like that name best." She sniffs, "Especially when you kiss me after saying it."

I survey the skin of throat, which seems unbroken, thank fuck.

"How dare that bastard threaten you with a knife." I trace my thumb over the pulse that flutters at the base of her throat. "When I get my hands on him—"

"You will not go after him," she scolds.

"I must," I reply. "He came after what belongs to me."

"Do I belong to you?" she asks.

"Of course, you do." I run my finger down the hollow between her breasts, around her nipples.

"What are you doing?" Her voice is breathless.

"Uh, taking care of you."

"He didn't hurt me there."

My vision tunnels, "Bastard touched you. I am going to kill him, I—"

She grips the 'V' of the shirt—my shirt, and tugs. The buttons pop and the shirt gapes to reveal the creamy curves of her breasts.

"What are you doing?" I stare at the curves, the nipples that she reveals when she shoves the shirt down her arms.

"Cookie," I breathe, take in the spread in front of my eyes. My throat closes. I stare at the blush that colors her gorgeous skin, her pink nipples that harden into plum-colored pebbles. I bend down, close my mouth around one, and tug. She moans. I bite down and she cries out. I suck on her sweet flesh and she sinks her fingers into my hair. I kiss one breast, then the other, straighten and peer into her face. "You're mine, Princess, my woman."

Her pupils dilate and her breathing grows shallow.

I pull away and she frowns, "Where are you going?"

"To lock the door to the apartment."

"No." She scissors her legs around my waist. "Don't go." She grabs my arms. "Please." Her lips tremble, "Stay with me."

"You're safe, Cookie."

"Only as long as I am with you, Wes." She leans in, drags her tongue around my nipple. I groan. She bites down on the nub with her sharp teeth and I feel it all the way to my cock. My dick lengthens in my pants. The tent at my crotch stabs into her core, still covered by my shirt and her panties.

"Fuck," I growl, "I really should secure the place first."

"You really should check out how wet I am for you."

I reach down between her legs, push aside her panties, and my knuckles graze her melting core.

She pants and I groan, "You're mine, Amelie. Only mine."

I lower my zipper, grab my cock and position it at the entrance to her channel.

"Mine to make love to, to bring to climax over and over again, mine to claim." I kick my hips forward, thrust inside her moist channel. My balls slap against her inner thigh, pressure builds in my groin.

Then the doorbell rings.

49

Amelie

"Expecting someone?" He pulls out of me, the head of his fat dick poised at the entrance to my pussy.

I groan, dig my fingers into his tight flank. "Ignore it!" I plead.

His nostrils flare and the skin pulls tightly across his cheeks. "Sure you're not expecting any lovers? Anyone I need to know about?" He massages the curve of my hip.

I shiver. "You're the only one in my life, Doc," I moan.

"Damn fucking right." He pounds into me again, with such force the entire table shakes. The mixing bowl crashes to the ground, rolls, then comes to a stop.

In the silence that follows I can't stop the giggle that bursts from my throat.

"You think it's funny?" He frowns.

"No," I chuckle.

He pulls out, then sinks back into me. "Yes," I gasp, "yes, it is actually."

"Clearly, I am not doing this right, if you are thinking about something else other than how I am going to tear your pussy apart, how I am going to sink inside you so deep you'll feel like you are splitting in half."

He pumps his hips forward, rams into me, and his balls slap against my inner thigh. *Oh, hell!* A moan spills from my lips. I reach up, wind my arms around him... Well, as much as I can reach, that is. This man is so broad, I reach maybe halfway around his back.

"Wes." I pant... "Please."

"You're fucking killing me, Princess." He bends his knees, loops his arms under my knees, and pulls my legs up and over his shoulders.

Instantly, he slips deeper inside, the crown of his cock hitting that secret part of me—one I didn't even know existed until now. "Oh." I open and close my mouth. "Oh, my," I gasp.

"When I saw that motherfucker with his hands on you, my heart stopped." He growls, "I swear, if you do that to me again, I'll—"

"You'll?"

"I'll chain you to my bed and never let you go until I've fucked every hole in your body over and over again, until I've covered you under layers of apple pie and licked them all off of your skin, off every gorgeous curve, from between your legs, from the tops of your breasts, the slope of your butt, the turn of your ankles, the valley between your arse-cheeks. Then I'll fuck you until I take you to the edge, but I won't let you come. I'll start all over again, this time with chocolate, then cream, then work my way through every ingredient of your dessert repertoire."

"Oh." I blink. My pussy clenches around his dick.

"You like that, hmm?"

"I..." I gulp, "I..."

He smirks, "I am going to fuck you now."

I blink, stare up into those hard features—a flush smears his cheeks, those gray eyes are pools of desire, of lust, of everything I've always wanted and hoped for but never thought possible. I see myself reflected in them—him, me, us... Our future. "Wes," I groan, "don't stop, don't—"

He thrusts forward, impaling me. His shaft fills me, stretches me, his girth imprinting every ridge, every hard inch of him against every millimeter of my sensitive channel. Goosebumps flare on my skin, and pinpricks of pleasure and sparks of heat shoot out from the contact. He slams into me again and I cry out, throw my head back, hold onto him and wait, wait— He begins to fuck me with domination, with precision, with that complete self-assurance that is so Weston. "Oh, my God. Oh, my God. Oh, my God," I chant.

"That's me, baby." He pulls out. "Never forget."

He propels his hips forward, sinks into me, hitting that place inside again and I howl, "Wes, please. I'm, I'm going to—"

"Come with me, Princess," he growls, and I shatter. The climax screams over me, and I cry out again. He kisses me, absorbs the noise I make, as he continues to fuck in and out of me, before sinking into me once more. He tears his mouth from mine. "Look at me," he growls.

I force my eyes to open, meet his gaze as he spills himself inside of me with a grunt, his features contorted into an expression of dominance and ecstasy that is so very Wes. He leans his forehead against mine.

My eyelids flutter shut as I float down from the space he always takes me whenever we make love, where everything is golden and happy and peaceful, save for my heart that hammers. The blood pounds at my temples; it mirrors the thump-thump-thump in his chest.

There's more banging, then the sound of the door to the apartment being pulled open.

"You there, Amelie?" A woman's voice calls out.

I snap my eyes open, "Oh, hell—" I gasp, "It's—"

"Amelie!" The voice sounds closer, "Where are you? My flight got in earlier than expected, I'm—Oh... OH!" There's the sound of a startled exclamation, "Oh, I'm sorry."

I turn my head over my shoulder and heat flushes my face. "Julia," I exclaim.

"Ah..." My friend glances from me to Weston, then back at me, "Umm... I'm so sorry..." She averts her eyes, "Ah, my flight just got in... I came in straight from the airport...uh! Why don't I go get coffees for all of us? I'll be right back."

"Wait, Julia..." I shove at Weston who, of course, doesn't budge an inch.

"It's fine, don't worry." She turns away, waves her hand in the air, "It's all good, honest. I'll, uh, be right back." She scampers off.

I turn to Wes, "Let me go." I slap at his shoulder.

"No," he smirks, "in case you've forgotten, I'm still inside of you."

His dick pulses inside of me and I blink, "You're hard again? How's that possible, you just ah, came..."

"So?" He bends his knees and kisses me, "Merry fucking-Christmas, by the way."

"You can say that again." I throw my arms around him and kiss him back, "Please can we get dressed, before she returns?"

• • •

Ten minutes later, I watch him in the mirror in my bedroom. He'd jumped in the shower a few minutes ago, and now he shrugs into the shirt I'd rescued from the kitchen floor.

He does up the buttons—the one's that had survived when I had ripped it off earlier. Gah! Had I actually done that? Around him I seemed to turn into some kind of sex addict. But can you blame me? I stare at the gorgeous planes of his chest being hidden by the fabric. My throat dries. The pleasant ache between my legs intensifies. I'll never get enough of him, never.

He tugs on the lapel of his shirt. "I can keep this off, if you prefer." His lips curl.

"Not a chance." I close the gap between us, then stab my finger into his rock-hard abs, "I don't feel like sharing right now. Besides, this picture-perfect cut physique belongs to me, you get me?"

He chuckles, "My, my, how possessive you sound, little Red?"

"All the better to scratch you with." I drag my fingernail down the demarcation between his pecs. Why the hell can't I keep my hands off of him?

"I can't wait to see you in scrubs," I mutter.

"I am sure I can oblige." He smirks, " kinky doctor-patient games are my specialty."

"And here I thought it was food kink that got you off." I widen my gaze.

"When it comes to you, babe, everything I do takes on another dimension." He runs his big palm down the curve of my waist and slaps my butt.

"Whoa, whoa," I protest. "What's that for?"

"Keeping you warm." He massages my arse, then cups the other cheek with his free hand and squeezes. My sex instantly clenches. He drags me up on my tiptoes, and the tent in his crotch pokes me.

"You're hard," I mumble.

"You're soft." His grip on my backside tightens and my nipples instantly pucker. Moisture pools between my thighs. "This is not the time," I half protest. "Julia will be back any moment."

He groans, "I think I much prefer the cabin. At least, I could have you to myself there."

I chuckle, "I'll always remember it as the place where I walked in on you naked."

"If I had my way, you and I would be naked for a month, on an island in the middle of nowhere."

"Just as long as there is an oven where I can bake." I warn.

"I'd rather see you baking in the sun... Naked, of course."

I shake my head, "Don't you think of anything but sex?"

"Do you?" He chuckles.

"I think you're fast becoming my favorite dessert, Doc Kincaid," I reply.

"You know you are always mine." He laughs and his features light up. His hair is all mussed up, thanks to me—I'd clung to it, when he'd insisted on going down on me, one last time before he'd released me. Seriously, the man is insatiable. The soreness between my legs is testament to that—and the hickeys on my neck, the bitemarks on my breasts—which is why I am wearing this long-sleeved turtle-neck sweater and a fresh pair of jeans. I glance down at his bare feet, "Did you lose your shoes?"

"Gave them to the homeless guy outside the apartment building."

A warm feeling seizes my chest. "You did that?" I ask. "You gave the shoes you were wearing to someone who needed them?"

He raises his shoulders, then widens his stance. "Don't go reading anything into it," he mutters. "It seemed like the thing to do; no big deal."

I scan his features, "I don't know of too many people who'd do that, you know?"

He cracks his neck in a gesture I am beginning to recognize. He does it when he's embarrassed and trying to hide it.

"You're full of shit Dr. Kinky-as-hell-Caid," I say. "You try so hard to come across all dominant and hard-ass, but in reality, you're like... like..."

"Like?"

"A Jammie dodger."

"A Jammie dodger?"

I nod, "One of those cookies which is double-layered, and hard on the outside, but is filled with sweet gooey jam in the center."

"Hmm." His eyes gleam. "You can taste my jam any day, baby."

"Eeyugh," I make a gagging sound, "I left myself open to that, didn't I? Will I never learn?" I groan.

"It's too easy to tease you." He steps closer, "You're the jam to my cookie; the pumpkin to my pie, the chocolate in my toffee."

"Thought you hated chocolate?" I swallow.

He bridges the distance between us, draws me to him, "That's what I thought too." He searches my face, "But then I tasted you and —"

"And?" I whisper.

"I realized it was missing an ingredient."

"Which is?"

He lowers his face to mine. His breath mixes with mine, our eyelashes tangle, our feet bump, he parts his lips, and the doorbell rings again.

"It's Julia," I groan. "I have to get the door."

50

Weston

She twists her body. My grasp loosens and she pulls away, then pivots and scrambles for the door.

"You," I mutter to the empty room, "it was you that I missed."

Jesus, fuck, can you hear yourself? Did you just confess that you were incomplete without her? Was I? How much do I need her in my life? Could I go on without her? A future without her would be...bleak, dull, no patches of color, no scent of complex notes, no flavors that beckon and open up my senses. Without her... I am less than half the man I could be... I rub the back of my neck. What the fuck? What just happened? Why is my heart thumping? The blood pounds at my temples and my shoulder muscles knot.

Without her... There is no future... There is no me... Bloody hell. I rotate my head, dig my fingers into my hair and tug on it. I can't leave here without her, no way. I don't know what the future holds, but if I don't keep her close... I'll never have a chance of finding out either. As long as she is with me... I stand a chance, at having everything I didn't even know I had wanted... She makes me chuckle, lightens the load I've carried alone for so long. I want her by my side, in my house, in my bed. My ring on her finger, her hand in mine, her body writhing under me as I bury myself inside of her, as I try to tame her, hold her down and fuck her, as I open myself up to her and claim her. I am going to chain her to my side in a way that she'll never leave. I have to do it. Have to get her to see things my way. That her future is mine, that I am her future, that she is my... Everything.

The band around my chest tightens and a ball of emotions fills my throat. A pressure builds behind my eyes, fuck... This...this thing that tears me apart inside and twists my guts, that buries its weight in my stomach, knots my insides and coils in my chest...dries up my throat and hardens my balls. It has to be... It has to be...fucking love. I grab my hair and tug on it. I'd said it out loud earlier, but I'd shrugged it off as something you say in the heat of the moment. But this...this gasping for breath, this sensation of my heart having been scooped out of my body, this nervousness inside of me that grows and grows, even as a desperation tightens my skin, my shoulders, my spine... All of it points to the fact that I am a fucking goner. I am in love... Bloody fuck, I am... And there's nothing I can do about it. My heart begins to pound so hard against my rib cage, I am sure I must be having a cardiac... Except I know I am not... It's the emotional shock causing my palms to sweat. My thigh muscles bunch. I lower my hand, not surprised to find that my fingers are shaking. I stalk out of the bedroom into the tiny living room space.

She faces Julia, who offers her a coffee from the takeaway tray. "I don't want to impose," she mutters.

Amelie curls both of her palms around the paper cup. "It's no imposition," she says.

"No, it isn't," I agree.

Both women turn to me.

Amelie frowns.

Julia tilts her head. "We haven't met, I'm Julia," she says.

I walk forward, halt next to Amelie, "I'm Amelie's boyfriend." Yep, I am well and truly pussy whipped. Since when had my identity become secondary to my position in her life, eh?

Amelie draws in a breath.

Julia smiles. "Good to meet you, Amelie's boyfriend." She holds out the tray of coffee.

"Thank you." I accept one of the cups, swig from it. Damn, but why couldn't it contain a shot of whiskey, at the very least? I suck down more of the coffee.

"You two been dating long?" she asks.

"Yes," I reply.

"No." Amelie shoots me a glance, her gaze narrowed.

"Long enough for me to ask her to move in with me." I smile.

Julia looks between us. "Congratulations." She holds out a hand. Amelie ignores it.

"You... you..." She gapes at me.

"You're coming with me." I say simply.

"I'm not," she splutters, tries to pull away.

I tug her closer, tuck her into my side, and tiny thing that she is, she fits right there, plastered against me.

"Come on babe," I plead, "I can't leave you here, not after the break-in."

"Break in?" Julia exclaims.

"Yeah," I reply, without taking my gaze from Amelie's face. "Someone broke into the apartment earlier today."

"It...it was the same man who forced his way into my bakery." Amelie swallows.

"He was wearing a mask," I remind her. "How can you be sure?"

"I'm sure." She nods. "I... uh, recognized the scent of his cologne."

"You did, huh?" Something hot stabs at my chest. Whoa, what the fuck? Why the hell am I all twisted up inside because she smelled another man's aftershave? This is bloody ridiculous. "That settles it," I growl. "You're not staying here a second longer. You're coming with me."

Her gaze narrows, "I don't think so."

"Yes, you are," I snap.

Her features pinch and she sets her jaw. Fuck, I can't let her go all obstinate on me. Not that I don't mind whipping it out of her, but well, we have company—not that it would stop me, but Julia is her girlfriend, and the one thing I've learned from the rest of the Seven hooking up, is that, you did not show down your woman in front of her friends.

My woman. Mine. I draw her even closer.

She tilts her chin up, "What are you doing?"

"Convincing you." I lower my head, press my mouth to hers, keep the kiss soft, coaxing. I nibble on her lower lip, and when she gasps, I swipe my tongue inside her mouth, just a quick in and out, enough to remind her what is in store if she comes with me, enough to communicate that I need her, want her. A whine tumbles from her lips. My dick instantly lengthens. I tighten my hold on her shoulders, lessen the intensity of the kiss, pull back, brush her lips with mine one more time. "See, that's all settled."

"Oh." Her eyelids flutter, "Wes—"

"Don't say no." I peer into her face, "Come home with me."

She holds my gaze, her chin wobbles, then she nods. "Okay."

Okay! The breath I'd not been aware of holding wheezes out. *What the bloody fuck? Had I been nervous as I'd waited for her reply? Had I actually given her a choice?* And if she had refused? Would I have left...? No, I'd have parked myself here and ensured there was security around the clock. Not that I have anything against this flat... Except there is no telling if the intruder will be back. Besides, I want her in my space, in my bed. I have to be inside of her again.

I stare at her, and her pupils dilate. She licks her lower lip, and her breathing goes ragged.

"Right, get what you need," I say.

She turns, then gasps, "Oh, my God, Jules. I can't leave you here."

"What rubbish." Julia looks between us. "I'll be fine."

"No way, am I letting you stay here. What if the intruder returns?"

"I'll lock the door from the inside," she insists.

"It's not safe," Amelie shuffles her feet, "I don't feel comfortable leaving you here."

I frown. I can't allow her to stay on, but I don't want Julia to come with us either, not when I want Amelie to myself... No way, am I sharing her with anyone else... Not yet... Not for a while, which means... There is only one way out. "I have an idea."

51

Amelie

"Holy fuck." I stare out of the window at the view of Tower Bridge from the window of Weston's penthouse.

He'd informed me that I was on his guest list, so I could come and go as I please. Also, my fingerprints had been added to the fancy-ass security thingy on the front door to the apartment. So I had to simply touch my palm to the lock pad provided and—wowza!—the door would open to let me in. Oh, he'd let me try it and it had worked on the way in. Woo. That is some fancy shit. The kind of security only the seriously well off could afford.

Don't get me wrong, I knew he was loaded...and talented, and over-the-top dominant...but this... All this luxury that surrounds me... It's too much. When we were at the cabin, London had seemed so far away. It had been easy to forget about daily life, my debts, my growing business, the fact that he is so bloody out of my league. And at my apartment... Well, that had been my turf. I had felt more in control maybe... Which is a laugh, considering it has been broken into. It is also the place where he told me he loves me.

"Did you mean what you said?"

I hear the words and curse myself. *Why the hell can't you filter your thoughts, bitch? Why is it so important to know what he feels for you?* He wants

me. He was taking no argument about leaving me behind at the apartment either. So, he lusts after my body... I mean, that's good, right? It's a
start. The fact that he finds me attractive? Heat sears my back, then his
big arm wraps me around my waist. He pulls me back and flush against
his big chest. Instantly, I feel tiny and cherished and taken care of. Big
mistake. He is going to lure me in, fuck me senseless, keep me in a sex-
induced haze, and when I wake up from it, I will regret every little piece
of me I had shared with him.

"Do you actually want to know the answer to your question?"

Of course, he knows what I was referring to... And yeah, I definitely
want to know the answer.

"No."

I shake my head.

"Liar," He pulls me close so my back is plastered against his perfect
chest. Heat from his body cocoons me, sinks into my blood.

My toes curl. My thighs clench. *Get your mind out of the gutter, you slut.*
"Umm," I hesitate. "It was nice of you to have a security system put in
my flat, and on such short notice."

Yeah, he'd made one phone call and in half an hour, his security
consultant had arrived, armed with an array of devices. She'd checked
out the place, then rigged it with enough alarms and sensors to satisfy
his exacting demands. It had taken less than two hours from start to
finish, during which time, Julia and Weston had gotten along well. I'd
watched from the sidelines as he'd charmed her, put my friend at ease,
so that by the time it was time to leave, she was completely convinced
that this was the right move for me. Well, apparently, he saves that
hard-headed, demanding alphahole side of his for me... Not that I am
complaining. It is part of his appeal—I admit, that firm hand of his is a
bloody turn on for me. If only I could always live in this sex-haze of a
bubble, huh?

He wraps both of his arms around my shoulders, enveloping me in
that gorgeous scent of his. "You're deflecting, babe." He bends to nibble
on the shell of my ear.

I shiver.

"Didn't think you were such a coward." He blows in my ear, and I
shiver. Bloody hell, with him, every part of me turns into an erogenous
zone. Bet I've sprouted nerve endings where none existed before... *All
the better to sense you with, Mr. Wolf.*

He spreads his fingers over my stomach. The width of his palm is so wide that the tip of his thumb brushes the underside of my breast. My nipple instantly pebbles. *Stupid, stupid, that I am so responsive to him.*

I pull away from him. Of course, he doesn't let me budge, not a millimeter. Against his strength, I am helpless. His force of will, his confidence... How is it possible that he always seems to know what he wants? Unlike me. My entire life is a two steps forward, one back kind of scenario. "Let me go," I mumble.

"Not a chance," he growls. The edge of his voice shivers down my spine, sinks into my center.

"Wes," I plead, "you're making this very hard."

"I'll make it simple." He releases me, only to flip me around. "Look at me."

I stare at his chest, the smattering of hair that peppers the dent between his perfect abs. We'd walked in and I had headed for the view and lost my composure. Now, when I lean in and press my nose into his skin and inhale, notes of sweetness mixed in with his darker scent fills my senses. "You smell like us," I whisper, draw in another breath, then bend and lick him. "You taste like honey and chocolate bomb overlaid with cinnamon and cloves and a dash of vanilla." Yum!

A groan rumbles up his chest.

"Woman you've got to stop comparing me to desserts."

"Oh?" I glance up at him, "Shall I compare thee to a summer's day instead?"

"Shakespeare?" He tilts his head.

I stare up at that perfect visage, that strong jaw, the mean upper lip that hints at the dominance inside that drew me to him...those thick eyebrows, the eyelashes that fringe his keen gaze. Everything about him is right, more than right. He is the complete package — he fits me; body, mind and soul, and damn it... This is all wrong. I can never have him, could never keep him. What do I have that could hold his attention? Why does he have to understand me so well? Tears knock against the back of my eyes.

"What's wrong?" He frowns.

"I don't belong here."

"You belong with me.

"I don't want you."

"You do."

"I can't do...this."

"What?"

"Whatever this is." I wave my hand in the air, "Playing house...or rather playing mansion—or whatever it is the other half calls it."

"Is that what you think this is?" He seems perplexed.

"Isn't it?"

"Maybe," he concedes. "Maybe not." He releases me, then steps back. He'd changed clothes, and now his tailored slacks mold his thighs and cling to that spectacular butt as he paces the floor in his Italian shoes—how many of them does he have in his closet, huh?

He drags his fingers through his hair, drawing my attention to how his biceps bulge against his button-down shirt. My mouth waters. *Whoa down girl, haven't you feasted on his delectable body enough?* And that's the problem. I'd prefer to lick his sculpted abs—and uh, other parts of him —over chocolate. Shit, I am so screwed.

"I am not sure what this is between us," he concedes.

"You're not?" I blink. The alphahole is always bloody sure of himself. He rolls his shoulders now, then cracks his neck, then pivots to face me, with his eyebrows knitted into a look I can only describe as confusion. This is a first.

"I'm not," he confirms my suspicion. "When I walked in and realized you were in danger, when he held that knife to your neck, something changed."

"It did?"

"I thought I'd failed you. If something had happened to you, I could have never forgiven myself."

"You're not my keeper," I mutter. "I've taken care of myself for so long."

"And look where that has gotten you." He scowls.

"What?" I blink, "Did you just say what I think you did?"

"Look," He holds up his hands, "I'm not saying you haven't tried your best, but I could make things much easier for you with my money, my contacts."

I swallow and something hot stabs at my chest. My throat closes and my eyes burn. Why the hell had I thought anything had changed? Because he'd chased that goddam burglar from my apartment? No, hold on, I'd played a part in that too. Because he'd ensured that my friend would be safe in my apartment? That was because he wanted me close, where he could keep an eye on me, take care of me, control me. That's what this is about.

He wants me here so I can be his little fuck toy. He'd have his way with me... Oh, yeah, I'd enjoy every second of it too.. And then what? He'd throw me away? Well, he'd have paid me for my time...

And I don't want it. I'd rather live in debt for the rest of my life, than be obligated to him.

Not that it wasn't part of the arrangement. I mean, I'd gone into it with my eyes open, not realizing I was giving him what he needed—a way to manipulate me.

Whatever the future might hold for us, whatever there could be between us... As long as the money stands between us...the money I had accepted...it would always be a relationship which would be measured, a connection which had a number attached to it... It's too finite. Too tangible. Too...restrictive. Something that goes against how I had lived my life, the future I wanted for myself. I want him, all right, but not at the cost of my self-respect.

If I stay, and accept the money, and allow him to treat me like one of his other women, someone whose bond is tainted by the materialistic aspects of life... We don't stand a chance. Not the way I want.

"This...is all wrong," I say.

He closes the distance between us, "I don't agree."

"I don't want your money."

He stares, "Excuse me?"

"I don't like how it makes everything too easy."

"Are you kidding me?" He scowls. "That's what it is meant for—to pave the way, to achieve dreams, to help you get what you want."

"I can do it on my own." I tip up my chin. "I will achieve my goals, on my own merit."

"What are you saying?" He glowers, "You're not making any sense to me."

"For the first time since I met you, I am making sense to myself."

His gaze widens, "So you admit that I affect you?"

I throw up my hands, "That has never been in dispute. I mean, come on, it's clear we can't keep our hands off of each other. Put us in a room and we'll end up in bed. Hell, I hear your voice on the phone and I'm wet."

"You are, huh?" He smirks and his shoulder muscles seem to broaden.

"OMG!" I slap my forehead, "Of course, you'd choose to focus on the more obvious. Of everything I said, is that the only thing you heard?"

"You want me; I want you. We're good together." He raises his shoulders, "What else is there?"

"Everything." I swallow, "And nothing." I peer into his face, "After all that we've been through, you still don't get it, do you?"

"Is this about the money?" He scowls, "Because if that's the case, I'll double what I am paying you."

"Money?" A chill spreads across my skin. "You think it's about the money?"

"I'll triple it."

"Triple?" I stare, "You'll triple the money?" *Is he for real? Isn't he hearing anything I am trying to communicate to him? And I thought he got me?*

"That's eighteen million pounds in your bank account on New Year's Day."

I cough. That's a bloody hell of a lot of money. I'd never see that in this lifetime, for sure. If I accepted it, I'd never be able to live with myself. I'd hate myself every day for the rest of my life. Besides, what's the difference between one million and eighteen million, huh? Other than the zeroes? That's the thing with money. The more you have of it, the less it does for you. Nope, I may have been blinded by what the money could have done for me—could still do for me, but not anymore.

"I'll throw in this penthouse," he growls. "Hell, say the word and I'll sign it over to you."

I open my mouth, then purse my lips together, "Good bye, Weston."

I brush past him, spot my suitcases by the door of the living room. He'd had his driver deliver my suitcases to this address. Sneaky bastard had planned it all along... How did I miss it? How come I didn't see through him? I was an acquisition for him. A possession. Hell, he even dropped the 'L' word in the height of passion, hoping it would convince me to give in to him. Well, fuck him, and his money and his bloody view —which is spectacular, I've never seen that view of London in real life before and will probably never do so again. Tears prick the backs of my eyes. *Get out before you bawl your eyes out over that ass.*

I ignore my luggage; it will only delay me, and I don't want that. I have Peter's contact details; I'll ask him to deliver it home. I'm sure Weston won't stop him, will he? I hesitate. Too bad. I'll have to risk it then. I am not stopping here for one second more. I grab my chef's satchel from the coffee table, tuck my handbag into my side, then head for the door.

"Don't you want to check out the kitchen?" He calls out.

I pause. "What?"

"The kitchen," he says, "it's to your right."

I stare straight ahead. Focus my gaze on the double doors to this blasted, beautiful penthouse. *Get out of here, get out of here.* I take a step forward.

"It has a never-before-used double oven that you have to see."

"It does?"

"You bet." He walks past me, heads toward what I assume is the kitchen. "And all the ingredients you'd need to bake apple pies..."

I swallow.

"Macaroons," he drawls.

I tighten my grip on my bag.

"Triple chocolate cake," he adds.

I turn to him, "Nothing I can't do in my kitchen."

"With this view?" He jerks his chin toward the kitchen, "Not to mention, the complete range of baking tools that you'll need to whip up your specialties."

"You know how I feel about your flaunting your wealth in my face, right?"

"Who said anything about money? This is simply a fully-equipped kitchen, crying out for the right chef to inaugurate it and give it purpose."

I frown. *How the hell does he know exactly how to get to me?* I mean, his words... They are like coffee in the morning, like oats for granola bars, like custard for fruit salad, argh! Stop it...your comparisons suck. Besides, I don't plan to stay. I'll take a peek, check out the kitchen... I mean, it's only a few minutes more, right?

52

____

Weston

She glances at the big-ass oven—the sleek, professional one, perfect for a baker to use at home, the one I'd had installed yesterday... Whew! She hates my money, but fuck, if it doesn't have its advantages. I've never given the money a second thought, to be fair. Perhaps, it's what comes from being born into wealth... And my career as a heart surgeon? Let's just say, it pays well. And I had invested with the Seven. We had chosen our ventures carefully, especially FOK media which had been a passion project and an investment, which is already paying dividends. So, fuck if I am going to apologize for the money that was mine by birth and which I had helped multiply through my hard work. I get where she's coming from though. She wants to strike out on her own... And I am not stopping her. I'm simply removing obstacles from her way, giving her the best chance of success. Doesn't she realize that? Why can't she accept the fact that everything that is mine is hers? If I could serve up the world on a platter to her, I'd do it. I stiffen. Do I think that? All that emo shit that I'd been sure was not for me...? Clearly, I'm rolling in that shit, thanks to Ms. Chocolate Cookie... Hell, I've even accepted the presence of chocolate in my life, and Christmas, and all that shit that has never mattered before? I want it all...with her. That's it. I need help—need to figure out how to solve this conundrum that I have worked myself into.

I pull out my phone, pace the floor of my bedroom, as I dial Damian's number.

"Motherfucker!" he says as his greeting.

"Merry fucking Christmas to you too, asshole," I reply.

"Yeah, yeah, same to you with knobs on." He yawns, "What are you doing on the phone with me? I thought you'd be shacked up with your bride in the penthouse."

"Jesus, I'm not married man. Far from it."

"Why aren't you?"

"What the fuck are you talking about?"

"Straight question, man." He yawns again. "Why don't you put a ring on her finger, put the two of you out of your misery, and let the rest of us get some sleep, huh?"

"Whoa, whoa." I cough. "You're not mincing any words here. What's up? You got a woman there you're eager to get back to?"

"What do you think?" He chuckles.

Yeah, he's with someone.

"Look I need your advice," I mutter.

"I gave it to you already. Don't expect me to make your decisions for you."

"Christ," I mutter, "what's prompted this level of candidness."

"Maybe it's the Christmas spirit, bro." I hear him move around. "Maybe I am tired of watching you screw up over and over again." His footsteps thud on the wooden floor, then the rustle of clothes reaches me. "Hold on." I hear the sound of muffled voices, then he comes back on the call. "So, where were we?"

"You sent her away, huh?" I ask.

"Bros before hoes and all that... " he replies, "Also, she's not the one, so..." I sense him raise his shoulders.

"How do you know that she isn't?"

"When you know, you know," he says, "and you do know, you just don't want to accept it."

"You're full of platitudes," I grumble.

"And you're full of shit," he retorts. "Why the hell don't you have a conversation with her?"

"I've tried, believe me."

"Have you, though?"

"What?"

"Told her how you feel. Have you done that?"

"I told her I love her."

There's silence, then he says, "How did you say it?

"What do you mean?"

"I mean, did you say it like you meant it?"

"Of course," *I think...* "only she didn't say it back."

"She didn't?"

"Nope." I begin to pace, "Maybe she doesn't feel the same way. I mean, I'm not the easiest when it comes to matters of the heart."

He bursts out laughing, "Says the heart surgeon."

"Har, har." I continue, "It's because I am so intimately conversant with that particular organ that I am wary of it."

"Have you thought of the possibility that maybe she doesn't love you?"

"What do you think, I'm stupid?"

"Do I need to answer that question?"

"Don't bother." My stomach ties itself in knots. "She probably doesn't, man, and that's fine. Perhaps in time, she'll develop feelings for me."

"Who are you and what have you done to Dr Asshole Kincaid?"

Heat flushes my neck, "Fuck off, man. If you have something to say, say it."

"You're pussy-whipped."

"You have no idea." I squeeze the bridge of my nose, "It's why I offered to triple the money I'd agreed to pay her —"

"What?" he explodes. "You did what?"

"You heard me," I mumble. A hollow feeling coils in my chest. I squeeze the bridge of my nose, "Fuck, I shouldn't have done that, huh?"

"The opposite, man. You need to take the money out of the equation."

"What do you mean?"

"Change the tone of the relationship."

"How?"

"Replace it with something...that means more to you than money... Offer that up to her... Something that you'd never have imagined giving to anyone else, or giving up for someone else." He pauses, "It could also be something that's ingrained in you... perhaps a habit which you'd change for her?"

I blink. "That...that's profound, bro."

"Sometimes I surprise myself." He laughs. "It's easier to be objective when it comes to other's problems, know what I mean?"

"Yeah," I blow out a breath. "I have to do this, right?"

"You bet," he replies, "it's time you left behind the boy who was kidnapped for good."

53

"Q: What do you call a lamb covered in chocolate?
A: Candy Baa."
-From Amelie's diary

Amelie

I slide the tray of chocolate cookies out of the oven. Yeah, I've been here for a half hour already. What can I say? I'm a sucker. And it doesn't take me much time to mix up the cookie batter. Not when all of the ingredients, and more, are available... And the oven...? Whoa!

I rake my gaze over the sparkling steel surface of the top of the range oven... The man has his faults, but he hadn't compromised when it came to the kitchen. I turn to glance out of the window; the evening light of the city pours in through the large panes. I can see the Thames and the bridge. OMG, Tower Bridge gleams as it picks up the rays from the setting sun. The entire scene is almost surreal, and beautiful, and completely not what I am used to.

But you could...you could stay here, bake in this kitchen every day, sleep in his bed every night, have him fuck you and bring you to orgasm. Hell, bet he'd even proclaim his love again and probably mean it this time... You could have everything you've dreamed of... So why the hell are you holding out? That fucking independent spirit of mine... Why the hell do I have to be this adamant?

It had seemed all right to take his money earlier... But that was before I realized I want more, want him to want me for who I am. A cakehead, who has to figure out things her own way, without help or interference... At least, he'd left me alone to get on with the baking. *Where is he anyway? Why hasn't he checked in on me yet?*

I place the cookies on the cooling trays I'd found.

I had been on the verge of leaving and he'd managed to stall me. Clever man — he knows me too well. I smile at the thought, until I realize it's not true. If he really knew me, he'd know what I want from him. He wouldn't be trying to buy me. Suddenly, I want to cry. I need to get out of here.

I walk toward the door, then pause. I wonder what else he has in this big-ass place? Should I explore? Shouldn't I leave instead? I pause... But the cookies. Okay, I'll stay until the cookies have cooled.

I set the alarm on my phone, pocket it, then creep out of the kitchen. I head for the living room; he's not there. Turn and walk into the next room. It's a playroom, filled with toys. Bet Phe spends a lot of time in here.

I walk into the next room — a study filled with books where an eleven-year-old pre-teen would love to spend time. Yep, this is Skye's. I guess his family comes over to visit often. Does he babysit his nieces? Of course, he does.

I head into the adjacent room. The scent of cigar smoke and something else — his scent, those heavy testosterone notes tease my nostrils. This is his space, a study, more of a man-cave, complete with volumes of medical journals on the shelves.

I peruse the titles, glance down. Huh? He has an entire shelf filled with the Harry Potter books. So, he liked to read them for pleasure? Aww. A warmth trickles through my chest. I stiffen. No, you cannot allow yourself to soften. Damn it, maybe this hadn't been such a good idea.

I'd hoped to find something that would incriminate him, allow me to nurture my need to have a low opinion of him. Instead, all signs confirm that this is a man who loves his family, who has the kind of quirks I enjoy. And yeah, he is a surgeon, and he does save lives. I hunch my shoulders. The man is bloody complex and too attractive, and I don't stand a chance. This had been a bad idea. Speaking of, where the hell is the Doc? Had he been so confident that I would stay, that he'd left? Had he done it to give me some down time? To cool off maybe, and come to my senses? Typical male manipulation. I huff. He knew if he left me alone in his space, I'd investigate it. I reach the doors to his bedroom, hesitate. Go on, do it. A quick peek, that's all it is.

I shove open the doors, enter a room which I swear is as big as my apartment. My feet sink into the carpet that stretches out toward a massive king-sized bed in the center. To one side, sliding doors open onto a terrace, beyond which is the inevitable spectacular view of Tower Bridge. And at the far end? That has to be a walk-in closet. I march toward it, push open the doors and peek in. It's filled with an array of his pants, shirts, ties, suits, scrubs, his designer shoes. No watches, of course. I know, now, why he doesn't keep those accessories. Also, one entire side of the closet is cleared out. For what? Did someone else just move out? Or had he been so sure that I'd move in with him? Presumptuous, much?

As I near the kitchen, the scent of freshly baked cookies teases my nostrils. My mouth waters and my belly grumbles. I hasten my pace, head for the oven. Ha, life's so much better when you have cookies in your hand. And really, I should have left, but procrastibaking is my specialty. You know, when you have a million things to do, but you put it on the back burner and prefer to bake? I snort, then brush my hand over the apron that I'd pulled on. It's a designer piece, that much I can tell. Who makes designer aprons? More to the point, who buys them? Weston fucking Kincaid does, that's who.

I lean over the cookies, inhale the heady perfume. OMG, almost as good as fucking... Well, that's what I used to think. Then I'd met Weston and okay...baking is my second favorite pasttime now, the first being, riding his monster dick, licking the frosting off of his penis... Stop, stop. Enough already. Change of topic, focus on something else. I reach for a cookie and bring it to my mouth.

"Is that for me?"

His voice sounds so close, I squeak. The cookie slips from my fingers. He swoops down catches it.

"Good save," I mutter as he straightens and turns to me.

He glances at the piece of cookie in between his fingers, then raises it and holds it to my lips.

"Open." His gaze is fixed on my face. He peruses my features, searching... searching for... What? My compliance? That I'll throw myself at his feet and ask him to fuck me? That I'll reveal my feelings? Tell him how I've fallen for him, that I want a future with him? Have I allowed him to distract me because I don't want to leave? Because I already miss him—his large body that pins me down and allows me to be weak... Secure in the knowledge that he'll catch me. He'll take care of me... I know that...but I want more. I part my lips and he pops the cookie in. I bite down. The soft texture melts in my mouth. I lick my lips. He lowers his gaze to my mouth, watches me with that intensity that's so Weston. I chew, swallow, open my mouth. He feeds me more of the cookie. I chew, swallow again. This time, his breath catches. The tendons of his throat move, his shoulders bunch. "Amelie," his voice is harsh and soft at the same time.

"Don't." I should turn away. This is where I walk away and never look back. Write off the past few days, count this Christmas as a lost cause, then go home to my apartment—now secure, thanks to him—and bake until I can't see straight. Then swallow down enough wine that I don't remember much of the immediate future. Go through the motions in life... Move on... Pick myself up again and plod forward, one freaking step at a time.

He holds up the last piece of the cookie.

I shake my head, "You have it."

He glances at it then pops it into his mouth. He chews on it and that's when it sinks in.

"It has chocolate," I mutter.

He raises his shoulders, "So?"

"Thought you didn't like it?"

"Told you I was coming around to it." He bends his knees and peers into my face, "In fact, it's fast becoming my second favorite dessert to eat."

My heart stutters. One stupid bit of praise from him and my heart literally seems to melt, like the chocolate in those stupid cookies.

Don't ask him. Don't.

"What's the first?" I mumble.

"What do you think?" His lips curve.

My cheeks heat. My belly flutters. *Don't blush. Don't let him see how much that compliment pleases me.* I swipe my hair over my shoulder. "Don't think that you can get back in my good graces by praising my cooking."

"Baking" he corrects me.

"Right." I drag my fingers through my hair. *Why the hell do I get the feeling that everything is out of my control, right now?* "It's time I left."

I brush past him.

"Stop," he calls out, then softly adds, "Don't leave, Cookie."

I hunch my shoulders, keep my gaze trained on the door. *You don't want this, don't want him like this. You are a big girl; you can move forward on your own. You don't need any alphahole to jerk you around and think he can buy you with money.*

"Princess," his coaxing voice follows me, "I'll let you take the lead."

54

Weston

What the fuck? Did I actually say that? And I meant it, too. Anything to make her stay.

Why can't you tell her how much she means to you? Well, I am about to show her that. And isn't showing better than telling, and all that fucking emo stuff that women believe in?

She pauses at the door, hesitates.

"I mean it." I keep my voice firm. "You can do what you want with me, and I won't stop you. I'll let you take the lead in bed."

She turns to glance at me, "You will?"

"Yep." I jerk my chin.

"Right now?"

"The deal's valid for the next ten seconds."

"Deal, huh?" She frowns.

Fuck, seems I can't change my vocabulary that easily. Go on, you can do this, for her sake. Tone it down, asshole. Keep it easy; don't show how much you need her to retrace her steps, and return to you. And once she does... I'm never letting her go. I am going to find a way to tie her to me. Yep, I have to. Don't fuck this up! I loosen my shoulders, force my muscles to relax. "Okay, not a deal then, an open invitation."

"Invitation?" She chews on her lower lip. Damn her, why does she have to seem so enticing? I force my attention off of my throbbing groin, narrow my gaze on her.

"Anything you need, babe." I hold up my hands in what I hope comes across as an unthreatening gesture, "You name it, you can have it."

She frowns, "What's the catch?"

"No catch."

"I don't believe it."

"Better believe it." I allow my lips to curve.

She stares at my face.

"What?"

"Did you actually smile without smirking?"

"I don't smirk..." I protest.

She arches an eyebrow.

"Okay, maybe sometimes," I concede.

"All the time," she grumbles. "I've never known you not to smirk, not that it isn't hot in a mean kind of way—"

"Aha, so you do find it hot?" My mouth curls.

"I rest my case," she snaps.

Bloody fuck, what the hell does she want me to do? Change my personality overnight? It's taken thirty-three odd years to cultivate this dickface persona. But for her... I'd give that up too... Only with her, that is. To the rest of the world, I'd still be the asshole surgeon with the bad attitude... But for her... I'd do anything.

Does that include letting go of control...for a tiny window in time...allowing her to have her way with me? My balls tighten; my skin crawls. Giving up choice? Not something I'd ever imagined doing...not before her. Only for her.

She is my woman and she'll get her satisfaction when, where and how she needs it. Everyone else will deal...and that includes me. Fuck. I wipe the smile off my face. "Better?"

She raises her shoulders. "Maybe," she takes another step forward, "maybe not."

"I know something that will make it better." I begin to smirk again.

She scowls.

I grimace, school all expression from my face. Best to keep my mouth shut, lock my muscles, dig my feet into the floor. I stay still... Wait... Wait for her to come to me, to tip her head back and meet my gaze.

"Anything, huh?" She drags a finger down my chest, down to my waistband, in the direction of where my cock tents the crotch of my pants.

Blood rush to my groin; pinpricks of heat follow in the path of her touch. "Anything," I growl.

She unbuckles my belt, and my dick thrusts against its restraints. Fuck, at this rate, I am going to come in my pants and she's barely touched me yet. My fingers tingle. I raise my hand.

She glances at it, then at me, "You promised," she reminds me.

I curl my fingers into a fist, then raise my hands and lock them behind my neck, "Indeed." I keep my gaze trained on her face.

Her pupils dilate and color pinks her cheeks. She lowers the zipper, then shoves my pants and my boxers down in one sweep.

The breath catches in my chest as I kick aside my clothes.

She reaches down and winds her fingers around my throbbing dick. My groin hardens, my balls tighten, and I grip my hands together. *Don't release them. Don't reach for her. Don't push her down onto her knees. Don't ask her to take you inside that gorgeous mouth and don't ask her to suck you off... Don't.* She reaches for her shirt and whips it off.

I stare. "What are you doing?"

"What do you think?" She pulls off her bra, then shoves off her boots, and wriggles out of her jeans and panties. Her full tits jiggle as she straightens. She runs her hand down her stomach, to where her pink pussy glistens. She strums her lower lips and my cock jumps in response.

"Huh?" She stares down at her crotch, then drags her fingers up to the swollen bud of her clit. My dick lengthens, I bunch my shoulders, and my balls grow impossibly hard.

"Jesus," I snarl.

"You shouldn't swear using his name on Christmas Day."

"If you don't get on with what you have in mind, I am going to—"

"Going to?" She flutters her eyelashes, "What will you do?"

I narrow my gaze. Why that sassy, little sex kitten. Apparently, giving Princess Buttercup a long leash means she thinks she can run away with it, huh? I glare at her. She pales, but doesn't break the eye contact. "Well," she asks, "shall I continue?"

"Do it," I growl.

"Hmm." She pushes a finger into her cheek, "You don't seem like you're having a good time."

"Doesn't matter." I dig my fingers into the palm of my hand, draw in a breath, count down the time.

Twelve o'clock.

Eleven o'clock.

Ten —

"What are you doing?" she frowns.

"Counting down the time in my mind.

"Why would you do that?"

"It's a technique that helps me find equilibrium."

"And yet clocks trigger you?"

"They used to."

"But not anymore?" She nods, "You didn't flinch when the egg timer rang in my kitchen."

"I may have been too busy saving someone's arse to notice." I mutter.

"You mean someone's gorgeous arse, right?" She wrinkles her nose at me. Fucking adorable. My heart stutters... It bloody stutters. Damian was right, I am pussy-whipped... And I want to whip her pussy too, every chance I get.

"Someone's curvy, beautiful, egg-shaped bottom, to be precise," I reply.

"My butt isn't egg-shaped."

"Wanna bet?" I drawl. "It's as smooth, and as curvy as that blasted egg timer you have—which, by the way, is a hideous piece of kitchen-ware, with no aesthetic sense."

"Are you saying my butt is ugly?"

"You are not butt-ugly, no," I clarify. "But if you don't get on with your seduction routine—I promise the marks I'll leave on your backside will not be pretty."

"You promised that I could lead," she scoffs.

"But you're not," I snap. "You're talking your mouth off, when you could be putting said orifice to much better use."

She throws up her hands, "Are you going to let me do this my way or not?"

"Fine, fine." I crack my neck. "What fucking ever. Take your time, dawdle, say whatever comes into your mind, while I suffer in silence."

"Hardly suffering and it's not like you've stopped speaking either."

True. I scowl, "You seem to bring out the worst in me, Buttercup."

"As do you." She chuckles, then glances around her before heading to the refrigerator. She pulls out a bottle of milk, then shuts the door and walks toward me.

"Anything, huh?" She asks.

I glance at the white liquid in the bottle, then up to her face, "Anything."

She holds up the bottle, tilts it over my chest.

55

Amelie

What the hell am I doing? I should have left an hour ago. Yet, here I am—first seduced by his kitchen, and now, by the man himself, who stands in front of me, naked as the day he was born, cock thrust up and out at me. OMFG, his dick... I've seen it up close, I've had it down my throat, inside my pussy, my arsehole... And yet, I swear as the milk pours down his chest, pools in the nest of hair at his groin, and drips down from his balls... I've never seen something this... erotic. This hot. This...gorgeous...almost as orgasmic as the sight of a triple chocolate cake lathered in freshly whipped cream.

A moan wells up my throat and my breathing goes ragged. I empty the rest of the milk on him, place the bottle on the island, then lean in and trace a path between the demarcation of his pecs, down his concave stomach. I dip my tongue inside his belly button; his abs ripple. Holy fuck. This... This is too much fun. The way his body responds to my touch? Wow... That's power. All six-feet four-inches of alpha hunk, at my mercy. Mine to do with as I want. Mine to tease, mine to hold and squeeze. Mine to climb up and wrap myself around him, if I want.

I bring my palm up and weigh his balls; a groan rips out of him. Every muscle in his body solidifies. I drag my tongue along the hair that arrows down to his shaft. His dick jumps and his thigh muscles spasm. I circle around to the underside then trace the path to its logical end, the tip of his dick. I close my mouth around him and he swears, "Fucking fuck, you're killing me, Princess."

I haven't even started.

I straighten, then turn and march back to the refrigerator. The hair on the back of my neck rises, and I know he's stalking me, watching my every move, waiting for me to push him to the edge, and I will...but first, I want to have some fun. He'd teased me and taunted me and I am going to return the favor.

I pull open the refrigerator. Oh, yeah! I straighten, pivot with the bowl of Jell-o—who'd made it? A housekeeper? Does he have a housekeeper? Of course he does. He's rich, remember? Filthy rich. Well, fuck that. I'm rich too, when it comes to talent. I can bake like a goddess and I can tease like a slut.

I bump my hip against the refrigerator door to shut it, then run a finger around the rim of the bowl. His gaze narrows and his nostrils flare. He glances at the quivering gelatin, then up at my face. He tilts his head, a warning look in his eyes. A shiver runs down my spine. Oh, he's going to get back at me for this, I'm sure... But whatever... I'm not going to stop, not when I am having so much fun. I amble over to him, wriggle my hips when I stop in front of him. His chest rises and falls. I dip a couple of fingers into the gelatin, scoop some of it out, and hold it up to his mouth. "Open," I command.

"Lick or suck, Princess?" he growls.

"Whatever you please," I breathe. A bead of sweat runs down his temple. Moisture beads my upper lip. Hell, is the heating on in here, or what? He lowers his head, closes his mouth around my fingertips. I feel the tug all the way down to my cunt. A moan spills from my lips. His mouth curves, he licks his tongue about my fingertips, swallows, then nips on my fingers. Moisture oozes between my legs. Oh, shit. I'm as turned on as he is. This was supposed to be his punishment... Ha! How stupid of me. The only person who will come out at the losing end of this bargain is me. I turn, place the bowl of Jell-o on the island, then grab my panties and pull them on.

"What are you doing?"

I don't reply, shrug into my jeans, find my bra and pull it on.

"Princess?"

"Shut up," I mutter, "I know what you're doing."

"Oh?"

I nod. "You're trying to lure me into staying."

"Am I?" he growls.

I snatch up my blouse, shrug into it. "Yes, you are." Tears knock at the back of my eyes, and honestly... I don't know why. I mean, why the hell should I feel like the entire world is ending? I could stay; he wants me to stay... But that would be empty, wouldn't it? I'd still be only a possession to him, something he had bought.

"Amelie, talk to me." He frowns. "What the hell is going on in that pretty head of yours?"

"Nothing, asshole." I toss my hair over my shoulders. "You can take your...your penthouse and fancy kitchen and oven, and all your privileged-as-hell shit, and stuff it where the sun don't shine."

"Princess..." he takes a step forward; I hold up my hand.

"Don't you dare," I snarl. "Don't you fucking say anything. Don't try to stop me. At least this once, would you stick to your word, and stay right there, until I am gone? This once, can you allow me to leave with a modicum of self-respect?"

He stares at me, his features wearing an expression of frustration. "Amelie, please."

I flip him my middle finger, then grab my phone, snatch up my chef's satchel and my hand bag from where I had placed them on the kitchen island and march out.

56

Weston

I squeeze my eyes shut. The woman I love walked out. I hadn't had the
balls to tell her how much I cared for her; all I'd been worried about was
emptying said balls into her. I lower my arms to my sides.

I should have stopped her; should have hauled her over my shoulder
and marched into the bedroom, where I'd have thrown her on her back
and thrust into her, kept her pinned down until she forgot all about
leaving me... About the money, and her business and my bloody ego,
which, as per usual, stood in the way. Jesus, couldn't I have said something...anything to stop her from leaving?

Woulda. Coulda. Shoulda. Since when had I begun to over-analyze
my reactions, huh? Gone are the days when I'd forge ahead, not caring
who I offended. Hell, I had never cared about how my actions affected
those around me.

Apparently, she affects me in more ways than I care to admit. Not
the least of which is how my groin knots, my cock thickening as I yearn
to be inside of her. I grab my shaft and squeeze, swipe it from root to
head with practiced skill. Only, it's not doing it for me at all. I need
something more, something warmer, moister, something that would
clasp me the way her cunt had when I had thrust into her and taken her.

I glance around, take in the empty milk bottle, the bowl of Jell-o —

my cock jerks, bombarded by images of how she'd scooped up the gelatin and offered it to me, her lips parted, tongue caught in concentration between her teeth.

The princess had challenged me. *Me.* The alphahole who has never allowed *any* woman to take the lead... I'd handed it to her, and she had left me. I hunch my shoulders, reach for the Jell-o, scoop up some from the center. Hmm, this has possibilities, huh? Except... I tilt my head. The damn Jell-o is too bouncy and it's bound to fall apart. No, I need something else. I plop the Jell-o back, glance around, and spot the basket of fruits in the center of the island... Hmm... I reach for a peach, glare at it. Apparently, doing it to the apple pie had not been enough. Here I am, searching for more substitutes for her pussy. The last time, I'd resorted to such desperate measures, I'd been...fifteen? And horny as fuck. Nothing has changed...

Except, now I know how it feels to make love to my woman. Jesus, the fuck is wrong with me? Getting soppy and sentimental over her? Thankfully, I still have my balls... Time I put them to good use, huh? I stare at the peach, what if I were to scoop out some of the pulp in the center along with the stone? Hmm... This won't do at all... One more thing that has changed since I was fifteen... My bloody cock is twice the size it had been... Okay, three times if you measure the length of the hardon that I'm sporting. Fuck.

I toss the peach aside, reach for the watermelon. Desperate times and all that... I glare at it, pump my cock again. Am I going to do this? Fuck a bloody watermelon? Would it be cheating on her if I did? A fruit is an inanimate object, right? As in, it doesn't have feelings, in the technical sense of the word, so it can't reciprocate sentiments... So, it does not constitute being unfaithful if I stick my dick in it, does it? I frown down at the offending fruit, massage its curved circumference. It's smooth...too smooth... Too cold... Nothing like the living flesh of her butt, the slight indentation of the dimple in the center of one arsecheek, that I had caressed before I'd cupped her backside and squeezed, then hauled her up so she could wind those gorgeous legs around my waist, before I'd pushed her up against the nearest hard surface and —

Fuck. Stop this line of thinking, you prick. It should be her heart you're focusing on. Her needs. The fact that she had thrown my money back at me... Hell, no one had done that before. But she isn't like anyone else I've ever encountered. Amelie...with her sass and her wit, and her habit of swearing by using names of desserts. Jesus, she is more delectable than any creation I've ever sampled. And I had let her leave. Again... I...

If I had stopped her, she'd have never forgiven me. She'd pleaded with me to let her leave...and I had... I'd stood there and watched her flounce out. What do they say? Something about, if you love someone let them go. If they return, they belong to you... And if they don't...?

Fuck that. No way, am I going to stand around here while she...*figures out her feelings*... I take a step forward, then stop. Wow, even my thoughts are dismissive of her feelings. And if I go after her...? I'd coerce her, bulldoze over her feelings, her choices... Hell, I'd ensure that she comes around to my way of thinking...and that... Fuck... This is not the time for my alphaholish, caveman-ish behavior. I mean, that's what I am. No excuses but... I hadn't become a surgeon without knowing when it was time to pull back.

I can't lose her.

I have to be strategic.

Have to trust...hope that she'll come back. And she will. She has to. I snatch up my phone from the corner of the island, dial my banker's number. When he comes on the line, I tell him to cease all further payments to her accounts. I am not surprised when he informs me that the money I'd sent through earlier had been returned electronically by her already. Yeah... Buttercup knows how to get a move on me.

I toss my phone aside, roll my shoulders. She'll return to me; she has to. The connection between us is too strong. She wouldn't ignore it... Would she? Nah! She'll get my message, get what I've been trying to communicate to her... Which is...that I can't live without her. She'll figure it out. She is smart, switched on. The love of my life has a razor-sharp mind. Surely, she'll glean what I was trying to communicate with her. Meanwhile... I glance toward the liquor cabinet. Only one thing a man can do when forced to bide his time. I stalk toward the bar, grab a bottle of whiskey and twist it open. I raise it to my lips.

57

Amelie

"Past pleasure doubles present pain,
  To sorrow adds regret,
  Regret and hope are both in vain,
  I ask but to — forget."

I take in the words scrawled on the board held by the homeless man. I'd ridden the elevator down, and walked out of the apartment building.

Every step I'd taken had echoed the thumping of my heart. I am doing this. Really doing this. I am leaving him. Good thing I had gone online and returned the money already. A few days ago, I'd checked my bank account and the zeroes in my account had brought home exactly how much I stood to gain from this relationship. I could pay off my debts, expand my business, ensure my parents are taken care of for the rest of their lives... And he'd always take me for granted. He'd known that I could be bought. Next time we came to an impasse... He'd know how to get his way. Throw more money my way...

And no, it's not only the money that binds us. There is so much more

—emotions and conflicts and a buzzing physical attraction that shows no sign of abating. There is so much there to build on... But the money...would always be a barrier... Unless he looks past it. Unless I take a risk, and leave him... Give him space to figure out his shit, while I do the same thing. I'd pushed forward, and had almost stumbled across the outstretched legs of the homeless guy.

"Excuse me," I mutter and step around him... Which is when I spot his shoes: tailormade, Italian leather, spotless, and polished to within an inch of its life. They seem familiar. Huh? I stare at them. Where have I seen them before?

"Pretty fancy, huh?" Homeless guy chortles, "Think these will impress the ladies?"

I glance up at his face. "I am sure they'd have an impact," I say. "Where did you get them?"

He frowns, "You mean, what's a man like me doing with shoes like these?"

My cheeks heat. Hell, that hadn't come out polite at all, had it? "I meant, uh... They seem familiar. Someone I know had a similar pair."

"Boyfriend?" He asks.

"He's...ah, currently no friend," I mutter.

"Ach!" he cackles, "Had a fall out with your man, huh?"

"Maybe, probably." I raise my shoulders, "He's an arrogant so-and-so. Know what I mean? He thinks he can buy anything."

"Not you, obviously." He nods.

"Exactly... See?" I flick my hair over my shoulder, "And he claims to love me."

"Do you?" he shoots back.

"Huh?" I frown, "Do I what?"

"Do you love him?"

"Yes," I reply. "Wait, I mean... No... I mean, yes...but..."

"No buts." He tilts his head up, pulls his legs up to sit cross-legged, "You gotta tell him that."

"I do?" I scowl.

"Absolutely," he jerks his chin, "better to take the risk and be sorry than to be a coward and—"

"Regret it," I complete his statement. "Yeah... Well..." I glance away. A pressure builds behind my eyes and my heart begins to race. What the hell is wrong with me? This constant back and forth... This not knowing my own mind... It's bloody tiring. So much easier to plan out a menu and bake. Even though the outcome of a dish is not completely in my hands, at least I can control the environment... Decide the ingredients. And if I change something, hell, I know the risks of what I'm doing. But with him...? I can't predict a thing. Not my reaction to him, not his ability to throw me off guard... Well, except for that sizzling attraction between us that throbs and ties us together. For better or for worse — that is one thing I can count on. The one ingredient that would never fail to liven up the dish... I mean, the relationship... I mean... I blink, turn to him. "I should, right?" I ask.

He lowers his board to the ground, then glances toward the apartment. "Go on, then."

I take in his features, those intelligent eyes undeniable, despite his unkempt whiskers.

"Who are you?" I frown. "What are you doing here?"

"All the world's a stage and we are but actors," he chuckles.

"First Byron, then Shakespeare?" I stare at him. "You have a thing for poets?"

"Or for pompous wankers who churned out pretentious shit."

"Sounds like someone I know," I mumble.

"Don't we all?" He rises to his feet, sketches an exaggerated bow, "Don't delay, young lady." He snatches his hat with the change inside and slams it on his dreadlocks. "Goodbye." He hauls the board over his shoulder and walks off.

"Bye." I turn, retrace my steps toward the apartment. What a strange man. He was well educated, no doubt about it. And his accent... I could have sworn he sounded almost posh. And when he'd smiled...his teeth were perfect. Which is bloody odd in England. I mean, when was the last time I'd met anyone with even teeth... Other than the alphahole... And the Seven...who had clearly spent a fortune on the dentist. But normal people like me... Hell... We can't afford that kind of dental work. So how had the homeless guy swung that, huh? I turn to call out, but the sidewalk is empty. Geez, he must have doubled his speed to get away from me or something. I shake my head. The shoes did fit him though. Chalk it up as one more good deed for Dr Grumpy McDick. He has his redeeming points... A lot of them, actually.

Too bad it isn't enough... Is it? I shake my head. *Stop overthinking this. Just march back for the last time and tell him how you feel.* As easy as baking banana bread, which would be done in double-quick time in his oven. Fine, fine... Don't think about his kitchen, or his equipment... No, definitely don't think about the tool he hides in his pants either. *Get on with it; don't back out, bitch.* I stomp inside the apartment, and head for the elevator door, which glides open. Shit, even the elements are working with me on this.

I reach the penthouse, push the door open and walk in. I cross the living room, pause only to place my satchel and handbag on the center table, then peek into the kitchen. There's no one there. Hmm. I pivot, head for the bedroom, when I spot movement. I pivot head toward the sliding doors at the far end of the living room, pulling them aside. I step outside and onto the terrace, walk another few steps and spot the hot tub... This one's sunken into the decking with steps leading down, and at the other end of it...is him. I'm drawn to him like chocolate to a clean surface... know what I mean? I pause at the tub.

He's sprawled in the water that froths around his waist, the bubbles covering the bottom half of his body. Not that I have any doubt about the state of his undress. He leans back, raises a bottle of whiskey. His biceps bulge and his shoulders flex. He brings the bottle to his mouth, swigs from it. The tendons of his throat move as he swallows.

I am instantly wet.

He raises his other hand, places a cigar between his lips. I rake my gaze over his features, watch him watch me with unblinking eyes, as I take another step forward. I reach the edge of the tub. The water writhes below me. My heartbeat writhes in my chest.

He glares at me from under hooded eyelids. He lowers the cigar, blows out a cloud of cigar smoke. The scent of cloves and spices, of darkness and lust, passion and fucking... Hell... I'll always associate the scent of cigar smoke with wild, out-of-my-head desire.

He doesn't move, doesn't say a word.

I shuffle closer, my toe brushing against something smooth. There's a plop as it falls in. I glance down to find an egg timer floating on the surface.

I bend my knees, reach over and scoop it up.

He glances down at the object, then up at my face. His lips twist, he swallows and opens his mouth, and I'm sure he's going to say something. Instead, he takes another swig from the bottle of whiskey. The skin across his knuckles stretches white... Huh? I peer across the distance and at his features... Lines radiate from the corners of his eyes, and the hollows under his cheekbones seem more pronounced. Why had I not noticed that before?

He keeps his gaze focused on my face, the skin around his mouth tightening. That's it—something's on his mind. But what? Why would the most confident man I have ever met seem unsure of himself.

"Why are you so on edge?" I laugh nervously. "I'd think you were going to pop a marriage proposal or something," I mutter, "if I didn't know you better."

His face pales. My gaze widens. I take in the way he holds onto the whiskey bottle. The skin of his knuckles stretch white. Then the bottle slips from his grasp, hits the decking and rolls away... "Fuck." He swears, then straightens. His lips twist. An expression I can't fathom grips his features.

"Holy shit." I gasp, "Is that what you are going to do...? I gulp. "No way. You aren't, are you?"

Again, he glares at the stupid egg timer I am holding. What the hell? I stare down at the curved object, raise it, fiddle around with it. I twist it and it comes apart in my hands, revealing something shiny, something with a perfectly-cut sapphire that winks back at me.

My throat dries. My heart begins to thud. "What...what is this?" I squeak.

"A fucking gummy bear," he growls, "what do you think it is?"

"I... I..." I glance at the ring, then back at him, then at the ring again.

"How... how long have you been planning this?"

"Since I met you?" He tilts his head, "Strike that. From before I met you. The ring was my grandmother's."

"Oh!"

"You mean oh, yes, don't you?" he drawls.

"Wait, wait." I draw in a breath. *Stay calm, don't lose it now.* Need time to think, just a bloody second here. I tip up my chin, train my gaze on him, "How did you rig the timer to accommodate it, considering I was gone for less than half an hour?"

He yawns.

"Of course. You repair clocks, so you could adjust a stupid egg timer, huh?" I pout.

"Not apologizing for the fact that I pulled off an almost-miracle, babe." He thrusts out his chest, "Besides it is Christmas."

"Wow," I stare. "Seems you're getting into the spirit of the season, after all?"

"As you are coming around to the idea of our wedding."

"Yes." I nod.

"So, it's settled then." He grins.

"What?" I shake my head. "No, no, no, I didn't mean it that way. I mean, not yet... I mean... What the hell!" I exclaim. "This can't be happening."

"It is." He shakes out his palm—the one with which he'd gripped the whiskey bottle.

"Did you hurt your good hand? I ask.

"I've been hurting in other places since I met you," he grumbles.

"Anyone ever tell you, you have the manners of an oaf?" I scowl.

"Only you, babe." He rises to his feet—the water pours off of those sculpted abs, his concave stomach, drips off of that spectacular cock. *Oh, my God!* I swallow, take a step back, stumble, drop the ring, let go of the pieces that formerly constituted the egg timer, swoop down, catch the ring. I straighten the ring, slip it onto my left ring finger. I blink, open my eyes in surprise. "It fits."

"Of course, it does," he snaps.

"Presumptuous, much?" I huff, turn my hand this way and that. The heart of the ring glows with silver sparks. Wow. My pulse thuds at my temples; my stomach bottoms out. OMFG, does this mean, what I think it does?

"You're marrying me," he growls. "What's so presumptuous about that?"

"I haven't said yes."

He looks at my hand then back at my face. "You're wearing the ring. Are you saying no?"

"You haven't asked...you...you...ass!" I yell.

He blows out a breath, stalks his way across the length of the sunken pool to where I stand. He glances into my eyes. Despite the fact that I am standing on a higher level, we are at the same height... That's how fucking big my alphahole is. I gulp; he frowns. His chest rises and falls, then he reaches out and takes my left hand.

58

———————

Weston

"I won't take no for an answer," I tell her.

She scowls, tugs at her hand. I hold on. *Fuck, get a grip, asshole. Stop thinking about yourself. Get rid of the fear that she'll refuse you and leave...* Nope, not this time. I'm not going to fuck this up, nope. I've conducted quadruple bypass surgeries... This...this should be a cakewalk... Not.

I shake my head, bring my other hand up, and enclose her slim palm between my much larger ones.

I clear my throat. She glances at me, and suddenly, my scalp feels too tight. My heart hammers and my muscles tense. I rotate my shoulders, bend my knee and press it into the side of the pool.

"Amelie," I peer up into her face, "will you be the chocolate to my whiskey, the caramel to my bourbon—?"

She blinks.

"—the spice to my tea, the fruit filling to my pie—"

Her lower lip trembles... *Huh? Is that a good sign?*

"—the butterscotch to my toffee," I raise one eyebrow, "the cookie to my coffee?"

She giggles, then slaps a hand over her mouth.

I allow a smirk to curl my lips, lower my head and brush my mouth over her knuckles, "Well?" I tilt my head up at her, "Amelie, will you marry me?"

"Not good enough," she replies.

"What?" I blink.

"You can do better than that."

"What the fuck?" I growl.

She shakes her hair from her face, "Go on, Mr, Alphahole. Why should I marry you?"

"Because I'll make you happy?"

"So can others."

"Because you can cook in that bloody kitchen with the oven I had installed specifically for you?"

"You...you did?" Her gaze widens. Damn, if I don't see heart-shaped little icons in place of her irises.

"It was nothing," I mumble. Why the hell had that popped out? Hadn't meant to blurt that out.

She looks away, then back at me. "What else?" she asks, her voice an octave lower than earlier. That's good. I am on the right track... *Go on, motherfucker, lay it out. It's now or never, you loser.*

"Because every time I see you, I can't see a way around fucking you, giving it to you until you're a whimpering gooey mess in my arms?"

"Oh!" She trembles. "Keep going," she says, her voice breathy.

I turn her palm face up in mine, bend and lick the skin between her fingers.

She shudders.

I drag my tongue down to her fingertip and kiss it.

"Because we're going to fuck right now in this pool, then on the decking, in the living room, in my bed, on the bloody kitchen island...on every surface in my home, and when the sun comes up tomorrow, we'll know every nook," kiss, "cranny," kiss, "crevasse of each other's bodies."

She makes a humming sound deep in her throat.

"You like that hmm?" I smirk.

"Much better," She agrees. "You're getting the hang of it, Mr. Alpha Claus, but it's not enough."

"You're right," I agree.

"I am?" She frowns.

"I haven't told you yet, how I'm going to walk you places, my Buttercup, up the aisle, into each day of our future lives...ease you into bed every night, wake you up with my tongue inside your melting pussy every morn—"

She chokes out a laugh, "And you were doing so well."

"Right?" I grimace, "I can't help myself, my sweet Cookie. When I see you, I lose sight of myself. When I scent you, I ache to be inside of you. And when I see you in pain," I swallow, "I want to turn the world upside down until I soothe it all away."

"Oh," she stutters, "that...that was romantic."

"I'm not done yet."

"No?"

"Not even remotely." I allow my lips to curve, mirror the happiness that filters through her gaze, "I'll take care of you, I'll love you, shield you from the elements, ease obstructions from your path—"

She frowns.

"Because that would be my prerogative." I declare.

"If that's not what I want?"

"We could discuss it," I say slowly.

"We could?"

"Perhaps."

Her forehead creases and she tugs on her hand again. My heart rate gallops. "I won't do anything you don't want me to," I add.

"Hmm."

"I promise." I hold up my right palm, "We can fight over it, then kiss and have hot make-up sex."

"As long as you don't steamroll me into agreeing." She frowns.

"As long as we agree to disagree," I say at the same time.

She huffs.

I twine my fingers through hers, "Come on, babe. Allow me to help; it's what I do best."

"I want to build my business on my own merit, you know?"

"And I understand and completely get that...but if I can pave the way so you spend your time on the actual creation and less on fighting through roadblocks?"

She shuffles her feet, then glances at me. "For every pound you spend on paying off my debts, you'll also put one toward a scholarship for someone less privileged who wants to study baking at a school of their choice."

"Done," I blow out a breath. "You can manage this each year

through FOK media, a division of 7A investments that was set up for exactly such causes."

She blinks. "You agree?"

I straighten my shoulders, "If that makes you happy..."

"This makes me happy." She sinks down onto the decking, sticks her legs into the hot tub and, parts her legs. Finally, fuck! I move into the 'V' between her thighs.

"You make me fucking happy," I hold her gaze, peer into those baby blues which mean more to me than life itself. "It was a time bomb," I say. "They wrapped a timebomb around me and left me in a locked room for days."

Her chin wobbles, her face pales. "The kidnappers?" she whispers. "They did that?"

I nod. "If I so much as moved or breathed wrong it could go off, so they said."

"What...what happened next?"

"My kidnapper... I couldn't see his face because I was blindfolded... Which didn't help, because I could imagine the moving hands of the clock in my mind." I swallow; my fingers tremble.

She grips my hand, and warmth chases away the ice that had crept into my veins. I focus on her beautiful face, those flushed features. "He kept coming in and torturing me, sometimes beating on my legs, sometimes hooking me up to electricity. Each session was timed, it lasted precisely an hour, all of which was counted down precisely by the clock." I chuckle, the sound harsh. "The torture went on for days I thought, but it was really only for forty-eight hours, so I found out later."

She gasps, "Oh, Wes." She places her palm over my chest, "Baby, I'm so sorry."

I focus on her gaze, the silverly sparks in her eyes. "That last time..."I force out the words, "he said he'd be back in twelve hours. I counted down the time, past the twelve hour mark. He was late. I knew then, he was going to kill me. He came in and started raging at me, told me he was going to kill me. He hooked me up to the electrodes. I sensed him move away to start the electricity. I knew there was no way I was going to survive that session. I prayed that my heart would give out before the pain got too bad. He switched on the electricity, and left."

"Wes, no." She throws her arms about me, "Oh my God, that's terrible." She presses her cheek into my chest and moisture dampens my skin. She's weeping, for me? Something inside of me dissolves. I fit my knuckle under her chin, tip up her head.

"The cops arrived within minutes of that... They broke through, switched off the electricity, had their best bomb disposal expert dismantle the one around my chest. Turns out, it was a hoax all along."

"What?" She gasps, "I mean it's a good thing, but still... That bastard."

"Yeah." I cup her cheek, "I escaped with no outward scars... I was lucky, unlike some of the Seven."

"It's why you guys are so close."

"Close? Ha!" I smirk, "The only person I want to be close to is you, baby."

I lower my head, brush my lips over hers. "You're welcome, by the way," I whisper.

"For what?"

"For the three words you were going to tell me earlier, but didn't, and which you are going to reward me with now."

"Reward you?" She pouts.

"Yep." I reach down, lower the zipper on her jeans. She grips my shoulders, rises up, and I yank down the pants and panties, ease them over her hips, then step back and pull them off of those gorgeous legs. I stare at the pink flesh between those beautiful thighs. "For the orgasms I am going to bring you to in the next hour."

"So sure of yourself. If you think you can trick me into—"

I step between her legs, hook her knees over my arms, pull them up and over my shoulders, then notch my dick against her pussy, "Into?"

"Saying that I want you—"

I lunge forward, impale her in one motion. She stutters, then her pussy clamps around my dick.

"Say it," I growl.

"I... I need you," she gasps.

I pull out of her, stay poised at the entrance to her channel. "Look at me," I pant.

She raises her head, sears me with those beautiful blue eyes.

"Princess," I lower my head to hers, share my breath with hers, brush my lips over hers "I want to hear you scream out those three words." I kick my hips forward, sink into her.

She curves her spine, throws her head back, "I love you," she yells. "Love you, love you... Only you."

My vision tunnels; blood beats at my temples. I haul her to me, kiss her hard. Then, I begin to fuck her in earnest—thrust into her, bury myself in her sweet pussy again and again. Bring my arms around her, pull her to me as, with a last ferocious drive of my hips, I sink inside of her. "Come," I growl.

59

Amelie

His command slices through my mind. His voice echoes in my subconscious. Heat from his body slams into me, sinks into my blood. Everything in me snaps tight, then I shatter. Moisture gushes out from between my thighs as the climax sweeps me up, higher and higher. I throw my head back and scream, *I love you, I love you.* Or maybe I just chant that in my head.

Black specks flicker at the edges of my vision. Above me, his shoulders draw back, his chest muscles harden, his body shudders, his cock thickens inside of me, then with a harsh groan, he comes inside of me. I slump against his chest, am half aware that he hauls me up in his arms, steps out of the hot tub and carries me inside. I must have snoozed, for when I open my eyes next, I am tucked into his side in his bed. I rub my cheek into his hair-roughened chest. "I would have told you anyway," I mumble.

"Hmm?" He rubs lazy circles over my upper arm.

I glance up to find him sprawled against the sheets, eyes closed. He has one hand flung behind his neck. A slight smile curves his lips. So, this is how it is to see the brute relax... In his den, surrounded by his possessions, in the arms of his woman. *His woman.* I reach up, cup his cheek.

"I love you," I whisper.

He smirks. "I know."

I hit his shoulder.

He laughs, cracks open his eyelids, "I adore you, Princess."

"Oh." I open and close my mouth, shake my head.

"What?" he grunts.

"Nothing."

"Say it," he drawls, "I promise I won't bite."

I purse my lips, scan his relaxed features, "I can't get used to this emo version of you."

He sighs, "No pleasing some people."

"Not that I don't want you to be nice to me and all that," I explain.

"Actually, I think you don't." He grins, then lowers his gaze to my breasts.

"What's that supposed to mean?"

"It means." He flips me over onto my back and my breath hitches. His eyes gleam and his big shoulders seem to swell further, if that is even possible. He glances up at the headboard, then back at me.

"Don't you dare," I huff.

"You challenging me?"

"Maybe," I mumble as a frisson of heat runs up my spine.

He glances around, then rolls off of the bed. I lower my arms. He turns to me, points his finger, and says, "Stay."

"Bossy," I grumble.

"You ain't seen nothin' yet."

He stalks over to the walk in closet. I hear him rummaging around, then silence. A few seconds later he walks out.

I gasp. "Oh my."

"Like it?" He stands there in his scrubs. The green material molds to his torso, outlines the cut abs of his chest, tents at his crotch—ha! so what's new?—and clings to his powerful thighs.

"You look—"

"Hot?"

"I was going to say yummy."

"Is everything a food reference to you?" He laughs.

"Is everything about getting the last word with you?"

He tilts his head, "Except with you."

"Oh?"

"You know it's true, babe. After all, I let you get away with chocolate."

"Someone had to change your mind about the devil's food." I chuckle.

"So you decided to feed it to the devil himself?"

"Are you the devil?"

"Where you are concerned, I am your lover and your protector, your lord and master, your to-be husband."

I curl the fingers of my left hand around the ring, "I haven't said yes to marrying you yet."

"Oh, you are about to." He raises his hand, and I spot the black ties he holds in his grasp.

"What...what's that for?"

He grins at me and his eyes glint. He stalks around the bed, then places his knee on the bed, throws his leg over my waist and straddles me.

"Wes." I draw in a breath.

"Trust me, Cookie." He leans over and ties my wrists to the headboard. Then rolls off of the bed and walks away again. What the hell?

He returns holding an egg timer in his hand.

"How many of those things do you have?"

"Enough." He grins. "Since you seem to have a penchant for the blasted thing, I figured I'd buy enough to see us through the rest of our lives together."

My heart stutters. OMG, did he use all the words that I've wanted to hear from him? "You're awfully confident." I tip up my chin.

"Nothing I can't deliver on, Princess." He winds up the egg timer. The ticking down of the timer fills the room.

"Doesn't that sound trigger you?" I ask.

"I'm changing it's association in my head." He places the timer on the side table, then climbs onto the bed and straddles me. "Close your eyes." he raises the second necktie he holds in his hand.

"B... but." My heart begins to race. My mouth dries. I can't stop the trembling that runs up my spine. "Wes."

"Trust me." He leans in and kisses me, a hard reassuring kiss, that sinks into my blood. I am instantly wet and he hasn't even started.

He peers in my features, "Okay?"

"Okay."

He leans over and wraps the tie around my eyes. Darkness engulfs me. My senses pop. The ticking of the timer heats my blood. "W...Wes?" I whine.

"I'm here." He cups my cheek, then his lips meet mine again. He licks my mouth, then whispers. "I forgot to tell you one thing."

"What?"

"You won't come until the timer rings."

60

Weston

"Not fair," she gasps, craning her neck toward me.

"All's fair in bed." I lower my head and kiss her breast. She moans; the sound travels down my spine and my guts churn. My heart begins to race. I cup her other breast and my fingers tremble.

The ticking of the clock grows louder; my stomach hollows out. Maybe this had not been a good idea. I close my mouth around her nipple and bite down.

She gasps.

My groin hardens.

I drag my mouth down her stomach, to her belly button, flick my tongue in and out of the indentation.

She moans. Her thighs tremble. I grip the curve of her waist, nibble kisses to the apex between her legs. I blow on her pussy and her body bucks, "Weston," she pleads.

The sound of her voice slices through the noise in my head. This time it is about her. Not about what the bastard did to me. Not about how he'd tied the ticking timebomb to my chest and left me. I hook my arms under her knees, pull her legs over my shoulders.

I smooth my hands down her trembling thighs, and cup her pussy,

"Mine," I growl, "only mine." I lower my head, swipe my tongue up her lower lips.

She whines.

I curve my tongue around the swollen bud of her clit; she shivers. Slide my hand down to squeeze her arse cheek.

Her entire body shudders.

I slide my finger inside her backhole; she bucks.

I insert my tongue inside her channel, ease it in and out of her. Bring my free hand to her clit and pinch it.

"Oh, hell, oh, hell." She digs the heels of her feet into my back, thrusts her pelvis up and into my face. The sweet scent of her tugs at my nostrils, the warmth of her juices coats my tongue. My belly clenches and my dick lengthens as the ticking of the clock counts down in the background.

I need more, more.

"Wes?"

The tick-tock of the clock grows louder. My fingers clench; a bead of sweat slides down my back. I drag my mouth up and to her face and kiss her deeply. She opens her mouth to me, and I thrust my tongue inside. I drink from her, that addicting, honeyed essence of her, mixed with the taste of her cum. My belly trembles, I dig my knees into bed, ease a finger inside her channel and bear down.

"Weston," she screams, "Oh, my God, Wes."

More, I need more. I need her warmth, her happy-go-lucky nature, her sass and fire. I need all of her, subsumed into me. I need her to ground me. I release her lips, then reach up and tear the blindfold from her.

She blinks, then her gaze narrows on me.

"What's wrong?" she asks. "Wes?"

"Nothing." I mumble.

"Something is."

"I need..." I frown.

"Me, take me, Wes." Her chest heaves, "Please, baby, come inside me."

Her blue eyes gaze into mine, the silver sparks in their depths similar to the sapphire I'd bought her... Except she is here, vital, real... Nothing else in my past, or my future, matters. Only her.

I loosen the drawstring on my pants, then grasp my dick, and notch it against her wet opening.

"Amelie." I brush my lips over hers. "I love you," I say. "I love it when you smile at me. I love it even more when I am the reason for your smile."

Those sappy words? Yep, that's me. Alphahole extraordinaire felled by a woman who is the sassiest, brightest, most special woman I have ever met.

"Oh, Wes," she sighs, "I love you too."

I slide inside her; she trembles. I stay there, allowing her to adjust to my size. I ease my tongue inside her mouth, tangle my tongue with hers, bring my other hand up to untie her bindings. She wraps her arms about my shoulders, pulls me closer. I prop myself on one elbow to keep my weight off of her. I hold her gaze, keep the connection, as I pull out of her, then thrust back in. Her pussy clenches around me. She digs her fingers into the back of my scalp, tugs on my hair. My cock jerks, thickens, and I begin to fuck her in earnest. In and out of her, as I slide a finger inside her backhole.

She groans and I swallow the sound, continue to kiss her, as I kick my hips forward, impale her to the bed. My balls harden, a pressure building in my groin. I don't stop. I thrust into her, again and again. She arches her spine, pushes up to meet me. Locks her ankles around me, flattens her breasts against my chest planes, strains against me, consumes me.

The ticking of the clock fades. I tear my mouth from hers, "I'll never get enough of you. Not until every inch of you is married to every inch of me, and not even then. Not until I've broken you completely, and myself. Until every part of you bears the imprint of me, every cell in your body recognizes that you are mine. Mine. Only mine, you get me?"

She nods. "Only yours," she whispers. "Always yours, love you Wes—"

I kick my hips forward and bury myself inside her with such force that the entire bed shakes. The headboard slams into the wall; somewhere something crashes to the floor. The timer rings as I growl, "Come with me, Princess."

Her mouth opens in a silent cry. She holds my gaze as she shatters, as her body trembles under me, as my orgasm takes hold and I come inside of her.

Her chest heaves, sweat beads her upper lip, and I bend down and lick it up. "Yum." I smack my lips. "How the hell do you manage to taste so sweet?"

"How the hell do you manage to turn sex into an orgy each and every time, my love?"

"Hmm." I bump my neck to hers. "Love it when you talk dirty to me, babe."

"Love it when you—" She blinks. "Did you hear that?"

I frown, "What?"

"Did somebody call your name?"

I angle my head, "Don't hear anything."

I reach down to kiss her again, when, "Weston, where the fuck are you, arsehole?" Damian's voice reaches me from the direction of the doorway.

I groan, "The fuck?"

She giggles, "Looks like your friends decided to pay you a visit on Christmas day?"

"Something I can do without." I grouse.

"Weston... Hey...oops. Sorry, man," Damian apologizes.

I turn, glare at where Damian stands in the doorway, face averted.

"I didn't see anything. I promise."

"Fuck off," I growl.

"A bit too late, old chap."

"Where the fuck is the wanker?" Another voice—Arpad's calls out.

"If he thinks he can spend Christmas on his own, he's got another think coming. What's he up to— Oh hell, did we interrupt something?" *Is that Edward?*

I grab a pillow, throw it in the direction of the doorway. "Back the fuck off, you tossers."

"Sorry."

"Didn't mean any harm."

"You ah—finish what you started. We'll be at your bar."

The voices fade.

"Close the fucking door behind you," I call out.

The door slams shut.

This is what happens when your friends have unrestricted access to your apartment, something I intend to rectify at the first opportunity. I draw in a breath, glance down at my fiancée, "Where were we, babe?"

"We need to get out there." She stabs a finger in my chest.

I lower my head to hers, "In good time."

61

Amelie

I walk into Weston's living room just as the doorbell rings.

Weston—who's changed into slacks and shirt— opens it as Saint, Sinclair and Jace walk in carrying a massive Christmas tree wrapped in a net. Weston leads them to the far corner of the room, where they cut off the net and proceed to set it up.

Weston turns to me, crooks a finger. I frown; he smirks. I mentally throw up my hands, walk over to join him. He wraps his arm around me tugs me into his side.

"Did you plan this?" I ask.

"What?" He grins.

"All this." I jerk my chin toward the Christmas tree currently being set up by his three friends, then to the bar where the other three are having an argument about the latest cricket scores.

The doorbell rings again, then the door is pushed open, and Isla walks in, followed by Sienna—Jace's wife, who pushes a pram with their newborn son.

Victoria follows her.

She smooths her hands down the green dress, as always, looking like she's stepped off a catwalk. She pauses halfway into the room, when Saint looks up. He closes the distance between them and pulls her into a kiss. His large hand covers her stomach protectively. Yep, these two are next in line to have a baby.

"Oh! How romantic." Isla waves a hand in front of her face. She turns to me and her face cracks into a big smile. "Well then, did you two make up your differences?"

"What differences?" Weston smirks, pulling me in for a kiss.

She chuckles, then her gaze widens, "Oh wow!" She gasps, then walks over to us, "Is that what I think it is?" She stares down at my hand.

I hold out my palm. She grabs my fingers and squeezes. "Ouch," I gripe.

"That's one big-ass ring, you bitch." She leans back, glowers at me, "You were holding out on me?"

"Relax," I assure her, "It happened only a few hours ago. He proposed—"

She squeals so loudly that everyone else in the room turns to us.

"Omigod, omigod." She claps her hands, " This is awesome! Another wedding to plan."

"Ah...no." I shake my head.

"What do you mean?" she asks.

"No way, am I going in for the whole song and dance of a society wedding."

"But Amelie," she whines, "you only get married once."

"Which is why it's going to be something low key, and romantic... Something with a specially-crafted menu of desserts."

Weston, bends his head. "Will it have cock pops?" he whispers.

"Chocolate cockups," I correct him.

"What-fucking-ever," He grumbles, "as long as you bake them only for us, and only you eat them."

"Possessive, hmm?"

"Just don't want anyone else's mouth on my penis, except yours."

"You got a deal." I grin.

"What did I miss?" Summer flounces in, hair flowing around her. She's in a festive onesie with glitter threaded through almost every inch of it.

"Woman, you're too bright for me." Sinclair prowls toward her. He makes a grab for her, but she evades him and giggles. He swoops down, hauls her close and she melts into his arms. They kiss, until her phone begins to ring. She tries to pull free, but he doesn't let her go. "Sinner," she mumbles against his mouth, "I need to get this."

"Fuck it," he responds.

"It may be Karma. I've been hoping that she'd call."

He releases her lips, but holds her in the circle of his arms.

She pulls out her phone from her bag, "Hello?" she says. Her face brightens. "Karma!" she exclaims. "Where have you been? I was beginning to get worried."

She listens for a second, raises her gaze to Sinner.

He frowns down at her. *Everything okay?* He mouths.

She raises her shoulders. "You sure, you're fine?" she asks, then listens to the reply. "So you won't be home for the New Year either?"

Her lips curve down. "Aww honey, I miss you." She listens some more. "Well if that's what you want..." She tips up her chin, a worried set to her features. "Right, okay. Well I'll see you soon, I hope. You take care, sweetheart, oh! And Merry Christmas." She cuts the call.

"How is Karma?" I call out to her. "When is she coming back?"

Summer turns to me, "She sounded... Fine... I guess." Her forehead furrows. "She's staying on in Sicily for a while longer."

"Ooh." Isla rubs her hands together, "That's so romantic. Maybe her new boyfriend doesn't want to let go of her, huh?"

"Maybe," Summer says slowly. "I wish she'd come home. I want to meet him, you know? Make sure he's treating her right."

"I'm sure she's fine, babe." Sinclair kisses the top of her head. "He's probably being possessive, that's all."

She snorts, "You should know."

"You bet." Sinclair smirks, "Once you find the woman of your dreams, you never let her out of your sight, or out of your bed. You make sure you keep her satisfied enough that she never wants to leave your side; you —"

"Enough." She turns in his arms, slaps a hand on his mouth, "Honestly Sin, you have no filter."

"Not when it comes to you, I don't." He grins down at her.

"But when it comes to you, I know exactly what turns you on."

His eyes gleam, "And what's that?"

"You're all about the chase, my love."

"Am I now?" His lips curl.

"Yep." She tips up her head, "Like now —"

She yanks back in his grasp. His grasp loosens, and she pivots and takes off toward the inner rooms.

"What the —" He seems startled. "You come back here Summer, and finish what you started," he growls.

"Not happening." She laughs, "You going soft, Sin? Worried you've lost the edge? Bet you can't catch me." She disappears around the corner.

His jaw drops, "Why you little..." He takes off in hot pursuit.

There's another knock on the front door; it swings open, then Julia walks in. She glances around the room, then spots me. Her face brightens.

"Jules." I wave at her, "What are you doing here?"

"I invited her." Weston brushes his lips over my hair. Seems Dr. Alpha Claus can't keep his hands off of me, huh? I snuggle into his side. "Thanks," I say. "And by that, I assume you knew this little get together was happening?"

"I had an inkling."

"Is that my Christmas gift?" Damian draws abreast. I look up to find his gaze arrested by Julia.

"She's my friend," I warn him.

He tilts his head, a considering expression on his features. "She's hot," He declares.

"She's off-limits to you, douche," Weston glowers at him.

"Shouldn't the woman have a say in that?" Damian interrupts.

"As long as Amelie gives you the go ahead..." Weston raises his shoulders.

Damian turns to me, "Well?" He smiles, "What do you say?"

"Do you promise to treat her right?" I scan his features. "Promise you won't hurt her."

"I promise to treat her however she wants me to." He smirks.

"Hmm." I frown. "Julia doesn't suffer fools gladly."

"And, rock stars?" His grin widens, "what does she think of them?

"Why don't you ask me directly?" Julia's voice interrupts us.

Damian pivots to face her, "Better still, how about I show you...?"

To find out what happens next read Damian and Julia's story in Marrying the Billionaire Single Dad. This book also features Weston and Amelie's wedding.

Turn the page to read The Christmas Surprise Hunter & Zara's story

THE CHRISTMAS SURPRISE

L. STEELE

1

Zara

"No."

"What do you mean, no?" The man sitting next to me in the driver's seat of his car, the man who represents so much of what I hate on every level, glares at me.

"Exactly that." I glance out my window. And why did I agree to him taking me out to dinner? Why didn't I turn him down? Why did I rise to his challenge when he asked earlier if I was scared? I may find him attractive, but I'll never find him appealing—not even if he were the last man on this planet. And especially not when he stands for everything I hate.

Hunter Whittington is the very embodiment of entitlement. He comes from old world money and has been groomed to take his place as the Prime Minister of the United Kingdom. He belongs to that class of Oxbridge educated, elitist, stuck-up, pain-in-the arse, wankers who thinks it's their right to rule and dominate. A grumphole who's highly popular with the old-boy's network, perceived as cunning, ruthless and lethal, while also appearing to not give a damn about anything. Well, except for being very insistent I attend this dinner with him.

"I thought we were agreeing to a truce for this evening?" Mr. Posh-tosh drawls.

I toss my hair over my shoulder. "I agreed to have dinner with you; doesn't mean I'm going to be all docile and pleasant."

"Pity, because when you smile, you're actually quite charming."

I scoff, "That the best you can do? Your compliments leave me cold."

"When I compliment you, you'll know it," he drawls. "That was simply me, stating a fact."

"And this is me, stating that I'm already regretting being here with you."

He flips on the indicator, then turns off the motorway and onto a secondary road. He's rolled up his shirt sleeves, and the veins pop in his arms. Oh, yeah, I forgot to mention that the arrogant prick has very well-defined forearms with sculpted muscles covered with tanned skin and a peppering of dark hair. My fingers tingle.

How would it be to trail my fingers over them and feel the scrape of those rough strands against my skin? How would it be to have his blunt fingertips trail up my arm, over my shoulder down the curve of my breasts and—why am I thinking along these lines? Sure, Hunter Whittington has the sort of features that wouldn't look out of place on the cover of GQ, his build resembles that of a Hollywood action hero, and his broad shoulders invite me to snuggle into his chest. He makes my knees go weak, makes my throat dry, makes a pulse flare to life between my thighs… None of which negates the fact that he stands for the kinds of values I've always hated. He's an egotistical wanker who was born into one of the richest families in the country. The kind of family with bloodlines related to royalty. The kind who'd never have to work for a day in his life if he didn't want to. The kind who had everything handed to him on a silver platter. The kind who is the exact opposite of how I grew up. Plus, I hated him on sight.

The first time I met him was at 7A Club, an outfit run by JJ Kane and Sinclair Sterling, two of the most powerful men in the country, and founders of the club intended to help identify talent and invest in them. They invited me to be a founding member, and I was the only woman at the table. Given the career I've chosen, that's not unusual. What threw me, though, was the visceral reaction I had to this man. How I took an instant dislike to him and he toward me. How we barely managed to be civil to each other in that first meeting. It was only exacerbated when we met at work.

He filed his candidacy to run for the position of Prime Minister, and I'm the fixer. A well-known PR spin-doctor who the country's tastemakers—from influencers to politicians—come to when they need to salvage their reputations. Which makes things messy, to say the least. Because, no way, can I personally be involved in a scandal.

His ride to Downing Street depends on his track record being free of scandal. And my job depends on my not becoming the scandal. I need to always be seen as an impartial party by the media. My ability to manipulate the news depends on that. Which means, I can't let my association with him be seen as anything but professional; i.e. I need to be courteous toward him when we meet in person.

If the media gets wind of just how much we hate each other, it will only become the topic of debate. Not to mention, hating someone at a personal level never bodes well. It would only encourage people to see me as someone who can't be objective when it came to those in the news, and I can't afford that. I've built my career as someone who is never pulled into media clashes, and I need to stay that way. Which means, I need all of my wits about me. Ergo, I need to defuse this...situation between Hunter and me that's becoming increasingly untenable.

It's why, when he asked me to dinner so we could try to come to some kind of an understanding, I agreed. It's not like I had a choice, either. When my instinct was to turn him down, he challenged me by saying, perhaps I was too scared to spend time with him one-on-one, that I might find I actually like him. I knew I was being played, that he was appealing to my competitive spirit. And yet, I couldn't say no. That's my weakness. I never can resist a confrontation.

So here I am, in the car that he's parked in front of a building set back from the road.

Behind us, the security car—with his security detail—that has been following us, comes to a stop. Another pulls ahead and parks in front. I gather my things and reach for the handle on my door, but Hunter has already walked around to hold it open. My stomach folds in on itself. A stutter swirls about my chest. So annoying that he has to shove his good manners in my face.

I slide out, then straighten. "You didn't have to do that. I can open my own doors." I scowl.

"My mother taught me better."

I sniff, brush past him and head up the path leading to the restaurant without waiting for him. Footsteps follow as his long legs eat up the distance. He walks past me and is holding the door to the restaurant open by the time I reach it. I scowl up at him, then step through the entrance and up the short hallway. I reach the restaurant and pause. The lighting is dim, and the walls are painted a pale ivory. Both sides of the restaurant are glass walls. To my right, past the glass wall, is what seems to be a forest of bamboo trees. And beyond the glass wall on my left is a manmade fountain. The entire effect is soothing, like being in a Zen space. Strangely, all of the tables are empty.

"Where is everyone?"

"Everyone who matters is here." He takes my coat, hands it over to a maître d' who materializes out of nowhere, then shrugs off his own jacket and gives it to the same man. He guides me to the table in the center of the room—to the only table set with silverware and candles. He holds out my chair and I slide in. There's a third chair set on one side of the table between us.

"Is there someone else joining us?" I frown.

"That's for your bag."

Eh? I blink, then lower my eyebrows. "Care to explain?"

"I'm aware of how much you love your accessories, especially your shoes and purses. And I know you'd never place your bag on the floor. And putting it on the table is simply gauche, so—" He raises a shoulder.

"So, you arranged for an extra chair for my Birkin?"

"Was I wrong?"

"You were..." I hesitate. I don't want to admit he's right. That he correctly anticipated that I do take great care of my shoes and my handbags. They're an extension of me. They project who I am to the world. They are more than a brand statement; they are a declaration of how much I value myself. Somehow, I hadn't expected this…uppity, almost-royalty twat to understand that. But in one fell swoop, he's done that and more. Probably just a lucky guess. Maybe I'm reading too much into it. I place my handbag on the chair and tip up my chin. "Thanks," I murmur.

"You're welcome." He inclines his head.

I glance about the restaurant again. "So, we're the only ones here?"

"And the bodyguards."

In my peripheral vision, I spot my security detail positioning themselves at strategic points in corners around the room and standing by the entrance. It's dim enough that their black suits blend with the shadows. Only, I can't forget they're there, of course. It's a necessary evil I've lived with since I took on this position.

"You know I don't mean them, either."

"There's also the service staff." He waves a hand in the air, and as if by magic, a waiter materializes next to him with a bottle of champagne.

"Are we celebrating something?" I scowl.

"You agreed to have dinner with me —"

"I agreed to give you two hours to convince me why I shouldn't hate the idea of you" —he begins to speak, and I raise a finger— "of which, you now have eighty minutes left."

He curls his lips. "Are you always this…blinkered?"

"Are you always this…carefree?" I snap.

His grin widens. "Appearances can be deceptive."

"You don't say."

He arches an eyebrow at the waiter who pops the cork on the champagne. The sound ricochets about the space, emphasizing, again, that we are the only ones here.

"You still didn't tell me where everyone else is," I murmur.

The waiter pours the bubbly into my glass, then Hunter's. He places the bottle in the ice bucket perched on a stand next to the table that I only now notice. Then he fades away into the darkness.

"Given the potential speculation seeing the two of us together could cause, naturally, I had to find a solution to take you out to dinner in a public space while ensuring we had privacy."

"Ergo, you used your money and influence to buy out the place?"

"I simply asked the owner, who happens to be a friend, if he could accommodate us. And he did."

"Is it always this easy for you? To wave your hand and have all of your needs met? To incline your head and have minions jump to do your bidding? To ask and always receive?"

"Except with you."

He narrows his blue-green gaze on me from across the expanse of the table. The candlelight highlights the golden-brown specks in the depths of his eyes and haloes his dark hair, turning it almost blue. The hollows under his cheekbones seem more pronounced, the dip in his chin seems more delicious.

I try to tear my gaze from his, but it's as if he holds me in a tractor beam. Awareness tugs on and stretches the air between us. My heart begins to race. This is ridiculous. So, he's good-looking. I knew that already. What I hadn't realized is that hidden behind that polished mask he presents to the world is an untamed animal. A beast lying in wait to unleash that darkness inside of him. An edginess, a sharp wickedness that I never would've guessed he'd be capable of, but which I sense now lapping at the restraints that he's placed on himself.

I curl my fingers around the stem of my champagne glass. "I didn't say I wanted champagne."

"You love champagne. It's your drink of choice," he declares.

My eyebrows shoot up. "And you guessed this, how?"

"Nothing a little bit of research didn't reveal."

I stiffen. "You had me investigated?"

"Something you already knew about." He continues, "As you did me."

I blink, then surprise myself when laughter tumbles out from between my lips. "Touché." I raise my glass.

He seems taken aback, himself. Then his lips curve up in a smile that's so open, so real that something flutters deep inside. It's probably ripples of hunger, that's all. I had very little for lunch and no breakfast. That's the reason my stomach seems to be bottoming out.

"Also, your acting skills need leveling up."

"Excuse me?"

"You knew you were being followed, considering you gave my investigator the slip a few times."

I raise a shoulder. "So, get a better investigator."

This time it's he who barks out a laugh. "Keep up this banter, and I'll begin to think it's our brand of foreplay."

"You wish," I scoff.

His grin widens. "Of course, the fact that you evaded the detective I had on you makes me wonder what you have to hide."

The blood drains from my features, then I tip up my chin. "Maybe I have a lover."

"No, you don't."

I pull back my shoulders. "You seem awfully confident about that, Minister."

He stares at me. "Why is that so sexy coming from you?"

Heat flushes my skin, and my mouth dries. Why is it so hot to hear him say that particular four-letter word? Why is the thought of this man talking filthy to me such a turn on? I toss my hair over my shoulder, then tip up my chin. "Hold your horses. I only called you, Minister, not *Prime Minister*, which you're not—"

"—yet," he adds smoothly, then narrows his gaze. "You can't belong to anyone else."

"Oh?"

He nods. "You're mine, Zara, and I'll do everything in my power to make you accept that."

My belly quivers. My pussy clenches. I feel the tickling sensation between my legs that tells me I'm getting turned on, and I squeeze my thighs together in an attempt to soothe away the itch between them. Why is his declaration of intent so erotic? Why is the focus in his eyes as he fixes his gaze on me, and only me, make me feel like I won the lottery by becoming the cynosure of his attention?

I square my shoulders and grip the stem of my flute glass tighter. "And if you can't?" I tip up my chin. "

"I've never lost... And I don't intend to start now." He touches his glass to mine. "To us."

"There is no us," I scoff.

"Not yet."

"Excuse me?" I widen my gaze. "I'm not sure I heard you correctly."

"Oh, you did. You just don't want to admit it."

He brings the flute to his lips and takes a sip of his champagne. The tendons of his throat move as he swallows. My pulse rate speeds up.

Stupid. This is stupid—really stupid. I underestimated him. I thought I hated him. Oh, subconsciously, I'd noticed how my body reacted to his nearness, but I'd simply set that to one side. I'm not the kind who will allow my desires to lead me. Not after I've worked so hard my entire life to get to where I am. To break stereotypes. To make a difference to my community and to my country. This is what I've always wanted. This is why I studied so hard, why I got a scholarship to study law, then started my own PR firm. Why I've been so focused on my goals, to the exclusion of everything else. Why I accepted his challenge to spend time with him. I was confident I'd come out on top of our encounter. But now, I'm not so sure. And one thing I'm not is stupid. I know when to stage a strategic retreat. "Excuse me, but I have to leave."

I place my glass of champagne on the table and begin to rise to my feet, but he swoops out his hand and grabs my hand. Electricity shoots out from the point of contact. My breath catches in my chest. I look at where his fingers are wrapped about my wrist, then glance up to find his gaze locked on my face. Some of the color seems to have drained from his features. He releases me, and I sit back down. We stare at each other. The silence stretches.

Then the waiter wheels in a cart of food. What the—? He ordered ahead and decided to order for me, as well? Overbearing wanker. The waiter places a dish in front of me, then another in front of Hunter before, once more, retreating. All this time, we haven't taken our gazes off of each other. My throat closes. My pulse thuds at my temples. Moisture pools between my legs, and I clench my pussy and wriggle around in my seat.

"That..." He inclines his head and smirks. "That is what I'm talking about."

"What?" I laugh, or at least try to, but all that emerges is a thready sound.

"You sensed it, same as I did. This chemistry that sizzles between us."

"We've only met a few times in person."

"And yet, every time I enter a room with you in it, my gaze instantly finds you."

Heat flushes my cheeks, but I manage to school my features into an expression of nonchalance. "Not my fault." I raise a shoulder.

"Don't shrug it off. If we don't address this" —he points to the space between us— "it's only going to build and become so monumental, it'll hurt something or someone. Possibly, both of us."

I pretend to yawn; except when I pat my mouth, my fingers are shaking. "I have no idea what you mean."

His eyebrows draw down, and for a second, he looks disappointed. "Funny, I had you pegged as the kind of woman who wouldn't hesitate to speak the truth, no matter how difficult."

"I'm also someone who knows when I'm better off ignoring the obvious."

"So, you'd rather lie to yourself than face the fact that the chemistry between us is explosive?"

"You said it; not me." I bite the inside of my cheek.

"I have a better idea. A way in which we can both be truthful to ourselves and walk away from this with our careers intact."

"Oh, so you do understand how dangerous it is for the two of us to even be seen together, let alone having dinner?"

"Which is why I've ensured privacy." He waves his hand at our surroundings. "And I have absolute trust in the restaurant staff, as well as my security detail. Additionally, I had my security detail ensure you weren't followed here by anyone else."

I stare at him. "I'm not sure if I should be impressed by your thoroughness or creeped out by how rigorous you've been in thinking through the possibilities."

"One thing you should realize about me... I'm always one step ahead of the obvious," he murmurs.

"One thing you should realize..." I lean forward in my seat. "I'm always thinking ten steps ahead of my rival."

This time, he's the one who laughs. "Am I your rival?"

"Aren't you?"

"When it comes to our jobs, yes, we don't see eye to eye. But I do believe we can use this intense hostility we feel toward each other to our advantage, when it comes to our personal lives."

I tip up my chin. "My personal life is my own business."

"Not anymore. Not since you caught my eye. Not since you can't stop tracking me with your gaze when we're in the same space and stalking me online when we're not."

"I don't stalk you—" I firm my lips.

He smirks. "That's what I thought. You're as obsessed with me as I am with you."

I open my mouth to protest, but he holds up his finger. "Don't even try to deny it. You and I both know, the fact that we never seem to get along when we meet is more than because we belong to opposing sides. It's because we are both aware of the other to an extent which is unhealthy."

"I am not going to dignify that statement with a response."

"All you need to do is accept my offer."

"Which is?"

"Let's fuck it out."

2

____

Hunter

"You're kidding me... aren't you?" Twin spots of color burn high on her cheeks. Her features wear an expression of surprise and shock, but her pupils are dilated, the black bleeding out until only a thin circle of gold can be seen around the circumference. Her chest rises and falls. She's flushed and angry, and also, turned on. I didn't think it was possible to shock her, but clearly, I have. Which is what I'd hoped for, of course. Except, I hadn't thought I'd be able to achieve it.

Since the moment I first laid eyes on Zara Chopra, she's fascinated me and also surprised me. Truth be told, I'm not even sure I like her. For one, she's curvy, with the kind of hourglass figure I didn't think I found alluring, until her. My previous girlfriends have been slimmer; mostly models and actresses, or those who've earned a living through their looks.

Zara, on the other hand, has striking features and is clearly more than a pretty face. In fact, she's the exact opposite of the kind of woman I normally date. Not only have we fought each time we've met, but she's also made it clear the dislike is mutual. Which I admit, is a blow to my ego. I've never met a woman who has been able to resist me. Until her.

Perhaps, that's why I made that offer to her. Perhaps, the fact that we don't see eye-to-eye makes her the kind of challenge I relish.

I didn't bring her here with the intention of doing so, but when she sat opposite me and seemed unmoved by my presence, I had to test her. I wanted to catch her off guard—which I did. And perhaps, also, myself. For until I heard my own words, I didn't realize just how much I mean it. How much I want to bend her over this table right now and explore what it means to have her writhing under me, impaled on my cock, as I bring her to orgasm over and over again.

"Do I look like the kind of man who'd say anything I don't mean?"

"You're a politician," she scoffs.

"And you aren't?"

She firms her lips. "I'm a fixer, I solve problems. I am not the one who makes them, I leave that to you politicians."

"Spoken like a true salesperson."

She blows out a breath. "I didn't come here to be insulted."

"That wasn't an insult. Salespeople are some of the most persuasive, some of the cleverest people I've met."

"You'll forgive me if I don't agree with you. You ask me to dinner, then tell me you had me investigated, then order my favorite drink and" —she glances down at her plate, then back at me— "my favorite food."

"So, I did my homework." I raise my shoulder.

"Then" —she raises her forefinger— "you tell me you want to fuck me."

"I said we should fuck each other."

"No, thank you."

I lean forward in my seat. "You scared you'll like it too much?"

"I'm not going to answer that. I'm not falling for that again."

I survey her still-flushed features. "You are worried that you might be spoiled for anyone else after our encounter."

"Your ego knows no bounds."

"And your ego would never settle for anyone with balls smaller than mine."

She stares at me, then throws her head back and laughs. It's a full-bellied laugh that comes from the depths of her being. Her eyes are squeezed shut, and her mouth is open. It's not a pretty laugh; it's a wicked, full-of-life laugh. It's the laugh of a woman who knows how to enjoy life.

"Let's enjoy ourselves, Zara. One night. You and me. Let's find out why it is, that even though we can't stand each other, we also gravitate toward each other."

She lowers her head and fixes me with those glowing, tawny eyes of hers. The candlelight dances over her skin, highlighting her high cheekbones, her upturned nose, her stubborn chin. She's going to be a handful. She'll never give in without a fight. She'll resist me every step of the way, and fuck, if I don't find that thought exciting. Nobody has piqued my interest, or drawn my hackles, or made me want to both spank her and kiss her at the same time, as this woman has.

"What do you say? Twelve hours. Until the sun comes up, we explore why it is that we're so drawn to each other, even as we also hate the other's guts."

One side of her lips kicks up. She reaches for her champagne and takes a sip. "Very clever. You think by outlining all of the reasons this is going to make our relationship exciting, you'll tempt me?"

"So, you agree that we're going to have a relationship?"

A crease appears between her eyebrows. "That was a figure of speech."

"Or a Freudian slip."

"Or a slip of the tongue." She trails her finger around the rim of her champagne glass, and my balls tighten. Goddamn! Now she's teasing me, while she still continues to deny the attraction. Every little action of hers is calculated to tease me. She has the way of a seductress, a siren song on her lips, and the look of a huntress in her eyes. She's unharnessed, unbridled, a wildling come to turn my world upside-down. An untamed vixen who'll steal my heart and my soul, and whose name will be stamped into every cell of my body.

The hair on the back of my neck rises. Something like a forewarning ripples up my spine. Get away from her. Leave. Get out as soon as you can, before things get too complicated.

A-n-d the very fact that I have that thought, that for the first time in my life, I, Hunter Whittington, am thinking of leaving the battlefield without even trying to engage with my opponent, gives me pause. I'm not a coward. It takes balls to embark on a career in the public eye. It takes nerves of steel to decide to run for the highest office in this country. It takes courage of conviction and a special kind of crazy to embark on the journey I have. And I wouldn't have done it if I didn't love a challenge. If I didn't relish the opportunity to win a confrontation. If I didn't enjoy finding my way through obstacles. All of which she seems to personify. I drag my finger across my lower lip.

"I'd love to slip my tongue inside you," I murmur.

Her gaze widens. A pulse throbs to life at the base of her neck. She bites down on her lower lip, and I feel the tug all the way to the base of my cock.

I tighten my grip about my own glass of champagne. "You liked that, didn't you?"

She huffs. "I expected better than a cliché from you."

"Clichés exist because they're true."

"And I thought you were capable of more original thinking?"

"You don't want to know what I'm thinking right now."

She holds my gaze boldly. "Why don't you tell me?"

I release the hold on my flute, then lean forward and slide her glass from her grasp. I turn it to where the mark of her lips graces the rim and take a sip of the sparkling wine. "Are you sure you want to hear this?"

Her lips part, then she raises one brow. "Try me."

"I want to touch your curves and fondle the dips in your body. I want to hold you and kiss you and bite you and suck on you. I want to lick you, taste you, sink my fingers inside you. I want to take you to the edge over and over again, until your blood is coursing with pheromones; until you're so high from the experience, you'll be spoiled for anyone else; until all you can think of is me, all you can taste is me; until your every breath belongs to me; until" —I place my hand over hers— "I bring you to your knees and have you begging me to show you every depraved thing I can do to you; until I bring every secret, perverted dream of yours to life; until you're begging me to show you just how far I can push you; until you surprise even yourself."

Her breath hitches.

"I want to arouse you to the point you have no other thoughts but how it will be to have my cock buried in your pussy, my fingers in your arse, my tongue in your mouth, and how I'll take you to the edge until you beg me to come and even then, I won't let you—"

"Unless?" she breathes.

"Unless you submit to me."

3

Zara

His words are filthy and explicit, obscene and so damn hot. I shouldn't find them so hot. I shouldn't find his lack of filter in outlining exactly what he wants to do to me such a turn on. But it is. I enjoy sex. I enjoy men. I enjoy how it feels when my body is treated like it was made for another's pleasure. I want to find out how it feels to be dominated. But I'll never let anyone close enough for that.

It's why my persona is that of a confident woman who's aware of her sexuality and of the effect she has on men, most of whom are threatened by how I come across. A powerful career woman. It's why the kind of men I attract are more than happy for me to set the agenda in bed. It's something I both hate and relish, for then, I'm in control. And if I'm in control, I can't be threatened. It's what I'm comfortable with, and perhaps, it's why I prefer to bed the kind of men I can hold sway over.

This man, though, is nothing like anyone I've faced before. Not in my work life, and not in my personal life. He's not threatened by me, and each time I challenge him, it seems to make him determined to confront me right back. And it's invigorating, to say the least. It's also annoying. Because I don't want to like anything about this man. But the very fact that he can look me in the eye and lay out what he wants to do to me is exhilarating, but also makes me want to defy him. The hair on my forearms rises. My guts clench, and that's only because I'm angry with him. That's all it is.

"Submit to you, huh? If you think I'm going to give in to you, you can think again."

He holds my gaze for a few seconds, then smirks. The jerkface curls his lips. "Is that a challenge?"

Oh, I'm so not walking into that one. "I don't care how you take it. This conversation is over." I jump to my feet and snatch my handbag.

I turn to leave when— "So this is what happens when you come up against your match? You pivot and run?" he drawls.

I draw in a breath. *I will not lose my temper. Will not lose my temper.* I take another step forward, when he speaks again.

"I guess I was right. You're too chicken to find out how good things could be between us. Bet you're worried you'll be spoiled for anyone else, you—"

I spin around and stab a finger in his direction. "Please, don't make this about me. I'm leaving before I say or do something that will blow up into something neither of us will be able to handle."

His grin widens. "Oh, please. By all means, speak your mind. It's why I brought you here, so we could clear the air."

"By you propositioning me?"

"That's one route we could take. The most enjoyable route, too." He smirks.

"Are you listening to yourself?" I fume.

"Are you listening to yourself?" He leans back in his chair. "You're angry at me."

"Thanks for noticing, Captain Obvious."

"When was the last time you got angry at anyone?"

I scowl at him. "Is that a trick question?"

"Think about it, Zara. When was the last time someone pissed you off so much, you decided to leave a meal without even tasting the food?"

I glance at the dish sitting at my abandoned place. It has fish and chips, my favorite dish. And he ordered it for me.

"It's spicy and the fish is halibut." He refers to the lean white fish that's not easily available. The side dish is a salad with baby lettuce, rocket leaves, and pomegranate seeds. It's a combination I love, and one which is not available on most menus. I know because I made up the salad recipe myself.

I glower at him. "How did you know—"

"That you like this specific type of fish, and you prefer your fish and chips extra spicy? That the only time you eat your greens is when it's spiked with pomegranate seeds?" His lips curve up in a smile that's half-wicked, half-satisfied. "Did I surprise you?"

I sniff. "Probably just something else that came up in the reports you had ordered on me."

"Why don't you sit down and finish it, hmm?"

"I think not." I eye the fish and my stomach growls.

He must hear it because he laughs. "Come on, Zara. You have to admit, the interaction over the past half hour is the most stimulation you've had in conversation with another person in a while."

"Don't flatter yourself," I mutter. He's right, though. I've never felt more alive than in the time I've spent with him. It's a combination of nervousness and excitement, with breathless anticipation thrown in. A feeling I only get when I'm faced with a new challenge. Which intrigues me. Which is the only reason I am still here and haven't walked out on him. That, and this chemistry between us, which I can't understand. A problem I need to resolve. I'm a fixer, after all. Nothing engages me more than a puzzle that needs to be put together.

"Sit. Eat." He leans back in his seat. "I promise, I won't even point out that you still haven't answered my earlier question."

I shake my head. "Seriously, and I thought I had a big ego, but yours just might be more colossal."

"Not the only thing that's colossal." He smirks.

I make a gagging sound in my throat. "How very unoriginal of you."

"Have dinner with me, and I promise, I'll reveal more creative ripostes."

I take my seat and plant my bag on the adjacent chair, then reach for my knife and fork. I cut into the fish and place a small portion in my mouth. The delicate, almost flowery notes of its flesh melt on my tongue. That, combined with the sizzle of the spices in which it's been marinated, makes it seem like the two different parts of my heritage have coalesced on my palate. "Wow." I chew and swallow. "That's amazing."

"Right?" He digs into his own food. He's ordered a burger and fries —another surprise. I hadn't thought this man was capable of eating anything so ordinary. But then, I don't really know him at all, so guess I shouldn't be surprised. Maybe I shouldn't have been so hasty in judging him. And maybe that's the reason he's brought me here—so he can soften my opinion of him. Well, it's going to take more than a plate of fish and chips, even if it's possibly the best fish and chips I've ever had, to alter my viewpoint. So what, if he took the time to find out what my tastes run to and ordered accordingly? He still decided to do it without consulting me, thinking I'd fall in with his plans. It shows just how egotistical he is. How much he's taking me for granted. And I can't wait to show him that I know my own mind. I'm not one of those easily maneuverable bimbos he, no doubt, likes to hang out with.

He forks up a piece of the burger and holds it out to me. "Here, taste this."

"Umm" —I glance from the food on his fork to him— "you want to feed me?"

"Humor me." He half smiles, and it's a smile devoid of any agenda. Well, in as much as that's possible for a twathole like him. When I hesitate, he brings it closer to my mouth so the food brushes my lips. "Go on, you know you want to."

The scent of the burger is so aromatic, my mouth waters. *Oh, fuck this. It's only food.* Letting him feed me doesn't mean I'm submitting to him. I'm only pretending to play along with his agenda. I'm trying to lull him into a false sense of comfort, so he'll let down his walls and share a little more of himself with me.

And he's trying to entice you to do the same. Sure, he is, but I'm too smart to fall for his moves, no matter how smooth they are.

I open my mouth, and he feeds me the morsel. I close my lips and wipe the tines clean as he slides the fork back. The whole time, he holds my gaze. His blue-green eyes deepen until they are almost azure. My belly clenches, the pulse between my legs speeds up, and somehow, the simple task of feeding me has turned into a seduction. Damn, but he's good. Then the flavors overcome my senses. The meat is so tender, it seems to dissolve on my tongue, and the herbs woven through are so fresh, I can feel the wind in the trees and the slither of grass between my toes as I walk barefoot through a field somewhere far away from this city.

I flutter my eyelids open—when did I close them? —and stare at him in amazement.

"I know," he laughs. "James Hamilton is the most talented chef in the country."

I gape at him. "You called James Hamilton and had him shut down his restaurant for us?"

He arches his eyebrows. "Have I finally managed to impress you?"

"You got the most sought-after chef in, perhaps, the world to cook for us, so yeah, I'd say, yes."

"So, food is the way to get through your defenses, eh?"

"I never said that."

"You don't need to. The very fact that you're more relaxed after eating speaks for itself."

"Good food, good drink—" I raise my glass. "Despite present company, I admit, I'm not as wound up as I was. Let's just say I was hangry."

He chuckles. "Go on, you can complement me for my efforts. It's allowed."

"Fine, it wasn't a bad effort." I admit.

He smirks. "It's going to be interesting to up my ante with you."

"You don't have to up your anything with me, Hunter."

His grin widens, "I could up a lot of things, but in specific, one thing, when it comes to you, Zara."

I blink. The flesh between my legs clenches. *I did not find that hot. I did not. I did. OMG.* That was a cringe-worthy remark from him—not particularly original but damn, it seems to be working on me. *How am I going to live this down?* I raise my hand, palm facing him. "Don't try to distract me from what I'm going to say."

"Which is?"

"That we're different. We have nothing in common. And it's madness to even think we could sleep together and get away with it. But I got to taste James Hamilton's food, so it's not a completely wasted evening."

"Say that again." He studies me with a strange look in his eyes. Like he's realized something but is trying his best not to acknowledge it.

"Umm, that it's not a completely wasted evening?"

"No, before that."

"That we have nothing in common?"

"Prior to that."

"Huh?" I try to think back. "Prior to that I said.. That we're so different, and before that I said... Your name?"

"Say it again," he murmurs.

"This is madness." I place my fork back on my embarrassingly empty plate. "I really should leave."

"Zara," he lowers his voice to a hush, and a frisson of anticipation sizzles up my spine. My nerve endings seem to spark. My pulse rate shoots up. And all because he said my name in that tone... That very dominant tone of his.

I rise to my feet. He narrows his gaze. "Sit down, Zara."

My backside hits the chair, and I blink. What the—? Did I just follow his order? Did I obey him, without intending to? When was the last time that happened? When has that ever happened as an adult? No man has ever dared to command me to do his bidding. I've never followed someone else's orders. Not like this. Not in my personal life. Even worse, I don't feel guilty about it.

I feel queasy, like I've stepped off a cliff, and instead of falling, I'm being pulled higher in the air, and I'm waiting for my stomach to catch up with the rest of my body. My blood begins to pump harder through my veins. The pulse between my legs becomes thicker, harder, stronger. And all because he directed my actions. This...is...insane. I feel so out of my depth. Like someone has cut off the cords that ground me and now I'm floating...floating.

I draw in a deep breath, then another. Draw on an ember of anger low in my belly. I fan it until it spreads through my stomach, my blood, my arms. I reach for the glass of champagne and toss it in his face.

4

———————

Hunter

One second, we're engaged in that now familiar battle of wills, where our gazes are clashing and holding, and neither of us is ready to back down. The thrill of the chase unfurls in my chest. My blood begins to thump through my veins. My vision narrows. Adrenaline laces my blood, but before I can act, she's thrown the champagne in my face. The liquid stings my eyes, drips down my cheeks, and I react on pure instinct. I jump to my feet, lean forward and grab her arm before she can withdraw it.

"Let me go," she snaps.

"No."

I tighten my grip on her wrist and the empty champagne flute slips from her fingers. It hits the table with a soft thud and rolls once, then stills.

"You shouldn't have done that," I say slowly.

"You deserved it," she spits at me.

"You're gorgeous."

She stills. "Excuse me?"

"You heard me. You're magnificent when you're angry. Your eyes flash fire. Your cheeks turn a gorgeous color that makes me want to close the distance between us and lick you up."

She shakes her head. "Am I dreaming? I must be dreaming that I'm in this restaurant with one of the people I hate the most holding my hand."

"Hate fuck. Think of how explosive it will be when we come together."

"Keep dreaming." She tosses her hair back from her face.

"It can be a reality, Z."

"Don't call me that."

"I feel like we've blown past the preliminary part of our relationship already."

She raises the forefinger of her left hand. "One. There is no relation-ship. And two" —she holds up her middle finger— "you can go fuck yourself." She lowers her forefinger and keeps only her middle finger upright.

"There she is. You turn me on when you get enraged."

"Didn't you listen to me?" She thrusts her middle finger forward. "I want nothing to do with you."

"And I want everything you can give me." I grab her free hand and pull so we're both stretched across the table with our faces so close our noses almost bump. I bring her outstretched middle finger to my mouth and close my lips around it.

She draws in a sharp breath and her pupils dilate. Those golden-brown sparks in her eyes glitter until they lighten to silver shards. I curl my tongue around her digit and suck harder.

A moan bleeds from her lips. The taste of her floods my mouth, sinks into my blood. My groin hardens. The crotch of my pants tightens. She lowers her gaze to my mouth and swallows. Her lips part. The scent of her, orange blossoms and vanilla with a hint of pepper, floods my senses.

She leans in closer, until our eyelashes tangle. She raises her gaze to mine, and lust flares in the depths of her eyes.

The blood beats in my ears, and goddamn, I want to kiss her. And I will... Just not yet. First, I need to tease her, taunt her, seduce her... Perhaps, court her. Coax her, so she comes willingly. Here, kitty, kitty.

"Maybe next time." I release her so suddenly, she falls back into her chair.

"What the —?" She gapes at me.

"You wanted to leave? This is your chance."

"After that...that..." She seems at a loss for words.

I mentally fist-pump. Rule number one in any negotiation is to catch your opponent off guard, and that's exactly what I've done. Question is, what's she going to do next?

She seems to get control of her emotions. "You're an asshole."

"Alphahole." I smirk.

Her gaze narrows. "Do you play chess?"

"Eh?" It's my turn to be surprised.

"Chess, Whittington. Do you play chess?"

"Do you wish to be beaten at your own game?"

She narrows her eyes. "You wish." She squares her shoulders. "Let's move our encounter to a more equal footing."

"Ah, so you're going to see me again?"

She firms her lips.

"You said it, not me," I remind her.

"I didn't mean to, but you got me so pissed-off, I didn't realize I was committing myself to seeing you again."

"Are you backing out?"

She tips up her chin. "I don't go back on my word."

"Neither do I."

"Good." She sniffs.

"Good." I widen my smile.

"Wipe that grin off of your face. You don't need to look so satisfied."

My phone pings a warning. "A-n-d, our two hours are up. Time sure goes by fast when you're having fun."

She makes a rude sound. "Whatever."

"Ah, the famous word that's the last resort when no other insults come to mind." I smirk.

She picks up her bag and slides it over her shoulder. "Goodbye, Whittington."

"Not so fast." I round the table and tuck her arm through mine. She trembles a little. Good. She's responding to my proximity. Which means, she'll miss me when I'm not around. Which will help build up anticipation for our next meeting.

When we reach the maître d's station by the entrance, he steps up with our coats. I hold hers up, and she slips her arms through the sleeves. I smooth it over her shoulders and lean in enough to sniff her hair. Orange blossoms and vanilla tease my senses. My cock lengthens at once. It's as if I'm hardwired to respond to her at every level. Which is…interesting, to say the least. When the chemistry between us finally explodes, it's going to be incendiary.

I step back and slide my arms through the sleeves of my jacket the maître d' holds out for me.

"Thank you, Charles."

"Pleasure, sir. Madam." He tips his head and melts back into the darkness.

Our security detail walks ahead, and I lead her to the door. By the time we step out of the restaurant, my Aston Martin is waiting for us. I open the door, and she slides in. I round the car, slip into the driver's seat, then ease the car forward.

We drive in silence for a few seconds, then I jerk my chin in the direction of the glove compartment. "Open it."

She glances at the built-in door in the dash, then back at me with a frown. "I'd rather not."

"I promise, it's not what you think," I coax.

The groove between her eyebrows furrows. "You have no idea what I'm thinking right now."

"You're thinking how much you'd like to slap me, then kiss me." I smirk.

Her jaw drops, then she laughs. "So damn cocky."

"With good reason."

"Not going there now," she warns.

"Go on, open the door and look inside, Alice."

She shoots me a glance from under those thick eyelashes, "Only because you referred to Alice in Wonderland."

"Do you know *The Matrix* was inspired by it?"

She blinks. "Was it?"

"Nah." I grin.

She scowls, then chuckles again. "You can be charming, if a little cringe-worthy, I'll give you that."

"And you want to open that door." I nod in the direction of the glove compartment again, "Go on, do it."

"Hmph." She leans over and presses the button on the panel, and it slides down. There in the middle of the space is a colorful rectangular packet. She reaches for it and draws it out, then holds it out to me.

"Haribo?" she asks in a dazed voice.

"They're your favorite," I say simply.

"You bought me Haribo gummy bears?" Her voice has a breathless quality to it now.

"Open it," I urge.

She tears open the small packet and pours out a few in the palm of her hand. "They are all the same color."

"Gold."

I say at the same time as her.

"They're your favorite," I add.

"You never get Haribo bears all in one color in one packet."

"I do."

She looks up at me, then back at the packet. "Not sure what to make of this." Her voice now has a touch of panic to it.

"It's only candy, Zara; don't read anything into the gesture."

"You're doing this to throw me off-kilter."

"Am I succeeding?"

She squares her shoulder. "Of course, not."

"Good, so why don't you eat one?"

She looks down at the splash of gold in her palm. "Maybe I will."

She pops one into her mouth, slides the rest back into the packet, except one. She drops the pack into her bag, then reaches over and holds it out in front of my mouth.

Without taking my eyes off the road, I open my mouth and she slides it in. I close my lips about her fingers and lick the gummy bear off her digits. The taste of her, more complex than the sweetness of the candy, goes straight to my groin.

I draw in a sharp breath; so does she.

She leans back, and out of the corner of my eye I watch as she brings the fingers to her mouth and sucks on them. A white flash of heat zings through my chest. I tighten my fingers about the steering wheel.

Her chest rises and falls, and I sense a ripple of something pulse through her body. The air between us grows heavy with lust, charged with the kind of lust that could detonate at any second. I knew the chemistry between us was explosive, but this is taking things to another level of combustion.

For a few seconds, neither of us says anything, then she reaches forward and touches the panel on the dash. The haunting strains of Mozart's "The Queen of the Night" flood the space. Some of the tension eases… Only because I'm going to let this go for now.

"Didn't take you for someone who listens to classical music," she murmurs.

"My mother loved listening to it. My fondest memories are of her knitting while listening to classical music, while my father worked on his papers in the study."

"That sounds like a very cozy scene."

"She was a home-body. She loved her husband and her sons." At least, until it all went to shite.

"You have a brother?" She turns to look at me.

I nod.

"Is he older than you?"

"Younger."

"I guess he's not in politics, or I'd have heard of him."

"He's not. He prefers not to be associated with the Whittingtons. He turned his back on his family and currently lives in Thailand, or at least, that's where he was when I last heard from him."

"Ah, so he's the rebel, and you're the obedient son?"

"Do I look like an obedient son?" I scoff.

"You look like no one can make you do anything you don't want to do."

"Very astute, Councilor." I shoot her a sideways glance before turning back to the road. "Why did a lawyer decide to get into the big bad world of PR?"

"You mean, the only professions worse than that of a lawyer are being a journalist or a spin-doctor, and I opted for the last?"

"You said it." I smirk.

"I got into law because my parents asked me to choose between becoming a doctor or a lawyer, and I knew I wasn't cut out to be a doctor, so—" She raises a shoulder.

"And PR?"

"I have the gift of gab and I've always been fascinated by media. Besides, I think becoming a lawyer prepared me for the cut-throat world of PR, don't you think?"

"As a politician, I'll be the first to admit that I loathe spin doctors while also knowing I can't do without them."

"You said it," she says lightly.

I laugh. "You're a breath of fresh air."

"You mean, as opposed to the models you normally date?"

"Was this a date?"

"You tell me."

I ease to a stop for a red light, then turn to her. "If this were a date, I'd have dismissed our security detail from the restaurant and told the staff to leave us undisturbed. Then, I'd have bent you over the table and fucked you so hard, you'd have felt the imprint of my cock for days."

Her breath hitches. Even in the dim light, I can see her pupils dilate.

"Does that excite you, Zara, hmm?"

"As propositions go, that wasn't very original."

"That wasn't a proposition. That was a statement of intent."

She laughs, then leans back in her seat. "I'm never sleeping with you, Whittington."

A familiar excitement zings through my blood. The hair on my forearms rises. My fingers tingle, and before I can change my mind, I reach forward, wrap my fingers about the nape of her neck, and pull her forward.

"Wait, what are you—"

I kiss her. I press my lips to hers and inhale her breath. For a few seconds, she remains stiff, either from surprise or because she's holding herself back. Tension vibrates off of her. Her entire body is one coiled mass of rigidity. I soften my mouth. I nip on her lower lip, and with a groan, she parts her lips. I sweep my tongue inside, tangle with hers. Suck on her, draw from her. Pull her as close as the seatbelts we're wearing will allow. I tilt my head and deepen the kiss. A moan bleeds from her. The blood in my body drains to my groin. The crotch of my pants tightens. A hot sensation wells in my chest. A shiver runs down my spine. All the cells in my body seem to come alive at once. Fuck, I need to get closer, need to be inside her, need to—

The blare of a horn cuts through the haze, and we break apart. Her pulse beats at the base of her throat; her glorious hair flows about her shoulders. Her lips are swollen, and she's staring at me with a dazed expression on her face. She's not the only one who's surprised. I hadn't thought it was possible for me to want a woman so much, so quickly. Especially a woman I had a strong reaction to on sight—something that doesn't happen often.

I thought I hated her. Turns out, my response to her is more complex than that. It's not black or white. It's more layered... More complicated. It's more... Everything. It's definitely unexpected. The car behind us honks again. I step on the accelerator, and the car moves forward. We drive in silence until I turn off the main road onto the side street leading to her apartment.

"If you think that kiss changed anything, *you're* mistaken."

"If you think that kiss *meant* anything, you're mistaken."

"Oh, trust me, I know exactly what it was. A chauvinistic way for you to shut me up. I told you I wasn't going to sleep with you, so of course, you took it as a challenge. You wanted to prove to yourself, and to me, that I want you, and I assure you, even if I did—which I don't— I'd get someone else to scratch the itch."

I brake so suddenly, we're thrown against our seat belts. I park the car, release my seatbelt, lean over, unlock hers, and once more, grip the nape of her neck and pull her across the partition between our seats.

"Wha—"

I don't let her complete the word. I close my mouth over hers and kiss her fiercely. She slaps her hand against my shoulder, then keeps it there, palm flattened against my jacket. I tighten my hold on her, bring my other hand up, and bury my fingers in her hair. I tug on it, and she shudders. I deepen the kiss, and with a groan, she grips the front of my shirt with her free arm and tugs me even closer. She bites down on my lower lip, and my cock jerks. My thighs harden. I thrust my tongue inside her mouth, dancing it over hers. Her chest rises and falls, her breasts crushed into my chest. The taste of her coats my mouth, the scent of her sinks into my skin, her curves melt into me, and my head spins. My breath comes in pants. A bead of sweat slides down my spine. My stomach muscles harden until it feels like I've been sucker-punched. I release her mouth and stare into her eyes. She holds my gaze, the look in hers dazed and angry. She moves, and I guess her intention, but I don't stop her as her palm connects with my cheek. My face snaps back with the momentum, but I don't look away.

She searches my features, with something resembling panic on her face. "Don't ever do that again," she spits out.

"Worried you won't be able to stop next time?"

"If I were you, I'd be worried about keeping my balls," she retorts.

"I told you we should have simply fucked it out."

"You're irredeemable." She raises her hand again, and this time, I catch her wrist. In a flash, I twist it behind her back so her breasts are thrust out. I take my time perusing her features, down the arch of her slender neck to where her tits are outlined against the coat she's wearing. By the time I raise my gaze, her face is flushed.

"I'm not going to apologize for what I did," I drawl.

"You're conforming to your image of being an inconsiderate twat," she snaps.

"Keep talking dirty, and I won't be responsible for what happens next."

She tries to pull away, but I tighten my grip on her.

"You may be physically stronger than me, but I promise you, I'll never give into you." She bares her teeth at me, and goddamn, all of my senses home in on her. I want nothing more than to throw her over my lap and spank her curvy behind before I take her so hard, we both see stars. Unfortunately, though, that will have to wait.

"That remains to be seen." I lift her back over to her seat, then straighten.

"You're an animal," she snaps.

"Only with you."

She blinks, then barks out a laugh. "That should sound trite, but somehow, coming from you, I almost believe it. Almost."

I rake my fingers through my hair, then drum my fingers on the wheel, "Believe it. I don't normally get this handsy on a first date —"

"Not a date."

"I took you to a restaurant, we ate, we kissed. Twice. It's a date."

She draws in a breath, and for a few seconds we sit there in silence. Then she murmurs, "You also bought me Haribos."

"I did."

"Thank you for that."

I tilt my head. "You're welcome."

"I suppose you're right." She straightens her spine, "It was a date, but believe me, it's never going to happen again."

We'll see.

She snatches her bag from where it's fallen on the floor. By the time she's shoved her door open, I've walked around the car. I hold it open for her as she steps out.

"You don't have to walk me to my door."

"On the contrary." I nod to my security detail who are poised on either side of the vehicle, then I walk her up the driveway. She uses her keycard to open the front door and I follow her in, up the wide staircase and to the door of her apartment.

"I'm not going to invite you in."

"I didn't expect you to."

She opens her door, then steps inside and turns to me. "I'm not going to thank you for tonight, either, except maybe for the champagne and the food which, I have to admit, were exceptional."

She goes to shut the door, and I plant my foot in the way. "See me again."

She laughs. "No fucking way."

"I'll get my way, one way or the other."

She sets her chin. "Not if I can help it."

"Don't underestimate me." I narrow my gaze. "When I want something, I go after it."

"Don't patronize me. Once I make up my mind, it's very difficult to change it."

A sizzle of excitement zips up my spine. Adrenaline laces my blood. Fucking hell, this thrust and parry of words, this matching of wits is as potent as foreplay.

"And what if I get you to come out with me again?"

She snorts. "Not gonna happen. But if it does, I promise you, next time, I'll be the one to initiate the kiss."

I hold out my hand. "Deal."

5

Zara

"So let me get this right. Cesar Underwood's car was caught speeding on camera, but he claims his car was stolen and it wasn't him?"

Steve, my right-hand person nods. "We suspect it's either because he was visiting someone he shouldn't or because his car really was stolen."

It's been three months since that dinner with Hunter. Two months in which I have seen Hunter's growing profile in the media. Clearly, he's being groomed by his party to take on the role of the next Prime Minister. The country will be going to the polls soon and rumor is the sitting Prime Minister is going to resign with Hunter tipped to take his place as the lead candidate. Keeping aside my personal issues with Hunter, I have to admit that he makes for a charismatic contestant.

His relative youth in comparison to his opponent, his presence, which the camera loves, the force of his personality, that comes through almost as strongly through any media platform as in real life, and the fact that when he speaks you are compelled to listen means his approval ratings in the polls have sky rocketed in the months since I met him. And all this time, there hasn't been a call or a text from him. Not that I had expected it. Okay, maybe I had…

A little. A man doesn't take you out to dinner then eye-fuck you the way Hunter did, only to back off because you turned him down. A man like that doesn't take no for an answer. If anything, my declining his overtures will only push him to be challenged. To find a way to come back at me faster and harder than ever, and in a way that will take me by surprise. Which is the only reason I've been following his media coverage. It's best to keep an eye on your opponent, track their every move, and not let them out of your sight. And trust me, I've been following his media appearances. Following his social media feeds, as well as the regular appearances he's been making at various industry shindigs, each time with a different woman on his arm. Not sure who's advising him, but that's the only glitch I could spot in his otherwise constant media presence. He's top-of-mind with the voters, all right, but not always for the right reasons. However, he doesn't seem to be worried about it. Entitled asshole that he is, he probably doesn't care how he comes across to the people. Or maybe he's confident he can smooth over any perceived mistakes with that blindingly bright smile of his.

Either way, I'm not his PR manager so I didn't need to worry about it. Right? Of course, given I am a crisis manager, a spin doctor, and a lawyer, all rolled into one, I'm the best in the business. The one sought after by celebrities, media personalities, and politicians in distress—like Cesar Underwood, who's one of the hottest actors on both sides of the pond right now. Second only to Declan Beauchamp, who I also happen to know personally.

I fold my arms across my chest and glance around the table in the conference room of my office. "Anyone believe Cesar is telling the truth?"

The team shake their heads.

"Anyone believe he was having an affair and was en route to see his mistress?"

The looks on the faces of my team give them away.

I blow out a breath. "That's what I thought."

"You'd think celebrities could, at least, try to be original when they come up with lies," Casey, my social media specialist murmurs without taking her gaze off of the device in her hand.

"I assume the media isn't buying it, and neither is the rest of the internet."

"No surprises there." She winces.

"That bad, huh?"

"Worse." She finally tips up her chin. "He cheated on everyone's sweetheart, who is pregnant at home with their first child. Her fans are baying for blood."

"He's in an impossible situation." Kate, my senior associate and crisis media manager, drums her fingers on the table. "Who'd want to cheat on his pregnant wife who is one of the biggest Hollywood stars and girl next door, within the first year of their marriage?"

"Someone who clearly doesn't know a good thing when he sees it." Casey rolls her eyes.

"Or someone who is running from something and didn't give a damn about being caught," Steve interjects.

"He's not that stupid." Kate sniffs.

"I don't know. When men are in love and trapped, they can go to great lengths to get a semblance of freedom." Steve murmurs.

Kate blinks. "You mean, he's feeling trapped by marriage to the kind of woman every man fantasizes about, which is why he's running out on her?"

Steve raises a shoulder. "Or maybe he just needed space to breathe. A monster hit in Hollywood, followed by marriage to someone the fans adore, with a child on the way, and all in under one year."

"You just listed all the reasons for him not getting an ounce of sympathy from the media or the fans." Kate sniffs.

Steve raises his hands. "So many changes can be an emotional burden for anybody. Then, try living it out in glare of the spotlight where the public scrutinizes your every move, and it's almost understandable why he jumped into his car and ran. If he hadn't been caught by a speed camera, he'd be free, and none of us would be the wiser."

"So why did he lie about it? Why not admit that it was him and pay the fine?" Kate raises her chin.

"Now, that's the big question." Steve touches his fingertips together.

"It's because he was under so much pressure that he decided to have an affair," Casey offers.

Both Kate and Steve look at her.

"What? I'm not making excuses for him, but if we go by what Steve said, it lays the case for him reaching the end of his tether and doing something crazy. Although, in the bigger scheme of things, it's not that crazy, compared to what others before him have done."

"I tend to agree with you," Steve says slowly.

"Whatever the reason may be, we can agree that he acted like a guilty person when he lied." Kate purses her lips.

"And that's the point. We're not here to judge our clients. We're here to solve their problems. It's why the wealthy and the powerful come to us." I slap my hands on my hips. "So, where's Cesar Underwood now?"

"I put him in the Zen meeting room," Mandy replies.

Now, it's my turn to wince. We only use that room when the client who comes in through the door is so stressed out that normal methods of calming them down don't work.

I square my shoulders, then turn and head out the room, Kate and Steve on my heels. I reach the door to the conference room and tap once before I push it open.

The soft sound of flutes and bird song piped in through the speakers fills the air. Underneath it, the tinkling of water from the small water-feature in the corner lends an air of peacefulness. Together with the simple wooden chaise pushed up against one wall, the deep-cushioned chairs opposite it, as well as a lava lamp in another corner and the bamboos growing from a pot near the window, the room manages to retain a semblance of tranquility. This, despite the waves of tension pouring off the man who's standing by the window. I step into the room, and he turns to face me.

"Zara!" He looks exactly like the face on the billboard I pass every day on my drive to work. Almost six foot three, broad shoulders, thick hair that flows back from his face in waves… With his square jaw and sharp cheekbones, he's handsome enough to have been called the most handsome man in the world, only he's nowhere near as charismatic as Hunter. Huh, how weird I should think that. I'm certainly not saying Hunter's handsome—not at all. Okay maybe he is. From some angles. And why am I thinking of him right now?

"Cesar." I nod in his direction.

"You have to help me, Zara, please." He closes the distance to me in a few strides and grabs my hand.

"And I will, I promise, Cesar." I try to extricate my arm, but he holds onto it. "I didn't do anything wrong, Zara, I swear."

"Except you were at the wrong place at the wrong time," Kate mutters under her breath.

I shoot her a sideways scowl, and Kate wipes the disbelieving look off of her face. She's every inch the professional; it's why I hired her straight out of college six years ago. She's grown with the firm, and I know I can count on her loyalty and her discretion. As I can with all of the other members of my team. Now, she steps forward and pats his shoulder. At least, my team is impervious to his looks. Which is nothing more than I'd expect of them.

It should be difficult to resist the lure of fame and beauty. But when you see the price people pay to stay in the public eye; the dirty laundry that gets aired by the celebrities, media personalities and politicians who pass through these doors, you realize, behind each pretty face lies the seamier side of celebrity popularity. No matter how well-known or how gorgeous the person in front of the camera is. It's only confirmed my belief that those with access to money and power are normally the ones with the most to hide. And Hunter… What is he hiding, I wonder?

"Zara, did you hear what I said?" Cesar's voice cuts through my thoughts.

"Whether we believe you or not, is not the point. It doesn't matter what you did; we'll do our very best to spin it and ensure the media buys into it so you can walk away from this and to your wife—" I search his features. "—assuming that's what you want."

"Yes!" He shakes my hand—which he still hasn't let go of—up and down. "Yes, that's what I want."

There's a knock on the door, and I turn to find Mandy has popped her head through the door. "Uh, Brittney Ward is here."

"What?" Cesar's face pales at the mention of his wife's name. His knees seem to buckle, and now it's me who reaches over and grips his shoulder with my free arm to steady him.

"Cesar, you okay?"

"Yes! No!" He glances about the room with the whites of his eyes showing. "I'm not ready to see her."

I resist the urge to roll my eyes. Of course, he isn't. I turn to Steve, who's already backing out of the room. "I'll keep her occupied for a little while."

I nod with gratitude. I trained him well. Steve's a one-time commando, who defied his superiors when they asked him to open fire on a target in Afghanistan where the fatalities would have included women and children. He was court-martialed and tried. When I learned of his case, I intervened and helped him out, and defended him success-fully. I got him off free and have had his unswerving loyalty ever since. He's happy to work for me, and happy to do what I ask him to do without asking questions.

The door snicks shut behind him.

"Why don't you have a seat?" I guide Cesar to the chaise. When I pull back my hand, he releases it. I sink down into one of the chairs opposite him. Kate pours him a glass of water and hands it over. He drains the glass, and when he lowers it, his arm trembles. Kate tops up his glass then shoots me a look before she sits down in the other chair.

Cesar swigs the second glass of water as if it's something stronger, then places it on the side table. He seems to have regained his composure, for when he looks at me, his features are calmer.

I lean forward in my seat and fix my gaze on him. "So, what's the real story?"

6

Hunter

"When do you plan to announce your candidacy for Prime Minister?" Declan Beauchamp, one of my closest friends and now a well-known film star, takes aim, then sinks his pool ball in the pocket. He straightens, walks around and takes aim again.

We're at the 7A Club in Piccadilly Circus. Sinclair Sterling and JJ Kane are the joint owners of the space with Sterling having paid enough to get the name of his company affixed to the club. When JJ Kane came up with the idea of a physical venue where he could encourage those who were contributing to the city in any form to be considered for membership, I wasn't sold on it. But in just a few months, it resulted in Liam Kincaid investing in a startup that was born in this very city and is now the toast of Silicon Valley; a startup that's going to earn him many times his original investment. Not only has it made Liam much richer, but it's also made the entrepreneur behind the idea the darling of the business circuit. So, perhaps he has an inkling of what he's doing.

Also, the club has proven to be one of the few places outside my own home where I will be undisturbed. And the moment I declare my candidacy, I can say goodbye to any semblance of quiet. I'll probably have to stop coming to the club, as well. Mainly because my every move will be scrutinized, and I don't necessarily want to draw attention to my friends. While each of them is well-off in their own way, I won't impose the kind of scrutiny I draw from the media on them. I tap my cue on the floor, then narrow my gaze on Declan.

"What's the hurry?" I drawl.

"Thought this was the dream of your lifetime?"

I incline my head and watch as he lines up his next shot.

A seemingly innocent statement but one which has haunted me, of late. Is becoming Prime Minister the dream of my lifetime? Or am I living someone else's dream? More specifically, that of my father. As the oldest son of the Whittingtons, it was assumed I'd walk in the footsteps of my old man, and his old man before him. Indeed, I've taken it as my inevitable future and embraced the certainty of it. I've never questioned it. Not until the last few months.

Maybe it's because I'm so close to achieving the dream I've spent so long pursuing. Maybe because, increasingly, I'm questioning how much I actually want it. Maybe it's because working late nights, focused on myself, and coming home to an empty house, one evening with a dark-haired, amber-eyed goddess made me realize I don't want to do it on my own. I want someone to share my thoughts with. Someone who'll match me word for word. Who'll challenge me, call me out on my bullshit. Someone who'll stimulate me in more ways than one. Someone whose features have haunted my dreams. Someone whose scent I carry, tucked away in my memory. Whose laugh I still hear when I close my eyes. Whose face I imagine waking up to, with my cock at full mast, and it's not just morning wood.

It's a painful, physical yearning that seems to come from a place deep inside. A place I've never acknowledged, and an intensity of sensation I've never expected. It's because of that, I decided not to call her. Not to approach her. Not to have anything to do with her... Not until I arrive at a decision about what to do with this new state of my emotions.

It's not that I like her more than I used to. I still consider Zara Chopra a hindrance in many ways. A distraction? Maybe. A diversion? Definitely. An interference in my well-planned life. A disturbance to my peace of mind.

Until a few months ago, I'd been confident about what I wanted, about where I was headed, about the kind of woman I wanted in my life. Then, I met her, and the sparks between us flew, and it confounded me.

Like any sensible man, I proposed to her that we fuck it out of our systems. Which would have been the best course of action. For both of us.

But the fact is, she turned me down, and her memory is still an itch I carry with me, an itch no amount of jerking myself off has managed to scratch. An itch no other woman I've gone out with has come close to touching. An itch which has since grown to consume every cell in my body, every fiber of my being, every waking thought, every sleeping breath. An itch that, even now, makes me hard just thinking of her. And I'm nowhere near her. I hadn't seen her in three months. I haven't spoken to her. I've avoided any gathering of friends where she could have been present which, considering the number of people we have in common, is an achievement in itself.

Given that I'm entering an important phase of my career, I can't afford distractions. Now more than ever, I need to focus. I needed to plan, strategize, spend time analyzing my opponents and drawing up scenarios. I need to brainstorm with my party colleagues, schmooze them, and win them over. I've tried my best to stay centered, but despite my best efforts, I've found myself unable to harness the single-mindedness that's been my hallmark. It's the reason why, at only thirty-nine, I'm on track to become the youngest leader of this country. Assuming I win the election, which I have no doubt I can do. If I can simply keep my head in the game.

The cue ball cracks against the object ball, which slides into the pocket. "Yes!" Declan fist pumps. He walks around, positions the cue across the table and sinks another ball, and another. When he finally misses, I line up my shot… And miss.

Declan bursts out laughing. "Your concentration is shot."

"Don't sound so happy," I grumble as he positions his cue, and of course, sinks his last ball.

"Can't blame me for enjoying your misery. In all the years I've known you, I've never seen you this distracted."

He straightens and rests the head of his cue against the floor. "Want to play again?"

"Yes, do you want to play again?" A new voice asks.

I turn to find Zara leaning a hip against the doorway.

Heat flushes my skin. Awareness crackles across my nerve endings. I take in the dark locks that curl about her shoulders, the way she has her chin tipped up, the stubborn glint in those gorgeous sunbeam eyes, and my entire body seems to turn into a whirlpool of desire. Fuck, she looks even better than I remembered. She's wearing one of those skirts that clings to her hips and comes to just below her knees. It's supposed to look professional but hell, if it doesn't bring out the perfect guitar shape of her body. Teamed with a jacket that she's buttoned up with the red of her blouse peeking from under the neckline, she resembles a gift I can't wait to unwrap.

She pushes away from the door and glides toward us. When she reaches the table, she turns to Declan. "Good to see you again. You were amazing in your last movie."

"Why, thank you. And the pleasure is all mine." He flashes her a smile, then takes her hand in his and brings it toward his mouth. Or at least, that's what I think he's going to do. Before I can stop myself, I've stepped forward and between them, forcing him to drop her hand.

He arches an eyebrow in my direction and snickers. *Asshole.*

"What are you doing?" Zara snaps.

I jerk my head toward the exit.

Declan's grin widens. "It would seem my friend here would rather not have anyone monopolize your time."

"Out," I snap.

He laughs, then walks around us. "Good seeing you, Zara." He tosses his cue in her direction, and she snatches it neatly from the air. "Good reflexes." He jerks his head in my direction. "Can't say the same about you, wankface." He holds his middle finger over his shoulder and strolls out.

"Wankface?" Zara coughs.

"He can be creative when it comes to his insults," I admit.

"So do you wanna play?" She nods toward the pool table.

I peer into her face. "What are we playing for?"

"Whatever you want," she says lightly.

"Whatever it is, you're going to lose."

"You were the one losing when I walked in," she points out.

"I won't lose with you."

"Oh?" She tosses her cue from one hand to the other. "And why is that?"

"Because of the stakes I'm playing for."

7

Zara

"Stakes, huh?" I'm pleased my voice comes out in a low, modulated purr.

I'm one of the board members of the 7A Club. I'm also the only woman on the board; something I intend to rectify. Meanwhile, I decided to swing by to conduct a meeting with a prospective client. I completed the meeting and was on my way out when I heard Hunter's voice as I passed the billiards room. My instinctive response was to avoid him and keep walking, a response which annoyed the heck out of me. If it were anyone else, I'd pop in and say hi, so why am I treating him differently? Why am I so worried I'll give away just how much he affects me? He's only an arrogant twat. So what if he's sexy as hell? Surely, I've embellished our last encounter in my head. And that kiss... Oh, my god, that kiss. It can't be as good as I remember it, right?

There was only one way to find out. I had to walk into the room and face him. And that's exactly what I'd done. I entered the room and assumed my persona of the confident career woman, the one who'll never shrink from a challenge. It's a role I've perfected over the years. Only, I've always recognized when to back down. That's the reason I'm successful.

I know when to cede ground and when to push my advantage, and this entire situation is one where my instincts scream I need to get the hell out. Away from him, before I get in way over my head. But I've missed seeing him. Missed the high cut of his cheekbones, the meanness of his thin upper lip, offset by that puffy lower lip that seduces me to lean in and nip on it to find out if he tastes as dangerous as he appears. He's taken off his jacket and rolled up the sleeve of his button-down, and those veiny forearms—good god, they're enough to make my panties self-combust.

As it is, I'm aware of the throb between my thighs, the sweet ache in my lower belly that flared to life as soon as his gaze locked on mine. It's like a tractor beam pulled me toward him, and at the very last moment, I managed to tear my gaze from him and greet Declan. And then, Hunter stepped right in front of me. He blocked the other man from my line of sight, and for a second, I was shocked, and I hate to say it, but it also aroused me.

That's the move of an alpha staking his claim. A primal instinct he harnessed to make very clear to the other male that I'm out of bounds. It was both unnecessary—for I regard Declan as a friend and nothing more—and also, so primitive, so elemental in its rawness, it left me breathless.

My thighs clench, my core spasming in on itself with the keen awareness that I'm so empty inside. I've never felt like this before, not in relation to a man, and the sheer suddenness and strength of my reaction has left me unable to protest. Also, damn, but it's so good to see him. I didn't realize how much I've missed him until just now, while he's standing there, all power and grace and so much masculinity, I'm sure my ovaries are opening up and welcoming him to stamp his name on them.

Whoa! This is unexpected. I know I'm attracted to him, but to think of pursuing something with him is career suicide, to say the least. He's in the public eye, and if the chemistry between us were spotted by the tabloids, my reputation would take a nosedive. I'd be the woman the Prime Ministerial candidate has a thing for. Forget what I've achieved on my own merit so far. It's a narrative I'm determined not to have thrust on me. It's why I'm going to come out on top of any encounter with him. It's why I'm going to win this game with him.

"Remember what you said the last time?" He leans forward on the balls of his feet. "If you come out with me again, you'll kiss me of your own accord."

"I'm aware," I murmur.

His lips curl. "If you lose this game, you come out with me on a second date."

"I won't lose."

He chuckles. "You're very confident of yourself."

"Is that a problem?"

He narrows his gaze. "The only problem is that the more I try to keep away from you, the more I can't stop thinking of you."

I blink. "Excuse me?"

His gaze intensifies. "You sound surprised," he drawls.

"I... I am. I wasn't expecting you to—"

"Say what's on my mind?"

I nod. "It's not the kind of candor I thought I'd hear from a man who comes from a privileged background."

The skin around his eyes creases. "There you go, passing judgment on me again."

I stiffen. "I'm not passing judgment."

"Aren't you?" He shoves his free hand in the pocket of his pants. "Since we've met, you've told me you hate my background, you don't trust my upbringing—"

"I didn't—"

"'You belong to the kind of entitled, snobbish, rich pricks who think the world owes them.'" He inclines his head.

Heat flushes my cheeks, but I don't look away. "You remember what I said word-for-word, eh?"

His lips twist. "I remember everything about you, Fire."

The heat spreads to my chest, and down to that traitorous core of me. My toes curl. I like his nickname for me. A little too much, maybe. I tip up my chin. "Don't call me that."

"You're fiery, stubborn and light up everything around you. You snipe at me, and I want to turn you over my lap and spank you. You scowl at me, and I want to kiss you. You challenge me and give no quarter, and that only turns me on more. You constantly try to—"

"Stop," I say through gritted teeth. "If you think you can sweet talk yourself into my pants—"

"I'm not just thinking; I know I'm going to fuck you."

"Oh?" I scoff.

"You can deny it as much as you want, but there's enough chemistry between us to light a bonfire without matches."

"A-n-d he's poetic, too." I tap my finger to my cheek. "But that's not going to make a difference."

"Hmm." He looks me up and down. "How about we play for it? You win the game, and I'll let you leave. I win the game and—"

"And?" I snap.

"And you kiss me, right here, right now."

"I thought you said, if I lose this game, I come out with you on a second date."

"Oh, that, too—" He smirks. "But first, you kiss me."

"Keep dreaming, buster. I'm not going to lose."

I toss my cue in his direction, and he snatches it.

I slide the button of my coat out of its eye, and his breath catches.

This is the true power I hold over him, and I am going to enjoy every single moment of his annihilation in this game.

I undo the next button, and his gaze follows my movement. I release the last button on my jacket, and the front falls open. I ease the jacket down my arms slowly, slowly, then hold it out to him. He transfers my cue to his other hand so he's holding both my cue and his in the same hand, then takes my jacket from me. He brings it up to his face and sniffs it. A hot sensation springs to life between my legs. It's not like he sniffed my panties, but oh, god, he might as well have. One side of his lips kicks up. He walks to the side and drapes it over the back of a chair. Before he's done, I'm walking over to the pool table. I rack the eight balls, then position my ball in apex position.

I straighten, turn and gasp, for he's standing next to me. And he's only holding one cue. Huh?

"Aren't you going to play?"

"I already am, baby." He lowers his voice to a hush, and my nerve endings crackle. A cloud of heat seems to spool off of him and smash into my chest. I draw in a sharp breath, and he smirks. *Jerk.* He probably knows exactly what his nearness is doing to me. He holds out my cue, and I take it from him; or at least, try to, for when I wrap my fingers about it and tug, he doesn't let go. For a second, both of our fingers are wrapped about the stick, his fingers mere centimeters from mine. He hasn't touched me, but the way he rakes his gaze over my face… Well, it doesn't bear contemplation. His scent is a deep, woodsy bouquet that teases and weaves its fingers through my hair, about my neck, down my spine. I tug on the cue, and this time, he releases it.

I spin around, then line up my shot. I bend over the table, knowing the skirt is pulling tight across my butt, knowing the hem has slid up the length of my thighs, knowing the cut at the side has pulled apart and bared an expanse of skin for his perusal. I sense him stiffen. I haven't moved my head, but I can feel the tension that radiates off of him. Good! Two can play this game, and if jerkwaffle here thinks I'm one of those girls who'll be taken in by his charm and a few words of flattery, he is sadly mistaken.

With a clack, my ball breaks the formation and I sink two of them. I straighten, turn in time to see him raise his gaze from where he'd fixed it previously—in other words, on my arse. I'm not Kim Kardashian, but I'm not being immodest when I say my rear end is almost as spectacular.

My figure bloomed as soon as I hit puberty. While I was elf-conscious about it, I soon realized boys loved my behind. I'm not flat chested, either, but while my bust is what an ex called 'neat,' it's my butt that captures the imagination of men and keeps it there. And this asshole is no different.

I stretch a little, thrust my arse out, then walk around the table, making sure to put an extra swing into my hips. I twitch my backside, then bend over again, positioning my cue so that I am almost halfway across the table as I line up my next shot. I take my time, focusing on the ball. Once again, I sense his gaze track down my spine to my behind and lower to where my skirt has ridden up almost to my arse. It's still decent; I'm sure my panties aren't showing or anything. I'm equally sure the material has pulled across my butt enough to show off the mounds of my arse-cheeks. I focus on my shot, then swipe my cue forward. My cue ball hits the one on the far side with a thwack, when thwack, a slap heats my backside. The shock zings up my spine. What the—!

I straighten and swing around with the cue stick raised. He shoots out his arm and grips my wrist, stopping me. The feel of his palm print seems to be etched into my behind. A snarl boils up my throat. I try to pull my hand away, but his grip tightens. My fingers loosen their grip on the cue stick which clatters to the floor. I raise my free arm, but he grabs it and twists it behind my back. He yanks me forward so my breasts are smashed into his chest. So I can feel the planes dig into my curves. I struggle to break free, and he hauls me even closer, until we're joined from chest to pelvis to thigh. Until the hot thick column at his crotch stabs into my lower belly. Until a shiver zigzags down my spine. Until my core clenches. Until wetness coats my lower lips and my toes curl.

"Let me go," I snap.

He curls his lips. "After you teased me like that?"

"I wasn't teasing you."

"What do you call laying across the pool table until you were all but making love to the play field?"

"That's called trying to get a competitive advantage." I bare my teeth.

His grin widens. "And this is called pushing my advantage."

8

———————

Hunter

I lower my head to hers, slowly, slowly, giving her enough time to move her head. I'm holding her hands so she can't move, but I'm giving her the freedom to turn her face away from mine. I pause with my lips so close to hers that our breaths mingle. We're so close I can make out the golden flares that jump deep in her eyes.

"I'm going to kiss you now."

I'm not sure why I warn her. It's not like me to announce my intentions. I want something, I take it. But with her, somehow, it's different. I need her with me every step of the way. And maybe I say it aloud because I expect her to take advantage of the choice I'm giving her and turn away. Instead, she tips up her chin and rises up on tiptoe so her lips brush mine. A jolt of lust zips down my spine. My balls harden. She must feel it, for a groan slips from her mouth as she pulls back.

The next moment, we move toward each other. I open my mouth over hers. I suck on her lips. I hold her gaze as I deepen the kiss—as I swipe my tongue across the seam between her lips, as I nip on her mouth, as she thrusts her breasts further into my chest, as her hips cradle the column that throbs between my legs. The blood drains to my groin. Those golden sparks in her eyes lighten until they seem to resemble flickers of static. The hair on the back of my neck rises. I release her, only to grab handfuls off her butt cheeks. She moans, and the sound arrows straight to my cock. I squeeze the soft flesh and she yelps. Color flushes her face. Her eyes resemble pools of liquid gold, and fuck, if that isn't the hottest thing I've ever seen.

I hoist her up and onto the pool table. She winds her arms about my neck, and I plant my bulk between her knees, forcing her legs further apart.

"Wait, my skirt—"

There's a ripping sound, and suddenly, I'm standing between her thighs.

"My skirt—"

"Fuck the skirt." I close my mouth over hers and swallow whatever it is she's been about to say. She freezes for a second, and I take advantage of her temporary complacency. I sweep my tongue between her lips, and when she parts them, I swoop inside. I dance my tongue over hers, tilt my mouth and deepen the kiss. I suck from her, swallow her breath and knead my way up those gorgeous thighs of hers, the sight of which has been driving me crazy over the past fifteen minutes. I bring one hand up and wind my fingers about the nape of her neck. With the other, I coax her to wind those spectacular legs of hers about my waist. A shudder grips her. I nip on her bottom lip, and with a groan, she melts into me. She swings her legs up and locks them about my waist. I release my hold on her neck, only to cup the back of her head. I deepen the kiss and lean forward and into her. She resists for a second, then allows me to guide her onto her back on that damn pool table which I had been so jealous of earlier when she'd leaned over it. I ensure my palm cushions her head, then with my other hand pinch her chin to hold her in place. Still holding her gaze, I kiss her deeply. And she kisses me right back.

She digs her fingertips into my hair and tugs. My cock jumps. Her chest rises and falls, and she squeezes her thighs pulling me even closer into the valley between her legs. I'm so hard now, my dick is going to stab straight through my boxers and my pants. I release my hold on her chin and cup her breast. I squeeze, and her entire body jolts. I tug on her nipple, which stands to attention, outlined by the fabric of her silk shirt. I pinch her nipple, and she tightens her hold about my waist. And still, she hasn't closed her eyelids, but neither have I.

If we could talk without speaking, then surely, that's what is happening now. My body is communicating with hers, my eyes holding hers, my breath mingling with hers, my lips fused with hers, and my cock aching to be inside her. My heart stutters; that warning beat is back, pounding in my chest. For a second, I stay where I am with my palm cupping her breast, then I tear my mouth from hers.

We stare at each other, my blood pounding in my temples, my throat dry, a ball of emotion forming in my chest and growing until it seems to weigh me down. I step back and pull her up with me. She blinks and looks between my eyes, then lowers her legs. I hold her shoulder until I'm sure she's stable, before I move away from her.

"That shouldn't have happened. I'm sorry."

"Excuse me?" Her voice is soft, her expression open. The look in her eyes is one filled with lust. I feel myself leaning toward her and stop myself. I am doing the right thing.

"It was a mistake. A moment of weakness, which I allowed myself to be overcome with. It won't happen again."

"Wait, hold on—" She raises a hand. "You're calling what we just did a mistake?"

"Yes."

"You bastard." The lust clears from her gaze. Her features harden. Her eyes snap golden fire, and goddamn, she's a sight to behold.

She glances around, then snatches up a pool ball.

"What are you—"

She lobs it at me. It's thanks to my quick reflexes that I duck. The ball grazes past my cheek. I straighten in time to see her sling another one, and another. I weave to the left, then right. I close the distance to her and wrap my arms about her, holding her captive. "Let me go," she snarls.

"Not until you calm down."

"Calm down? I'll show you how calm I am." She straightens up and sinks her teeth in the side of my throat. Goddamn, my cock twitches. Pinpricks of heat radiate out from where she's bitten me. She leans back, and I spot the blood that coats her teeth.

"Fuck!" I bend my head and fix my mouth on hers. She struggles in my hold, tries to kick out, but I don't let go. I kiss her and keep kissing her, absorbing the taste of my blood from her mouth until she stops trying to escape. Muscle by muscle, she relaxes in my arms. I soften my kiss, draw on that drugging taste of hers that swirls on my palate. A groan wells up. I loosen my hold on her. The next second, she's pulled free. She pulls back, flattens her palms on my chest and pushes. She's not strong enough to move me, but I pause. We stare at each other. I see the same confusion in her gaze that I feel.

"I'm sorry, I didn't mean that." I murmur.

She opens her mouth as if to say something, and I press a finger to her lips. "Don't, baby."

She swallows, glances between my eyes, then flicks out her tongue and licks my digit. A flash of fire coils low in my belly. My thigh muscles bunch. "Jesus, Fire, this is crazy."

"You can say that again." Her voice comes out hoarse, and she clears her throat. I bring my finger to my mouth and suck on it. Her gaze intensifies.

"You're right, we shouldn't be doing this. It was a mistake." She swallows.

I nod. "A temporary insanity."

She glances away, then back at me. "It won't happen again."

"It can't," I agree.

We glance at each other, and the air between us grows thick. Sparks seem to shoot out from our joined gazes. The blood in my veins pumps harder. We move toward each other when— "Hunter, good to see you here." A voice I recognize as JJ Kane's calls out.

I jump back; she stiffens, then smooths down her skirt.

I stay where I am, hoping I've blocked her from the line of sight of the door. She brushes the hair back from her face, then smooths her features into what I've begun to realize is her 'media face.'

"If you know what's good for the both of us, you'll stay away from me." She turns and heads to where I've hung her coat over the back of the chair. The rip in her skirt is barely noticeable, and the confidence with which she walks deflects from the flaw in her outfit.

She shrugs into the coat, then turns to JJ. "I was just leaving."

He looks from her to me, then back to her. "It's nothing urgent, I can come back."

"No, really, we're done here." Without another look at me she marches toward the door. "Nice place you have here. Can't say the same about the members you've opened it up to though." She brushes past him and leaves.

"Ouch." JJ winces. "What did I interrupt?"

"Nothing." Everything. I bend and retrieve the fallen cue stick, then walk over to the case and stow it next to mine. At least our cues get to spend the night together. I shake my head. Did I actually think that? Clearly, I'm going out of my head. I need a change. Need to do something different. Maybe call one of the models I've been out with recently —and all of them were dull, boring, perfectly turned out, and completely vapid.

"Hunter?"

I shut the door to the case and pivot to face JJ. "You were saying?"

"That you need to unwind, you're wound too tight."

"Exactly what I'm thinking." I head past him when he speaks again.

"I thought I couldn't be with her, but then I realized the only thing stopping me was myself."

I pause and glance at him over my shoulder. "I assume you're speaking about you and your girlfriend?"

"Lena, she was my son's girlfriend before we got together."

I'd heard so but hadn't really concerned myself with the details.

"I thought we were all wrong for each other. I'm twenty-six years older than her, you know?"

"There a point to this conversation?" I scowl.

One side of JJ's lips kicks up. "Humor me." He slides two cigars out of his jacket pocket and offers me one. I hesitate, then walk back and accept it. He heads for the bar on the far side of the room and picks up a cigar cutter from the corner top. He snaps off the cap end of his cigar, turns and takes my cigar and does the same before handing it back to me. He picks up a lighter, leans over and lights my cigar, then his own. We puff for a few seconds. Then he raises his cigar in my direction. "I tried to give her up. God knows, I did, but each time I tried to leave her behind, it's as if a part of me shriveled up and died. I realized then, the most important part of me was her. Living without her was like living without air...or water...or any of those things that are life-critical. Know what I mean?"

"If you mean you seem to have a romantic core that, I admit, surprises me, then yes."

He chuckles. "You remind me of myself when I thought sharing my emotions was a sign of weakness. I didn't realize how ballsy it was to share what was on my mind with her. I didn't realize how life-changing it would be to go after her. The moment I stopped fighting my instincts and embraced my reality, everything flipped on its head. I knew I was going to find a way to be with her, no matter what it took."

"You didn't have the media spotlight on you. You weren't going to embark on a campaign for the top leadership spot in the country."

"You're right, I didn't." He places the cigar between his lips and takes a puff, then blows out a cloud of smoke. "I only had the relationship with my son at stake. She and Isaac were living under my roof. Of course, they were already having problems, but still… She was, technically, his girlfriend. I was also her boss. The relationship was forbidden on so many levels. Of course, she found out later that he'd cheated on her, but still…" He glances at the tip of his cigar. "All the external signs indicated even thinking of having anything to do with her was so wrong."

"But you couldn't stop yourself."

He barks out a laugh. "Everything within me insisted she was it for me. That I couldn't let her go. That I was going to fight for her any which way, even if I had to play dirty."

"With your own son?"

"There was that. I'd been estranged from him. A possible relationship with Lena meant I might lose him…" He winces. "But that didn't happen."

"It didn't?"

He glances up at me. "Turns out, we found our way through it, after all. Isaac and I are far from the best of friends, but at least he stays in touch with me. It's more than I could say about the state of our relationship before. I wouldn't have found my woman, and gotten my son back, if I hadn't put aside my doubts and focused on what my heart said was right for me."

I take a drag of my own cigar, and the sweet cherry-laced scent reminds me of Zara. Hell, everything reminds me of her. Which is crazy. We don't have a future together. I'm going to become the Prime Minister of this country. That's where I need to focus my attention. Nothing can come between me and the goal I've held for so long. Even if it wasn't my dream to begin with, somewhere along the way, I adopted it for myself. I've internalized it enough that it's a part of me. One I can't cast off. And if I have to bury thoughts of her deep inside to fulfill my ambitions, so be it. I place my cigar on the lip of the ashtray and straighten. "Good talk." I turn and head for the door.

"Hunter?" JJ calls after me. "Sometimes, you only get one chance at finding real happiness. Don't screw it up."

9

Zara

"What if this is my one chance at true happiness and I blow it?" My friend Solene's face fills my phone screen. She's an up-and-coming pop star whose last song hit number one on the charts. When that happened, it seemed like her life changed overnight, and she's still coming to grips with it. Especially the impact it's had on her personal life.

I met Solene through my other friend, Isla, who's a wedding planner. I met Isla via a work gig a few years ago and we hit it off right away. I met Lena through her as well, and the four of us ended up hanging out a lot. Then, after Lena met JJ and moved in with him, Solene, Isla and I gravitated toward each other.

Now Isla, too, is married—which really leaves me and Solene as the last singletons standing in our social circle. Strike that. Solene has a boyfriend—who also happens to be one of the hottest stars in Hollywood. And clearly, while both of their careers are taking off, it's not all smooth sailing in their relationship, as evidenced by her pinched features.

"What if I've already blown it?" She hunches her shoulders.

"Why, because you decided to go off on your tour rather than stay home with your boyfriend?" I scoff.

"We've only been together for six months; it's still early in our relationship," she says softly.

"Six months is not that young a relationship. And if the two of you love each other, then it shouldn't matter how far apart you are, right?"

She places her phone on the side of her dressing table and begins to apply her make-up. "I guess so."

I narrow my gaze. "What does that mean?"

She pats the foundation onto her cheeks as she answers, "It's just, sometimes I'm not quite sure what we feel for each other."

"Umm. You either love each other or you don't. There's no gray area here, is there?" Not that I'm the one to give relationship advice, considering I have no idea what the hell that last encounter with Hunter was all about. I walked in there intending to prove to him—and myself—that I was impervious to his efforts. I spectacularly failed. Sure, I flaunted my body at him, and I expected him to react, but I was also confident I'd be able to resist him. Boy, was I wrong. Did I say that already? Well, it's true. And I just can't stop thinking about it. I'm so mad at myself.

The moment his lips touched mine, the moment his breath mingled with mine and his scent teased my senses, it's like I descended into a fugue state. My body insisted I lean into his and absorb his taste, and his touch, and the indentation of his hard muscles into my skin. I came undone, my panties soaking wet as he leaned into the space between my legs.

That was two months ago, and I still haven't forgotten how that thick, fat column in his pants stabbed into the softest part of me. How his fingers felt wrapped about the nape of my neck, around my wrist. How it thrilled me when he grabbed greedy handfuls of my butt and squeezed and—

"Zara? You there?"

"Eh?" I glance at the screen. "Of course, I'm here."

"Hmm..." Solene looks at me closely. "Seems to me like you're distracted."

I laugh. "Moi? Distracted? You know that's not possible."

She picks up her eyeliner wand and scans my features. "I don't know. For a second, it seemed like you drifted off."

"I'm very much here."

She continues to survey my features. "You have dark circles under your eyes. Have you been sleeping okay?"

"I've been sleeping just fine," I lie. No, I *haven't, actually*. The twathole is haunting my waking thoughts. I tossed and turned last night, and when I finally fell asleep, I dreamed of Olly. Something I haven't done in a while. I thought I finally put his passing behind me, but maybe something like that never truly leaves you. Maybe all that happens is that the grief settles somewhere deep inside you where you can't see it, only to unfurl when you're feeling more vulnerable. Which I am now, thanks to Hunter-knobhead-Whittington.

"You sure? Is there something you want to talk to me about?"

"Not right now." I mean, what am I going to say? That I have a huge crush on the one man I need to steer clear of? That the more I try to not think about him, the more it seems my body is unable to forget how it feels to be around him? Nah. Best to pretend nothing happened. And nothing *did* happen. We had dinner. *And you let him all but fuck you on the pool table in a place where anyone could have walked in on the two of you, and damn, but that had been hot.* Not only how he made me respond, but also the fact that he didn't give a damn that we could have been discovered at any moment. And somehow, his confidence, his not giving a damn about what that could do to his reputation, and the fact that the entire situation is so forbidden… It only turned me on even more. Ha, even thinking about it makes it all seem insane. "I'm good, really." I paste a smile on my face.

Her lips curve. "Not fooling me, but fine. If you're not ready to talk about it, I'll let it go."

"Thanks. I promise, I'll tell you more when there's something to tell, okay?"

"Hmph." With a last look at me, she turns to her mirror and begins to outline her eyelids. "We haven't really gotten around to declaring our feelings for each other."

"That's normal, right?"

"Is it?" She completes one eye, then turns to the other. "When my sister Olivia got together with Massimo, they declared their feelings for each other within weeks."

She's referring to Massimo, who was once part of the notorious Cosa Nostra. However, in the past few months, he and his brothers have gone legit. They funneled their assets into the formation of CN Enterprises and Massimo's the CFO.

"By all accounts, coming clean about your feelings and marrying each other within weeks of meeting is the exception, rather than the rule," I point out.

"I know." She sets down her eyeliner, then reaches for her mascara. "Guess their relationship raised my expectations. I keep thinking Declan will announce his feelings for me, but so far, there's been nothing."

"The two of you did take to each other right away though. You left for the US with him within days of meeting him, didn't you?"

I wait while she finishes applying mascara. "I was bowled over by him. Once I saw him, nothing else existed."

"So, what changed?"

She picks up a lipstick and puckers her lips. "Both of us becoming so successful so quickly. He was already on the rise when I met him, and now, with his second big hit, he's a hot Hollywood property. He needs to capitalize on his success and sign the best offers he can get his hands on. And then my big hit—which was completely unexpected…"

"So, the two of you have had to focus on your careers? It happens, right?"

"I always knew it would be challenging when both of us have such demanding careers. What's complicating it is being in the media eye."

"You mean #solan?" I chuckle.

She pauses to smear the color over her lips, then when she's done, sets down the tube. "We've barely had the chance to get to know each other, and now the media's all over us. The paparazzi are everywhere. We can't step out of our house in LA without being snapped. I don't mean to sound ungrateful. This is why I moved to LA, to make a name for myself. And Declan is so talented, too—"

"So are you."

"Thank you." She lowers her mascara wand and turns to me. "It just hasn't been easy. And now, he's shooting in London, and I'm about to embark on my tour."

"Which has already been getting amazing reviews, by the way."

"It's been better received than I expected."

"Don't sound so surprised. You're amazingly talented, and that video of your song with the both of you is adorable."

She blushes. "Thanks. It feels so good to hear it from you and—"

My phone vibrates. I glance at the message that pops up on screen. "Oh, my god, the baby's coming."

"The baby? Whose? Summer's, or Karma's, or—"

"Summer's."

My phone vibrates again. I read the second message from Lena.

"And Karma's," I murmur.

"What? Both of them?" Solene screeches.

I hold the phone away from my face. "Yes, apparently. Gotta go, babe."

"Message me and keep me posted."

"I will." I blow her a kiss and disconnect the call, then grab my bag and run out the door.

I burst into the waiting room of St George's Hospital and come to a stop. The room is crowded. Summer's husband Sinclair has close knit friendships with the rest of the Seven of 7A Investments, and Karma's husband Michael is one of seven Sovrano brothers, and the former Don of the Cosa Nostra.

The wives of the Seven have become friends with those of the Sovranos. And...given the fact that Summer and Karma are sisters, it means there are a lot of people invested in the arrival of these two babies. Still, I hadn't expected quite so many of them to be here.

It's through Isla that I met the rest of the Seven and the Sovranos. Summer has included me in various get-togethers. While I initially turned her down, she was persistent that I attend—that's Summer for you, as I've discovered—and eventually, I gave in.

Now I take in the familiar faces of Arpad, who is one of the Seven, and his wife Karina, as well as Weston's wife Amelie who's talking to Karina. Then there's JJ and Lena, who jumps up from her seat as soon as she spots me. I walk over to her, and we embrace each other.

"You came!" she gushes.

"Of course, I came." I lean back and gaze into her face. "How much longer do you expect it's going to be?"

"We don't know. These are babies, remember? They set their own schedules." Amelie reaches us, and while I'm not one for group hugs, this occasion definitely calls for one. I wrap my arms about the other two women.

"Isla, did you—"

"I messaged her, and told her not to rush back from her fourth, or is that fifth, honeymoon?" Lena laughs.

Liam and Isla got married six months ago on Liam's island near Venice. Since then, the couple has split their time between the island and London. It seems like they rush back to the island every chance they get.

"And Karma? How's she doing?" I glance between Lena and Amelie. "I thought there were a few more weeks to go before she gave birth."

"The baby's premature. But hopefully, everything will be fine," Lena says in a soft voice.

"Weston is with her now, along with Michael," Amelie adds.

Karma suffers from a heart condition that was exacerbated by her pregnancy. Michael has been very worried about her, all through the pregnancy. It's why they moved from Sicily to London—so Karma could be close to Summer, and the sisters could support each other through their pregnancies. Weston, who's a heart specialist, has been monitoring Karma through the last few months.

"I'm sure she's going to be okay." I pat Amelie's shoulder.

"Oh, I hope so," Lena says and lowers her chin to her chest.

"She's a fighter. I'm sure her baby is going to be running circles around us very soon," I say firmly.

"I agree." Karina joins us. "Medical science has advanced so much, and the baby is only a few weeks early. She is in safe hands."

I shoot her a grateful look. Normally, in situations like this, it falls to me to be the strong person in the group. It's my default setting—to bury my doubts and be the person everyone else can lean on. And I sense a kindred spirit in Karina. Her background, too, is slightly different from the others. She comes from a Russian family, and her brothers form the Bratva. She also runs a top-notch security firm that the Seven and the Sovranos have turned to when they need additional safety measures in place. She nods in my direction, then wraps her arm about Amelie's shoulders.

The door bursts open, and the hair on the nape of my neck stands to attention.

10

Hunter

I burst through the doorway of the waiting room, and the first person I see is her. She's standing in the circle of women, with her gorgeous dark hair flowing down her back. She's wearing a dress this time—a dark blue number that clings to the dip of her waist and stretches across the lushness of her behind before it outlines her strong thighs and comes to below the back of her knees. She's also wearing stockings— netted stockings, with a seam running up the back before it disappears under her dress. The blood instantly drains to my groin. The fuck? Oh, and I almost forgot, she's wearing four-inch heels which make her legs appear even longer, accentuate the muscular lines of her calves, and push out that spectacular butt of hers so I can't take my gaze off of it. I am here to lend support for the delivery of my friends' wives' children. Instead, I seem to have sprouted a boner that most assuredly tents the crotch of my pants. I stalk inside and she turns toward me. Those amber eyes of hers gleam. For a second, something like happiness flashes across her face. Her gaze widens. Her lips part. She takes a step toward me, then stops herself.

I cross the floor until I come to a stop in front of her. Even with those fuck-me heels, she only comes up to my shoulders. She's not short, by any means, but she's also not a tall woman. She's five feet, seven inches, at the most. The perfect height for me to lift her up and coax her to wrap her legs about my waist as I bury myself inside her hot softness… As if she's reading my mind, she tilts up her chin. Those amber eyes turn molten gold. Sparks of silver flash in them. But her breathing is erratic, and her chest rises and falls. Her orange blossom and vanilla scent teases my nostrils, and my heart thuds against my rib cage. I raise a hand to touch her cheek when —

"Hunter, you're here!" Arpad draws abreast and slaps me on my back. "Where's Declan?"

"I messaged him. He's on his way."

"Don't you have a campaign to run?" Zara scoffs. The earlier delight I glimpsed on her face is replaced by that haughty aloofness I now recognize as her mask.

"I have two months to go before I file my nomination," I say mildly.

"Well, don't you have to do whatever it is rich pricks like you do in the run up to the nomination?" She flips her hair over her shoulder.

"Does it bother you that I'm here?"

She seems taken aback, then laughs. "Of course, not."

"You sure?" I scan her features. "Because you seem to be rattled to see me."

"That's your ego speaking. Not everything in this world revolves around you."

"Except that —"

Arpad clears his throat. "Umm, guys, maybe you want to take this outside?"

"No need," I say at the same time as Zara. I narrow my gaze on her, and she scowls back at me.

"We're done here." She turns to leave, when I shoot out my arm and circle my fingers about her wrist. Pinpricks of heat shoot out from the point of contact. She must have the same reaction for she stiffens.

"Actually, I think we do need to speak."

She scowls at me over her shoulder, and I drop her hand at once.

"We have nothing to say to each other," she snaps.

"On the contrary. I think we need to discuss our last meeting."

"Our last meeting?" She scowls.

"Unless you prefer to talk about it here?" I glance about the assembled group of people, all of whom are now watching our interaction.

She follows my line of sight, and her lips tighten. She scowls at her friends, but it doesn't seem to have any impact. Amelie smiles sweetly at her. Lena leans an arm on Amelie's shoulder and grins. Karina has a wicked smile on her face.

"I don't think it's right to leave. What if the babies come while we're away?"

"I'll text you if I hear anything," Amelie says brightly.

"Hmm." She blows out a breath and turns to me. "Fine, let's go, but I'll choose the space."

"This is where you want to speak?" I glance around the bustling cafeteria located on the ground floor of the hospital. Many tables are occupied by doctors in scrubs; others by nurses in uniform. Still other tables have people in street clothes. Either staff, or people who have come to visit patients. The buzz of voices fills the air.

"You have a problem?" she retorts.

"I know what you're trying to do."

"Oh, so now you're trying to read my mind?"

"You think it's safer to have this conversation in a public setting. That's why you brought me here, didn't you?"

"I brought you here because I heard the coffee here is good."

I shoot her a disbelieving look. "At a hospital cafeteria?"

"Don't mock it until you try it." She walks over to the buffet counter and places a salad on her tray. I pick up my own tray, then select a plate of pasta. By the time we reach the payments counter, I've added some fruit and a slab of chocolate cake.

"That all you're having?" I glance at her tray which still has only the salad on it, in addition to two cups of coffee.

She gives me a withering look. "You have a problem with it?" She reaches for her handbag, but I lean over and tap my card on the machine on the counter.

"I can pay for my own food," she says in a hard voice.

"Too late." I smile at the cashier, who smiles back at me.

"You look familiar." She scans my features.

"It happens sometimes. I have the kind of face that people seem to think they've seen before."

She continues to stare at me as I watch the machine process the charge, then her face lights up. "Oh, I know who you are: Hunter Whittington." Her smile widens. "You were so good on Newsnight last night on the BBC."

"Thank you."

The machine spits out the receipt which she hands over to me. I turn to leave, but she pulls a strip of blank paper from the register, grabs a pen, rounds the counter, and thrusts them at me. "Please, can I have an autograph? It's for my son."

"Your son knows who I am?" I frown.

"No, but you're famous, aren't you?"

Next to me, Zara snorts. A reluctant smile tugs at my lips. I place my tray on the counter and take the pen and paper napkin from the woman.

"I'll grab us a seat." Zara turns and walks away. I can't take my gaze off of the sway of her hips.

"Are you two dating?" the woman asks.

"Can I pay for my food please?" An irate voice pipes up behind me.

"So sorry for holding you up." I quickly dash off my signature and hand the paper and pen back to the woman.

"Excuse me." The woman opens her mouth to speak, but I grab my tray, then spin around on my heels and head toward where Zara is seated. I slide into the seat opposite her, facing away from the crowd, and once again, glance at my full tray and the lone salad bowl on hers.

"You sure you don't want to share some of my food?"

She slides a cup of coffee in my direction. "Very sure."

I glance at the coffee then back at her. "Really?"

She inclines her head. "Don't you trust me?"

I hold her gaze. "I do." I reach for the coffee and, without breaking my gaze from hers, take a sip. An intense aroma fills my mouth, followed by a sweet flavor tinged with just the right edge of bitterness, all coated with richness that makes me groan.

I blink. "Whoa!"

"Told you."

I place my cup back on the table. "Question is, do you?"

"Do I what?"

"Do you trust me, Zara?"

She lowers her gaze, then stabs her fork into the salad and spears some leaves. "Not on your bloody life."

I blink, then bark out a laugh. "Jesus, woman, can you be any more perfect?"

She shoots me a glance laced with disbelief. "Umm, did you hear what I just said?"

"Did you hear what I said?" I smirk.

"Do you always have to answer my question with a question?"

"Do you always have to pretend you don't enjoy our verbal sparring?"

Her lips twitch, then she schools her features into an expression of haughty indifference. "What did you want to talk to me about?" She lifts the leaves to her mouth and closes her lips around the tines of the fork. I watch in fascination as she licks some of the dressing off her lips. The sight of her pink tongue sends a shiver of lust down my spine. My pants grow tighter at the crotch. Fuck, this is so not the time. I really should tear my gaze off of her mouth, instead of imagining how much I'd like those lips wrapped about my cock. A-n-d my balls tighten. If my dick grows any thicker, I'm risking an embarrassing accident the likes of which haven't happened since I was sixteen.

"Hunter?" Her lips form my name and warmth pulses through my veins.

"Once more," I order.

"Excuse me?"

"Call me by my name again," I murmur.

"Are you serious?" The edge in her voice cuts through my thoughts. I raise my gaze to find her glowering at me.

"Very. I haven't been able to forget what happened between us, Zara."

She scoffs. "I have no idea what you're talking about."

"You mean to say you haven't thought about what would have happened if we hadn't been interrupted by JJ that day at the club?"

She holds my gaze for a second, then glances away. "What happened that day was a mistake."

"Look at me and say that."

She swallows, inhales, then turns to hold my gaze. "It was a mistake."

I look between her eyes, but the mask she wears for the world is back in place. She's almost as good at hiding her feelings as I am. She's just as much of a professional who can play the media. We're so evenly matched, I couldn't have found a woman more in tune with my needs than her.

"Zara—" I reach over and place my hand over hers. "You don't mean it."

Once again, a zing of electricity shoots out from the point of contact. My throat closes. A weightless feeling flutters in my chest. And all I'm doing is holding hands with her in a crowded cafeteria. The noise fades away. The rest of the people disappear. It's as if we are cocooned in a world of our own where all that exists is her and I. And this…jolting awareness that joins us.

She must feel the same sensations, for color suffuses her cheeks. "You haven't called me once in the two months since that day," she says in a low voice.

"Two months and fifteen hours, to be precise," I murmur.

Her gaze widens. "How did you…" Her voice trails off. She scans my features and her lips firm. "Why didn't you call me, Hunter? Once again, we meet, and then I don't see you for two friggin' months. It's as if you're committed to only running into me after long intervals of time."

"I was traveling. Also, if I recall correctly, you're the one who told me to stay away from you."

"I know what I said, and that's beside the point. You didn't even message me."

"You could have called or messaged, too," I point out.

"Why would I do that?" She begins to pull back her hand, but I grip her wrist and hold on. "Don't do that, Zara. Don't shut down on me."

"This won't work, Hunter. We both have too much to lose."

"I, more than you."

She firms her lips. "Oh, you're going there, are you? Because you're the man in this relationship—"

"The man who's standing for elections to be the leader of this country."

"And I've built my career as a crisis manager. Someone who can be relied on to defuse tricky media situations for my clients. Imagine if it got out that I was involved with you."

"We'll cross that bridge when we come to it."

"Easy for you to say that. You're not the one whose competence will be questioned."

"Because you're dating me?"

"Who said anything about dating?" She tugs on her hand again, and this time, I release her.

"I'm saying it. Now. I want to try and see how it would go if we were to formally date."

11

Zara

"Date? Did you just ask me out on a date?"

"It would seem that way, yes," His lips twist, and damn, but that smirk of his is so hot. As is the invisible print of his fingers around my wrist that I can still feel. He forgets about me for months on end... Again. And when we run into each other, he thinks he can pick up from where we left off?

"No," I snap.

He blinks. An expression of surprise forms on his features before he smooths it away. "Okay." He picks up his fork and digs into the bowl of pasta.

"That's it? Okay?"

He licks the pasta sauce from his fork, and my core clenches. How would it feel to have him stab that tongue inside my cunt. *Oh god, you did not just think that. Did not.* I stab my fork into my salad and shovel some of the cheese into my mouth.

"You don't want to date me. I can respect that."

"Hmm." I fork more leaves between my lips, watch as he digs into the pasta with gusto. He chews and the tendons of his throat flex as he swallows. My stomach stutters, and moisture pools between my thighs. Damn it, I should be impervious to him. Especially after how he ignored me for the past few months. In fact, come to think of it, there's a strange pattern to our meetings. We run into each other, apparently by accident, and the attraction flares. I end up doing something crazy, like kissing him, or he fingers me, or I get a sense of what he's packing between his legs... And then, he's gone. Poof. Just like that. It's almost like he's showing me how it could be between us, then vanishing so that I'm left wanting. And then I have to stop myself from stalking him online. Except for the headlines he makes when he attends some social event or another with his models. Something which I'm sure he wants me to see so he can make me jealous. I push away the salad.

"Not hungry?"

"Nope."

He finishes off his pasta—which he seems to have inhaled, by the way—and reaches for his chocolate cake. He scoops up a spoonful of the icing and slides it between his lips. He licks the spoon and my core clenches. My toes curl.

I reach for the coffee and take a sip. The bitterness of the brew laced with a tinge of nutty sweetness sinks into my palate. "Mmm." I close my eyes to savor the liquid, letting the warmth envelop me.

When I open my eyelids, he's watching me with those blue-green eyes of his, which now resemble a stormy sea. His nostrils flare. His jaw is tight. He seems to be trying his best to get control of himself.

Good. Two can play this game, and it's not one I intend to lose. I take another sip of the coffee, and he draws in a breath. I swallow and his gaze narrows.

Then he scoops up a sliver of the chocolate and offers it to me.

"You're going to feed me here?"

"No one's watching us."

"There's always someone watching. You should know that."

"Indeed. But I'm willing to take the risk. Question is, are you?"

My heart flutters in my chest like the wings of a dragonfly. Am I willing to take the risk? Am I? That's the big question. One for which I don't have an answer. I glance about us and find, sure enough, no one is paying us any attention. Also, our table is set to one side in an alcove, so we're somewhat hidden from the rest of the room.

"Where's your security personnel?"

"They're around."

Once again, I scan the people at the other tables but don't see anyone who resembles his security team.

"They're good at their job," he drawls.

"Indeed. How about you? Are you good at what you do?" Shit, hadn't meant for that to come out quite that suggestive. My subconscious is getting ahead of me.

His lips kick up and he gives me a full, blinding smile that lights up his features and positions me at the receiving end of all of his charisma. Even though I know exactly what he's doing, it doesn't stop my pulse from drumming at my wrists, at the base of my throat, between my legs. He is potent. All he has to do is turn on his charm and few would be able to resist him.

He looks at the spoon of chocolate he's holding out, then back at my face.

I scowl.

"Zara." He lowers his voice to a hush and a thrill of anticipation grips me. No one, no man so far, has been able to command me, to tell me what to do. Yet this man, with simply an intonation of his voice, has me salivating to fulfill his every demand. He's good, I'll give him that. Am I going to give in to him. Am I?

He holds my gaze, and the air between us grows thick, charged with everything unsaid, tinged with the lust that has colored our every encounter. A cloud of heat seems to plume off his body and slam into my chest. I gasp. He leans forward and slides the spoon between my lips.

The creamy dessert melts on my tongue. The acrid taste of cocoa combined with the sweetness of sugar coats my taste buds. I swallow, and it slides down my throat, and seems to head straight for my core. He has a direct line to the most intimate parts of me, and I'm not even sure how that happened.

He brings the spoon to his mouth and sucks on it. A million fires seem to erupt under my skin. I grip the edge of the table, my breathing erratic. I need to look away from him, now. I try to tear my gaze away from his, but it's like we're connected, entwined, linked, affixed together. It's as if some part of him has hooked into me and is now reeling me in.

I lean forward; so does he. He places the spoon down, leans across the table. Closer, closer. I can see the fine lines that radiate out from the edges of his eyes, the flashes of gold deep in his irises, as if he's drawing on that secret fire power that lights him up from inside. That haloes him and attracts people to him. I am but a helpless insect caught in his web and he's reeling me in. We're so close, his breath grazes my cheek. I glance down at his mouth, part my lips.

My phone buzzes. I ignore it and flutter down my eyelids. His phone rings, and I sense him hesitate. I snap my eyes open to find he's looking at me with so much longing that my breath catches. His phone continues to ring. My phone buzzes again.

"The babies!" I exclaim at the same time as him.

"He's so cute." I touch the tiny fingers of the baby that Summer is holding. Twelve hours of contractions, followed by five hours of labor in the hospital, and the baby finally burst into the world. Weighing in at nearly nine pounds, he's also bigger than expected.

"I can't believe you pushed him out without an epidural." I wince.

Karma's baby was born a few minutes after Summer's, but he was nearly four weeks premature, so they rushed him to the neo-natal unit. Karma's still sleeping off the emergency cesarean. Michael opted to stay with her. We were told that we can see her tomorrow. Both sisters gave birth to boys.

Summer had a natural birth, with both her and the baby in good shape. She bounced back quickly after the birth and was eager to show off her son to the rest of us. Now, I watch as she kisses her son's forehead. "I confess, it's the hardest thing I've ever done. But it's worth it."

"He is," I say softly. I draw my fingertip over his tiny knuckles. "He's perfect."

"He is." Summer sniffs.

Sinclair, who's sitting next to her, kisses her forehead. "You did well, baby. I'm not sure I could have gone through what you did." His voice is tinged with awe.

I glance up at him and realize, under his tan, he's pale. Summer, on the other hand, is glowing. There's an ethereal light in her eyes that tells me she still hasn't come down from whatever endorphins flooded her system during the birth.

"I hope you're giving her a 'push gift' that makes up for everything she went through." I narrow my gaze on him.

Summer laughs. "This" —she glances at the baby— "is enough of a gift. I don't need anything else."

Sinclair rubs his cheek on her hair. "You know I'd pluck the moon from the sky and place it at your feet if I could, baby. You showed me what it means to feel. Without you, I was lurching from one disaster in life to the next. Then you came along and taught me what it is to belong. I love you, Summer."

"Aww," Summer raises her head for a kiss.

I look away and my gaze clashes with Hunter, who's been standing on the opposite side of the bed.

All of the others came by and saw the baby in pairs, so as not to crowd the newborn, until it was only Hunter and me. When we were ushered in together, I didn't protest. It seemed silly to say I'd go in separately. But being here with him, and watching Summer and Sinclair cuddle as they enjoy their first few moments as a family with the baby is, somehow, more difficult than I expected.

"Do you want to hold him?" Summer's voice interrupts my thoughts.

"But he's just been born." I blink.

Summer laughs and holds him in my direction. My stomach coils in on itself. I glance blindly in Hunter's direction.

He must sense my panic, for he steps forward. "I'll take him." He scoops up the little bundle from Summer and cuddles the baby close to his chest. The sight of the tiny infant against his big broad chest as he holds him carefully is unexpectedly poignant and hot. So hot. I've never found the sight of men carrying babies sexy, until now. For that matter, I've never consciously gravitated toward babies.

I have friends who've been obsessed with their biological clock and swore they needed to have children to feel complete, but I've never been like that. Maybe it's because I had to be the strong one in my family, and was used to taking on responsibility from a very young age. Or it's because my father always encouraged me to be independent. Because I wanted to break stereotypes from the time I was little. Because I had to protect my twin brother and be strong for him. Because I was so focused on my career.

Either way, having children has never been a priority for me. So why am I so shaken at seeing Hunter with a baby? Why is my mouth dry, my stomach churning, and my heart pumping so hard, I'm sure it's going to break through my ribcage? "Excuse me." I rise to my feet and stumble toward the door.

12

———————

Hunter

"Zara, wait!" I hand the baby over to Summer and follow Zara out of the hospital room. One second she was fine. The next, she jumped to her feet and bolted for the door. I'm not sure what upset her, but I plan to get to the bottom of it.

She hustles down the corridor and toward the waiting room at the far end. By the time I enter the space, she's standing by the window looking out.

"What's wrong?" I draw abreast with her, but she refuses to look at me. "Zara, why are you upset?"

"I'm not upset," she says in a hard voice. But when I try to peer into her face, she looks away.

"You are definitely upset." I step around her, and she instantly looks the other way again.

"Zara… Fire."

"Stop already with your silly nicknames. Especially when you don't mean it," she bursts out.

"How do you know I don't mean it?"

"If you did, you wouldn't have just disappeared after the last time we met. Not a message, not a phone call, not even a goddamn dick pic."

I stifle a chuckle. "Do you want me to send you a dick pic?"

"No. I don't want anything to do with you. Can't you get that through your thick skull?"

"And yet, you're pissed off at me because I wasn't in touch with you."

"I'm not angry at you. I'm angry at myself." She locks her hands together in front of herself.

"And I'm trying to figure out why that is."

"I don't need to tell you anything." She pulls out a handkerchief from her handbag and dabs under her eyes.

"Zara, baby, don't cry. Please." I grip her shoulder and turn her to face me, but she averts her gaze. "Please, tell me what set you off. Please?"

"You don't get to ask that question—"

"—Because I wasn't in touch with you for the last few months?"

"I know, I'm the one who told you to stay away, and I was right. So I'm not really sure why I'm upset right now."

She tries to pull away from me, but I don't let go.

"Is it because of the baby?" I scan her features.

"What?" She stiffens. "What makes you say that?"

"Because I thought we came to some kind of agreement in the cafeteria. I thought you agreed to date me."

She tips up her chin. "You're the one who said you want to date me. I didn't agree to anything."

"So are you saying you don't want to date me?" I peer into her features. "Are you, Zara?"

She tips up her chin. "I'm saying, anything between us is impossible. I've worked too hard to get to where I am. I can't throw it all away by getting involved with you. I don't want to be seen as someone who sleeps her way to the top of her profession."

"I'm not even a client, Zara."

"But your party is. I've done work for them in the past. I've built my career on being someone who is a problem solver, someone who can defuse the trickiest media situations. I am a fixer. I am the expert media personalities, including pop stars and politicians, go to when they need help. I'm good at what I do."

"I know that."

"And I'm effective."

"What are you trying to say?" I frown.

"That my reputation rests on the fact that, while I've helped others with their PR campaigns, I, myself, have always stayed away from any scandal. I've kept my reputation intact by steering clear of any kind of involvement, with anyone or any situation. It's why the media has never found anything on me. It's why I am respected. It's why I am able to influence the influencers. It's why journalists and celebrities alike agree to be steered by me. The position I occupy in the minds of the media is my currency. I can't fritter it away."

"You're likening what's between us to the makings of a scandal?"

She looks between my eyes, then nods.

"But what if it didn't have to be that way?" I lean in closer to her. "What if we give this—whatever this connection is between us—at least, a chance?"

"It will have to come out at some point. You're going to be standing for elections. I've worked with other members of your party. At some point, people will connect the dots and know what's happening."

"Why don't we cross that bridge when we come to it?"

She laughs. "Typical. Of course, someone who comes from a wealthy background doesn't need to plan out. Maybe you can do things on the fly, but I'm not that way. I couldn't have gotten to where I am without having planned every step of my career. And that did not include—"

"Someone like me."

She swallows, then nods. "That's right. I didn't plan for someone like you coming along. I can't afford to have someone like you in my life on a personal level. You're a distraction I don't intend to dwell on for too long. We're too different, you and I, and there's no common meeting ground for us."

I tighten my hold on her shoulders. "Are you sure about this? Is there nothing I can do to change your mind?"

She looks between my eyes, then nods. "There is one thing you can do."

"Anything."

"Forget you ever met me."

A hot sensation stabs my chest. My stomach muscles clench. It shouldn't be so difficult to walk away from her. We barely know each other. So why does it feel like I am cutting off a part of myself I didn't even know belonged to me?

"Zara—"

She shakes her head. "There's nothing more to say Hunter." She pulls back, and I release her. She secures her bag over her shoulder, then pivots and heads for the doorway.

"Zara!" I call out after her.

She pauses.

"This isn't over."

"The coffee actually is quite good here." I slide the paper cup in Michael's direction. We're seated at a table which has been pushed up in the corner of the waiting room of the hospital.

"I think I should be with Karma." His gaze remains focused on the doorway. His shirt is crumpled, and for the first time since I met him, he's not wearing a jacket or a tie. His hair is mussed, his chin shadowed with whiskers with hints of gray peeking through. There are dark circles under his eyes and hollows under his cheekbones. He looks like someone who's wife has given birth by emergency cesarean to a four week early premature baby.

He insisted on sitting by Karma's side, his fingers entwined with hers as she slept. It took the combined efforts of Sinclair and me to get him out of her room. He only agreed when Zara, who dropped by to see her, insisted that she'd stay with her. A Zara who refused to even acknowledge my presence, much to my annoyance. Not that I expected anything more, given how we parted yesterday. I left the hospital soon after and returned this morning to check in on Karma and Michael.

I found the waiting room, once again, full—this time, with Michael's brothers who had taken to keeping watch outside Karma's room and the nursery. Not that there's any danger to Karma from anyone, given the Sovranos have made peace with most of their enemies—and, rumor has it, neutralized those who didn't accept their offer to end any clan wars.

Still, given the newborn is Michael's heir, the first in the next generation of Sovranos, they feel duty-bound to stay alert and ensure no one gets through to mother and child. The hospital didn't protest about their presence, which isn't a surprise, considering the kind of weight the Sovranos carry with those in power. And while I'm confident that same influence extends to keeping their presence out of the media, I don't particularly want to tempt fate by being seen with them in public. But

Michael's my friend, and I want to be here for him and Sinclair. Which is why I grabbed a couple of coffees on my way in and insisted he join us for coffee in the waiting room. Now, I train my gaze on him.

"She's in good hands," I reassure him.

"Weston is the best in his field." Sinclair leans forward in his chair. "Along with the Chief Consultant of Obstetrics from the hospital, they won't leave any stone unturned when it comes to her safety."

Michael drags his fingers through his hair. "The doctors have been wonderful, and the baby is going to be fine. I just worry what impact going through the delivery has had on Karma."

"The challenging part is over, and she has a new baby to look forward to. She's going to be back on her feet and healthy very soon." Sinclair takes a sip of his coffee, and an expression of shock skims his feature. "What the—" He glances at the coffee, then back at me.

"Told you." I try not to recall sitting here with Zara when she said the same thing to me just yesterday. Yesterday... When she reiterated that I shouldn't try to keep in touch with her, while her actions conveyed the opposite. She was upset that I hadn't messaged her or called her since the time we last met. Yet, she was as insistent that nothing could develop between us. She's not even willing to give us a chance, which is bloody frustrating.

"Did you hear me, Hunter?" Sinclair's voice cuts through my thoughts.

"It's Zara who introduced me to the coffee." I roll my shoulders, trying to dispel the niggling ache that has settled there.

"Zara, huh?" Michael seems to grow alert and narrows his gaze on me. "So, you and Zara—"

"Me and Zara, nothing," I add quickly.

"I think he's protesting too much. Don't you think he's protesting too much?" Sinclair turns to Michael.

"I think he's protesting too much," Michael agrees.

I scoff. "Since when did the ex-criminal and his victim begin to see eye-to-eye?"

Both of them stiffen. "Tread carefully, Whittington. Spouting bullshit to your constituents seems to have loosened your tongue," Michael says in a low voice.

I raise my hands. "You're right. I'm sorry. I crossed a line there." I glance between them. "Still, you have to admit the two of you sitting across the table from each other and ganging up on me is a far cry from when you two were essentially on opposite sides."

The two of them exchange glances. Something passes between them, then Sinclair cracks his neck. "It's true that Michael's family was behind the incident when the rest of the Seven and I were kidnapped. But now that I'm a father, I've realized no child should pay for the sins of the father. I haven't exactly lived a blemish-free life, myself… And it's true what was done to us changed the course of our lives forever. It left us emotionally crippled, and if we hadn't met the women who've given each of us the courage to allow ourselves to feel again, things would have looked very different. But we did meet them, they did change us, and here we are today, with both of our wives having delivered newborns next to each other in the same hospital ward."

"Also, our wives are sisters." Michael rolls his shoulders.

"Summer would never forgive me if I held a grudge against her sister's husband," Sinclair admits.

"And I am deeply apologetic for what happened to the Seven."

I glance between them. "I assume this apology also had a monetary aspect to it."

"It did cross my mind that an offer of investing in Sinclair's company would help ease the pain of what had happened, but then Karma told me to put myself in Sinclair's shoes. She asked me how I'd feel if I had been the one who'd been kidnapped and emotionally tortured as a child, and then had my perpetrator's family tell me they'd make it up to me with money." He winces. "Rest assured, that put things in perspective."

Sinclair inclines his head. "And Summer asked me how it would feel if someone held a grudge against my child because of something I did." He raises a shoulder. "It's time to move forward. Our sons are cousins."

"I don't want any child of mine to be tainted by my past," Michael agrees.

"And I don't want any of my children to carry on the quest for revenge that dogged most of my life," Sinclair confirms.

I rub my chin. "If only politicians could see eye-to-eye on important policies." I draw in a breath. "I say that because I'm one of them. Sometimes, it's difficult for me to see things from the opposition's point of view. And hearing the two of you, my instinct says it's best for my country if I try to find common ground, rather than take issue with them."

"Perhaps that might not be a savvy move though. It would dilute your message," Michael points out.

"Perhaps," I reply, and tap my fingers on the table, "but the only reason I went into public service is so I can make a difference to the community and my country."

"You having second thoughts about running?" Sinclair narrows his gaze on me.

"Maybe."

"Does it have anything to do with a certain dark-haired woman who's been able to stand up to you and who clearly takes no bullshit from you?" Michael drawls.

"Possibly." I glance at the cup in front of him. "Also, have you tasted the coffee yet?"

He glances at it, then lifts the cup to his mouth and takes a sip. He blinks, then does a double take. "And that came from the hospital cafeteria?"

"Good, right?" I smirk.

"Almost as good as the espresso in Italy, and far superior to the swill they serve at most coffee shops in this country." He takes another sip, and the muscles of his shoulders seem to unwind. "Give my thanks to Zara for introducing you to this brew."

"On that…" I rest my elbows on the table and place the tips of my fingers together. "I need your help with something."

13

Zara

"How are you feeling now?" I take Karma's hand in mine.

Her lips curve slightly. "I do feel like I've run a marathon, or many marathons, but it's all worth it."

I squeeze her fingers. "Spoken like a true mama. You are so damn brave, Karma."

"Because I gave birth?" she asks a tad dryly.

"Not only, and you know what I mean."

She glances to the side, then at me. "It was stupid of me not to have mentioned my heart condition to Michael."

"Maybe. But you wanted the baby, and I can understand why you didn't want to worry Michael about your heart condition complicating things further."

She blinks. "You do?"

I chuckle. "Don't sound so surprised. Granted, I'm not the most maternal person around, but I respect how important being a mother is to you."

"You're wrong, you know." She scans my features, "You are maternal."

"I'm not," I scoff.

"You helped Isla through the ups and downs leading up to her wedding with Liam. You're the first to stand up for the underdog. As soon as you heard about Summer and me, you dropped what you were doing and raced to the hospital. If that isn't being empathetic—-which is really what a mother is—then I don't know what is."

Heat flushes my cheeks. "I did what any good friend would have done."

"You went beyond the scope of friendship. You're here holding my hand so my husband can take a break."

I dip my chin so my hair covers my features. "It's not a big deal. Anyone else would've done the same."

"You have an incredibly busy life, an agency to run, and some very tricky PR disasters to mitigate, as we speak. In fact, if I asked you to pull out your phone, I bet I'd see innumerable missed calls, text messages, and an overflowing email inbox, and yet, you're here sitting with me instead. Not once, have you glanced at your phone in all the time you've been talking to me. And I've heard it buzz."

I laugh. "I'm here because I wanted to see you. Of course, I'm not going to look at my phone while I'm talking to you. It would be disrespectful to do so, not to mention, discourteous."

She stares at me.

"What?" I scowl back.

"How many people do you think would say what you said just now?"

"I don't know about anyone else. This is just my mindset, you know."

"Precisely." Her smile widens.

"Now what? Spit it out, woman. Clearly, you've spent some time thinking about this. Whatever it is." I resist the urge to roll my eyes.

"Actually, no, but you're easy to read, at least, for me."

"Oh?" I incline my head.

"You hold your feelings in check, and think showing them is a sign of weakness."

"Isn't it?" I shuffle my feet.

"See?" She jerks her chin in my direction. "That's what I mean. Bet you have a gamut of emotions running through you right now, but to look at you, one would think you're the very epitome of grace and beauty and sophistication. Which you are, of course—"

"Of course," I deadpan.

"It's just… You don't like showing your feelings to the outside world. Maybe not even to your close friends."

I shrug. And yet, I revealed more of myself to him than I intended.

"Hmm." She purses her lips.

"Now what?" I tug on my arm, and she releases it.

"It's just—" She surveys my features.

"Just what?" I squirm a little, trying to find a more comfortable position. I would've never guessed Karma's this insightful or this intuitive when it comes to sussing out the feelings of others.

"Just… When you meet the right man, you're going to fall really hard." Her lips kick up, once more, in that smug smile. You know the kind—where someone who is married and has a baby smiles, hinting that they know a secret, something to which you're not yet privy.

But even she doesn't know exactly how much Hunter occupies my thoughts, and I plan to keep it that way. I wave my hand in the air. "That person does not exist."

"So they all say. I—" She winces.

I stiffen. "Are you okay? Do you need something? Should I call the doctor?"

"Stop, now you're acting like my husband. It was just a twinge from the stitches."

I grimace.

She chuckles. "I bet, when it's your turn, you'll be the one to deliver without an epidural."

"God forbid I ever get pregnant," I exclaim in horror.

"And, I bet you'll be back on your feet the next day."

"Umm… I'm not Superwoman."

"You sure?" she says smugly.

"Wait." I blink. "Was that a trap? I feel like I walked into a trap."

"I'm not sure what you mean." She releases my hand and lays back against the pillow with a sigh.

"You sure you're okay? I can call the nurse if you want more painkillers—"

"You need more painkillers? Why do you need more painkillers?" Michael strides into the room. He rounds the bed and drops into a chair next to Karma. "You okay, Beauty?" He takes her hand in his, then leans forward and surveys her features. "Are you in pain?"

"No, I'm not, Capo," she says softly.

His chest rises and falls, and he seems to be controlling his emotions with great difficulty.

"Are you sure? If there's anything else I can do to make you more comfortable..."

She shakes her head. "I'm fine. Have you seen him yet?"

He holds her gaze. "I'm looking at you now."

A shadow crosses over her features. "He looks so much like you."

He swallows. "I almost lost you."

"But you didn't. I'm not going anywhere, Capo. I plan to live to a ripe old age, and have more kids with you, and nag you so much you'll wish you'd have never married me."

"There's not a single day that goes by when I don't thank God for bringing you to me. As for more kids—"

She lifts her fingers to his mouth. "Let's not argue about that yet."

He seems like he's going to argue, then shakes his head. "Fine, we won't talk about that now. But Karma, you have to realize, I can't let anything happen to you. If anything had happened to you—"

"Kiss me, Capo," she murmurs.

A-n-d that's my cue. I pick up my bag, rise from my seat, and head toward the exit. I spot Hunter talking with another of the Sovrano brothers. It's Luca. I know who he is because Karma introduced us earlier.

All of the brothers I've met so far are tall, dark and good-looking in that swarthy, slightly exotic way that Sicilian men seem to possess. They're also stone-faced. And while Luca comes across as testy as them, he also possesses a streak of wickedness that marks him out as more unpredictable than the others.

Hunter is as tall as Luca, and on the face of it, more easy-going, but I'm coming to realize that's a fallacy. His brand of charisma is more lethal, for he can hypnotize you into thinking you're making your own decisions while, in actuality, you're following his lead. Hunter's brand of dominance is more dangerous, in that sense. You think you have a choice in the actions you take, but actually, it's him influencing you to do what he wants, without you having an inkling of what he's doing.

In a way, it's similar to how I operate. Which is why I recognize his technique. We're more similar than I realized; it's what makes him such a dangerous adversary. I can anticipate his moves, as he, no doubt, can mine... I have a sense of how he thinks. And while he may often be two paces ahead of me when it comes to planning his move, I'm going to do my best to outwit him.

"Excuse me." I jut out my chin.

Luca steps aside at once. Hunter, on the other hand, stays where he is.

I glower at him.

He shoots me a lazy smile.

My blood pressure spikes. "May I pass through?" I say through gritted teeth.

"Not stopping you," he drawls.

"This isn't the time, Hunter."

"On the contrary" —he slides a hand into the pocket of his slacks— "I'll take any time I meet you as the best time to try to convince you to date me."

"That ship has sailed," I snap.

"You're still standing here, aren't you?"

I pull back my shoulders. "Let me go, or I'm going to kick you in the balls."

Luca chortles.

Both Hunter and I glare at him.

He glances between us, then backs up a step. He turns and engages one of his brothers in conversation, keeping his voice so low I can only make out the odd word in Italian.

Hunter turns back to me. "You won't knee me, Fire." His lips twist. "You have a vested interest in my balls, remember?"

A chuckle bubbles up, and I bat it away. "Ha! Keep dreaming."

He looks between my eyes. "And my dreams are always of you."

My heart jumps in my chest. My stomach flip-flops. Stupid, stupid, school girl crush that I have on this guy. I'm acting like I'm sixteen again. Strike that, I've never had such a crush on anyone, not even when I was sixteen. I was too busy laughing at boys who'd fall for me and ask me out, and then I'd turn them down. Like I did with him. Only this time, I can't stop thinking of him. All the more reason to put this madness behind me and move on with whatever is next on my agenda and in my planned career trajectory.

"Hunter," I say in a low smooth voice. "Let me through."

"Nope." His smirk widens.

"If you don't, I'll—"

"You'll—?"

"I'll, uh, have to go through you."

"Please." He leans forward until the heat of his body envelops me. I shiver. My blood pressure elevates, until I can hear my heart pounding in my ears. Sweat beads my palms, but my mouth is annoyingly dry. To hell with this. I turn sideways, then ease myself through the gap between the door frame and his heavily muscled arm.

14

Hunter

She brushes past me, and for a moment, I want to turn and pin her in place against the door frame. And perhaps, she expects it, too, for she glowers at me. It turns into a look of surprise as I step back, then follow her down the corridor to the elevator doors. She stabs the elevator button, then turns on me. "What are you doing?" she hisses.

"What do you think I'm doing?"

Her gaze narrows. "Don't do that."

"Do what?"

"Don't think you can change my mind about our dating."

I tilt up my lips. "Wouldn't dream of it."

"So, why are you standing here with me?"

"Why, I'm waiting for the elevator, of course."

She tightens her lips. "You—" she begins to speak but the elevator dings. The doors open to reveal an empty cab.

I clap my hand on the doors to hold them open, then jerk my chin toward the cab.

She opens her mouth as if to protest, then changes her mind and walks through. I follow her in and press the button for the ground floor. The doors close and the elevator begins to descend.

We stand in silence for a few seconds, watching the numbers count down. The orange blossom, vanilla scent of her seems to intensify. I curl my fingers into fists at my sides. Do not do this, do not. You're going to stand for elections; you're on track to become the Prime Minister of this country! You don't need to screw everything up by risking your reputation. And what choice do I have? If I let her go now... I may never see her again. And then I'll have lost the opportunity I had to feel her, hold her, touch her, kiss her.... Kiss her.

I swing my arm out and slam the stop button. The elevator jerks to a stop.

"What are you doing? Are you crazy?"

She reaches for the control panel, but I grab her shoulders and push her up and into the wall of the cage. Her jaw drops. "Have you lost it completely?"

"Would you blame me if I had?" I flatten my palm on the wall next to her face. "Do you have any idea what being in close proximity to you does to me, Zara? Do you know just how much I need to feel my skin against yours, my lips on yours, my breath mingling with yours, my hands cupping, squeezing, kneading your curves as I bury myself in your hot, tight pussy?"

Color flushes her cheeks. Her chest rises and falls. She opens her mouth, then raises her gaze over my shoulder and at the camera in the far corner of the cage.

"It's not working."

"Eh?" She swivels her head in my direction. "How do you know that?"

"I have my means," I assure her.

Her gaze widens. "You mean to tell me that you knew how to get to that camera, in this lift, at precisely the time we are here and ensure the camera is out of order?"

I thrust out my chest, hold her gaze.

She draws in a sharp breath. "So this is how you use your power—"

"—And my connections." *Thank you Michael.*

"—To make sure you get what you want?"

"Only when it comes to you." I glance between her eyes. "I'd use any means possible to make you see the fallacy of your ways."

"And that includes accepting help from the Mafia to shut off the camera in this lift?" she snaps.

Very good. She's smarter than I gave her credit for, but a part of me already knew that. She and I, together? We'd be unbeatable. But first, I need to tame my Fire. Not that fire can be tamed; contained maybe, temporarily. And I certainly don't want to douse my Fire, but won't that battle of wills be thrilling? A flush of anticipation pulses through my veins. My balls tighten. I widen my stance to accommodate the column that throbs between my legs, then incline my head. "If needed."

She seems taken aback, then squares her shoulders. "While I have to credit you on your ingenuity, I must warn you, you'll never succeed in changing my mind."

"Is that a challenge, Fire?"

"It's reality, Hunter." She tips up her chin. "Your background gives you the confidence to walk on the morally gray side, with the blind faith that you'll get away with it, knowing that you are risking your career... And for what?"

"For you."

Her gaze widens. She reads my features, and she must see something there that gets the message home. She swallows. "Hunter, don't make this more difficult for both of us."

"It's very simple, Zara. We'll be good together—more than good, we'll have the kind of sex that comes along once in a lifetime—and you know it."

"Excuse me, are you hearing yourself?"

"Are you, Fire?" I search her features.

"I'm not sleeping with you, Hunter." She firms her lips.

"You will."

A shudder grips her shoulders, and her pupils dilate. Oh, she feels the certainty that has every part of me thrall. She senses the truth in my words. Her subconscious does, even if her rational mind is unwilling to accept it.

She tips up her chin. "No." The pulse at the base of her throat beats faster.

"Yes," I murmur.

She leans her head back against the wall of the elevator car. "Not sure what you're high on—"

"The nearness of your body."

She chuckles, then rubs at her temple. "Jesus, can't believe I actually allowed myself to laugh at that. Hunter, you have to stop this. You can't keep—" She waves her hand in the air.

"Can't what?"

"You know—" She gestures between us.

"No, I don't."

"You're going to make me spell it out, aren't you? Fine, here it is. You can't go around making these sweeping statements like you mean it."

"I do mean it."

"No, no. Stop right there." She shuffles her feet. "Enough already with the cheesy platitudes."

"Nothing cheesy about the truth, Fire."

"Oh, my god." She squeezes her eyes shut. "Are you seriously hearing yourself? You sound delusional, obsessed—"

"I am, about you." I lean in closer until my chest brushes hers, until my breath raises the hair on her forehead, until her scent intensifies, and I draw it in and hold her essence deep in my lungs.

A trembling grips her. "Hunter, this is all wrong. I can't let you do this. I can't let you jeopardize your career…and mine."

I tuck a strand of hair behind her ear. "Or maybe, this is how we take the leap to finding a path that's different, but much more satisfying for the both of us."

One side of her lips twists. She opens her eyes, and in the depths of her gaze, I see pain and regret…and something else. Something that gives me hope and squeezes my heart at the same time. It's a kind of wistfulness, a forlorn yearning, a longing for something that is so within our grasp. Something that she is going to turn her back on. Again.

"Don't do it," I snap.

"It's already done." She lowers her gaze and, this time, when she raises her eyelids, there's only calm acceptance, and a steely resolve. One that makes the band around my chest tighten further. I tighten my hold on her, and she stiffens. "Let me go, Hunter."

"I can't."

"Oh?" Her lips thin.

"If I did, you'd hate me for not pushing my advantage when I had the chance."

"If you don't release me, I'll hate you more."

"I'll take my chances." I lean into her, and she begins to struggle. Every brush of the sweet cradle of her hips sends a thrill of piercing lust radiating out from the point of contact. I pin her with my hips, and she gasps. A flicker of heat bursts to life in the depths of her gaze. Finally, fuck.

What I wanted to do earlier? I only temporarily managed to control my impulses. But being with her alone in the enclosed space of the elevator car, combined with her stubbornness in not wanting to give us a chance, has pushed me over the edge. I have no regrets that I manipulated the situation to essentially trap her here with me. I have no compunction that I'm holding her against her will right now. I'll take every opportunity I can get to convince her to give us a chance.

I lower my head until our breaths mingle. I draw in her scent, pulling it deeply into my lungs, letting it sink into my cells, and allowing it to slide down to my cock, along with most of the blood in my middle section. My head spins. My muscles harden. I am so engrossed in her that it isn't until my head snaps back and pain slices across my cheek that I realize she slapped me.

Anger pulses through my veins. Lust streaks under my skin. I glare at her, and the pulse at the base of her neck skitters. Her breath comes in pants, her pupils dilate, and something seems to snap inside of her. Thank fuck. It's the same animal instinct I've tried to hold in check since I met her. We move at the same time.

15

Zara

He moves at the same time as me. Our mouths fuse. Our teeth clash. A growl rips up his chest. The next second, he grips me under my butt and lifts me up. I wrap my legs about his hips. There's a ripping sound, and I stiffen for a second. Then he pushes his pelvis forward, and the long, thick column in the crotch of his pants stabs into my core. My pussy clenches, my clit throbs, and my nipples are so hard, I'm sure they'll tear through my blouse and jacket.

I have too many clothes on. I throw my arms around his neck, plaster myself to him. Mold myself to his hard planes and angles and gradients, and that very manly chest of his, which is so wide, it never fails to make me feel dainty and utterly feminine. Which is a first. It's not that I haven't been attracted to other men. No one has been macho enough, strong enough, secure enough, dominant enough to not feel intimated by my personality. With Hunter, that has never been a problem. He's so masculine, so virile, so completely male. And I don't mean just the fact that he is six-foot-three with shoulders so broad, they never fail to make my breath flutter and my ovaries clench. It's his mindset, his gaze, the way he surveys the space around him with a confident manner that is downright sexy and potent and so...so... Hot. It makes me want to climb him...and lick him...and punch him...and slap him...and then kiss him... The way I am right now.

As if he senses the roiling emotions running through me, as if he feels the surrender from deep inside of me, as if he's aware of the slippery slope of my thoughts, he tilts his head, opens his mouth over mine and devours me. He nips on my lower lip, and when I moan, he thrusts his tongue over mine, draws on my breath, sucks from me, and it feels like he's consuming me completely. A whine slips from my lips, the sound so needy, so wanting that it turns me on even more. My panties are soaked, and I can smell the sweetness of my arousal in the air.

As I cling to him—with my ankles locked about his waist, and my arms locked around his neck, with his cock jabbing into my pussy in a gesture so demanding, I'm tempted to rip off my panties and take him inside—I know, for sure, I've met my match.

A shudder grips me. My stomach seems to bottom out. My entire body turns liquid, and he squeezes the flesh of my arse to hold me up. My breasts are crushed into his torso, and my mouth is full of his tongue. My head seems to have dissociated from the rest of me. I have an out-of-body moment when it's as if I'm looking down on the titillating image we present. Then he releases my mouth, only to whisper kisses up my jaw and down my throat. He brushes aside the neckline of my blouse, buries his nose in the curve of my shoulder and inhales deeply. The action is so salacious, so much more sexually explicit than anything else he has done to me so far that my eyes roll back in my head. My clit throbs, my core melts, and I begin to grind against the hardness at his crotch with abandon. Oh, god, I'm going to come. I'm going to... A ringing sound slices through the haze of sensations that grip my body. I stiffen; so does he.

What the—? I try to get my brain cells to form a coherent thought.

"Ignore it." He digs his teeth into the curve of my shoulder and my pussy clenches. Moisture pools between my legs. Heat surges out, from where he's bitten me, to my extremities. Every part of me is hardwired to follow his command. To become his. *His. His. His.*

The ringing blares through the space, and I snap my eyes open. I take in the confines of the elevator car and a cold sensation clutches at my heart. I slap against his shoulder. "Let me go!"

He doesn't move.

"Hunter, let me the hell go!" I wriggle against him, and his cock lengthens; it grows even bigger. *Oh, my god.* My fingers tingle to hold that part of him, my mouth waters to taste him, my clit swells, and I push my pelvis up and into the tent at his crotch, yearning for release.

The ringing starts again, and Hunter swears. Without letting go of me, he reaches over and grabs the phone from the control panel of the elevator car. "What?" he barks.

He listens to the voice at the other end and draws in a breath. "No, we're good." He listens again. "Yes, Ms. Chopra is with me."

I stiffen. *Who is that? His security personnel? So now they know we've been trapped in the elevator for how long? Five minutes? Ten? More?* I struggle against him, and he leans more of his weight into me, rendering me immobile. *Asshole.* Still, he hasn't even broken a sweat, and he's holding me up with one arm—and his cock…umm, not quite, but you get the picture—while talking on the phone, and that is impressive.

"I'll see you on the ground floor." He slaps the phone back into the cradle, and the elevator car begins to move.

"Hunter, let me down!"

He scowls down at me. "You're the most annoying woman I've ever met."

"Ditto."

"And the most stubborn."

"Pot, meet kettle."

"And the most gorgeous."

"Same," I snap, then freeze. "You're a jerk."

"Yep."

"Let me go, you piece of—"

He moves back, and I hit the floor of the elevator, on my arse. *What the hell?* I shove the hair from my face and jump to my feet. "You let me fall? How could you let me fall, you—"

"You asked me to let you go."

Anger twists my guts. I take a step toward him, and he jerks his chin in the direction of the indicator above the door. We're on the second floor. *Shit!* I smooth down my skirt—my second ripped skirt, and this one is Chanel, argh! —then pat down my hair. I grab my Birkin from the floor and hook it over my shoulder. To think, I had been so caught up in our mutual lust that I hadn't realized I'd let it fall to the floor of the elevator… That's something. To be honest, a bomb could have gone off next to us and I wouldn't have noticed. That kind of distraction is epic, a once-in-a-lifetime occurrence and… Nope, not going there. It was a kiss; just a kiss. A mind-blowing, panty-melting, London Fashion Week kind of kiss… It was…something significant, all right.

This is so unfair. Why am I so attracted to him? Why is he so irresistible? And hot and sexy, not to mention charismatic, and he wants to do something for his community and his country. Yes, I've listened to some of his speeches in Parliament, and observed how he doesn't hesitate to raise tough issues with his opponents and doesn't think twice about questioning measures he doesn't agree with. He's known for taking risks, for speaking his mind, for challenging those whose outlook opposes his. He's seen as somewhat of a champion of the underdog—something which I find really attractive, too.

I hate to say it, but if there were a man powerful enough to hold his own against me, it's him. And he doesn't even need to try. It's both annoying and hugely seductive. That he could just be, and I'd gravitate to him; that he could reel me in without any protests on my side, and not much of an effort on his. It's frustrating and oh, so erotic. Tantalizing and completely exciting. And I can't afford to dwell on it.

I am going to put it behind me and move on. Stay focused. Stay centered. Keep moving forward. I draw in a deep breath, then another. When the elevator doors open, I hustle out, with Hunter on my heels. I brush past his security detail, then increase my pace. Of course, he keeps abreast. I reach the double doors leading out of the hospital and walk out, only for a flashbulb to go off in my face.

16

Hunter

"Mr. Whittington is Zara your girlfriend?"

"Zara, are you dating Mr. Whittington?"

More flashlights go off.

What the fuck? How did the paparazzi know I was here? Not that I'm trying to hide my movements, but it's not like I broadcasted to the world that I'd be here today. Perhaps, someone spotted me entering earlier?

My security detail brackets us in, one to my right and another on the other side of Zara.

"This way," David, one of my bodyguards says, and leads us through the throng of news people. One of the paps steps in our path and aims his camera in our faces. I reach out to cover the lens. "No photos."

"How about a comment then?" He lowers his camera. "Are you two dating?"

"Ian, isn't it?" I smile and hold out my hand. "How are you today?"

Ian hesitates, then takes my hand. "You still haven't answered the question. Is she your girlfriend?"

"She is a...friend."

"Was that a hesitation I sensed there?" Ian's gaze narrows.

"Have I ever lied to you before?"

He slowly shakes his head.

"We are here to see a mutual friend, and you caught us leaving together."

"Hmm." He doesn't look convinced.

"When I do have a girlfriend, if I ever have a girlfriend, I'll be sure to let you know."

He releases my hand. "I'll hold you to that."

I nod, then brush past him and reach for Zara's hand, both to guide her forward, and because I want to protect her from the pack, but she shakes it off. She flounces past me, a smile pasted firmly on her features. Her gaze is calm, certainly calmer than what I'm feeling now.

We reach my car, and I hold my door open.

"I am not leaving in the same car as you."

"Get in, Zara."

"They're still watching us," she hisses.

"And I'm giving my 'friend' a lift."

"I have my own car."

"David will follow us with it."

She scowls. I glare at her. "Fire, do this, please."

Maybe it's because I say please, or because she can't wait to get out of there, but she pulls out her key fob and slaps it into my outstretched hand. I hand it over to David. She slides inside the car, and I follow her. One of my security detail gets in the front seat next to the driver and we're off.

"We'll drop Ms. Chopra off at her apartment first."

My chauffeur nods, and I raise the barrier between the front and back seats.

She arches an eyebrow. "Fancy."

"Have I impressed the hard-nosed Ms. Chopra?"

She raises a shoulder. "Never seen a Range Rover with one of these." She nods toward the now raised divider.

"It's custom built."

She shoots me a sideways glance. "I assume it's also armored."

"And has a self-contained oxygen supply."

"Should you be telling me all this?"

"It's not a secret; you can look it up on Wikipedia. But even if it wasn't there, I'd share it with you."

She shakes her head. "Don't do that."

"Do what?"

"You know what. You're trying to pretend we have a future together and we don't."

"But we could."

She squeezes the bridge of her nose. "You're not listening to me."

"I am, but I don't agree with you."

"We were in that hospital together and you saw what happened. Already the newshounds are circling."

"And you and I are veterans at playing the media," I point out.

"Which is why I can't believe I allowed myself to be caught coming out of there with you."

"You couldn't have known that they'd have sniffed a story so fast."

"There's no story." She lowers her hand and locks her fingers together in her lap.

"Not yet."

She tips up her chin. "Never will be."

"You're stubborn."

"And you're a pain in the wrong place."

"I can do a lot to alleviate any pain in any part of your body, baby."

She groans. "Ugh, that was terribly corny."

"So, why are you smiling?"

Her lips twitch. "Am not."

"You are, too."

She covers her mouth with her palm.

"That's cheating."

The skin around her eyes crinkles.

I smirk. "Now you really are smiling."

She drops her hand and folds her arms across her waist. "You're good at distracting from the topic at hand. A born politician."

"And you do a fantastic job with your PR agency."

"You sound surprised."

"It was a genuine compliment." I raise my hands. "Honest."

"Hmph." She finally turns to scan my features. "Apparently, you do mean it," she finally says.

"Of course, I mean it. I've always admired your work ethic, your focus, and how you've defused the trickiest of media situations for your clients, including how you handled yourself back there." I jab my thumb over my shoulder.

"I'm a PR consultant." She angles her head. "Though I admit, being in the eye of the camera, rather than the person pulling the strings, has a very different feel to it. It's a good lesson to take away. I often demand a lot of my clients when they come to me with their problems. I've forgotten how you have to think on your feet while you are caught in the crosshairs of the paparazzi."

"You are inherently empathetic—"

"No, I'm not," she bursts out.

"—however you may try to hide it," I finish my sentence.

"Stop trying to find good traits in my character," she mumbles.

"Stop putting yourself down so much."

We stare at each, and a reluctant smile pulls at her lips again. "You're persistent."

"I am."

The moment stretches, the space between us, once again, charged with that connection that's shimmered between us from the moment we met. I reach over and rub the edge of her lips. She pulls away from me.

"Your lipstick; it's smudged."

"Oh, god, and that's how the photographers saw me?" She dips into her ever-present bag—now placed on the seat between us—and pulls out her lipstick and compact. She paints her lips with the color, and heat tightens my groin. She smacks her lips together, and fuck me, I almost come in my pants. I guess I make a sound, for she shoots me a sideways glance. "You okay?" she asks in an innocent voice.

"Don't push it, Fire."

She tilts her head. "Should I call you Brimstone then?"

"You may call me yours."

Her features harden. "Don't do this, Hunter."

"Now that you've refreshed your make-up, I think it's time."

"Time for what?"

"This." I reach over, clamp my fingers about the nape of her neck, and pull her close.

Her gaze widens. Her chest rises and falls. She swallows, but doesn't pull away.

"Do you want this, Zara?"

She doesn't answer.

"Tell me you don't want my lips on yours. Tell me you don't want to feel my breath entwined with yours, my fingers squeezing your arse, my cock in your pussy as I pound into you and take you to the edge but don't let you come... Not until I've pulled out and taken your arse; and even then, when you beg me, I won't let you orgasm—not until you agree that you belong to me and then—"

"Then?" she whispers.

"I still won't let you orgasm—not until I've shown you how explosive it is when you're in my arms. Until I've convinced you how good we are together. Until I've taken every hole in your body and shown you the kind of pleasure you've never felt before. Until every part of your body belongs to me. Until your curves cry out for my ministrations, your flesh yearns for my touch, your mind can no longer resist me, and your emotions and senses are honed in on me. Not until you acknowledge you are mine."

Her pupils dilate. The gold in them lightens until they seem almost silver in color. She lowers her gaze to my lips, and the pulse at the base of her throat speeds up.

I tighten my grasp about the nape of her neck. "Tell me to stop, Zara, and I will."

"Hunter, I... I can't." She raises her gaze to mine. "But if you kiss me, I'll never forgive you."

Zara

That's the last thing I said to him. In the back of his car, with the shaded glass of the windows hiding us from the outside world. He held my gaze for a second longer, his hold on the nape of my neck seemed to tighten almost imperceptibly, and then he loosened his fingers. He pulled back his arm, turned his head away, and it was as if a physical wall came down between us. He rolled down the screen that had hidden us from his chauffeur and bodyguard in the front seat, and for the rest of the journey he didn't look at me or acknowledge me again. He pulled out his phone and began to scroll through his messages. A first.

He never did that before. He always focused one-hundred percent of his attention on me, and now that I don't have it, I miss it. A few seconds earlier, he had his hands on me, his gaze locked with mine. And now, it's as if he's withdrawn from me. Completely. Of course, he did. The horrible, sinking sensation in the pit of my stomach tells me I've lost him. Irrevocably. I told him I'd never forgive him; it never occurred to me he might not forgive me.

I pushed him away once too often, and now, he's never going to look at me the same way again. It's really over, and he's never going to pop up in my life the way he'd been doing. The fact that it's been more than three months since that incident confirms it.

I glance through my office window and see the throng of shoppers on the streets of Soho. The Christmas lights were lit a few weeks ago. Christmas decorations began appearing in shop windows a few months ago. When autumn turned into winter, with the temperature plunging and warnings of early snowfall, I had no idea. I buried myself in work after that last run in with Hunter.

A new client—another impossible media disaster—a well-known politician turned down claims from a woman who insisted she was his illegitimate daughter. This time, I not only helped him navigate the barrage of negative publicity that followed his daughter's interviews with the press, but I also brokered a meeting between the two. I banked on the fact that when he came face-to-face with her he'd accept her, and sure enough, that's what happened. He even agreed to appear on her social media feed and publicly apologize for the emotional distress he'd caused her. He also publicly embraced her as his daughter, and the two hugged in a very touching moment on screen. Now that, I count as a win.

And perhaps, a few months ago I wouldn't have been so insistent that he meet with his daughter. Perhaps, I'd have focused only on the job he'd engaged me for, which was to redeem his reputation—which, by the way, I delivered in spades. But I knew I could make a difference, so I insisted he meet his daughter. In fact, the public claiming of his daughter helped to soften his reputation and make him more popular. It all worked out, and it wasn't all planned by me.

I'm…softening? Thawing? I can feel myself wanting to do better, to do good where I could. Oh, make no mistake, I'm still a cut-throat career woman, but somehow, something inside me insists I do more. The part of me I denied since my younger brother died… That emotional core of me came alive. And maybe, I have Hunter to thank for it.

I'm not going to admit that I miss his presence in my life, sporadic as it may have been. But I've been counting on him making an appearance two months to the day I lost him. In fact, I ensured I met up with Summer and Karma and their friends in the hope that I'd see him…

And also, so I could test myself. Did I actually miss him? Or was it my ego, bruised because he no longer seemed to want to pursue me? Maybe the fact that he'd been so insistent, and not taken no for an answer was more than a little flattering. It was the first time a man had been so persistent, and I enjoyed it. So now that he backed off, it was sobering. I felt a little deflated.

Or maybe it was the Christmas season which I admit is not the most favorite of times for me. It reminded me of how much I missed my younger brother. I was going to meet my parents and my twin of course, but this season is always a reminder of another year that Olly was no longer in our lives.

My phone vibrates. I turn to my table, look at the name of the caller in surprise. I raise the phone to my ear. "Lord Alan, what can I do for you today?"

"Zara, how are you?" My mentor's plummy voice fills the airwaves. He comes across as a crusty, old English gentleman, but his views have always been ahead of the times. No doubt, that's why he saw the potential in me and in my company, and hired me for my first project—to salvage the reputation of a bad boy rockstar after he trashed his hotel room and was caught urinating out of his window. A picture the paparazzi had a field day with. I not only helped turn around his reputation, but I also introduced him to a few charities which he supports to this day. Another win.

"I'm very good. How is Heather?" I ask after his wife.

"The same. She wants me to work less, but you know me. I'll rest when I'm dead."

"And not be around to trouble the rest of us? I can't see that happening anytime soon."

"Very true," he laughs, then quietens. I sense him gather his words and wait for a few seconds. Sure enough, he clears his throats then says, "I do have a very interesting project for you… Something which, if you deliver on it, will establish you as the go-to person when it comes to media management."

"Sounds intriguing," I narrow my gaze on a young couple walking arm in arm down the sidewalk. They stop to admire a window show-case. The girl leans her head into the man's shoulder, and his arm tightens about her. It's no different than hundreds of couples I've seen before but somehow, the way her dark hair flows down her back, as well the man's confident stance, the way he pulls her even closer as if he wants to hide her from the sight of the world, reminds me of Hunter and myself.

"Zara, are you there?" Lord Alan asks.

"Yes, of course." I turn away from the window and begin to pace my office. "So, it's a confidential project, and you can't tell me who the client is?"

"Not until the day you start."

I chew on the inside of my cheek. "Isn't that highly unusual?"

"Not in situations like this where we can't afford any information leaking."

"Hmm." I walk over to the couch in the corner of the room and lower myself onto it. "Of course, it's related to something political?"

He stays quiet.

"Is the top leadership of one of the political parties in trouble?"

"I didn't say it was political." His voice is cautious.

"You didn't have to. When Lord Alan, who's been retired from the industry and public life, calls me, I know it has to be about something more than a celebrity being caught with his pants down or a sportsman caught having an affair with a reality TV host."

"You did enjoy managing the positive spin campaign on that one though," he chuckles. He's referring to one of my previous successes, where I brokered an understanding between said sportsman and his estranged wife, so she didn't open up to the media about his other kinks. True story.

"That was one of the more satisfying campaigns I've worked on. The wife walked away with a massive settlement, and he later married his mistress, so everyone was happy."

"And if you take on this campaign and deliver on it, you'll consolidate your position as Kingmaker within the UK media circuit, a position which I know you're aiming for."

"So it definitely has to do with politics," I state.

"I can neither confirm nor deny that, Councilor," he laughs.

"So that's a yes."

"I never said that."

"Right." If there's one thing Lord Alan is good at, it's evading an issue. He can't be drawn into an argument at all. Not unless he intends to put forth his point of view which, at the moment, he is not in a mood to do. It's from him, I learned how to steer a conversation so it benefits me.

"So you'll do it?"

I blow out a breath. "You know I'd never turn you down."

"I know. And perhaps it's wrong of me to ask this of you, but I think, in the end, you'll thank me."

"Is there nothing else you can tell me about it?"

"Graham!" I hear a woman's voice call out his name over the phone.

"I'll call you when the details have been hammered out, my dear. Give my regards to your brother." He signs off.

I lower my phone to the table. My brother who's been overseas the last three months playing cricket matches and shows no sign of coming home, *that* brother? The last time I'd heard from Cade, was a rushed call before he'd left the locker room to get on the pitch. I doubt I'll hear from him again before the new year, if that.

Of course, I could go spend Christmas with my parents. But they still run the corner shop in a little corner of Leicester, so they'll likely be working through the holidays. Not even on Christmas, will they take time off. I've often told them they could afford to employ people to cover for them, but they won't even consider it. It's an unbroken tradition of forty years that the shop has stayed open. The only times they shut it was the day my father had a heart attack—not that he slowed down after that. And he insisted my mother open the shop the next day, which she had, reluctantly, leaving him in the hospital. And the other time was when the Queen passed away. They are staunch royalists, my parents. They admired the Queen for her work ethic, tenacity, and dedication, values they tried to instill in the three of us. And which my brother and I rebelled against, in our own ways.

My father's parents immigrated to the UK from the Indian subcontinent. My mother is English, but having married my dad, she seemed to have converted completely to his style of thinking and living, which equals embracing the need to equate your worth with your work. Despite my best efforts to rebel, some of their mindset must have sunk in because obviously, I inherited my workaholic tendencies from them.

Why else would I be at my desk in my office, at four p.m. on Christmas Eve? I definitely do need to get out of here.

I reach for my bag, when my phone rings again. Amelie's name lights up the screen.

"Hey you!" I say by way of greeting.

"Are you still in the office?" Amelie's wide-eyed gaze stares back at me from the rectangle of my phone.

"I was just leaving."

"Oh, are you coming over to our place for our Christmas Eve party?"

I wince. "Umm, I wasn't planning to, if I am being honest."

"Aww, Z!" Amelie pouts. "Everyone is here, including Karma and Summer." Karma's son had been kept in the neo-natal unit for nearly a month before being discharged. Since she brought him home, the boy has thrived and seems to grow bigger every time I see him.

As for Summer's kid, he looks exactly like a mix between her and Sinclair, and is the sweetest little boy I've ever seen.

"Victoria and Saint will be here with their new baby too," she adds.

She's referring to Saint, who's one of the Seven, and his wife Victoria, who had her baby at home. I love hanging out with them, but right now, I just need some time alone.

"I'm thinking of leaving London for a bit over Christmas."

"Really?" She tilts her head.

"Yeah." I rub the back of my neck. "I'm exhausted, and I think I could do with some down time."

"You've been working so hard lately," she says as she scans my features. "I understand why you want to get away, though I do wish you could come here. It would be nice to have you over. Why, even Hunter Whittington has promised to come by."

"He has?"

"Yep. Haven't seen him, either, since the day he arrived in the hospital after Summer's delivery."

"Oh?" I murmur, schooling my features into what I hope is an expression of disinterest.

"He hasn't announced his candidacy for Prime Minister. I wonder why that is?"

I do, too. And it's not because I've been following his appearances in the media or on his social media. Not at all. It's only because he's a newsmaker and my team keeps me briefed on all of the goings on when it comes to key figures in UK entertainment and politics, that's all. "I have no idea."

"You sure you don't want to come?"

"Nope." And especially not since what's-his-face is going to be there. I've been so good thus far. Coming face-to-face with him will only tempt me, and I can do without that. "I think it's best I get away for a bit. Re-energize, clear my head and all that, you know?"

"So where are you planning to go?"

"Umm… I… To be honest, I haven't thought it through. I only, just now, came up with the idea."

"Hmm." She looks at me speculatively.

"What?" I scowl back. "Do I have something on my face."

"No, but I may have something for you."

I tilt my head.

"I know the perfect getaway place for you."

"You do?"

"Uh, it's a little cottage just two hours out of London. Set in a beautiful little village which is right out of *The Holiday*."

"You're referring to the Kate Winslet and Cameron Diaz movie?"

"Yep. The cottage is also where Weston and I hooked up for the first time last Christmas."

"Really?" I laugh. "Now this is a story I have to hear."

"I'll tell you more another time. If you go now, you'll have enough time to get there before it's too late."

"Umm okay." She seems awfully keen to get me to go. Maybe she can see how tired I am. "Are you sure it's okay? Who does the place belong to?"

"Oh, it's jointly used by all the Seven. It's been refurbished recently. They have a caretaking service that keeps it in readiness, in case any of them wants to pop over for a weekend away. In fact," —her features brighten— "we keep it fully stocked. The caretaker is scheduled to go there this afternoon to add some fresh items. Text me a list of some of your favorite foods and we'll make sure they're included. You'll be able to cook something special for Christmas."

I laugh. "Me and cook?"

"Or not." She raises a shoulder. "There should be enough in the kitchen that you could whip up a something simple to eat, if you prefer."

"It sounds ideal," I admit.

"It's a gorgeous space. You'll love it."

"Hmm." I chew on my lower lip. "And no one's going over there this weekend?"

"Everyone's here for Christmas. Unlike someone I know, who'd prefer to be on her own."

I hunch my shoulders. "I know, and I don't mean to go all Scrooge on you. It's just, since Isla and Liam decided to move to the island near Venice…"

"You miss her, huh?"

I rub the back of my neck. I miss Isla more than I realized I would. I hadn't realized how close a friendship I built up with her and Solene. And with Solene on tour and rarely able to call me, I became dependent on Isla for female camaraderie. But with her married now, and also in a different country, I guess I'm feeling a little more lost than I thought. Normally, I'd be working. It's when I'm out of the office and need to unwind that I feel a gap in my life. That's when thoughts of Hunter occupy my mind, which I hate to say, happens more often than I'd like. Which is why this getaway is going to do me good.

"I do miss her, but she deserves her happiness."

"So do you," Amelie murmurs gently.

"And I'll find it with a nice bottle of wine tonight."

"And a hot tub."

"A hot tub?" I stare at her. "This place has a hot tub?"

"On the back porch. It's covered, and you can enjoy the view of the fields stretching out in front of you." Her gaze turns dreamy. "It's so… Rejuvenating."

Did her tone turn tongue-in-cheek there? I gaze at her closely, but her features remain open, even if she does look a little flushed.

"Is it really as picture-postcard perfect you make it out to be?"

"More than you can imagine. If I could, I'd love to go back there, but we've already committed to hosting this party, so…" She raises a shoulder.

Someone calls out her name. She turns and waves at someone over her shoulder, then glances back at me. "If you don't want it then—"

"You convinced me. Where is this place, how do I get there and, more importantly, don't I need keys to get in?"

17

____

Hunter

I ease the car up the short driveway of the cottage and into the garage at the back. I noticed a garage in the front of the house, but Weston mentioned it was being used for storage at the moment. I switch off the engine and quiet descends. The kind where it's not just silent, but the type of silence where you can hear yourself breathe, sense the tension slide off of your shoulders, feel the lack of vibrations brought on by traffic, overhead flights and traffic helicopters, and the sound of eight million souls drawing breath in the metropolis called London.

A city I grew up in. A city I love, despite the ups and downs I've faced there, in a life which, admittedly, has been more up than down so far. Some would say a privileged life. One where I was groomed for the top position in this country. The one my dad occupied at one point, and which I'd known with certainty, I would one day, too. I never questioned that belief, was content with my choices—or the choices made for me by default, and which I adopted as my own—until I met her.

She told me she'd never forgive me if I kissed her that day in the elevator car, but I'd done it anyway. After all, the last time she'd asked me to stay away, I had, and she'd been pissed off at me. So it made sense to push aside her objections and kiss her… Or so I'd thought.

But then, I held her gaze and sensed the struggle inside her. Sensed, also, that she was going to use that kiss as an excuse to walk away from me. And that's something I'm not going to allow. I'd kissed her to show her what she was missing out on. And I'd been right. It had been mind-blowing, earth-shaking, pulse-pounding, a balls-tightening kind of kiss. And she'd felt it too. And if I had continued kissing her I'd have taken right there in that damned elevator car. Which is the only reason I had let her go. Not because it wouldn't have filled that dark yearning inside of me to take her right there, in a place where both of us could have been compromised any moment; for I didn't give a damn about being discovered. But she clearly did. And I couldn't risk hurting her like that. Indeed left to myself I'd have fucked her right there and then and walked out and told the journalists outside that she was mine… only that'd have pissed her off no-end, and while the make-up sex with Zara would be every bit as explosive as the hate-sex we're no doubt going to indulge in soon—fact is I want her to want to be with me.

When we come together, and we will, it will be because she needs it as much as me. Because she admits to yearning for it as much as I do, and decides to throw caution to the wind and be adult enough to own up to this insane chemistry between us.

Only, it's more than simple chemistry. It's the kind of connection that one rarely finds with another person. That click inside that signals once you've been with this person, it will spoil you for anyone else.

She knew it. I knew it. But she refused to accept it. And while patience isn't my strongest virtue, this time, I had no choice but to sit back and bide my time. And trust me, that is so against my personality, so against my natural instinct of chasing after her, that it's been far more stressful than preparing to launch my campaign to become Prime Minister. Something I can't put off forever, either. But I have a plan for it, and hopefully, it should all come together very soon.

Meanwhile, I needed to get out of London. I arrived at Amelie and Weston's place to find it was packed with friends and pets and kids. And it was nice to hang out with them, and shoot the breeze with the Seven and the Sovrano brothers, and play with the babies, but seeing the waves of domestic contentment wafting off of them had made me realize, for the first time, what I was missing. And the very fact I was thinking that surprised me.

Perhaps, I was more tired than I'd realized. Perhaps, I definitely did need a break. I mentioned it to Weston, who told me he knew of the ideal place where I could unwind undisturbed. He gave me directions to the cottage a few hours outside of London, where he first hooked up with Amelie last Christmas. I was unsure about it, but he told me about the packed bar, the fact that it was stocked up so I wouldn't have to worry about provisions, and then he mentioned the hot tub on the back deck. And that settled it.

I took the directions and the passcode to the front door, which they put in recently, then headed home to pack my bag, fielded calls from my parents, who were disappointed I wasn't coming home for Christmas, and headed over.

Now, I push open the door of my Jaguar — my preferred make of car when I'm driving — and step out. I managed to give my security personnel the slip on my way here. It may not be my smartest move, but I needed a little time with no one breathing down my neck. Just an evening to unwind; I'm sure they'll track me down by tomorrow. Meanwhile, I'm on my own, with my thoughts — and with thoughts of her, of course — and an entire evening, and if I'm lucky, the entire day tomorrow, with no calls, no disturbances, and no intrusions. I open the back door, reach for my duffel bag, then lock the car. I head up the steps, key in the passcode to the door, and it clicks open. I step in, switch on the lights and glance about the place.

Weston wasn't exaggerating when he said it was renovated recently and has every convenience under one roof. The starlight pours in through the windows on the right to illuminate the space. A fireplace in the center, that dominates the space, is not yet lit. To my right, is a sectional couch. On the opposite side, is a wet bar. All the fixtures are gleaming.

I walk into the room, and my booted feet sink into plush carpeting. I reach the fireplace and throw the switch on the wall next to it. The flames instantly ignite. I round the fireplace, then head through the door and down a short hallway that leads to the kitchen. To my right, a door opens into what I assume is the bedroom. I head through, drop my bag on the carpeted floor and stretch. A drink, and then a long soak in the hot tub, sounds perfect. I strip off my tie and shirt, then kick off my shoes and socks, my pants and my boxers. I grab a towel and wrap it around my middle before I head back to the bar. I reach over to grab the bottle of whiskey — Macallan 24-year-old; the Seven wouldn't stint on their alcohol, of course — and pour myself a drink. There's also a cigar box. I flip it open, snip a cigar and light it, then clamp it between my teeth. I grab the glass and head back through the hallway and past the kitchen to the back porch and the hot tub.

I move toward the sliding doors at the back when the strains of music reach me. Huh? Also the glass is fogged over. Which is why I hadn't noticed the flicker of light that gleams through. I take a step forward, and the notes grow louder. I reach the doors and ease them open.

The music resolves itself into the chords of a song that sounds familiar, but which I can't place. I can, however, place who the person in the sunken hot tub is. Her back is to me and she has piled her dark hair on her head in a messy bun. Tendrils have escaped to stick to the slim line of her neck. Her shoulders are bare and she has an arm spread out over the edge of the tub. As I watch, she wraps the fingers of that hand around the stem of a wine glass and brings the glass up. She turns her head at the same time, so I can see the curve of her eyelashes, her upturned nose, and those lush lips as she wraps them around the rim of the glass and takes a sip.

The blood drains to my groin. I don't need to look down to know that I'm already hard. Her throat moves as she swallows, and I wonder how it would feel to have it move around my cock. The light from the candles she's lit about the place lends an ethereal, dreamy feel to the tableau.

The woman's voice coming through the speaker she's placed on the platform near the tub warbles about getting lost in translation, about asking for too much, and generally, clearly, blaming herself for the inevitable breakup that so many pop-stars seem to sing about. Still, I'll admit, the tune is haunting.

I take a drag of my cigar and blow out smoke a second before I realize she'll probably smell it and realize I'm here. Not that I was planning to spy on her like a creeper. Although, being able to watch her without her knowing I'm watching her is a treat. And perhaps, I'm beginning to sound like one of those pop songs I despise.

She leans her head back, and though I can't see the rest of her, I can sense how relaxed she is. How she's communing with herself in the moment, and how I hope she's imagining me in whatever scenes she's playing out in her head. I take a sip of my whiskey, and the liquor burns its way down my gullet, setting off a pleasant warmth in its wake. None of which will compare to the heat of her pussy when she clenches about my shaft. I almost groan aloud at the throb of lust that tightens my groin.

I leave the city to escape thoughts of her...and run straight into the object of my obsession.

I came so close to taking Michael's suggestion, planting cameras on her phone and computer so I could track where she was. And if I'd done that, I'd've known she was here, and perhaps, not have accepted Weston's invitation. Of course, it would've taken me from being in the zone of 'morally gray' to straight up 'black,' not that I have any illusions about myself. I've always had that streak of darkness in my center, hidden carefully from the world; and it would have stayed that way, but for the fact I met her.

She brings out that primal, animalistic side of me that I've tried to deny even existed, but something about her makes me want to share it with her, if only to test her response. To see if it'll make her hate me further, or if I guess correctly, brings out a different side of her. The one I've sensed, but never seen unleashed in full. That sadistic, needy part of her that resonates with me, that pushes me to make her submit to me.

I blow out another puff from my cigar, then walk around the tub, drop my towel, and take the steps leading down into the hot tub. I lower myself into the bubbling water and place my glass of whiskey on the rim next to me. "Hello, Fire."

18

Zara

One second, Taylor Swift is warbling about her lost love with Jake Gyllenhaal, and how he called her up again just to break her heart; the next, a familiar, hard voice that has haunted my dreams, and if I'm honest, almost my every waking moment, reaches me.

I snap my eyes open, and he's there, in the hot tub, the light from the candle flames highlighting the hollows of his cheeks and turning his skin into a golden, candied surface that I'd like to lick and suck on. He has a cigar clamped between his teeth, a tendril of smoke wafting up from the lit end like the forked tail of a devil. And damn, if the tufts of hair standing up on his head don't resemble horns. His torso is bare... The carved planes of his chest and those broad shoulders make the hot tub, which had felt too big for one person, now too small for the both of us.

Both of us? What the hell is he doing here? I thought I smelled the sweet, cherry scent of cigar smoke, but had dismissed it as my imagination. Except, it hadn't been. The jerkhole who's haunted my dreams is sitting opposite me in the hot tub. He plucks the cigar from between his lips and holds it out and away from the water. With his other arm he reaches for his glass of whiskey and holds it in my direction.

"Salut, Fire."

I curl my fingers into fists. Yep, no doubt about it. He's really here. I am not dreaming. Not that I doubted it earlier—for I'm not given to flights of fancy, where my mind conjures up illusions which seem too real—but until he spoke, a part of me wondered if I'd thought about him for so long and with so much intensity that, perhaps, the images in my head had come to life. At least, now I know I'm not at fault. He's here and—I lower my gaze to his chest again—he's not wearing clothes. At least, not on the top part of his gorgeous, shapely, muscle-bound body.

The steam condenses on his chest. The droplets glisten like dewdrops on leaves in the early morning. Maybe I should say like the spots on a leopard because, sprawled there, with his eyes half-closed, as if he's waiting for the inevitable explosion of anger from me, he resembles a predator...a beast...a sleek feline...a sexy specimen of masculinity who's at rest and yet, ready to pounce at the least provocation.

Also, did I mention he's not wearing anything on his torso? I swallow. One side of his lips ticks up. His eyes gleam. Bastard's enjoying this. No doubt, he thinks I'm going to throw a fit and act all pissed-off—which I am—but damn, if I'm going to let him have that satisfaction. I reach for my glass of wine and raise it. "Cheers, Brimstone."

He seems taken aback for a second, then he chuckles. The sound grates over my already sensitized nerve endings and seems to travel straight to my core. A hot, heavy sensation thickens between my legs. My toes curl. Jesus Christ, and all this because the wankface chuckled?

Maybe it's not such a good idea to pretend I'm cool with his sudden appearance. Maybe I'd be better off throwing a fit. This is supposed to be my getaway. Why is he here? Either way, it's clear I can't stay here, now that he's here. Time to get out of here. Why are all of my sentences ending with here?

I clap my half-filled glass onto the platform of the hot tub with enough force that wine spills over the sides. Then I begin to rise to my feet, but his arm whips out and he locks his fingers about my wrist. A flash of electricity zips out from his touch. A-n-d here we go again.

Apparently, nothing has changed over the last few months. If anything, my body is even more responsive to his touch. If anything, the throbbing pulse between my legs has grown bigger, wider, stronger... Until my entire body seems to be weighed down with an overwhelming heaviness, even as my head feels lighter, like I am floating above my body and watching this bizarre situation unfold.

I glance at his grasp on my arm, then back at him, but he doesn't let go. "Stay," his voice rumbles across the distance. His gaze is intense, his blue-green eyes lightened to an impossible shade I can only describe as colorless? It's as if all of his emotions have been swallowed up and are churning inside, ready to be hurled back at me in a ball of sensation so intense, I won't stand a chance. I clear my throat, but still, it comes out as a croak. "Hunter—"

"No, don't speak. Let's just enjoy what's left of the evening, okay?"

I glance between his eyes, then nod. "Okay."

"Okay." His grip loosens, and he seems to release me with great reluctance. I sink back in my corner, reach for my glass of wine, and take a sip. I place the glass back on the rim of the tub, then lean back again. With nothing to do with my hands, I place them in my lap. His gaze follows the movement, and his eyes flash. I'm wearing my skimpiest bikini, which barely covers my nipples, and the bottom is a string thong. To be honest, I wouldn't even have worn that, since I thought I was on my own. It's just... I'd changed into my swimsuit and already immersed myself in the tub before I realized I needn't have bothered with wearing a suit, at all. By then, I was too lazy to change. Thank god... Or maybe not. Maybe I would've enjoyed shocking him if I hadn't worn anything—not that he'd have been shocked. He's probably been with enough women. A hot sensation stabs at my chest, and whoa... What's that about? I don't have a claim on him. Though I could have one. If I want to.

"I can hear you thinking," he drawls.

"And I wish I didn't have to hear your voice, at all."

His lips curl. "I can't wait to hear your voice when you finally scream my name as you come."

That hot sensation in my chest balloons into this massive explosion of lava that travels to my extremities. My arms and legs tremble. A shudder grips me, and I have to fight to not squeeze my legs together. Oh, my god, Hunter talking dirty is... The stuff my dreams are made of. And I'll be honest, I've groaned his name many times in all of my sordid fantasies where he's done exactly that to me.

"Let me guess, you had no idea that I was here?" I murmur.

"If I had known you were here... I'd have—" He searches my

features. "I still would've come. For the record, I didn't see your car outside. I had no idea there was anyone inside the house."

"I parked my car in the garage." I firm my lips.

"Which would explain why I didn't see it. Guess we're stuck here for the night." His eyes gleam.

My gaze widens in horror. *No, no, no. I can't spend the night with him. I can't.* If I do, there's no way I'll be able to resist the pull between us. "You have to leave, now." I burst out.

"Have you looked outside lately?" He glances to the sky beyond the enclosed patio. I follow his gaze to find soft flakes of snow floating down.

"You're kidding me."

"There's a storm on the way, heard it on the weather forecast on the way here."

"You sure you didn't arrange for it just so we both had to spend the night together?" I scowl.

"Are we spending the night together?" He tilts his head.

My thighs clench. Every cell in my body seems to go on alert. Every pore on my skin seems to open in anticipation. I am so fucked. Well, maybe not yet. But let's be honest, I will be.

"Zara?" His voice is low and soft, and yet, there's a hard edge to it. A tension coils under his tone. It reaches out to me and lights the ball of heat that's taken up residence in my belly. Flickers of awareness sizzle through my blood. My toes curl.

"Fire?" he murmurs, and this time, the question in his voice is tinted with desperation. The skin around his eyes tightens. His stance is relaxed, but every muscle in his body is wound tight. The muscles of his shoulders are rigid and defined and oh, god... I want to reach out and trace their shape and feel their dimensions. I want to rub myself against him and lick off the droplets of sweat that roll down his temple and... I want to lower myself onto his thick, long, large cock and get myself off, then clench down on him until he abandons all control and fucks me so hard I can't think any further —

"You're killing me," he growls, and something snaps inside of me.

I surge to my feet.

19

Hunter

The water pours off of her shoulders and slides off of her hips. She stands there for a second, a cross between a mermaid and Artemis the huntress. That slip of fabric she's wearing barely covers her nipples, which are peaked and outlined through the top of her bikini. Her waist is tiny, her hips wide enough to form that classic hourglass figure that's driven me crazy since I first laid eyes on her. Her thighs are thick and strong. My fingers tingle, my palms ache and... I want to squeeze her flesh and mark her so every time she looks at it, she'll know who she belongs to.

She covers the short distance between us, then stands in front of me. I tilt my head back and watch as she reaches over and takes the cigar from my fingers. She brings it to her lips and closes her mouth around it, and goddam, my cock stands to attention at once. Who am I kidding? It was already standing at attention, but now it's... More so? She draws on the cigar, blows out a puff of smoke.

"You're playing with fire, Fire," I growl.

"What if it's because I want to be burned tonight?"

"Do you want to be burned?"

She searches my features. "Only if you burn with me."

I reach up, pluck the cigar from her fingers, and brush mine over hers. She shivers, and a fierce sensation tightens my chest. Without breaking the connection of our gazes, I place the cigar between my lips. The taste of her—something spicy and pungent and so fucking familiar—crowds my senses. I glare at her, but she doesn't flinch. Fucking hell, I am going to enjoy taming her.

"There is one thing, though," she murmurs.

"Oh?" I move the cigar to the corner of my mouth. "Are we negotiating?"

"Maybe." For the first time, she looks unsure. My heart stutters. Goddamn, what insanity is this that the very thought of her not being at ease is making me want to soothe away her uncertainties?

"What is it?" I snap, my voice coming out harsher than intended.

Her forehead furrows. "It's only for one night."

"Eh?"

"You. Me. We fuck. But it's only for tonight. Tomorrow, we go our separate ways."

"Weather permitting." I nod toward the snow that's begun to come down harder.

"Weather permitting," she agrees.

"And if it's still snowing tomorrow, the deal continues."

Her eyebrows knit. "I have to get back tomorrow."

"So do I. But if it's too dangerous to drive..." I raise a shoulder.

"Then I leave when the snow clears, no matter what time it is."

"Only if you let me drive you."

"I have a car—"

"I'll arrange for it to be dropped back," I retort.

She firms her lips, then nods. "Fine."

I look her up and down. "Of course, you'll let me do anything I want to you tonight."

She blinks. "What does that mean?"

"You'll let me do what I want to do to you, when I want to do it to you, and you do everything I tell you to do—"

"Within reason."

"Choose a safe word," I order.

"Excuse me?" She snaps back her shoulders. "I'm not into S&M."

"I am."

"Ah..." She opens and shuts her mouth. "What if I don't like it?"

"Oh you will," I smirk.

She flushes. Her eyes spark, and I almost jump to my feet and throw her over my shoulder and walk inside and to the bedroom, but... Patience. Patience. Wouldn't do to spook the tigress.

She bites the inside of her lip and sweat pops on my brow. This waiting and enticing game is not one I normally play with women. But when you're wooing a magnificent goddess, you do what it takes.

"What kind of S&M are you talking about?" she finally asks.

"It can be anything." I blow out a cloud of smoke. " You'll have a safe word, and the moment you use it, I stop."

"Just like that?" She scowls.

"Just like that. But remember, the moment you use it, the night is over."

"Huh." She purses her lips. "So I use the word, and that's it, no more sex."

"Something like that."

"You have a lot of confidence in your ability to turn off your libido."

My grin widens. "You won't want me to stop; this, I promise you."

She scoffs. "Don't make promises you can't keep."

"Do we have a deal?"

She narrows her gaze.

"Do you know, when you're thinking through all the pros and cons, you get a divot in the corner of your lips?"

"I do?" She rubs the left corner of her mouth.

I crook my finger at her. "Come 'ere and I'll show you."

She leans over slowly, slowly, until her face is just above mine. I reach up and rub my thumb into the other side of her mouth. She swallows but doesn't move away.

I drag my thumb across her lower lip, and a moan bleeds from her lips.

"Say yes," I murmur.

"And if I don't?"

"You will."

She shakes her head. "That goddamn cocky attitude of yours. I hope you have the equipment to back it up."

"Is that a yes?"

"Yes," she whispers.

"Choose a safe word."

"Do I need to?"

"You agreed, Fire."

She glances into my eyes, then nods.

"Did you settle on a word?"

"Pomegranate."

I tilt my head. "The symbol of fertility and abundance. The seeds that led to Persephone being tied to Hades."

"Didn't ask for a lesson in mythology," she scoffs.

I lower my hand, then jerk my chin toward her side of the tub. "Go back to your corner."

"Excuse me?" Her jaw drops. And fuck me, but the expression on her face is worth every bit of clash of wills that's going to follow. I am going to win her over, I have no doubt. And I'm going to make sure she enjoys every second of our time together. And if she hates me during the process, it's only going to make our inevitable union so much more satisfying.

"You heard me." I reach for my glass of whiskey and drain it. "Also, I need a drink."

She looks at me blankly, so I repeat myself, enunciating each word, "I. Need. A. Drink."

She rolls her eyes. "I heard you the first time, wankhole. If you need a drink, you can damn well get it yourself."

I glare at her, and she scowls back at me.

I tilt my head, and she slaps her hands on her hips, which only has the effect of making her breasts, barely covered in that itty-bitty bikini, jiggle. Her nipples are outlined against the fabric, while droplets of water cling to her chest and in the valley between her tits. My cock thickens further, and if I glance down, I bet it's going to be emulating submarine action. Not that I have anything to hide right now, but I'd prefer to pretend to have the upper hand. For the moment, anyway.

"Fire," I lower my voice to a hush and she swallows.

A shudder grips her and she throws up her hands. "Fine, I'll do it, and only because I don't go back on my word."

"I'm counting on it."

She reaches for my glass of whiskey, then turns and steps out of the hot tub. For a second, she's poised there with her curvy figure silhouetted against the flickering candlelight. That arse of hers? Fuck, it's the most phenomenal, jaw-dropping butt I've ever noticed and damn, if I don't want to sink my teeth into that ripe peach of a behind right now.

"You're staring," she murmurs without turning around.

"Are you complaining?"

"You're the one delaying gratification with this stupid exercise in trying to put me in my place."

"It helps to increase erotic arousal, baby."

"Why don't you admit that you're doing it to have control over me?"

"Or maybe I'm simply into self-torture."

She pauses, then turns to glance at me over her shoulder. "Are you always this...honest?"

"Did you think I was going to deny the obvious? When it comes to you and me, I aim to give you the truth... Unless there's a specific reason to hold back something."

She narrows her gaze. "So you're holding something back from me?"

"The sooner you get the whiskey, the sooner you'll find out."

"And just when the wordplay between us was heating up," she scoffs.

"Not the only thing that's heating up, baby."

She lowers her gaze to my crotch, and her gaze widens. Color flushes her cheeks.

I can't stop the smirk that twists my lips. "Does that answer your earlier question about my endowments?"

"How you use it remains to be seen, Brimstone." She picks up her own glass then flounces off in the direction of the door; but not before infusing an extra twitch into her arse. Heat flushes my skin, and sweat beads my shoulders. At this rate, I'm the one who'll give in to my needs before I've made any headway in getting her to submit. And no way, am I going to let that happen. I need her to open herself up to me, to become vulnerable enough to sense what I feel for her.

She disappears through the doorway into the house, only to appear a few seconds later, with both my glass and hers. She walks down the steps and into the bubbling water, which rises to her waist by the time she reaches me. She holds out my glass. I take it from her, once more allowing my fingers to brush against hers. Her breath hitches. The pulse at the base of her throat flutters like the wings of a butterfly.

"You okay, Fire?"

"Why wouldn't I be?"

I widen the space between my thighs, then jerk my chin toward it.

"You want me to sit...there?"

"You have a problem with that?"

"Of course, not." She turns around, then places her glass on the rim of the tub. Naturally, she has to bend over, which means that magnificent arse of hers is squarely in my face. My fingers itch, my thigh muscles grow rigid, and every brain cell in my head temporarily short circuit. Jesus H. Christ, I'd give anything to bury my teeth in that luscious behind—a reaction she, no doubt, expects me to have; which is why she's flaunting her asset at me. But I am not going to give her the satisfaction. Still, I must have made a noise, for she peers around with a gloating look on her face. "You alright back there?"

A-n-d that's the last straw. Two can play this game. And I don't intend to lose. Not this round. I plant my hands on her hips, then lean in and bury my face in her lower cleavage.

20

Zara

"Oh, my god." The glass of wine topples, but I manage to catch it at the last moment. His face. He's got his tongue between my arse cheeks. Heat flushes my cheeks. My *other* cheeks. I try to wriggle away, but his grip on my waist pins me in place. I'm not a prude; not by a long shot. I'm a strong, independent woman who has always believed that the right guy is an illusion, that the only person I can rely on is myself. That the person who'll appreciate me 'as is' has yet to be born. It's something I have believed in firmly, and no one I've ever met has made me revisit this assumption. But the way this man is worshiping my body by licking that very intimate, very forbidden part of me is making me question every one of my beliefs. And it's not only because of how my body is responding to his attention, how my heart is thudding against my ribcage like my favorite vibrator on its highest setting, how my nipples harden and my thigh muscles quiver, how I can't stop myself from clenching down and pushing back into his face, and holy hell, that's not what I want to do. I don't want him to realize how turned on I am because he's eating my arse. "Hunter, stop," I gasp.

It only spurs him on to drag his hands down to my cheeks and squeeze them apart even further. He pushes aside my bikini bottoms, then swipes his tongue over my puckered hole and my eyes roll back in my head. He twists his tongue inside my back channel, and I shudder. Pleasure contracts my lower belly, and my thighs squeeze together. My eyes roll into the back of my head, and I'm going to come. Oh, god, I'm going to—

He pulls out his tongue. "Don't you dare come, Fire." I hear his voice as if from far away. And he's stopped torturing me with that magic tongue of his. I push my butt back, trying to chase that sensation that brought me to the edge, and he laughs.

The twatwaffle snickers, and the lust recedes from my thoughts. I pull away—and this time, he lets me. I pivot around, straighten my bikini bottoms then raise my hand; but he catches it. Then he wipes the back of his free hand across his mouth. The gesture is so erotic, so salacious, that my pussy clenches. The shudder of lust that had retreated rushes forward in a wave again. My knees knock together, and I'd sink down into the water if it wasn't for the fact he has a tight grip on my wrist.

He scans my features. "You okay?"

"No, I'm not. Why did you stop?"

"Told you I wasn't going to let you come. Not that easily, anyway."

Jerkhole. I try to pull away from him again, but he tightens his hold on my wrist.

"Let me go."

"When you're no longer angry."

"You can't tell me how to feel," I snarl.

"Wanna bet?"

"Fuck you." I shouldn't allow him to see how much he's unnerved me, but damn it, I'm allowed, aren't I? First, finding him here, under the same roof, in the same hot tub as me, when I'd been thinking rather randy thoughts about him. Then, having him come through on said randy thoughts in the randiest way possible…was not what I'd expected of him. To be honest, I'm not sure what I expected, but it wasn't quite that. Definitely not Hunter Whittington squeezing my arse like it belongs to him. Not Mr. Stick-in-the-mud, stabbing his tongue inside my forbidden place and bringing me to the edge, only to not let me orgasm.

"I will, just not yet." He smirks.

"Go to hell."

"Only if you come with me, baby."

"Aargh." I squeeze my eyes shut. It's not like me to lose my cool when I'm dealing with a man. Definitely not Mr. Douchekabob, who denied me my climax. "Do you always have to have a ready comeback?"

"Only with you, Fire."

Something in the tone of his voice, a gentleness at odds with the ruthless restraint with which he pulled me back from the throes of a mother of a summit I came so close to peaking, has me opening my eyes.

He's looking up at me with a strange light in his eyes. A possessiveness? A hunger, perhaps. More like a proprietorial look that, combined with his dominating presence, has me going weak in the knees. *Shit, shit, shit.* I knew I shouldn't have agreed to this one-night stand arrangement with him. He's manipulated his way into making me agree. Doesn't mean I have to go through with it. I take a step back, and he rises to his feet.

Just like that, he unfolds himself and straightens. The water cascades off of his shoulders like he's the model from the Old Spice commercial I watched growing up. No, he's more like Chris Hemsworth in *Thor: Love & Thunder*, or Chris Pine in that nude scene in *Outlaw Knight*. Ooh, la, la, and now, I'm resorting to French in my thoughts. That's it, I am truly flustered…but, in my defense, he's standing in front of me and he isn't wearing a stitch of clothing.

Those carved-out-of-rock chest planes extend to a lean waist, flat stomach—no, concave stomach—which, in turn, dips down to meet a humongous, monstrous, enormous, gargantuan, colossal, massive—you get the idea—appendage that points straight up toward his belly button. And ladies, I wish I could say it was grotesque, or hideous, or repellant, but the truth is, it's the most gorgeous, most beautiful, most immense cock I've ever seen.

My knees buckle all over again. I stumble forward, and he stops me with his other hand on my shoulder before I can fall against that wall of goodness—otherwise known as his chest. Before I can feel the hardness of all that male virility in that column he carries between his legs. And his balls, oh, his balls are a work of art.

They should have their own installation at the Tate Modern, along with the upthrust of his dick between them. A sculpture I'd call Hunter's Pillar, or a phallic representation of what it is like to be hunted by the owner of said appendage. Right, I've officially gone into meltdown then, and all because I saw his penis? Again, in my defense, I've seen the male member before, but none as prodigious as his.

The heat that had retreated toward my core turbo charges forward, until it seems to have flooded every part of me. My nipples tighten until it feels like they're ready to torpedo out of my bikini. As for my pussy...? It's in pussy heaven, with threads of moisture lubricating my cunt, readying itself for an imminent penetration—which I'm not going to let happen. Not yet.

I twist my arm and tug. This time, he releases me. I stumble back, right myself, then tip up my chin. "I'm going to take a shower."

21

Hunter

She scampers up and out of the tub and disappears through the doorway before I can call out to her. I saw her gaze lower to my groin, knew she saw the evidence of my aroused state. Then, her gaze widened, the color surged through her face, and still, she continued to stare hungrily at my cock, which grew even more erect under her perusal. Well, at least, now she knows I have the apparatus to back up my ego.

What I hadn't expected was for her to make that quick retreat. Apparently, she hadn't expected to see me naked. It had the effect I was hoping for. I took her mind off of the thoughts buzzing through her head. I'm almost certain she was going to call off our deal for the night, and no way, would I accept that from her. So, I opted to distract her instead, and by the looks of it, I succeeded... Maybe too well.

I sink down into the hot tub, then duck my head under completely, before coming up again. I do want to give her time to cool off. On the other hand, if I give her too much time, she's likely to develop cold feet, which I'm not going to allow.

I rise to my feet, step out, then walk through the doorway. My wet feet slap on the wooden beams as I walk past the kitchen, down the hall-way, and into the bedroom. I notice the luggage stowed away inside the walk-in closet at the far end, something I missed the first time I walked in.

I push open the door of the bathroom and enter. The shower is running, and through the steamed-up wall of the cubicle, I can make out her figure. I head toward the sink, brush my teeth, rinse out my mouth, then head toward the cubicle. I push it open and walk in. She stiffens but doesn't turn around. Instead, she tips up her chin so the water pours over her face and down her hair, which sticks to her back in long twisty coils.

I walk over to her, take the shampoo, and pour it into my palm. I begin to massage it into her hair. Her shoulder muscles grow rigid, but she doesn't stop me. I dig my fingers into her scalp and knead it in circular motions. A moan spills from her lips. She leans back into my touch as if she can't help herself. I continue to massage her scalp and she slumps back further. I lean into her so her back is flush against my chest. Her eyes are closed, those long eyelashes spiky with moisture. I drag my fingers through her hair, then down to her shoulders. I dig my knuckles into her shoulders, and she groans. The sound is so sexy, so hot, my groin tightens. My balls harden, and my cock jerks from where it's nestled between her arse cheeks. Her muscles clench, and I press down on her shoulders. "Relax, baby."

She draws in a breath, then bit by bit, her muscles loosen. I continue to squeeze her shoulder muscles, working my way down her biceps, then back up. I drag my knuckles down either side of her spine and she groans again. "That feels so good." Her voice is relaxed, the words almost slurring together. I tilt her head so the shampoo suds slither down her back. She leans her head into my shoulder, and I bend and kiss the curve of her shoulder.

She wraps her arm about my neck, and I drag my chin up the side of her neck. She shivers. I cup her breasts and squeeze, and she arches further into me. Her eyes are closed, her breathing shallow. I glance down the slope of her waist to the hollow between her legs. I reach down and strum her pussy lips, and she gasps. I stuff two fingers inside her, and she rises up to the tips of her toes. She turns her face in my direction, and I close my lips over hers. I lick her mouth, and she parts her lips at once. I slide my tongue over hers, suck on her lower lip, and her pussy clenches around my fingers. My shaft throbs, my balls grow heavier. Fuck, I need to be inside of her. I release her lips, then reach for the conditioner. I step back and pour it between her butt cheeks.

"What are you —"

"Shh." I kiss her again and she opens up completely. She moves into me and I position my cock against her back opening.

She begins to protest, but I deepen the kiss and absorb her words. I work my fingers in and out of her until she widens her legs, allowing me to add a third finger inside her cunt. I fuck her even harder with my fingers, and her entire body trembles. That's when I thrust my hips forward and breach her puckered hole. She's so relaxed that I slip inside her and through her resisting ring of muscles in one smooth thrust. She gasps into my mouth, and I feel her shudder. I continue to kiss her as I allow her to adjust to my size. When she relaxes again, I soften my kiss. I press little pecks to her mouth, then up her jawline and to her ear. I lick inside her ear and she moans. "Hunter, please."

"Tell me what you want, baby."

"You're so big," she groans.

"All the better to fill you up, Fire."

"It hurts." She scowls up at me.

"Good."

"What the hell? How dare you —"

"Relax darling, it's only going to get better."

"Easy for you to say, you're not the one with a monster cock stuck up her backside."

"You mean this?" I pull out a little, then slip back inside her, and her entire body jolts. I pinch her clit, and she gasps.

"Oh, god. Oh, Jesus."

"You mean oh, Hunter, don't you?"

"You're so fucking smug, you twatarse."

I chuckle. "I'm the one inside your arse, baby." I pull back, then propel my hips forward again, sinking deeper inside. At the same time, I slide my fingers in and out of her pussy, and her head rolls forward. I ease her forward, then coax her hands out from behind my neck and place them flat on the wall. "Hold on, baby."

I grip her hip with one hand. With the other, I continue to finger-fuck her. Then, I begin to fuck her arse in earnest. Each time I sink deeper, she moans. When I pull back, she follows me, chasing the feeling of fullness that she's already adjusted to. I stay there for a few seconds, and she scowls over her shoulder. "You better finish what you started this time."

"You mean like this?" I propel my hips forward with enough force that my balls slap against her butt. She slaps the wall with her palm, then spreads her legs even wider, taking even more of my length. "Oh, god. Oh, god. Oh, god," she chants.

I tilt my hips and pound into her. This time, I sink all the way inside of her. I bottom out, and the tension at the base of my spine coils into a ball of tightness. Her entire body trembles. Her knees seem to give way again. I squeeze my hold on her hip, holding her upright, then tilt my hips and begin to fuck her in earnest. She clenches down on my cock, and I see black spots. Fuck, I'm so close. I grind the heel of my palm into her clit, and she cries out.

I lower my head until my cheek is pressed to hers. "Come with me, right now."

22

Zara

Barely are the words out of his mouth when that tension inside me explodes. The vibrations zip up my spine and crash between my ears. "Oh, my god, Hunter!" I'm aware of clenching down on his cock, while my pussy clamps down on his fingers, and I shatter. I hear his muted growl and he follows me over the edge. I slump forward, but he wraps his arm around my waist and pulls me in for an embrace. I sense him throb inside me and when he pulls away, I can't stop my moan of protest. He reaches over and shuts off the shower, then scoops me up in his arms. "What are you doing?"

"I'm taking care of you, baby."

I scowl up at him. "I can take care of myself."

"I have no doubt but humor me."

I glower at him, and he chuckles. "You're fucking cute, you know that?" He leans down and kisses my nose, and it's such a tender gesture that I gape at him.

"You don't need to look so surprised. You are eminently endearing when you forget to be prickly and put on that tough as nails mask that you like to show the world."

"I am as tough as nails," I insist, then yawn and spoil the effect.

"Of course, you are." He carries me out of the shower cubicle, then lowers me down next to the bathtub. He reaches for one of the folded towels and wraps it over my head. He dries my hair quickly, then my body with brisk strokes. He rubs the same towel down his body, then tosses it aside. Why is it so intimate that he used the same towel on his body as he used on me? It's just a towel. Doesn't mean anything. He scoops me up in his arms and walks over to the bed. He lowers me to the ground, yanks the covers up, then jerks his head in the direction of the mattress.

I slide in and scoot over, turning over on my side. He pulls the sheet over me. The bed dips, and the next moment, the heat from his body envelops me. He slides his arm under my neck, wraps his other arm about my waist, and pulls me close. Then he spoons me. He freakin' spoons and, OMG, it's the most incredible sensation in the world. I can feel his hard body embracing every inch of my back, his cock—still semi-rigid—lays in the valley between my arse-cheeks, his thighs cradle mine, and his feet, oh his feet are so warm. I tuck my own freezing toes between his feet, and he chuckles. "Woman, your feet are like ice, and you just got out of the bath."

"So are my hands." I place my palm over his, and it feels so right. It's just for one night. Doesn't mean anything. Heat cocoons me and sinks into my blood. My muscles are so relaxed. My head feels so light. Clearly, the sex helped me relieve a lot of the tension I've been carrying. My eyelids flutter down, then I snap them open. "We didn't use a condom," I exclaim.

There's silence, then. "I'm clean. I can show you the paperwork tomorrow."

"I'm clean, too," I say slowly.

The silence stretches, then, "It's not that I didn't remember that we needed to use a condom, but I didn't want to," he finally admits.

I stare at snow falling outside the window. "You didn't want to use a condom?"

I sense him shake his head.

Then, "Are you okay if we don't use a condom when I fuck you next?" He asks.

"What if I want you to use a condom?" I swallow.

"Do *you* want me to use a condom?" he parries.

Of course, I anticipated he'd answer my question with a question.

Only, I hadn't wanted to answer his question because... I don't want him to use a condom. And damn, if that doesn't surprise me.

I turn in his arms and glance up at him. "I've never allowed anyone to fuck me without a condom."

"I've never fucked a woman without a condom," he replies.

We glance at each other. His blue-green eyes are a dark blue in this light. He holds my gaze, then bends and kisses my nose again. "Don't think too much about it. It's you and me, baby, in this cottage. There's no one else. Forget the outside world for the next few hours. It's just us. You can be yourself. I promise, I won't tell anyone."

I half smile. "As long as you'll be yourself, too."

His gaze grows earnest as he replies, "Always, and only with you."

Why does that seem like a promise? Nah, it's my imagination. Probably because I'm tired from the day.

"Okay." I nod.

"Okay." He kisses me on the lips, then tucks my head under his chin. "Sleep, so I can wake you up in the sexiest of ways."

My eyelids flutter down.

The images seem to flit over my mind almost as soon as I close my eyes. I know I'm dreaming, but I'm powerless to stop it. It's always the same thing. Me chasing after Olly, who's giggling and laughing as he runs from me. He steps on the road. I yell at him. He stops in the middle of the road and turns as a car bears down on him. He turns to see the car, and his gaze widens. "ZaraDi!" He yells my name with the honorific 'Di' added on at the end to symbolize his respect for me. Because I'm his bigger sister. Someone who should have been watching out for him. Someone who should have never let him escape my hold and stopped him before he stepped in the path of the car. Olly, my little squishy, smooshy Olly. Gone in the blink of an eye.

"Zara, open your eyes."

I snap my eyes open to find Hunter scowling down at me. His features are pale underneath his tan or maybe it's just the moonlight that's turning his face into an effigy carved out of marble? So smooth, yet so hard, and soft on the inside. He scans my features. "You were dreaming," he murmurs.

I swallow.

"I'll get you some water."

He begins to pull away, but I grasp his arm. "No, don't leave me."

He looks between my eyes, then nods. "Want to tell me about it?"

I shake my head.

Hurt flashes across his features, and my chest tightens. A burning sensation coils behind my ribcage. "I will, just not yet." I bite the inside of my cheek. "Please, can you trust me on that?"

He draws in a breath then lowers his head and brushes his lips over mine. "Anything you want, baby."

Tears prick the backs of my eyes. It's not like me to cry—not in front of another, and definitely, not in the bed of a man I let fuck me. But then, there have already been so many firsts with Hunter, I'm beginning to lose count. Is that good or bad? Or maybe, here under this roof, and with him, as we are snowed in over Christmas, it doesn't matter?

As if he senses the train of my thoughts, he cups my cheek and says, "I'll do anything to make you feel better, Fire."

"Anything?" I tilt my head.

23

Hunter

"Anything," I murmur.

She blinks away the brightness in her eyes, then offers me a slight smile. "There was this one thing."

"Oh?"

She releases her hold on my wrist, only to trail her fingers up my forearm. Goosebumps pop on my skin. My shoulder muscles tighten.

"I have this burning sensation in my center," she murmurs.

"Was that here?" I kiss the tip of her nose.

"Not the center of my nose." Her lips tip up.

"Is it here, perhaps?" I lower my head and kiss the hollow at the base of her neck. Her scent—that blend of orange blossoms and vanilla, with a tang of pepper, instantly goes to my head. My cock thickens. "Or maybe here?" I press tiny kisses down to the space between her breasts.

Her breath hitches. She grips my shoulders, and I can't stop the rumble of satisfaction that wells up my throat. I continue to kiss my way down to her belly button. "Was it here, you think?"

"No," her voice trembles.

"Or maybe here?" I drag my chin down her lower belly to the flesh just above her clit.

She writhes under me, then digs her fingers into my hair.

"Not there." Impatience threads her voice, and I chuckle.

She tugs on my hair, and pinpricks of heat zip down my spine. My balls tighten.

I press a kiss into her inner thigh, and she moans. I nibble on the skin over her thigh and she pushes up her core, chasing my tongue.

I laugh and she makes a noise at the back of her throat. "Are you teasing me, Whittington?"

"Always, Fire."

She rears up, but I flatten my palm in the center of her chest and hold her in place. "Patience, Fire."

"Fuck patience," she snaps.

"Now, where's the fun in that, hmm?"

"I'm beginning to wonder if you can even find my cli—" She gasps as I swipe my tongue up her pussy lips. I wrap my tongue around the swollen nub hidden there, and she yanks on my hair. "Oh, god, Hunter."

Finally, fuck. "If I knew this is what it took for you to say my name, I'd have gone down on you as soon as I met you."

"As if I'd have allowed it."

I ease my tongue inside her channel, and she groans.

"You were saying?"

She pants. "I was saying that—" She yells, for I've slid my palms under her butt and squeezed the flesh. At the same time, I bite down on her clit.

She thrashes her head from left to right, yanks on my hair with such force, I'm sure she's pulled out tufts of strands. "Ohmigod, ohmigod!" She pushes her pelvis into my face as I continue to fuck her with my tongue.

Her entire body shudders.

I pull back for a moment, only to throw her legs over my shoulders. I cup her arse cheeks and position her so when I stab my tongue inside her next, she groans. Color smears her neck, her cheeks. Her eyelids are squeezed shut. Her mouth is open and she pants. Her entire body is an arc of desire, a bow of lust, and I'm the arrow that's going to slot into her center and make her come so hard, she's not going to be able to see straight for days. I continue to eat her out, and when she squeezes her legs about my neck in a vice-like grip, while her pussy clenches down on my tongue, I know she's close. I apply pressure on her thighs, so she parts them enough for me to rise up and crawl up over her. "Open your eyes," I order.

She flutters open her eyelids and her pupils are so expanded, there's only a circle of gold around the black. I sit up on my knees and she frowns.

I position myself over her so my hips are over her face and her pussy is directly below mine.

"Open your mouth."

She instantly complies.

"You okay with this, baby?" I look between her eyes.

She holds my gaze, then wraps her fingers around the base of my cock and slides it between her lips. No hesitation, she takes me down the column of her throat, holding my hip with her other hand. A groan rips out of me. I grit my teeth to stop myself from fucking her mouth. I dig my elbows into where I have them positioned on either side of her thighs, then force myself to open my eyelids.

"Do you remember your safe word?"

She nods.

"Anytime you need me to stop, tap my thigh."

Her gaze widens. Then she pulls back, allowing my cock to slip to the edge of her mouth, before she tips up her chin and takes it down her throat again

"Oh, fuck." I watch as, without breaking the connection with my gaze, she pulls back again and rolls her tongue up my length.

"You're fucking gorgeous, you know that?"

She merely swallows me down her throat, then gags. Saliva slides down the edges of her mouth, and maybe that's when I fall in love with her a little. So, I'm a cliché, but goddamn, if she isn't the most perfect woman in the world right now, as she massages my balls while swallowing my cock, like she was born for it.

I lower my face to her pussy, then squeeze her thighs apart and begin to eat her out in earnest.

She stutters. Her hold on my hip tightens. She's even more aroused than a few seconds ago. Fat drops of cum pool between her legs, and I lick them up. So fucking sweet. She tastes like honey and cloves. An amalgamation of tastes I'm never going to forget. I tilt my head, glide my tongue inside her, then out, then in, out, in. As I find my rhythm, her entire body jolts. Her movements become frantic, and she stuffs me down her throat, then out. And again. The blood rushes to my groin. Sweat beads my shoulders. I rub my whiskered chin down her clit, and she gasps. She arches up so my cock slides impossibly deep down her throat. The ball of tension at the base of my spine tightens and my entire body shudders. Fuck, I'm too close. Too fast. And this time I'm coming inside of her. I pull out of her, then flip around. I settle between her legs.

"You ready for this, baby?"

She nods.

I wrap her hands around the headboard, then throw her legs over my shoulders. "Hold on."

24

Zara

Maybe I should have asked him to use a condom. But I don't want him to use a condom. If this is the only night I get with him, I want to feel all of him. With nothing separating us. So, I've never felt this way before, and that makes this entire situation dangerous, but... It's only one night. I'll walk away tomorrow. I'll make sure our paths don't cross—it will be difficult with all the friends we have in common, but that's fine, I can manage it. I can.

That's when he brackets me with those massive arms, and positions himself at my entrance. He holds my gaze, propels his hips forward and breaches me. I know he's big, I've taken him in what is a smaller channel, not to mention, I just had him down my throat, but this...

Oh god, he feels so huge. So massive. So enormous. So damn good. A groan wells up, and he closes his mouth over mine and swallows the sound. He pulls back, then rams into me with such force the entire bed moves forward. The headstand smashes into the wall, and something crashes to the ground. Then he begins to pound into me.

He still hasn't released my mouth, and his gaze, locked with mine, is intense. His blue-green eyes, now a startling color that resembles the stormy seas, bore into mine. His shoulders are so huge, his body so large, so solid, the heat from his chest pins me in place, and it feels like I'm being consumed by him. The next time he pulls out of me, he releases my mouth and stares between my eyes. "You feel so fucking good, Fire. I'll never get enough of you."

I want to agree with him. I do. I open my mouth, but all that comes out is a groan. One side of his lips kicks up. He wraps his hand over my hip, then lunges forward. He tilts his hips and bottoms out inside me. He touches a part of me deep inside. One that sets off a series of reverberations that zip up my spine. My head spins. Sweat clings to my shoulders. I dig my heels into his back, curl my fingers into the headboard. "Hunter," I gasp. Not sure what else to say. What else can I say?

He seems to understand, though, for he lowers his head until his eyelashes brush mine. "Come with me, Zara." He thrusts into me once more, hitting that same spot. "Come right now."

I orgasm instantly. The climax slams into me, and I cry out. Sparks sweep across my vision, and as I black out, I hear his hoarse cry.

When I come to, I'm curled on his chest, his arms about me. His heart beats at an elevated rate against my cheek, and the heat from his body surrounds us like our own personal patch of beach in the sun.

I turn my face into his chest and lick up a bead of sweat.

"Did you just lick me?" he rumbles.

"I want to do more than lick you." I turn over to rest my chin on his chest. He folds his arms behind his neck and the movement makes his biceps bulge.

"For someone who spends most of his time in Parliament, defending your government's policies, you sure are built."

"I also spend time on the road with my constituents. And I work out most mornings."

"Let me guess. Up at five a.m. to work out, while listening to the morning news —"

"Four-thirty a.m., and also, the stock markets," he corrects me.

"Then run five miles on your treadmill."

"Ten miles, and normally outside." He smirks.

"And you eat political arguments for breakfast."

"I'd rather eat you."

I blink. "You have a one-track mind."

"You and public service. Nothing else has intrigued me as much in my entire life."

"Hunter, don't." I begin to pull away, but he flips me over and leans over me.

"Why is it that you don't like to talk about us?"

"It's only one night."

"Are you sure?"

"What do you mean?" I scowl.

He jerks his head in the direction of the window. I turn to find the gray light of dawn filtering through the window. Also, it's snowing, the flakes coming down so hard that it forms a sheet of white past the windowpane.

"Oh, no."

"Oh, yes."

I turn to find an expression of satisfaction on his face. "You knew this would happen. You knew we'd be snowed in today."

"I'd hoped for it, yes."

"So technically, our one night stand was never going to happen."

"Technically, today is a continuation of our one night stand, if you never leave the bed." His smirk widens.

"I think your logic is faulty."

"I think it's time you stop thinking." He lowers his weight onto me, and the thick column between his legs nestles against my pussy.

"Oh." I swallow.

"Indeed." He leans down and kisses my nose.

"I wish you wouldn't do that."

"Do what?"

"Go all tender and sweet."

"You don't want me to be tender?" His eyebrows draw down.

"I'd rather you fuck me hard."

He tilts his head. "So you don't have time to formulate your arguments on why we shouldn't be together? So you can put the blame of your agreeing to be fucked by me on me?"

When he says that, it feels so wrong. Like I'm putting the onus of our being together like this on him, and somehow, it's not fair to him. But neither is the fact that I'm pulled so strongly toward him, and after how we fucked, I know it's not going to be easy to forget about him. Maybe impossible. So, I don't deny what he says. But I don't agree to it, either.

The seconds stretch, then he tucks a strand of hair behind my ear. "You know what I think we should do?"

"What?"

"Have breakfast."

He places the breakfast tray on the bed between us. He insisted I stay in bed and snooze while he cooked breakfast. I protested half-heartedly, but when he'd reminded me that it was a one night stand, which was valid only as long as I didn't leave the bed, I agreed. Also, I love sleeping in, and I never allow myself to do so. All those years of my parents waking me up, along with my twin brother Cade, to study in the mornings because it was the best time to practice our math before we went to school, instilled a sense of discipline in me I've never been able to shake off. Trapped in this room and this bed, with the storm raging outside, it feels like I've found a liminal space that doesn't belong to my normal life. A space and time where no rules apply. Besides, getting thoroughly fucked last night relaxed me to the extent that when I cuddled into his pillow and drew in his scent, it instantly made me close my eyes and drift off. I awoke when he placed the breakfast tray in the center of the bed.

Now, I sit up, tuck the sheets under my arms, and eye the monstrosity of a breakfast. On the tray is a plate piled with two eggs over easy, bacon, baked beans, sausages, hash browns, and toast. There's butter in a bowl on the side, a glass of orange juice and a cup of coffee.

"That's a lot for one person," I murmur.

"It's for both of us."

He slides onto the bed. At some point, he pulled on a pair of gray sweats. But that glorious chest is shirtless. A-n-d I'll never get used to seeing that ripped torso, those eight pack abs, that trim waist with the trail of hair that arrows down to that very distinctive part of him. The one that I had my fingers around not very long ago. The one I had taken down my throat, and felt thicken and fill my mouth—and earned me that compliment from him.

"Men are suckers for blow jobs, huh?"

"You mean, you don't like it when I go down on you?" He smirks.

My belly clenches. What is it about this man talking dirty that touches something primal inside me? Still, I manage to meet his gaze without blushing, "Feel free to eat me out anytime." I reach for a piece of toast, but he gets there first.

"Let me." He butters the toast, holds it out, and I crunch down on it. Then he feeds me some of the baked beans, followed by hash browns, and finally, the crunchy bacon.

"Mmm." I lick my lips. "You can cook, apparently."

"Surprised that the entitled, poshhole can get his hands dirty?"

This time, I can't stop myself from blushing. "Poshhole, I like that." I reach for my cup of coffee, and once more, he gets there first.

"Now, now, no cheating, Fire." He raises the cup of coffee to my lips. I sip from it, and his eyes flare. He brings the cup to his mouth and sips from the same spot I did. When did the action of drinking from a cup become so pornographic? He places the cup down, then feeds me more of the hash browns. "You like your potatoes, eh?"

"What's not to like? It's my fave vegetable. I can have it in any form. Fries and crisps are my downfall."

He feeds me more of the hash browns, and the shredded potato pieces melt in my mouth. I've had hash browns before, and let me tell you, that's gourmet level cooking right there.

"Did you study cooking?"

"That obvious, huh?" He cuts up a piece of the sausage and offers it to me. I chew on it, and once more, the intense green of chives, with the bite of peppercorns, combines with the chewy texture of the meat and fills my mouth.

"I'm not a great cook, to be honest. But this food could come from a very fine restaurant." I lick my lips.

His gaze is fixed to my mouth, and he feeds me more of the sausage. "I could spend all day watching you eat."

I redden. I'm good with accepting compliments; I really am. So why is it that these remarks from him make me blush?

"I briefly entertained the thought of becoming a chef." He picks up a piece of the sausage and chews on it.

"You? A chef?"

"That's how I met James," he adds.

"You mean James Hamilton, the chef?"

He nods. "I even went to culinary school with him. But then, my father had a heart attack. I came home to find him weak and almost at death's door. He told me his one wish was for me to follow in his footsteps."

"And you did," I point out.

"I always knew I was going to go into public service eventually; the cooking was a hobby I enjoyed. I loved experimenting with ingredients almost as much as I enjoy putting the right people together to create a group that will draw on the strengths of the individuals and make the combined team much more than the sum of the parts."

He glances up, then tilts his head. "That's a very thoughtful look you have there."

"My father was very demanding of me and my brother. He never treated me as a girl, actually. He always told me, anything my brother could do, I could do better. I found the weight of his expectations both crushing and exhilarating. And maybe, I felt more compelled to rise to the challenge. Maybe I felt I had to deliver on his dreams for me."

"Hence, you became a lawyer?"

"I did." I tuck the sheet firmly under my arms. "And then, I started my own PR firm."

"A gamble, maybe?"

"No more than you going into public life."

"I'll be the first to admit that following in the footsteps of my father, and his father before that, opened doors for me that otherwise might have remained closed. It also invited comparisons with my father and grandfather, which I was prepared for. I took it as a compliment that people contrasted my style to theirs. I knew I had to focus on my strengths, that with time my style would shine through, and I'd develop my own approach, my own modus operandi."

"Your own brand appeal," I murmur.

"Indeed. As have you, Councilor. You're one heck of a ballsy, fearless negotiator, who'll go to any lengths to ensure your client is protected. You have single-handedly steered tough journalists into writing stories from the angles that benefit your principals."

"Why, thank you," I dip my head. "And you have a strong brand, Minister. Not only are you charismatic, but your confidence comes across as a self-assuredness which is very attractive."

"Is it now?" He smirks.

"Clearly, it's going to swell your already oversized head, but since I've opened this particular line of thought, I may as well tell you that you also speak sense. Which is more than I can say of many of your colleagues."

He laughs—a full belly laugh that wells up from deep inside, rumbles up his chest, and brightens his features. With his tousled hair and days-old growth on his jaw, not to mention, those gray sweatpants and bare chest, he could well be a sex god. Correction, he is a sex god, who not only has the equipment but also delivers on the promise.

He lowers his chin and watches me with a speculative look.

"You haven't eaten much breakfast." I gesture to the half-full plate.

"That's because I'm saving my appetite for something else."

25

Hunter

Her eyes flash and her breathing grows rough. She moves restlessly under the covers, which dip down between her breasts. I slide my legs off the bed, take the tray and stow it on the side-table. Then I quirk my finger. "Come 'ere."

Her color heightens. For a second, she stays still, then she shakes her head.

"Zara," I lower my voice to a hush, and she shivers. But she still doesn't move.

"If you don't do as I say, I'll have to interpret that as a sign of battle lines being drawn."

"Oh, good." She rises to her knees, then shuffles toward the edge of the bed, and I click my tongue.

"Remember what I said? You can't leave the bed."

"I have to use the bathroom." She protests.

"I'll take you."

She scowls at me over her shoulder. "I'm not an invalid."

"And you agreed to a one night stand, an agreement which *is* invalid the moment your feet touch the floor outside the bed."

"I'll have to touch the floor of the bathroom," she points out.

"That's allowed."

She scoffs. "Who makes these stupid rules anyway?"

"I do, babe, you should know that by now."

"Doesn't mean I have to follow them." She puts out a leg to jump off the bed, and I throw myself across the length of the mattress. I grab her around her waist, and she yells as I pull her to the bed and clamber on top of her.

"Let me go." She begins to struggle under me, and each time she moves, her thigh brushes against the hardening column between my legs. She must feel it, for she freezes. Her color is high, and her entire body vibrates with a nervous energy that tells me she's both afraid of what I'm going to do next, and excited about it.

"You're being bratty, hmm?"

"You're being all dominating, hmm?" She tips up her chin.

"It's who I am, baby, and you find it appealing"

"Do not."

I lower my head and run my nose up the side of her throat; she shudders.

"You can try to deny it as much as you want, but your body responds to my every touch."

"Doesn't mean much when my mind's not in it, does it?"

I stiffen, then pull back. "Are you saying you don't want me to touch you, Zara?"

She holds my gaze.

"All you have to do is use your safe word, and I'll stop."

She swallows.

"Well, what's it gonna be Zara?"

She firms her lips. "I'm not using my safe word, am I?"

A hot sensation stabs my chest. A flush of triumph sweeps under my skin. *Huh? Was I so afraid that she'd use her safe word? And would I have allowed her to leave if she had? Would I have gone back on my word?* Good thing I don't have to answer that question. I search between her eyes, then roll off the bed. Once on my feet, I scoop her up in my arms.

"What are you doing?"

"I'm taking care of your needs." I pivot, head for the ensuite, then deposit her next to the toilet bowl. She makes a twirling motion with her finger. I simply fold my arms across my chest.

"Why aren't you turning around?"

"You don't get to ask the questions, Fire."

She flushes. "You can't coerce me into doing anything I don't want to."

"But I can seduce you into it."

She blinks, then chuckles. "You have me there. And why is it that every time I want to stay angry at you, you say or do something that makes me laugh instead?"

"Maybe it's because we're on the same wavelength."

"Not bloody likely. Also" —she turns around and sits on the commode— "if you think I am shy about peeing in front of you, think again."

She holds my gaze, and then the tinkle of a stream of water hitting the pot fills the air. Color sweeps up her throat and her cheeks, but she doesn't look away. This woman has nerves of steel.

If there's anyone who can stand by me through the upcoming campaign I'm embarking on to become the Prime Minister of this country, it's her. Question is, how do I convince her of it? Do I want to convince her of it? Am I really thinking of binding myself to someone after years of never wanting to be tied down? I'm well aware of the optics related to a Prime Ministerial campaign. Having my woman by my side will send the message that I'm grounded and reliable. A serious person who's ready to settle down. But that's not why I want her. It's because it feels right to be with her. To have her by my side feels like the completion of a journey I hadn't even been aware I was on. I set out to tame her, but somewhere along the way, she began to tame me, and I wasn't even aware it was happening.

The sound of the water being flushed pulls me out of my reverie. She walks over to the sink and washes her hands. I close the distance to her, wrap my arm about her waist, and tuck her head under my chin. She dries her hands, then glances up. Our gazes catch. The contrast between us couldn't be starker. She's not tiny, but not too tall, either. She comes up to the level of my heart, and fits into me like she was made for me.

Her skin is flushed, and I know it's soft to the touch. Her eyes sparkle with intelligence, with that awareness of her own self that I've always found so appealing. There's something about her confidence that turns me on. It makes me want to own her, possess her. To pit my wits against her, and to celebrate her when she wins an argument, too. A-n-d whoa, that's a first. I've always been confident about my ability to win, but to acknowledge another person's intellect, to recognize their strengths, to own their successes as mine? That's definitely a first.

She turns around in my arms, then reaches up and straightens out the fold between my eyebrows.

"Whatever it is you're thinking has you disturbed," she murmurs.

I tighten my hold on her. "Only because my thoughts have gone down paths never traversed before."

She tips up her chin. "Is that a confession?"

"It's an observation."

"Oh." She bites down on her lower lip, and my cock twitches. I reach over and slide her lip out from between her teeth. "No one can hurt you, Fire. No one except me."

She scoffs. "Have you any idea how you sound?"

"Like a demented, possessive bastard who can't get enough of his woman?"

"I'm not your woman." She tips up her chin.

"You are for one more night."

"Only you could define a one night stand as one that extends over two nights."

"Whatever it takes to keep you with me, baby." I smirk.

"You're so full of yourself."

"And you like me for that."

She glances between my eyes. "It's true. It's not that I like you, and yet I can't keep away from you."

"It's not that I like you… No… My emotions are too strong to be called like," I parry.

She laughs. "Neither one of us can win a war of the words."

"Only because I'm letting you get away with it."

"Oh, yeah? You're letting me get away with it, you—" She gasps in surprise as I lift her up and throw her over my shoulder.

"What are you doing?"

"I'm making the most of the time we have left."

"You're using brute force to win the argument." She wriggles in my hold, and I place my arm over her waist to hold her in place.

"Let me go."

"You know better than to say that, Fire."

"And don't call me by that nickname," she snaps.

"I'll call you what I want, when I want, and you'll answer to it, *Fire*."

She groans in annoyance. "And if I don't?"

"Are you sure you want to find out?"

"Are you sure you want to find out?"

26

Zara

"Do your worst, you twathole."

No sooner have the words left my lips than a white jolt of heat screams up my spine. I yell, "You spanked me, you…you…jerkass."

"You're beginning to repeat your insults," he observes, right after which he brings his palm down on my other arsecheek.

I scream, wriggle about over his shoulder. He simply swings around, heads for the bedroom, then toward the bed.

"Let me go, Hunter. Right now."

"If that's what you want." He throws me down on the bed, and before I've even completed my first bounce, he shoves off his sweatpants —no briefs—and follows me down. He covers my body with his, digs his elbows into either side of my head, and presses his hips into mine so there's no mistaking just how turned on he is. The thick pole between his legs nestles into the valley between mine. His weight pins me down, and he lowers his chest to mine, the carved planes digging into the softness of my breasts. The heat of his body slams into mine, and it's like I'm in a sauna.

Goosebumps pop on my skin. Moisture pools between my thighs.

He stays there, holding my gaze, not moving, simply allowing me to feel every inch of his hard body against mine. Letting the rightness of us being together in this moment sink in. My nipples peak, and my clit throbs. That emptiness in my belly unfurls and grows. All of the cells in my body seem to open and ready themselves to be invaded by him. He's all around me, enveloping me. I've never felt this fragile, this intensely conscious of just how much bigger than me he is.

Our bodies seem to communicate without words. Our gazes lock. The thickness at my core grows even more prominent.

"Do you remember your safe word?"

His voice is hard; there's a meanness to it that reaches that part of me deep inside I've never wanted to acknowledge. The part that yearns for a male strong enough to overpower me. A man who is as determined as me; someone intelligent enough to pit his wits against mine, quick-witted enough to trade words with me, dominant enough to command me, skilled enough to manipulate my body, and considerate enough to bring me to orgasm every single time—an area in which all of my previous lovers have failed.

"Zara, do you?" He peers into my eyes.

I nod.

"Say it aloud."

"I remember my safe word." My voice sounds like it's coming from far away. My mind seems to have detached from my body, floating somewhere above while I watch this entire scene unfold. I shouldn't find it so hot—oh, god—but I do. I push up my chest so my nipples stab into his unforgiving chest planes.

His lips twist. "Good girl."

I shudder. Pleasure sweeps through my veins, and I almost orgasm. And all because he praised me? Jesus, what's he doing to me?

He pushes away from the bed and stabs his finger at me. "Stay right there."

I couldn't move if I tried. The primitive part of my brain has acknowledged he's the master. And I'm his to do with as he wants... For now. All of my senses are focused on him, on how his powerful thighs ripple as he stalks over to his bag in the corner and rummages around before turning to face me. A few strips of silk dangle from his hand.

"What's that?"

"Relax, Fire, I promise you're going to enjoy this."

"That's what you said when you fucked me in the arse... For our very first time together."

He reaches the bed then glares down at me. "Did it hurt?

"What do you think?" I scowl.

"That you screamed my name as you came so hard that you could barely move afterward. And now, you're embarrassed about it."

"I'm not embarrassed about anything."

"Then why is your face so red?"

"It's not—" I firm my lips. "Fine, I didn't expect to enjoy it so much. Also, I definitely didn't think that the first time we fucked you'd enter the wrong way."

He chuckles. "That's a quaint way of referring to anal."

"I believe in social, political and economic equality of the genders; doesn't mean I'm not well-mannered," I say primly.

"Seems to me you also believe in the anal quality of pleasure."

I laugh. I can't help it. Here I am, trying to make him feel guilty for jumping right into having anal with me. I've never allowed any of my partners to take that liberty with me. Not even my longest relationship, which lasted all of three months. And Hunter here, hunted me down and boldly went where no one had dared to before.

"Hold on a second." He scrutinizes my features. "Was that your first time?"

My cheeks heat. "What? Don't be ridiculous."

"It was your first time with anal."

My face is so hot now, I'm sure there are flames leaping up from it. "Can we stop this discussion?"

"Is it because four letter words are an issue for you?" he asks slowly.

"Fuck, no." I tilt up my chin. "But I do have an issue with your having opened your innings with anal."

"Not to worry, baby. I'm a believer in marathons and five-day long cricket matches." He places a knee on the bed.

"Personally, I prefer working in short quick bursts." I choke out.

"And I prefer to keep my stamina, when it comes to both the campaign trail and my sexual performance."

"Did you just compare politics to sex?" I gasp.

"There's a similar high when you win over a particularly stubborn opponent in both, wouldn't you say?"

I widen my gaze. "And now you're comparing me to a political rival?"

"You're, by far, the most beautiful, most vital, most intelligent adversary I've ever taken on."

"So, we've covered cricket, politics, and sex in the space of a few sentences." Three things I am passionate about. "That's a—"

"First," he says at the same time as me.

The air between us thickens and swirls with unsaid words. The kind you don't dare blurt out for fear of where they might lead. And yet, you also can't ignore it. When was the last time my pillow talk with a man covered such a large spectrum of interests?

"I don't know of many women who're familiar with cricketing analogies," he says as if he's read my mind. And it's no surprise I am. Cricket is the one game that we watched as a family when I was growing up. It's the one time my father allowed my brother and me to slack off our studies—when there was a cricket match on the TV. Also, my brother now plays cricket for England, something I don't publicize much.

"My brother plays cricket for England," I say, then squeeze my eyes shut. Did I say that aloud? I said that. Not even my closest friends know about Cade.

It's not that I have anything to hide. It's more to do with the fact that, given the kind of job I do—being a fixer, that is—it's simpler to keep my family out of the limelight. Also, Cade attracts his share of attention, given the high-profile nature of his sponsorships. So, it's simpler not to draw the media's attention to our relationship. I've even managed to keep it off of my Wikipedia page. And now, I shared it with this man. This man, who I've known for barely a few days... Okay, more than that. But the sum total of time we've spent together amounts to a couple of days or less. Although it will be more than that by the time this interlude is over.

"Zara, you okay?"

I nod, still keeping my eyes shut.

"What are you afraid of?"

I snap my eyelids open. "Who said anything about being afraid?"

"Why are you upset?"

"I prefer not to tell people about my family. It's how I protect them."

"Understandable, given the nature of your job. But it doesn't explain why you're so pissed off with yourself."

"I'm not—" He tilts his head and I firm my lips. "You're right, I am upset with myself." I glance away then back at him. "That was my first time."

His eyebrows shoot up. "Your first time with anal sex?"

My cheeks heat further, if that were even possible. "Why don't you yell it out so the neighbors can hear you?"

His lips kick up. "Our nearest neighbor is miles away. And you have nothing to be embarrassed about enjoying it, baby." He scans my features. "Do you know how it makes me feel to find out that I had one of your firsts?"

Did I hear him correctly? It shouldn't mean anything to me, what he just said, and yet my body insists otherwise. My thighs quiver, and my knees threaten to turn to noodles. My toes curl and I have to reach deep inside myself to find the strength to stay standing. "H...how does it make you feel?" I finally manage.

"It makes me want to fuck you for days so you'll not be able to walk straight. In fact—" He bends his knees and peers into my eyes. "I promise, before I'm done with you, you're going to come at least ten more times."

"In the space of eighteen hours?" I scoff.

"Fine, so eighteen, then."

"An orgasm an hour?" I throw my head back and laugh. "Not even you can deliver on that."

"Make sure you keep count, baby."

He holds out his hand. I look at his outstretched palm, then at his face. "What are you going to do?"

"Don't pretend you don't know what I'm going to do," he retorts.

"Can you give me a straight reply, for once?"

"Can you honestly say you don't know what's coming next?" He glares at me, and the threat in his tone slithers down my spine. He's right about one thing—there's a special thrill in pushing him, in being bratty and getting him to act all dominant with me. It fulfills that masochistic streak in me. Hold on, masochistic? Did I just label myself as masochistic? Did I just agree that I want him to be a sadist with me?

I'm not a prude when it comes to sex, honestly. But something inside of me stopped me from exploring S&M and everything it has to offer. And it wasn't my strict upbringing, either.

My parents were very strict and did not allow me to date as long as I was under their roof. What they didn't know about was the boys I smuggled into my room when they were away at the shop. My brother, too, had his share of girls parading through the house. By mutual consent, we never spoke about it. Then, when I was sixteen Olly was born, and all that stopped.

Once I left for university, I celebrated my freedom by hooking up with a variety of boys, and one of them was into S&M. I made it very clear I wanted nothing to do with that. And he never pushed the point, something that told me our relationship was going to be short-lived. He's the guy with whom my relationship lasted for three months. I was the one to break up, as was normally the case. All of the men I've been with have respected my wishes. Not one of them pushed me to re-evaluate my boundaries, like Hunter has.

"What if I say I'd rather be surprised?"

"Do you want to be surprised, Fire?"

I hold his gaze, then place my hand in his.

27

Hunter

"Good girl."

A shiver streaks down her body. Her pupils dilate. Oh yeah, she loves being praised, and I am only too happy to oblige her on that. Of course, she'll have to earn it, as she's already realizing, but that should only make the praise, when she receives it, so much more satisfying.

I twist her arm over her head, then loop the scarf about her wrist and tie it to the headboard.

When I hold out my other hand, she places hers in mine without hesitation. I tie her hand to the headboard, then slide off the bed. I walk around to the foot, then circle her ankle with my fingers.

She tries to pull her leg away, but I hold on. "You remember your safe word, don't you?"

She nods.

"Are you going to use it?"

She shakes her head.

"Then let me do this for you, Zara. I promise you're going to love it… Eventually."

"That wasn't very reassuring."

"You're doing so well, baby, just put yourself in my hands."

She swallows, then nods.

"That's my girl."

This time, a moan bleeds from her lips. The scent of her arousal fills the air. My groin tightens, and I bend and tie first one leg, then the other, to the footboard. I straighten, then fold my arms over my chest. I take my time perusing her—from her flushed features to her upturned breasts, her narrow waist, and the flare of those gorgeous hips, she's a vision I'm going to carry in my head long after today.

"You're so beautiful, baby," I murmur.

She swallows, and goosebumps pop on her skin.

"Have you ever been told just how gorgeous you are? How spectacular your body is? How incredible you look laid out there for my delectation?"

I wrap my fingers about my cock and squeeze. Her body jerks. She writhes, tugs on her bindings, and that only tightens her restraints further.

"Untie me, so I can touch you," she pants.

"Not yet."

I massage my dick from base to crown, and her pupils dilate. Her gaze is fixed on my crotch, her lips parted.

"Do you want to taste me, baby?"

She nods.

"Do you want my shaft down your throat?"

"Yes." She licks her lips.

"Are you going to swallow every last drop and then lick me off?"

She tugs on her ties again, then scowls. "Why are you torturing me?"

"Because you love it."

"I didn't sign up to be taunted."

"Oh?" I continue to swipe myself from base to crown, and again. Her thigh muscles clench. She's trying to squeeze her legs together, but of course, she's unable to pull free of her bonds.

"Hunter," she snarls.

I laugh.

Her frown deepens. She still hasn't taken her gaze off of my throbbing and very erect cock.

"You want this, don't you, Fire? You want me to fuck your face, then your pussy, and your arse… Or preferably, have me fill all of your holes at the same time, don't you?"

"Fuck you, Hunter," she snaps.

"If that's how you feel, then..." I turn as if to leave, and she gives out an angry cry.

"Fine! You plonkface, you jerkass, you prathole, fine. You win."

"I love it when you speak dirty, baby."

She draws in a breath and lets it out. "I told you, you win."

"Not the words I was looking for."

"What do you want me to say, you…you…wanker?"

I arch an eyebrow. "You know what."

"I'm not a mind reader," she snaps.

I raise a shoulder. "But you have an IQ of 160. I'm sure you can figure it out."

"Too bad I can't say the same about your EQ. You…you…"

"Charismatic, attractive, magnetic man. Isn't that what you were trying to say?" I smirk.

"You wish," she spits out.

"Okay, then." I turn and head toward the doorway.

I've almost reached it before she calls out, "Fine, fine. Yes, that's what I was going to say."

"What was it? I didn't quite hear you."

She blows out a breath. "I said you're an intelligent, intuitive, charming man," she finally says.

I turn to glance at her. "Do you mean that?"

"You know, I do."

"Then prove it." I walk over to the bed and straddle her. "Take my cock like a good little slut and suck me off."

The pulse at the base of her throat accelerates. Her chest rises and falls. Her hair crackles about her face like a medieval goddess. She's so fucking magnificent, I almost undo her ties and pull her to me, but that won't help; I want every orgasm she has to be better than the previous one. I want the endorphins to fill her blood. I want her to be so drunk on the happy hormones that she remembers this time for the rest of her life. I want her to feel this connection between us as intensely as I do. I want her to experience just how connected we are, how in tune our thoughts are, how on the same wavelength our emotions are, how good it is when we both open up to each other, how there's nothing like the sensations our fucking evokes in both of us. I want all of her. I want…

I crawl up her body, then position myself over her face.

"Open your mouth, baby."

She does.

I drag the crown of my weeping cock over her lips, and she licks them. My balls tighten, and I squeeze the base of my shaft to stop myself from coming right then.

"Remember to tap my hand if you want me to pull out."

She nods.

"You have the most perfect mouth, you know that? The first time I saw you, all I could think was that I wanted to have those beautiful lips around my shaft."

"We're even then. The first time I saw you, I knew I wanted to sit on your face and pull your hair."

I blink, then bark out a laugh. "And you will, I promise. I'm going to give you so much pleasure you'll forget everything else but my name."

"Promises, promises—"

Her words cut out because I've slid my dick between her lips. "Open wider still," I order.

She extends her jaw, and I glide my cock inside and down her throat. She breathes through her nose as tears squeeze out from the corners of her eyes. Then she breathes through her mouth, and I pull out until, once more, my cock is balanced between her lips.

"You okay to continue?"

She jerks her chin.

"You sure you don't want to stop?"

She scowls at me, then tips up her chin and drags her tongue up my dick. She closes her mouth about the head, and heat squeezes my chest. She begins to pull back, and I dig my fingers into her hair to hold her in place. She moans around my cock, and my balls throb. I ease the head back until I'm positioned between her lips, then once more, I slip my cock over her tongue. She draws in a breath, and my head spins. I wrap my fingers about her throat, and goddamn, the feel of my cock moving down her gullet is the most erotic thing I've ever experienced.

Her golden gaze widens; her eyes blaze with a combination of lust and heat, and that edge of defiance that draws me to her over and over again. This queen of a woman agreed to suck me off, and fuck, if that isn't both humbling and titillating. She has me by my balls, literally. I'd do anything she asked. It's good that she doesn't know that... Yet.

"I'm going to fuck your face, baby."

She swallows, and the suction around my shaft drives me a little out of my head. I grit my teeth, forcing myself to slow down. To focus on the pleasure. Just enough pain to make sure she's on edge. Enough friction to get her all hot and bothered, so she can't stop thinking how it'd feel to have my dick inside her hot, melting pussy.

"If I feel between your legs, I bet you're going to be so fucking moist. One strong tug of your clit, and you're going to detonate, aren't you, Fire?"

She groans, and the vibrations travel up the column of my cock. Sweat beads my forehead. My balls draw up. I increase the intensity of my back-forth-back motions. Inside her mouth, down her throat, and out, and again, and again. Her entire body shudders, and I know she's close, so close. I pull out of her, then slide down her body. I bury my face between her legs, and she screams.

I slide my hands under her butt and squeeze as I stab my tongue inside her slit. I draw her clit into my mouth and suck on it, and she shatters. She throws back her head and yells as she climaxes. I lick up her cum, then crawl up and position myself over her face.

"You ready for me, baby?" She cracks open her eyelids, and the drugged, contented look in her eyes cuts me to the core. So, this is how it feels to put someone else's pleasure ahead of my own. It's the most fulfilling, most sexy feeling, almost as good as shooting my load. Almost.

I ease my cock between her lips and hold her gaze as I pull her hair behind and over her head so I can watch my dick disappear into her mouth. I pull out, then slide back in, again and again. She closes her mouth about my girth, and the suction shudders up my cock, squeezes down on my balls, and I empty myself down her throat.

Her eyelids flutter down and her body slumps. I reach over, untie the bonds from around her wrists, then release the restraints around her ankles. I lay back, pull her on top of me, and hold her until her breathing quietens. Finally, she tips up her chin and raises those gorgeous eyes to mine.

"Wh...what was that?"

28

Zara

"I do believe that was your first of eighteen orgasms. And I'm only getting started."

"I came...again." My voice is awed, as if I just discovered sex. Which, in a way, I have. Sex with someone you have this connection with is a completely different ball game—pun intended.

"That you did, Fire." He tucks my hair behind my ear. "How do you feel?"

"A little light-headed, like someone shot me out of a cannon and I'm floating down to earth." I yawn.

"You're tired."

"Just sated." I try to keep my eyelids open, but they seem to be too weighed down. "Maybe I'll nap just for a few minutes." I press my cheek into his chest.

When I open my eyes, I'm alone in bed, and the light outside has that gray-blue which hints at it being late afternoon. Did I sleep the morning away?

I yawn, then sit up and gasp when I find him sitting at the foot of the bed.

"Sorry, didn't mean to scare you." He reaches up and cups my cheek. "Did you sleep well?"

I nod, unable to speak. The words seem to dissolve within me… My brain cells don't seem to be able to put the words together to form a sentence. Heat flushes my cheeks, and he watches my face with interest.

"Did you just blush?"

"I don't blush," I protest.

"Hate to say it, but I've seen your face turn all shades of red in the last few hours."

"Only because you're a filthy, dirty, man." I try to pull up the sheet but am unable to budge it because he's sitting on it.

"Don't cover yourself up. I love your body."

I lower my hands to my sides and take in the T-shirt he's pulled on over the same gray sweatpants he was wearing earlier. What a pity I can't see those chiseled abs. On the other hand, Hunter in a worn, black T-shirt that clings to his shoulders, and hair mussed about his face, is both sexy and adorable, and so endearing.

"Come 'ere." I crook my finger at him.

His lips quirk, but he obliges. He leans forward, and I dig my fingers into his hair, pull him even closer, then brush my lips over his. I mean it to be just a quick kiss, but Hunter being Hunter, deepens the kiss until it feels like he's sucking my breath from my body. When he finally releases me, my heart is pumping, my blood thudding in my ears, and the heat between my thighs threatens to streak up my spine. "Wow." I swallow.

"Indeed," he says with a smirk. "You didn't think I was going to let you off that easily now?" He rubs his nose against mine. "You hungry?"

"I could eat," I concede.

"Good." He straightens, then walks to the closet in the corner of the room. When he returns, he's holding a silk bathrobe.

"I think I'd prefer to get dressed."

"I think you should wear this." He holds it out to me.

"You're not going to take no for an answer, are you?"

He smirks, and it's so sexy, I can't stop my heart from doing that little flip-flop in my chest. "Fine, but only this time."

He places the robe around my shoulders, and I shrug into it. Barely have I finished tying the knot around my waist, when he scoops me up in his arms.

"I really can walk." I try to sound angry, but my words come out in a giggle. Multiple orgasms can do that to a woman, I suppose. Also, the dick providing the orgasms is memorable. And as for the man attached to said dick? He's proving himself to be irreplaceable. I'm reluctant to admit it, but always being the person in charge, and the one who makes the decisions at work... Well, it's refreshing to lean on someone else for a change. I'll probably question my train of thought later, but for now, I hold onto his shoulders as he strides into the kitchen. There are pots and pans in the sink, and going by the various open bottles of spices, the chopping board, the bags of half-used vegetables he's been cooking. I sniff and draw in the heavenly scents of cooking. "You've been cooking again," I murmur.

"Indeed, I have."

He lowers me into a chair. A crisp white cloth is spread on the dining table. On it are plates, cutlery, two lit candles, as well as a bucket of ice with a cooling bottle of champagne. "And you laid the table?"

"You have to stop sounding so surprised." He laughs.

"You are Hunter Whittington. London's most notorious bachelor, alphahole extraordinaire, GQ's man of the year and one of Time's most influential people of the year. Not to mention, the person tipped to take the leadership role in this country. To find you cooking and laying the table is—"

"Just another aspect of me. One I don't show to the world—" He straightens.

"But which you are showing to me."

"But which I am showing to you," he agrees.

"Why are you doing this, Hunter?" I tilt my head back, and further back, to meet his gaze.

"Why am I cooking for you?"

"Yes, why do all this?" I beckon to the beautifully laid out table.

"Because I want to. Because it's Christmas, and I'm happy to be spending it with you."

I blink. "Oh shit, it's Christmas."

"Indeed, it is." He moves around to the bucket, places a white linen napkin over his arm, then uses his other to lift the bottle of champagne. Moet et Chandon Brut. He pops the cork, and the cheerful sound thuds through my veins. He pours the fizz into my glass, then his own. He places the bottle back in the bucket, then lifts his glass. "To us."

"Is there an us?" I narrow my gaze.

"You know there is..." More softly, he adds, "For this moment."

Okay, guess I can live with that. And maybe it would be churlish of me to point that out when he's gone to such lengths to cook a late lunch for the both of us. But if I agree to it without pointing that out, it could raise expectations—for both of us—and that wouldn't be fair to either of us. It seems even more important to remind the both of us that this—whatever this is between us—is temporary, fleeting, just two people who found themselves double-booked for the holiday in a cottage, with one bed between them. I wince. A-n-d that sounds like a cliché. One of those situations that the hero and heroine of a romance novel find themselves in. And of course, they end up together.

Unlike us. We're going our separate ways, come the morning. But for now... In this moment... Yeah, there's an us. And seventeen more orgasms to go. I raise my flute. "Salut."

"Salut." He takes a sip without breaking the connection of our gazes, and it's as if he's dipped his tongue back into the cleft between my thighs.

One side of his lips quirks, but he refrains from remarking. Instead, he bends, presses a hard kiss to my mouth, then straightens and stalks off to the counter. He pulls on a pair of oven mitts and slides out a tray from the oven. He walks over and places it in front of me. The tangy scent of spices wafts up from the dish.

"Roast turkey flavored with cumin, ginger, garlic and five spices, with orange and rosemary sprigs," he declares with a flourish. "And that's only the main course."

"There's more?" I exclaim, but he's walking over to the second oven in the corner of the kitchen, which I only now notice. He pulls out another tray then walks over and slides it over.

"Beetroot & red onion tarte Tatin."

"Wait, hold on." I glance between the dishes. A tickling sensation teases my nostrils. My head feels too light for the rest of my body. "You knew that I like spicy food, so you flavored the turkey accordingly; and beetroot is my favorite vegetable, after potatoes, that is, but how did you —" I glance up at him. "How did you—"

"Know it was your second favorite vegetable? Told you, I have my sources. And really, it wasn't anything to flavor the turkey to your taste."

"Still." I look back at the dishes. I texted the names of my favorite foods to Amelie. But for Hunter to not only know what I like but to also use that knowledge to cook the dishes accordingly? That shows attention to detail. It shows he cares. It shows he's been paying attention to my likes and dislikes. It shows that he wanted to do something special for me. And I can't remember the last time someone did anything like this for me.

"Zara, baby, hey!" He places his glass on the table, then hunkers down next to my chair. "Are you crying?"

"Of course, not." I sniff.

"You're crying."

"It's just dust in my eyes," I lie without looking at him.

"Hey, Fire, don't cry, please." He notches his knuckles under my chin and turns it, so I have no choice but to hold his gaze.

"I still can't believe you cooked all of this."

"I told you, I love to cook."

"And I was fast asleep. I didn't even help you." More tears run down my cheeks, and he wipes them away with his thumb.

"I looked in on you a few times, but you were so adorable with your eyes closed and burrowed under the covers, I didn't have the heart to wake you up."

"I don't even have a gift for you."

"You're here. That's my gift, Fire."

"A-n-d you also know the right thing to say." I throw up my hands. "You can't be this perfect. You can't."

He leans back on his haunches. "So, you're upset because I'm perfect?"

"It's not fair. I'm trying to resist you, and you go and do all of these things that make it impossible to resist you."

He laughs. "And I haven't even gotten through the rest of the orgasms."

"Don't remind me." Clearly, I don't stand a chance. By the time he's done with me, I'll have no resistance left in my body. I'll be a pile of mush—gooeyness without the ability to think straight. I'll have become his sex slave, not to mention a slave to his cooking.

"You're thinking so hard, you're giving me a headache." He takes my glass of champagne and hands it to me. "Have your drink and enjoy. I promise, you're not going to regret agreeing to stay here with me."

I know for a fact he's right, and that pisses me off even more. It wasn't supposed to be like this. It wasn't supposed to feel this good with him. It wasn't supposed to feel like I'm going to miss him when we leave. And he cooked for me. Jesus, he cooked for me. A warmth sweeps through me. It's almost as pleasurable a feeling as the orgasms he's given me. Almost.

I lift my glass and finally take a sip. The bubbles burst on my tongue. Flavors of peach and cherry, citrus and almond, cream and buttery toast. The notes merge, and the confluence of it all sinks into my palate. My head spins, and a burst of happiness sizzles through my veins.

"This is exquisite."

"No more than you, baby."

I chuckle. "You sweet-talker, you."

"Glad you're feeling better."

"I'm actually really hungry." Maybe I was hangry, or *horngry*? That could explain the tears. Yep, I'm sure that's all it was.

He peers into my face, then nods before he rises to his feet and takes his seat again. He carves out a piece of the turkey and places it on my plate. At the same time, I carefully slice a piece of the pie and place it on his.

He tops up our champagne, then grins. "Shall we eat?"

29

Hunter

"That was really, really good." She leans back with a sigh.

Her eyes are glazed over with what I recognize as the classic signs of food coma. A warm sensation floods my chest. My heart feels like it's expanding until it fills my ribcage. Satisfaction—that's what it is. A feeling of contentment so different from anything I've experienced before, it takes me a little time to understand the root of it. I may not have hunted down the food for my woman, but I cooked it and made sure she enjoyed it. It's the single most significant thing I've accomplished, except for when I made her come. It's more rewarding than winning the election in my constituency, more enjoyable than anything I've done for myself in the past. And all I did was make sure she was well fed. What is it about this woman that makes me want to take care of her every need?

"You did say that you trained to be a chef, but this was exceptional." She tilts her head back.

"I'm pleased you liked it." I polish off the rest of the food on my plate, then reach for the champagne bottle. I top her off, then myself.

"Are you trying to get me drunk, Minister?" She peers at me from under her eyelashes.

"Am I succeeding?"

"And I thought I was the lawyer." She chuckles.

"Oh, you know us politicians. We have to be part entertainer, part statesman, part every other profession that needs to be people-facing. And in my case, it's woven through with the need to do good for the country."

"Where does it come from? This need to do good for the country?"

"That's a good question." I look into the depths of my flute. "When I first decided to stand for elections in my constituency, I did so because it was expected of me. My father held down the seat, and my grandfather before that, so it was expected of me. I'd been preparing for it my entire life, yet when I got elected, no one was more surprised than me."

"I'd have been surprised if you hadn't been elected to the parliament," she murmurs.

"Two compliments in the space of two minutes, I do believe you may be thawing, Councilor," I drawl.

She raises a shoulder. "I may not always see eye to eye with you, but I'll be the first to admit that of all the politicians on the scene today, you stand out as being the most well-intentioned."

"Why, thank you, Fire."

She flushes, and goddamn, that's adorable. She might come across as a hard-headed career woman, but I can see the woman she really is—soft-hearted, generous, loyal. I know her better than she realizes.

"I'm not saying anything the critics haven't pointed out already." She scoffs.

"But it's you saying it; that means a lot."

She places her glass of champagne on the table with a clink. "Don't, please."

"Don't pay you a compliment?"

She nods.

"So, you can pay me a compliment, but I can't return the favor?"

She locks her fingers together, a sure sign that she's flustered. "I don't want you to get any ideas."

"Ideas, hmm?" It's my turn to place the glass of champagne on the table. "I wonder what you think these ideas may be?"

"You know. Me, you" —she flutters her hand in the space between us— "this thing between us."

"What thing?"

"You know this…this attraction, chemistry, lust, whatever you want to call it."

"And if I say it's more than that?"

She stiffens. "It's not more than that."

"You sure, baby? Because whatever we did last night touched the both of us, and I don't think that's happened to either of us before."

"It was just sex."

"I see." I drag my finger below my lower lip, and her gaze drops to my mouth. Her pupils darken, until the black bleeds out into the iris and there's only a circle of gold around the circumference. She swallows. The pulse at the base of her throat flutters like the wings of a humming-bird. "Just sex, hmm?"

She blinks, then glances away. "Just sex." She reaches for her glass of champagne and knocks it back, then slides it in my direction. "More."

"I live to fulfill every one of your wishes, Fire." I rise to my feet and her gaze widens. "Where are you going?"

"To get dessert."

"Dessert?" She frowns.

I head toward the counter and whip off the cover of a dish that I'd left to cool.

"You made dessert?" Her voice rises in pitch.

"Made would be a stretch. I merely pulled off the wrapper and slid it into the oven to warm up."

"And actually remembered to pull it out, counts as a win."

"You don't cook at all, I take it?" I scoop out the dessert onto two plates.

"Nope, much to my mother's chagrin." She pushes her hair back from her face. "My mum works side-by-side with my father, but she always finds time to cook for her family. It's just not something that interests me, I admit."

I place the dish on the table, then half bow. "Voila."

"Is that Christmas pudding?" She gasps.

"Cranberry and chocolate Christmas pudding."

She pales a little. "That's my favorite."

"I know." I scoop out some of the pudding and hold it out. "Open," I say in a hard voice.

She pales, looks like she's about to protest, then complies. *Thank fuck.* I slide the spoon of pudding between her lips. She closes her mouth around the spoon and wipes it clean. A dab of cream sticks to her lower lips. I reach over, wipe it off with my thumb, and bring it to my mouth. When I suck on my thumb, her breath hitches.

I scoop up more of the pudding and, once more, offer it to her. Again, she leans forward, closes her mouth around the spoon, and licks up the dessert. She swipes the tip of her tongue across her lower lip, and the blood drains to my cock.

I put the spoon aside, then drag my finger through the pudding and pick up a dab of the pudding. I lean over and spread it across her lips, before dragging my finger down her chin, her throat, to the valley between her breasts.

"What are you doing?" Her voice sounds breathless.

"I think I'd prefer to eat this dessert off your skin."

"You're crazy."

"And you agreed to do everything I asked." I raise my gaze to hers. "Unless you want to use your safe word?"

She stays silent for a second or two, then shakes her head again.

"Good girl."

Her features flush. She licks off some of the pudding from her lower lip, and I click my tongue. "I didn't give you permission to do that."

She scoffs. "Seriously?"

"Don't defy me, baby."

She tilts her head. A considering look comes into her eyes, then she reaches over, swipes up the pudding, and brings her finger to her mouth. She sucks on her digit and flutters her eyelashes at me. "Oops."

My heart begins to race. Adrenaline dumps into my bloodstream. "You've done it now, Fire. I'm giving you until I count to five."

"Eh?" She lowers her hand and blinks. "What do you mean?"

"Run, baby. If I catch you, I'm not letting go of you—not until I make you come the remaining sixteen times."

"Seventeen, actually." Her lips kick up.

"So, you were keeping count?"

"I take my orgasms very seriously."

"So do I." I rise to my feet; so does she.

"If you want a head start, I suggest you run, now." I jerk my chin in the direction of the door.

"Ooh, I'm so scared." She mock shivers.

"You should be."

"Five."

"What are you doing?"

"Counting down." I smirk. "Four."

She narrows her gaze. "Thought you didn't want me to touch the floor of the house with my feet?"

"Change of rules. Three." I roll my neck, and her entire body stiffens.

She looks at the doorway, then back at me. "Are you being serious about this?"

"I'm always serious with you, Fire. Two." I crack my knuckles.

She gulps, shuffles her feet. "I think this entire thing is stupid. You seem to change the rules at any time, and with very little warning."

"My rules. I change them as they suit my needs. Except for one thing. Are you going to use your safe word?"

She shakes her head slowly from side to side.

"Good girl."

A tremor shakes her shoulders.

"Your time just ran out, Fire. One." I lean over the table.

30

Zara

My heart somersaults into my throat. I push away from the table so fast, my chair crashes to the floor, and even then, his fingers brush against my bathrobe. I scream, then jump and race toward the door. Footsteps sound behind me, and I know he's on my heels. How can he move that quickly? He warned me he was going to chase me, but I didn't take him seriously. I thought he was joking... I underestimated him.

Surely, this is some kind of a twisted game for him—one which I don't intend to lose. I increase my speed and reach the doorway. Almost there, almost... If I can only get out of the kitchen and get to the bedroom, I can shut the door behind me, and then— Something latches onto the belt I tied around my bathrobe. I yell and pull away, leaving the bathrobe behind. Cool air touches my skin. *Shit, shit, shit.* And now, I'm naked, to boot. Footsteps thud behind me, and my pulse raps against my temples. Sweat pools under my armpits. My knees tremble, but I keep going.

I reach the bedroom and thrust one foot over the doorway when his fingers lock around my upper arm. I yell and try to wriggle away. The next second, the world turns upside down. Huh? Where the hell am I?

What the—? My hair flows down my ears—or is it up? I don't know. I'm upside-down. Down is up and up is down—and over my face—not under. That would make me inside-out. And why the hell am I having these nonsensical thoughts? What is wrong with me? Clearly, I'm delirious.

I stare at his backside—his very spectacular arse hidden by those sweatpants.

"The fuck! What are you doing?"

"I caught you, fair and square, Fire. Now you're mine." His voice rumbles from somewhere above me; the vibrations travel down his back, and my chest, which is pressed up against his spine. I wriggle and writhe. He places his arm across the back of my thighs.

"Let me go, Hunter," I snap.

"Not a chance, baby." He strides away from the bedroom and through to the kitchen. He approaches the dining table with the over-turned chair next to it and comes to a halt.

"What are you doing?"

"I haven't had my dessert yet."

"Excuse me?" I squeeze my thighs together. He can't mean… Surely, not. "Hunter, don't you dare," I yell.

"Don't challenge me, darlin'." He lowers me down onto the table. I spring up at once, but he presses his palm into the center of my chest. "I love it when you stand up to me. And when you defy me, it fucking turns me on, you know that?"

I glance at the tent in his crotch and then up at him. "I can tell." I push into his palm and he steps forward until his knees brush against mine.

"Part your legs for me."

"No."

His eyes gleam. "Fuck, if that doesn't turn me on even more."

"You're a psychopath, you know that?" I snarl.

He tilts his head as if considering my statement. "Only when it comes to you. Although right now, what I am is really fucking horny. Also, I think the word you were looking for is sadist."

I swallow. That part of me that yearns to have him handle my body as he sees fit, that hidden side of me that can't wait for him to do to me as he wishes, that submissive woman inside who wants to open her thighs for his tongue, his fingers, his cock—ideally, each and every one of those parts, in different holes of my body, at the same time— rises to the fore. He must sense it, for he bends his knees and peers into my eyes.

"Open. Your. Thighs."

I widen the gap between my legs.

"Good girl."

He plants himself in the space between my thighs, and my core clenches. He reaches past me and his neck brushes against my nose. I draw in a breath—only because I have to breathe—and my lungs fill with Hunter. My head spins. I hear the sounds of the dishes being pushed to the side, then he pushes down on my chest. I lay back until the back of my head meets the table.

"Jesus, look at you." His voice is harsh, the tone gravelly, as he rakes his gaze from my face to my stomach to the space between my legs. "Fuck, you're aroused, aren't you, baby?"

"I'm not."

He laughs, then shoves two fingers inside me. I groan as my core clenches down on his fingers. He pulls out his glistening fingers, then brings them to my lips. "Suck it off."

I scowl at him.

"Now," he commands.

And I don't want to do it; I don't. But that feminine core of me, the one that yearns to be his, the one that's riding me hard, takes over. I open my mouth, and he places his fingers on my tongue. I lock my lips about his digits, and he slides them out. I pop my lips together, taste myself and…and him.

"How do you taste?"

"Like you."

His eyes darken until they seem like the depths of the sea. I can see it clearly. I'm going to dive in, and when I surface, I'll be changed. My stomach knots. My chest hurts. *Am I really going to go through with this?* "Hunter, I—"

"Shh, baby, let me take care of you."

He looks into my eyes, and in his, I see lust and need and something else. Something more intense. That emotion he's been hinting at over the last day. That…sensation that's bound us together from the moment I laid eyes on him. The connection I've been trying to deny, knowing it's going to take root in me. The one that's already tying me to him. No matter how much I deny it, he's crawled under my skin, and when I leave here, I'm going to feel empty. I'm going to miss him… But for now, I have him, and I intend to make the most of the time we have.

I force my muscles to relax, one by one, not taking my gaze from his.

He nods, as if he senses my submission and accepts it as his right. Then he reaches behind and pulls off his T-shirt displaying those perfect chest planes. He throws it aside, and before I can say anything else, he leans over, scoops up the pudding, and smears it across my chest.

31

Hunter

I glance at the sticky pudding that smothers her breasts, except for her nipples, which peek through the gooey mess. They're like blackcurrants, enticing me to close my mouth around them. The next second, I do just that. I squeeze one nipple and nip at the other one. A moan spills from her.

"Hunter," she gasps and winds her arms about my neck. I lick the dessert up from her breast, the complex sweetness of raisins and almonds mixed with the salty taste of her skin is a perfect blend of opposing flavors. I lick the last of the sauce from one breast, then turn my attention to the other. I eat my way through the pudding before I lick her nipple, which hardens further. I drag my teeth over the bud, and she shudders.

"You're so damn responsive." I raise my head and stare into her eyes. "I want to eat you up."

"Thought you were already doing that."

"I haven't even started."

She chuckles. "It shouldn't feel this right, Hunter. Why does it feel so right?"

"Because it is."

"But it can't be. You and me… It'll never work."

"Trust me." I press a hard kiss to her lips. She opens her mouth, and I suck on her tongue. The taste of her is deeper than chocolate, more complex than nutmeg, more flavorful than citrus, and as contradictory as politics can sometimes seem on the surface. She pushes up and into me so our skin sticks together. She digs her fingers into the hair at the nape of my neck and tugs on it. Goosebumps pepper my skin. I manage to lift my head and gaze into her face. Her eyelids flutter open.

"Eyes on me, baby. I want you to see me as I eat you out."

Her gaze widens. She opens her mouth, but I've already slid down until my face is above her pussy. I blow on her lower lips, and her hold on my hair tightens. I sink to my knees and bury my mouth in her cunt, and she groans. "Hunter, please, please, please—"

She cuts out with a gasp when I stab my tongue inside her soaking wet channel. I twist my tongue inside her, and she screams as she orgasms. Her cum soaks my tongue and runs down my chin. I glance up to find her eyelids fluttering down. I squeeze her thigh. "Eyes on me, baby."

She raises her eyelids and glances down as I lick her pussy lips. I circle the swollen nub of her clit, then tease it with my teeth. Her entire body jolts.

I straighten, then grip her arms and twist them over her head. I lock them around the edge of the table. "Hold on."

I take a handful of the pudding, slap it over her pussy, and her gaze widens. She bites down on her lower lip as I sink back to my knees. I throw her legs over my shoulders, then bend my head and swipe my tongue from her puckered hole to her clit.

She writhes under me, locks her thighs about my neck, and I begin to eat her out in earnest. I nibble on her clit, lick her pussy lips, then stab my tongue inside her slit. I close my mouth over her cunt and her eyes roll back in her head.

"I can't come; not again."

"You can."

I fit two fingers inside her pussy and scissor them in and out of her. I suck on her clit, add a third finger inside her, and her entire body jolts. I curl my fingers inside her, and she shudders.

"Ohgodohgodohgod," she chants.

I tease her puckered hole and she cries out. Her entire body jolts as she orgasms. I lick up the cum from her slit, from the crease between her pussy and her inner thigh, then surge to my feet. Her chest rises and falls, and her eyes have drifted closed. I press her thighs further apart, position her legs so she can lock her ankles about my waist, then shove down my sweats. I fit my cock into her slit, and she flutters open her eyelids.

Her golden eyes are almost colorless, her features are flushed, and her hair flows about her face like the halo of a goddess.

"Again?" She draws in a breath and lets out a sigh.

"And again." I plant my hand next to her head, then thrust my hips forward. Her gaze widens, and in one smooth move, I bury myself inside her. She parts her lips, and I close my mouth over hers. I absorb her scream, then thrust into her with enough force that the entire table moves forward. Cutlery falls to the floor, and one of the plates hits the wooden floor and rolls away. She jerks, but I don't release her. I deepen the kiss as I pound into her, again and again. I slide my palms under her hips, angling her just right, then slam into her. My balls slap against her inner thighs. I tear my mouth from hers and check her face. "Open your eyes."

When our gazes clash, I pull out of her, then plunge forward again. I slide my hand between us, then grind the heel of my hand into her clit. "Come with me," I order.

She opens her mouth, and with a silent cry, she shatters. I thrust into her once, twice, thrice, then follow her over the edge.

"Umm, what was that?" She rubs her cheek against my chest.

After she came with me, I carried her to the bathroom, where we showered. And I went down on her and made her come again, then turned her into the shower wall and fucked her in the arse, and she came. Twice.

"That, baby, was me warming up."

She laughs, then groans. "Shut up, you egoistical monster."

"It's true. I'm only now finding my stride."

"Right." She turns her face into my chest and inhales deeply.

"How do I smell?"

"Like sex and mint and lust and something sweet. You smell like us."

I lock my arms about her and pull her closer. She melts into me.

"How many, baby?"

"How many what?" Her voice is muffled. Her muscles relaxed. Her still wet hair lies in long coiled strands about her shoulders.

"You know what."

"No, I don't." She clears her throat.

"It's the reason why you've been screaming my name over the past few hours."

"That's because you like it when I call your name."

"Which I do, of course. Guess you've forgotten why you did it though. Maybe I need to remind you?"

I begin to turn, and she slaps my shoulder. "Fine, fine, you asshole. Fine. That was because you made me orgasm."

I make a circular motion with my fingers, indicating she should keep speaking.

She huffs. "That was five orgasms—"

"Six—" I smirk.

She throws up her hands. "Fine. It's six so far, are you satisfied?"

"Not until I make you come another twelve times."

<hr>

I made her come another three times, back-to-back, after which we both napped for a few hours. I woke up with a raging hard-on a few minutes ago and reached for her, only to find she, too, was awake. I reached over and kissed her deeply. She wrapped her arms about my shoulders and pulled me even closer. Now, I position myself between her legs, and she draws in a breath.

"I can't, Hunter. I can't," she whimpers.

"You can, baby. Lift your hips; let me in."

She obliges, and inch by inch, I slide inside her.

"Oh god, you're stretching me, you're so damn big," she groans.

Even after I've buried myself inside her again and again, it still feels like it's the first time. I plant my elbows on either side of her head and peer into her eyes. I hold her gaze, tilt my hips, and sink further inside. Her gaze widens.

Strands of hair are stuck to her forehead. Her face is flushed, and her eyes, those gorgeous golden eyes, had turned silver and now, they're a shimmering, translucent gray. The purple smudges under her eyes cause my heart to stutter. "I should let you sleep." I begin to pull out, but she locks her ankles about me.

"Not so fast, buster. You owe me another nine orgasms."

I rub my thumb over her cheekbone. "You could always take a rain check on it."

Her face pales. She looks away, then back at me. "I'd prefer to cash that check in now."

It was worth a try. I hoped to seduce her into agreeing to meet me again, but maybe it's too early to get that commitment from her.

I brush my mouth over hers. "You sure, baby? You look tired."

Oh? She flutters her eyelashes at me. "Or maybe it's you who's tired."

"Oh?" I rotate my hips so my hardening cock slides even deeper inside. Her breath stutters. My lips kick up. "Does that feel tired to you?"

"That feels…so good." She wraps her arms about my shoulders. "Why does it feel like it's the first time every time you fuck me?"

Her words echo my thoughts from earlier. I run my nose up her jawline, and she shivers. I curl my tongue around the shell of her ear, and she moans. "Hunter, please."

"What do you want, baby?" I nibble little kisses down her cheek to the edge of her mouth. "Tell me."

"You know what I want," she whines.

"Not unless you tell me, I don't."

"I want you to fuc—" She gasps as I pull out and thrust back into her with enough force that her entire body moves up the bed. I lunge forward again, then bottom out inside her. Her back curves, her body stretched so tight, her muscles vibrate with tension. She's close, so close.

I pull back, then peer into her eyes. "What are you thinking of now?"

"You."

"Who are you going to dream about, Fire?"

She swallows. "You, Hunter."

"Whose cock are you going to fall apart around?"

Her features flush, and her lips part. "Yours, Hunter, only yours." I lower my face to the curve of where her neck meets her shoulder, then bite down.

She moans, "Hunter, oh god, I'm going to—"

"Come with me, baby."

32

Zara

I drift on a cloud of warmth. My muscles are so relaxed. I try to move, but my arms and legs feel weighed down. My thigh muscles ache, and my shoulders hurt. There's a pleasant thrum under my skin, like I've spent the night plugged into a low-key electricity generator. Or had a rather large, monster cock plugged into me, shooting me up with cum. *Ugh, I didn't just think that. Did I think that? Of course, I did. It's not as if there's someone else controlling my thoughts.*

I turn on my back, and my entire body protests. My core clenches down on the emptiness, then protests at the movement. I'm alone in bed and already, I miss him. And I'm sure there's no way I can bear to come again. Not after how he fucked me in every position I can imagine—as much as the bed, and the table, and the shower would allow, that is.

Of course, he's not going to allow my feet to touch the floor of the bedroom. Another of his rules—-which he could change at will. The man makes them up at the drop of a hat, and leaves me breathless and unable to keep up which is… Another first.

Every time I think I have him pinned down, Hunter Whittington surprises me. It's what makes my interactions with him so interesting.

For a cynical media whore who spends so much of her time interacting with people for whom appearance is everything, and who assumed that Hunter was one of them… Well, he's definitely proved me wrong. For one, he's more caring than he comes across. More humane. And he can cook. God, the man can cook. And he knows how to use his cock, and his fingers, and his tongue, and he's focused on my pleasure. Indeed, he didn't stop until he made me come over and over again.

I'd have lost count, except after each one, he asks me how many orgasms I've had, and I have to recount the tally to him. And each orgasm has been delivered creatively. On my back, on my front, on my hands and knees, me on my side and him standing behind me, him kneeling and me balanced on his thighs, pretzel style, flatiron style, me with my legs thrown over his shoulders G-whiz style, me riding him, me riding him reverse-cowgirl style, and then the wheelbarrow style, where he made me balance on my arms as he planted his feet on the floor, positioned himself between my thighs and took me from behind… And… then there was the magic mountain pose. Oh, my god. I've read about it, but never tried that one before. He positioned me leaning back on my arms, with my legs bent, then mirrored my pose and inched toward me, then slid his dick into me.

And then, the most memorable one. The eighteenth one was just as the dawn light filtered through the windows. That time, he held my gaze and spooned me, but from the front, so we could maintain eye contact. And that made it so much hotter, so much more intense. He caressed my butt, then squeezed the back of my thigh, and encouraged me to slide my leg between his. He took his time as he buried himself, inch by inch, inside of me and penetrated me while maintaining the connection of our gazes. The position allowed him to thrust into me so that he hit that spot inside of me every single time. Then he pulled me close enough for my clit to grind against his pelvis, and it set off a long, slow, deep orgasm. A shiver snakes down my spine at the recollection. Oh, god, that had been incredible. I came and came and then I must have blacked out for when I awoke I was in bed alone.

My stomach grumbles. The activities of last night, clearly, gave me an appetite. The only thing that would make things even better is having pancakes for breakfast.

I should move, should swing my legs over the bed and get dressed and leave. This one night stand is well and truly over. I try to force my body to respond, but it seems to have developed a mind of its own.

Everything you hear about body memory is true. I can still feel the touch of his fingertips on my skin, of his breath on my cheek, the sound of his breathing speeding up as he buries himself in me, the vibrations of his heart thundering against his ribcage, and into my chest as he thrusts into me, the echo of his groan as he empties himself inside me...

I rub my cheek against the soft cotton of the pillow. The remnants of sleep tug at my eyelids, and I try to sink back into my dream. If I do, I won't have to face the future...

A day when I won't be with him. When I have to go back to my world, my career—the one I spent so long building. A world I love, but where there's no space for love. No room for someone like him. He only makes me weak. He makes me want to lean on him. He makes me want to abandon the rules I created so long ago for success. He makes me want to redefine the idea of success and—

Whoa, I can't do that. I can't let a man change my mindset, my reason for living. I can't let the future Prime Ministerial candidate of this country transform me into exactly the kind of woman I swore not to become. A woman like my mother, who allowed her life to be defined by her husband. That isn't me.

I owe it to myself to rise above the events of the past few days. To keep it where it belongs—in my thoughts, in my deepest memories. To never be looked at again. A hot sensation knifes my ribcage. My guts churn. A tell-tale pressure stings the backs of my eyes. Nope, I'm not crying, not now. Not when I didn't allow myself to become weak when Olly was diagnosed as having autism spectrum disorder. I didn't shed a tear then, and I certainly won't now.

I'm a strong, independent woman. I know what I want. I know what makes me happy, and Hunter makes me...feel at odds with myself. He brings out the hidden, vulnerable parts of me that I never even knew existed. And that will only prevent me from doing my job well. So no, there's no space for him in my life. I had my fun with him, and now it's time to move on. I push back the sheets and sit up. That's when the door opens and the object of my thoughts strides in.

33

Hunter

One look at the furrow between her eyebrows, at the downward tilt of her lips, at those eyelids still weighed down by the weight of the pleasure I wrought from her body, even as those golden eyes flicker with awareness of what passed between us the last two nights—and I know she's come to a decision about us.

"Don't do this." I stalk over to her.

She begins to swing her legs over, but I push her back into the bed and cover her body with mine.

"Hunter," she half-laughs, half-tries to push me off of her. "What are you doing?"

"What do you think I'm doing?"

"Do you always have to answer every question with a question?'

"Do you?" I lean enough of my weight into her, and she stops struggling.

She glances between my eyes, then tips up her chin. "It's over."

"It's not over until we say it is." I growl.

"It was a one night stand that stretched to two," she murmurs. "And now the sun has come out."

As if to mark her words, a ray of sunlight beams through the window and across our faces. It picks out the flickers of silver in the depths of her eyes. The ones that captivated me from the moment I first spotted them. The ones that tell me her emotions are nowhere as settled as she'd like me to believe.

I cup her cheek, and she blinks. "Hunter, please."

"You know I'm not going to be able to let you go." I hold her gaze.

She looks away then back at me. "That was the deal. We had this time together, and now it's time to leave."

"Not before you promise it's not over between us."

"I can't." She swallows. "We can't be seen together. It will only get people talking."

"So let them."

"We've been over this. I can't afford to be linked with you."

"Why not?"

"You know why." She firms her lips.

"I'm not sure why."

"You're the Prime Ministerial candidate—"

"And you'd be the woman I'm seeing."

"There, that's what I mean. You'll be the leader, the man in charge, the one in power and—"

"You'd be my equal. In public, I may be the future Prime Minister. In private, I'd be the man who makes you orgasm so hard you can't have a coherent thought for days."

She laughs, and her features light up. She looks so goddamn beautiful, I lean in and press my mouth to hers. She parts her lips, and I deepen the kiss. By the time I raise my head, we're both breathing hard. I press the tent between my legs into her. "See what you do to me, Fire? How do you expect me to not pursue you after this?"

"Because your career is important to you—"

"Not more than the woman I want by my side."

"What?" Her gaze widens. "What did you say?" There's a thread of panic in her voice. *Fuck, I shouldn't have said that. Why is it that when I'm with her all my careful planning goes to pieces?*

"You heard me. I want you to be with me on the campaign trail."

"No. That's not going to happen. I can't allow anything to tie the two of us together. I won't allow my personal life to become the fodder of gossip blogs and political commentators."

"Why not? What are you so scared of? Why do you always want to stay behind the scenes, Zara? Why is it you never want to face the issue that's standing right in front of you? What are you hiding?"

She pales, then shoves at me again. "Let me go."

"No."

"Let me go, Hunter." Her voice is so cold, it stabs through my heart like a bloody knife. I'm going to lose her. I'm going to lose her. That's when the phone in my back pocket vibrates. Fuck, I shouldn't have switched it on earlier, but I thought I could get through some of my work while she was still sleeping. I hoped to buy myself a little time before the inevitable demands of the campaign pulled me away. The very fact that I didn't switch on my phone for the last forty-eight hours, no doubt, sent the rest of my team into a panic. No matter that it was Christmas and the day after, which is also a public holiday in this country. There's no time off when you're running to be Prime Minister. Something I knew and pushed aside because I wanted to spend time with her.

"You need to answer that," she points out.

"I don't need to do anything I don't want to."

The doorbell rings, I swear aloud. She tilts her head. No way, am I going to move. If I do, I'll lose her. And if I don't? She'll hate me anyway, for keeping her here against her will.

My phone vibrates, and the doorbell rings again. The sound of someone pounding on the door reaches us. My phone pings with an incoming message.

"I think that must be your security team?"

"Fuck that," I growl.

"I think we've done enough of that, don't you think?"

"When it comes to you, it's never enough."

She draws in a sharp breath. Her pupils dilate. I lower my head and my phone vibrates again and doesn't stop. At the same time, the doorbell rings, a series of long bursts of noise that tear through the liminal space we created.

"This isn't over yet, Zara." I press a hard kiss to her mouth, then roll off her and off the bed.

She begins to rise, and I stab a finger in her direction. "Make sure you're dressed properly before you come out there."

Turning, I stride out.

"I strongly advise that you not attempt to lose us again, sir. We are only doing our jobs in trying to protect you, and if you leave without telling us, and then disengage the tracking device on your phone, you put yourself at risk and—" Ralph, the head of my security team breaks off halfway through his tirade as Zara sweeps into the living room where I've been talking with them for the past forty-five minutes.

I told her to get dressed properly, and I have no doubt she hated the fact I ordered her to do so. It wouldn't have hurt to tack on a please at the end of my statement, but had I done so? Of course, not. I was pissed with myself that I hadn't found a way to get her to agree to see me again. At least, when I had her under me, I used my cock to seduce her into submitting to me, but with the length of the room between us, all I can do is watch as she looks away from me.

"Zara Chopra," she says, and holds out her hand as she approaches us.

"Ralph Sanders, Mr. Whittington's Head of Security." Ralph reaches to shake her hand, and I stiffen.

Before I can stop myself, I step in between them, forcing him to retreat. I cut off his view of Zara and glare at him. "Shouldn't you be out doing a search of the perimeter?"

"Already done," Ralph replies.

Behind me, Zara tries to peer around my back, but I shift my position.

"And checking my car to make sure it's safe to drive back," I snap.

Ralph's eyebrows draw down. "My men are on it."

"Ms. Chopra's car..."

"Is parked in the front garage." She shoves at my arm, but I don't move.

"You're parked in the front garage, huh?"

"So?" She frowns.

"I'm parked in the one at the back."

"Your point being?"

"Weston told me, specifically, to use the garage at the back," I murmur.

"Huh." She purses her lips. "Amelie texted me to say that I should use the garage at the front."

"Jesus." I roll my shoulders, "You don't think—"

The creases in her forehead clear. "I do think."

Our gazes meet, hold.

"I can't believe they did this," she says finally.

"I guess I owe Weston one." I allow my lips to curve.

Ralph clears his throat.

I stiffen, then turn my gaze on him. "Once you're done checking our cars, could you wait outside?"

"Of course, sir; ma'am." He walks out the front door, and Zara punches my arm.

"The hell is wrong with you?"

"What are you talking about?" I strive for what I hope is an innocent tone.

She stomps around to stand toe-to-toe with me. "You were acting like a Neanderthal. You planted your ugly arse—"

"Didn't hear you calling it that when you had your fingers squeezing down on that part of my body last night," I murmur.

"—in between us. You forced that man back. You didn't let him see my face while I spoke to him."

"Trust me, if I could control myself around you, I would, but apparently, I'm not ready to allow the outside world to look at you."

"Deal with it." She throws up her hands. "Have you heard yourself? You sound deranged. Like an over-the-top, overprotective, dominant, possessive, wankhead."

"All true, except that last descriptor. Not sure I agree with that."

"This is no laughing matter, Hunter."

"Do you see me laughing?"

She glowers at me. "You're smirking; that's close enough."

"Fine, I accept maybe my behavior was a little extreme." I raise a shoulder.

"A little extreme?" She snaps her shoulders back. "And you told him we were having a discussion. A discussion!"

"Isn't that what we're having now?" I incline my head.

"This is not a discussion. This is our—"

"First argument as a couple?'

"We're not a couple."

"Strange, that's not what it seemed like to me last night."

"One night—okay, two nights of sex, no matter how mind-blowing, how out of this world, orgasmic, how—"

"So, you admit it was mind-blowing and out of this world?" I ask.

"Of course, it was, you numbskull. And you don't need me to confirm that to you, and oh, you keep interrupting me." She tucks her elbows into her sides. "Hunter, what are we doing?"

"We" —I place my hands on her shoulders— "are going to leave here, have breakfast somewhere nice, and then drive back to London."

34

———————

Zara

I glance down at the stack of pancakes on my plate, then toward his plate, which holds a pile of waffles dripping with syrup and ice cream on top.

"You found the only diner in the UK that serves American-style breakfast dishes?" I ask. We're seated at a table at the far end by the window. A table where he pulled up a third chair for my Birkin. In that moment, I felt something inside me melt all over again. I opened my mouth to tell him that maybe I would see him again, after all, when the waitress arrived to take our orders.

Hunter's back is to the door, and he's big enough and broad enough that I'm hidden by the width of his shoulders. Also, he's wearing a cap and had on a scarf and sunglasses, which he took off once we were seated. Not that he was trying to disguise himself. He's well-known among the media, but perhaps, not as much with the general public, though that will change once he hits the campaign trail.

The waitress didn't recognize him, either. If she did, she didn't let on. And the place is charming. I glance around the wooden fixtures, the large fireplace, the wooden tabletops with the gleaming cutlery, the bar at the other end where, despite it being Boxing Day morning, there are still a few people—clearly regulars—seated. It has a homey feeling, and the food looks amazing.

"You should know by now; I'll always find a way to fulfill your heart's desires." Hunter lowers his chin.

"I never told you I wanted to have pancakes for—" I cut off my words because he fixes me with an all-knowing glance.

"How did you know I wanted pancakes for breakfast?" I scowl.

"A lucky guess."

"Don't bullshit me, Whittington. Did you find out my tastes from having me investigated?

He merely shoots me a look. I guess that's a yes, then. He cuts off a big chunk of the waffles and shoves them into his mouth. Some of the ice cream sticks to the side of his mouth.

"Umm, you have a—" I nod my chin in his direction.

"What?"

I lean over, scoop up the dab of ice cream, bring it to my mouth and lick it off. "There, you're fine now."

"Am I, though?" His eyes turn a stormy shade of green. Like there are emotions roiling around inside him, and he's not sure how to give them words.

"You have to be. I have to be. Don't you see that?"

His gaze intensifies, and a dull ache gnaws behind my breastbone. I tear my gaze away from him and pick up my knife and fork. I cut off a small portion of the pancakes and pop it in my mouth. It melts on my tongue. "Mmm, this tastes even better than it looks."

"So do you."

I cough, then reach for my glass of water and wash down the food.

"Hunter, seriously, stop doing this. You really have to stop."

"Give me one reason why," he shoots back.

"Because there's somewhere I need to be."

"Right now?'

I glance at my phone, then back at him. "Someone's waiting for me."

His lips firm. "Someone more important than whatever it is between the two of us?"

"Definitely more important. Also..." I set down my cutlery and fold my arms across my chest. "Let's not forget, you said one night. I gave you two."

"You gave me two? As if you didn't get anything out of it? Besides, you stayed a second night because of the storm," he points out.

I glance away, oddly ashamed. "Agreed, and now we have to go back to our daily lives."

He looks between my eyes. "Is that your final decision on the matter?"

I swallow, force myself to meet his gaze. "Yes." I clear my throat. "Yes, it is."

He stays silent for a few seconds, then nods. "Okay." He pulls out his phone and begins to scroll the screen.

I blink. "Did you say okay?"

"I don't repeat myself, Zara."

Zara, not Fire. He called me Zara earlier, but not like this. Not with his attention focused on something other than me. Not with his jaw hard. Not with an invisible barrier he seems to have pulled down between us. What happened? Did I finally succeed in pushing him away? It's what I want. It's what I've been trying to achieve since I met him. I succeeded and now, I already miss him. He's sitting in front of me, but it's as if he's not with me anymore. This is how it feels to not be the cynosure of Hunter Whittington's attention. It feels like all the warmth in the room has drained out. Like an avalanche has dumped ice all over me, and now I'm frozen, unable to feel my limbs, while my heart flutters in my chest like a caged bird.

He glances up from his phone suddenly, and our gazes connect. And his eyes? Oh, god, his eyes are a cold blue, a glacial frostiness in them that I've only seen reserved for others. And now, he's aiming that aloof politeness at me.

"Don't you want the rest of your breakfast?" He glances at my plate, then at me.

"Not hungry," I murmur.

He seems like he's about to protest, then catches himself. "Fine." He rises to his feet and brushes past the table.

My jaw drops. I watch as he stalks out the door of the pub without waiting for me. He didn't wait for me to finish. So, I told him I wasn't hungry, but he could have, at least, asked me if I really meant it. Is this how it's going to be from now on? Isn't this how I want it to be from now on?

I jump to my feet, grab my bag, and march through the doorway. I walk outside and into the parking lot to find him talking to Ralph. When

I reach them, Ralph nods at Hunter. "I'll follow you back to the office, Sir." He nods at me and says, "Ms. Chopra," then walks toward one of the two black SUVs parked next to the car Hunter drove us in.

"You're heading to the office?" I turn to Hunter, who slides my car's key fob from his pocket and holds it out.

I take it, and he retrieves his hand before our fingers touch… And why do I feel so deprived?

"Goodbye, Zara." He takes a step back.

I want to jump forward and grab his sleeve but stop myself. "It doesn't have to be like this, Hunter."

"Like what?"

"Like… Like this…" I point between us.

"I don't know what you're talking about."

"If you're going to be so immature about this—"

"I'm merely giving you want you wanted. You don't want us to have a relationship? You don't want to be seen with me? This is how it looks."

"Can't we be friends?"

"Friends?" For the first time since he took his phone out in the restaurant, his eyes turn more green than blue. "With what I feel for you, we can never be friends."

35

Zara

"That's what he said? That the two of you can never be friends?" Solene asks from the screen of my phone.

"That's what he said." I pour myself a cup of coffee and carry it to the window of my office.

It's been three weeks since Hunter threw those words at me and took off in his car. He left one of his security detail behind, who insisted on following me on the drive back to London. They ensured I was safely inside my house before they left. I felt protected by Hunter's gesture, that despite the fact we parted on what were not the friendliest of terms, he insisted on making sure I got home safely.

At the same time, it's not like he asked me if his team could escort me home. He simply assumed I'd be fine with it and ordered his team to to it. I could hardly tell the team not to do so when they approached me. To do so would have made me appear churlish. Besides, I was glad they were following me home, given how treacherous the roads still were after the snow last night. So, I accepted their offer.

Which meant, ultimately, he won, even though he agreed to walk away from me, just as I asked him to do. And he did. And now, I feel his loss so deeply, I feel like the biggest loser of all. Instead of feeling joyful to have escaped his clutches, I feel empty inside. Like I had a chance and wasted it away. Like all that's remaining in my life now is empty evenings and nights in a bed that feels too big and too cold, like… I've lost a part of me, a part I could have had but refused.

"Zara, you there?"

"Eh?" I turn to my phone. "What did you say?"

"It's not like you to be so pissed off over a man's words."

Only, he's not just any man. He's Hunter. He's the man who I can't stop going toe-to-toe with, the man who I was sure I didn't like; the man who gave me the most memorable night—okay, nights—of my life.

This is what happens when orgasms addle your brain. You can't think straight. Not that it seems to have affected the day-to-day life of the jerkhole. He's been in the news almost every week, spotted at openings and galas, each time, with a new woman on his arm. And he hasn't called me. Not once. Nor texted. But neither have I.

"It must have been some weekend break with him. The sex must have been phenomenal."

I flush. Her jaw drops. "OMG, did you just blush, Zara?"

"So what?" I flip my hair over my shoulder, trying to school my features into an expression which I hope is casual.

"So what? I've never seen you blush."

"I blush." *Especially when I'm in the presence of the poshhole.*

"Not when it comes to talking about sex, you don't."

I raise a shoulder. "Yeah, so I have a liberated view about sex, in general."

"And a rather low opinion of men, in particular," she points out.

"I did—" I admit.

"So, not anymore?"

"I mean, I still do," I say hastily.

"Umm, I think not." She chuckles.

"Can we change the topic?" I scowl.

"No way. In fact, I'm going to dial in Isla."

"No, wait! Don't. What are you—"

My screen changes view, and a third window pops up with Isla's eager face. "What's happening? What did I miss?"

"Hello to you, too. I assume you are finally back from honeymoon number five?" I ask in a droll tone.

"It was our sixth, actually. Although, since we decided to move to the island, every day with Liam feels like a honeymoon," she says in a dreamy voice.

Solene and I exchange glances. It's almost funny how much Isla is in love with her husband. Truth is, he seems just as crazy about her. And the few times I've seen them since they got married, they couldn't keep their hands and their gazes off of each other.

"Anyhoo" —Isla beams at both of us— "I didn't jump on the call to talk about myself. Tell us about your latest man."

I look down my nose at her. "Why does it have to be about my man?"

"Because I'm married, and Solene is, more or less, in a relationship." Isla's referring to Solene dating Hollywood heartthrob Declan Beauchamp.

"I'm not," Solene butts in.

"Okay, so she's not, at the moment, but given we know their ups and downs last until one of them misses the other and they get back together—"

"Or not," Solene chimes in again.

"Or not, which I don't believe for a moment. Either way, it's not as if she's interested in anyone else. You though" —Isla's smile grows broader — "you are Zara Chopra, Ms. Shark herself—"

"I'm a tough negotiator." I shrug off the title the media seems to have thrust upon me.

"Indeed. And you are not easy to please. So, if you have a new man in your life —"

"I don't," I snap.

Both women look at me.

"Okay, fine. So, I may have had a dirty one night stand," I finally admit.

"I knew it." Solene does a mock fist pump.

"It's Hunter, isn't it?" Isla bursts out.

When I don't reply, Solene chimes in, "It is Hunter. Also, he told her they could never be friends."

"And when has that bothered you?" Isla asks.

"It doesn't bother me."

She scans my features. "Hmm."

"What's that hmm for?" I glance at my coffee. It's only four p.m. If only, I could have something stronger. Only it's dry January, and I'm trying to detox. And not just when it comes to alcohol, apparently, because since that night with Hunter, I haven't wanted to sleep with anyone else. Or been attracted to anyone else, for that matter. In fact, I haven't been able to stop thinking about Hunter, which is, honestly, not great.

"Just hmm," Isla's voice has a sly tone to it.

"What's going on in that head of yours?"

"Me? Nothing." She widens her gaze and I sigh.

"'Fess up, will you."

"Oh, I'm just thinking that the two of you make a good couple. Of course, not that you are together or anything, but if you were, then you could help him with his leadership campaign."

"It would be a disaster. The two of us would not be able to agree on anything. He wants someone who's more submissive, and I'm not someone who likes to be told what to do." Except in bed, and only by him, apparently.

Isla blinks. "Umm, are we talking sex, or are we talking about getting on the campaign trail here?"

"Both," I shoot back.

There's silence, then Solene presses a finger to her cheek. "I think it's the fact that the two of you challenge each other that makes you both so well-suited for the other. In fact, I think you are exactly the kind of person he needs to help him during his candidature."

"What do you mean?"

"Ever since my track went viral, the number of people who've crawled out of the woodwork and want to become part of my entourage has multiplied. In fact, the only people it hasn't affected are the two of you—"

"And Declan," Isla points out.

"And Declan," Solene agrees, but her tone is hesitant.

I narrow my gaze. "Is it all the publicity surrounding your success that's made it difficult for the two of you to be together?"

"One of us being in the public eye is difficult enough," she replies and blows out a breath. "But add in the fact that Declan's last film was a big hit, and the media speculation on our every move, can make things challenging, to say the least."

"Oh, honey, I'm so sorry," Isla says in a soft voice.

"Media intrusion is never easy. The trick, though, is not to give any weight to what they write. Don't respond to them, don't engage with them. And never, ever google yourself," I add.

"It's not easy, though, when you are in the eye of the storm —"

"You find the calm," I murmur.

"Wise words." Solene chuckles. "But again, we're not talking about me, and neither Isla nor I are letting you off that easily." She waggles a finger at me. "So, going back to sex and the hot Prime Ministerial candidate to-be, you were saying —"

"Not much. I don't have anything to do with his campaign, or with the man himself."

"Is that why you're moping?" Solene tips down her chin.

"I'm not moping."

"You refused to come out and meet any of us on New Year's Eve."

"I was busy." I fold my arms across my chest.

She firms her lips. "How many New Year's Eves have you spent on your own at home before this?"

This was the first one. It really is not like me to be a shrinking violet. To prefer my own company to that of my friends, or indeed, a roomful of strangers I could socialize with. But I've been feeling so tired and under the weather, nothing has felt as good as watching the News at ten on BBC, then crawling into bed. On my own. Jeez, am I growing old before my time? My face falls.

Solene's features soften. "Didn't say that to make you feel bad. It's just that you have dark circles under your eyes. Also, I think maybe you've lost weight."

"Gee thanks," I drawl.

"Solene's right." Isla's gaze narrows on my face. "You do look a little peaked. Are you coming down with something?"

"I'm fine." I bring my cup of coffee to my mouth and my stomach churns. Ugh, nothing worse than coffee gone lukewarm. I pivot, head back to my table and place the coffee on it.

"So, when do I see the two of you again?"

"I'll be in London in a few weeks. Liam's board meeting is coming up, and he needs to be there. Also, I have a few new wedding planning clients I'd like to meet in person." The scene behind Isla changes. She climbs up the stairs at the mansion on the island she and Liam now call home.

"I'll try to stop over on my days off between gigs," Solene chimes in.

My phone buzzes again with an incoming call. I recognize the caller ID and frown. "Can't wait to see the both of you. So sorry guys, I have a call coming which I can't not take."

"See you soon."

"Can't wait."

Both women disconnect. I switch to the other call. "Lord Alan?"

"Zara my dear, how are you this very fine morning?" His familiar voice reverberates over the phone.

"I am well, sir, and you?"

"Never been better." There's a pause, then, "Remember our last call? I now have more details regarding the project I spoke to you about. I assume you're up for it?"

36

___

Hunter

"So, you're launching your campaign bid?" Sinclair leans back in his chair.

"I am," I confirm.

"About fucking time." JJ Kane smacks the table in front of him.

"The question I have is, why did it take you so long to make up your mind?" Michael places his fingertips together. This is the first I'm seeing him since Karma's delivery. He's spent the last few months at home with her and the new baby. Given Karma's delicate health and the baby being born prematurely, he was, understandably, very stressed about them, but both mother and child are doing well, which is why he agreed to meet the three of us for a meeting at my office.

"Politics is all about timing and" —I glance about their faces— "about who you have in your corner."

"And other than the three of us, I assume there's one more person who's support you need to put your best foot forward?" Sinclair drawls.

I lean back on my heels. "You could say that."

"And does this ace up your sleeve happen to be the shrewdest fixer this side of the pond?" Michael smirks.

"And does she happen to be a dark-haired spit-fire who's known for defusing scandals related to well-known personalities?" JJ Kane's grin widens.

"It's no secret that Zara and I ah…have a connection, and it's true that I've been waiting to ensure I had her on my team before I declared my candidacy."

"And is that wise?" Declan's voice interrupts from the phone.

I turn to where the device is balanced against my glass of water on the table.

"It would have been unwise to not have included her. I need her insights to plan my roadmap to the foremost leadership position of this country."

"But does she know that?" Declan retorts.

I rub the back of my neck. "Not yet."

"And when were you planning to tell her?" He scowls.

"At the right time?"

"I suggest you not delay that, not if you truly want her working with you," JJ murmurs.

I raise my hands. "Point taken, chaps. Though, that's not why I asked you here today."

"Could there be anything more important than figuring out your personal life and how it's going to impact your professional life?" Sinclair drums his fingers on the table.

"My personal life is my own. I take all of your advice and consider it, but ultimately, it's my decision how I decide to take things forward."

"Yours and hers," JJ reminds me.

"The callousness of the man who's lost his heart but is not yet aware of it." Sinclair scoffs.

"Hold on. I have feelings for her. That doesn't mean I've lost my heart, thank you very much."

The three men look at each other, then burst out laughing.

"Wait, what did I miss?" I scowl.

The three continue laughing, and I turn to Declan. "Do you know what they're laughing about?"

He rubs his hand across his face. "I'm not married, mate, and at the rate things are falling apart around me, I won't be for a while."

I pause, then pick up the phone and peer into Declan's features. His eyes are bloodshot, his hair mussed, and he's sporting days' old growth on his chin. "You all right, ol' chap?"

"No, but I will be. Fame is a double-edged sword, isn't it? You spend your career pursuing it. You think you want it. Then when you have it, it bites you in the arse."

"Anything you want to talk about?" JJ calls out.

I place the phone back in position on the table so the rest of the men can see the screen.

"Not that we're the best source of advice, considering we're scrambling to get our heads out of our arses after the birth of our kids." Sinclair yawns. "Sorry, the boy kept fussing last night, and it was my turn to feed him the bottle. So, as I was saying—" He looks around the table with a puzzled expression. "What was I saying?"

"That you're not the best source of advice." Declan chuckles. "Right now, you seem more tired than I feel."

"It's losing sleep at night that's wrecking me. You'd think raising a child would be a cakewalk. Everyone does it, after all, but after the fifth consecutive night of lost sleep, I swear, I'd give anything to find a way to put him to sleep so I can hit the sack by ten p.m."

"Ten p.m.?" I smirk. "Is this the same Sinclair Sterling who partied 'til dawn with the rest of the Seven?"

"Most of whom are probably spending an evening at home cuddled on the sofa watching Netflix and ordering a curry with their wives." He points out.

"Yep, I'd do anything for a good curry." Michael nods slowly.

"Man, I'm all for a good curry. The spicier, the better." JJ smirks.

I look at the three of them. "I'm definitely missing something aren't I?"

"Of course, not. You'll know when it's time for an exceptional curry. Nothing like getting your own recipe right for it, too." JJ's grin widens.

"What are you guys talking—"

The door opens and Lord Alan walks in. "Gentlemen, Minister." He nods his head in the direction of the assembled men.

JJ, Michael and Sinclair exchange glances, then as one, rise to their feet. "We were on our way out." Sinclair yawns, then shakes his head as if to clear it. He looks like he's about to keel over any moment.

JJ walks over and shakes Lord Alan's hand. "Good seeing you here. I'll leave the Minister in your capable hands."

He heads toward the door, when it opens again and Zara steps in. Her gaze arrows straight to mine, and her face pales. She opens her mouth, then shakes her head. She glances at Lord Alan, then at me, and understanding dawns on her features.

JJ dips his chin in Zara's direction, then walks out. Sinclair and Michael, too, shake Lord Alan's hand. They nod toward Zara before they follow JJ out.

"Good chat, Hunter, keep me posted how things develop." Declan signs off.

Lord Alan waddles over and lowers his bulk into one of the seats facing me. He waves his hand in Zara's direction, "I do believe the two of you have met?"

Zara's gaze narrows. "I believe we may have met on one or two occasions." She squares her shoulders and walks into the room.

"Ms. Chopra, a pleasure." I tilt my head.

She pauses next to the empty chair opposite me and next to Lord Alan. "Mr. Whittington." She jerks her chin.

"Please take a seat."

"I'm not sure I'll be here long enough for that."

"Oh?" I cross my arms over my chest.

"I plan to be out of here as soon I have a word with Lord Alan." She turns to the older man. "I'm not sure I'm the right person for this project."

Lord Alan places his elbows on the arms of his seat, then locks his palms under his chin. "So, you're going to let your ego get in the way of managing a campaign that's going to put a breakthrough candidate in Downing Street?"

She swallows. "I'm not right for this role."

Lord Alan barks out a laugh. "I don't mentor fools, nor losers. And you are neither of the two. You're not the type to give up without a fight, Zara, so what's making you do so now?"

"I'm not giving up," Zara splutters.

"Aren't you?" Lord Alan lowers his arms to his sides.

"Of course, not. It's just, I don't want to work with him." She stabs her thumb in my direction.

I drag my thumb under my lower lip. "I'm afraid, I have to admit, the two of us are incompatible."

"Or maybe you haven't dug deep enough to find common ground." Lord Alan glowers in my direction. "We need you in number ten, Whittington. And you" —he jerks his chin in Zara's direction— "we need your brains, madam, and your spin doctor skills, not to mention your acumen in getting the media to dance to your tune."

Zara flushes. "You give me too much credit, Lord Alan."

"Oh, take the praise when it's due."

She draws herself up to her full height. "You're right. I'm damn good at what I do. There's no one better placed than me to run the Minister's PR campaign. Without me, he may as well give up any hope he has of closing in on the leadership position."

"Now, hold on a second—"

"No, you hold on a second." Lord Alan glowers at me, "This woman is all that's standing between a good campaign and a brilliant campaign that'll put the wind under your wings and sail you right into number ten."

I raise my hands. "I defer to your wiser counsel, sir." I allow my lips to quirk. "Of course, if Ms. Chopra doesn't want this opportunity—"

"Ms. Chopra would relish this opportunity, but I have a few conditions."

"Oh, good, I can leave the two of you to sort out the details then?" Lord Alan pushes up to standing, then glances between us with a thoughtful look on his face. "Of course, I don't have to warn the two of you that anything beyond the lines of what is proper could be damaging to not only the two of you, but also the party?"

I blink. Lord Alan is the chairperson of the party, and as such, it's within his right to ensure that all of us toe the line. Indeed, anything that could harm the Party's image comes under his purview. But to hint at the possibility of anything that isn't within the margins of being 'proper' is surprising, to say the least.

I exchange glances with Zara, who has a similar confounded look on her face. I signal to her with my eyes that we need to agree and that we can sort out what he meant later. She nods subtly. "Of course, Sir Alan, nothing I say or do will hurt my client's image."

"And you know me, Sir Alan, I'll only ever do what is in the interests of the Party."

"Good." He raps on my table. "I'll take my weary bones out of here and let you two thrash out the rest of your agreement."

He brushes past Zara, and the door snicks shut. For a few seconds, we look at each other. The silence stretches. Then she places her bag on the chair closest to her, reaches for a book on my table and hefts it in her hand. "So, you had no idea this was coming, did you?"

I glance at the book, then at her. "You mean about Lord Alan asking you to join as Communications Manager for my campaign? Of course, not."

"Liar." She raises her arm and pitches the book at me.

37

Zara

He ducks, and the book flies past him. Anger churns my guts. "You think I'm going to believe you when you say you didn't know Lord Alan was going to ask me to become your PR manager?" I shoot out my arm and grab the paperweight. Who keeps a paperweight on a desk anymore? This stuck up, privileged prick does, and isn't that helpful? I pitch the paperweight at him. He moves so fast, he's almost a blur. The paperweight misses him and crashes to the wooden floor and rolls away.

"Zara!" he growls.

"Don't even start." I reach out blindly. My fingers encounter a ceramic mug which he must have drunk coffee from earlier. "You knew he'd ask me, and that I wouldn't be able to refuse. You told him to keep your name out of it so I wouldn't know it was you he was talking about; not until I walked into this office and saw you." I launch the cup at him. This time, he swoops out his hand, catches it, and places it on the table.

The slow burn of anger erupts into flames of rage. The blood pounds at my temples, and my heart catapults into my throat. I grab a book from the table and chuck it at him. Then snatch up a pencil, a pen, a stapler, and throw them at him, one after the other. He easily evades them and slaps his hands on the table. "Zara, stop that. You're acting unreasonable."

"You think this is unreasonable? You haven't seen anything yet." I reach for his phone, and he rushes around the table. I raise my hand, but he reaches up and circles my wrist with his fingers.

"Let me go."

"You need to calm down first."

"Don't tell me to calm down, you twatworm!" I burst out.

He chuckles. "Where do you pick up your gutter language, baby?" He grabs my other arm, then twists both of my hands behind my back.

"Don't you dare 'baby' me, you conniving piece of shit." I try to pull free, but his hold on me tightens. He squeezes my wrist just enough that I loosen my fingers. The phone slips from my hand. He releases my wrist and catches the phone before he places it on the table. At the same time, he draws me flush against him so I can feel all of him from chest to groin to thighs.

"Hunter, don't you dare."

"You know I can't stop myself from rising to a challenge." He thrusts forward, and the unmistakable bulge in his crotch stabs into my arse.

"Fuck you," I spit out.

"I will, but only if you ask me nicely." He leans his weight into me so I'm pushed up against his desk. Then he circles my wrists with the fingers of his one hand; the other, he plants in between my shoulder blades. He applies pressure, and I find myself folded over his table, my arse jutting out and flush against the column in his pants. He's even more aroused than a few seconds ago, if that were possible. Heat spurts in my lower belly. A shudder of need ladders up my spine. He must notice, for he pulls the hair back from my face and drapes it over one shoulder. Then he bends and nips on my exposed earlobe.

I shiver. "Hunter, stop."

"Do you remember your safe word?"

I swallow.

"Do you, Fire?"

I nod.

"Unless you use it I'm going to keep going."

I draw in a ragged breath. My heart is beating so fast, I can feel the pulse between my legs, behind my knees, at my ankles, my temples, even behind my eyelids.

"Do you want to use your safe word?" he growls.

I hesitate.

His entire body goes solid. I feel the tension flow off of him. His muscles are so hard, I can feel every individual chest plane outlined against my back. His heart canters against my back, the speed so fast it echoes my own.

"Do you, Zara?" He releases me and steps back. "If you want me to stop use your safe word, now."

I squeeze my eyes shut. My knees feel like they're going to turn to jelly. He's giving me a choice, and that makes it so much worse. Because what I'm going to do now is only going to show me how reckless I am. How totally seduced I am by his touch, the feel of his skin on mine, his eyelashes brushing my cheek, the feel of his hard thighs gripping mine. The length of his cock stretching me, while his fingers probe that forbidden place between my arse cheeks.

"Zara, do you want me to stop?"

I shake my head.

"I need you to say it aloud, baby."

"I don't want you to stop."

"Open your eyes and say it like you mean it."

Jerkhole. I snap open my eyelids and glower up at him from the corner of my eyes. "I want you to fuck me, you bastar—"

He's on me so fast, I gasp. He rolls up my skirt so it's over my hips, then tears off my panties. A moan falls my lips. My pulse rate is so fast, it's as if I'm competing in a sprint. "What if someone walks in?" I manage to get out.

He lowers his head until his gaze is on level with mine. "You'll just have to come fast enough so they won't catch us."

A tremor of heat coils in my underbelly. My pussy clenches, and my thigh muscles quiver.

"That turns you on, doesn't it?" he growls.

"Of course, not."

"Oh?" He straightens, then kicks my legs apart. He shoves his fingers inside me—rough and hard and with no consideration for me, just how I like it. He pulls out his fingers and holds them in front of my face. The unmistakable white liquid stretching between his digits reveals just how turned on I am. "Your body never lies to me, baby." He thrusts them in my mouth. "Lick them clean for me."

I don't need a second urging. I am a slut for punishment. That's who I am at my most basic. God help me. I lick myself off his fingers, and a tremor grips his body. Apparently, I'm not the only one who's excited. A calm descends, and my normal heart rhythm resumes. This is going to happen. I'm going to let this happen because I want it. Because he wants it, too. Because when we're together, we're as combustible as dry wood and fire.

He lowers his fingers. I hear the jingle of his belt, and another spurt of heat pumps through my veins. Then the blunt head of his cock teases my slit.

"I'm going to scream," I warn.

"I'm counting on it."

"Won't be so good if the rest of your office listens to it."

"It's soundproofed, baby."

I scowl. "How many women have you fucked in here before?"

He stills, then lowers his head again so he's on eye level with me. "Jealous?"

"Not at all."

"Liar." He tucks a strand of hair behind my ear. "And you're the first woman I've taken on this desk."

My heart seems to open in my chest. A thrill of joy bursts through my veins. He straightens, grips my hips.

"The only woman I plan to fuck again and again on this surface."

"Wait, what? This is not happening agai—"

I gasp as he pistons his hips forward and impales me. Oh god, that familiar thickness, the way my pussy expands around his girth; it hurts and yet, it's also so very erotic.

He leans over and wraps my fingers about the edge of his desk. "Hold on."

He pistons his hips and sinks into me with such force that the entire table jolts. I slide forward and his hold on my hips tightens. He pulls back, then thrusts into me and his balls slap against my inner thighs. He reaches under and rubs on my clit, and the climax sweeps out from my core. He releases his hold on my hips only to slap his hand down next to my face. He's rolled up his shirtsleeves and the veins on his forearms flex. That, along with the smattering of dark hair on his arms, sends me over the edge. The next time he crams himself into me, my entire body jolts. He bends over, his wide chest covering me as he presses me into the table. Then he places his cheek next to mine and growls, "Come for me, Fire. Come right now."

A cry spills from my lips and I orgasm instantly. He fucks me through the aftershocks, then with a groan, empties himself inside me.

He stays that way with his weight pinning me down, with the heat of his body holding me captive, the cum running down my leg— a combination of both of us—and my head floating somewhere above my body. He pulls out, and I wince at the loss of his heat. I hear him walk away, and know I must move, but my legs seem to have lost the ability. Then I hear his footsteps, and something cool brushes between my legs. He pulls down my skirt, then pulls me up and turns me around in his arms. "Are you okay?"

38

Hunter

She raises those heavy eyelids, and her sated eyes hold my gaze. "This can't work."

"I thought that worked very well, actually."

"We can't work together. Not when every time we meet, you want to fuck me, and I can't stop you from fucking me."

She pulls away from me and begins to pace. I ball up the paper towel with which I wiped her and am about to toss it, then bring it up to my nose and sniff.

She turns just in time to catch me do so and her gaze widens. "You're an animal."

"Only when it comes to you."

"See?" She stabs a finger in my direction. "This is what I mean. We can't even have a normal conversation without it turning into this sexual gameplay."

"One which I enjoy."

"One which your team is going to notice," she retorts.

"Not if we're careful."

She plants her palms on her hips. "You really think they won't notice the chemistry between us?"

"No," I admit. "But that chemistry is precisely why it makes sense for you to be my PR manager. You know what I am, how I think. No one knows me better than you. And you can use that to your advantage."

"You're not going to budge on this one, are you?"

I shake my head.

She glances away, then back at me. "I can't do this, Hunter. I'm sorry. I'm putting myself and you at risk. I can't allow our relationship to become media fodder. It would remove every last bit of leverage I have with the news people."

She smooths her skirt down over her hips, pats her hair into place, then reaches for her bag. She turns and heads toward the door when I call out, "Where do you think you're going?"

"We can't work together, Hunter. Even though I owe this to Lord Alan, I'm sorry, but I can't deliver on it this time. Please give him my apologies."

I reach for my phone and swipe up the screen, then tap a button. The sound of her moans, and the unmistakable impact of flesh on flesh fills the room.

She pauses, then pivots to face me. "What's that?"

"Why don't you come and see for yourself?"

She heads toward the desk, then rounds it and stands next to me. On my computer the scene playing out shows a woman stretched out over a desk, with her entire body moving forward. The man's hand is in view, the rest of him is hidden. Her face, though, is in full view of the camera.

She spins around, arm raised, and I catch her hand before it can connect with my face. "Careful, Fire, there's a limit to how much leeway I grant you."

"Limit? And what about what you're doing?"

"That's self-preservation."

"You'd use it to blackmail me?"

"If it means you'll be working for me, then yes."

She firms her lips. "You're more despicable than I thought you were."

"Is that a yes?"

Her gaze narrows. "I'll never forgive you for this."

"You haven't answered my question yet."

"Goddamn you, yes. I'll work for you. Now, will you release me?"

"On one condition."

"You're a real piece of work, aren't you, Whittington?"

"Only when it comes to you."

"Stop saying that."

"But it's true. There's no limit to what I'd do to make you mine, Zara."

She looks between my eyes, then tips her chin. "There's no limits I'll go to avoid becoming yours."

I twist my lips. "We'll see."

"Okay."

"Okay."

The door swings open. "Oh, sorry Mr. Whittington, I didn't realize you were with someone."

I release her hand and step back.

"It's fine, Daniel, come on in. Meet Zara Chopra, my new PR manager. Zara, this is Daniel, my campaign manager."

"That went as expected." Zara pushes back from the conference room table and rolls her shoulders.

After the meeting with Daniel, I called a team meeting and introduced Zara to all of them. She, of course, was impressive, and within minutes of meeting everyone, began to draw up a PR strategy for the campaign.

"I thought that went better than expected."

"You mean at least one-fourth of your team doesn't resent me for having marched in here and redrawn half the campaign strategy?" She snatches up her notepad and pen, then her phone, and slides them into her bag.

"I mean, you cut through the clutter and came up with a coherent strategy. You did in an hour what my team and I have been trying to pull together for months."

She turns in her chair to face me. "Is that why you never launched your campaign? Because you weren't happy with the strategy so far?"

"Among other things."

"Why else would you hold back when every day you didn't declare you were running would make it tougher for you to win?"

"I'm still launching before the deadline."

"If you mean twenty-four hours before the final deadline, then you're barely squeaking through. As it is, you've lost so much time—"

"But I'll be off to a strong start and that's more impactful than simply announcing my campaign in order to be seen."

She tilts her head. "Sometimes, I'm forced to agree with you."

"As I recall it, when you were stretched out across my table earlier you were very vocally in agreement with me. In fact, I recall precisely you saying that you didn't want me to stop, that I should fu—"

"Shut up, Hunter." She glances around the room, then back at me. "How can you be so careless?"

"There's no one here. There are also no cameras or bugs in here."

"How can you be sure?" She frowns.

"I have the premises swept every morning."

"Except your office where you have cameras placed so you can film anyone who comes in to meet you," she says bitterly.

"I do have cameras in my room. It's a precaution, and only I have access to the footage."

"So you can blackmail people into doing what you want?"

"If need be."

She tips up her chin. "Are there any other indiscretions you need to tell me about? Anything I need to be prepared for as your PR manager?"

I close the distance to her, then grip the arms of her chair and bend until I'm eye level with her. "I've never used the filming to blackmail anyone else before."

"So only I'm subjected to your machinations then?"

"Not letting you go so easily, Fire."

"We're working together now; it's best to keep our relationship professional so I can do my job."

I hold her gaze, and she doesn't glance away. I see the hurt in the depths of her eyes, and damn, I already hate myself for what I did. But if it's the only way to have her close to me, then I'll take my chances. But I also know when not to push further.

"I won't touch you again; you have my word. Unless—"

She swallows "Unless?"

"Unless you ask me to."

"That'll be the day," she scoffs.

"Don't underestimate how much you enjoy being with me, in every way."

"You're underestimating how easy it is to piss off a woman. One wrong move, and they'll never forgive you. Not unless you grovel and go back to them with your hat in your hands, and sometimes, not even then." Liam leans forward in his chair. "And you've crossed the line here with what you did."

Don't I know it? "I had no other choice. She was going to walk out the door."

"And you should have let her."

"Eh?" I blink. "Did I just hear the man who's never backed down from a corporate takeover tell me that I should have given up without a fight?"

"In matters of the heart, the boardrooms don't apply."

I tap my fingers together. "If you mean I don't know when to back down—"

"What I mean is, the rules of engagement are different when it comes to affairs of the heart."

"We talking about Hunter's non-existent love life, then?" Declan prowls in. He collapses into the chair between us and kicks out his legs. He's wearing jeans torn at the knees, a hat on his head, and a sweatshirt with the hood pulled over the hat. He pulls off his sunglasses, revealing dark circles and hollowed cheekbones.

"You look like shite, mate," I offer.

"Fuck you very much." He reaches for the bottle of Macallan, lifts it to his mouth, and takes a swig.

"Last I checked, we're still civilized enough to drink out of a glass," Liam chides.

"You do the whole proper English gentleman thing. Right now, I need sustenance to get me through the rest of this shitty day." He raises the bottle of Macallan and chugs down more of the liquor.

"And I thought I was in the doldrums." I raise my cigar to my lips.

He lowers the bottle, wipes the back of his mouth with his hand, then places the bottle on the table. "Never fear. When it comes to lessons in how to ruin a relationship, you can consider me the fore-runner."

"Surely, it can't be that bad?" Liam leans back in his seat. Bastard looks all relaxed, with that happiness radiating off him that men who are settled in relationships seem to have. He's temporarily back from his sojourns in Italy, and clearly, living abroad suits him.

"No, it's worse." Declan lowers his arms between his legs. "But that's what happens when you're trying to juggle not one, but two careers, not to mention, a burgeoning relationship in the media limelight."

"Speaking of, should you even be here? Won't your adoring fans have surrounded the club by now?"

"Nah, it's a little better in London, as long as I keep my face hidden. I even took the tube over here."

"Impressive."

He reaches for the bottle again, and Liam moves it out of reach. He pours out a glass and slides it over to Declan who tosses it back. "Enough talk about me, anyway. How's it going with your spin doctor?"

"She's now the official PR manager for my campaign." I study the ash building up on the tip of my cigar.

Declan straightens in his seat. "That's good, right?"

"Not the way he got her to accept the role, it isn't," Liam interjects.

"Do I want to know?"

"No," Liam and I say simultaneously.

"O-k-a-y, but if it gets you time with her, perhaps it's worth it?"

"I sure hope so."

"So what are you doing here?"

I narrow my gaze on him. "What do you mean?"

"If you want her, you need to go after her. Why are you wasting your time here with us?"

"Our relationship is now professional." I take a puff on the cigar and blow out a cloud of smoke. "So, I can't exactly pop into her place without reason, the optics on that wouldn't be great."

"But a work meeting wouldn't attract the same scrutiny, would it?"

"Hmm." I place the cigar in the notch in the ashtray, then lean over and grab him by the scruff of his neck. Which, mind you, was easier when he was a skinny junior who always got ragged by the rest of the boys for being the scrawniest of the bunch. Now, he's six-foot-three, with shoulders like a quarterback, yet I can't get over the habit of treating him like a cheeky younger sibling.

"Hey, watch it, man." He grabs my neck back in return.

Yep, he's definitely grown up. Doesn't mean I'm going to stop behaving like a protective older sibling. "Sometimes you do have words of wisdom to offer."

Liam snaps his fingers. "The V&A Ball. That's the one you need to attend, and invite her to it, as well."

I glance between them. "I'll go on one condition."

39

Zara

"How do I look?" I pop out a hip and the light bounces off of the Swarovski crystals that decorate my shimmery-silver, one-shoulder dress. It clings to me like it was made for me, which it probably was, considering it arrived in a box by special delivery just a few hours ago. I almost turned it away, until I noticed the label on the box. Armani. Only a fool would turn away the chance to wear an Armani original, and a fool, I am not. Still, I hesitated when the courier handed over the second box. This one bore the Manolo Blahnik label. And if I had any doubt, the third box—this one sporting the Birkin brand—sealed the deal.

"Well?" I quirk an eyebrow at the phone which I've propped up against the mirror.

"You look gorgeous and that dress might as well be painted on," Solene replies from the screen.

"That's what I thought, too." I turn sideways, running a hand down my stomach.

"You look amazing, Z."

"It's the dress," I demur.

"It's the woman in the dress. Your confidence shines through."

"That's the glitter of the Swarovski crystals." I laugh weakly.

"The man knows your weakness." She chuckles.

"Doesn't he ever." If I had any remaining doubts about accepting the dress, they vanished as soon as I slid it on. Something about the gunmetal color, and the one-shouldered cut, lent a regal air to the outfit. As for the fit… It's clear he memorized my curves. There's no other way the dress could have fit without my having tried it on in advance. I thrust out a leg and the slit, which slashes almost up to my waist, parts to reveal the line of my thigh. As for the heels, the Manolo Blahnik's have a bondage-type strap that clings lovingly to my ankle.

"Those shoes alone are going to make the man combust."

"I hope so." I look at myself with a critical eye. I'm dressed to bring a man to his knees. And he must have known this would be the outcome when he sent me this specific combination of clothes to wear.

"You sure about this, though?" Solene's voice pulls me out of my reverie.

"You mean about wearing the clothes he sent me?"

"It's your favorite designers, and creations you couldn't possibly buy off the shelf, so I'm not surprised you didn't turn it away. It's just… won't he misinterpret your wearing the clothes he sent you for your encouraging him?"

"He might." I run my palms down the Swarovski studded fabric. "And if I had turned it away, he'd have won, and I can't allow that."

"This thing between the two of you isn't a game," she cautions.

"Sure could have fooled me," I murmur

"Just don't want you getting hurt, babe."

Might be a little too late for that. I turn to face her image on the phone screen. "I'll be careful, I promise."

"Good. You're a strong woman, Zara, but you have a heart that can be hurt easily."

Damn, when your friends see you so clearly, it's humbling. "You're a good friend, Solene."

"Because I'm looking out for you?" She laughs. "If our roles were reversed, you'd do the same. You know that."

"You bet I do."

The doorbell rings.

"That must be Liam and Isla." I blow a kiss at the phone. "I love you, babe; can't wait to see you in person."

"Same, and don't forget to tell me all about it."

"I promise" I disconnect the call, then drop the phone into my clutch with my lipstick and house keys. A last look at myself, and I grab my coat and head for the door. When I throw it open, he stands there with one hand against the doorframe.

I open and shut my mouth. "What are you doing here?"

"Liam and Isla are running late, so I offered to pick you up."

"I didn't hear anything from Isla." I scowl.

"Have you checked your messages?"

I pull out my phone, check my messages, and sure enough, there's one from Isla.

ISLA:

> So sorry babe. Liam's mom wasn't feeling well—she's fine now—but Liam wanted to look in on her before we went to the ball so we're running late. I hope you don't mind that Hunter's coming to pick you up. I know things are rough with you two, but you do work together now, and he offered. We won't be long, I promise. See you soon.

Guess in all the excitement of the new clothes and accessories, I missed her message. I pull up the app for the cab company, and he places his hand on mine. Tendrils of heat flicker out from the point of contact. Both of us pull back.

"What are you doing?"

"I'm ordering a cab."

"It's Friday evening; you're not going to get one in time."

"We'll see." I type out my destination, press the relevant buttons and the app stalls. "Damnit." I try again and again; each time the app crashes.

"I have a car waiting, Zara."

I ignore him and continue to try the app with the same result. "Bloody hell." I drop the phone back in my bag and scowl at him. "You planned it all, didn't you? Inviting me to the ball—"

"As my PR official; nothing personal about this."

"Then making sure, somehow, Liam and Isla couldn't pick me up."

"You think I orchestrated Liam's mother falling sick?" His gaze widens. "Not even I could pull that off."

"Hmph." I scan his features. He's combed back his hair and is wearing a tux which outlines his broad shoulders. His crisp white shirt stretches across his chest. His jaw is freshly shaven, the bowtie at his neck turning his entire look from sophisticated to positively deadly. Why does he have to look so edible? So hot? So sexy, so everything. I frown. He arches an eyebrow.

"Something wrong?"

"You have a—" I lean up and press my thumb to a dot of blood at the edge of his jawline. I show him the drop of scarlet, then bring the digit to my mouth and suck on it.

His nostrils flare. His blue-green eyes darken until they resemble pools of midnight blue. "I must have nicked myself shaving."

"Right." I swallow, glance away, then back at him. "If I'm to travel in the same car as you, we need rules."

"Rules?" He arches an eyebrow.

"No touching without permission."

"Goes both ways," he points out.

I flush, then draw myself up to my full height. "That was an instinctive reaction."

"So was mine."

I nod slowly. "Moving on, no looking at me like you want to—"

"Fuck you?" he interjects.

Heat sweeps up my back. "Exactly. You need to be on guard when we are together in the open."

"I'll have my game face on."

"No kissing."

"Not unless you ask me to."

"No moving into my space."

"You mean like this?" He moves in until the lapels of his jacket almost brush my dress. Until his breath kisses my cheek, until the heat from his body wraps around me, and his scent—that gorgeous spicy, testosterone-laden scent of his permeates my pores and my cells, sinks into my blood, and arrows straight to my core.

"You promised," I whisper.

"You set the rules; I didn't agree to anything," he says, his voice as hushed as mine.

"We can't, Hunter, please." I swallow.

He glances between my eyes, then nods, and to my relief, takes a step back. "Shall we?"

"You pulled out all the stops, didn't you?" I accept my flute of champagne and glance about the interior of the Jaguar. It's definitely custom-made, complete with the bar and the panel between the front and back seats, which is now currently up.

"No reason not to travel in style." He slides the bottle of Moet & Chandon Espirit du Siecle Brut into the ice bucket then raises his glass. "To the evening ahead."

I clink my glass with his and raise it to take a sip. The clean notes of citrus and pear, shot through with licorice, tickle my nostrils. My stomach churns. I raise the flute to my mouth and take a sip. That churning sensation grows stronger. I manage to swallow down the champagne without gagging, then place the glass back on the table.

"Good?" he asks.

"You know it is." I heave an internal sigh of relief as my stomach settles. I forgot to eat lunch. I should remember not to skip meals.

"Nothing like hearing the appreciation first-hand."

I chuckle. "You're smooth."

"As smooth as the champagne?"

"Smoother, and stop fishing for compliments."

He laughs, and his entire face lights up. That square jaw, that aristocratic nose, those high cheekbones, and in the designer suit he's wearing, he's the most gorgeous man I've ever met.

"You're staring, Zara."

I glance away. "My mind was a million miles away."

"Oh?" I hear the disbelief in his voice.

"An upcoming family reunion, which promises to be as stressful as the ones before." And that's the truth. Though I only brought it up as a means to divert attention away from that slip up. So, the man is sex-on-a-stick, but I already know that. So why am I so flustered being this close to him? Especially since I've been much closer to him in the past.

"I take it, you don't get along with your parents?"

"I do, until something sets one of us off, and then it all descends into pandemonium."

"You have a brother?"

I hesitate. "He's my fraternal twin, but you know that already."

Now, it's his turn to hesitate. "I do, but it's different hearing it from you than reading it in a folder."

I reach for my flute and take another sip. "My grandfather arrived from the Indian subcontinent when he was five years old. He met my grandmother, who's also Indian, here in the UK. My father was born here. My mother's English. She met my father at the grocery shop that his father established. It's the same place that she and my father now run. When my parents had us, they were determined we would make a mark."

"And both of you have."

I glance away, then back at him. "They weren't very happy when, after qualifying for the bar, I moved into this 'ungodly' profession." I make air quotes with my fingers.

"Parents normally come around when they see their children are happy."

"Oh, and let's not forget, I'm past my prime and not married. So, I've doubly failed them."

"How old are you?"

"Twenty-nine, but you know that—"

"Already, yes, but can we pretend I don't, for the purposes of this conversation?"

"A little tough, considering, as your PR manager, I have access to the most intimate details of your life."

His lips quirk. "Not all of them."

"No?"

"No." He taps his temple "Not the ones I carry here or" — he taps the place over his heart— "here."

I blink, then glance away.

He blows out a breath. "I didn't mean to say that. But when I'm with you, it seems, I can't stop myself."

"Well try harder, Hunter. You seem to forget, it's both of our careers on the line."

"And I promise, it'll be game-face out there."

I throw back the rest of the champagne, then place the glass back on the table.

"So your brother's going to be at this family reunion?"

"He will be, and he's the darling of my parents. As you know, he plays cricket for England. He's famous, and in their eyes, a success. And of course, they don't care that he's not married or doesn't have kids. It's the daughter who always bears the brunt of that particular line of thinking."

"I'm sure you'll persuade your parents otherwise."

"Oh, when I'm with them… All these PR skills? They go out the window. I seem to go back to being five and I'm unable to do much but listen to them rant." I begin to flick my hair over my shoulder, then remember I've put it up for the evening. I settle for locking my fingers together and looking out the window.

"It's because they care about you," he murmurs.

"You don't say."

"They seem like they were very hands-on parents."

"Too hands-on, when they were around. They were always trying to make up for the fact that they couldn't be there at all times since they were running the store." I snort.

"I'd have liked mine to be more hands-on."

I shoot him a sideways glance. He's looking into the depths of his champagne flute, a furrow on that perfect forehead.

"Your parents weren't around as much as you'd have liked them to be, I take it?"

"More like, not around at all." He glances up and holds my gaze. "Yep, I'm the poster child for the poor little rich boy," he says in a self-deprecating voice.

"Did they also leave you *Home Alone*?"

He blinks, then barks out a laugh. "Very good, Chopra."

"Why do you call me by my surname when you think I'm being particularly witty?"

He raises a shoulder. "Shouldn't I?"

"It's like when I'm unexpectedly witty you, somehow, attribute my intelligence to the patriarchy."

His gaze widens. "And all this, because I referred to you by your surname?"

"Think about it. When you're turned on, you refer to me by my nickname, when you think I'm being bratty, you scold me by calling me by my name, and when I say something particularly witty, you refer to me by my surname."

"I still don't get it." He shakes his head.

"That's the problem. With all you private school educated, entitled prats, your background fosters emotional austerity and fierce clique loyalty, not to mention the misogyny that runs through you lot."

"You mean, I spent the formative years of my childhood in boarding schools being looked after by adults who didn't love me," he drawls.

"Are you trying to make a play for my sympathy?"

"I'm merely letting you know that you judge me and my lot" —he makes air quotes with his fingers— "too harshly."

My gaze narrows. "You think I need to re-evaluate my opinion on you and your lot who never grow up. You, who forever remain boys; who think they can do anything and get away without consequences."

"I think" —he tilts his head— "I think you need to see it from my point of view. I remember my childhood as long stretches of desolate homesickness, of having my attachments to home and family broken abruptly several times a year. I lost everything—parents, pets, toys, younger siblings… Of course, I could cry if I liked, but no one was going to help me."

He drags his thumb under his lower lip, and my nipples harden. I shove aside the traitorous reaction of my body and tip up my chin. "So you learnt to cultivate the stiff upper lip. You could either be yourself— homesick, vulnerable, lovelorn, and frightened—or you could perform being loyal, robust, and self-reliant. Wear a brave face and distance your feelings, growing the hardness of heart of the educated.

"And you chose the latter. You convinced yourselves early that you had no great need of love. You decided to act grownup, even when you were very young, for that meant you needed no one. In fact, your experiences toughened you enough that, later in life, when you saw other people cry, you felt no great need to go to their aid. That's what you're getting at, aren't you? That it's not your fault how you turned out. It was circumstances that made you what you are."

"Didn't your circumstances make you what you are today?" he counters.

"I hardly think our backgrounds have anything in common."

"On the contrary." He places the champagne flute on the small table and turns to me. "You understand me so well because you've been through the same experiences I have, albeit in a different milieu."

I scoff. "Are you contrasting my upbringing with that of your privileged lifestyle?"

He looks between my eyes. "We're both the products of over-ambitious parents who wanted their children to become over-achievers."

"And here we are," I murmur.

"Indeed. Both of us, high-performing goal-setters, never happy with the status quo. And" —his gaze grows intense— "I've never been happier than I am right now, sitting next to you."

I swallow, then set my lips. "You forgot to add, we're never meant to be."

"You're here now, aren't you?" His shoulders are relaxed, yet a nerve pops at his temple. His body is sprawled out against the rich leather seat, but his gaze is wary. This man is so full of contrasts, it makes my head spin. He's such a puzzle. It both energizes me and chips away at my reservations—all of the hurdles I've been throwing in my own path of why I can't be with him.

"You're so—"

"Clever, witty, erudite?" he drawls.

"—full of yourself," I snap.

"And soon, you'll be full of me."

I blink, then make a gagging sound. "I can't believe you just said that."

"Believe it. It was a good comeback, though, admit it." He smirks.

"You have a one-track mind."

"Don't tell me you aren't, right now, thinking of straddling me as I thrust up and into you."

My belly clenches. My pussy hums. I can feel the evidence of my arousal gnaw at my lower belly and...oh, god, my breasts hurt, my thighs feel so very heavy, and my core? It feels so empty, so aching, so yearning for that sensation when his beloved thickness has me impaled and stretched and skewered around his gorgeous cock. A-n-d, did I just think of his penis as 'his beloved thickness'? Why do his words turn me on so? Why am I so unable to resist him? I squeeze my thighs together, then pretend to frown at him.

"Hunter," I say in a warning tone.

He laughs and raises both of his hands. "Just kidding you, Fire."

"So now it's Fire, is it?"

"You set my world on fire."

I half-laugh, then turn away. I shake my head, try to gather myself, and I'm all too aware of his big body taking up so much of this small, enclosed space, of his dark scent that envelops me, the cloud of heat that spools off of his chest and pins me in place, the strength of his dominance which is a palpable presence, one that turns my throat dry, that wrings my insides into coils of tremulous anticipation, and oh, god, I'm losing myself. I'm going to hell for what I'm going to do next, but I can't fight this... Can't fight us anymore.

I square my shoulders. "So..." I turn to him. "That scenario you painted earlier, do you want to recreate it?"

40

Hunter

"Which one?" I take in her gleaming eyes, her thick hair put up in some intricate hairdo that I've been itching to get my fingers into, just so I can pull out the pins and see her hair down in thick strands about her face again. Clearly, she's been processing our conversation and come to some kind of conclusion in her head, the results of which I'm about to experience.

"This one." She rises to her feet. Then, in a move that has my breath catching, she hitches her dress above her hips, and straddles me.

My heart slams into my ribcage. My pulse rate shoots up until I can feel the blood thudding in my ears. I slide my palms up her thighs to squeeze her hips.

"Fuck, Zara, you don't have any panties on," I growl.

"Oh, so it's Zara, is it? Is that because you're trying to scold me for being impudent? I wonder."

"You're playing with fire, Fire."

"And maybe, this time, I need you to be brimstone. To allow both of us to burn in the time it takes us to reach the gala."

"Sir, Mr. Whittington, it's eight minutes until we reach our destination, sir." My chauffeur's voice comes through the speaker.

She frowns.

I raise my fingers to her forehead and smooth out the wrinkles in that beautiful brow.

"I told him to give me a warning when we were close."

"Because you expected us to be in this situation?"

"Maybe?"

"Oh, for fuck's sake, and just when I thought, perhaps, you weren't as much of a tosser as you made yourself out to be." She begins to slide off, but I hold her in place.

"Just kidding you again, baby. No. For once, my intentions in wanting you with me were purely so I could spend time with you in a legitimate fashion, on a professional basis."

"Being photographed arriving together is barely going to make it seem professional."

"You're with me as my PR specialist. Sure, you're my plus-one for the evening, but we're not hiding anything. If anything, being seen together openly will only make it even more obvious that there's nothing between us."

"Or maybe, people will pick up on the chemistry between us." She frowns.

"If you were that concerned, why didn't you say anything earlier?"

"It was the dress...and the shoes... And the bag." She glowers at me. "You blindsided me with my favorite brands. I'm a proud woman, but even I bow at the altar of Armani. Add Manolo Blahnik and Birkin to the mix, and you knew I was not going to return them." She stabs a finger into my chest. "Especially not, after I tried on this dress."

"I prefer you even more dressed in only the Blahnik's and nothing else." I wrap my fingers about her delectable arse cheeks and massage the rounded flesh.

It's her turn to groan.

I pull her even closer so her soft core grinds down into the tent over of my crotch.

This time, both of us exhale sharply.

"I'm going to leave a damp spot on your pants," she protests.

"Fuck that." I tilt my hips so the tent at my crotch stabs into the apex of her legs.

She moans; my balls tighten. "Baby, I need to be inside of you," I growl.

"You have less than eight minutes to make me come." Her voice breaks, but her gaze is alert. Her color is high, but anticipation radiates off of her. It sinks into my skin, ignites my own need.

"I'm going to make you come at least three times before we reach our destination." I wrap my fingers about the nape of her neck and pull her in. Our lips meet, teeth clash, tongues entwine. I kiss her, and she kisses me back. I lick into her mouth, and she bites down on my lower lip. My cock stabs into the fabric of my pants. I tear my mouth from hers. Holding her gaze, I reach between us, unfasten my belt, slide down my zipper, and take out my cock. I position her over the head of my shaft, then thrust up and into her. I breach her, and her gaze widens. Her mouth opens in a soundless gasp. Her golden eyes catch fire, and for a second, it's as if I'm gazing into my destiny. Into a future that belongs to the both of us. It's scary, and so fucking right, it turns me on even more.

"I'm going to fuck you, Fire."

She grips my shoulders and swallows. "Don't you dare spoil this dress."

"I'll buy you a hundred more."

"I prefer to buy them for myself," she says primly.

"And I prefer when your attention is solely on me."

"Aww, feeling left out, are you?" She flexes her inner muscles, and the reverberations seem to travel up my spine.

"You're so hot, so tight, so fucking wet for me, baby." I pump up and into her, hitting that spot deep inside of her that makes her cry out. She throws her head back, and I bite the curve of her breast. She moans, and the noise goes straight to my head. Something snaps inside of me.

"Look at me." I apply pressure to the nape of her neck, and she opens her eyes.

I hold her gaze, then slide my hand down between us. I pinch her clit, and she explodes. The orgasm seems to take her by surprise, for her entire body jolts. Moisture bathes my cock, and she shudders and places her forehead against mine.

"Oh, my god."

"You mean, 'Oh, Hunter,' don't you?"

"Why do I find your arrogance such a turn-on?"

"Because you like a man who's confident enough to dominate you, baby."

She opens her eyes and stares into mine. "Your ego is going to be your downfall."

"Right now, it's on the ascent, Fire." I piston my hips up, and my shaft drills up and into her.

She groans. "Ohgod, ohgod, ohgod."

"Hunter."

"What?" she whines.

"Say my name."

"No."

"Oh?" I pull her off my cock, and she glances down at where my dick stands up at attention between us.

"Why did you do that?" she wails.

"So I could do this." I pull her back further, then bring down my palm on her pussy.

"What the—" she howls. "What are you doing?"

"Making you say my name."

"Don't you dare, Whittington."

I spank her core again.

Her back arches. "Fuck you, Hunter."

"Just my name."

"No way."

I slap her on her clit, and again, and she orgasms.

41

Zara

Holy hell. I've never orgasmed simply by being spanked between my legs. But there you have it. Another first for me. The other being, I decided, of my own volition, to put my career at risk and agree to ride with him, and then, because that wasn't enough, I decided to fuck him enroute to the event. But I don't regret it. Not yet. Not when the added edge of the time running down to reaching the gala is clearly accelerating my ability to orgasm back-to-back. The climax punches through me, then dies away, just as suddenly. I begin to slump, but he holds me up.

"Eyes on me."

I open my eyelids, which must have fluttered down of their own accord, thanks to that last orgasm. Then, I'm gazing into his now midnight blue eyes, and all other thoughts vanish from my mind.

He releases his hold on the nape of my neck, only to squeeze my hips and position me, once more, over the swollen head of his cock. He nudges my opening and my legs tremble. My toes curl. A shiver squeezes my lower belly, and he's not even inside me yet.

"Hunter," I rasp.

His eyes flash. An expression of satisfaction sweeps over his features. He yanks me down and onto his cock. "You are" —thrust— "mine. You hear me?"

I can only gasp as, once again, that thickness… Oh, that incredible girth of his, which still feels like it's the first time, and yet, it's also so familiar how my channel struggles to adjust to his size. The sweet pain of his intrusion convulses up my spine, and it's so right. So hot, so everything, I can't stop myself from leaning in and placing my lips on his.

He instantly takes control. Of course, he does. He wraps his mouth around mine and sucks on me as if he's trying to absorb my very essence into himself. Then he fucks me. He tunnels up and into me with such force, the entire cabin of the car seems to shake. He drives up and crams himself fully inside of me, once more, hitting that spot. This time, the trembling begins somewhere at my toes and spirals up, up to my core. He pulls back, thrusts up and into me, and at the same time, he wraps his fingers about my throat. "Come with me, Zara," he orders.

I do. I orgasm right there, for the third time, and still holding my gaze, he empties himself inside of me. I begin to slump again, and this time, he rests his forehead against mine. For a few seconds, we stare at each other then— "Two minutes to arrival, Mr. Whittington, two minutes." The chauffeur's voice fills the space.

He kisses me hard. I nod. We haven't spoken, but the understanding between us is seamless, as I move, and he helps me to lower my legs onto the floor of the limo. I reach for the paper towels by the window but he curls his fingers around my wrist. "I want you to feel my cum dripping out of your cunt as you meet and greet people tonight."

I flush. "You're a filthy beast."

"And you love it."

I begin to protest, then stop myself. Unfortunately, he has a point. Instead, I reach over, pull at his collar and bite the side of his neck. "Now, we're even."

I slide the dress down over my hips and take my seat next to him. He rubs his thumb across the reddening patch of flesh, then pulls off his bowtie and throws it aside.

I gape. "What are you doing?"

"Wearing your mark with pride, baby."

"B-but, that'll only raise speculation."

"I can live with it, if you can."

His gaze lowers to my chest. I glance down to find there's what can only be described as a twin reddening mark on the slope of my left breast. "Oh, hell." I glare at him. "You did that on purpose."

"No, you did this on purpose." He points to what now clearly looks like a hickey on his throat.

I reach up, pull out the pins from my hair, and the strands flow about my shoulders. I pull a couple down over my breasts. Hopefully, that will help deflect from the mark.

"Smart." He inclines his head. "You think on your feet, Councilor. A true PR pro."

"And you, sir, live dangerously. You need to be more careful, or your campaign will be over before it starts."

"Will it?" He smirks.

A-n-d there's that confidence I love and hate, and goddamn, I'm beginning to fear is going to be my downfall. There's something so seductive about a man who knows what he wants and who doesn't hesitate to go after it. In this case, it's me he's set his sights on, and the sinking sensation in my stomach tells me he's close to getting what he wants. Somehow, though, it doesn't feel like it's a loss for me, or a game between us, anymore. It's turned into so much more, without my even realizing it.

"You okay?" He reaches over and tucks a strand of hair behind my ear.

"I will be."

He holds my gaze, nods. The limo comes to a stop. He glances to the window, through which I can make out the shapes of the paparazzi lined up on either side of the red carpet.

"You ready?"

As it turned out, I needn't have worried about the paps because, apparently, being seen together and out in the open means they accepted his answer that I was there with him as his work colleague. This, despite the fact that when we left the hospital together, they instantly speculated that we were together 'together'. But now that we were formally attending an event together, we didn't have anything to hide, did we? The media truly is a fickle creature. You never can predict how they'll behave.

When they asked me why I was with him, I replied with, "You know me, guys. I'm the PR consultant, and he's my client, and I'm here simply to make sure Mr. Whittington gets a great start to the campaign."

After which, I stepped aside, despite Hunter indicating I should stay with him. I left him to the mercy of the cameras and reporters—he's good at talking his way out of any situation, politician that he is. Plus, he deserved to be sacrificed to the wolves for a little longer, after that stunt he pulled in the limo. Luckily, the collar of his shirt was high enough to cover the hickey I gave him, and if anything, not wearing a bowtie added to his rakish appeal.

And no one noticed the love-bite on my cleavage. If they had, I know for a fact, I wouldn't have gotten away with an easy explanation. I can moan about it as much as I want, but the fact is, the media, and the public, still view and judge women with a different lens than it does the men. The double-standard persists.

All I can do is try my best to correct the status quo and hope my daughters will have an easier time.

My footsteps slow and I almost stumble before I catch myself. My daughters. Did I just think about 'my daughters'? Why am I thinking about 'my daughters?' I've never thought about having a child or getting pregnant. Now I'm suddenly thinking of having offspring, and in plural? My head spins.

I manage to keep my wits about me as I check my phone at the entrance. That's right, the event is a phone-free zone. Given the profiles of the attendees, the organizers insisted this was the only way to allow guests to relax, and apparently, they wanted to maintain secrecy around the silent auction that came at the end of the event.

I head inside the massive ballroom. It's a beautiful room, but I barely manage a glance at the frescoes which decorate the ceiling. Instead, I glance around for a place to sit down for a bit, catch my breath, and get something to eat, perhaps. A waiter passes by with canapés. I beckon him over, relieve him of a few of them and—whoever is watching be damned— scarf down the hors d'oeuvres.

They're as insubstantial as party canapés are reputed to be. Why is it that the booze at such gatherings is top-notch, but when it comes to the food, the portions are miniscule? I glance around for another waiter to flag down, when a plate piled high with food—the non canapé variety, i.e. the real stuff—is thrust in front of me. "Looking for this?"

I follow the arm attached to the plate and turn to find familiar features beaming at me.

"Isla!" I exclaim.

"You seem starved," she says and grins at me.

I lean around the plate and hug her. "I missed you, babe." We've been talking via FaceTime a lot, but nothing beats seeing your friends in person. With Isla in Italy and Solene's career taking off, and the rest of the Sisterhood of the Seven—which is what the wives and girlfriends of the Seven call themselves—either pregnant or having given birth recently, as in the case of Karma and Summer, I didn't realize how lonely I had been. Tears prick the backs of my eyes, and I blink them away. How strange. First I think of my own kids for the first time in my life, then I get emotional when I see Isla. Things are getting weird.

"I missed you, too." Isla pats my shoulder.

I sniff. She stills. "Zara, you okay?"

"Of course." I step back and tip up my chin. "Let me see you." I scan her features. Glowing eyes, glowing skin; in short, glowing everything. She's the picture of contentment.

"Marriage suits you."

"I know, right." Her smile widens. "Liam is the absolute bestest husband ever. He waits on me hand and foot, takes care of me, refuses to let me out of his sight, and the sex—" Her gaze turns dreamy.

A stab of something... Jealousy? No, more like a want, a need to feel what she's feeling, to be in that slightly blissful state where it feels like you have someone in your corner, your partner, someone who has your back, no matter what... Someone like Hunter. The hell? Just because I have his cum running down my thigh doesn't mean I've developed 'feelings' for him. Especially not now, when he's my defacto boss. Who I fucked on the way over in his limo. Jesus, what a mess.

I must make a noise for Isla, once more, peers into my face. "You sure you're okay Zara?"

"Just hungry." On cue, my stomach growls. I reach for the plate of food, then glance around for a place to put it down.

"Over here." Isla guides me to one of those high-top tables which are at a perfect height to lean on, specifically, one that was pushed to the side behind a large potted plant.

I place the plate of food down on it, then reach for the knife and fork she placed on it, and tuck in. I shovel in the fried mozzarella sticks, then the goat cheese crostini—yum—followed by the glazed pecans, and the turkey avocado pinwheels.

I hail a passing waiter and grab a glass of apple juice from him.

"You're not having champagne?" she asks, surprised.

"My stomach's been a little funny with alcohol, of late. With coffee, too, come to think of it. I might have overdone it over Christmas."

"Christmas was nearly three weeks ago," she points out.

"Guess it's taking a while for my system to stabilize." I raise a shoulder.

"And how long have you had this upset stomach?"

I bite the inside of my cheek. "About a week?"

Silence.

I glance up to find Isla staring at me.

I swallow down the morsel in my mouth and frown. "What?"

"Your stomach seems to tolerate the food okay, though."

"Huh." I glance down at the almost empty plate in front of me. "You should have seen me after I tried to eat breakfast this morning. I couldn't keep anything down. Actually," —I place the now empty glass down on the table— "it's been that way this entire week."

"You've been sick in the mornings?"

I nod.

"And you haven't been able to tolerate coffee or alcohol?"

I shake my head slowly.

"Hmm."

I grip the edge of the table with clammy fingers. "Oh, no, no, no. It's not what you think it is."

"I never said anything," she murmurs.

My heart seems to stop beating for a second, before starting up again. "It can't be. It can't be." I glance about the quickly filling room, then back at her. "Can it?"

"You tell me, honey. I assume you've been careful with all the horizontal action you've indulged in with—"

"Don't say his name," I rasp.

She raises her hands. "Okay."

"I'm on birth control." I grip the table tighter. "I can't be, I really can't be..." I can't say the P word. If I do, it will all seem very real. Besides, I don't need to say it aloud. "I'm not...you know." I tilt up my chin.

"Didn't say you were. But maybe it's worth testing?"

"Testing?" I feel the blood drain from my face.

"A—that word that I should not speak right now— test?" she says gently.

"Right." My head feels like it's dissociated from my body. I'm having an out-of-body experience. That's the only explanation for this strange conversation I'm having.

"Zara, babe. It's going to be okay." She wraps her arm about my shoulder. "You're going to be okay."

"There you are." Liam materializes next to Isla, then glances between us. "Everything okay?"

"Of course," both of us say at the same time.

His forehead furrows, but he doesn't push it. "There's someone I want you to meet," he tells Isla.

"Oh, but I want to stay with Zara," she protests.

"Nonsense, I'm fine, you go with Liam." I insist.

"It's not urgent," he starts, but I wave him off.

"Please, take your pretty wife and go mingle. That's what this shindig is for, after all."

"But—" Isla starts.

I turn and hug her. "I'm fine, and if I need anything, I'll message you."

She hugs me back. "Promise?"

"I promise."

She steps back and squeezes my shoulder. "You let me know how everything goes, okay?"

I swallow, knowing she's referring to the thing-I-shall-not-call-by-name test. "Okay," I manage to say in a voice that sounds nothing like the little butterflies of nervousness that have taken wing in my stomach.

She nods, then Liam takes her hand, and they walk away.

I stand at the table for a few more seconds. This is so not like me, hiding in a corner. I need to follow my own advice and get into the thick of things and live up to my reputation as The Shark. The woman who loves to mingle and talk to people, and keep her ear to the ground and find out the latest gossip doing the rounds—which at the moment, is not me, yet. My stomach curls in on itself. No, no, no, I'm not going to be sick, not now. I drain my glass of juice. To my relief, my stomach rights itself. Okay, that's good.

I grab my little bag and walk toward the crowd. The orchestra has struck up a waltz, and some of the guests have taken to the dance floor. The chandeliers in the ceiling pick out the colors of the dresses worn by the women. Tiny lights strung up at intervals turn the entire space into a fairytale setting. The architecture of the building is in the style of the Italian Renaissance, and it lends a storybook feel to the event.

Someone steps up to me. "Would you like to dance?" a voice asks from somewhere above me.

I turn to face a man whose features are familiar. He's tall, with broad shoulders and dark hair. Dressed in the obligatory coat tails, he looks dashing. Of course, he's not Hunter. Maybe it's time I stop thinking of Hunter for a while.

I take his proffered hand. "Why not?"

<h1 style="text-align:center">42</h1>

Hunter

"You're doing well in the polls," JJ Kane says as he puts his arm around his girlfriend. His much younger girlfriend who, at one point, was his son's girlfriend. But to see how happy he and Lena are now, you'd never know the journey they went through to get here.

The younger woman looks up at him with adoring eyes, before turning to me. "You have my vote, Minister."

"Thank you." I tilt my head.

"Your strategy to launch your campaign a little later than the other candidates paid off."

"Thanks to the hard work put in by my team," I demur.

"They've done a stellar job in getting you off to a good start." Sinclair Sterling joins with his wife Summer. Lena and Summer embrace. Sinclair takes two glasses of juice from the hovering waiter and passes one to Summer.

"Thanks, darling." She takes a sip while Sinclair places his own glass on the table between us.

I glance at the glass, then back at him.

"Summer's nursing; I'm keeping her company." He raises a shoulder.

"I told Sinclair he can drink for the both of us, but he insists he'll start drinking once I wean off the baby completely." Summer laughs.

"He's right." I raise my glass in their direction. "Parenting is bloody hard work, not that I know anything about it. But hats off to you guys, you're doing an incredible job."

"Sinclair's been so helpful. He insists on waking up at night when the baby starts crying and is really good at putting him back to bed."

"Good on you." JJ, too, raises his glass in their direction.

"This is our first night out in" —Sinclair shakes his head— "in forever. Speaking of," —he takes his wife's hand in his— "I'm going to take my wife dancing."

"Go for it." I laugh and take a sip of my champagne.

Sinclair pulls away with Summer. JJ turns to Lena and asks, "Want to dance?"

She shakes her head, then wraps her arm about his waist. "I'm happy to watch."

He pulls her even closer. "And I'm happy to watch you."

They share a look, and it's such an intimate moment, I feel like I'm intruding. "I think I need to get around and press the flesh and all that." I shuffle my feet.

JJ and Lena look at me. "You sure, you—" He looks past me and his jaw firms.

"What is it?"

Lena follows the direction of his glance and her gaze widens.

I begin to turn, when JJ shakes his head. "Don't."

I arch an eyebrow. "Meaning, I really need to look at this."

I glance over my shoulder, and all of my muscles coil. The hair on my forearms rises. I curl my fingers so tightly around the stem of the glass that it cracks. "Fuck." I swipe out my other hand and catch the thin bowl of the flute before it can roll over the side. I place it back on the table upside down so it doesn't fall, then shake out the champagne that's fallen on my hand. Luckily, I didn't cut myself. I pull out the handkerchief from my pocket and dry my fingers before stuffing the cloth back in my pocket.

"Excuse me."

I turn to leave, when JJ grips my shoulder. "Don't do anything stupid."

I hesitate.

"The paps are salivating for gossip. Your enemies can't wait for you to take a wrong step. It's your career at stake."

I set my lips.

"And hers," he adds.

I draw in a breath and force my muscles to relax. When I nod, he releases me. At which point, I turn and stalk toward where she's dancing with someone else. I know she has to circulate among the guests. It's her job. It comes with the territory of being a fixer. Of keeping an ear to the ground and staying abreast of events. I get that. But this... This is where I draw the line. She came to the event with me and now she's dancing with another. How dare she dance with another man?

There's something familiar about his stance, his features, but I'm positive I've never met this man before. He's much taller than her—as tall as me—and in comparison, she looks tiny, fragile. His swarthy looks complement her delicate ones. With his head of full dark hair, and Zara's dark locks that flow behind her, they make a striking couple.

My chest seizes. My heart pumps so hard, the beats reverberate through my cells. The bastard has his hand around her tiny waist, the other holding her hand. As I watch, he releases her waist, only to twirl her out then back toward him. She laughs, that full-bodied, hearty laugh that arrows straight to my cock. He leans forward, until his face is close to hers, until his mouth is close to her ear, until it feels like his entire body is a hair's breadth from enveloping hers. That's when something inside me snaps.

I weave through the people standing around the edge, then past the other dancing couples, to stand beside them.

For a second, they don't notice me, so engrossed are they in each other, and that only fuels this burning sensation that's flared in my chest.

"Let her go." I hear my words, and only then, do I realize I've spoken.

Both of them turn to face me.

Her features pale. "Hunter, we were just dancing."

I glare at her, then back at the motherfucker who still has his hands on her.

"Let her the fuck go."

He looks between us. "Are you with him?"

"I'm not," she snaps at the same time that I growl, "She is."

He frowns. "Maybe it's best I step back."

"That would be best for all of us, motherfucker," I growl.

"No need to swear." The man's lips firm. "I'll leave once I make sure Zara's okay." He turns to her. "You all right, Z?"

"The fuck?" He called her by a nickname? How dare he call her by a nickname. No one gets to do that, except me.

I glare down at where the bastard still has his hand on her hip. "Let her the fuck go."

"And if I don't?"

I raise my fist and bury it in his face.

<hr>

"Really? Really?" She paces back-forth-back in the small room up the corridor from the ballroom where the gala was being held. "What were you thinking, Hunter?" she snaps.

I wasn't thinking.

I saw his hands on her and I swung and connected with his face. The stranger took the hit, staggered back, only to recover and swing at me. I ducked, of course, and growled at Zara to step aside, which she did. When I was sure she was at a safe enough distance I swung at him again, and we both went tumbling to the ground.

"You were lucky that Michael Sovrano happened to be there and caused a diversion by pulling the fire alarm," she rages at me.

Which also opened up the sprinklers in the ceiling of the ball room, and water rained down on us. It hit me with the impact of a cold shower. Literally. I pulled back; so did the stranger. We stared at each other, chests heaving, breath coming in pants. Logic dictates that's when I should have apologized to him for starting the fight. Which I hadn't.

"'Stay away from what's mine'? You growled at him to 'Stay away from what's mine'?" She turns on me, eyes spitting golden sparks, her hair clinging in long damp tendrils to her shoulders, and that gorgeous dress showing off the curves of her spectacular hips. "Who says something so Neanderthalish?"

"Is that a word in the English language?" I ask in a mild tone.

Her already pink cheeks now flush red. "That's what you take away from what I said?"

"Not only."

"Oh?" She plants her palms on her hips.

I nod. "I also know now that I can't bear it if anyone else dares touch you. If any man dare look at you again, I'm going to kill him."

She throws up her hands. "You've declared you're going to run for the top leadership position in this country. You can't afford to lose your temper at such a trivial matter."

"Trivial matter?" Anger punches my guts with such force, specks of black dot my vision. I rise to my feet and prowl toward her. "He. Had. His. Hands. On. You." I stop in front of her and glare into her features. "He was dancing with you. You were laughing at something he said, you—"

"He's my brother, Hunter."

I still. "Eh?"

"He's. My. Brother. Cade Kingston."

"That was Cade Kingston, aka the King, the Captain of the English Cricket Team?"

She nods.

I shake my head. "He looks different from his pictures."

"He shaved off his beard and his hair."

Of course, I know Cade Kingston is her brother. And there was something familiar about him... But I was so consumed by anger, and he looked so different from his pictures, I never, in a million years, would have recognized him as her brother.

I rub the back of my neck. "Fuck, fuckity, fuck."

"Indeed." She folds her arms across her chest. "If you had paused to think for one minute, or better still, decided to think with something else other than your dick—"

"Which is very difficult for me to do where you're concerned."

"—you'd have noticed that he had his hands on me, not in a lover-like fashion, but in a brotherly manner."

I lower my hand to my side. "He still had his hands on you."

"Didn't you just hear what I said?" She scowls up at me. "He. Is. My. Brother."

"He was a man. He was someone other than me. And he was touching you."

She throws up her hands. "So?"

"So?" I bend my knees, peer into her eyes. "I will not tolerate you being with anyone else. I will set fire to the world before I let anyone else touch you, and that includes any sibling of yours."

"Jesus Christ, give me patience." She draws in a breath, then stabs her finger into my chest. "This passion of yours? This obsessive attention to what you want, this forgetting everything else except the one thing most important to you? This…this…all-consuming fervor is what you need to bring to the campaign trail."

I blink. "You're comparing what I feel for you to the emotions I need to bring to the campaign trail?"

"Absolutely."

I glare at her. She pales but doesn't look away.

"This fire inside of you, this need to go after what you want, this absolute focus that you have for me, it's the most flattering thing in the world.".

"It's how I feel about you," I growl.

"It's the true you." She flattens her palm against my chest. "The one you need to show to your constituents. To this country."

This woman, only she could take my words and turn them on me, and yet…a part of me wonders if she doesn't speak the truth. Is this what's been missing in the run up to my campaign? Why I haven't been able to galvanize my efforts behind this program? Why it felt empty, even to me, like something was missing? Why I feel alive only when I'm with her? Why I need her beside me to feel whole?

"You're right."

Now, it's her turn to look taken aback. "I am?"

I nod. "Since I met you, something inside of me, something I didn't even know I had, came to life. Until now, I'd been following the path that was expected of me. Well also, my instinct dictated this was right for me. That deep inside I do want to serve my country. But it's only when I'm with you that I feel inclined to follow my truth. Because you are my truth, Zara."

The color drains from her face. She pulls her hand back, but I curl my fingers about her wrist. "Don't. Don't deny what's between us."

"Hunter, but—"

"No buts. You saw me out there. You saw how I'm unable to control myself around you. And you're right. I need to bring that passion, that visceral feeling when you want something to the exclusion of everything else, that ruthless determination to succeed, that aggressive, tenacious urge for domination that I feel when I'm with you, that I sense only when I'm with you. I need to become it. I am all of this when you are with me, by my side. When I'm in your presence, I am alive. It's your proximity that fires me up. It's your look, your touch, the feel of your skin on mine, your breath entwined with mine, the thud of your heart echoing mine, the drumbeat of your pulse mirroring mine… It's always been you."

"Hunter, don't," she whispers.

She tries to pull away, but I hold onto her.

"I'm only truly me when I'm holding your hand, Zara."

I lower my gaze to where I clasp her wrist.

She follows my gaze.

I place my other palm on hers, enfolding her smaller one between both of mine, then I go down on bended knee.

43

Zara

"Wait, what? He proposed to you?" Solene screeches.

I hold the phone away from my ear and glance toward Isla, who's seated in the chair opposite mine. Isla raises a shoulder in a gesture that embodies the confusion I'm feeling right now.

"It would seem that way." I turn back to the screen.

"And what did you tell him?"

"Nothing."

Solene's gaze widens. "You didn't give him an answer?"

"Nope." Strictly speaking, I couldn't have given him an answer before, I was too busy gathering my jaw off the floor. He went down on one knee and asked me to marry him in this very room, and I was dumbstruck. A first. I stared at him for a few seconds, then pulled my hand from his. And this time, he let me. I backed away from him until the backs of my knees hit this very chair—where I'm still seated—and I sat down heavily.

Thankfully, I was saved from replying because Liam and Isla burst through the doorway immediately after.

Isla had one look at my face, walked over to me, and took my hand in hers, while I tried and failed to look anywhere but at Hunter's face. When I finally made eye contact, his blue-green eyes seemed almost colorless. His features, as if hewn from a material that gave no inkling of what his thoughts were.

"I'll be waiting for your answer," he bit out, then walked out of here, with Liam on his heels. I began to tell Isla what had happened, and she told me to stop and dialed in Solene so I could bring them up to speed on the soap opera that is currently my life.

My phone vibrates, then again. Yep, I have a second phone hidden away in the secret compartment of my bag. What? I'm a PR professional and the media is my lifeblood. You didn't think I was going to stay without my electronic lifeline for even a second, did you? Only this time, I haven't dared check my inbox, or my messages, or any of the social media channels...yet.

Given the crisis of Mount Everest proportions I walked out of earlier, I know things must be going crazy on the internet. But it's not going to help if I get drawn into the online speculation. Right after Hunter left, I called my team, briefed them, then told them to reach out to key influencers for damage control. If things were really bad, they'd call me, but considering fifteen minutes have passed and there've been no SOS calls to me...yet... Maybe we managed to nip this thing in the bud. I'm not holding my breath, though. While the hours and days after a slip-up like what happened earlier between Hunter and Cade is the stuff bloggers and social media users around the world are waiting to broadcast to their followers, the long-tail effect of it surfacing in the future at the most inopportune moment is nothing to be sneezed at.

"So, what are you going to tell Hunter?" Solene asks.

I exchange glances with Isla, then shake my head. "I don't have the foggiest."

"What does your instinct tell you to do?" Isla murmurs.

"To get the hell away from here. To refuse to be his PR manager. To cut all ties and move to another country and reinvent my life."

There's silence for a second, then Solene laughs. "You'd never do that. You're not the type to do a runner. You're the strongest woman I know, Zara. In fact, I've always aspired to be you when I grow up."

I flush a little. "Don't be daft, Sabatini, I'm hardly the poster child for how to live your life."

"You're doing a fabulous job of it so far, Zara."

"That's why I had a one night, which became a two night stand, with the possible Prime Minister to be of this country, and I might be pregnant with his child."

Silence descends on the room.

Isla looks at me with concern in her eyes. Solene stares at me with a shocked expression.

A woman clears her throat. "Umm, sorry, don't mind me. Cade sent me in to make sure you were okay. But uh, I'll just tell him you're fine."

I glance up to find a woman standing at the doorway. I scowl at her, and she raises her hands, palms face up. "The door was open."

Fantastic.

"Who're you again?" I manage to choke out.

"Uh, I'm Cade's friend's sister. Cade didn't have a date to the gala, that's the only reason he asked me to the ball and… Oh, god, I'm talking too much, aren't I? I swear, I didn't mean to barge in and listen to your secrets. And no, I didn't just hear you say that you're pregnant—I mean, possibly pregnant—with the child of the man who might be our next Prime Minister and… Hey, are you going to marry him?" She seems to run out of steam, finally, and glances between me and Isla. If Isla's face looks anything like mine, it's a combination of shock, horror, surprise, frustration, and maybe even a glimmer of humor—because, let's face it, there's a touch of absurdity to the proceedings.

Isla is the first to recover. She rises to her feet, marches to the door, shuts and locks it, then gestures to the sofa. "Take a seat please—what's your name again?"

"Abigail. My friends call me Abby... But you guys are not my friends... Yet... But I'd like you to be. You're Cade's sister, after all." She looks at me with big doe eyes that carry more than a touch of hero-worship in them. Oh, god, she has a crush on my brother, and it seems, by transference, on me.

"Umm, Abigail—"

"Call me Abby, please." She locks her fingers together in front of her in a gesture that hints at her nervousness.

"Abby, please do sit down." I nod toward the sofa.

"Of course." She heads for the sofa, sinks into it, then glances between the two of us again.

"So, you're Zara's brother's girlfriend?" Solene asks from the phone.

Abby presses a hand to her chest. "Oh, no, no, no, not his girlfriend." Her cheeks pink. "I'm, uh, his friend's sister."

"And you came with him to the ball," Isla murmurs before taking her seat again.

"Yes, and I saw what happened." Abby turns to me. "That was some fight, huh? They both held their own."

"Is Cade okay?" I ask.

"He has a shiner, but that only makes him look even more dashing." She bites the inside of her lip.

Isla and I exchange another glance.

"So, about what you heard when you walked in —"

"Oh, you don't have to worry." Abby waves her hand in the air. "It's been forgotten. I promise. In one ear, out the other. Nothing to it. Also, I know how to keep secrets." She mimes zipping her lips.

"Hmph." I look closely at her. Her gaze is open. Her expression indicates she has nothing to hide.

"No, really. I know when a person says that, you think the next thing they'll do is turn around and blab out the secret to everyone. But I understand how difficult it must be to conduct a relationship when all the media attention is on you. So, you can count on my discretion."

I press a finger to my cheek. Can I believe her? Should I believe her? More to the point, when did I become so cynical that I couldn't take a person at face value? Oh, wait, that's because I work in a cut-throat profession, where I'm trained to disbelieve the words of people, and normally, they deliver on my suspicions. Still, my instinct says Abby made an honest mistake, and she means it when she says she's not going to tell a soul. Doesn't mean I'm not going to find a way to ensure she sticks to her word. "So, Abby, what is it you said you do?"

"Uh, I work at a communications agency."

"Oh?" I tilt my head. "And are you looking for a career change?"

44

Zara

"Smart thinking, offering her a job," Isla says after Abby has left.

Solene, too, signs off—after asking me to keep her posted on the results of the pregnancy test I promised I'm going to take as soon as I fire-fight the fall-out from the impromptu sparring session that my brother and my boss—who's also my lover—indulged in.

"That old adage about keeping your enemies where you can see them? It's a technique I've used more than once." Not that Abby is my enemy. Far from it. The girl almost fainted when I offered her a job as an executive in my agency. A step up from the unpaid intern position she's held for the past six months. She thanked me profusely and promised to do her best. I took her up on the offer by telling her to research all media mentions—if any—from the earlier incident. I lean back in my seat and place my hands over my stomach, which hasn't felt very steady over the past ten seconds.

Isla levels me with another look of concern. "Do you think you really are—"

"Pregnant?" I force myself to say the word. "I haven't taken the test yet, but my instincts are screaming that I am. Considering I'm already a week late."

"It might just be all the stress you're under."

"I thrive on stress. I've never had a day that hasn't brought with it new stress, and I've never been late."

"Hmm." She taps her fingers on the armrest. "Will you tell him?"

"I don't know," I say honestly.

"I suppose it's opportune that he proposed to you?"

I scowl at her. "I'm not going to marry him just because I'm pregnant."

"It's as good a reason as any."

"When—if—I marry, it will be because not only am I in love with the man, but I also see him as a partner in every way."

"And you don't with Hunter?"

I squeeze the bridge of my nose. "I don't know."

"I think you do know, but you don't want to accept it."

"Eh?" I lower my arm and stare at her. "What are you talking about?"

"You've been prejudiced against Hunter from the beginning. You've held his background against him."

"No, I haven't." I gape at her.

"Haven't you?" She half-smiles. "It's normal, though. You've worked hard to get to where you are, and a part of you resents that he seems to have gotten everything so easily."

I squirm in my seat. Is that true? Do I begrudge Hunter his success so far? Have I held him up to a standard of my own making and found him lacking? Just because he was born into money... Do I hold that against him? Is his success less credible because he, seemingly, didn't have to jump through the hoops to get to where he is, unlike me? I lower my chin to my chest. "Oh, god, Isla, do you think I've misjudged him? Do you think I'm holding him up to a standard that he could never match?"

"Zara, I—"

A knock on the door interrupts us. Then Liam pops his head through. "Everything okay in here?"

"Hey, babe," Isla beckons to him. Liam walks over to Isla and leans a hip against her armrest. The two of them kiss, and they've only been separated for half an hour. Gosh, they're so sweet together, it's almost too much.

I hear footsteps before Hunter enters the room, followed by my brother. Cade sports a shiner, which only adds to his good looks. The two of them stop halfway inside the room, then glower at each other. O-k-a-y, so apparently, whatever they were discussing didn't go down well.

Isla rises to her feet. "I think Liam and I are gonna leave now." She walks over to me and kisses my cheek. "Keep me posted on everything," she says in a low voice. I nod and hug her back. She steps back, then heads for my brother.

"I'm Isla, Zara's friend."

Cade's features break into a smile. "My pleasure." He brings her hand to his lips and kisses it.

Liam instantly closes the distance to them and wraps his arm about Isla. "Well played on your last innings. That was some record-breaking century you made." He's referring to the last cricket match, where my brother scored enough to win the tournament for his team.

"Thanks, man!" He releases Isla's hand, and nods in Liam's direction.

Liam holds out his hand, "Liam Kincaid."

"Cade Kingston."

The two men shake hands.

"Looking forward to seeing you play at Lord's next month." Liam refers to the upcoming match at the well-known cricket grounds.

"Can't wait to play there; it's my favorite venue," Cade acknowledges.

"We'll be off then." Liam heads toward the door with Isla in tow. He and Hunter exchange chin jerks in the manner of friends who know each other enough to say a lot to each other without saying anything. The door snicks shut.

I glance between the two men who are resolutely not looking at each other. Which means both of them are glowering at me. I blow out a breath. "Care to take a seat? Or do the two of you prefer to stand there and ignore each other?"

"Prefer to ignore each other," they reply at the same time.

A dull ache stabs behind my eyes. My stomach jumps in response. I rub at my temple and resist the urge to rub at my stomach. Oh, god, I can't really be preggers... And if I am? Best to wait until I have a positive test before I begin to panic, though truth be told, a part of me already knows.

"Zara, you okay?" Hunter's voice reaches me. I open my eyes, take in the concern on his features.

"What do you think? My boss beat up my brother, and you've probably made tabloid headlines with that asinine stunt."

My brother winces. "It's not pleasant to get on her bad side," he says in a conversational tone.

"So I'm learning." Hunter's lips twitch.

They finally look at each other, twin expressions of wariness on their features. Apparently, they're in agreement about something, and naturally, it involves their opinion of me. I make a sound at the back of my throat, and both men look at me in alarm.

"You sure you're okay, Z?" My brother—the clunkerhead asks.

"Don't keep asking me that as if I am an airhead who needs to be mollycoddled."

Cade raises both his hands. "Just brotherly concern, is all."

"And where were you all these months? You take off touring the world on your job, then show up at a gala. You could have told me you were going to attend."

"I didn't know you would be here," my brother protests.

"The biggest event of the season, with influencers, entertainers and politicians in attendance, and you didn't think my job would demand that I be all over it?"

My brother drags his fingers through his hair. "You're right. I should have thought it through. Should have reached out and checked how you were doing. I took the easy way out and stayed away so I wouldn't have to visit the folks. And calling you would have reminded me that I haven't been in touch with them, either." He raises a shoulder. "That was cowardly of me; I'm sorry."

I deflate a little. It's tough when your sibling is being all reasonable.

Hunter looks from Cade to me, then back to Cade. "How did I not spot the similarity?"

"Probably because you had your head stuck up your arse?" I retort.

Cade whistles. Hunter seems like he's having a difficult time controlling his mirth.

I glower at him. "You won't be laughing when your reputation is all over social media, and the two of you become a meme."

He leans forward on the balls of his feet. "No phones in the ballroom, remember?"

I scoff. "Do you think everyone in there followed the rules? There's bound to have been someone who had a phone stashed away. Someone who, at this very moment, is uploading footage from your faux pas to the internet, as we speak."

The knobhead grins. He actually grins. "You forget, I have the best PR manager in town who will, undoubtedly, stop anything like this from happening," he murmurs.

"You could have saved me the headache and simply used your grey cells—which I assume you have, considering you're vying for the topmost post in the country—and stopped yourself before landing that first punch," I snap.

Hunter draws himself to his full height. "I saw a stranger with his hands all over you. What the hell would you have me do?"

"You should have trusted me."

"I cannot look the other way when my—"

"Stop," I bark, darting my brother a glance. Thankfully, like most men, he's clueless enough about the undercurrents in the room. If anything, he looks uncomfortable.

"Uh, Abby's waiting for me outside. I think it's best I leave so the two of you can sort things out."

"No," I burst out.

"That would be a good idea." Hunter nods.

Hunter and I glare at each other for a few seconds.

This is when the penny drops for Cade, for he suddenly squares his shoulders. "Hold on, are you—" He glances at Hunter. "You're not—" He looks at me. "Are the two of you— Are you—"

"No," I snap.

"Yes." Hunter nods. "Your sister and I are in a relationship. In fact, I asked her to marry me."

45

Hunter

"You're marrying him?" Cade asks.

"I haven't answered him yet," Zara interjects at the same time.

"Right." Cade drags his fingers through his hair. "I guess I'd best let you two figure this out, but first…" He lowers his hand, and in a move I didn't see coming, he steps up to me and grabs me by my collar. "You hurt her, and you'll have me to contend with."

I curl my fingers into fists at my sides, more out of instinct than out of a need to avoid picking a fight with him again. Also, he's her brother. Of course, it's natural he'd threaten me. Especially, now that he realizes I'm not just a jealous boyfriend, but a potential husband.

"You hear me?" he growls.

"Crystal clear." I step forward so the toes of our boots collide. "You and I need to have a catch up, separately."

"No, you don't." Zara jumps to her feet.

"You bet," Cade says at the same time.

"Bloody hell." Zara seems to sway, then sinks back down in her chair.

I twist myself out of Cade's grasp and leap toward her. "Hey, Fire, you okay?" I squat down in front of her. "What's wrong? Are you dizzy? Is it because of the stress from what happened? I'm sorry it came to that. I promise, I'll never pick a fight again—not unless I absolutely have to." I take her hand between mine, and her fingers are cold.

"Fuck!" I turn to Cade. "Dr. Weston Kincaid—he's on my phone list. Call him; tell him he needs to get here pronto.

"No doctor," Zara says weakly.

"Save your strength, baby." I pull out my phone, unlock it, and toss it at Cade. He snatches it out of the air, then steps out of the room.

"Stop with the histrionics." She scowls. Her voice is stronger, but her color is still pale.

"I will not make any compromises when it comes to your health."

"Do you have any idea how cavemanlike you sound?" she murmurs. Her expression is far from being angry though. If anything, there's a softening around her eyes.

"I'm glad I'm living up to my reputation."

"Also,"—her brow furrows—"how do you have your phone with you?"

"How do you have yours with you?"

Her lips curve, and god, her smile is so beautiful, so bewitching, so everything. I bring her hand to my mouth and kiss her fingertips.

Her phone buzzes. She reaches for it, but I get to her bag first. I hold it up and out of her reach.

"Hey, gimme my phone."

"Not until the doc has checked you out and pronounced you okay."

"I really am okay, Hunter." She says softly.

"Let the doc give you a clean bill of health."

She looks between my eyes, then blows out a breath. "Fine, if he says I'm okay, then I walk out of here, on my own steam, and you don't follow me."

"No fucking way. You came with me, and I'll drop you back home."

"Let your chauffeur drop me off, but I'll ride alone. After all the speculation that is, no doubt, circulating amongst the guests, it's the least we can do to ensure no other gossip spreads."

"I don't fucking care what people say."

"But I do. I care about your campaign. I want to see you elected, Hunter."

I set my jaw, then take in the expression on her features. They mirror the stubbornness that is my hallmark, and which I'm recognizing is also second nature to her. "You're not budging on this, are you?"

"So, she's okay then?" JJ leans over and tops up my glass of whiskey. When he offers the bottle to Sinclair, he refuses. As does Michael. Both men are not drinking for the duration that their wives are still nursing.

"She seemed fine when I dropped her home, but I don't understand why she didn't allow me to be in the room when the doctor examined her." I peer into the depths of my glass.

Cade had reached Weston, who'd turned up in the next ten minutes. At which point, Zara insisted I leave. I refused and she grew increasingly agitated. Weston pulled me aside and told me it was best to respect her wishes. I didn't want her to get more stressed—her health is of paramount importance—so I removed myself from the room.

I paced outside for the half-hour it took for the doctor to complete the examination. Cade watched me with curiosity on his features, but he didn't ask me any further questions about my relationship with his sister. Thank fuck. Meanwhile, her phone vibrated non-stop, as did mine. I refused to look at either of the screens. Truth is, I wasn't able to focus on anything, until Weston finally came out of the room. He had a strange look on his face, and for a second, my stomach plummeted to my toes. Then he smiled and reassured me that she was fine. Maybe a little exhausted. Nothing that a good night's sleep wouldn't cure.

The tension drained out of my shoulders and I felt faint. Only then, did I realize how overwrought I'd been about her condition. Somewhat reassured, I thanked him and walked into the room to find her on her feet. Adamant woman insisted she was fine. She then told me I needed to tell my chauffeur to drop her home. I was having none of it.

No way, was I letting her be driven back on her own. Much to her consternation, I told her I was breaking my word and driving back with her. Cade supported me, and it was both of us against her, so she finally backed down.

I had the car come around to the back door so we could get in without any prying eyes. Then I took her to her apartment, insisted on seeing her up, and tucked her into bed. By then, she was so exhausted, she didn't protest. She fell asleep as soon as her head hit the pillow. I covered her up and placed her phone—after putting it on silent—next to her bed. I stayed there watching over her until the wee hours of this morning, then I came home and put in a full day's work, before arriving at the 7A Club. I walked into the private room which has become the unofficial meeting place for me and the rest of the Seven, as well as the Sovranos, and those known to us.

"You respected her privacy and left the room when the doctor examined her? I'm assuming you have eyes on her." Michael tips his chin in my direction.

"I'm running for office. I need to uphold the highest levels of ethics" —I glance between the faces of my friends— "but when it comes to her, there are no rules. I'll do anything to ensure she's safe. Even if it means protecting her from herself."

"So, you have eyes on her." Michael nods.

"On her phone, her laptop, in her house." And now, I'll finally find out why she kept evading the investigator I had on her. Y-e-p, that's me, wading out into the morally gray area.

While Zara slept, I called in Axel Sovrano and his security team. Axel is Michael's younger brother. An ex-cop, he now runs an agency and can be counted on for discretion. I explained what I needed, and he obliged. His team moved in within the hour and put the security measures in place.

After the team left, I brewed a fresh pot of coffee for Zara, and left a plate of breakfast for her. Woman needs to eat to keep up her strength, after all. Only then, did I leave.

"You do realize, this doesn't bode well for you? What you did is bound to come out, at some point. And when it does, she's going to be pissed." Sinclair drums his fingers on the arm of his chair.

"That's a bridge I'll have to cross when I get to it."

"I understand why you did it, but don't put off sharing what you did with her for too long. It's best to come clean."

"Shouldn't the leader to-be of this country keep his reputation clean at all costs?" A new voice announces.

I glance up, spot Cade at the door and groan. "The fuck you doing here?"

"I could ask the lot of you the same question." He glances about the table. The shiner around his eye is an interesting shade of purple. Not that I regret putting it there, in the first place.

Only, he's Zara's brother... Her twin...which means, I need to repair the relationship between us. That's the only reason I jerk my chin in his direction. "Have the rest of you met Cade?"

JJ is the first to beckon him in. "Great last inning at Lord's."

"Thanks." Cade walks over to JJ and holds out his hand. "Cade Kingston."

JJ shakes it. "JJ Kane."

"Sinclair Sterling."

"Michael Sovrano."

The men shake hands.

"Cade also happens to be Zara's brother," I interject.

The men glance at him, then at me.

"Ah." JJ lights up his cigar. "I can see the resemblance. Why do the two of you have different surnames though?"

"I took my mother's surname. Zara took my father's." He raises a shoulder. "Family dynamics can be complex."

"Tell me about it," JJ says in a self-deprecating tone. I have no doubt he's referring to the relationship between him and Lena, and his son. "These things have a way of working themselves out though," he offers.

"You haven't met my family." Cade shakes his head. "Speaking of...how's Zara?" He turns to me.

"She seemed fine, last I saw her." Which was through the camera app on my phone, which showed she was back at work in her office. She seemed fine, on the face of it, at least. Checking in on her, making sure she's okay, now that I could see her with the swipe of the screen, is getting to be a dangerous addiction. At least, I've managed to curb myself from doing so since arriving at the Club.

"And the fallout from the V&A Ball?"

"Seems to have been minimal." I also authorized Axel's team to track down anyone who got a hold of clips from the event and pay them to take them down. He'll be the front for all of the proceedings; my name will be kept out of it completely. Not that I don't trust Zara and her team to handle it, but if I can spare her the stress of finding any reference to the bout between Cade and me, then it could only be helpful for her, right?

"I assume that's where the shiner is from?" Sinclair jerks his chin in Cade's direction. I filled them in on what went down at the ball but left out the fact that Cade is Zara's brother. Now, all three men dart me knowing looks. Yeah, so it was stupid of me to swing without thinking, and I'm loathe to apologize for it. Except, he's Zara's brother. So…

I square my shoulders, "If it's any consolation, you got in a few good ones, too." I move my jaw from side to side.

"I should hope so." He flexes his fingers. The skin over his knuckles is raw.

"I owe you an apology." I hold out my hand.

He stares down at it, then at me. "This doesn't change anything. Zara may come across as strong, but she's fragile inside. She's one hell of a survivor, and you don't deserve her."

"In this, I am with you." I tilt my head.

His scowl deepens. "Hurt her, and I'll break your jaw next time."

"If I hurt her, I won't stop you," I concur.

He finally takes my hand. "For Zara's sake," he mutters.

We shake, then both of us pull our hands back. That's when my phone vibrates. I glance at the camera app, then rise to my feet.

"Good meeting you." I manage to infuse a note of sincerity in my voice, then turn to the others. "Later ol' chaps."

I head out of the club, then direct my chauffeur to take me to her place. Twenty minutes later, I'm pressing the doorbell to her apartment.

I hear movement behind the door before it swings open. "You?"

46

Zara

"Expecting someone else?" Hunter smirks from his position against my door frame.

"A grocery delivery, actually." I tip up my chin.

"Lying, Fire?" His smirk widens.

"You're the politician, not me, remember?"

He chuckles. "Touché, Councillor."

"Wish you wouldn't call me that. I'm not a practicing lawyer anymore."

"Your skills at verbal comebacks remain as sharp."

I widen my gaze. "Is that an honest-to-god compliment?"

"Not the only one I've given you." He lowers his voice, and his tone is so intimate, I can't stop the shiver that crawls up my spine.

"What are you doing here?"

"I've come to take you out."

"I don't recall agreeing to come out with you." I scoff.

"It's a last-minute…work thing." He schools his features into an expression of absolute innocence.

Work thing, my arse. "Is that what they're calling it nowadays?"

"Not my fault if your mind went to places it shouldn't."

I flush. "I'm not going anywhere with you."

"Are you saying you're refusing the candidate for whom you're running a PR campaign, and your defacto boss, to meet him on an important work situation?"

I blow out a breath. "The groceries—"

"Message them and delay the delivery to tomorrow," he orders.

"Oh, so now you're changing my grocery schedule to suit your needs?"

"Wouldn't you change your schedule to suit my needs?" he murmurs.

"Now who's mind is in the gutter?"

He raises his hands. "I'm simply asking you out to a business meeting, is all."

"If I postpone the grocery delivery, I won't have anything to eat tonight." My voice sounds whiny, even to me. Jesus, when did I become such a complaining little bitch?

"Which is why I'm taking you out to dinner."

"How did you pull this off?" I glance down at the blanket he's laid out on the floor of the House of Commons, in the Palace of Westminster. Yep, the same House of Commons which is covered so often on TV when the members of the ruling party face the opposition during Question Time, which takes place from Monday to Thursday during working hours. Today is a Friday. It's also after office hours, so the entire Parliamentary building is deserted.

"You should know better than to ask me that." He places the picnic basket at the edge of the blanket. He hauled it in from his car and up many steep flights of steps, all without breaking a sweat or getting out of breath, annoyingly.

I take a slow turn, taking in the galleries on either side of the floor. The benches, as well as other furnishings in the chamber, are green in color, a custom which goes back 300 years. The adversarial layout— with benches facing each other is, in fact, a relic of the original use of the first permanent Commons Chamber on the site, St. Stephen's Chapel. There's so much history in this room. If I shut my eyes, I can almost hear the echoes of the voices of a debate between the ruling and opposition parties.

"You had a picnic basket in the trunk of your car when you came to my apartment?"

He straightens, then fixes me with that trademark Hunter look—raised eyebrow, smirk on his lips, and that part-innocent, part-wicked gleam in his eyes, which seem to imply all the world's a stage, he's a player, and everything is done in the spirit of good fun. Also, if he's done anything wrong, then he'll be happy to ask forgiveness… After the fact.

"You have quite the ego about you, don't you?"

"Which we have established many a time." He pulls out his phone and swipes his finger over the screen. The lights in the chamber dim.

"No way." I shake my head. "You arranged for mood lighting?"

"Not only." Another flick of his finger, and a melodic aria wafts from his phone speaker. He leans the phone against the basket, then straightens and holds out his hand.

When I hesitate, he chuckles. "I won't bite."

"Don't you?" I murmur.

His nostrils pulse. His blue-green eyes take on a midnight hue, a tell-tale sign he's aroused. A cloud of heat wafts off of his chest. It slams into me and seems to pin me in place. I gasp, unable to move, unable to do anything other than appreciate his sheer assuredness—this complete sense of rightness that fills me whenever we are together. He must sense some of the emotions running through me, for he closes the distance between us. He wraps his arm about my shoulders and pulls me in. I rest my forehead against his chest, then after a second, fold my own arms about his waist. We sway in place, as the haunting notes from the classical ditty fill the space.

"La fleur que tu m'avais jetée from Carmen, otherwise known as The Flower Song," he murmurs.

"It's beautiful." I close my eyes, and for the first time since I woke up in my bed and found him gone, my muscles relax. The stresses of the day fade away, and I lean closer. His arm tightens around me. He tucks my head under his chin. The thump-thump-thump of his heart is a reas-suring vibration against my cheek. His dark scent is as familiar as my own. Some time, over the last few months, he crept under my skin, into my blood, and occupies my every thought and dirty fantasy. He's become a part of me, without my realizing it. Or maybe, I was very aware of it and did nothing to stop it. Either way, I can't deny the fact that I've come to depend on him. When I opened the door earlier and saw him, a flush of joy spread through my chest. Oh, I hid it behind the smart words I lobbed at him, but deep inside, I felt as if it were Christmas all over again. Pun intended. He rubs his palm over my back in slow circles, and a tingling grips my limbs.

Neither of us speak, and the notes of the aria replace any lingering stresses that may have hidden in my cells. The last strains fade away, and we continue dancing, slowly...slower...until we come to a stop, arms about each other. Neither of us seems to want to move. I wish I could capture this hushed silence, so full of everything in my heart, so I can take it out later when this moment is gone, as time inevitably does.

"Baby, I think we need to feed you." His voice rumbles under my cheek.

I shake my head, not wanting to pull away. Not wanting to separate from him yet.

Then my stomach grumbles.

"Definitely need to feed you." His eyes flash, and I wonder if what he's thinking of putting in my mouth is something more than what's in the basket.

I slide my hand between us and place it on the thickness between his thighs that made itself known a little earlier.

His nostrils flare. Then he leans down and presses a hard kiss to my lips. "First food, of the nourishing variety." He pulls back, then urges me to sink down onto the picnic blanket

---

"That was some spread." I pat my mouth with the paper towel that was packed into the basket. We ate from plates of the ceramic variety, with cutlery that wasn't plastic. He offered me champagne, and when I declined, he didn't push it. Or asked questions. He simply poured me some sparkling apple juice, which was delicious.

"I still can't believe you arranged for all of this." I place my now empty plate on the blanket and glance about the room.

"It had to mean something to you."

I narrow my gaze on him. "Am I that easy to read?"

"You trained to be a lawyer, then got into PR because of your love for the media. And you come into your element when trading arguments with me. You've also taken on some high-profile politicians as clients and prevented their names from being marred by scandals. It doesn't take a genius to realize you love politics."

I look away. How can he see me this clearly? When my own family, and perhaps, many of my friends have not.

"Hey, don't hide from me." He reaches over and tucks a strand of hair behind my ear. "Why didn't you get into politics yourself?"

I shoot him a startled glance.

"I'm sure the thought crossed your mind." He holds my gaze.

"I did think about it," I concede. "But the timing didn't feel quite right."

"When you marry me, you'll have the chance to set that right."

I place my glass on the blanket and scowl at him. "I haven't agreed to anything."

"You will."

"A-n-d there he is. Just when I thought we were getting along so well."

"Don't change the topic. You were born for a political career. With your communication skills, your intelligence, your background—"

"You mean my working-class credentials will complement your privileged one and portray a more holistic dimension to the voters."

He frowns. "I meant you are a product of modern British society. You stand for everything that is right with the system. You are a role model for so many young girls. Your being by my side will send a positive message across parties."

I shake my head. "It will never work."

"Why won't you give us a chance? Just once, why can't you open your mind to the possibility that this could work?"

"Because..." I shake my head. "Because I can't."

"If you mean Olly—"

"Don't mention Olly." I rise to my feet so quickly, my head spins. I must stumble, because the next second, he's gripping my arms and steadying me.

"You okay, Zara?"

I shake my head. "I'd like to go home now."

"Look at me." He takes me by my shoulders. "I'm sorry if I distressed you. That wasn't my intention at all."

I glance away.

"You don't give me much to go on. You don't share anything with me. It's why I keep trying to push you, even though I know it's wrong."

When I refuse to meet his eyes, he blows out his breath. "Zara, please, I really didn't mean to hurt you."

"And yet, you did." I turn and narrow my gaze on him. "Can we go back now, please?"

47

Hunter

"Are you sure she's okay?" I barked down the phone.

"Are you questioning my professional judgment?" Weston growls back.

I drag my fingers through my hair, then squeeze the bridge of my nose. "No, of course not. I'm sorry I woke you up so late."

There's a pause. "It comes with the territory," Weston finally says. "I can assure you that there's nothing wrong with Zara's health. As for the rest, it's up to her when she chooses to confide in you." He cuts the call.

I stare at my screen, then place my phone down on the table. So, she's all right. There's nothing wrong with her. Yet, she definitely seemed to pale when she rose to her feet too quickly earlier at our impromptu picnic. And then, she got upset when I mentioned Olly. Which was a tactical mistake. But she had to have known I'd have found out about her youngest sibling's death due to an accident when he was three years old.

She was only nineteen when he died, and she left home shortly after. I didn't mean to bring it up, but I wanted to reassure her that whatever's in her background that might be stopping her from considering a future with me, it doesn't matter. I didn't expect her to get so upset when I mentioned Olly. Which, I now realize, is understandable. Losing a sibling, especially one that young, would have been devastating for her. And I brought it up without any consideration for her feelings. After that faux pas on my part, we packed up the remnants of our picnic dinner. I dropped her off at home, made sure she locked her door behind her, and returned to my office, knowing there'd be no sleep for me tonight.

I lean back in my chair and stare at my blank computer screen. Something doesn't compute. Why is she so resistant to a relationship with me? Sure, she's my PR manager and part of my campaign team, but I want to be open about our relationship. Yes, it would bring a whole new level of scrutiny of us. It would mean changing the scope of her role from being only responsible for PR to weighing in on the bigger decisions, by my side. A warmth fills my chest at the thought. She would be perfect. She was made for that role. No, fact is, she was made for bigger things than being campaign manager. By my side, she could impact larger decisions. She could carve out a role for herself, one that complements my political career and which, no doubt, would be much more fulfilling than being a fixer. So, what's stopping her?

I squeeze the bridge of my nose, when my phone buzzes. At the same time, my computer screen springs to life with the ding of an email, then another, and another. My phone buzzes again, then rings. I pick it up, spot Zara's name and answer it at once.

"Everything okay?"

"They found us out, Hunter." Her face fills the screen. "We're all over social media," she cries.

"What?"

"Yes. There's a picture of us—"

"What picture?"

"I'll send you a link." She looks down into the screen, then my phone vibrates. I click through the link she sends me to the news in a tabloid. There's a picture of her and me, shot through a window. It's grainy, but clear enough. There's no mistaking the two faces in profile. Zara is reaching up to wipe something from the corner of my mouth. We're both laughing and looking at each other in a way that leaves no room for doubt. It's a picture of two people who have feelings for each other.

"It's from the breakfast at the diner," I murmur.

She nods grimly. "What are we going to do?"

I rise to my feet. "I'm coming to you."

"No—" she cries out. "I mean, there are already paparazzi pulling up outside my door."

"All the more reason that I be there."

"But—"

"No buts. You stay where you are and—"

"No, you listen to me. I'm the PR professional here—"

"And you're my—"

"My—?" She narrows her gaze. There's something like a dare in her voice.

"You're my everything, Zara. Whatever we have to do, we'll face it together."

Her face crumples. A tear slides down her cheek.

My heart stutters. "No, don't cry, baby. I promise, we'll come out of this."

She sniffs. "I know. I'm the PR professional here, remember?"

"It's okay to lean on me, baby."

She brushes away her tears. "Are you coming here, or are you going to waste time talking to me on the phone?"

I chuckle. "I'm on my way."

"Are you and Zara Chopra together, Minister?"

"What impact will this have on your candidacy?"

"Are you and Ms. Chopra getting married?"

"Minister, how long have you been seeing each other?"

The questions come thick and fast as I shoulder my way through the throngs of reporters. Just as I reach the main door of the apartment building, it slides open. Zara must have been tracking me from upstairs. I take the steps two at a time, then walk down the corridor to her apartment. Before I can press the doorbell, the door swings open.

"Hey." I peruse her features.

"Hey."

I follow her into the apartment; the door snicks shut behind me. She walks to the window and peers through the crack between the drapes. "There's more of them there than there were a few minutes ago."

"How are you holding up?"

She turns to face me. "I expected something like this to happen, just not so quickly."

I take in her pale features. "You look peaked."

"I'm fine," she says and slashes her hand through the air. "We're going to deny it, of course."

"Excuse me?"

She begins to pace. "We'll deny that there's anything going on between us."

"The picture suggests otherwise," I say gently.

"We could say we're friends."

"You're rubbing off a dab of something from the corner of my mouth. It's an intimate picture."

"Fuck." She halts, then locks her elbows at her sides. "Of course, it's an intimate picture. It looks like exactly what it is. The morning after a night spent fucking."

"Two nights, actually."

She turns on me. "Are you even taking this seriously?"

"I'm here, aren't I?"

She crosses the floor, then comes to a stop in front of me. "You don't seem put out by what's happened."

"Should I be?"

"Don't!" She throws up her hand. "Don't give me that. You know this means it ties you and me together. It means, it casts doubts on my talent, on my career, on everything I've worked to achieve."

"All that picture shows is that we are in a relationship. It doesn't take away from your talent because you've already built an outstanding profile as a fixer. You did this before we met. Of course, I'd want to hire you because of your abilities. You're not a newbie. This image doesn't take away from your abilities as a PR consultant at all."

She looks into my face. "This is what you wanted, isn't it? You wanted it to come out that we're together, so you could push me into making an announcement with you. So you could announce to the world that we're getting married. I can just see the headlines." She mimes a rectangle with her fingers. "The love story of the decade." She lowers her hands to her sides. "It's the kind of story that could propel you all the way to Downing Street."

"You have to admit, it's going to thaw the most cynical of hearts. Nothing like a marriage to give you a poll bounce," I admit.

"In fact," —she narrows her gaze— "I wouldn't be surprised if you're the one who leaked the picture."

I try to wipe all expression from my face, but I must be too slow. Her jaw drops. "Oh, my god, it was you. You slipped that picture to the media. And you did it to force my hand."

I shuffle my feet. I could deny it, of course, but it's not my style to hide behind lies. Besides, I don't regret doing it. If this is the only way to get her to marry me, then so be it. Once we're together, I can smooth over everything else. I can take care of her, ensure that she doesn't get too stressed, ensure that she has the kind of career she deserves—one beyond merely being the fixer to becoming the person who makes the news, who has a positive impact on society and the community. She has so much potential, this woman. All she needs is someone to help unlock it for her… And that's what I'm going to do, I'm—

"No." She takes a step back.

"Eh?"

"I'm not doing it. I'm not going to marry you. I'm not going to make a joint announcement with you. I will not be manipulated into a place where you make me feel like I have no options. I always have a choice, and I choose not to fall in line with your plan."

48

Zara

"Oh, my god, Zara, how are you holding up?" Solene's face wears an expression of absolute horror mixed with sympathy. She's the media darling, the upcoming music superstar. Of all my friends, she's the one most likely to understand what it means to be in the eye of a media shitstorm.

"Umm, I'm not sure, actually." I roll my shoulders, where a permanent ache seems to have taken up residence. "I've only ever been on the other side of the scandal. I'm the fixer. I'm not the one who's supposed to be in the eye of the storm."

I glance out the window of my apartment, where I've been holed up the last forty-eight hours. The crowd of paparazzi has only grown since that showdown I had with Hunter. After which, he left without making a statement, which only sent the journalists into a tizzy.

The speculation about our relationship has grown in an exponential fashion. From online blogs and social media, to tabloids, to the broadsheet newspapers, and today, the headlines of the leading financial daily. Everyone is asking if we're together, and if so, what we have to hide since we haven't bothered to address the rumors. One of them asked if I was pregnant. I read that article, then promptly rushed to the bathroom and got sick.

After that, I stopped checking the internet for the latest developments on the story. Instead, I have my team keeping track of the coverage. Abby keeps me up to date, shielding me from the details, but sharing highlights as they unfold, without going into the gory parts. She's only been on the job for a few days, but she's a fast learner. Kate and the rest of my team have warned me that every minute I delay only adds fuel to the conjecture around our relationship. As if I don't know that. It's PR 101 to address the postulations around a theory head on, in order to kill them. If you shut your ears to it and ignore the rumors, they rarely go away. More often than not, they take on a life of their own, which will snowball to affect other areas of our lives. As is happening to Hunter.

The speculation is affecting his ratings, as evidenced in the latest polls. His approval has dropped by five points since the picture of our being together broke. Of course, you could argue that he brought it down on himself. And yet... He did it because he wanted me enough to risk everything. He risked my ire, risked his career, risked so much... Just so he could coerce me into marrying him. Of course, he could have just asked... But when he did, I refused to give him an answer. I still haven't given him an answer. I can't give him an answer, not when there's so much unanswered in my own life.

I glance around my apartment. I need to get out of here. Need to go to the one place where I'll find some peace of mind so I can think. Which means, I need to leave without drawing the attention of the paps. I need a diversion.

I pick up my phone and make a few calls.

"You sure about this?" Isla asks.

"It'll work, won't it?" Abby shuffles her feet nervously.

Only Kate seems completely unruffled by what I proposed. The woman's cool in the face of pressure. Almost as collected as I normally am—when it's a situation that does not have me at the center of it. It's so much easier to take stock of a crisis when you're not the one in the eye of the storm. I'll never underestimate the courage of my clients after this.

I just need perspective on the situation. A chance to get my bearings and feel myself again, and then it will be fine. I trust myself to make the right decision. I simply need a little space to get to that point.

"It will work." I glance between them. "All you have to do is hold them off long enough for me and Isla to slip out the back."

"You sure you want to risk going, today of all days, when there's a good chance you'll be followed?" Isla interjects.

"I need to go there. I need to be there... Just for a little while."

"Okay." She nods.

"Okay." I blow out a breath, then turn to face Abby and Kate. "You guys ready?"

———

In the end, it worked fine. Kate and Abby went out onto the steps of my apartment building and gave a statement—full of sound and fury, signifying nothing. Essentially, it was a holding pattern statement that gave the press some words to embellish but did not cast any light on the situation. Which they knew. And they knew we knew. And the more astute of them weren't happy about it. But everyone went along with the charade, happy to have something with which to fill the pages and posts.

I pulled on a baseball hat and wore glasses, as well as the biggest pair of sweatpants—shudder—that Isla brought for me, along with a sweatshirt and trainers. It was a get-up very unlike what I'd normally wear. It did the trick, though, for we slipped by the lone, enterprising journo who was loitering around the backdoor exit to the building, but who let us pass without glancing. It was only when Isla pulled away in the car that I noticed him give us a second glance, but by then, we were well on our way.

Now, I glance at the squat, gray building she's stopped in front of. The sign on the gate said Presley Academy.

"You good?" she asks for the fifth time since we left home.

"I will be." I turn to her, then lean over and kiss her cheek. "Thanks, Isla."

"Anytime, babe." She shoots me a smile. "You sure you don't want me to wait?"

I shake my head. "I'll call for a ride home."

She scans my features. "So, this is it?"

I nod, then push the door open, and walk into the school.

"Hey Naz," I greet the man behind the reception counter.

"Hey, Zara. You made it!" He flashes me a huge smile.

"Of course, I did." I walk up the corridor, up the steps, and toward the gym on the first floor of the school.

"Zara, glad to see you." Debs, the session coordinator greets me. I place my bag in the classroom next to the gym, then join the rest of the volunteers in the gym.

"We'll be doing warmups, followed by basketball, then a spot of cricket, where we'll be dividing ourselves into two teams. If all goes well, we'll play Duck-Duck-Goose, finish off with the Hokey-Pokey, and then the Parachute Game. If, at any time, you need help in communicating with the athletes, you can use the visual support cards." Debs looks between us. "Remember, coaches, you are role models for the athletes. At the same time, make sure you have fun. Any questions?"

I shake my head, as do the rest. Then I pair up with Samira, my partner coach, and we begin the warmup exercises. Soon, the first child bursts into the gym.

"Jeremy, hello." One of the other coaches approaches the boy, along with his partner and they follow the child as he tears around the gym before making a beeline for the small playpen that's been erected in a corner of the gym with toys that the children can use to entertain themselves during the session.

Tracy, my athlete, soon arrives, and I spend the next hour-and-a-half, along with Samira, playing with her, letting her be when she needs space, coaxing her to join the group activities, which she finally does when we approach the last twenty minutes. Tracy loves Duck-Duck-Goose, and soon, we are all seated, and the children take turns walking around the circle, tapping each player on the head until they finally tap someone and say 'Goose.'

The hair on the back of my neck prickles. I glance up and am almost not surprised to see him standing by the door to the gym.

That's when one of the children decides I'm 'It.' I hurry after the child, but he takes my spot. I slow down, then walk forward until I tap one of the other athletes as 'It.' When I'm seated, I look toward the doors of the gym, which are now shut. He's no longer there. Huh, did I imagine that?

For the final ten minutes of the session, we play the Parachute Game, and the children sprawl on the floor as the adults float the large colorful cloth up and down over them. The kids stare up at the colors.

Some have smiles on their faces. All of them are calmer than when their parents dropped them off earlier. Then we wrap up the game.

The doors to the gym open, and the parents trickle in. Tracy's mom arrives smiling. Tracy jumps up and races toward her. I head for the bench at the side of the gym, pick up Tracy's bag and jacket and hand them over to her mom.

"How was she today?" Tracy's mom asks me.

"She was gold."

"Thank you so much." Tracy's mum clutches at my hand. "What you volunteers do every weekend is a godsend. It gives me some much needed me time where I can catch my breath, knowing she is in good hands."

"Yes, this is the only place my Yacine can be himself and not be judged," another mom nearby agrees.

"It's all thanks to Debs and the team who founded this charity and have kept it going for ten years." I jerk my chin in Debs' direction.

The parents leave with their kids, and we head into the classroom next door.

"Don't forget to fill out the feedback forms before you leave. It helps us in tracking the progress of our athletes." Debs points toward the tablets on the table near the doorway. "Thanks everybody, that was a great session."

Samira and I fill out the feedback form for Tracy. Then I say goodbye to the rest of the volunteers, pick up my bag and retrace my steps to the front door of the school. I step out, and my gaze instantly zooms in on him.

49

———

Hunter

She steps out of the school entrance, and her gaze widens. Her body tightens, then she squares her shoulders and heads in my direction. Her scent teases my nostrils, then she walks past me. I follow her out of the school gates then down the sidewalk until she comes to a coffee shop. She walks inside with me in tow. I take the seat opposite her. She ignores me and scans the menu. When the waitress comes, I order her a chai tea latte and a black coffee for myself.

After the other woman leaves, she narrows her gaze on me. "Is there no part of my life that you don't know about?"

"I didn't know you were volunteering with children with special needs."

She glances away, then locks her fingers in her lap. "How did you find me? Did you bug my phone? Is that how you tracked me down?"

When I don't reply, she jerks her gaze in my direction. She spots the expression on my face and her jaw drops. "No way."

"I had to make sure you were safe."

"What did you think was going to happen to me? We live in a first-world country, or have you forgotten?"

"You forget, you are involved with me. The media attention on me is only going to grow, and it's going to bring all kinds of people out of the woodwork. I had to make sure you were protected at all times, which is why I have eyes on you. As long as you are fine, I can focus on my work."

"I assume you also have security on me?"

I tilt my head.

She draws in a breath, then squeezes the bridge of her nose. "This is so fucked up, Hunter. Have you heard yourself? You're obsessed with me. You're stalking me, and you're possibly the next leader of this country."

I set my jaw. "As long as you are kept from harm, I can focus on other things."

"So, you bug my phone and, I assume, my computer, as well? What about my apartment and my office?"

I raise a shoulder.

Her eyes widen. "You bugged my apartment and my office?"

"I have cameras on you, yes."

She stares at me, then holds up her hand. "You've lost it."

"I have. I can't think. Can't focus on my campaign. Can't sleep at night unless I jerk off to images of you under me. Can't eat unless I recall the taste of your pussy when you come all over my tongue."

Her breath hitches. Her eyes flash.

"I compare every woman I meet to you and find them all wanting. Your grit, your tenacity, and your strength fascinate me. I always knew you had a big, giving heart, and what I saw today only confirmed that I have been right all along. There's no one for me but you, Fire. I'd rather spend my days loving you than spend my time pursuing a calling that feels meaningless unless you are by my side."

Our gazes catch and hold through the interval when the waitress arrives and places our drinks on the table.

"I should resent you for intruding into my life. I should hate you for leaking that photo of us and destroying my reputation. I should" —she bites the inside of her cheek— "abhor you for how you fucked me so hard, you've spoiled me for anyone else, how you manipulated me into a place from which the only way out is to join forces with you, to accept your proposal… And yet, I can't find it in myself to do so." She glances between my eyes. "Why is that, Hunter?"

I hold out my hand, palm face up. "You know why."

She swallows, then places her hand in mine. I weave my fingers with hers, and a sense of rightness grips me. A sense of peace envelops me. A sense of…never wanting to let go of her makes me tighten my hold. She squeezes my hand, and my heart stutters. That iron band around my chest—the one I hadn't been aware of—loosens. I draw in a breath, and the rush of oxygen to my lungs makes my head spin.

"I volunteer at the school, at least once in two weeks. A small local charity runs these sports sessions where they train us volunteers to play games with special needs children."

"Because of Olly?"

She nods. "He had ASD, Autism Spectrum Disorder, and he was the most beautiful little boy I've ever known. I was only sixteen when he was born, and he became my entire life.

"My parents were busy with the shop; Cade was already a budding cricketer with the junior English cricket team and traveling to matches. I spent every spare minute I had with Olly. I was responsible for him. That day" —she blinks rapidly— "that day, I took him to the park to play. But I had just gotten my first phone and couldn't stop messing with it. I took my gaze off of him for a few seconds, and when I looked up, he was gone. I searched for him all over the park, and as I reached the exit, I heard the screech of brakes. I knew it right away. I knew what I would find before I even reached the road. He died in a car accident. He'd dashed out into the path of an oncoming vehicle." She firms her lips. "He never had a chance." She pulls her hand from mine. "But you had me investigated, so you probably already know all of this."

I hesitate. "I knew you had a youngest sibling who died in an accident." A tear rolls down her cheek.

My heart feels like it's going to splinter apart. "Zara, baby, please." I wrap my arm about her, and to my relief, she lets me pull her close.

"It was my fault," she says in a low voice.

"It was an accident."

"I should have been more vigilant." Her chin quivers.

"You were barely an adult yourself."

She opens her eyes and looks up at me. "I was nineteen." She sets her jaw. "I knew my responsibilities and I failed him."

"You've been punishing yourself ever since." I lean in, bring her hand to my mouth and kiss her fingertips. "That's why you work so hard. That's why you're so focused on your career."

"You've spent a lot of time analyzing me, haven't you?" She scowls.

"Obsessed with you, remember?"

Her lips kick up. "And I'm obsessed with you, too."

"I know."

"Damn, but that swollen ego—" she murmurs.

"Is not the only thing that's swollen at the moment."

She scoffs. "Keep it in your pants, buster, especially since we're going out there to face the paps, who've already begun to hover outside the door."

I fold her fingers in mine. "Found us, did they?"

"Took them longer than expected. They must be losing their touch."

"Or you're too smart for them."

"You smooth-talker, you."

"Comes with the territory, baby."

I lean in; so does she. I hold her gaze as I lower my lips to hers. I kiss her softly, slowly, gently, and a sigh wafts from her lips. I begin to tilt my head and deepen the kiss, then stop myself.

"You sure you want to do this now?"

She holds my gaze for a second more, then nods.

"Okay."

"Okay."

I rise to my feet, and she follows me, hand-in-hand, as we head out of the café. We step outside, and the questions hit us.

"Are you two together, Mr. Whittington?"

"Are you marrying Zara, Mr. Whittington?"

"Are you pregnant, Zara?"

"Yes."

I hear her answer, and for a second, it doesn't register. And then, it does. It must take the journalists by surprise, too, because for a second, there's silence. I glance at her, trying to keep all expression from my face, and hoping to god I succeed.

"Congratulations, how many weeks are you along, Zara?"

"Are the two of you already engaged?"

"Where's your ring, Zara?"

"Will you be by Mr. Whittington's side when he campaigns, instead of behind the scenes?"

I squeeze her hand, and she returns the pressure. She's pregnant. With my child. And she didn't think to tell me about it? Is this her way of getting back at me for coercing her into a situation where she has no choice but to marry me? And considering she's pregnant, isn't that best for the child, too? I raise my hand and wait until the journalists quieten.

"Zara and I are together. We haven't set any plans for a wedding. When we do, we'll let you know. That's all I'm going to say right now."

I begin to shoulder my way past the first rows of paps, but she tugs on my arm. I turn to find she hasn't moved from her place. She tips up her chin at me. "I have something to say."

"Now?"

She nods.

I frown, trying to read her features, but unable to understand what that look in her eyes means. When she stays silent, I turn to the journalists and, once more, raise my hand. When they fall silent, I gesture toward Zara. "My soon to-be wife wants to share a few words."

I step back by her side. She squeezes down on my hand. Her fingers are cold once more. A tremor runs down her body. Then she lowers her chin. "I'm sorry, Hunter, but it's best for it to come out all at once."

Before I can ask what she means, she's turned back to the journalists.

"I became pregnant when I was sixteen and lost my son when I was nineteen."

50

———————

Zara

"You didn't trust me enough to tell me about this before you broke it to the media?" Hunter glares at me from across his office.

After I'd ripped open my past and shared it with the press, we were bombarded by questions. Hunter, however, shouldered his way through the throng with me in tow. His security pulled up in a car, and we made a speedy getaway. All through the trip, we neither looked nor spoke to each other. Our phones vibrating off the hook, but by mutual, unspoken consent, neither of us checked our devices. He also did not let go of my hand.

We drew up to his office, and he led me through a path between desks occupied by his team. Most of them were hard at work, regardless of the fact that it was a weekend. That's the nature of an election campaign. There are no 'off' days, not until the poll results are declared —and not even after that, when the real work begins. Most of them, however, fell silent in our wake. No doubt, seeing their leader pull me along with his fingers threaded through mine was enough to make them realize things had changed.

He barked at his assistant to not let anyone in, then he ushered me inside his office, shut the door, and locked it for good measure. Only then, did he let go of my hand. I avoided his table and the chairs around it and walked over to the sofa pushed up against the wall. I sank into it, placed my bag on the seat next to me, and folded my hands in my lap. Now, I watch as he paces back-forth-back on the carpet.

"I thought you already knew," I finally offer.

He turns on me. "Is that the best you can do?"

"It's a reasonable assumption. You had me investigated. You know everything about me, right down to my hot beverage of choice. Of course, I assumed you knew about my past."

"Apparently, my investigators failed to discover the sibling who died was not your sibling but your son."

I wince, then squeezes my eyes shut. "I suppose I should be grateful that the people I hired to wipe out that particular detail of my past came through." I rub my chest. "My son. I gave birth to him, then watched as he was buried. Then wiped out his connection to me. I am a terrible mother."

"You're not, Zara. You are the strongest, bravest person I have ever met."

Heat flushes my cheeks. I lower my hands to my sides then tip up my chin. "You forgot to say I'm a fixer; it's what I do best. What better use of my talent than to fix my past. I covered up the fact that Olly was my child like it was a dirty secret." My heart squeezes in my chest. My guts churn. "I am a terrible person. I wiped out all existence of my own son. What mother does that?"

"You did what you thought was right. You did what it took to survive. You loved your son. It's evident in how you talk about him. You tried your best to take care of him. You're not to blame for what happened to him."

I chuckle. "Don't go making me out to be something I'm not. Have you forgotten that I didn't tell you about Olly? That I broke the news of him to the press without doing you the courtesy of telling you first?"

"Olly was your secret to tell, when you thought it was the right time. And you did it before you lost your nerve." His gaze softens.

There's so much understanding on his face. So much love. So much everything. The pressure behind my eyes builds. My heart feels like it's going to burst. "I... I could have told you first, when we were on our own." I choke out, "I'm a bad person. You deserve better, Hunter."

He leans forward on the balls of his feet. His blue-green eyes turn that stormy shade of green I now know means he's pissed off. And he has reason to be. If I were in his shoes, I'd break off all relations with me right now. I tip up my chin, and the groove between his eyebrows deepens.

He finally says, "I know what you're doing here."

"Oh?"

He nods. "You think because you sprang that surprise on me, and in front of the media, I'm going to call off our relationship. But you're wrong."

I blink. "I… I am?"

He walks over, then squats down in front of me. "You forget how tenacious I am, Fire. I didn't come this far, only to walk away from you over something that happened in your past."

I jut out my chin. "I kept a lot of things from you, Hunter. I didn't tell you I had a child, that I was a teenage mother of a special needs boy who died because I couldn't care for him."

"You did your best."

A tear squeezes out from the corner of my eye. "You have no idea what I did or didn't do."

He leans forward and scoops up the trail of moisture from my cheek. "In all the time I've known you, you've never—not once—shirked your responsibilities." He brings his moist finger to his lips and sucks on his digit, and my heart feels like it's going to burst.

"You take time out to volunteer with children." He holds my gaze.

"It's nothing."

"You give them your time. It's not like you write a check and forget about it. That means something." He takes my hand in his. I try to pull away, but he tightens his hold on me. "You've gone above and beyond the call of duty. I know how you've supported your friends when they've needed you, how you've given your best to each of your clients and helped them through situations which would have caused anyone else to lose their nerve. But not you, Zara. You face each challenge head on and come out on top. I'm proud of you."

The hot sensation behind my eyes intensifies. "I didn't tell you I was pregnant."

"I knew."

My jaw drops, again. The number of times this man has taken me by surprise is almost as many times as I have tried to pull the rug out from under him…and failed. "You mean—?"

"You refused champagne the last two times. Also—"

"The bug in my mobile phone." I slump into the sofa. "Of course, you knew."

"I'm sorry I spoiled your surprise." He quirks his beautiful lips and a slow fire ignites low in my belly.

"I should be the one saying I'm sorry. I should have told you everything—about being pregnant, about Olly. All of it. It's just"—I glance away, then back at him—"it was all too much for me to process. It was such a shock to find out I was pregnant."

He rises to his feet, then sits down next to me. "You should have let me be there for you."

"I've been having morning sickness the last few weeks, so I had a strong suspicion I was pregnant. The test was merely a formality, but seeing that pink line—for the second time in my life—I'm afraid it brought back memories."

He wraps his arm about my shoulders and pulls me close. "I'm sorry you had to go through it alone."

I allow myself to relax against him, muscle by muscle. "I wanted to do it at my own pace. I kept putting off taking a pregnancy test, until I couldn't put it off anymore. And when I saw the positive test this morning, I needed some time to get my head around it all. That's why I knew I had to go to the school and spend time with some of my favorite people."

"The kids."

"The kids," I agree.

We sit quietly for a few more seconds, then I look up at him. "Guess I'm going to marry you after all, huh?"

"Do you want to marry me, Zara?"

"Do you want me to marry you, Hunter?"

He chuckles. "So damn stubborn, but I'm going to wear you down yet." He slides down onto his knee for the second time in our lives, then pulls a ring from his pocket. He holds out his palm, and I place my hand in his. He slips the ring onto my left ring finger. The yellow-gold stone in the center is surrounded by tiny diamonds. I tilt my palm and the light from the window picks up the golden sparks at the heart of the sapphire.

"Fire for my Fire."

"Hunter," I breathe. I'd expected a ring, but this…is beautiful. It's unique, and very much the kind of ring I'd have chosen for myself.

"It's an antique." He rubs his thumb over the shining, golden ball of fire on my finger. "It belonged to my grandmother. She was the one person in my life who truly loved me. She left it for me with instructions to give it to the woman of my dreams. The woman who's my dream, my wish, my fantasy. The woman who's everything I need. You're my hope, my love, my beginning and my end. You're everything I need. I love you more with every breath. You're my reason for living. You give my life meaning. And I want to spend the rest of it giving you and our children" —he places his other palm on my belly— "everything you'll need."

"Hunter." I swallow. There's so much I want to say, but my brain cells seem unable to bridge the connections needed to form the words. "Hunter." Another tear slides down my cheek, and this time, he leans in and kisses it away.

"Marry me, Zara. Marry me, and I'll stand beside you through the years. Although I'll make mistakes, I'll never break your heart. I promise to make you so happy that the only tears you cry will be happy ones. Marry me because I'd rather have one kiss from your lips, one touch of your fingers on mine, one brush of your hair on my skin, hear your heartbeat against mine, than spend any time away from you. Marry me—"

"Yes." I press my lips to his. "Yes."

51

Hunter

"Minister, have you and Zara set a date for the wedding?" The journalist asks.

We're in the small conservatory attached to my townhouse in Primrose Hill. We agreed the best way forward was to hold a press conference to which we'd invite a select number of news people.

We drew up a list of those who we knew would be sympathetic to our cause, as well as those we knew would have tougher questions. It was Zara's idea to do that. She also said it would be best to hold the press conference in a location that was personal. It would mellow the media and make them feel like they were our guests, rather than adversaries. I suggested the gazebo attached to my living room, and she agreed. I was delighted. It meant she'd be on my turf, in my house, even though she hasn't yet agreed to move in with me. Something I'm working on. This, I'm sure, will give me a head start in convincing her.

I left it in her capable hands to manage the entire event. She's still the Head of Communications for my campaign. In addition, she's also my partner. After I proposed to her the second time, and she accepted, we ended up kissing and making out, right there in my office—again. The best use I've put my desk to in all the time I've had it.

When we emerged from my office, my entire team clapped. They'd seen the clips from the impromptu catch-up with the journalists at the entrance to the café, followed by me hauling Zara to my office, and had come to their own conclusions. Then there was the ring she was wearing. The ring that announces to the world she belongs to me. That she's mine, under my protection, joined to me, and that I'm never letting go of her. So, it's clear to everyone that we're together.

Now, I turn to my fiancée, who's seated on the chair next to me. "That's for Zara to decide."

The journalists' gazes swing in her direction.

"Given that I like dropping surprises on the minister—"

A titter runs through the group.

"I would only be conforming to my tendency to shock and awe him by saying that I have, indeed, set a date."

Everyone holds their breath. I watch her with pride.

This woman—she could rule the world if she wanted. Yet she's chosen to rule my world, instead. Every day, I thank the powers responsible for making our paths cross. She makes it all worthwhile. She gives me purpose. She's the thread through my thoughts. The rhythm to my walk. The cadence to my words. The color in my dreams. The only reality worth living in. She…belongs to me and that makes me the luckiest man in the world.

"Hunter?"

I blink, realizing she's looking at me. "Whatever you want," I murmur.

"So, you're okay if we get married right now?"

I blink. "Now?"

"We have our attendees" —she nods toward the assembled journalists— "and as for friends…" She smiles at someone past me. I turn my head to find Liam and Isla entering the gazebo from the side door. They also seem to have brought along their dog—a Great Dane who strains at the leash held by Liam.

Behind them are Sinclair and Summer, then Michael and Karma. Weston and Amelie—both of whom confessed to me and Zara that they'd set us up, and who couldn't be more delighted at how things turned out— wave at us.

Behind them are JJ & Lena and Saint & Victoria.

Bringing up the rear is Cade Kingston, on his own. His gaze is fixed on something—or someone—on the other side of the podium. I follow his line of sight to find Abby scowling at Cade. She tilts her chin. Then, in a deliberate snub, turns her back on him. She leans in to speak to one of her fellow team members, Steve, I think. I glance back to find Cade's brow is thunderous. His jaw tics, and he seems to be having a hard time controlling himself. He takes a couple of steps forward, but just then, Lena turns to say something to him. He tears his gaze off of Abby and replies to Lena. A new face, one I've not seen in many months, walks into the room behind Cade.

"Is that—"

"Edward Chase, one of the Seven," Zara confirms.

"What's he doing back in the country?" The last I'd heard from Sinclair, Edward had renounced the priesthood, and left to travel the world.

"He happened to be visiting, and considering I decided only this morning that we should get married today, it seemed like a sign to ask him to officiate the wedding."

"He's no longer a priest."

"He can still marry us," she points out.

"And as soon as I can arrange it, we're going to the registry office to get our marriage validated."

Her lips curve. "Not taking any chances, are you?"

"Not gonna stop until you're mine in every possible way."

Her golden eyes spark. The pulse at the base of her throat beats faster. I lean in closer, and so does she. Our breaths fuse. I lower my head until my eyelashes brush against hers.

Someone clears their throat. I glance up to find Abby glancing between us. "Uh, we're ready for the both of you."

Zara frowns. "I hadn't planned on anything else."

"But I have." I rise to my feet and hold out my hand. "You're not the only one who can pull surprises, Fire."

She looks taken aback, then chuckles. "I wouldn't have expected anything else from you."

We walk out of the gazebo and into the garden.

"Oh, wow!" She takes in the heaters that have been placed at strategic locations around the lawns. Chairs have been placed in rows, with an aisle in the center. It leads to an arch made of pampas grass, with yellow and purple flowers dotted at intervals.

"When did you do all this?"

"Technically, it's Abby and your team who helped set it up." I nod my thanks at Abby, who clasps her hands together. "I hope you like it."

Kate walks over to join us. "And if you don't, too bad; it's the best we could do in the little time we had while you guys were in the press conference."

"Oh, shush!" Steve draws abreast on the other side of Abby. "We had a fun time doing it, didn't we?"

Kate rolls her eyes. "If you say so. But it's for your wedding, Zara. Never thought we'd see the day, by the way—but since you are planning to be married, I'd say choosing the person who could be the leader of the country is a damn good move."

Zara chuckles. "Thanks, Kate."

The journalists begin to pour out onto the lawns; Abby, Kate, Casey and Steve guide them to the chairs. Our friends take their seats in the front row, and Edward walks around to wait for us at the top of the aisle.

I take Zara's hands in mine and bring them to my lips. "See you on the other side."

52

Zara

Had I really thought I could pull another surprise on my man and get away with it? He's known as the sharpest politician of our times for a reason. All along, I thought I was a step ahead of him, but he's outwitted me at every turn. He bugged my phone and my computer, placed cameras in my apartment and office—and I hadn't been aware of any of it. Sure, I got back at him by springing the surprise of my past to the press, and revealing I was pregnant. But he'd already guessed I was.

He proposed to me, and I accepted.

Once more, he's gotten ahead of me. He guessed I had something up my sleeve when I agreed to have the press conference at his place. He roped in my entire team to help with the arrangements for the wedding. Good thing I have this last chance to catch him off guard.

I nod toward Abby, who walks over to Cade. She engages him in conversation. He frowns as she gestures in Hunter's direction. Finally, with reluctance writ in every angle of his body, he follows her to where Hunter is speaking with Edward. The four huddle in conversation. I step back, and head inside, toward the guest room at the end of the corridor. I step in and, shutting the door behind me, I walk over to where my dress is laid out on the bed. It's a simple white sheath created by an up-and-coming British-Asian designer. Someone whose career I've been following with great interest and whose designs I love. I strip off my pantsuit and step into the dress. As I slide the sleeves over my shoulders, the door opens.

"Am I too late?" Abby bursts in and comes to a halt behind me.

"You're just in time."

She zips me up. I step into the white-satin stilettos, by the same designer. I pat my hair, which I put up earlier this morning, then place the one-tier vintage style veil on my head. Abby helps me fasten it. I draw the netting down over my eyes, then freshen up my makeup.

"How do I look?" I glance at my reflection in the mirror.

"Gorgeous. You look both sexy and understated. Hunter is a lucky man."

"I think we're both lucky we found each other." I meet her gaze in the mirror. "Not to mention, it's a miracle we made it to the altar without killing each other."

"I think you're both going to be very happy," she says in a soft voice.

"As you will be, if you and my brother decide to look past your differences."

"Eh?" She blinks rapidly. "There's nothing like that between us." She waves her hand in the air. "Also, he's my brother's best friend. No way, can we get together."

"Hmm." I decide not to push the point. Each of us has a journey to get through to find our HEA, and given how Hunter and I put each other through the wringer... Well, I'm not sure I'm the best person to give her advice. Still, I can't help but say, "Anytime you want to talk, I'm here, and not just as your boss."

She seems taken aback, then nods. "When I first met you, I thought you were a scary figure. Now, I realize that under all that woman-of-the-world persona, you have a soft heart. You take care of your friends and your team. I'm lucky you took me under your wing."

"Don't count your blessings yet. We have a lot of hard work to be done for the upcoming campaign."

"I look forward to it." She hands me my bouquet. "But first, we have a wedding to attend."

"Zara, you look—" Cade shakes his head. For once, my cocky, smartass brother seems to be at a loss for words. "You look absolutely gorgeous." He leans forward and kisses me on my cheek. "I'm sorry Mum and Dad chose not to attend."

I raise a shoulder, trying to pass it off, but in truth, it did hurt that, once again, my parents chose the shop over me. You'd think their daughter's wedding would be more important than keeping the store open, but apparently, not.

"They did message me to say I'm most welcome to visit and bring my new husband with me," I murmur.

"That's something, huh?" He tucks my hand through the crook of his arm. "It's not that they don't love you."

"They just weren't happy about me becoming a teenage mother, and then turning my back on the legal profession to pursue what I love."

"They did support you, though. They were ready to adopt Olly as their own."

"Not that I'd have allowed it." I shift my weight from foot to foot. "You're right, though. When all is said and done, they didn't disown me. They were there for me when I most needed them. They're just not happy with my life choices, that's all."

"Will you go visit them with Hunter?" Cade asks.

"When he's won the election and becomes Prime Minister. He'll probably be good enough for them as a son-in-law then."

We both laugh.

Footsteps sound. Abby reaches us. "We're ready for you." She ignores Cade and addresses her remark to me.

"Thanks, Abby."

She nods, then turns and leaves. Cade watches her go with a frown on his forehead.

"What's that all about?" I nod in her direction. "Something up with the two of you?"

"Nothing's up between us. My best friend, Knight, is her brother. Trust me, he'd be more than pissed off if there was anything between me and Abby."

"When has that ever stopped you?" I scan his features. "Or wait. Maybe you actually feel something for this girl. Is that why you prefer to trade smoldering glances with her than act on what you're feeling?"

"Smoldering glances?" He shakes his head. "Just because you're in love doesn't mean the entire world has to follow suit."

"Aha!" I smile smugly "So you are falling for her?"

"Eh, no, of course not. I don't intend to be romantically involved with anyone, anytime soon."

"Famous last words." I pat his hand. "I'll remind you of it when you're standing in my position."

"I don't think my tastes tend toward white, gowns."

I laugh. "You know what I mean."

"I'm not getting married. Not for a long, long time. And speaking of" —he turns toward the doorway leading to the lawns— "you don't want to be late for your wedding."

53

Hunter

The crowd quietens. The hair on the back of my neck prickles. I turn to find her stepping onto the aisle, and my breath catches. Goddamn, she's a vision. A goddess come to life. I'm not sure how she managed to change outfits so quickly, but all of her efforts are worth it. The white gown covers her shoulders then dips slightly to hint at her cleavage. The fabric nips in at her waist then flares over her spectacular hips, before dropping down to her toes. The lace outlines her arms, and her gorgeous skin peeks through the netting. As Cade escorts her up the aisle, she's breathtaking, sublime, exquisite. And I'm the luckiest man on this planet.

They reach me. Cade kisses Zara's cheek, shakes my hand, then places her hand in mine. I kiss her fingertips, and the crowd oohs and aahs. Zara smiles up at me. I lower our arms, then both of us turn toward Edward.

He glances between us and a smile tips up his lips. I see his lips move and must make the appropriate response, as does Zara. Then, I'm turning to face her again. I pull the platinum band from my pocket and slide it onto her finger next to her engagement ring.

She does the same.

"Guess we both had the same idea, hmm?" I smirk.

She laughs. "Seems we're finally on the same page."

"Does this mean you're going to stop your verbal sparring?" I step closer; so does she.

"What do you think?" she murmurs.

"I think" —I wrap my arm about her waist and pull her into me— "that you'll never stop keeping me on my toes, and I wouldn't have it any other way."

She looks up into my eyes. Her golden eyes lighten until they resemble pools of sunlight. "I love you, husband."

My heart fills my chest. Warmth pulses through my veins. I pull her closer, then dip my head until my lips brush hers. "I love you more than myself. I promise to respect our differences. I swear I'll put you and our family before anything else."

Her chin trembles. "Your country needs you, too."

"And I promise to serve with passion and dedication and do more than my best to steer the course of our future."

"You make me proud." She tips up her chin, and I close my mouth over hers. I kiss her deeply. She parts her lips, and I sweep my tongue over hers. I suck on her mouth, until a moan spills from her lips, until she sways into me, until she melts in my arms, and I pull her even closer into my chest. I kiss her and kiss her until, finally, the sound of clapping reaches me. Then I soften the kiss, brush my lips once, twice over hers, before I pull back. Her chest rises and falls, her skin flushed. Her breathing is ragged, and when she finally flutters her eyelids open, her eyes are more silver than gold.

"That was some kiss." She clears her throat.

"A promise. A pledge. My allegiance to you and my child you carry in your belly."

She swallows. "You're going to make me cry."

"Only as long as they are tears of joy." I cup her face. "I love you, Zara."

A chair crashes to the ground, then, "Tiny!" a woman's voice yells. We look up to find the Great Dane has broken free from Isla's grasp. He's galloping toward where the drinks are being poured at a table halfway up the garden.

"Tiny!" Isla lifts her skirts and races after him. "Tiny, stop."

The man pouring the champagne into the glass pauses midway. Then

Tiny leaps onto the table, which crashes under his weight. The man jumps back. The bottle falls from his hands. Tiny snatches it out of the air, tips it upside down, and into his mouth.

"Tiny, you're a bad boy!" Isla grabs the bottle and tugs it from Tiny's jaws. Liam reaches her and seizes Tiny's collar.

"Did that dog neck a bottle of champagne?" Edward asks in a dazed tone.

Zara and I share a laugh. I turn to Edward. "We have much to catch you up on."

***

"Does that Great Dane have a taste for champagne or am I seeing things?" Edward looks from Isla to Liam.

"It's her mother's dog." Liam raises his hands. As if that explains everything.

"We're baby-sitting him, while my mother is on a trip with her knitting club." Isla explains.

"And he has a fondness for bubbles?" Edward asks in a disbelieving voice.

"From the very first time we opened a champagne bottle in front of him. And it doesn't seem to hurt him, at all." Isla raises a shoulder. "Occasionally, he has a hangover, which is when my mother gets really upset with him."

"He's so cute, though." Abby bends and hugs the Great Dane. Liam's tied Tiny's leash to his chair, and for now, at least, the dog sits on his haunches watching the humans with a long-suffering look on his face.

"He's a darling, except when he's in proximity to champagne," Isla agrees.

"Not that I'm encouraging him or anything, but he can have my share, considering I'm not drinking," my wife announces.

"Oh, my god, I totally forgot to congratulate you." Solene, leans over and hugs Zara.

From across the table, Declan watches Solene with a frown on his face. The two turned up separately to the wedding, have not exchanged a word since, and are seated at opposite ends of the table. Interesting. Not that it's my business. Still, now that I'm married, I can't help but wish the same for my friend.

"I'm so excited for you." Isla flashes my wife a smile. "Marriage and a baby, back-to-back. Who'd have thought you'd beat me to the baby side of things?"

"Umm, it was an accident," Zara mutters.

"But one I'm really excited about," I interject.

Isla straightens, then glances between us. "It's going to be good for the polls as well, right?"

Zara and I look at each other. "It can't hurt," Zara says finally.

"Actually, the coverage has been very positive." Abby waves her phone in the air. "I didn't want to bother either of you, since this is, technically, still your wedding, but the press has lapped it up. There are already gushing accounts of the wedding and the upcoming baby. And the latest polls see elevated approval ratings for Mr. Whittington."

"Call me Hunter."

Abby flushes a little. "Yes sir, Mr. Hunter."

"Just Hunter."

"That's what I meant. Your idea of a surprise wedding with the press invited to it is a hit. Of course, some of them are complaining that they'd have liked to have been told beforehand so they could have dressed accordingly, but other than that, it's one big love fest."

"It's a good way to start our honeymoon, huh?" I tuck a strand of hair behind my wife's ear. *My wife.* How did I get so lucky?

"Our working honeymoon," Zara raises her sparkling juice to her lips and takes a sip. "You still have a campaign to run."

"You're going to keep me on the straight and narrow, hmm?"

"You know that's impossible. You have a mind of your own, baby. All I'm trying to do is give you options. I know you'll always make up your own mind, but it's not going to stop me from sharing my viewpoint."

I take her hand in mine and kiss her knuckles. "I want you to actively campaign with me. I want you to talk about the causes that are dear to you. I want you to head up a fund that supports the needs of the women, the vulnerable, and children with special needs."

Her features soften. "Are you sure about that?"

"More than anything in the world."

I lean in to kiss her, when someone clears their throat. I look up to find Abby standing next to us. She darts a half-smile in Zara's direction. "Uh, I guess I'm going back to the office."

"You're going back now?" Zara frowns.

"The campaign is still underway, and there's a lot of follow up to be done from the coverage generated by the wedding. It's best to do that now, while interest is high on what the two of you are going to do next. I thought I might—uh— draft a strategy to share with you."

"A strategy?" Zara lowers her chin.

Abby nods. "If that's okay? If you don't mind, I mean—"

"I think it's a great idea."

Abby's features lighten. "You do?"

"Absolutely. I" —she looks at me— "*we'd* be happy to hear your thoughts on how to leverage the publicity for the campaign."

"Absolutely," I agree.

"Oh, great." Abby pulls out a phone from the pocket of her pants. "Let me call for a car pick up."

"There's no need for that, I can drop you." Cade rises from his place on the other side of the table.

"What? No." Abby jerks her chin in his direction. "I mean, you must have had a lot of champagne to drink, so surely, you can't drive."

"I've been nursing water." Cade raises his glass of water in her direction. "I'm in training, so no alcohol."

"Oh—" Abby glances to the left, then the right. "But you must be busy."

"I have nothing on for the rest of the day." He smirks.

"Surely, you have something better to do than drive me to the office."

"Actually, I can't think of anything better than playing chauffeur."

54

Eight months later

Zara

"I promise to serve the country with integrity, humility and compassion. I promise to do my best for my country and for you who voted me in. I will deliver on the promises I made to you during my election campaign." The newly elected Prime Minister of the country, who also happens to be my husband, glances about the crowd. "There will be challenges, of course, but I am not daunted. I hope to live up to the demands of my office and deliver on the trust you have placed in me. I stand here before you, ready to lead our country into the future. To put your needs above politics. Together, we can achieve incredible things. We will create a future worthy of the sacrifices so many have made, and fill tomorrow, and every day thereafter, with hope. Thank you."

He moves away from the podium and holds out his hand. I walk over to him, balancing the weight of my swollen belly.

It's been eight months to the day we got married.

Eight months, during which time, I worked side by side with him, campaigning across the country. I continued on as the Head of his PR strategy, until the day he won the elections. At which point, I sold my PR agency to Kate. It was a difficult decision, but the right one. No one knows more than me how all-consuming taking on the leadership role of this country will be. Being married to the Prime Minister means any client I took on would come under a lot of scrutiny. And while I wouldn't be doing anything wrong in holding down a separate job, it could present a conflict of interest with the office my husband holds. So, I decided to make a clean break and embrace my role as the First Lady of the country. I also accepted Hunter's offer of launching a project aimed at looking after the interests of women, the vulnerable, and children with additional needs. That's my passion, and it feels right to use my energy to help those who are weaker.

And all the time we were on the campaign trail, the child I carry in my belly has grown. By now, I'm massive. I should hate just how big I am, but every time I see my stomach, I feel this huge rush of tenderness. This big gush of love that makes my heart swell until I'm sure it's bigger than my stomach.

I promised him I'd hold out until after he was sworn in. Now, as we pose for pictures, he has one arm around me, and the other over my belly. Our wedding and my pregnancy raised a lot of media speculation, but the voters embraced us. Many of the journalists lauded my courage for coming forward with my teen pregnancy and subsequent loss. Of course, there were those who called me unfit to be the wife of the future leader of the country, but overall, the feedback was supportive. Most of the media were excited about our child, and from the time I first made my appearance at Hunter's side, I've been inundated with good wishes.

I'd like to think our child has brought in a rush of good fortune for us, one that paved the way for Hunter to take on the responsibility of being the leader of the country. I smile and wave at the journalists calling to us to pose for them. This goes on for too many minutes. I'd managed to squeeze my swollen feet into heels, and now I'm regretting it.

Sensing my discomfort, Hunter gives a final nod toward the news people. Then, he scoops me up in his arms. Instantly, flashlights go off behind us as the journalists rush to capture the moment.

"Whoa, Hunter, what are you doing?" I gasp.

"Carrying my wife over the threshold, of course." He walks inside 10 Downing Street, and his aides come forward to greet us.

Heat flushes my cheeks and I turn my face into his shoulder. "I think you should put me down now," I say in a muffled tone.

"When I'm ready."

"Hunter, please." I half-laugh, then glance up at him. "Why am I not surprised by your over-the-top gesture?"

"Because you love me?" He smirks.

"That I do, Mr. Prime Minister, so very much."

His features soften. He bends and captures my lips. The kiss is soft and sweet, and firm, and so very hot. I lean into it, open my mouth, and he nips on my lower lip. He deepens the kiss, and that familiar weakness invades my limbs.

Someone clears their throat, and I stiffen. Hunter kisses me for a few seconds more. By the time he raises his head, I'm flushed and my breathing is erratic.

He surveys my features, then nods. "You going to be okay?"

"I'm more than okay as long as I have you by my side."

"You have me baby, always and forever. I love you so very much." He kisses my forehead, then lowers me to my feet.

I take a step back, then nod toward his team. "Go on, your country needs you."

"You always come first, Fire." He searches my features. "You sure you're going to be okay?"

A twinge tugs on my lower belly. I resist the urge to rub my stomach, then nod. "You know I am."

"Hmph." He holds my gaze for a second longer, then bends and kisses me on the lips again, before turning to speak to the assembled people.

I fall back to watch as they line up to speak with him. He shakes each person's hand, giving them his full attention. The full impact of those magnetic blue-green eyes that change with his moods. The country may have his attention now, but I'll have his attention always. I'll have to share him with the world for as long as he's Prime Minister, and probably longer, since he's going to be in some form of public service for most of his life; but I have no doubt, he'll always place me and our family first.

Another spasm squeezes my belly, this time, with enough force that I gasp. I glance around, but no one has noticed me. For once, it pays not to be the center of attention. Hunter is probably the only one I wouldn't begrudge that. After all, I got into PR not only because I like building up the media profile of my clients, but also because I'm an attention whore. The most satisfying time of my life was the last few months, not only because I got to spend so much time with Hunter on the campaign trail, but also because there was a personal connection to the work I was doing. Of course, I gave my best to every client, but with Hunter, I put everything of myself into the PR for his campaign.

I wanted him...needed him to win. I had gotten to know the man behind the public facade, and it was clear to me he would do his best for the country. He has the vision for a future that he will try his best to make happen. More than that, he's genuine and loyal and wanted to use his intelligence and everything he has at his disposal to create a better future for the newer generation.

Sure, he comes from a moneyed background, but it is precisely that which made him selfless. For so long, I held his money and his privilege against him. I judged him, and by doing so, I was guilty of the same kind of mistake that I've berated others for when they've tried to pigeonhole me. I can't be put into a neat category, and neither can Hunter. We're both complex individuals, with many facets to our personalities. Our backgrounds are only one of them.

Now, I realize I was too quick to form an opinion of him when we first met, but Hunter has completely overthrown any preconceived notions I might have had about him. I know now that he's the most tender, most possessive, most protective man I'll ever meet. I also know he's willing to cross the line between right and wrong to take care of me. Perhaps that should bother me, but somehow, I can't hold it against him. The shades of grey to his personality only make him so much more interesting. Am I worried that it will spill over into his professional life? No, because it's only me who brings out that part of his personality.

A third stab of pain cramps the entire lower half of my stomach. The pain is so hard, it's as if I've been buffeted by a wave. I gasp and bend over. Simultaneously, liquid gushes out from between my legs and pools about my feet. I glance down at my now-drenched skirt in horror. I look up to find Hunter has turned toward me. He takes in my stance, and the way I'm gripping my sides. I straighten, draw in a deep breath. In two bounds, he reaches me and sweeps me up in his arms, again.

"Hunter, what are you doing? You'll dirty your suit."

"Fuck that, I'm taking you to the hospital."

To say the next few hours were dramatic would be putting it mildly. He asked for the Prime Ministerial car—a massive Jaguar Sentinel—to be brought around the rear entrance. He placed me in the back seat, followed me in, and ordered the driver to take us to hospital. The security vehicle in front flipped on its siren, and I knew we were being followed by another vehicle. Two other members of his protection team on bikes flanked us, and we reached the hospital in under ten minutes.

He insisted on carrying me out of the car and into the emergency room, where we were instantly waved through. He held onto me until the doctors insisted he place me on a bed so they could examine me. They pronounced I was six centimeters dilated, and that we had time for the baby to come. That was ten hours ago.

I've spent the time alternating between the agony of the labor pains and the times in between when I've gathered my energy for the next push. And through it all, he's held my hand, fed me ice chips, and wiped the sweat from my forehead. He didn't even blink when I cursed him soundly for putting me in this position.

Karma and Summer, followed by Isla and Abby, popped their heads around to let me know they were waiting with me. I told them to go home—it could be hours still, before the baby was born—but they refused. My brother's away on another cricket tour, but Abby mentioned she messaged him, and he's on his way back.

I glance at Hunter's face as he sprawls back in the chair next to my bed.

"You should go get a coffee."

"Not a chance," he growls.

"It could be some more time before—" I wince.

He leans forward, concern in his eyes. "You okay?"

I breathe through that now familiar pain traveling up my spine. Only this time, it builds and builds until it's like a wall that's pushing into me, shoving into me, cutting through me. I gasp, and must scream; perhaps, even black out a little. When I open my eyes, Hunter's features are pale. The shadows under his eyes are pronounced, and there's a drop of blood on his lower lip. "You hurt yourself, did you bite down on your lip?"

He opens his mouth, then closes it. "I'm never putting you through this again." His voice is hoarse.

"Famous last words." I laugh, then gasp again when the pain begins to build once more. "Oh, no, no, no, that's too close."

His gaze widens. He reaches for the switch next to the bed. "I'm calling the midwife."

"He's gorgeous." Hunter's warm voice cocoons me like a balm.

After he called the midwife, it took another three hours for the baby to emerge screaming into the world. I was shattered, numb, and shell-shocked. My entire body feels like it was put through a concrete mixer. My insides felt like they were torn out…which, in a way, they were, I suppose. And then, the midwife placed the baby over my chest.

I touch his little nose, take in his eyelashes, the little snub nose, those pink lips, and I fall head-over-heels in love… For the third time in my life. I hold him, and a tsunami of love fills every fiber of my being. I miss Olly so much. He would have loved his younger brother.

I've been given a second chance with this little boy, and I'm going to do everything in my power not to screw it up. The tears slide out of the corners of my eyes. I'm unable to stop them as I gaze at my son. Hunter wraps his arm about me and pulls me into his chest, and that only makes me sob more. Then, the baby opens his eyes and looks at me; my breath catches in my chest, and I nearly swoon. Blue-green eyes. Hunter's eyes look back at me, and I fall for my husband and my son all over again.

When the doctor places my son at my breast for his first feeding, he latches onto my breast with only a little coaxing. The sensation of him suckling at my breast brings forth a fresh round of tears. Hunter holds me until the sobs subside, and my son falls asleep while feeding. I carefully wipe his mouth, pull my hospital gown shut, and both of us stare at the wonder we created.

A buzzing sound fills the room. Hunter ignores it. It stops, then starts again. "I think you should get that," I murmur.

"If I do, it means I'll have to go back to my responsibilities." His eyebrows draw down.

"You can't keep putting it off." I shoot him a sideways glance. His hair is mussed, his shirt creased. A day's growth of stubble shadows his cheeks. He looks crumpled and tired, and so damn delicious.

"You're beautiful, Mr. Prime Minister."

He chuckles. "You, calling me by that name, in that husky voice of yours, might become my new ki— thing," he corrects himself.

"Glad to see you're managing to hold back your four-letter words."

The buzzing of his phone fills the room again. "You really need to get that, Hunter."

"I never should have turned on my phone, is what I should have done." He peers into my face. "I'll never forget what you did for me, for our family. You are the bravest, most courageous person I've ever met. I'm honored you became my wife. I thank the powers that be for the day our paths crossed. If I'm born again, Fire, I hope you'll do the honor of being my wife in that life, and in all our future life's together."

Tears prick the backs of my eyes. I swallow down the lump of emotion that squeezes my throat. "Stop, you're going to make me cry again."

"Don't cry, baby. This is your time to be happy." He leans in and kisses my forehead.

"Oh, hope I'm not interrupting?"

We glance up to find Abby lurking in the doorway of the room. "I could come back." She turns as if to leave.

"You're not interrupting." Hunter rises to his feet. "Actually, I'd be reassured if you kept Zara company while I make a few calls."

With a last glance at me, he prowls out.

"Come on in." I gesture to the girl. She walks over with a big bunch of flowers that she places on a table already overflowing with bouquets and toys. "Wow, this room smells like a garden," she exclaims.

"All of the Seven and their wives have sent me flowers and toys for the baby," I murmur.

"You mean the Seven who run the 7A company—"

"Yes, and the Sovranos."

Her gaze widens. "The Sovranos, as in, the Italian Mafia?"

"As in the Cosa Nostra," I nod.

Her eyes grow even bigger. "Aren't they criminals, of sorts?" she whispers.

"Doesn't everyone have skeletons in their closet?" I retort.

She flushes a little, glances away, then back at me. Huh? That was a guilty look, if ever there was one.

"You're not good at hiding your thoughts, are you?"

Her cheeks grow brighter, if that's possible. "It's the curse of having such fair skin."

"Or a pure mind." I half-smile. "It's okay to be innocent. In fact, it's preferable one retains a core of innocence at heart. Just don't be naive when it comes to making decisions, okay?"

She nods. "Thanks, Zara, I really appreciate you taking me under your wing."

"You've more than pulled your weight over the past few months on the campaign. Without your efforts, my husband couldn't have been elected Prime Minister."

She hunches her shoulders. "Th-thank you so much."

"Raise your chin."

"Eh?" She blinks.

"Raise your chin, girl, and accept the praise. Own it like a mother—ducking—fitch." I stumble over my words. Guess Hunter's not the only one who has to watch his language around the little ears.

Abby laughs. Then peeks down at the little bundle in my arms. "He's sooo small."

"He didn't feel that small when I pushed him out of my va—a—ah—ina. You know what I mean?"

"Jesus, that's too much information," a new voice declares.

I glance up to see my brother inside the doorway. His familiar features wear an unfamiliar, uncomfortable expression.

"You're perfectly aware of how the birthing process takes place," I scold him.

"Yes, but so far, births and anything to do with them have only been a concept. Just like the fact you're a mother now is something I'm still getting my head around."

He walks over to stand on the side of the bed opposite Abby. In his hands, he's holding one pink and one blue balloon, which say 'baby boy' and 'baby girl,' respectively.

"Covering all my bases," he explains to me, then glances down at the baby. "Wow, you really are a mom."

"And you're an uncle."

Cade's face lights up. He thrusts out his chest, pulls back his shoulders, and folds his arms across his chest. "I can't wait to teach him how to play cricket."

"Would you like to hold him first?"

Cade looks alarmed. "Me?"

"Yes, you."

"Umm. He's too fragile. Maybe when he's a little older?" Then he takes a step back to punctuate his words. The balloons flutter above him. "I guess I should tie these somewhere?" He pivots and crosses the room to one of the chairs, then ties them to the back. Apparently, it's going to take my brother a little longer to be completely comfortable with the idea of holding his nephew.

"Oh, now I realize what's wrong, the pink says baby boy," Abby explains.

"I'm aware." Cade spins around, then walks back to take his place on the side of the bed opposite her; this time, putting more distance between the bed and himself.

"Shouldn't it… I mean… Shouldn't it be the other way around…?" Abby chews on her lower lip, and I notice my brother's shoulders tense. His gaze is fixed on her mouth, and there's a look of something I can only define as lust in his eyes. Talk about TMI.

I clear my throat, and my brother seems to snap out of his reverie.

"Who am I coming to visit, hmm?" He addresses his question to Abby.

"You're coming to visit Zara." She frowns.

"Who is…?"

"Your sister?" she replies hesitantly.

"And?"

"Uh, she's very much a feminist, a strong woman, ah—" Her brow clears. "I get it now. You were making a statement that you knew she'd approve of."

My brother smirks. "You're smarter than you look."

Abby's lips firms. "And you're not as dumb as you look, either."

My brother blinks. "Dumb? Did you just call me dumb?"

"You know what they say, when you have a good-looking face, chances are good, there's nothing between the ears."

Cade's jaw hangs open, then he chuckles. "Very good."

"You talk as if you didn't think I could hold my own in a conversation." Abby huffs.

"Oh, I'm sure you can. If not, my sister wouldn't have hired you."

"I took her on because Abby showed a lot of potential. In fact—"I turn to Abby. "I see something of me in you."

Abby's features light up. "You do?"

I nod. "You have the same hunger, the need to prove yourself. That thirst for success that pushes you to try harder, to go that extra mile—"

"Which is why I think you'll be perfect for the role of my new Communications Manager," Cade steps in smoothly.

Abby jerks her chin in his direction. "Wh-what do you mean?"

"I need help managing my social media profiles, as well as my PR, and you heard my sister, you're among the best on her team. So, I've decided you can come work for me."

Abby stiffens. She folds her arms across her chest, mirroring Cade's earlier body language. "And if I refuse?"

To find out what happens next read Cade and Abby's story in The Agreement, HERE

Turn the page to read The Pretend Christmas Bride, Edward & Mira's story in which Edward gets his HEA

THE PRETEND CHRISTMAS BRIDE

L. STEELE

For the g00d girls who
love a morally grey man
who'll t1e y0u up and
worship y0u like
the goddess y0u are!

Because you asked,
here's a count of relevant words:
The 'F' word = 96 times
The 'p' word = 55 times

*No of times he calls her "**my wife**" = **87 times***
No of pages with groveling = 50!!!!

Chapters with sp1cy scenes
Ch. 23, 25, 26, 29, 30, 31, 32, 33, 35, 36,
37, 40, 41, 48, 49, 50, 51, 52, 53, 55

SPOTIFY PLAYLIST

Pray - Jaden Hossler *(L. Steele's note: I see this as Edward's anthem)*

Jealous Guy - The Weekend *(L. Steele's note: This... this song... is everything Edward feels for Mira)*

All the Good Girls Go to Hell - Billie Eilish

Ceilings - Lizzy McAlpine

Maria Maria – Santana ft. The Product G&B *(look up the Fabio Rodrigues cover too)*

Wake Me Up When September Ends - Green Day

New Year's Day - Taylor Swift

Old Money - Lana Del Ray

Lithium – Evanescence

Somebody Else - The 1975

Something in the Way – Nirvana

Sleeping Beauty Waltz – Tchaikovsky

Angels & Demons – Jaden Hossler

Whispers – Invadable Harmony

Fallen Angel – TIX

SUN SIGNS

Edward Chase - Scorpio

You are deep, emotional, and loyal.
>You are single-minded in achieving your goals.
>You can be painfully honest and obvious in your intentions.
>You can be mistrustful, possessive, controlling and jealous.
>You are aggressive when looking for vengeance.

Mirabelle 'Mira' Young - Pisces

You are a hopeless romantic.
>You are kind, intuitive, and very giving.
>You experience intense emotions in the heat of the moment.
>You are creative and imaginative.
>You have a big heart and respect honesty.

1

Mira

"You're with child?" I yelp, then flush when everyone at my friend Gio's wedding turns to stare at me. We're at the bookshop her husband gifted her, because that's where Gio wanted to hold the ceremony. And the brew of choice? Coffee. Also, there are cupcakes, because what else do you need when you're a smuthead getting married in your favorite space? Talk about marriage goals. Tiny, the Great Dane, who's currently being dog-sat by one of Gio's friends, parks himself next to me. He looks at me with melting eyes, and I swear, he has the only sympathetic gaze in the house.

I tighten my grip on the mug of coffee in my hand, flash a smile at Gio, and say, "I mean, *you're going to have a baby*!" I take a step forward and stumble across Tiny's flag-like tail. *Oof!* The cup goes flying from my hand, and the contents spill over a man standing nearby. The cup bounces off his chest and hits the ground, then spins away.

"What the —?" He glances down at the coffee stain he's wearing across the front of the tailor-made jacket which, by the way, molds his shoulders while his pants cling to his powerful thighs.

My heart stutters. My pulse booms at my temples. I draw in a sharp breath, and under the bitter whiff of coffee is the sharp tang of something more complex, something spicy and savory and so laced with that tingle of electricity, it arrows straight to my center. My toes curl, and goosebumps pepper my skin. I glance up and into his face, and tawny-brown eyes blaze at me. The anger in them cuts through the noise in my head. I flinch, take in the mess that was once what I'm relatively certain is his ten-thousand dollar three-piece suit. I should know the price; it's the world of privilege I come from, too. Which indicates he can afford another with ease. But to see the loathing in his features, you'd think otherwise. I manage to get a hold of myself and gasp, "Oh god, I'm so sorry."

I remove the scarf from around my neck and dab at his suit lapel, then at his thigh then—*stay away from his crotch. Not his crotch*—I brush my scarf over the impressive packet between his legs. His thigh muscles bunch. Anger vibrates off of his big body, and I flinch, retrieving my arm.

"Am I always such a klutz? I'm not. Do I often ask questions of myself aloud and reply to them? Only when I'm nervous." I chuckle, making sure to keep my eyes averted. "What comes first, though? Being nervous leads me to being a klutz? Or does being a klutz make me nervous? Or maybe one leads to the other in an endless feedback loop." I nod. "Yep, that's what happened. Which is why I tripped over Tiny's tail. But Tiny didn't mean to cause the accident, did you?" I look down at Tiny.

The dog woofs, then head-butts me. The momentum causes me to tumble forward. The man catches me around the waist. I look up, and this time, when our gazes meet, gold fire sparks in his eyes. A lick of fire, a whip of mahogany, a sheen of amber—all polished to a burnished, searing flame that could burn you on contact. The air between us seems to ignite, drawing in all the oxygen in the room. I try to breathe, but my lungs protest. I sway, and his hold on my waist tightens. His jaw hardens. The sharp contours of his cheekbones lend a stark, almost cruel quality to his features. I've never met this man before, but I've heard about him from Gio. Edward, that's his name, and he's a former priest. He walked away from the church and embraced a life in pursuit of money—or so I heard from the girls—not that I tend to gossip. Okay, maybe a little.

When you don't have a choice in your future, you take pleasure in the little things in life. And gossip happens to be one of those treats I refuse to deprive myself of. Besides, I want to know why he walked away from what was, surely, his calling. It takes strength of conviction to become a priest, but to then leave it behind? Why would he do that? On that count, my girlfriends were mum. It's his story to tell, they said. Which led me to speculate, it had to have been because of a woman. Did he break up with the church to be with her? Though, from what I've heard, he's single. So, does he still think of her? And why is my mind racing at a million miles an hour? Why are my palms sweating, my stomach twisting and turning? Why is my heart banging into my chest like thunder crackling across the skies before a storm?

A heavy weight pins me in place. I can't move. Can't speak. Caught up in the tractor beam of this man's gaze, I'm a butterfly trapped in a bell jar. Then Tiny woofs, and both of us jump back from each other.

"Sorry, sorry, oh my god, I am so sorry." I wave my hands in the air. "And I sound like I'm a broken record, stuck on repeat. You do know what I mean by a record, right?" I peer up at him. "Of course, you do." I take in the threads of grey at his temple. "You're older than me—not dinosaur age, but close to it. I mean you're not Santa Claus old. No way I'd mistake you for him though, given your build is much more streamlined. Not to mention, your whiskers are jet black. Although, this time of the year is the most wonderful time, don't you think?" I beam at him because… *Who doesn't love Christmas?*

"I hate Christmas," he snaps.

This guy, apparently. Just my luck. Of all the men I could have spilled my coffee on, it had to be the grumpiest, growliest, meanest…sexiest looking man I've ever met.

His diamond-hard jaw grows more rigid. A nerve throbs at his temple. Fish on a tricycle, it should frighten me, but honestly, he's too yummy-looking. He can glower at me any time. He can fix me with those intense golden eyes and make my panties melt with his smoldering gaze.

The tension coiled in his muscles thickens the air between us. I swallow around the ball of lust in my throat and attempt a smile. "Just so you know, I didn't mean to imply you're ancient. I mean, you're, what, twenty years older than me?"

He scowls.

"Okay, fifteen, at least." I cough. "Not that I don't like older men. I have a soft spot for them." I shuffle my feet. "No, no, not that kind of soft spot. I find older men much more confident. You know what you want, and don't hesitate to get it. You guys have your shit together, you know?"

His scowl deepens.

"I don't mean I find you attractive. Not that you're not good-looking. You have that whole tall, dark, and intense look going on, which I admit, is a turn on. Not that *you* turn me on."

The blood drains from my face.

"Oh my god, I didn't mean to say that. Also, whoa—you'll have to dry-clean your suit. I'll pay for it, of course."

Utter silence follows my proclamation. Even Tiny is quiet. Guess I shouldn't have offered to pay? Maybe, I should have kept quiet. But his demeanor is daunting. Why is he standing there, silent, except for his body language, which screams his displeasure? A muscle works above his jaw. If he grinds his teeth any harder, he's going to crack a molar or two. Why is he so annoyed? It was an honest mistake, after all. "At least the coffee was decaf," I offer.

Someone titters— then turns it into a cough. Someone else chuckles, then manages to stifle it. But the man in front of me stays silent. His shoulders are bunched, and the tendons of his neck stand out in relief. He might as well be carved out of stone but for the rise and fall of his impressive chest.

I shuffle my feet. "You're not saying anything. Why aren't you saying anything? Are you pissed-off? Oh god, you're pissed-off. I'm sorry, you make me nervous. Can you tell? Haha, I tend to fill the silence when the person I'm talking to stays quiet. I do like to talk; ask anyone. The only time I clam up is in church, because it would be rude to talk while the—" *don't say priest, don't say priest*—"priest," *oops*—"is talking…"

I had *not* meant to say that out aloud. *No shit, Mira. Why did you think of the P-word in his presence? You know you have no filter between your brain and your mouth, or where he's concerned, between that space between your thighs and your mouth. No, don't think of how moist you are down there. Not right now.*

Edward's shoulders swell. The tendons of his throat are so pronounced, he's beginning to resemble the Hulk. Only his face is utterly emotionless, which is, frankly, terrifying. I gulp. At my side, I sense Gio trying to smother her laugh, but I don't dare look at her. I draw in a ragged breath and want to turn and run out of there. But one thing I'm not is a coward.

It's why I didn't run out on my family, either. That would have hurt them too much. Instead, I bargained with them—a few months of freedom in exchange for returning to the fold. Helplessness squeezes my chest. Any day now, I'll get the call and have to go back home, to the arranged marriage that will follow. Until then—I can live life the way I want.

I found work at a preschool, made enough to rent my own apartment, and everything was going well. Until it went out of business. But I'm going to find another job soon. I'm not going to give up and go back home. Not until my father calls for me. I have the strength to face my uncertain future, knowing I won't have control for much of it. But this, here? In this moment, I hold the power.

I straighten my spine. "I didn't mean to talk about your past. I was warned not to. Not that I'm a gossip—" I pause. "Okay, maybe a little." I hold up my thumb and forefinger. "And only because gossip is good for you. It helps to de-stress. And you look like it would help if you were to relax. I'll bet you keep it all locked up inside. Which makes you a prime candidate for a coronary. Not that it's any of my business. It's your heart, after all."

"Heart?" he asks in a dark voice.

"The organ that beats in our chests? On the other hand, looking at your grim-faced countenance, I'm guessing you don't have one." I squeeze my eyes shut. "I've crossed the line, haven't I?"

When I look at him again, his expression veers between fascination, disgust, and anger.

"Okay, that's it. I will not speak anymore. I'll wipe you down and be on my way." I lean forward, then brush my scarf over the lower part of his jacket which covers his crotch. And again. His thigh-muscles coil. The fabric of his pants stretches until I'm sure they're going to pop at the seam. I sense his gaze boring into the top of my bent head, but I don't dare look up.

"You done?" he finally growls through gritted teeth. And his voice—it's gravelly and hard, and carries the promise of all the delicious, unforgivable things he could do to me. And I want him to.

I swallow around the ball of emotion in my throat. "It's not getting any better, is it?" I ask in small voice. "No, it's not. Am I making it worse? Of course, I am." I slowly tip up my head and meet his gaze. "Can I make it up to you?"

His lips thin, he looks ready to bite my head off, then a cunning look comes into his eyes.

"How are you at obeying orders?"

2

———

Mira

"Orders?" I blink slowly. "What kind of orders?"

Not the kind you read in your smutty books. Definitely can't be those kinds of orders.

The skin around his eyes tightens. "What are smutty books?" he rumbles. My nerve-endings spark. Oh my god, that caramel-velvet voice of his brushes up against my skin, and every cell in my body seems to come alive. *Also, no, no, no, did I say the S-word aloud?*

"I meant, slutty books." I cover my face with my hands. "I said that aloud, as well, didn't I?"

I peek through the gaps in my fingers in time to see him nodding slowly. He doesn't say a word, though. He merely glares at me like I'm a puzzle to solve, or maybe, an annoyance, or an irritant, or a pest he'd prefer to swat away.

The silence stretches. Our gazes catch. The air between us crackles with awareness. The fine hairs on the back of my neck rise. A heavy feeling pushes down on my chest. I swallow, and my throat feels like it's lined with sharp glass. *What's happening to me?*

"Do you always say whatever comes into your mind?" he asks in a voice that's both detached and curious, in the way a scientist might be while observing an animal in the wild.

I frown. "Of course, not." I wave a hand in the air, striving for casual. "Only when I'm nervous. Not that I'm nervous now. And do you make me nervous? Of course, not."

"Also a liar." He drags his thumb under his lower lip, and my gaze is drawn to his mouth. Gorgeous mouth. Hard mouth. A mean upper lip that hints at his authoritarian nature. That puffy lower lip that might signify his pursuit of pleasure. A hedonist. A savage. A fiend. He's all of them. Does that make him a heartless monster? Or a merciless lover? One who seeks gratification, but not in an instant way. This man would wait months…years, if needed. This man would pursue what he wants with a singular focus. And oh, to be at the receiving end of that intensity.

What I'm facing now is a tiny insight into how it would be if he were to get fixated on me. I shake my head. Fixated? I don't want that. Not at all. I don't know this man. All I know is the passing reference to him within the circle of my girlfriends, whose husbands he's a friend of. I've never seen him with a woman, though.

"I've never seen you with a woman." *What the —!* "Did I say that out loud?" I ask weakly.

His features harden until they look like they could be carved from a diamond-hard material, whatever that's called.

"Oh, shit," Gio says in a soft voice from behind me.

Indeed.

"Umm, sorry? Did I say something wrong? Of course, I did. But why is it wrong? I have no idea. No one has ever seen me with a man before today, either. So, it's not odd not to be seen with someone of the opposite sex. By the same token, it's allowed for a woman to have friends who are men and a man is allowed to have woman friends. Besides, you're no longer a priest, so…" I swallow, for he's leaned forward on the balls of his feet.

It's a slight movement, but it brings him close enough for his spicy scent to crash over me. A tingle of electricity runs up my spine. It's as if I've been bathed in a cloud of aphrodisiacs—oh wait, those are his pheromones! A-n-d my stupid stomach goes into free fall. "Sooo, what I'm trying to say is, it doesn't matter if you have women friends. Or girlfriends. Or ladyloves, as they called it in the regency era. I mean, you look stuffy enough to belong in an historical romance. All you need is a ruffled shirt..." I hum thoughtfully. "Yep, a white ruffled shirt, which would stand out against your skin and be the perfect foil to your cut-glass cheekbones. Does that mean you're good-looking? Of course, not. I mean, if you smiled a little more... Now—"

"Smile?" he asks in that dark, dangerous voice, and that swirling sensation in my belly intensifies. My toes curl. Goosebumps pop on my skin.

"Smile," I say in a dazed voice. "You know, when the sides of your mouth curve up because your sense of humor is tickled, or when you feel the urge to show your appreciation of a situation, like this." I project my most confident, school-picture-day smile. "Not that either of those have crossed your mind for a decade."

"How do you know that?" he asks in a curious voice.

"Oh, b-b-b-because your lips have been set in a firm line since I saw you earlier. And there's this wrinkle between your eyebrows which seems to have been etched in permanently, and then the frown-lines that radiate out from the corners of your eyes, which are, no doubt, because you're old—er,"—I cough—"older and distinguished. Anyway, you have that dark-cloud-brewing-over-your-head look that only adds to your charm. From far away. I mean, it's understandable you don't have a girl-friend or any significant woman in your life. You look like you're angry at the world, and there's an internal war going on inside, and you're all scowling and brooding and menacing. Which is all fine in a smu—I mean, romance novel. But in real life, no one wants to be around a man who's an alphahole."

"Alphahole?" He says the word as if he's trying it on for size, and it fits. Speaking of fits, from the looks of it, he'd need an XL condom, given the size of the resting-package at his crotch. A-n-d, my gaze slides downward. It...it's bigger than what it was earlier, so the tent under that coffee-stained fabric is... because he's aroused? Am I thinking in ques-tions? That's a first. That's how rattled I am in his presence.

Tiny woofs. I jerk my chin up to find this tempting package of yum is looking at me with a glint in his eyes.

"Was I caught in the act?" When he only raises an eyebrow, I continue, unabated. That's me, I keep digging that hole. "I was. So what?" I tip up my chin. "A man can stare at a woman's chest, but a woman can't ogle a man's package?"

One of my girlfriends—Summer?—gasps, before turning it into a cough.

"Hear, hear," Gio calls out.

Someone else titters, then the sound cuts off.

I don't dare look around the room, though. Can't take my gaze off those tawny eyes of his—burnished gold, glistening copper, hard like topaz gemstones. They could sear me, look right through me to decipher my secrets. They could turn soft like melted butter which… is not me. He's an unfeeling brute, a vicious beast. The devil incarnate. The kind of man who'd be all wrong for me.

Besides, I don't like him. I don't like the fact I can't read him. I prefer someone who's open and honest with his feelings, who can be sensitive to my needs. This man… He'd break me down, then leave me. I'd be better off keeping my distance from him.

"Oh, look at the time." I raise my hand and pretend to gasp at my empty wrist—*no, I don't wear a watch, but so what? It's the intent behind my gesture that counts, right?* "I need to be someplace else, somewhere urgent. Nice meeting you, Mr. Former-Priest who shares his name with the man whose side I was not on in Twilight."

I turn to leave, when he drawls, "Team Jacob, are you?"

I pause, then scowl at him over my shoulder. "Is that a problem for you?"

"Is it for you?" he shoots back.

"Of course, not."

"Good." He nods with satisfaction. "Remember, you asked how you could make things up to me?"

I nod slowly.

"Come work for me."

My jaw drops. "You're kidding."

"Am I?" His eyes glint.

My heart crashes into my rib cage. This is a joke—him asking me to work for him. Only, it doesn't feel like that. His harsh features indicate he has not one funny bone in his gorgeous, sexy, chiseled out of granite, body. And to have him as my boss? This brooding, unfriendly, severe man, this…dark, handsome in an uncompromising manner man, who'd relish ordering me around, is not something I want. Of course, not.

"Of course, you are." I turn to face him. "You don't know me. You have no idea of my qualifications. Why would you want me to work for you?"

When the expression on his face doesn't change, I swallow, spare a glance around the room, and find no one willing to meet my eyes.

"You *are* joking?" I ask in a small voice.

He tilts his head. "What I am, is offering you a job."

"A-a job?" I manage to choke out.

"I assume you need one?"

"What makes you think—" I shut up because there's a knowing look on his features. *What gave it away?* I'm still a plus-size woman. Never mind, I've been surviving on dry ramen for the last week, ever since the preschool went bust. My body shows no signs of losing these stupid curves. Good thing Gio had already moved out of the apartment when I lost my job. There's no way I would have wanted to bother her with my problems or allowed her to buy my food. And I know she would have insisted. It's not that I don't want to burden her, because I know money isn't an issue for her and Rick, but I'm too ashamed to admit I need help. I need to do this on my own. But what hurts the most is not being able to see the kids I used to take care of.

Between my aching heart and my empty stomach, I've only managed to make it to two interviews, both for jobs I didn't get. I'm running out of options. And there's no way, I'm calling up my family. My stepmother and half-sisters would be only too happy to tell me, again, I'm a failure. I had enough of that when I lived with them. I am not subjecting myself to that misery again. So yeah, I need a job.

He sees the expression on my face, and a flash of satisfaction colors his before he schools his features back into a mask. He reaches into his suit pocket and pulls out a card before handing it to me. "Be at my office, eight a.m. Monday morning."

3

———————

Edward

"You think she'll turn up?" Sinclair spots me as I bench press twice my body's weight. My chest squeezes down, my shoulders scream in protest, my biceps threaten to tear apart, but I ignore it. Breathe through it. In and out.

"She will."

"And if she doesn't?" He assists me as I push the barbell up and over my head.

"She will," I grunt.

"There's a chance she won't."

"If she doesn't, there are more fish in the sea, but she will." I lower the weight down to my chest, hold, then he assists me as I hoist the barbell up again. The tendons on my throat strain, and my triceps feel like they are being shredded. I push the barbell up and hold. And hold. Sweat runs down my temples, between my pecs. My stomach muscles harden, my thighs contract. I push my feet into the floor and brace. Brace. *You need to bear the weight. Bear the mistakes of your past. Bear how you were abandoned by your parents when you needed them most. Bear how she decided you were not the one.* Not that I blame her. Baron would be—has been—a better husband for her. And now, they have a child. A family. Moisture trickles out from the corners of my eyes, joining the beads of sweat on my face.

"You okay, mate?" Sinclair murmurs.

"Why wouldn't I be?" I begin to lower the barbell down, and he doesn't let go. He helps me as I push up and through the pain again. *Work through it. Keep riding it. At some point, you'll find the calm in the center of the storm.* At some point, I'll figure out my life's purpose.

It's the only reason I took the meeting with my grandfather. My father's father, who I never met before. Never even knew existed. Imagine my surprise when he called me and introduced himself. My father never spoke about him.

After the incident, the communication with my parents broke down. They were at a loss for how to deal with what had happened to me. And I took refuge in whatever helped me find oblivion from the emotional pain I was carrying—am still carrying—inside.

I almost hung up, but he pleaded with me to meet him. Just once. Ten minutes of my time. I finally agreed because, why not?

Being the General Manager of the London Ice Kings has given me some focus. Working with Rick Mitchell, the captain of the team, we steered the team to victory in the League. From being the underdogs to one of the highest paid teams in the world, and in one season. It was unheard of. I'd accepted the position as a favor to Knight, the owner of the team. But in working toward a greater goal, I discovered some measure of satisfaction. You can take the priest out of the church, but you can't take the need to help people from him. It's also the reason I agreed to my grandfather's request.

"You've been through a lot in the past week." Sinclair helps me ease the bar onto the rack. I draw in a breath, feel my heart thunder in my chest, and the blood pounds in my ears, drowning out all thoughts for a few seconds. It's the main reason I work out. Pushing my body in a way I can't push my mind. Controlling how much I can lift in a manner I never can control my thinking.

All those restraints, the limitations I imposed on myself. I lived my life according to the directives of the Church. Found some modicum of peace in the routine, the daily prayers, the sermons... All the while, knowing the storm brewing inside me would break loose, and ignoring the warning signs. Until it did. I sinned, and punished myself by leaving the house of God.

Unmoored, I left everything behind. I travelled until I managed to ground myself. And by the time I returned? It was too late. She had turned to Baron. And they were—they are—happy together. And me?

The empty shell that constitutes me, Edward Chase, lives from moment-to-moment, not quite sure what I wanted out of life. I feel un-needed, unwanted, useless to everyone, even myself. Maybe, that's why I grasped onto Grandfather's ask. Maybe, I could be of help to someone, after all.

I don't need a shrink to tell me I'm going about this all wrong. I don't need a shrink to tell me the person I see when I look in the mirror is not the person I was. Or the person I want to be. I don't need my friends to point out I'm on a one-way trip to a crisis again. Hell, I'm living from one crisis to another internally. Every minute I get through without doing something I'll regret is a win. As is the deal I made with my grandfather. It gives me a reason to…keep going.

I sit up, then reach for my bottle of water and chug from it. I lower it and raise a shoulder. "I'll live."

"For how long?" he asks softly.

"For however long it takes, I assume."

He searches my features. "I'm worried about you."

I bark out a laugh. "Since when did you start going soft?" I raise a hand. "Forget I said that. All six of you are married, and most of you with kids… Who'd have thought?"

His mouth curves in a smile, the kind I never thought I'd see on Sinclair fucking Sterling's face. The meaner they are, the harder they fall, apparently. The seven of us are united by an incident that changed our lives forever. And each of my friends went through their journey and found their soulmates. That's not my path, and that's okay. I'm happy they're happy. All of them. Including Baron. He makes her happy, and in her happiness is mine.

"Speaking of,"—he tilts his head—"what time is your girl coming to the office?"

"Not my girl, merely a—"

"Cog in the wheel?" His smile grows sly. "A piece in the puzzle. A—"

"Stepping stone to my larger plan? Yes," I say dryly.

"Hmm." He snatches up a bottle of water, twists open the cap and chugs from it.

"The fuck does that mean?"

"Nothing. Why should it mean something?"

I frown. "No, of course not, but if you have something to say—"

He caps the bottle, then wipes his hand over his face. When he lowers his arm, his eyes gleam. "It would be lost on you. Ergo, you need to learn your lessons yourself."

"Thanks. And to think, I'm the one who gave the sermons."

"You know what they say? Even a doctor needs another when he's unwell."

I lower my eyebrows. "Are you saying—"

"Nothing. You do you, Ed. Find your way. I have every confidence that you will."

I snort. "What-fucking-ever."

He laughs. "The classic rejoinder of a man who's at a loss for words. Also,"—he nods toward the clock on the wall—"you need to rush if you don't want to be late."

I *am* late but not for the meeting with her. I left instructions with my HR manager to get her settled in. I'm on my way to a much more important meeting. When I walk into the conference room adjoining my new office, the five men in the room turn to glare at me. Once again, I'm the outsider, but I prefer it this way. They're brothers. Some of their blood runs through me, but I've never met them before today.

"Knox." I jerk my chin toward the man standing in the far corner. The sunlight streaming in casts his face in shadows. The other four are at strategic positions around the conference room. None of them are seated. And I'm sure their locations weren't chosen by chance. These five are united in a way that tells me I am the opposition. The enemy. The one who came in from the cold to take over their business. The one chosen by their grandfather to take over as the CEO of their company.

"Edward." Knox tips up his chin. "Or should I call you Priest?"

There's a challenge in his tone—one I don't rise to. I've come across enough men who've decided it's best to go on the offensive when they're backed into a corner, as my half-brothers, no doubt, are at this moment.

"I prefer Priest."

"Yet, you left the church?" This from Ryot who's standing closest to me.

"Funny how you only value something when you don't have it anymore," I murmur.

"Like your girl who's not your girl anymore?" Tyler, the brother standing on the other side of the table drawls.

Anger squeezes my guts. My pulse begins to race. "Better than not knowing your child was not your own."

The moment the words are out of my mouth, I regret it. I raise my hands.

"Sorry, that was a low blow."

Tyler's jaw tics. A nerve pops at his temple. He folds his fingers into fists and takes a few steps forward, as if he's about to jump over the table and hit me.

But the brother standing near him—Connor—moves forward and touches his shoulder. Tyler seems about to shake it off, but the other man says, "Don't. Arthur won't be happy if you fuck up this meeting."

Arthur. So they do refer to our grandfather by his first name? He's the chairperson of the company, so it stands to reason it's easier for all concerned to call him by his name at work, and he asked me to do so the one and only time we met. But I'd have thought when they were among family, they'd refer to him as Grandpa? Or Grandad? Not that he looks like either of those.

Tyler lowers his arms to his sides but continues to glower at me.

The fifth man who, so far, stands in one corner of the room reading, looks around, then snaps his book shut and walks over to the table. From my research, I know that Brody is the quietest of the five, and the one I know the least about. He keeps to himself and does not participate in the day-to-day running of the company. The only reason he's here is because Arthur asked him to come.

Brody pulls out a chair, and seats himself. The rest of the brothers look at him, their expressions ranging from anger to frustration. All of their gazes are tinged with stubbornness. Do I really want to take over the company and deal with their egos, not to mention, the roadblocks they'll put up to obstruct any plans I want to execute?

If it's a challenge I'm looking for, being the GM of the London Ice Kings provides me plenty—or rather, did provide me plenty—right until the time they won the League, and on their first attempt. I played a role by helping to put the team together, but the glory belongs to the players. And they won the championship.

I have the option to continue as GM, but I'm ready to hand that off. I paved the way for someone else to take over and build on the founda-tion I set up. That's me. I prefer to do the hard work, the dirty work, the work that requires the most obstacles to be overcome. And once that's done, I move on.

The only time I stayed consistent was when I was part of the church. The routine, the discipline, and the regulations ensured I could focus on the only thing which mattered—my devotion to the Lord. And then I left it behind, and with it, my ability to have a focal point in my life. I hoped being the GM of the Ice Kings would provide me with that anchor, and it did. Briefly. But something was missing. The position always felt temporary. I loved building something with the team, but like I said, something was missing. Something I hope I'll find as the CEO of the Davenport group of companies.

It's why I accepted Arthur's offer to take over this role. The fact that it means working with my half-siblings is something I've both been looking forward to, while also dreading it.

It's not every day a man finds out he has an entire biological family he never knew anything about. Turns out, my biological father and my mother had an affair, and when she broke things off with him, she didn't realize she was pregnant. By the time she did, she was married to my adoptive father, his older brother.

My biological father went on to marry and father my half-brothers.

My adoptive father, who is technically my uncle, fell out with his family, changed his surname to his mother's maiden name, and never spoke to them again.

But when Arthur found out about my existence he wanted me to rejoin the family business. He also wants to groom me to become his heir.

Now, I glance about at the faces of my half-brothers, then pull out the chair at the head of the table and drop into it. The men stiffen. None of them move for a few seconds. Then, Knox steps forward into the light. I take in the scars on his face as he crosses over to the chair at the other end of the table.

He sits down, and once his brothers follow suit, he leans forward in his seat. "You have something to tell us?"

4

———————

Mira

"He had nothing to say to you?" Gio scowls up at me from the screen of my phone.

I shake my head. "I didn't see the man the entire day."

She taps her finger to her cheek. "Maybe he was busy? He is the CEO of the company."

"And he asked me to get to his office for eight a.m., which I did, but he wasn't there. He palmed me off to his HR manager who onboarded me. She also told me one of my roles, get this, is to ensure his favorite coffee is stocked, as well as his sparkling water."

"So he did instruct someone to show you around?"

I pop a shoulder. "There was no reason to ask me to report for eight a.m. if he wasn't going to be around."

"But the office hours are from eight a.m. to five p.m.?"

"Eight a.m. to eight p.m." I grimace.

"He's a workaholic." She shrugs.

"I don't want to work for him."

"So don't."

"Don't think I have a choice. I need this job."

"Join me. I've resumed PR for The London Ice Kings. Also, the bookshops are booming. I need someone who can help manage the workload."

"I don't know anything about PR," I protest.

"You don't know anything about being an assistant."

"How difficult can it be? I have experience taking care of three-year-olds. Surely, pandering to the needs of a CEO can't be as challenging?"

"You have a point." Gio pushes the hair back from her face.

Since she married Rick, she's taken to wearing her hair down. She also seems less stressed; there are no wrinkles on her forehead. She's glowing with health and seems a lot more relaxed. "Most men, in my opinion, don't develop beyond being five years old anyway. You need to treat them like they're children. Humor them, but also don't hold back the truth from them. You have to be upfront, but also selective, when necessary. It's a fine balance."

I chuckle. "Is that how you manage Rick?"

"Now, there are always exceptions to the rule. Rick was one of them. Nothing I said or did could sway the man, stubborn as he is. He's one of the only men I've met who's so secure in himself, he wasn't threatened by my self-confidence. That's what made me hate him, at first, but also intrigued me enough to find out more about him."

There's a soft smile on her face. Almost as if talking about him has conjured him, I hear Rick's voice in the background.

"Do you have to go?" I ask.

"Not until you tell me what you're going to do next."

"Not much I can do. It's noon, and I'm stuck here behind this assistant's desk. I have a ton of emails which have landed in my inbox. I've tried to reply the best I can, but without his direction, I'm not sure how much further I can go, and—"

A baby's shriek breaks the silence of the office.

Gio frowns. "Was that—"

"A child, yes." I glance around the floor. This is the executive floor, so it's only the senior management who are here, along with their various assistants behind desks similar to mine. And no one seems to be bothered by what I've heard. Maybe, it's from someone's computer or phone? But it didn't seem that way and—there's another cry, and this time, the sound doesn't stop. And yet, nobody else on the floor seems to be reacting.

"I need to find out what's happening. I'll talk to you later, Gio." I disconnect before she can protest, then rise to my feet, pocket my phone, and walk in the direction of the crying child. As I pass each cubicle, I find people glued to their computer screens. Many are wearing earphones; others are typing into their tablets. No one seems curious about the child's crying. I pass an empty conference room, then a few offices with more executives staring at their screens. Gosh, this place is as cold and severe as my new boss. I reach the end of the floor and peek into the last cubicle to find the HR manager, the one who inducted me, changing a baby's diaper on her desk. The kid begins to cry in earnest.

"Not a fan of her diaper being changed, huh?"

Adela, the HR manager, shakes her head. "She hates it. I had to bring her in because the babysitter called in sick. I was hoping she'd sleep for most of the day, but clearly, I didn't think things through."

Just then, the baby flings out her leg and hits a pen holder which crashes to the floor.

"Andrea, no. Stay still. It's almost over, I promise." She manages to remove the used diaper, folds it and looks around for a place to deposit it.

"Here, give it to me." I grab it from her and head to the restroom that's in the hallway behind the cubicle.

I'm back in a few minutes and find Adela has finished changing Andrea's nappy, but the kid is still crying. She presses the child into her shoulder and rubs circles over her back. "There now, hush, baby. Everything is fine. You're fine."

The infant cries louder.

A man pops his head around the adjoining cubicle. "Keep it down. We're trying to work here. Also, you shouldn't have brought the kid here. You know this is a child-free zone."

"You think she had a choice?" I scowl at him.

He looks me up and down. "You're new, I take it?"

"I'm Edward's Chase's new assistant."

"Well, I'd say good luck, but it's not going to help where Priest is concerned. As for you"—he turns to Adela—"I hope you have your CV brushed up. You're going to need it."

I open my mouth to tell him off when a hard voice interrupts, "Ms. Young, am I paying you so you can waste your time babysitting?"

5

Edward

"Firstly, any time spent baby-sitting is not a waste. Babies are our future and take priority over anything else." She plants her hands on her hips. "Secondly, you haven't yet paid me, and thirdly—"

The baby's wails rise to a crescendo.

"—you're scaring the little mite."

With that, she flounces toward my HR manager and holds out her arms. The other woman hesitates; the baby screams louder.

Someone pops his head out of his room, while another woman looks over her cubicle. Both notice me and retreat without a peep. In the week since I've taken over as CEO of the company, my reputation has been cemented as someone not to be messed with. Except for this sprite of a woman who turns her back on me.

My HR manager hands over the baby to my new assistant. She rocks the kid, soothes it, but the child only cries louder. She pats the little one's back but the infant screams.

"Oh, for heaven's sake." I stalk over to her and hold out my arms. "Hand over the kid."

She gapes at me. "You?"

My HR manager looks at me with an expression of shock.

"I was a priest. I know how to calm a child," I say through gritted teeth.

The infant solves the problem by jumping into my chest. I hold the kid close, then rub ever widening circles over her back. Her crying slows down, turns into hiccups, then stops. The baby draws in a deep breath, and her eyelids flicker down. I smooth down the wisps of soft curls on her head, then rock her for a few more seconds, before I hand her over to my HR manager.

"Thank you," she whispers.

I nod, then turn to my assistant, in time to catch the dreamy expression on her face. Hold a child in your arms, and every woman in the vicinity takes it as a sign you're ready to procreate. Something I've sworn off. "Ms. Young, don't keep me waiting again," I snap.

She blinks then straightens her spine, "I'm the one who's been *waiting*. I came in at eight a.m., as instructed, but you weren't here." She smooths her hand down the skirt she's wearing. One which clings to her curves and outlines her full figure. Her hips are the most enticing I have ever seen. As for her thick thighs which stretch the fabric of her skirt? I'd do anything to squeeze them apart and—I stiffen, then curl my fingers into fists at my sides. She wore that skirt on purpose, knowing how tempting she'd come across in it. She squeezed into it, knowing exactly the effect it'd have on me. But I'm not going to give into my base instincts. I will not be distracted from my goal of becoming the CEO of this company. I resisted my impulses when I was a priest. Surely, I can do the same now?

"I've done what I could with your email inbox, but I need some direction." She sets her jaw. "And I couldn't stand by while the baby cried. Also, I had my phone with me so you could have contacted me anytime." She pulls out the device and waves it around.

I arch an eyebrow at her, and she blinks rapidly. "Surely, you didn't expect me to stand by while Adela needed help with her child."

"Speaking of"—I turn to my HR manager—"you're aware children aren't allowed in the building?"

"What?" my assistant screeches in horror. "No children in the building?"

I glare at her. "Look around you, Ms. Young. This is a workplace."

"So? People have families. And working women like Adela need babysitting facilities so they're assured their children are taken care of while they're at work."

"Does it look like I'm running a charity, Ms. Young?"

She juts out her lower lip, and my dick twitches. A zing of lust sizzles up my spine. I stiffen. There is no room for a woman in my life — not since the one I wanted decided I was not for her. I made a vow, then, never to be emotionally involved again. It's one I don't intend to break. Definitely not for a curvy woman who streaks her hair purple and with a figure like she's channeling Marilyn Monroe.

"Companies which provide childcare have seen productivity soar by fifteen percent," she announces.

"Is that right?" I drawl.

She raises a shoulder, then sighs. "I don't know if it's a fact, but I do know women need all the help they can get. And by going that extra mile for your employees, you'll ensure they stay loyal to you."

"I pay them. That's more than enough. If they don't like it, they can leave, as can you —" I stab my finger over my shoulder.

My assistant stiffens, "If I hadn't seen you with the baby, I'd believe you were an insensitive ass, but now —"

"Now?" I incline my head.

"Now, I know you *are* one, you —"

"I'm so sorry, this is all my fault," my HR manager cuts in, "my babysitter cancelled today, and I knew I had to get into work to complete the staff-training. I thought I'd get through things while she was asleep, but then she woke up. Then, I had to change her. And then, she started crying." She swallows. "I'm sorry, Mr. Chase, I know it's against the rules. It won't happen again."

I nod, "Emergencies happen, and we can't always predict circumstances when it comes to children, so I'm willing to overlook the incident. This time."

"Of course," Adela says stiffly.

"It's not what I want to do, but I have to set an example, you understand? If it happens again, I'll have to compensate for the drop in productivity by taking it from your salary."

My assistant gasps. "And will you pay her extra if productivity goes up?"

I shoot her a look. She scowls back, but thankfully, stops speaking.

"It won't happen again." Adela pats the now sleeping baby on her back, then turns to my assistant. "Thank you, Mira, you're a lifesaver."

My assistant smiles. "Anytime."

I make a warning noise at the back of my throat.

Of course, she ignores it. "What's your daughter's name?" she asks.

"It's Andrea," the other woman replies softly.

"I predict Andrea's going to sleep for at least another hour, enough time for you to get through whatever's urgent."

The HR manager shoots her a grateful look, then walks back toward the makeshift bed she has for the baby.

Silence descends. Mira stiffens then slowly turns to me. "I guess I can't delay any longer?"

I tilt my head.

She heaves another sigh, then lowers her chin to her chest. "Fine, whatever. I know you're pissed off. But I'm not going to say sorry."

"Good."

She jerks her gaze back to my face. "Did you say, good?"

"You passed your first test."

Her jaw drops. "Did you say, test?"

I raise a shoulder. "If you want to work as my assistant, you need to stand up to me."

She blinks slowly. "I thought you wanted someone who follows orders?"

I tap my fingers against my chest. "You arrived at eight a.m. today, didn't you?"

"Another test?"

I fake a yawn. "Enough of this prattle." I turn, walk a few steps forward, then turn back and scowl. "Are you waiting for a special invitation, Ms. Young?"

Her mouth firms, but she follows me down the corridor and into my office. I walk over to the floor to ceiling window that looks out over the River Thames. In the distance, the circle of the London Eye cuts a swathe through the rain. The dome of St. Paul's Church is almost hidden by the low hanging clouds, except for a curve at the top bared like the shoulder of a shy bride.

"You love this city, don't you?" she asks from behind me.

I nod before I can stop myself. *The hell?* I never talk about my likes or dislikes with my friends. Definitely not, with my employees. During the time I was General Manager of the London Ice Kings, I kept a strict demarcation between my personal life and my professional one. I prefer to keep my preferences and my secrets to myself. A hangover from the days I was a man of the cloth, maybe, but it's served me well. This way, I can keep my life straightforward. No emotions, no connections, nothing that could result in getting hurt.

The incident when I was a boy changed me forever. Then there's the broken heart, which I'm still not over. Which is why I've done away with messy sentiments. No more allowing myself to feel a connection with others. I did that when I was a priest.

I opened my heart to her, and she chose someone else. I don't hold it against her. How can I? I left her, with no explanation. She was right in choosing my best friend over me. He can give her everything I can't—emotional security, a grounding influence, the stability to put down roots and start a family. I curl my fingers into fists.

Last I saw Ava was at a gathering with Baron. She was glowing, and he had his arm around her. They looked at each other with adoration. And their love created a cocoon which enclosed them in their happy space. Surrounded by people, they remained separate, a unit tuned into each other's presence.

Then I knew, I'd done the right thing by walking away. I stepped aside so the two of them could be happy. And something inside me grew peaceful, knowing they were. I made the correct choice...for them. So what, if I'm to spend the rest of my life alone?

"Edward?"

I blink, then pivot to face her. "Whether I love this city or not is not your concern. You're here to do a job. You'd best focus on that, so you don't lose it."

Her mouth firms. "I haven't said I'd accept the role."

6

Mira

"Where are we again?" he drawls.

"We're in your office, why?"

"I rest my case."

He brushes past me and heads toward his massive desk.

"What do you mean?" I follow him.

"Let's cut the bullshit. You need this job to pay your rent." He slides into his armchair, his back straight. That soldierly poise of his hints at the strict control with which he lives his life. I can almost imagine him as a priest, at the pulpit, wearing the robes, standing upright and sermonizing to his congregation. None of which gives him the right to pass judgement on my life.

"Who told you that?" I jut out my chin. "It can't be Gio, or any one of my friends, for that matter."

"Does it matter?"

"Did you overhear me talking to them? No, that can't be. I know I tend to run my mouth, but no way, would I have turned to them for help."

"Why not?" There's a note of curiosity in his voice, but the expression on his face is bored, like this entire conversation is a chore.

I stiffen. "Does it matter?"

A spark of something lights his eyes, but he extinguishes it quickly. "I didn't get to be where I am in life without reading body-language. And yours indicated you were desperate at the event yesterday."

"I'm not desperate," I protest.

He stares at me steadily, and I hunch my shoulders. "Maybe, a little. No doubt, you saw me scarfing down the cupcakes at Gio's wedding yesterday. But they were free, and I hadn't eaten breakfast yesterday. Also, I ended up having ramen for dinner last night. Not that I'm—"

"Have you had breakfast today?"

I blink. "Why do you care?"

He continues to hold my gaze, and damn, I don't stand a chance. Those tawny eyes of his bore into me, and I'm sure he can read my mind.

"I ate breakfast," I say in a firm voice. My stomach chooses that moment to rumble. The sound seems to echo in the room, and I flush.

Without breaking my gaze, he picks up his cell phone, presses a key, and holds it to his ear. "Send in lunch for me and Ms. Young." He places his phone down on the table, then points to the chair opposite him. "Sit." The light glistens off the watch on his wrist.

I shake my head. "No, thank you."

"We need to go over your duties."

"Still haven't said I'm accepting the job."

His chest rises and falls. "I'm paying you £10,000 a month."

"What?" I squeak. "Why would you pay me that much?"

"Trust me, you'll earn every penny." His lips curl.

I scowl. "I'm not going to sleep with you, if that's what you're after."

He looks me up and down. "No fear there. You're not my type."

My jaw drops. "Were you born this rude?"

"No, it's a skill I've perfected over many years."

Wow, okay. "If you're going to be this obnoxious—"

"I haven't even started, Ms. Young."

"Mira."

"Excuse me?"

"That's my name."

"I know what your name is, Mirabelle."

I pick up my jaw off the floor, again. "H-h-h-how d-d-did you...."

"Mirabelle Young, living temporarily in a one-bed room apartment in Hackney. Father is Cyril Young, the CEO of the Young group of hotels. One of the most successful and wealthy families in the world."

My gaze widens. I open my mouth, but he holds up his hand. "Before you ask any predictable questions, I make it my business to know everything about people before I hire them."

"So, when you saw me yesterday at the gathering, you already knew about my background?"

He hesitates. "I had my investigator get me a file on you and—"

"You have a file on me?" I yell.

"I have files on all of my employees. It's standard HR procedure to do a check before you hire someone. It's why I didn't ask you for references."

"It's an intrusion of privacy, is what it is."

"Not when all your information is in the public domain."

I blink, then realization dawns. "My social media networks."

"Shouldn't have set your settings to public." He clicks his tongue.

I cross my arms over my chest. "Do you take pleasure in belittling people?"

"I don't care one way or the other."

I throw up my hands. "What *do* you care about?"

"That you do the job you're paid to do."

"Don't you want to know why I'm looking for a job, despite my father being one of the richest in the country?"

"Nope." He makes a popping sound at the end.

"You must also be aware my only experience so far has been working in a preschool."

"Where you also helped with the admin and running the place. In the short months you were there, you not only helped hands-on with taking care of the children, but also streamlined the processes. Too bad the owner didn't have deeper pockets. If he'd managed his cash flow wisely, the nursery would exist today."

Chills run up my arms, and I skim my suddenly sweaty palms down the fabric of my skirt. I struggled to zip it up this morning, and the jacket is a little too tight at the shoulders. That's what happens when you shop at the second-hand outlet. I can only find my size in the plus-sized brands, which are currently out of my budget, so I knew I'd lucked out when I found a half-way decent-looking ensemble in the thrift store. Unfortunately, it's one size smaller than what I normally wear. I thought I'd looked professional when I saw my reflection in the mirror. But with his piercing gaze on me, and that inscrutable expression in his eyes, I feel like I'm back in high-school and being rebuked by the principal. Though none of them looked anywhere as delicious as the glowering man on the other side of the desk.

"You seem to know everything about me."

"I know enough." He looks me up and down. There's a peculiar look in his eyes, which he banks again. "Only what's needed pertaining to your job. In my position, I need to be careful who I allow in my proximity."

"You've only taken this job recently, I understand?"

His gaze narrows.

"I heard from our mutual friends—"

"Friends?" he drawls in a tone which indicates he doesn't have many of them, which, given his attitude so far, is not surprising.

"I meant, the girls who are married to your friends. And I know you're close to the Seven—"

"What do you know about the Seven?" There's that hint of lazy curiosity in his voice again, one that signals he finds this entire conversation amusing.

My stomach tightens, but I force myself to relax. *You do need this job. Besides, it's only going to be for a few months.* That's as long as my family is going to let me be. And no way am I borrowing money from my friends or admitting defeat and returning home before that. This must be a test, his version of an interview. Yes, that's all it is.

"I know the Seven co-own 7A investments. They each are on the list of multi-billionaires on the continent. I know they're rumored to have links to the Mafia, so they know about all the big deals in the country. I know that six of the seven are married, leaving only one, who is among the most eligible bachelors in the country. And that person is you."

When he doesn't react, I'm emboldened to add, "I also know your half-brothers aren't too thrilled that you'll be taking over."

He seems taken aback by my knowledge.

"I do my research, too." So what if my primary source of information is The Daily Mail and Cosmopolitan? I have my ear to the ground as far as celebrity gossip is concerned, and the Seven used to grace the tabloids, until they found their ladyloves. Except for Edward—though speculation is rife that it won't be long before he settles down, considering his new position is that of the CEO of Davenport Industries. As for him not getting on with his half-brothers, that was a calculated guess. I may not be a cut-throat corporate shark, but even I know when an outsider is given the top position, the ones on the inside tend to be pissed off.

"Why is your surname different from the company you manage?"

"Didn't your research reveal that?" he drawls.

Heat flushes my cheeks. "My sources aren't as thorough as yours. All I know is your grandfather is Arthur Davenport, a business legend. I also know that, while he is estranged from your parents, he's decided to make you the CEO of his group of companies."

He doesn't seem surprised by the scope of my knowledge. "Did your investigation also reveal that Arthur wants me to get married?"

"He does?" I blink.

He nods. "Question is, do you have what it takes to be my wife?"

7

Edward

"You mean, do you have what it takes to be my husband, don't you?"
She huffs. "Also, if that was a marriage proposal, it sucked,"

"But you're considering it," I declare with satisfaction.

"No, I'm not."

"If you weren't, you wouldn't have mentioned it," I point out.

"What do you— Wait... You— I—" Finally, she throws her hands
up. "Aargh. Even if I were considering it, which I'm not, you'd be the
last man I'd marry."

"Oh?"

"Oh, *yes*." She tips up her chin. "You're too arrogant, too unfeeling,
too conceited. You're the kind of man—"

"—you'd prefer to fuck you."

Color flushes her cheeks. "Excuse me, did you use the F-word with
your employee?"

"Get used to it."

"You're breaking every rule in the employee handbook," she
informs me.

"I'm paying you enough to look past it."

She rubs at her temples. "This is all too much. I'm definitely not going to marry you. In fact, I'm not even sure I want to work for you—"

"Yet, here you are."

"You caught me at a vulnerable time." Her shoulders slump. "I suppose, that's what makes you good at your job. You see an advantage and move in. It's annoying; except, a part of me can't help but admire it, too." A determined look comes into her features. "I want to be more like you."

"No, you don't."

She sets her jaw. "Yes, I do."

"Trust me, you don't."

"You don't understand. You're confident and in control of your destiny. You can do what you want, when you want, how you want, and no one's going to stop you."

"Who's going to stop you?"

She opens her mouth, then seems to catch hold of herself. "Doesn't matter."

"Of course, it matters. Everything you say or think matters."

She flushes a little. "That's not a very professional thing to say."

You make me forget what it is to maintain a professional relationship. In fact, I'd rather we skip the professional etiquette and head to the more personal stuff and —what the—! I stiffen. *Why is it that talking to her tempts me to break the vow I made to myself?* In the three years since my last relationship, I haven't been with another woman. I haven't been interested in much else, except spending time on my own. I used to hang out with the Seven, but it became too painful to see Ava with Baron, so I reduced the amount of time I spent with them.

After leaving the church, and after fucking up the opportunity I had with Ava, I travelled the world, searching for a challenge, a focus, anything to get my mind off what I could not have. It's what led me to accept the post of the General Manager for the London Ice Kings, and now, the role of the CEO of the Davenport group of companies.

Perhaps that's what she is—a challenge. Is that why I haven't been able to get her out of my mind since I met her?

"You'd prefer for us to keep our relationship professional?"

"Is that a trick question?" She frowns.

"You want control over your destiny. This is me giving you the chance to define this relationship."

She rubs at her temple. "You're confusing me. There shouldn't even be a choice here. You're my boss. I'm your assistant, who's been working for you for less than a day. Of course, I want our relationship to be professional."

"Okay."

She seems taken aback. "That's it? Okay?"

"You seem disappointed."

"What? No." She shakes her head. "It's the right thing. The only thing possible between us is a professional relationship, after all."

I look up at her. "If you're going to work for me, the first thing you need to do is remove the idea that anything is 'impossible' from your vocabulary."

She thinks it over, then shakes her head again. "I disagree. Certain things are not done."

"Like what?"

"Like fraternizing in the workplace, for one."

"If you'd bothered to check the employee contract, you'd know that there is no clause that prohibits employees from engaging in a relationship. As long as it doesn't impact their performance, I don't care."

Her gaze narrows. "Everything has a consequence. You can turn a blind eye to everything but the money you're making, and it's only going to end up hurting you."

"Worried about me?"

She scoffs, "You can take care of yourself."

"But who's going to take care of you?"

She folds her arms across her chest. "I don't need you looking out for me."

"You're my employee. Of course, I'm going to look out for you."

"You don't seem to have the same interest or concerns about anyone else."

"That's because they are not you." *What the —? Where did that come from?*

A wrinkle appears between her eyebrows. "What do you mean?"

"That I ensure nothing impacts the bottom line. Ergo, I do what's needed to create an environment that results in optimal efficiency."

"I'm still not sure —"

There's a tap on the door before one of the kitchen staff wheels a food trolley into the room. "Where would you like this served, Mr. Chase?"

I rise to my feet and walk over to the seating area on the right side of my desk. "Here is good." I gesture to the coffee table.

He slides the two covered plates on either side of the table, then whisks off the dome shaped covers. "Enjoy." He half bows, then spins around and leaves.

Mira rises to her feet but makes no move to approach the food.

I take a chair and gesture to the settee on the opposite side.

When she stays unmoving, I tilt my head. "You need to eat."

"I don't understand you." She locks her fingers together in front of herself.

"What's not to understand? I ordered us an early lunch, since you didn't eat breakfast."

"But I told you I ate."

I stare at her.

"Well, anyway, that's not the point. What I don't understand is, why do you care whether I've eaten or not?"

"Because it's going to be difficult for you to focus on an empty stomach."

The sound of her stomach growling fills the room. She flushes. "Fine, have it your way." She stomps over, throws herself onto the couch, then stares at the food.

"It's not poisoned." I reach for my fork, scoop up some of the black truffle risotto from her plate, bring it to my mouth and wipe the tines clean. I glance up to find her gaze fixed on my lips. I run my tongue across the seam of them, and she swallows. I chew, swallow, then scoop up more of her risotto and offer it to her. "Open."

She raises her gaze to mine, then slowly parts her lips.

"Good girl," I murmur.

The pulse at the base of her throat kicks up. *Oh, she likes that.* I slide the fork over her tongue. She closes her mouth around it, and when I pull it back, the tines are clean. She chews, and her gaze widens.

"Good?"

She nods.

I scoop up more of the food and hold it to her mouth. Then watch as she closes her lips around the fork, as she flicks the tip of her pink tongue around the tines and picks off the food, as she chews and swallows. I place the fork down, then reach out with my fingers.

She flinches.

I pause. "You have a bit of food at the corner of your mouth."

"Oh?" She sweeps her tongue to the right-hand corner of her lips, and my cock, which already thickened from watching her eat, jumps in excitement. *Interesting.* This reaction of my body to her every move is fascinating. And unwelcome.

"Is it gone?" she asks in an anxious voice.

"May I?"

She hesitates, then nods. I close the distance to her face, scoop up the cream on the left corner of her lips, then bring it to my mouth and suck it off.

She draws in a sharp breath. "Why did you do that?"

"Do what?" I transfer the fork to my left hand, pick up my knife, and cut into the duck's breast on my plate.

"You fed me with your fork, then picked up the smidgen from my lips—"

"And swallowed it?" I shrug. "It was a reflex."

"Oh."

"Also, you're not eating."

She watches me for a few seconds, then picks up her own fork and eats a few mouthfuls. "You ordered risotto for me and duck for yourself."

I nod.

Her features light up, "You knew I'm vegetarian?"

"You mentioned it in the employee forms you filled out."

"Oh." She deflates a little and continues to eat.

"Thanks," she murmurs. When she's done, she places her hands in her lap. "That was delicious. Thank you, again."

"Don't expect me to feed you lunch every day; this was a one off."

Her lips stiffen.

"I order you to make sure you have your breakfast every day from now on."

"You order me?" Her gaze widens, "Who are you to order me?"

"Your boss."

"And if I don't want your job?"

I lean back in my seat and nod toward the door. "You're free to leave."

She glances toward the exit, then back at me. Her blue eyes spark, and color flushes her cheeks. She glowers at me, her features set in a mutinous expression.

"That's what I thought." I rise to my feet, head back to my chair and busy myself with the document open on my computer.

Footsteps sound, then she walks over to stand on the opposite side of the table. "Are you going to tell me what else is expected from me?"

"Your task list is in your inbox, Ms. Young, along with my expectations of the role. I assume you're able to read?"

She makes a strangled sound at the back of her throat.

My lips twitch. This has got to be the most fun I've had since preparing for my sermons. The thought wipes the smile off my face.

I managed to put the days of my being a priest behind me. I managed not to think of the absolute calmness which filled me then. How I was so sure I'd found my calling, my purpose… Only to find, it's not for me. And I haven't allowed myself to think back in such detail to that time in my life. I thought I'd managed to put it behind me and move on, but all it took was one conversation with her, and the gates to my past have been pushed open. My hard-won control over my thoughts has never been this tested. I was right. She is a test, a provocation, a problem poised to flush out the weakness in my defenses. And I'm not going to let her win. I'm going to resist her. I'm going to use her to strengthen my resolve. I will not be swayed from my path. I will not give in to this temptation. I will stay true to my promise to never be involved with anyone.

"I take that as a yes?" My voice comes out in a snap.

She flinches, then juts out her chin. "Thank you for sending through my job description. I promise I will not bother you with such trivial questions again."

She turns to leave, I call out, "Oh, Ms. Young? The zipper on your skirt is undone."

8

———————

Mira

"Oh, my god! What did you do?" My friend Abby cackles from the couch. We're in the townhouse she shares with her husband Cade. He's the captain of the English cricket team and currently on a tour of Australia.

"What could I do?" I look into the depths of my glass of Pinot Grigio. "I hauled ass out of there, then ran to the ladies room and checked."

"And," Gio interjects, "was your skirt unzipped?"

"Yep," I say sadly. "I must have tugged on the zipper a little too hard while I was trying to pull it on that morning. It must have broken at some point, and I didn't realize it."

"Oh, no," Summer, Sinclair's wife, gasps. "You were wearing a skirt with a broken zipper all that time?"

"Don't remind me." I tilt the wine glass to my mouth and polish off the liquid. The alcohol slides down my throat, hits my stomach and sets off a pleasant warmth. I hold out my wineglass.

Gio tops me up, then herself. "I can't believe he pointed that out to you."

"It might have been worse if he hadn't. I'd have ended up flashing the world. This way, I only flashed him. I hope."

"Oh, honey, I am so sorry." Summer rises from the couch and walks over to me. She hitches a hip on the arm of the chair I'm seated on and touches my shoulder. "I can only imagine how mortifying that must have been."

"It was." I press my head into her arm. My family is not the most demonstrative, to say the least. My ma died when I was little. My father married again, and my stepmother and half-sisters, have never been welcoming to me. Surprisingly, it worked in my favor when I wanted to leave home. My stepmom sided with me—probably because she wanted me out of her hair. Definitely, because she wanted me to get into trouble, in the hope I would spoil my chances of making a good marriage.

How I wanted to be able to do that, too. But I couldn't break my father's heart that way. Maybe he wasn't always available to me, but he loves me, in his own way.

That's me, the responsible girl, at heart, even though a part of me wants to break free and rebel so much. I tried to please my stepmom, went out of my way to be friends with my half-sisters, but that invisible barrier that comes from not being blood seemed to always be between us. The three of them were a unit, and I was always on the outside. I thought I'd never find my tribe, until I met Abby and her girlfriends. They adopted me, and for the first time in my life, I feel like I belong.

"Learn from it and move on, honey." Summer runs her fingers though my hair. "Don't dwell on it, or it'll drive you a bit crazy."

"I have been going around in circles in my head," I admit.

"I hope you, at least, flashed Priest properly," Gio drawls.

Abby spits out the non-alcoholic beer she's been drinking. She's six months along and glows with that radiance that pregnant women seem to exude.

"Really, Gio?" Summer says mildly.

"He probably got a glimpse of my stockings." I try to shrug in a nonchalant manner. *OMG, he saw my pantyhose, and probably a hint of my panties through the material.* "Though, I doubt it made any impact on that man." I glance up at Summer. "Has he always been this…inscrutable?" Of all of us in the room, she's known Edward the longest.

Summer straightens and slips into the armchair next to mine. "He's always been the quietest of the Seven, and the one who always seemed the most wounded from within."

"So, he was like that even before he left the priesthood?"

"He was, maybe, more hopeful when he was a priest." Summer twirls a lock of hair about her fingers. "He seemed to have a purpose then. But after what happened with Ava—" She firms her lips.

"Ava?" I frown.

She lowers her hand to her lap. "Pretend you didn't hear that name from me."

"But—"

"It's not my place to tell you, Mira. You understand that, right?"

I purse my lips. "I understand, but don't agree."

"Did she break his heart?" Gio asks.

"Is he still carrying a torch for her?" Abby muses.

Summer merely shakes her head. "Not fair guys. I don't want to speculate about his love life—"

"Aww, where's the fun in that?" Gio protests.

Summer sets her jaw. "It's Edward's story to tell," she insists.

"Well, give me something." I lock my fingers together in my lap. "He's my boss. It'll help me manage him better, considering it's so difficult to read him."

Summer seems conflicted.

"I need this job so I can prove to my family, and to myself, I can be independent. And I can't do that unless I have an advantage."

She glances around at our faces then sighs. "There was an incident," she finally says.

"An incident?" I frown.

She shuffles her feet. "When the Seven, including Edward and Sinclair, were in school, something happened. It's how they formed a bond that's lasted all this time."

"You're saying something affected all seven of them when they were young, and that's how they forged their friendship?" Gio narrows her gaze.

Summer nods. "And that's all I'm going to say."

"Aww, not fair," Gio begins to protest, but Abby pipes in, "I think Summer's right. Whatever happened to Edward, it should be his prerogative to share or not."

I take another sip of the wine. "I know you're right, but given how uncommunicative he is, not to mention how mean he was to me, it probably means I'll never find out what happened and"—my phone chirps from my bag —"and I guess that means I'm going to have to find another way to survive on the job."

My phone stops, then starts again.

"You going to get that?" Gio stares at my bag. There's a feverish look in her eyes. Woman has her own phone strapped to her palm, and thanks to her PR background, leaving a phone unattended is akin to a worldwide disaster.

"Fine, you can get it for me," I offer.

"Oh, thank you!" She springs up, pulls my phone from my bag, and holds it out to me.

I look at the screen and groan. "I don't want to answer it."

"Yes, you should."

"No, I don't want to." I sink back further into the chair.

"Don't be such a coward; it's only a man."

"Is that what you thought of Rick, when you first saw him?"

Her expression changes. "So, he's not just a man?"

"I didn't mean *that*."

My phone stops buzzing.

"You did compare your boss to her husband," Abby points out.

"It was a slip of the tongue."

"Like how your zipper slipped down your skirt?" Summer murmurs.

"You too?" I cry. "Girls, honestly, my boss is a hottie, but I am not attracted to him. I'm not."

"Then why didn't you answer the phone?" Gio looks at me with knowing eyes.

My phone starts buzzing again, and when she holds it out, I take it from her. "Hello!"

"Ms. Young, what's the use of having a phone if you don't answer it?" His hard voice sets off little tingles that slither straight to my core. I will not be turned on by the velvety depth of his tone, or that clipped British accent of his which brings to mind frosty mornings, and dewdrops on grass, and the clopping of horses on paved stone. *Lay off the historical romance books, Mira. This is Edward, your boss, the rudest man you've ever met.*

"Oh, sorry, uh… I had the phone in my bag… Which wasn't near me. I find holding a phone in my hand is so distracting, especially when I am with my friends and want to concentrate on them instead of on my device. It's such a shame people prefer to sit at the same table and focus on their phones instead of on the person opposite them, don't you think?

It's alienating, instead of bringing people together. You should know. You were a priest, so you must have seen how people are finding themselves even more alone, despite all the ways technology has enabled us to keep in touch. Imagine if they came to you for counsel and you happened to be on your phone instead of guiding them and..." I swallow down the rest of my sentence then squeeze my eyes shut. "I'm sorry I was prattling on, wasn't I?"

The silence on the phone could be the kind you face when you walk into a haunted house at an amusement park, right before the creepy crawlies reveal themselves in the light. I swallow. The silence stretches.

"Um... You there, Mr. Chase?"

"You done, Ms. Young?"

I open my mouth to reply, then don't dare let any words emerge from my lips because I might not be able to stop myself from another word vomit. I don't normally let my sentences get the better of me. Not really. It's this man whose presence and absence both disturb me in equal measure. I content myself with a nod, not that he can see it, but he must sense it, because he says in that stern tone of his, "I'm picking you up in thirty minutes."

9

Mira

"Some advance notice would have been appreciated." I scowl at the man in the driver's seat. Of course he'd drive his own car. He's too controlling to put his life in someone else's hands. A reluctant admiration fills me. He truly is the master of his life. A position I'd give anything to be in. Right now, I'm at his beck and call though.

When I complained, he reminded me that I signed away my life when I agreed to work for him. I'm sure he's doing this to test me, too. I might look weak, but I have more mettle than he imagines. Doesn't mean I'm going to take his springing this trip on me without making my displeasure known. Not that my questions have brought forward an answer from him. He focuses on the road in front of us. I glance out the window and notice we're on King's Road. At this time of the night, the high-end boutiques and yummy-mummy cafes are closed. He turns off the main street, and I notice the sign for Chelsea Pier.

"Are we taking a boat?"

He doesn't answer. I risk another glance at his profile, then wish I hadn't. Illuminated by the lights from the dials on the dash, the gold in his eyes glints like that of a predator. A beast at the top of the food chain, who is the master of all he surveys. His hooked nose and square jaw, once again, bring home how much his profile resembles that of the regency heroes I'm so fond of. Only, he's wearing a fresh three-piece suit with a new tie. This one is a dull gold, and the color lends a burnished glow to his skin. His well-cut jacket accentuates his biceps, and when he turns the wheel into the parking bay in front of the dock, I can't help but notice his thick fingers, the blunt fingernails, the capable way he steers the vehicle. He was born to rule, to command.

I can't imagine any woman turning this man down. How was he before he had his heart broken? Before he walked away from the priesthood? How was he with his flock? Was he good at giving advice? Is that why he prefers not to talk much now? Or is it only because I don't know him too well? Is he different with his friends? Although, from what Summer mentioned earlier, he hasn't been socializing much with them, either. The man's an enigma, a mystery which intrigues me, but which I doubt I'm going to be able to solve anytime soon.

Moonlight glints off the water of the Thames and he pulls to a stop in front of a jetty. He switches off the engine, and except for the ticking of the engine cooling, it's silent. The lights of the jetty illuminate the wooden boards, and at the far end, I notice a motorboat.

"A little late to be cruising on the Thames, isn't it?"

"I need to remind you that you signed an NDA, Ms. Young."

"An NDA?"

"A non-disclosure-agreement." His tone carries a touch of boredom, which rubs me the wrong way.

"I know what an NDA is."

"But you didn't read it before you signed it."

"Of course, I did."

He slowly turns his face in my direction. "Are you lying, Ms. Young?"

"Of course, not."

He reaches into the inside pocket of his jacket and pulls out a sheaf of papers. "I suggest you read it properly before we leave."

I shoot him a curious look, then take the papers from him. He flips on the interior light, and I take in the letters on the sheets. He's helpfully highlighted some of the passages, and when I read them—for the first time, I admit—my jaw drops.

"D-d-does...it say a-anal?"

"Not only."

I race my gaze across the page. *Ball gag, fellatio, edging, whipping, choking, dominant, submissive.* "Double penetration?" I squeak.

"Could be with two dicks or with one real dick and a vibrator."

"Vibrator." I swallow around the word.

"Surely, you've used one before, Ms. Young?"

"Of course." I lie around the ball of nervousness in my throat. "What does this have to do with me?"

"It has everything to do with you." He takes the sheets from my nerveless fingers and turning, slides them onto the back seat.

"I… I am your assistant."

"And the only other person who has so much access to me."

"O-k-a-y?"

"Other than Tiny, of course."

"Of course. Speaking of, where is he?"

"He gets seasick," he declares.

I blink slowly, "Tiny, your Great Dane, gets sea-sick?"

"I'm dog-sitting him. Also, the mutt can down a bottle of expensive champagne without any problem, but get him on a boat, and he begins to puke. So, I had to leave Tiny home today. Which works in your favor. It means we'll only spend half the night on the ship."

"The ship?"

He nods toward the windshield. I look through it to the lights I noticed in the distance, but which I now realize *is* a ship.

"You don't get seasick, I assume, Ms. Young?"

I shake my head.

"Ever been on a boat?"

"I'm from Brooklyn. Of course, I have."

"Brooklyn, huh?"

"And what am I doing in London, you ask? It's the furthest I could get away from my family."

"Don't get along with them?" His tone is mildly curious.

"My dad's okay. But I wanted to be on my own. Find out what I like and don't like, before—"

"Before?"

I bite the inside of my cheek. "Never mind."

"Never cut off your thoughts like that. If you have something you want to say, do it with confidence."

I blink. I've never had anyone tell me that. With my father, I've always minded my words because I don't want to disappoint him. With the rest of my family, I've preferred to keep my thoughts to myself because I don't want to upset them. With my friends growing up, I hid my true sentiments because I wanted to fit in. It didn't help I went to a private school where everyone was too busy trying to keep up with the latest trends. It all seemed so empty, so pointless. I bottled it all up, until one day, I rebelled in spectacular fashion.

For the first time ever, I skipped school to hang out with another girl. The funny thing is, she wasn't even my best friend, just someone who always seemed so 'with it'. So when she invited me out, I couldn't refuse. We were caught smoking pot and chugging down beer in her car. Looking back, it seems like a relatively innocent escapade. It's not like I was caught having sex. But my father was so disappointed.

The worst part? He didn't scold me. He simply drove me home in silence and told me to go to my room, and that made it so much worse. I vowed not to ever let him down again. Yet, here I am, an ocean away, in the car that smells of that dark spiciness and ozone with my boss, and I'm about to find out what the sexual acts I read about in the NDA mean in real life. This…is not what I had in mind when I wanted to claim my freedom. This is not what I envisioned when I said I wanted a say in how I live my life… Did I?

He must see the apprehension on my face for he arches an eyebrow. "Scared, Ms. Young."

"Please call me Mira."

"Ms. Young, don't change the topic."

I blow out a breath. "I'm not sure if I want to do this."

"Do what?"

"This." I stab a thumb over my shoulder to where he tossed the NDA. "Whatever it is."

"You don't have to take part in anything. You simply need to be with me and take notes when I tell you to."

"Take notes about the s-s-sex acts you mean?"

"About the kink you're going to witness, yes."

Heat flushes my cheeks. "You said that word simply to get a reaction from me."

He pauses to think, then nods. "You're right, I did."

"At least, you don't lie."

"Unlike you."

I set my jaw. "I am being honest when I say I don't want to witness sexy—huh—kinky stuff."

He stares at me steadily. His features are inscrutable, but there's a bend in his lips which indicates he's amused by this conversation.

"There's nothing funny about this situation."

"Except for the fact you're curious about said acts. Except, you've always wanted to know about kink but never had the courage to find out. Except, you can't wait to get out of this car and accompany me to the yacht, but you don't want to admit it."

"I don't."

"Hmm." He taps his fingers on his wheel. "Slide your fingers into your panties."

"What?" I stare.

"You can, of course, leave the car, and I'll have someone drive you home and we may never speak of this night."

"And I'll still have my job?"

"You will."

The expression on his face indicates he expects me to take the easy way out. The rebel at heart, who's headed for an arranged marriage, and who's never had the guts to seize the opportunity when it was presented to her, wants to prove him wrong. And I was so sure I wanted control of what I would do next. *What am I going to do next?*

I straighten my legs, then raise my hips to hitch up my skirt. It takes some wriggling to pull it halfway up, but finally it's bunched up my thighs. Good thing I noticed a tear in my stockings earlier and took them off. Or a bad thing… Depends on your perspective. I have to admit, it's with relief I slide my fingers down the front of my panties. My breath hitches. Fish on a bike, I'm soaking wet.

"Exactly." His voice is calm.

I search for any traces of triumph or satisfaction in his tone, but I only hear a methodical intent in them. It's as if he wants to prove a point and knew he wasn't going to lose. He baited me, and I walked into his trap. I could, of course, get out of the car and leave…but that would mean walking away from his challenge. I'd be conforming to the image my family created for me. Following through would mean, when presented with the opportunity to create my own experiences, the kind I could draw on later when I was trapped in a marriage I don't want, I'll have some satisfaction that I embraced my deepest desires. The kind the man next to me seems to bring out in me. The kind I heard gossiped about among my girlfriends, and to which I nodded along, pretending a first-hand knowledge I didn't have. The gap in my skillset is one I could fill now. He's giving me the opportunity to find out how it would be to feel my fingers inside of myself while he watches. When I still hesitate he stiffens. I sense the change that comes over him.

"You're a virgin," He declares.

"What? No." I jerk my chin in his direction, then gasp, for he's staring at me. And his amber eyes glow with a look of such intensity, I'm sure he's going to reach over and curl his fingers around my neck and pull him to me and—

"Touch your clit," he orders.

I don't comply.

"You do know where your clit is?"

"Of course, I do." He said it to rile me. He's trying to manipulate me… And I am going to let him. This time.

I circle the swollen bud between my moist pussy lips, and frissons of electricity zip out from the contact. "Oh," I gasp.

His gaze intensifies. "Run your fingers around it again."

I do. The pin-pricks of sensations deepen. Moisture bathes the area between my legs. My thighs quiver, and my toes curl.

"How does it feel?" he asks without moving his gaze from mine.

"Like…a storm is gathering in the most intimate part of me." *Like I've never realized what my body was meant to be used for. Like I want to be used by you. Like I want you to close the distance to me and replace my fingers with your thick ones.*

The air in the car grows heavy. The tendons of his throat stand out in relief. The muscles of his jaw flex and I realize he's not as much in control as he'd like to think he is. "Pinch your clit," he snaps.

A tremor of heat zips under my skin. I hold the tiny swollen nub between my thumb and forefinger, and when I bear down, a volley of sparks charges to my extremities. My nipples tighten. My scalp tingles. I throw my head back and moan. I hear the sound and realize how needy it is. It also turns me on more.

"Do you want to squeeze your tits?" he asks in that low heavy voice which courses another flurry of butterflies through my veins.

I nod, then begin to remove my fingers from my pussy, when he clicks his tongue. "Did I give you permission to do so?"

I shake my head.

"As a punishment, rub your clit."

The thought of the friction where I need it most is almost too much to bear. "I can't."

"You can. You will. Do it, Belle."

Wait? He has a nickname for me? A glow ignites deep within. I replace my fingers with the heel of my hand. The first stroke sends a surge of sparks spiraling down my legs. I groan, continue to swipe, and an avalanche of goosebumps covers my skin. My entire body shudders. My fingers tremble. "I can't. No more."

"Once more," he commands.

A whimper spills from my lips. I squeeze my eyes shut, draw in a breath, another, then brush up against my throbbing clit. This time, flames lick my nerve endings. A trembling begin at my toes, steps up my calves, my thighs, circles my lower belly, my pussy. "I think I'm... I'm going to—"

"You will not come without my permission."

"What?" I open my eyelids, turn to him. "Why?"

He merely jerks his chin. "Bring your fingers to your mouth and suck on them."

My breath hitches, my gaze caught by his fiery eyes, the look in them so insistent, I know I can't disobey. I raise my fingers to my mouth and suck on them.

"How does it taste?"

"Sweet, complex and tangy, with an underlying saltiness." I hold out my fingers. "Do you want to taste?"

10

Edward

Fuck, yes. The sweet scent of her arousal wafts over to me, and my already thickening cock extends further. My blood drains to my balls, and my thigh muscles are so rigid, I'm sure I'm going to split my pants. I've never wanted anything as much as I want to lick the glistening ends of her fingertips. And if I do, I'm going to hell.

I swore never to fall for another woman. Yet here I am, in an enclosed space, with the most dangerous woman I've encountered since *her*. Maybe even more than *her*. I can't remember feeling this out of my depths with *her*. But Belle… She is a constant surprise.

Mirabelle Young, daughter of one of the most powerful families in the world, a woman whose purple streaked hair indicates she's trying to change what's in her control—ergo, she can't change many of the bigger things in her life. The woman who's twelve years younger than me—not twenty, or fifteen, as she'd guessed. The woman whose beauty struck a blow to my chest the first time I saw her, so much so, those big blue eyes of hers had seared themselves into my soul.

The creamy expanse of her neck had made me want to dig my teeth into the skin and mark her where her shoulder met her neck; the flare of her ample hips had invited me to dig my fingers into them and hold her still as I bent and swiped my tongue across her cherry blossom mouth. She's perfect. From the top of her blonde hair, whose shine not even the purple streaks could hide, to the imprint of her nipples that can be seen through the layers of her blouse and her jacket, to the thick thighs that beg me to wear them as earmuffs—to sink to my knees and push my face into the delectable treasure between them. Fact is, since meeting Ms. Mirabelle Young, everything about my carefully structured life has been upturned.

The force of her beauty touches that dead organ in my chest, the one I thought would never revive—indeed, did not want to be revived. Her presence is grace and light, with an awkwardness that awakens my protective instincts. It's why I offered her a job as my assistant. This way, I can watch out for her. I can make sure she's safe. But I cannot allow myself to develop feelings for her. I cannot act on this attraction I feel for her. Besides, if she sees the truth of the man I am, she'll hate me. She'll never want to see me again. My only role is to ensure she's protected. That what happened to me as a boy never happens to her.

When I showed her the NDA, I was sure it'd discourage her from accompanying me on this little sojourn. But Little Miss Gorgeous—whose face I almost jerked off to twice today—surprised me… Again. It made me want her more.

Not to worry; I can resist her allures. I stayed celibate as a priest. Until I didn't, and see how that worked out for me. Nope. I'm not falling for a woman again. And definitely not for her.

I step out of the car, hit the electronic lock, then walk around to open her door. "Ready?"

"Always." She tucks her handbag under her arm and brushes past me, only to trip on a crack in the pavement.

My heart slams into my ribcage. I grip her shoulder and straighten her.

"Do I have Tiny to blame this time? Of course, not," she mumbles. She tries to pull her arm from mine, but I tighten my grip.

"You can let me go."

"Can't have you breaking your neck on my watch." My voice comes out harsher than I intended.

She winces, then a shudder grips her.

"You're cold."

"Don't be ridiculous," she huffs.

"What did I say about lying?" I glare.

She pales, then slowly, nods. "I am…a little."

I shrug off my jacket and place it about her shoulders. It's big enough to envelop her completely and comes to mid-thigh. She burrows into it. Then, as if unable to help herself, turns her face into the collar and sniffs. She draws in a long breath, holds it, then sighs. Then, as if she realizes what she's done, she whips her head around in my direction. "Did I sniff your jacket?" she bursts out.

When I nod slowly, the color on her face deepens.

"I… I didn't." She bites down on her lower lip, and goddam her, I feel the tug in my groin.

I step away from her. Pretending not to notice the disappointment on her face, I stalk forward, without waiting for her.

I sense her surprise, then hear the clopping of her heels as she hurries to keep up.

We reach the waiting motorboat. The man at the wheel nods in my direction. I jump down into it, then turn and, without asking for permission, grab her hips and haul her down. The warmth of her skin sinks into my blood. My cock thickens, and my balls tighten. She draws in a sharp breath, and I have no doubt she feels the connection, too.

Fuck. I thought I was being clever when I invited her to join me as my assistant. I hoped I could keep a few steps ahead of this—whatever it is she's doing to me. I thought I was being clever by taking the lead and nipping this attraction in the bud. I took that entire 'keep your enemies close' dictum to heart. Apparently, she's not the one I need to be worried about.

It's me and my reaction to her that I need to control. And I have the rest of the night to prove to myself how wrong it was to have anything to do with her.

"Sit." I point at the bench set into the side of the boat, then heave a sigh of relief when she complies. I grab a life-vest and place it about her shoulders. She begins to protest but I shake my head. "That's non-negotiable. I will not risk your life, Belle."

She looks between my eyes then nods. "What about you?"

"I'm good."

"I will not risk your life either, Edward." She sets her jaw.

A frisson of heat squeezes my chest. I bat it aside, then reach for another life-vest and shrug into it. Then, I take a stance beside her. Not because I want to act as her shield from the wind, and definitely not because I want to make sure she's safe. She's a grown woman; she can handle herself on a boat. The vessel leaps forward, and she lurches with it. I grip her arm until she finds her balance again.

"Thanks." She tilts her face up. Her hair flows across her features, and before I can stop myself, I've pushed the strands behind her ear.

In the moonlight, her blue eyes turn a translucent silver.

"Beautiful Belle," I murmur.

"Excuse me?"

I shake my head, stare ahead, but don't let go of her.

"I like it when you call me, Belle." She whispers the words, and I shouldn't hear it above the breeze, but I do. Only, I pretend I don't.

When the motorboat reaches the stern of the larger ship, the driver cuts the engine, then throws the line to one of the waiting crew on the yacht. He secures it, then signals that we're good to climb aboard. The man moves toward Mira, but when I glare at him, he pauses.

I reach for her and help her onto the boarding ladder. When I follow her up, I realize I made a mistake. From my vantage point, I have a clear view of her pear-shaped bottom in that too-tight skirt outlining her lush curves. My fingers tingle, and the blood roars in my ears. I raise my arm, needing to touch her twitching arse, then stop before I make contact.

Why is my control so fraught around her? Why does she reduce me to the most basic of instincts? Why does she turn my emotions inside out? Why does she affect me so? Why did I decide to bring her here? I thought I'd punish her for daring to tempt me, yet I'm punishing myself by her proximity. She reaches the yacht, and the steward helps her aboard. When he touches her, a burst of anger sweeps through me. I don't question my need to hurry up and reach her. I step between them, and steward's arm drops away. He looks between us, then lowers his gaze, signaling he understands my unspoken sentiment.

I shrug out of my life-vest, then help her slide off her own. I hand it over to the steward. He accepts it, then half bows his head, "Everything you asked for is ready," he assures me.

"Belle, are you ready?" I rap on the door to the room she disappeared into. I told her she'd find fresh clothes laid out for her. She protested, but I glared at her, and she paled. I softened then, and told her, since I'd spoiled her evening with her friends, the least I could do was make it up to her. She finally relented and walked inside to change.

That was half an hour ago. Truth be told, I'm getting impatient. I want to see how she looks in the clothes I chose for her. I want to see her features—those plump lips, those rosy cheeks, the vulnerable column of her neck, the pulse that beats at the hollow of her throat. Every part of her is enticing and alluring, and I want... No, need to smell her and see her and be in her presence again.

"Open up." I bang on the door. "If you don't, I'm going to break this down and—"

The door swings open. I stare.

11

———————

Mira

"I'm not sure this looks good on me." I run my hands down the silken fabric of the dress which clings to my curves like it's a second skin.

He runs his gaze from my feet, now clad in six-inch-Manolo Blahniks, up the gown which sweeps my ankles, over the slit which bares the length of my leg up to almost the top of my thigh, to the flare of my hips which are molded by the glossy material, to where it dips in the front to bare the valley between my breasts. His gaze stays there for a few seconds, and by the time he meets my eyes, I'm flushed to the roots of my hair.

"This wasn't made for someone with my figure," I burst out.

He frowns. "What do you mean?"

"Don't pretend you can't see it."

"Can't see what?"

"This." I gesture to myself. "I'm overweight. I always have been. Nothing I do has helped me get rid of the extra pounds I'm carrying on my body."

He slides his hand inside his pocket, which pulls the fabric across his crotch tight. It outlines the bulge which I'd noticed the time I spilled coffee on him. It only seems bigger… Ugh, I have no business noticing these things about my boss. Except, he's the one who asked me to get myself off… And I obliged.

How am I going to face him in the office tomorrow? How am I going to get through the rest of this evening, for that matter? "Forget it. I changed my mind. I need off this boat. Can you arrange for me to leave, please?" I turn away, but he curls his fingers around my wrist. A flare of sensations run up my arm. My nipples tighten. A thousand little bees have taken up residence under my skin. I sense him draw a sharp breath, then he releases me.

"Look at me."

The authority in his voice forces me to comply. I slowly glance over my shoulder to find he's looking at me with a strange fervor, one that raises the hair on the back of my neck. I'm trapped in the vortex of gold, which are his eyes.

"You are the most beautiful woman I've ever seen, and I don't say that lightly."

"Oh." I swallow.

"You're a real woman, earthy, sexy, voluptuous."

"You mean, I'm fat." I swallow.

"I mean, you're gorgeous. You're curvy, shapely, full-figured, as Mother Nature intended you to be. The swell of your hips mirrors the beauty of spring, the dip of your waist and the thrust of your tits, hint at the passion within, your luscious thighs promise that softness which is your appeal. Your eyes, your lips, your flushed cheeks, your every inch radiates the appeal of a siren calling to every man in the vicinity."

"Everyone, except you."

"Especially me." His throat moves as he swallows. He raises his arm, then pauses, before curling his fingers into a fist and tucking it back into his side. "You're perfect as you are, and never let me catch you saying otherwise."

I hold his gaze and sense the seriousness in his eyes, the sincerity writ in every hard angle of his body, the honesty which laces his expression and I know he means everything he said. "Thank you," I say softly.

He nods. Then slides his hand into his pocket and holds up a strip of leather with a circular disc in the center. "What's that?"

"Turn around."

I do so without hesitation, his earlier words having cut through any doubts I might have had about coming on board this yacht. He places the piece of leather around my throat and hooks it at the nape of my neck. I see our reflection in the mirror on the wall ahead, and the bees under my skin seem to take wing. Edward, in his black three-piece suit and golden tie is the perfect foil for the flaxen color of my dress. He's tall, stern, all straight lines and angles and dark shadows. I'm a glittering, glowing, shining bundle of sparks. His fingers brush my neck, and goosebumps crowd my skin. He looks up and meets my gaze in the mirror. The air thickens, pulsing with unsaid emotions. There's a wrinkle between his eyebrows as he peruses our reflection. I touch the engraving on the disc that nestles at my throat. "Is this a—"

"Fallen angel," he nods.

"It's pretty," I muse.

"It's essential, so everyone here knows you're mine."

A hot sensation stabs into my chest. "I'm y-yours?"

"For the next few hours. It's necessary."

"Necessary?" I frown. "Why would it be necessary?

"You told me it was necessary, not that it was a collar."

We're in the grand hall of the yacht. The light is low, and there's music on in the background. It's very faint and rhythmic, and filled with pounding, pulsing beats which surround me in an intimate, soothing, yet edgy ambiance. He led me through the hall without touching me, but making sure I was close to him at all times. We passed a few couples, and the men eyed me with interest, until their gazes alighted on the band around my neck. At which point, they turned their attention away. That's when I'd realized the necklace signified possession. I should have felt like an object—I *did* feel like an object—but I was being seen as *his* object, and somehow, that gave me pause.

Edward ushered me to a couch in a corner. A waiter served us. A glass of sparkling water for me and a glass of whiskey for him. When I asked for alcohol, he said he preferred me to have my wits about me. Which wasn't exactly reassuring. Also, I didn't notice him giving the waiter an order which means he must have messaged ahead.

Before I can ask him about it, I notice a woman halfway across the room. She's on her knees, next to a man who's seated on a couch. He's talking to a woman in a leather jumpsuit.

The kneeling woman has a strip of leather around her neck with a circular disc on the side. That's where the resemblance to my accoutrement stops. There's a chain hooked to her choker, the other end of which is in the hand of the man next to her. He's talking to the leather clad woman while she stays with her chin lowered to her chest. She's motionless, but for the rise and fall of her chest. She's wearing far less than me, and her skirt rides up high, enough for me to see the moisture glistening on her inner thighs. My face grows hot. She's aroused. And I'm embarrassed on her behalf.

"You don't need to be embarrassed. She's content." He takes a sip of his whiskey.

"How would you know?"

"Look at her face. What do you see?" He places his glass on the table in front of us.

"It's not polite to stare." The words come out in a prim tone, and I wince. The gap between me and this man has never seemed as insurmountable as now in this space. A very exclusive space which you have to be invited to, and only if you are of a certain profile, or so Edward informed me earlier. It's not about the money you have. It's about your ability to be discrete. Everyone here trades in something which entitles them to be here. When I asked Edward what he bartered, he stayed silent. I didn't bother to pursue that line of questioning. See? I'm learning fast. He only answers if he wants to, and he can't be swayed. I can only speculate, so I decided not to waste my time on it. I was too busy taking in the scene around me.

"She wants you to stare at her. She wants the world to know she belongs to him."

"You're a man. Of course, you'd say that."

He blows out a breath. "You're just like the rest—quick to pass judgement. Quick to view everything through a narrow moral compass, when the world is much more complex."

"You should know. You're the one who turned your back on your calling, after all."

His entire body goes rigid. The tension that always seems to cling to him intensifies. The static in the air shoots up, and the hair on the back of my neck straightens. "I'm sorry," I whisper without meeting his gaze, "that was uncalled for."

"Life is complex, Belle. It's not what you expect it to be. You think you have it all planned out, and then something happens that destroys everything you believed in. Suddenly, your past and the choices you made haunt you. The future's a long road, with an end you cannot see. And your present? It digs its claws into you and refuses to let go, no matter how painful your everyday is."

Tears prick the backs of my eyes. A ball of emotion chokes my throat. The bleakness in his voice drips onto my skin like acid and burns me to the bone.

"What's this?" He reaches forward and scoops up the moisture on my cheek. "Are you crying?"

If I didn't know him better, I'd say his voice carries a note of wonder, but this man is not capable of such emotion. More likely, he's laughing at me. And I'm not going to risk looking at his face to find out.

"Are you, Belle?"

I sniffle. "I didn't mean to. It's just…you sound so lonely."

"I enjoy being on my own."

"Yet here you are." I gesture to the large hall which is now considerably fuller than when we came in.

"This is a way to connect to the only part of me I still recognize."

"Which part?"

'The one I knew I always had but which I refused to acknowledge all that time I was a priest. The one that resulted in my losing everything I once held dear."

I stiffen. "You mean —"

"I mean, you haven't looked at her face and told me what you see yet," he interjects.

Of course, the moment it seems like he's opening up, he has to change the topic. Which is good. I don't want to get to know the man behind the facade. The man who's emotionally wounded. The man who's hurting and refuses to share it with anyone. The man who's an enigma…

Which I want so badly to solve. I focus my attention on the woman who hasn't moved from her perch on the floor. She's been kneeling all this time on the wooden floor without a word of complaint. Her hands are clasped in front of her, her gaze lowered. The light is dim in the space, but there's enough for me to take in her relaxed features. The slight upward turn of her lips. The man next to her runs his fingers through her hair, and she trembles. She licks her lips, and when he drags his knuckles over her cheek, her mouth opens. I'm not close enough to hear it, but I'm sure she's panting. She's even more aroused and she looks "blissful."

"She is."

Only when he replies, do I realize I said the word aloud.

"But he's demeaning her, by making her kneel, and not paying any attention to her," I protest.

"Is he?"

I bring my gaze back to his face and pout. "Of course, he is. She may seem happy, but looks can be deceiving."

"Everyone who is here is here by their own choice."

"But I—" I'm about to say I'm not, but he did give me a choice. And it was my decision to be here, too.

He nods.

"It doesn't seem right. Why should she be chained? Why is he treating her like—"

"His possession?"

His rough voice forming that word turns the flesh between my thighs into molten lava. I begin to cross one leg over the other, but he shakes his head. "Don't."

"Why not?"

"Because I want to smell your cunt."

12

———————

Edward

"What did you say?" she gasps.

"I want to smell your—"

"I heard you," she says hastily, "But did you have to use the C-word?"

"Did it turn you on?"

Her pupils dilate. Her breathing hitches. She seems taken aback, but also, she obeyed me. She's a natural submissive. Doesn't mean she's compliant. And the deepening azure of her blue eyes tells me she's going to deny my statement. She's feisty, likes to stand up for herself, and isn't easily cowed. She's curvy and perfectly formed, but only a fool would take that to mean she's malleable. This woman may not know what she wants yet, but she'll stand up for herself. She's diffident about her figure —but that's only because she doesn't realize how stunning she truly is.

She's spirited, plucky, a ray of light which illuminates those parts deep inside of me that I haven't wanted to examine closely. She…makes me want things I was sure were not in my future. She urges me to ignore the limitations I've put upon myself. She tempts me to break the rules I've decided to live my life by. She…is turning me into someone who's obsessed with her every move, her every breath, her every gesture. She makes me want to find out her every thought, her dreams, her deepest desires…and fulfill them. She makes me want to own her, keep her, possess her, make her *mine*. My belly churns, my heart slams into my ribcage, sweat pools under my armpits, and I rise to my feet. "Come on."

She rises to her feet. I indicate she should follow me. I march across the floor, retracing our steps out the door to the stairs. Taking them two at a time. I reach the landing and wait for her to catch up. She's panting by the time she reaches me. "What's the hurry?"

"You'll see."

I motion for her to go ahead, then curse myself once more when I'm unable to keep my gaze off her luscious behind as she climbs the next set of stairs. The twitch of her butt, the rhythmic sway of her hips, the pull of the fabric across her arse-cheeks, the way her waist flares out to meet her fleshy bottom… My throat closes. My mouth dries. The blood drains to my groin. I reach down and adjust myself, then follow her to the top of the flight of steps. I brush past her, cross the floor and hold open the door on the far end. Her footsteps are soft on the carpet as she approaches. She walks into the room, takes in the rectangular table, the chairs set around it, and the man standing on the far side with his back to us and looking out of the window onto the lights of the city visible in the distance.

"Is that?" She comes to a standstill. "No, it can't be."

I walk past her, pull out a chair. "You'd better sit down for this."

She doesn't take her gaze off of the older man. His shoulders froze when he heard her voice, but he doesn't turn to glance at us.

"Dad?" The color fades from her cheeks. "Is that you?"

He turns and her gaze widens. "What are you doing here?" She swallows.

He looks like he's about to say something, then he shakes his head. "I'm sorry, Mirabelle." His tone is clipped.

"Sorry for what? Why are you in London?"

"Belle, sit down," I order.

She shudders visibly, then manages to tear her gaze off of her father, and walking over, sinks into the chair. I push it in. My fingers graze her shoulder, and goosebumps scatter over her skin. I stay with my head bent, drawing in her sweet apple blossom scent. My cock extends further, and I straighten. This is not the time to be sporting a hard-on, especially not in front of her father. Not that the man particularly cares for her. If he did, he wouldn't have come to an agreement with me.

"What's happening?" She addresses her question to him. "Why are you here?"

"You mean, why is he here in an S&M club?" I drawl.

Her father flinches. His cheeks redden, but he manages to hold his silence. Good thing, too, because nothing he says can justify what he's about to tell her.

"Dad?" she prompts him. "What's going on?"

He rubs at his temple then slowly lowers his hand. "You know, I love you, Mirabelle, don't you?"

"Of course, you're my father." Her tone is impatient.

"And you know I want what's good for you?"

She sits up straighter. "What is it? You're scaring me. Is everything okay? Is it your health? Are you sick? Is that what this is about?"

His features take on a stricken look. "Nothing's wrong with me, honey." He swallows. "I'm here because"—he looks at me, then back at her—"because…"

"If it's not you—" She tilts her head. "Is everything okay back home?"

His features soften. "Only you'd be kindhearted enough to ask after your stepmom and sisters, even after the way they've treated you."

I lean forward, and before I can stop myself the words are out: "What do you mean? How did they treat her?"

"It's nothing." She waves her hand in the air.

"I know I've never openly taken your side, and I apologize for that." His lips turn up in a sad smile before he raises his gaze to mine. "My wife was threatened by Mirabelle from the moment she saw her. And after the birth of our daughters, that sentiment only grew worse."

"Dad, stop," Belle bursts out.

"I'm telling the truth." He glances at her. "It's not like I haven't been aware of how the three of them have tried to make your life miserable over the years."

Every muscle in my body tightens. *Why does it matter to me that she hasn't had an easy life? Why do I feel this angry that someone upset her, that her own family distressed her?* My stomach churns. *Why do I feel her pain like it's my own? If only I'd been able to prevent the emotional scars she carries from her growing years. If only I'd actually been there to help.* I draw myself to my full height. "Your wife and your daughters were unfair to her, and you did nothing?"

The violence in my tone must be evident, for her father holds up his hands. "I accept the blame. I knew they weren't being kind to her. I should have stepped in, but my head wasn't in the right space."

"Of course it wasn't. You'd lost a wife," she interrupts.

"You lost your mother," he replies.

Belle begins to speak again, but he shakes his head. "I thought I was doing the right thing by getting married again. I hoped she would be a stabilizing influence in your life. I was too consumed by my grief to put things right. I hoped to make it up to you by finding the right match for you, but I've failed you again."

The skin across her knuckles whitens. "What do you mean? You said you'd wait until the year was out. You said you'd give me a year to live my own life before you called me home."

He winces. "I said you could live your life until I called on you to come back home."

"And I asked you for a year."

"I never promised that. I agreed to let you go on the condition you'd return when I asked you to."

"Is that why you're here now?"

"I'm here because"—he swallows—"because—"

"Because he's arranged your marriage."

She looks at me, confused. "He has?" She leans back in her chair and locks her fingers together. "Dad? Is this true? Have you...have you decided who I'm going to marry?"

He nods but doesn't raise his gaze.

"Who is it?" she asks in a low voice.

He stays silent.

"Dad, please." She swallows. "Is it...is it someone I know? Is that why you're not speaking? Is it someone I don't like? Is it—"

"It's me."

13

———————

Mira

"What?" I jump up so quickly my chair almost topples over, except he grips it and straightens it.

"What do you mean, it's you?"

He rounds the conference table until he's standing on the opposite side of the room from me.

"You know what I mean."

"No, I don't." I turn on my father who's examining the carpet at his feet, because apparently, that's more interesting than confronting the future that lies ahead for me.

"Dad, what's he saying?"

My father sets his jaw. His lips thin but does he speak? Of course, not.

"Dad? Please, say something, please."

My plea must get through to him for he slowly raises his eyes, and then I wish he hadn't, for the expression on his face confirms my worst fears. "No, no, no, no."

"I'm sorry, Mira." An anguished expression comes over his features. "So sorry."

The fact that my father called me Mira, a name he's eschewed in favor of the more formal Mirabelle, confirms to me everything Edward said is true. That, and the fact my father looks torn. Cyril Young is too set in his ways. Too confident in his ability to make money, to steer the des*tiny* of his company and his employees and his family, to ever show any emotion or resort to niceties. The fact he apologized to me earlier is a sign the deal is done, and while he may not be in favor of it, as evinced by his reluctance to tell me about it, the fact is ,he's here. And we're talking about my future — *my* future — like it's a business transaction.

"How much did he pay for you for the deal?"

My father flinches, but he doesn't deny it. *He. Doesn't. Deny. It.*

"No." I begin to shake my head. "No. No. No." My knees give way. I sink down into the chair, and suddenly, Edward's standing next to me. He snatches up a bottle of water from the table, twists open the cap, pours it into a glass, and offers it to me. "Drink."

I shake my head.

"Belle," he lowers his voice to a hush, then holds the glass to my lips, "drink it. Now."

I take the glass, ensuring not to touch his fingers, then take a sip, another.

"Drink all of it." There's a command in his voice which insists I obey. I drain the water like the dutiful wife-to-be that I am, then place the glass on the table with a soft thunk. *Is this my future? To obey him? Is that why he's committed to this alliance?*

"Why?" I address my question to my father. "Why him?"

My father's shoulders stiffen. There's a look on his face I can't quite interpret. One that's a mixture of anger and irritation and helplessness. I've never known my father to be helpless. Never known him to be this silent. It's as if he's unable to form the words. "The least you owe me is an explanation."

Next to me, Edward stays motionless. His attention is on me. I feel his gaze on my face like he's run his knuckles down my cheek. Heat suffuses my skin. The hair on the back of my neck rises. It's like I'm caught in a quagmire of emotions that's pulling me under.

"Dad," — I swallow — "tell me."

He blows out a breath. "I needed the money."

"Money?" Of everything he could have told me, that was not what I expected. "You are a billionaire many times over. Why do you need the money?"

"I *was* a billionaire many times over." He looks away, then back at me. "A few of my investments in the last six months did not deliver the way they should have. I lost a lot of money. Enough that when Chase, here, approached me, I couldn't say no."

"You approached him?" I turn to meet Edward's gaze and flinch. The full impact of those smoldering embers which are his eyes sends a shiver of anticipation—no fear, it has to be fear—down my spine. I see the answer in his expression and a slow burn starts somewhere deep in my belly. "Why?" I clear my throat. "Why me?"

"Why not you?"

"There are so many other women out there. Anyone who would fit the bill and would gladly become your wife."

"I chose you."

Something hot coils in my chest. Satisfaction? Pride that he wants me? I could deny it, but the fact is, a part of me is taken aback that he decided on me—the plus-sized woman who's never had a chance to have a boyfriend, or managed to hold down a job long enough to know what it's like to be independent and live my own life. The woman who never knew the love of a mother. Whose own father decided her only worth was to barter her into an arrangement.

"I didn't choose you." I tip up my chin.

My father exhales sharply. He begins to say something, but Edward shakes his head. My father falls silent. That's a first. I've never seen him not win an argument, but apparently, today is a day for firsts.

The skin around Edward's eyes wrinkles, then a divot appears on the left side of his mouth, which is how I know he's smiling. Yeesh, I've worked for him only a day and I already know how to interpret his expression.

My father shuffles his feet. He begins to say something, when Edward nods his head toward the door without taking his eyes off of my face. "Leave."

"What?" My father blusters.

"You've served your purpose. It's best you go while you're still able to walk."

"Are you threatening me?" my father snaps.

"I should do more than that for your being a silent spectator to the emotional agony she was subjected to. In your home. In front of your eyes."

"B-b-b-but—" my father begins to stutter—another first, I've never heard him stutter, ever—but Edward shuts him down.

"You'd best get gone before I show you just how angry I am. And I don't want to do that, not when it's bound to upset my future wife."

Future wife. Wife? He said WIFE. My breathing grows shallow. Strange tingles make their way down my extremities.

I want to turn and take in the expression on my father's features. I want to see the regret on his face. I want to hear him admit that he did wrong by me. But a part of me is afraid that I wouldn't see that if I looked at him, so I won't. The way he allowed them to treat me is something I've never dared acknowledge to myself before today. Oh, I hoped he'd come to my rescue, that he'd tell my stepmother and half-sisters that I was a part of the family and needed to be treated with respect. I hoped, but never thought the day would come when he'd actually admit he wasn't fair to me. Not only did he do so today, but he also apologized to me.

And it's because this man put him in a position where he was no longer the most powerful man in the room. Where he was beholden to someone else… And you know what? He's beholden to me. I could have refused the wedding, and where would that have left him? I could still refuse the marriage, but that would mean my father would suffer financially. And while I've wanted him to show me his love, even though he never actively defused the situation with my stepmother and sisters, there was never any question he loved me. I can't stand by and let him face financial ruin. Not while I can make a difference and help him. Before this, I've never had the chance to contribute to our family. This is my chance to impact the outcome for my father in a positive fashion. This is my chance to… Marry this man who's fascinated me from the moment I set eyes on him. I don't know him well, but he's not a stranger. As the saying goes, better the devil you know than the one you don't, right?

"Mira, I—"

"You need to leave. Right now," Edward says in a voice which sounds casual but which has a steely undertone to it.

My father hesitates, then I sense him getting a hold of himself. "You'd better take care of her."

"You can bet I'll take a damned sight better care of her than you ever did."

"That's not fair. She's my daughter—"

"She's not yours anymore. She's mine."

14

Edward

Mine. Mine. Mine. The word ricochets around in my mind before swooping down to my chest where it sets off a fireball of sensations. How strange. I've never felt this, alive, this apprehensive, this nervous, and also…angry. I curl my fingers into fists at my sides. *How dare she walk into my life and turn it upside down? How dare she make me feel the emotions I locked out of my life? How dare she stare at me with those big blue eyes with hurt swimming in them and trailing down her cheeks? Fuck!* That ball of sensations in my chest shoots off flames which zip to my fingers, my toes. Every part of my body seems to come alive. Like a seed sprouting through the ground, the individual sentiments make themselves known.

I'm aware of her father walking out of the room. The door snicks shut. I go down on one knee, then scoop up the trail of moisture. I bring it to my mouth and suck on it.

She gasps. "What are you doing?"

"Why are you crying?"

"I'm not." She swats at her cheek. "At least, not on purpose." She bites her bottom lip before whispering, "No one's stood up to my father for me before today."

"I'm sorry for what your family put you through."

"It wasn't that bad." She half smiles. "I had a roof over my head, and designer clothes, and a team of staff who made sure my every need was taken care of."

"Everything except your emotional needs," I murmur. *And what do I know of that? Why am I unable to stop myself from comforting her? You can take the priest out of the church. You can even try to unlearn everything that you stood for by traveling around the world and trying to lose yourself amongst strangers... But it only takes a full-figured goddess with tears in her eyes to bring out that tenderness inside you which you thought you'd managed to wipe out completely.*

"He wasn't a bad father. He was just lost without my mother."

"You're defending the man who signed away your future in return for money?"

"Was it a big amount?" she murmurs.

"A few billion dollars."

"At least, it has a lot of zeroes." She chuckles, but the sound is weak.

"A lot of zeroes," I assure her.

"And you're the one he made the deal with."

"Does that make you angry?" I search her features.

"I'm angry that I'm unable to disobey my father." Her lips tighten. "I'm angry I was born into a family that believes in arranged marriages to further their business interests. I'm angry that the little time I thought I had to be independent and have a normal life was taken from me. As for the rest, I'm confused."

"Confused?" I tilt my head.

"I'm confused you asked me to work for you and you gave me a job. I'm confused how you connected with my father. How you knew he was in trouble, how—" She must notice my expression, for she slowly nods. "Of course, you knew. You have money and power and connections. You knew he was in trouble. You knew you could barter a deal with him."

"I need a wife. And contrary to your declarations, you do need a husband."

"I do not." She scowls.

"If it weren't me, it would be somebody else. Better a man you've already met than a complete stranger."

She blinks, then tips up her chin. "That's what I'm trying to tell myself. But I don't know you, either."

"A problem that's easily solved."

"What do you mean?"

"We'll get to know each other after we're married."

"And love, what about that?"

"I don't believe in love."

"Because you already gave your heart to someone else?"

I narrow my gaze. "I see you've heard about my past from our mutual friends?"

She shakes her head, then stops herself. "Only a little. It wasn't that I asked; it was mentioned in passing that you had your heart broken."

I firm my lips. I want to deny it, but that would be lying. And that's the one thing I don't do. The habit of always telling the truth, no matter the consequences, is one I haven't been able to shake. I settle for not saying anything, which she interprets correctly in the affirmative.

Her forehead wrinkles. "So, what I heard is true."

"My past is of no consequence to you."

"How can you say that when it will impact my future?"

"All you need to know is that your father and I came to an amiable agreement, and he has agreed to my proposal of marrying you."

"Do I have a choice in this?" There's a bitter note in her voice.

"You know the consequences of refusing."

"So, that's a no?"

I rise to my feet then pull out a chair and sink into it. "That's a—this relationship can work to both of our advantages."

"How's that?"

"You'll be my wife in name only."

"Meaning?"

"You'll take my name, you'll marry me, you'll wear my ring on your finger. You'll be civil toward my family. As far as they're concerned, this is a real marriage. But we will not sleep in the same bed."

"We won't?"

"I have no interest in having sex with you."

"You...you don't?"

"I'll take care of my needs...elsewhere."

"You mean in this club?" She gestures to the room.

"I'll be discreet, of course."

"Of course." That bitterness is back in her voice, and for some reason, that bothers me.

"You have no interest in being my wife, Belle. But you want to save your father from bankruptcy. You also need money to keep a roof over your head."

She begins to protest, and I cut in, "You and I both know if I hadn't offered you a job as my assistant, you'd have had to return home. This way, you don't need to stay under the same roof as your family again."

She sets her jaw but doesn't deny the facts.

"I am compelled to get married to ensure my grandfather confirms me as the CEO of his group of companies. This is a win-win, as far as I'm concerned."

"I can only see losses in my future."

"How's that?"

"I'll be stuck in a loveless marriage, with no intimacy. No intimacy,"—her features pale—"which means, no children."

"You want children?" I stare.

"Of course, I want children. The only reason I'd consider this marriage if I could have children." She sets her jaw. "I know this might sound lame, but I've never known a time when I didn't want to be a mother. In fact, it's the reason I decided to pursue a career in childcare. It's one way to be in the company of kids throughout the day. It's probably not the most ambitious of dreams, but—"

"Don't put yourself down. Your dreams are important, and you deserve to give them life."

"I... I do?" Her lips part.

I nod slowly. A soft sensation invades my chest. Belle, big with my child. Belle, playing with my son or daughter, taking them to school, making breakfast for them. Belle, holding him or her in her arms and—I shake my head. "You can still have children."

"How—oh!" The wrinkle in her forehead vanishes. "You mean, by IVF."

"If that's what you decide."

"And if I decide I don't want to be married anymore?"

I lean forward in my seat. "I'm afraid that's not possible."

"Meaning?"

"Once you marry me, you can't leave me. You'll be mine for the rest of your life."

"So, I marry you and that's it. I'm stuck with you?"

"Don't overwhelm me with your enthusiasm," I drawl.

She flushes. "You know what I mean. One day, I don't know you.

The next, you're my boss. And now, you're saying you want to be my husband, but not in the true sense of the word."

"There are worse options out there."

"So you keep saying."

"I'll make sure you have your independence. You can continue to work for me."

She frowns. "But wouldn't that be conflict of interest?"

"It's my company." I raise a shoulder. "Besides, we'll be married only in name, so—"

"So—" She swallows. "No sex."

"None."

"And I can stay in my own flat?"

"You're my wife; you'll have to move in with me. We'll share the same suite—"

"But—"

"We'll have our own rooms."

"So we won't share the same bed?" she says slowly.

"I sleep best on my own."

She locks her fingers together. "Can I think about it?"

"Afraid time is running out." I pull back the sleeve of my shirt and look at my watch. "My grandfather wants me married within the week."

"The week?" she squeaks.

"Is that a problem?"

"It's just… Things are moving very quickly, and I haven't said 'yes' yet."

Not that she has a choice, given her father has already committed her to the marriage. She knows it. I know it. But I'm enough of a gentleman to play along...for now. If an illusion of having a choice is what it takes for her to say yes, then I'm more than happy to humor her.

I tap my fingers on my thigh. "What are you waiting for?"

"I... I have some questions." She shuffles her feet.

"Shoot." I settle back in my seat.

"Why did you bring me to this club?"

"So you'd be aware of the inclinations of the man you'll be marrying."

"You mean BDSM?"

Not bad, she managed to get out the words without fumbling over the vocabulary.

"Among other things."

"You wanted to show me your needs are...a little extreme?"

I can't stop my lips from twitching. "Those are your words, not mine."

"So this was a test?"

"Maybe?" I yawn.

"Why hire me as your assistant?" The wrinkle between her eyebrows deepens.

I want to lean forward and smooth out her brow a-n-d nope, not going there. *Why do I feel so compelled to soothe away her worries?* I set my jaw. "I told you already. You needed a job. I did need an assistant. Besides, what better way for you to find out more about my habits than working with me in such close proximity?"

She rubs at her temple. "But when did you decide you wanted to marry me? Did you know about my father having business troubles already? Did you—" She searches my face. "You knew who I was when we met at Gio's place."

I nod.

She firms her lips. "You've been planning this since then?"

"When I met you, I needed an assistant. You're trusted by my friends. And I trust my friends, so it felt right to offer you the job. Turns out, I also need a wife, and—"

"You decided I fit that role, too?"

I wipe my thumb under my lower lip. "You're single. And when I had you investigated, I realized who you were."

"So, all the pieces fell together," she says flatly.

"It seemed the logical next step. You'll have to sign a contract, of course."

"I... I do?"

I nod. "Only you and I will know the real state of this marriage. To everyone else, we decided to get married because we're in love."

"So we met, and you decided I was the one, and we got married within a week?" She scoffs.

"When you know, you know." The words come out with more certainty than I intended. And for some reason I believe it, too.

She must, too, for her eyes widen. "You sure you used to be a priest and not an actor?"

I tilt my head. "A priest has to be an actor to take the pulpit, and an actor might well be a priest when he's on screen."

"How do you mean?"

"An actor is the mirror of the audience's desires. He or she accepts it without judgement, and in turn, grants them absolution."

She searches my features and hers soften. "Also a poet."

I hold her gaze and ensure my own are steely. "You must be mistaken."

She looks at me a second longer, then nods. "I must be."

I reach for my phone and message a number, then slide it back into the pocket of my suit. "The contract is for everything I outlined, including a non-disclosure agreement. Everything I've told you today is confidential."

"So you don't trust me?" She scoffs.

"I asked you to marry me, didn't I?"

"Only because I happened to be convenient. Not to mention, you had leverage over me." She wraps her arms about her waist.

"The NDA is a deterrent. So, if you're tempted to tell your friends, it will stop you."

She jerks her chin up, and I take in the guilt in her eyes.

"It's normal for you to want to consult with someone else on this, but I'm afraid I can't allow that."

"You can't?"

I shake my head. "Time is of the essence. As is the timing. I understand it's all sudden, but you need to trust me on this."

"How can I trust you when you used my father's circumstances to coerce me into a wedding?"

"You can leave, of course."

"We both know that's not an option." Her lips turn down. Her eyes grow haunted.

I want to go over and pull her into my arms and tell her everything is going to be okay. But that would be lying. And I don't say anything I don't mean. *Also, why am I so affected by her?* All the more reason to get through this sham of a wedding, make sure my grandfather and half-siblings believe in the veracity of my marriage, and then I can get on with my life.

There's a knock on the door, and a suited man walks in. He looks between us, then places an envelope in front of me. I nod, and he leaves.

She stares at the envelope with a look of apprehension. "What's that?"

"The agreement outlining our marriage of convenience." I pull a pen from the inside pocket of my jacket, then slip a sheaf of papers from the envelope and slide them over to her.

"Do I have to sign this right now?"

15

Mira

"You're marrying him?" Abby pales. "You barely know him."

I glance out at the pouring rain. It's a Saturday, so I didn't have to go to work. Gotta hand it to Edward. He planned it out so we didn't have to meet at work this morning. He gave me eighteen hours to arrive at a decision. Eighteen hours to make a decision that's going to impact the rest of my life. Should I be grateful he gave me this much time? Or is this a way for him to pander to me, safe in the knowledge I'm going to comply? Definitely the latter. Edward's too smart. He knows I will agree to his proposition. He knows I don't have a choice in the matter. This—giving me a few hours—is him creating an illusion I am in control when I'm not. A chance for things to sink in, so I'll go into this arrangement more willingly.

"Are you sure about this?" Summer asks quietly.

No. But of course, I can't tell her that.

The girls are in my tiny apartment. Abby and Summer are on the couch. Penny, has taken the sole armchair, and Gio's pulled up one of the barstools from the kitchenette. I've been too restless to sit still. I was moved that my girlfriends turned up so quickly, but I also knew it would be pointless telling them I was okay when it was clear from the expression on my face that I'm not.

Edward dropped me off at my apartment building yesterday. Neither of us spoke a word. He focused on driving, and I focused on trying to get my thoughts together. I barely slept last night. When dawn broke, I made myself a cup of tea and wondered how I was going to get through the coming few days. *How am I going to get through my life?*

Other than my father, the rest of my family won't care about my marriage. I want to talk things through with my friends, but I signed the agreement last night, which means, I have to keep the details confidential. The minutes ticked on, and with every passing hour, my panic increased. When Gio called me, I tried to appear normal, but she must have seen something in my expression because the next thing I knew, she was at my doorstop, followed by Abby, Summer, and Penny.

"His proposal was very sudden," I murmur.

"No shit. I knew he was up to something when you spilled coffee on him, and he responded by asking you to work for him. And now he wants to marry you." Gio looks at me with suspicion. "Is he holding something over you? Is that why you agreed to be his wife?"

I glance away, not wanting her to see the confusion in my eyes. Edward is one hell of a good actor, but I can't say the same about myself. And these are my friends. And now, I'm lying to them.

"It's nothing like that. I...uh... I fell in love with him. It's why I'm marrying him."

"You met him a week ago," Gio points out..

"It was love at first sight." I hear the defensiveness in my voice and wince. That isn't very convincing. Judging by the silence behind me, none of my friends believe me, either.

"If you're in trouble, you can tell us," Penny says in a soft voice. "We can help you. Our husbands—"

"Wouldn't hesitate to use their billions to rescue me from a sticky situation, I'm aware." I turn to face them. "And I appreciate the offer. But honestly, it's nothing of that sort. He... He loves me." *Don't look away. Don't look away.* I lower my eyelashes, and Gio instantly jumps to her feet.

"You expect us to believe that grumpass took one look at you and decided you were going to be his wife?" She stabs a finger in my direction.

I raise my gaze to hers and nod firmly. In this, at least, I'm not lying. The truth in my eyes must convince Gio, for she seems taken aback.

"It's not that I don't believe in insta-love. I'm the living embodiment of it, after all, but getting married to him within the week you go to work for him?" She shakes her head.

"I know it's a little rushed—"

"Try very rushed." Gio scowls.

"Give the girl a chance to speak," Abby admonishes her.

Gio firms her lips but continues to stare at me with a speculative look in her eyes.

"Is this what you want?" Summer searches my features. "Is it, Mira? Because if you have your heart set on it, then of course, we're in your corner."

"But if that asshat is holding something over you—" Gio begins.

"Didn't you agree when Rick asked you to marry him? And you knew him for a short period of time.

"I met him months before he asked, but yes, I only got to know him properly for a week before I agreed." She tosses her hair over her shoulder. "I suppose, I shouldn't be lecturing you about the need for caution, but I worry about you, Mira. You're—"

"Innocent?"

"In a good way. You're the best of us. You have a heart that is swayed so easily."

"Doesn't mean I'm stupid." I set my jaw.

"I didn't say that. I only mean, you lead with your emotions. You're the woman who volunteers at the senior citizen's center when you're not taking care of kids at the preschool."

"Nothing wrong with volunteering." I tip up my chin.

"But you went above and beyond the call of duty. You started a knitting club so those old ladies had something to look forward to."

"Only because they love reading smut, as do I."

"Wait, you started a smut club for grannies?" Penny gapes.

"And one grandpa, if you want to be accurate, but yes. We meet weekly and knit and talk about spicy books. You should hear them. Their vocabulary of four-letter words puts the rest of us to shame."

Gio chuckles. "That's what I mean. You're smart and sexy. You light up any room you walk into, Mira. While Edward—" She shakes her head. "Is not the easiest man to be with."

"Maybe that's why they work," Penny says slowly.

Silence descends.

"What?" She looks around the room. "It's why Knight and I are so good together. He's a grumpy-face, and I can't stop myself from having a smile on mine" She curves her lips to demonstrate.

"It *is* probably why I'm so attracted to him," I admit.

"Hmm." Gio shifts her weight from foot to foot. "Edward's a complex man."

"That's putting it lightly." I half laugh.

Abby taps the arm of the couch. "I think we all agree that our relationships with our respective husbands did not begin in the most traditional of ways—"

"—but it turned out well, and we're very happy," Abby murmurs.

"Blissfully." Summer nods.

"Doesn't mean you have to agree to marry him," Gio points out.

I set my jaw. "But what if I want to?"

"Do you?" Summer asks.

I nod slowly.

"If you do, then make sure you negotiate with him, before the wedding." Gio brushes off a speck of dirt from her Prada jacket. "Make sure you get what you want out of it before giving in to him."

"Like what?"

"Money? Houses. Whatever you want out of it."

"But how—" A knock on the door interrupts me. I glance toward it; so do the girls.

"Don't you have an intercom system?" Penny frowns.

"I do." I begin to walk toward the door when whoever is at the door knocks on it again. I look toward the peephole, then step back and pivot around to face them. "It's him."

"Who?" Gio asks.

"Edward," I whisper. Not that he can hear my voice through the door, but he's right there on the other side of it. "What should I do?" I wring my hands. "I'm not ready to see him.

"Belle?" He bangs on the door again. "I know you're in there."

I freeze, and I'm sure the look on my face is that of pure panic, for Gio rises to her feet. She marches past me and grips the door handle, before turning to me. "Should I tell him to leave?"

I shake my head.

She sighs. "You want me to buy you some time?"

I nod.

"Why don't you go on into the bedroom?"

"Thank you" I race past the other girls.

Behind me, I hear her throw open the door. "Edward, what are you doing here?"

16

Edward

"I'm here for Mira."

"Hmm." Gio purses her lips. "What are your intentions toward her."

I glance past her to where the other women look at me with varying expressions of displeasure and mistrust.

"Can I come in?" I hold up my hands. "I mean no harm."

"That's debatable." She purses her lips, then finally, stands aside.

I stalk past her and into the center of the rom. "Ladies." I tilt my head. "I'm glad Mira has friends looking out for her."

"Can we say the same about you?" Summer asks in a serious tone.

Of everyone in this room, I've known her the longest. I attended her wedding to Sinclair. I've seen the bond between them grow. Sinclair loves her more than his own life, and she reciprocates their sentiment. She's aware of my past. Of the incident that binds Sinclair and me and the rest of the Seven together. No one else in my family knows the true extent to which that incident scarred me. It's a secret, known to us, and now the wives of the Seven.

I keep my arms loose at my sides and nod. "You can."

I hold her gaze, and she must read the sincerity in my eyes, for her shoulders relax.

"She's my friend, Ed," Summer murmurs.

"I'm aware."

"Don't hurt her."

"I won't," I hear the vehemence in my tone. "I'll do everything to protect her."

"Including from yourself?"

I blink. *That's the plan.* The problem is, when I'm around her, I don't act in character. I tend to become unpredictable and unable to keep my gaze off of her. I'm also not able to stop my mind from wondering how it would be to have her under me, to bury myself in her softness, to have her scent wipe away the images from my past, to allow her voice to lead me out of the maze I am stuck in.

And I can't allow that to happen. I can't let myself fall for her. "I'll do everything in my power to give her what she needs."

She frowns. "That doesn't answer my question."

I square my shoulders. "Her happiness is important to me. I will ensure she is taken care of, that she wants for nothing, that all her wants are met—"

"Including her emotional ones?"

I hesitate. "I will do everything in my capacity to give her what she needs."

Summer rises to her feet and walks over to stand in front of me. She scans my features. "I know you've been through a lot, Ed. You deserve a chance at happiness. Mira can be the catalyst to help you move forward with your life, if you'll let her."

That's what I'm afraid of. That's what I have to guard myself against happening. I incline my head. "Do I have your blessings?"

She looks between my eyes, then nods slowly.

"If you do anything to upset her, you'll have me to contend with," Gio snaps.

"And me." Penny stabs her forefinger and middle finger in the direction of her eyes, then at me.

"And me." Abby gives me a considering look from the couch.

I look between the women and nod. "You won't need to because I'd punish myself if I did anything to make her unhappy. Now, can I go in and see my wife-to-be?"

Gio stalks past me, and raps on the bedroom door. "You ready to meet this asshat, honey?"

A few seconds pass, then the door opens. Mira stands in the doorway. She turns without meeting my eyes and walks away. I move past Gio, step inside the room, and shut the door behind me. I lean against it, cross my arms over my chest, and watch as she stands at the window with her back to me.

"I have a surprise for you."

She stiffens.

"Don't you want to know what it is?"

She shakes her head.

I stalk toward her. She hears me approaching and stiffens but doesn't turn to look at me. I pause behind her; then, because I can't stop myself, I lean in and sniff her hair.

She turns and stares at me. "Did you sniff me?"

Busted. "Me? Do I look like the kind of man who'd sniff you?"

The skin between her eyebrows wrinkles. She looks uncertain, but at least, she's looking at me.

"You said you have a surprise?"

I hold out my hand, palm face-up. She looks at it warily.

"I promise, I won't bite." *Yet.*

She places her left palm in mine with reluctance. I slide my other hand into my pocket, pull out a ring, and slide it onto her ring finger.

"Oh, my god, is that… Is that a—"

"Engagement ring."

She swallows, then slowly raises her hand. She tilts it this way and that. The light from the window bounces off the sapphire in the center. The diamonds surrounding it reflect the blue. Together they deepen the color of her eyes into a shade you'd only find in the depths of the Mediterranean.

"It's gorgeous." Her chest rises and falls. "And it fits."

"Of course, it does."

She looks up at me. "How did you know my size?"

"You are mine. I know everything about you."

The skin at the corners of her eyes crinkles. She scrutinizes my features like she's trying to solve a puzzle, then her forehead smoothens. "It's because you need to convince your family our marriage is real."

It's because I have this compelling need to know everything about you. What makes you smile; what makes you laugh? What makes you worried or scared?

What you like; what you hate? Why you always manage to bring the sunshine with you wherever you go? "Can't slip up. This is my one chance to make sure my grandfather confirms me as the CEO of the company."

"Is that so important to you?"

"Is that a question?"

She opens, then shuts her mouth. "Money isn't everything. Nor power. There's more to life than just trying to build your business empire."

"Been there, done that. All there is to life is money and power. It's what allows you to control your future."

"You don't believe that."

I incline my head.

She searches my features, then lowers her hand to her side. "Just because you had your heart broken once—"

"That is not up for discussion," I growl.

Hurt flares in her eyes.

My heart stutters. I'm unable to guard myself against her responses. I want to draw her close and tell her everything, and then what? I'll never break my vow to not allow anyone else in my life again. It's not right to give her false hope when I intend to always keep that emotional distance between us. I firm my lips.

She takes in the expression on my face, then squares her shoulders. "I am going to be your wife—"

"Fake wife."

"But real in front of everyone else."

"What's your point?"

"I need to know enough about you so I can ensure no one, especially your family, can question our relationship." She thrusts out her lower lip in that expression I'm coming to recognize as stubbornness, and damn, if that doesn't make me want to close my mouth over hers, dig my teeth into her lower lip and—

I clamp down on my errant thoughts. "You're right."

"I am?"

I nod. "It's why you're moving in with me."

17

Mira

"This is your room. Mine is next door; the ensuite connects both rooms." He stands at the entrance to the bedroom, one hand braced on the door-frame. It's a posture that declares his masculinity in no uncertain terms. When he said I needed to move in with him 'right now,' he meant it. He coerced me to pack what I needed in an overnight bag. He assured me the rest of my stuff would be sent over soon.

Then, he hustled me past my friends, who looked at us open-mouthed in surprise. He gave me just enough time to tell them I was fine, and that I was relocating to his place until the wedding, which is in approximately five days. Gio spotted the engagement ring. When she pointed it out, my friends gathered around me while Edward waited nearby, impatience writ in every angle of his body. Abby congratulated me, and Summer said she couldn't wait to help me choose my wedding dress. She's also recommended a wedding planner, who she said would contact me. Penny said her friend, Amelie's company would do the catering.

Only Gio remained unconvinced. She made me promise to call her if

I need any help. I hugged them all, managed to keep the tears from falling, and left with Edward.

And I know, he mentioned we'd have separate rooms, but looking around the space, which is almost as big as my entire one-bedroom, I'm overwhelmed. I'm getting married in a few days, to a man I don't know. And no one except me, him, and my father knows why. A shiver grips me, and I wrap my arms about my waist.

I hear footsteps, and the next thing I know, he's draped his jacket over my shoulders. The scent of woodsmoke and that faint tingle of electricity surrounds me at once. It's as if I'm surrounded by Edward. I'm not sure if I like him, but I could bottle his scent and sniff it all day. Not that I'll ever admit that to him. I snuggle into his jacket. The weight of his hand on my shoulders sends a flush of heat over my skin. I shiver again.

"You're cold. I'll turn up the heating in the room."

"No, I'm good, I—" I begin to protest, then turn to find he's pulled out his phone.

He plays with the screen. "All done."

"You're able to control the temperature of my room with your phone?"

He raises a shoulder. "I want to be sure you're comfortable."

"Right."

"I'll give you a tour of the apartment tomorrow."

"I wouldn't have envisioned you living in a penthouse." I nod toward the lights of the city which shine outside the floor-to-ceiling window.

"Why not?"

"You seem like a man who values history. I thought you'd live in a Victorian townhouse. Or in a heritage building."

A strange look comes into his eyes, then he banks it. "You don't know me at all."

"Which is why you asked me to move in with you before the wedding, so we can get to know each other."

He tilts his head.

"When do we meet your family?"

"Tomorrow."

"What?" I gape. "I… I'm not ready."

"You'll be fine."

"Easy for you say. You're not the one on display."

His features soften. "My grandfather will be relieved I'm settling down. As for my half-brothers, their opinions don't count."

"How can you say that. Aren't they family?"

"I'm the odd one out."

"Why is that?"

"Their father, who is also my biological father, didn't know of my existence until a few months ago. My mother fell pregnant with his child, but never told him. She broke up with him and married my uncle, his older brother, who adopted me. My adoptive father was estranged from his family. He changed his surname to his mother's—"

"Hence, your surname is Chase, while your family surname is Davenport."

He nods. "My grandfather, Arthur, found out about my existence a few months ago. He realized I was his oldest grandson and wanted me to take over as the CEO of the family."

"And you agreed."

"I want to make him happy." He raises a shoulder.

"You also need a goal, a focus in your life, and this gives you an anchor."

Once more, that strange look flickers in his eyes—it's a combination of puzzlement and surprise. Once more, he banks it, and his features take on that mask of polite disinterest. The one I'm coming to hate.

"If this is going to work, you have to be truthful with me."

"Are you accusing me of lying?" he asks in a low, hard voice. My core instantly clenches. My nipples perk up. When he uses that voice, it's as if he flips a switch somewhere deep inside me that controls my feelings of arousal.

"You don't lie, Edward."

He blinks.

"But you *are* evasive."

His gaze grows hard.

"I know the episode in your childhood hurt you, and then—"

"What do you know about the episode?" That uncompromising tone of his voice is like a diamond edge.

I manage not to flinch, manage to tip up my chin and peer into his face. "Just that it affected you and your friends. I don't know any of the details."

He searches my features, then slowly nods. "I'm not ready to talk about it."

"I understand."

"Do you?" He sets his jaw.

"Of course, I do. You're not a sharing kind of person. So, for you to say that you're willing to allow me to get to know you is huge. You're not as beyond redemption as you think you are."

A muscle pulses at his temple. "And you're the one who's going to redeem me?"

"I am going to be your wife."

"Only in name."

"So you keep telling me. It's as if you're trying to convince yourself." I look between his eyes. "Is that what this is about? Are you worried you're going to fall for me, Edward?"

His features shutter.

"Are you?" I ask again.

He sets his jaw and shoves his hand into the pocket of his well-cut pants in a gesture I'm beginning to see as a tell. "I will not fall in love."

"Will not?"

"I took a vow after my last…run-in with that particular emotion… that I won't allow it in my life again."

"You took a vow?" I ask in a dazed voice.

"Love is not for me."

"But you do love your friends. I know you're close to Sinclair and the rest of the Seven."

He nods slowly. "The seven of us have been through a lot. We have a bond that cannot be broken. I suppose, I do have a depth of feeling for them. Is it love?" He raises a shoulder. "Maybe. As for romantic love? That will not figure in my life again."

"Why is that? Don't you owe it to yourself to be happy? Don't you—"

"I promised myself not to fall for anyone again."

I gape. "You promised yourself?"

"And that's all you need to know."

"Wait, that's not fair. You—"

The door is pushed open, and Tiny pops his big head around the corner. He looks between us, then shoves the door open the rest of the way. He walks into the room, past Edward and plants his rump near me. He looks up at me with his melting brown eyes—so different from my fiancé's. Tiny may be a mutt, but there's something in his eyes that's heartfelt and soft, like he carries his heart in his eyes. My fiancé, on the other hand? Carries his emotions buried behind so many walls... And while I may have seen some flickers of emotion in his gaze, they've been few and far between. As if sensing the turn my thoughts have taken, Tiny makes a whining noise.

"Aww, did you miss Eddie? Is that why you're here?" I reach over and scratch Tiny behind his ears. He makes a purring sound and leans into my touch.

"Did you call me, Eddie?" His voice is shocked.

I risk a look at his face and find an incredulous expression there. It's so unexpected, I laugh. Tiny lets out a small bark at that. "He agrees." I nod.

"Agrees with what?"

"That it's the first time I'm seeing you taken aback."

"Hmph." He firms his lips and schools his features back into that emotionless mask.

"You don't fool me." I point my forefinger at him.

"Do I want to know what you mean by that?"

"Just that you're not as impassive as you make yourself out to be."

He seems taken aback, again, then inclines his head. "I decided a while ago there was no place for feelings in my life."

"We've established you feel something for your friends and also, for Tiny here."

Tiny woofs, then turns his soulful gaze on Edward. My fiancé scowls at the dog, then sighs. "Yeah, okay, that mutt has a hold of my heart. But that's it. There is no space for anyone else in my life."

Nice. Now I'm in queue behind a dog. No matter, it's a Great Dane who's so intelligent he might well be almost human, I'm not as important as he is to Edward. He must realize how his words sound, for he stiffens. "I didn't mean —"

"You did."

"You are my fiancée," he offers.

"Fake fiancée."

"Real to the outside world."

"But it's a charade."

"It is," he agrees.

"Okay." A heaviness tightens my chest. I wrap my arms about my waist, feeling so very lonely.

I thought when I got married, even if it was an arranged marriage as my father wanted, perhaps, I'd find companionship in it. Perhaps, I'd have my children make up for the loss of a true partner. And sure, I could technically still have kids, but the entire process is going to feel so clinical. I hadn't thought as far as sex with my future arranged husband… But maybe, a part of me had hoped he'd fall in love with me. That we could find love on the heels of the arrangement. Guess I was wrong. Tears prick the backs of my eyes. I look away. Tiny senses my sadness, and rising up on his feet, he brushes his head gently against my hand. I pat his head, then give in and lean forward to kiss his shaggy head.

Edward clears his throat and I look up. He has strange expression on his face but I'm too exhausted to decode it.

"What time do we leave tomorrow?"

18

Edward

"May I take your coat, Sir? Madam?" Otis, my grandfather's butler looks between me and my fiancée. I slide my coat off and hand it to him, then ease Mira's coat from her shoulders. I place it over his arm.

"This way please." He gestures toward the hallway that leads to the dining room.

"I can see myself in, Otis. Thank you."

He seems taken aback, then nods. "Of course, Sir."

I barely slept last night. And when I finally fell asleep, it was to images from my past. I broke my vows, walked away from my calling. I'd searched for that elusive peace, which I'd fooled myself into believing I had when I was part of the church. It's only after I left, I realized I'd been running all my life.

I'm still running now—except I've come up against a woman who threatens to stop me in my tracks. I don't like it. It's a feeling I don't relish. I don't want to be faced with the proof of my own vulnerability. And all it took was a pair of baby blues and a lusciously curvy figure on a woman who's all sunshine and rainbows, despite her own unhappy past. A woman who places the happiness of her father before her own.

What kind of person would push her dreams aside and bow to the call of duty? She reminds me of the man I thought I was. The man who put his vocation before anything else; the man who believed in the greater good; the man who wanted to redeem others.

He walks into the cloak room adjoining the hallway, leaving Mira and me alone. She glances up at the ceiling, which is three stories above us. The skylights are dark, but in the mornings, light pours into the entryway. In the center, two staircases curve toward each other to meet on the second-floor landing. Above that, the rooms on the third floor look down on the entryway. A massive chandelier descends from the roof, and the lights shine off the stained glass that adorns the windows on the first floor. The floor is made of marble, and there are satin drapes on the walls, interspersed with paintings of some of the great masters — all originals. The overall effect is that of wealth — the kind that has been in a family for generations. My parents weren't poor — not materially — but my grandfather's wealth makes them look like small business owners.

"I forgot it's almost Christmas." Mira walks toward the Christmas tree set between the two staircases. The focal point of the entranceway, it's almost as high as the roof and is lit up with Christmas lights and ornaments. The scent of pine is heavy in the air, but as I approach her, I detect her light, apple-blossom perfume below it. I come to a stop behind her, then lower my head and discreetly sniff. She doesn't notice it, too intent on taking in the decorations.

"It's gorgeous," she murmurs.

"It is," I murmur, looking at her.

"I loved opening my gift on Christmas morning. It was the one time my father was around, and I knew he'd always have something I loved."

"Gift?"

She turns to me. "Yes, my father would buy me a gift."

"What about your — "

"Stepmother?" She shrugs. "We always pretended it was from her too, but it was obvious she never gave me much thought. Given a choice, she'd have sent me off to boarding school so I wouldn't be around, and definitely not for Christmas morning. But it was the one thing my father refused to agree to. He'd promised my mother he'd keep me close. He also knew how much my mother had loved Christmas. And while he never had time for me otherwise, he made sure I knew I was loved during Christmas. What about you? Do you love Christmas?"

"I don't believe in Christmas."

There was a time when I did, but when I left the priesthood, I also turned my back on the rituals, and that's all Christmas really is.

"What?" She pivots to face me. "Are you serious?" She sees the expression on my face and her jaw drops. "You are serious."

"Always."

"You don't say?" she says in a droll voice.

"It's the one time of the year I ensure I'm away from this city."

"Christmas is the best time of the year in London. I arrived in this city last December and found it all lit up. There were decorations up in shop windows, the pubs were festive, people on the tube smiled at each other. I thought it was the most cheerful place on earth. Then came January, and I realized it's the only time of the year people walk around with smiles. But my first impressions remained. I ended up falling in love with the city anyway. Now I can't wait for December and the festive season. It's the one time of the year everyone in London seems almost happy."

"Exactly."

"Jeez"—she shakes her head—"should've guessed you're a Grinch."

"He's a chip off the old block, all right." Arthur's voice reaches us. Then my grandfather draws abreast.

"Edward." He nods at me.

"Arthur." I nod back.

"You made it."

I half smile. You don't turn the old man down. I haven't known Arthur Davenport that long, but even if he hadn't been my grandfather, his authority is writ large in everything he says and does. He's not the kind of man you say no to easily.

"You must be Mirabelle." He turns to Belle.

"Grandad." She closes the distance to him and throws her arms about his shoulders. "I am so happy to meet you."

Arthur stiffens. His gaze widens, and he gapes at me. If I didn't know better, I'd say the old man is shocked. And it takes a lot to shock him. I manage to keep the smile off my face, then watch as my grandfather recovers himself. He pats Belle on the shoulder. "It's nice to meet you, too."

She steps back and beams up at him. "Call me, Mira."

"Hmm." He scans her features. "I can see why Edward fell in love with you."

"Oh, but he's not—" she begins.

I cut her off. "I hope we didn't keep you waiting."

"You did"—he shoots me a glance—"but since you were showing Mira around, you're forgiven."

Belle laughs, a happy sound that infuses warmth into my veins.

"When Edward told me he was getting married, I was sure he'd decided to ask the first eligible woman he came across to be his wife. I'm relieved to see he's been much more discerning."

"Umm—" She shuffle her feet. "I… We…."

"We're very in love, Grandad. When I saw Mira, there was no question I was going to marry her. Your condition that I get married before I can be confirmed in my role as CEO spurred me to pop the question."

Arthur holds out his right hand, and when Belle places her left palm in it, he raises her fingers and kisses her engagement ring. "You gave her the ring your grandmother left you?"

"This is your grandmother's ring?" She glances at me in shock.

"It's the reason I found out about his existence," Arthur adds.

She tears her gaze away from mine and frowns. "I'm not sure I understand."

Arthur hooks her arm through his, then leads her down the hallway. I bracket her in from the other side.

"When my wife passed away last year, I was gutted."

"I'm so sorry for your loss," she murmurs.

I shoot him a glance in time to see his eyes shadow. "Thank you. I appreciate it. Greta and I were married for fifty-five years."

Her gaze widens until those blue eyes seem to fill her face.

"Seems like a long time, but it went by in a flash." Arthur's lips curve. *Holy shit, the old man smiled?* In the little time I've known him, I've never seen the hint of softness on his face, but a few seconds with her, and he's already in a better mood. Seems I'm not the only one susceptible to her sunshine nature.

"Time is funny." I narrow my gaze on him, then continue, "When you're having fun, it speeds by, and when you're dreading a deadline, it seems to be roaring toward you."

Arthur nods. "I'll bet the two of you can't wait to get married. It must seem like an impossibly long time until the ceremony."

I frown at my grandfather. Did he mean…? Nope, he means we're in love and can't wait to get married, and it seems like a long way off in the future, though it's only a few days.

Belle hesitates, then shakes her head. "You're wrong."

"I am?" He knits his brows.

I narrow my gaze on her. *What the hell is she doing?* Before I can say anything, she hooks her free arm through mine, and rubs her cheek against my sleeve. "Every day with Eddie is the best day of my life. He's so warm, so caring, and he has a great sense of humor." She beams.

I do? I blink.

"Oh, honeykins, you have a wicked, tongue-in-cheek wit, and your jokes crack me up." She pats my shoulder.

I stare at her, unsure of where she's going with this.

"Oh, Sweetie, you have such a sense of humor. I've never laughed so much as when I'm with you. In fact, the amount of tears I've shed—"

I growl loud enough for only her to hear me.

"—due to finding your jokes funny… Perhaps, I'm the only one who does, but you've made me burst out in hysterics until I cry, Eddie." She flicks an imaginary tear from the corner of her eyes.

She called me Eddie, again. I'm aware I'm glowering at her, and in front of Arthur, but what-fucking-ever. *No one calls me Eddie and gets away with it. Except her, apparently. Time I put an end to that.* I open my mouth to set her straight, but Arthur cuts me off.

"That's what my Greta used to say."

I manage to tear my gaze from that of my fiancée long enough to take in the wistful look on Arthur's face.

"She always found my jokes hilarious. Even after all those years of being married, she'd laugh at my jokes. She liked to say she was the only one who found my jokes funny after all that time." He swallows then turns to me. "I'm glad you took my advice to heart."

"Wouldn't dream of doing otherwise." I can't stop the note of sarcasm in my tone.

His shoulders tense. There's a flicker of anger in his eyes before he bats it away. "Then you also won't dream of turning down an old man's wish?"

It's my turn to stiffen. "Depends on the wish. I've already agreed to not only take on the role of CEO but also to settle down, as you dictated."

He doesn't seem satisfied by that. "You were wise to acknowledge when someone gave you good advice. All I ask is you do one more thing for me."

I scowl.

His forehead furrows.

I am only just beginning to get to know this man, but I see the same stubbornness in his expression that I recognize in myself. My footsteps slow; so do his and Belle's. We come to a stop at the threshold of the library he's been walking us to—not the dining room, as I'd originally envisaged.

"I think I've done enough. I—"

"G-Pa, can I call you G-Pa?" Belle chimes in.

Arthur shoots me a final look, then glances down at her upturned face. "I would like that very much. And both of you would make me very happy if you agree to my last wish. I don't have many days left on this earth, after all."

Why that canny so-and-so. The man has a strong enough constitution, he'll probably outlast all of us. My scowl deepens. I open my mouth to tell him off, but Belle cries out, "Of course, G-Pa." She turns to me. "I'm sure there's no harm in agreeing to what he wants."

I glare at her. Her color fades, but she firms her lips. The two of us lock gazes. The air between us heats. The pulse at the base of her throats kicks up and moves as she swallows. Another wall I've built around my heart crumbles, and a slow beat drums at my temples. If Arthur weren't here, I'd teach her never to defy me. My fingers twitch. I reach down and tuck a strand of her hair behind her ear. Her pupils dilate. She sways toward me. I begin to lower my head when Arthur declares,

"I want the two of you to marry right now."

19

———————

Mira

"What?" Edward whips his head around to look at his grandfather. Whatever he sees there has him turning to look at the conservatory. And that has him tightening his jaw. He's gritting his teeth so hard the muscles of his jaw flex. I follow his line of sight, take in the group gathered inside, a-n-d, the breath whooshes out of me.

"We…we're getting married, right now?" my voice comes out shaky.

"Why wait until next week, when you can tie the knot now?" G-Pa's tone is satisfied. He glances toward us, then seems to falter. "I hope it's okay I invited your friends and arranged for an officiant?" He waves a hand toward the be-spectacled guy I don't recognize at the far end of the library in front of the lit fireplace.

"I assume you didn't want a priest presiding, Edward?"

"Nice of you to take my wishes into consideration." His tone has a biting edge which cuts through me.

"You're welcome," G-Pa says in a mild voice. "Mira, I arranged for your friend to get your wedding dress made."

"My wedding dress?" I ask faintly. *What is happening? Are we getting married, right now?* Given I recognize the people in the room who're all dressed up in their finest and who're looking at us with big smiles on their faces, I'd say my question is rhetorical. *But I'm not ready.* I wasn't ready for getting married in a week. And I'm absolutely not ready to get hitched within the hour. I tighten my hold on Edward's arm. He must feel the pressure of my grasp, must sense the nervousness that, no doubt, vibrates off of me like I'm an off-balance washing machine on the spin cycle, for he places his big warm hand over mine, and it's at this point, I notice my fingers are freezing.

He lowers his head to mine, and under the pretense of pressing a kiss to my temple, whispers, "Breathe."

I try to comply, but my lungs burn. I shake my head. This must be a dream. We're getting married. *Right now. Right. Now.* My guts churn. A bead of sweat slides down my back. My muscles seize up.

"Take a breath for me." His hard voice cuts through the chaos in my head.

I suck in air, and this time, oxygen rushes to my head, and I sway.

He tightens his hold on my hand. "You will not faint."

His voice is harsh and emotionless, and exactly what I need right now.

"Keep breathing," he orders.

I do as he says. Focus on my breathing. In-out-in.

"Good girl." The words are spoken in a low voice only I can hear. My toes curl, and heat courses through my belly. I blink and manage to focus on the faces of the people in the room. Summer and Sinclair, Penny and Knight, Abby and Cade, Gio and Rick—the eight of them stand clustered in a corner. The women wear expressions that range from happiness to concern.

On the other side of the room are five men I don't recognize. Four of them wear dark suits; three of them with ties. The fifth wears jeans with a leather jacket and has his hair slicked back. All of them are broad-shouldered. The tallest of them has a scarred face which adds to the menacing air about him. He's glaring at us, as are his brothers—they're definitely brothers. Which means, these are the half-brothers Edward mentioned. He wasn't kidding about them hating him. The air around them might as well be painted black, thanks to the contemptuous vibes emanating from them.

A little distance from them is a very pregnant Karma with her husband Michael's arm about her. When she catches my eyes, she walks forward. "I have your dress ready for you. I hope you don't mind, I estimated your measurements, but I think you'll be happy with the results." She turns to Edward. "I'd like to take her away so she can get ready. No woman likes to be caught unawares on her big day." She shoots an admonishing look at G-Pa. "You're lucky to be getting away with this."

"Oh, pffft!" G-Pa waves his hand in the air, and the gesture is so authoritative, so much like Edward's, I have a snapshot from the future when Eddie's as old as him, and every bit as stern and forbidding, and only allows himself to unbend for our granddaughter.

Our granddaughter? Holy shit, we're not yet married, and by all accounts, I'm not going to be able to bear him a child unless I go the IVF route—which, I have to admit, I'm not completely comfortable with. But I may not have much choice if I wanted a baby of my own—and my mind is totally future-casting here by imagining a future where we have grandkids.

I must make a noise because all three of them turn to me.

G-Pa surveys my features and furrows his brow. "Are you okay my dear? I hope this wasn't too much of a surprise. I thought, since you two were getting married in a few days—"

"In a full six days," Edward growls.

"—in less than a week, we could short-cut the process and have the ceremony today."

"Why would we want to short-cut something like this? You could have asked," Edward says in a hard voice.

"Would you have agreed?" his grandfather turns to him.

"That's not the point." Edward scowls, "Maybe Mira had a dream wedding planned, and you're cheating her out of it. Besides, it's only six days away, I don't understand the reason for the hurry?"

G-Pa's face falls. "I'm so inconsiderate. I only thought of myself and how much I did not want to wait a day longer. At my age, every day is the equivalent of a year, and who knows if I'm going to be around when the two of you tie the knot. I wanted to be present for my oldest grandson's wedding."

"You're not in danger of dying anytime soon," Edward says drily.

I jab my elbow in his side. "That's not very nice."

"I'm sorry, truly. I hadn't thought of the fact it would deprive you of your dream wedding." G-Pa turns to me, "We can stick to the original plan and—"

"No, it's okay," I say around the ball of emotion in my throat. "It's not like I had a vision of what I wanted my wedding to be."

"You didn't?" Eddie blinks.

"I didn't." I tip up my chin. Knowing I was going to have an arranged marriage, I was too stressed worrying about who I'd end up marrying to plan the perfect wedding ceremony in my head. Not that I'm going to say that aloud in front of G-Pa.

"Hmm." Eddie surveys my features. "All the more reason to hold the wedding as planned in six days so you have time now to plan and—"

"No, really, it's fine. It doesn't matter to me if it takes place now or six days from now." *It's inevitable, after all, so maybe it's best I get it over with.*

He frowns. "Are you sure about this?"

"I am." I hold his gaze.

"I apologize, my dear. In my excitement to get the two of you married, I didn't take your feelings into consideration." G-Pa holds out his hand. I glance at it. Then, with reluctance, release my hold on Edward and place my palm in his. G-Pa's big gnarly hands engulf both of mine. "I did not mean to trample all over your dreams—"

"You're not."

"We can move the wedding to the original date, in six days—"

"Actually, I think it's better to have it today. You've gone to the trouble of planning everything, and all of my friends are here, and I think I'd rather not spend the next few days stressing over what is to come." *Besides, I don't have the energy to plan anything. The fact that someone else has stepped in and taken care of the arrangements is a weight off my shoulders.*

G-Pa, doesn't seem convinced.

"I mean it." I squeeze his hand. "I'd like to get married today."

"Don't feel compelled to agree," Eddie interjects.

"I'm not." I raise my gaze to his. "Unless, of course, you'd prefer to wait another six days to get married?"

He blinks, then slowly shakes his head. "I'd prefer we get married right away."

"It's settled then." I turn to G-Pa.

His eyes glisten with tears. He raises my hand to his face and kisses my fingertips. "You're an angel. I'm aware how all of this must be a surprise for you. I thought I had five grandsons. After my wife's death, I read a letter from her that told me about Edward. Our daughter-in-law swore her to secrecy, but my wife wanted me to do right by him. When I learned I had another grandson—my oldest—I realized a part of me always knew. I wanted to ensure he got his share of the inheritance. And when I met him, I could sense how deeply unhappy he was."

Edward makes a sound deep in his throat, but G-Pa ignores it.

"My son and his wife want nothing to do with me. I hoped they'd attend his wedding, but as you can see, they're not here."

"Neither are mine, by the looks of it," I say softly.

"I'm sorry. Your mother said it was too last-minute and too far to travel, and they had other plans. I suggested changing the time but…

"…but she declined…"

He nods sadly, then brightens. "But I'm here." G-Pa's eyes, more grey than brown, yet so much like Edward's, turn intense. "And I want to thank you for already changing him."

"Me?" I look at Edward, then back at his grandfather. "I've done nothing."

"By simply being who you are and being here, you've set events in motion."

"O-k-a-y?" I'm sure he's mistaken, but I guess this is not the moment to argue with him.

"The two of you have so much in common, my dear."

"We do?" I burst out.

"No, we don't," Edward says at the same time.

"Your stubbornness, to begin with." G-Pa smiles.

"Look who's talking," I say lightly.

"It's a family trait, which is why you'll fit right in."

Tears prick my eyes. I've never felt this welcome before. He's the patriarch of the family, and when Edward spoke about him, I sensed that he might be much more aloof and standoffish, but I was wrong. G-Pa, for all his faults—and I'm sure he has many—has opened his arms and his heart and made me feel at home in a way my own father hasn't done in a very long time.

I pull my hand from his, then throw my arms about him and hug him. "Thank you," I whisper.

I sense him clearing his throat, then he pats my back. "I should be saying thank you for your agreeing to marry my grandson."

I sniffle, then lean back and look up into his face. "Actually, he should be the one saying thank you to me.

Edward growls.

G-Pa laughs.

"I assume you took care of the paperwork needed for the marriage to go ahead?" Edward cuts in.

G-Pa snorts. "The Registrar General is my golfing buddy."

All right, then.

Karma smiles, then places her hand on my shoulder. "Shall we get you dressed?"

20

Edward

"The fuck am I doing?" I stare at my reflection in the mirror. Arthur made sure to get me a brand new suit, in the style I favor, and it fits me, too. The bastard thinks of everything. I knot my tie, then swear when it comes out wonky. I untie it, try to knot it again, fail. Anger squeezes my chest. I curl my fingers into fists, and am about to let it fly when I hear a familiar drawl. "The cool emotionless Priest losing his temper? That's a first."

Sinclair draws abreast and meets my gaze in the reflection. "Need some help?" He nods toward my tie.

When I don't answer, he steps around between me and the mirror and begins to fasten my tie. "There; all done." He nods in satisfaction.

"Thanks," I murmur.

"Do you remember when I got married?"

"That was what, two years ago?"

"Nearly three." His lips curve. "Remember how nervous I was?"

"I'm not nervous."

"Of course, not," he says in a soothing voice.

"Don't humor me, Sin."

"I wouldn't dare, Priest." He raises his hands. "All I'm saying is, it's natural to feel unnerved. A man doesn't get married every day."

"I shouldn't be getting married in the first place." I glance away.

"You deserve to be happy. You deserve a second chance."

Do I? I pivot and walk to the window of Arthur's manor. No other way to describe it. It's a ten-bed Victorian home perched on a hill in the center of Hampstead Heath. It has its own private driveway and swimming pool, and underground parking garage. Also, a home theater, a gym, and a den, which is where my half-brothers retired to wait for the ceremony to start. My entire life has turned upside down in the space of a few months. A family who largely hates me, except for Arthur—and he has his own selfish reasons for wanting me to take on the business. A fiancée who I should have never put in this situation. The only blessing is I have the company to focus on. Power and money—the two things ingrained into me as wrong when I was a priest. The two things I crave more than anything else now.

Wait. I can't lie. Now, there's her. She's quickly becoming my new obsession. It doesn't take rocket science to tell me I was wrong to offer her a job, in the first place. I wanted to keep her close, in the hope of controlling the damage she could do to my focus; but this time, I calculated wrong. I should have walked away from her. Instead, I invited her into my life, and she accepted. And I'm going to pay the price for it—

No. Once we're married, I can put distance between us, and everything can go back to being the same.

"You can't keep blaming yourself for what happened," Sinclair's voice sounds over my shoulder.

"Is that your expert opinion?" I scoff.

"When I met Summer, I was a heartless bastard." He stands abreast.

"Still are," I point out.

He ignores my comment and nods toward the city. "My only goal then was to amass as much money and power as I could, hoping to fill that void inside of me."

His words are so close to my earlier thoughts, I stiffen.

"Then, Summer swept in, with her pink hair and her optimistic nature, no matter that she'd been dealt some tough cards in life. She showed me it's okay to not always be uber-focused on my goals. She made me realize there's more to life than chasing the next billion. The thrill of seeing her smile is more satisfying than the next merger, more exciting than another acquisition. She's the only person who knows the truth about Max."

"Max, your Whippet?" I shoot him a sideways glance. "What about him?"

His mouth kicks up. "That's between us."

I shuffle my feet. A sliver of tension coils in my belly. I'm not jealous of his happiness. I'm not envious about his contentment. Or his absolute certainty that Summer is his soulmate. I had mine and I lost her. And Belle?

She deserves better than a man who'll never be able to love her the way she should be loved. Only, I'm not selfless enough to let her go. I can't have her. But I will not let anyone else have her, either. Does that make me a selfish bastard? I never claimed otherwise. I have more in common with my grandfather than he'll ever know.

"The reason I'm going all emo on you is because you need to pull your head out of your arse and recognize the good thing you have here."

"I'm not cut out for marriage." I rub the back of my neck.

"Who is? But then, the right woman comes along, and you willingly tie yourself to her, clip your wings, and remind yourself she's always right."

"Sounds torturous." I wince.

"With the right woman, there's a certain contentment, a peace of mind, a knowledge that she's your better half, that she rounds out your edges, compliments your strengths. It's the two of you against the world. A unit. And then you have kids, and everything changes again."

"Sleepless nights, and all the bullshit that comes with it." I roll my shoulders.

"You're only looking at it from the outside—"

"It's all I can do."

"You're choosing to ignore the obvious upsides."

"There's none— Oh, wait... In my case, I get to consolidate my role as the CEO of the Davenport group, so there's that."

"Money was never your motivator." Sinclair frowns.

"It is now."

"You're the last person to be power-hungry."

"People change."

"The Edward I knew was the most loyal, the most ethical of all the seven of us."

"And look where that got me."

"So, you got your heart broken. Shit happens. You deal with it and move on."

I squeeze my fingers at my sides. "You're beginning to piss me off," I growl.

"Good. I'd rather you *feel* those emotions you've bottled up inside since the incident."

"I don't want to talk about the incident."

"Or the fucking betrayal you feel you committed in leaving the church?"

"I had my reasons." I set my jaw.

"And have you shared them with anyone?"

I glance away.

"Thought not. It's not healthy to go through life without sharing what happened with someone else."

"Baron knows what happened." I swallow. It's difficult to talk about the man who was my best friend once without that familiar pit opening up in my belly. I thought I'd gotten over what happened, but the ghosts were merely lying in wait under the surface.

"Have you spoken to him or Ava since you returned to London?"

When I don't reply, his forehead creases. "You have to meet them at some point."

"Not if I can help it."

"We move in the same circles. He's one of the Seven; it's unavoidable."

"I've managed to avoid them this far."

"You can't do it forever," Sinclair points out.

"I don't see why not."

He sighs again. "Perhaps, being married will help you move on."

If being torn apart inside is how it feels to do so, then I'm not so sure.

"It will get better, Edward." He puts a hand on my shoulder.

If it were anyone else but Sinclair, I'd shake it off. But after I decided to limit my interactions with Baron and Ava, I ended up spending more time with him. The rest of the Seven are busy with their wives and families, and while they went through the same experience as Sinclair and I did, there's always been a kinship between us because Sinclair, like me, has other demons to deal with.

"They have a child." I swallow.

There, I've said it aloud. It's the first time I've acknowledged it to myself. I want Ava and Baron to be happy. I wish them well—*I do*—but when I found out Ava was pregnant, it gutted me. That's when I realized I might not get over what happened for a long time. That's when I knew every time I felt I was healing, it was merely my emotions lying in wait to ambush me again. That's when I vowed to find myself a new focus. Something to channel all my energies into, so I could occupy my every waking moment with something other than my past.

I need to move on. I know that, and the only thing that seems to help has been throwing myself into something bigger than me. First, as the General Manager of the London Ice Kings, and now, as CEO of the Davenport group. It's a temporary solution, but if it helps me move forward, I'm not complaining. It's also why this marriage is important. It's the only way for me to ensure Arthur hands over the decision-making power to me.

"I know you're hurting Ed, and I wish you didn't hide it. It's not healthy for you."

I snort. "You're beginning to sound like one of those new-age self-help gurus."

"And you're ignoring the obvious."

"Which is?"

"You need her, Edward, more than you realize."

21

Mira

"You ready?" Gio looks at me closely.

I tighten my grip around the bouquet, Rachel—the wedding planner—thrust into my fingers.

"I hope you don't mind that we worked with your soon-to-be grand-father to pull this wedding together overnight?" Summer asks softly.

My friends are standing with me in the guest room we took over. After G-Pa's announcement, things were out of my hands. Karma whisked me here, with my friends in tow. I was helped out of my clothes and into the gown that Karma had chosen and altered to fit my measure-ments, so it was ready for me in less than twenty-four hours.

"The only other time I had to stitch a wedding dress faster than this was my own," she murmurs.

I shoot her a sideways glance. "You stitched your wedding gown overnight?"

She laughs. "Let's just say, I was not a willing bride."

"And Michael, he—"

"Kidnapped me and forced me to marry him, yes."

I blink. "But the two of you are—"

"So happy? Yeah." She rubs her massive belly. I swear, the woman seems about ready to pop. She winces, and Summer touches her shoulder.

"You okay, sis?"

"Of course." She waves a hand in the air. "Baby's kicking, is all."

"And everything else is fine? Your heart—"

"It's all good," she insists.

I heard about Karma's heart condition and how being pregnant put her in the life-threatening zone. But Karma was adamant about carrying another child.

"At least, sit down." Gio drags a seat over and Karma sinks into it.

"Thanks, that's much better." She places her hands on her belly and surveys my mermaid dress. "If I'd had more time, I'd have designed you a more spectacular one. But given the urgency I had to go over the dresses I had in stock and choose one and alter it to your measurements."

"This is perfect." I turn around, glance over my shoulder and take in how the neckline dips down almost all the way to the crack of my butt. "Is it too sexy?"

"Nope," Gio says with conviction.

"The long sleeves down to your wrists and the modest neckline that only hints at your cleavage make the entire effect even more startling." Summer nods.

"And sexy." Gio's eyes gleam. "Priest is going to swallow his tongue when he sees you."

"I doubt he'll even notice," I murmur. I rub my fingers lightly down the silky fabric. I mentioned to Karma that I'd always wanted an unusual wedding dress. To consider it my last stand at being independent. I wanted to break from what's customary and have a dress in a shade of purple for my wedding. She'd used that as a guide and while the dress looks different from a normal wedding dress, her genius is such that the pale lavender color is both demure and sexy, at the same time.

"Oh, he'll notice all right." Summer laughs.

"You do realize, he couldn't take his gaze off of you earlier," Karma says slowly.

"What do you mean?"

"He went all protective when Arthur announced the wedding was today. If I'm not mistaken, he was upset on your behalf."

I don't comment. I sensed the same, but my thoughts were all over the place, so I wasn't sure.

"Arthur swore us to secrecy. I was tempted to break it, but the man has so much power and connections—" Gio shakes her head. "I should have told you what he was planning."

"I don't think it's advisable to go up against a man like Arthur," I say slowly.

"But it's your wedding, your life, Mira." Gio takes my hand in hers. "If you don't want to go through with it, say the word, and we'll get you out of here."

"We're on your side," Summer says softly, but there's a hint of steel in her tone.

"Only you know what's right for you." Karma rubs her belly. "No one knows what's happening in a relationship except for the people involved, so if this isn't what you want—"

"I do." I draw in a sharp breath. "I know it seems strange. But I believe Edward has—feelings for me—" It's half true. He's not impervious to my presence, as he's demonstrated, but he's good at hiding behind that wall he's built around himself. "I know he's not very demonstrative—"

"That's putting it kindly." Gio snorts.

I half smile. "But if it weren't Edward, my father would want me to marry someone else."

"You did mention arranged marriages are a norm in your family," Summer says slowly.

Gio stiffens. "Are you marrying him because you love him or because you think he's a better option than someone else your father would choose for you?"

"A little bit of both, I don't know. I mean, my father did choose him." I touch the petals of the flowers in my bouquet. "I think Edward will make a good husband. He's not very demonstrative, but I don't think he's the kind of man who'd knowingly hurt me."

"You sure?" Summer touches my arm. "The offer stands… If you want to call off the wedding—"

"—we'll march right out and tell Arthur." Karma nods.

"He doesn't scare us," Gio says with a fierce look in her eyes.

I sniff. "You girls are the best friends ever. I appreciate the offer. Truly. But I want to get married."

There's a knock on the door and Rachel the wedding planner, pops her head in. "Are you ready?"

I stand at the threshold of the library. Earlier, I got a glimpse of the skylight, the stained glass windows set high up in the walls, the floor-to-ceiling books, and the massive fireplace on the far side, before G-Pa's announcement scattered my thoughts. As venues go, this is exactly the space I'd have chosen to have my wedding. And my wedding dress could not be more perfect. It's only the bride-groom I'm not sure about.

"Love you, babe." Summer kisses the air next to my cheek—so she doesn't smudge my make-up, which she applied earlier—then pushes the door open and steps onto the aisle lined with the candles on either side. I draw in a breath. With the other lights in the room dimmed, and flower placements which were set up in the short time I was away, the space seems magical.

"You look incredible. Ed is a lucky man." Karma squeezes my shoulder, then follows her.

We agreed they'd be my bridesmaids. I'm so lucky to have my friends with me.

"You sure you don't want me to escort you down the aisle?" Gio scans my features with her all-seeing eyes.

"Actually, I was hoping you'd give me that privilege." G-Pa steps up on my other side.

Gio looks from me to him, and her forehead furrows. "I'm not sure—"

"I know, it's a little unusual, I'm from the groom's side, after all, but if you'd indulge an old man a little more, it would be my honor." G-Pa's features are serious. There's a plea in his eyes that goes straight to my heart. This man is responsible for my sudden change in status, from a single woman, to an engaged woman, to a soon-to-be married woman, not to mention, it's because of him that my year of freedom is being cut short. So, why is it, I can't seem to hold a grudge against him?

"Mira?" Gio frowns.

I clear my throat, then tilt up my chin. "I think I would very much like that G-Pa."

"You sure?" Gio touches my arm. "I can accompany you on your other side."

I half smile. "I'll be fine, I promise."

"You sure?" She looks toward the aisle. I follow her glance and spot Rick waiting for her.

"I'm sure." I give her a big, genuine smile. "Go on, your husband is waiting."

She leans in and air kisses me near my cheek. Then, with a last scowl at G-Pa, she leaves.

"Your friends are protective." G-Pa holds out his arm, and I hook mine through it.

"So are you," I murmur.

He pats my hand. "If I could've, I'd have given you more time to prepare for the wedding. But it seemed fortuitous that all of my grandsons agreed to be here under my roof at the same time. I wasn't sure if or when that would happen again. I didn't want to let the occasion go to waste. Also, I want to see Edward married." He looks between my eyes. "Do you understand?"

"I do." I swallow. "I can tell you love Edward very much."

His features soften. "I see a lot of myself in him. Of all my grandsons, he's the one who's had it the roughest."

I take in the troubled expression on his face and realize he knows about the incident. I could ask him about it, but that doesn't seem right. No, I need to wait for Edward to tell me, when he's ready. And he will be. He has to be.

"You want him to be happy."

"I know he'll be happy." He squares his shoulders. "Shall we?"

22

Edward

"Your grandfather never ceases to surprise," Sinclair murmurs. He's my best man, along with Knox, my oldest half-sibling. If Knox was surprised, he didn't show it. He merely nodded, then fell in line behind Sinclair. He's pissed off at this turn of events because it confirms I'm the CEO and not him. He hasn't spoken a word to me since that tight-lipped nod. I'm surprised he agreed to be my best man. I felt sure he would refuse me. Maybe, it was Arthur's presence that compelled him to assent. Although, from what I know about Knox, he's not the kind to be intimidated by anyone, not even our very charismatic grandfather. But then, he's had a relationship with Arthur which has lasted for the dura-tion of a lifetime. He can take liberties with the old man I can't. And it's not because I'm daunted by him. It has more to do with the fact he's newly-found family, and someone who already seems to understand me more than my own parents.

How would it have been to have had him in my life when the incident happened? Would he have helped me out? Would he have guided me in navigating the after-math of that one event that changed the course of my life? If he had been there, would he have stopped me from becoming a priest? Would that have meant I'd still be with Ava? At least, now, I'm able to refer to her by name, which is something I haven't been able to do for a long time. Having Belle in my life is changing me already, and in ways I'm not ready for.

"You're not going to turn and watch your bride approach?" Knox growls.

I stiffen and stare forward into the flames. The hair on the back of my neck prickles, and I sense her approach. My heart sends up a clamor in my ribcage. My pulse rate heightens. Every cell in my body is switched on and aware of her approach. And I want to. *I. Want. To.* And yet…if I do… If I see her face and take in her figure, I'll be a goner. The sense of events running away from me squeezes my stomach.

"Edward," Sinclair's voice cuts through my thoughts.

It's going to look suspect if I don't turn toward her. And the entire point of this charade is to convince my new family that this spectacle is genuine. I lengthen my spine, square my shoulders, turn… And the breath whooshes out of me.

She's a vision in lavender, the fabric clinging to her curves and stretching across her thighs with every step she takes. It embraces her lush figure until, in a dramatic sweep, it falls to her toes. Her purple-streaked hair is loose and in long curls. It streams out over her shoulders. The blonde strands catch the candlelight and gleam like burnished gold with threads of copper shot through it. And her eyes—the blue is deeper, almost indigo, taking its cue from the color of her gown.

In one hand, she holds a bouquet of white and purple flowers. The other hand is curved into the crook of my grandfather's arm. The old man took it upon himself to escort her down the aisle. He seems to be enamored with her, in their very first meeting. Enough to walk her to me himself. On the other hand, he's probably making sure the two of us are hitched without anything coming in the way.

Arthur reaches me, then places her hand in mine. "You keep her happy, boy," he says in a stern voice, before stepping back.

I tilt my head, unable to take my gaze from her features. The perfect arc of her eyebrows, the curve of her eyelashes, the tiny nose, the rosebud lips, the flushed cheeks—she's beautiful, ethereal. A goddess. And I'm a sinner. She's pristine. I'm tainted. I'll never be good enough for her. I release her hand, then turn toward the officiant. He begins the ceremony, and the words wash over me.

I must say the right things, for suddenly, he's asking us to exchange rings.

I glance at Sinclair, who jerks his chin in the direction of the aisle. Good thing, I acquired the rings after I proposed the arrangement to her.

Sinclair insisted I hand the rings over to him so he could hand them over to me at the wedding. And he knew about the wedding being pushed up. Obviously, all my friends did; that's why they're all here. I make my displeasure known to him. He shrugs. Looks like Arthur got to him, too.

I turn to find Tiny walking toward us. He's holding a cushion in his mouth, and it holds the two rings I chose. I assume he thought it fitting to have the Great Dane be the ring bearer. Which, judging by Belle's joyful exclamation of, "Tiny," was the right thing to do.

She bends and scratches his ear. He makes that mewling noise at the back of his throat, and she giggles. The sound is so fresh and young and innocent, my heart stutters in my chest. She should always sound like this. Happy and carefree, not weighed down by the past, like I am.

Tiny looks up at me with reproach in his eyes. I scowl down at him, and he makes a growling sound. Nice, now a mutt is telling me off at my own wedding.

I take my ring, hand it over to Belle, then take her ring and straighten. I wait for her to hand her bouquet over to Gio who's hovering nearby. When I hold out my hand, she places her palm in mine. I slide the ring onto her finger. It's a platinum band studded with blue sapphires, the companion to her engagement ring. She slides a platinum band, devoid of any stones, onto my left ring finger. When she glances up at me, her eyes are wide, her color pale. The pulse at the hollow of her neck draws my attention to the creamy expanse of her neck.

I want to sink my teeth into the curve where her shoulder meets her throat and mark her. I want to throw her over my shoulder and march her out of here so no one else will dare take in her delicate beauty. I want to—break the vow I made to myself to never have feelings, to never get involved in a relationship again. My throat closes. My heart rate soars. And when, from a distance, I hear the officiant say I can kiss my bride, I don't hesitate. I close the distance to her, wrap my fingers around the nape of her neck, and draw her up on her tiptoes. Her blue eyes dilate, her lips part—in surprise, I'm sure—but it gives me the perfect opportunity to close my mouth over hers.

23

Mira

I expect his kiss to be cold and biting and hard, and it's all of that, and so much more. His hold on the nape of my neck. The assuredness in his grasp, the way he hauls me to him with complete confidence, how he slants his mouth across mine, thrusts his tongue inside my mouth to dance over mine, how he then…slows…slows… Like we have all the time in the world, like we're not in front of our friends and his family, like he's not my arranged husband, like I'm his real wife… Wife. I'm *his* wife. A shudder runs down my spine. He must sense it, for his hold on the nape of my neck tightens. He runs his tongue across the seam of my lips, and my nipples tighten. My heart drops to the place between my legs. My core throbs. He softens the kiss even further, until his lips barely brush mine, until we're sharing breath, and his gaze, which hasn't wavered from mine since he captured my mouth, intensifies. Sparks of gold and silver light up his eyes. It mirrors the million little sparks bursting under my skin. I'm burning up from the inside, melting into a puddle at his feet. My knees give out. I sway, and he wraps his other arm about my waist and pulls me into his chest. My arms are around him. He tucks my head under his chin. I close my eyes and draw in a breath of pure, unadulterated Edward. The tension in my muscles fades; the throbbing between my legs increases. The sound of our friends clapping reaches me. Oh god, I forgot where we were. I try to pull away, but he doesn't let me. He holds me in place and rubs soothing circles over my back. A sigh of relief leaves my lips.

"Better?" he rumbles from somewhere over me. When I nod, he finally steps back, but continues to hold me about my waist.

Then he notches his knuckles under my chin, tips up my face, and surveys my features. Whatever he sees there must satisfy him, for he nods, then turns, guiding me to face the room and the group.

He leads me up the aisle, and our friends surround us.

Summer reaches me first. She clasps my shoulders and kisses me on both cheeks. "That was beautiful!" she sniffs.

Karma is next. Her swollen belly between us, she squeezes my shoulder, then leans in and whispers, "I hope both of you will be very happy."

Then it's Penny, then Abby, and finally, Gio. She holds out the wedding bouquet, and I take it from her. "Since most of us here are married, you might want to hand this over to Rachel. She's the only one not married."

I nod.

She leans in and kisses my cheek. "That was a very convincing kiss."

I feel myself blush, then nod.

"Is he taking you on a honeymoon?"

I blink, but before I can reply, there's a woof. Then Tiny pushes his way between Gio and Rick, who's congratulating Edward.

"Hey, baby, you played your role so well." I bend and rub him behind his ear. He woofs again and wags his tail with such force, he brushes against G-Pa who's walked up to congratulate us.

Gio steps aside, and G-Pa takes my hands in his. "That was beautiful." He blinks the tears from his eyes. "Edward is very lucky to have you in his life."

"I'm lucky to have him in mine," I murmur.

My husband must hear my words, for his muscles stiffen. He continues to accept the felicitations from his friends. Then, it's his half-brother Knox's turn. He jerks his chin toward Edward. "Congratulations."

Edward nods. "Thanks."

"Just because you're married and fulfilling the terms of Arthur's agreement doesn't mean I accept you as the CEO."

Silence descends as, one-by-one, people stop talking and train their attention on the exchange.

G-Pa slowly releases my hands. He looks between the two half-brothers but doesn't say anything. Apparently, he wants to see how this exchange will proceed.

Knox shoves his hand in his pocket. "I won't make it easy for you during your honeymoon, either."

"There is no honeymoon," Edward drawls.

G-Pa stiffens.

Gio gasps.

I'm not sure what I expected, but I think a part of me, somewhere, assumed there'd be a honeymoon. Isn't that what people do when they get married? But this is a fake wedding. And that's my fake husband. Let's ignore that he kissed me so I felt it all the way to my toes; it was all pretense.

Knox looks taken aback. "No honeymoon, huh?"

G-Pa looks at Edward with something like suspicion in his eyes. "You're not taking your wife for a honeymoon?" His forehead furrows.

"I'm the newly appointed CEO. I can't take time away from the job."

"Don't forget, you continue to stay CEO only if you consummate the marriage," G-Pa snaps.

"What?" Edward's usual mask-like features unwind enough for the shock to show in his eyes.

"What?" I squeak.

"Why do you seem surprised?" G-Pa looks at Edward steadily. "Were you planning otherwise?"

"I'm surprised because I didn't expect my grandfather to interfere in my personal life to this extent."

"Welcome to the family," Knox says drily. Then he steps toward me. "I assume it's okay to kiss the bride?"

Without waiting for Edward's response, he bends and kisses me, not on my lips, but so close, he might as well have.

There's a growl from Edward, and the next minute, Knox is shoved away. "Get away from my wife." Edward wraps his arm about my shoulder and pulls me close.

Knox's lips twist. It's not a smile so much as a grimace. Then he glances at G-Pa. "You have your answer; he has feelings for her."

"Did you plan this?" Edward growls at G-Pa.

"Give me some credit." G-Pa scowls at Knox. "You will apologize to your brother—"

"Half-brother," Knox sneers.

"And his bride," G-Pa thunders.

Knox glowers at G-Pa, then clears all emotions from his features. When he looks at me, he's wearing a mask that rivals Edward's. They might protest at the fact they're related, but clearly, they are, given the trait of masking emotions runs in the family.

"I'm sorry if I embarrassed you, Mirabelle." He smirks. "Though I'm not sorry I kissed you."

There's a low snarl, then Edward shoots out his fist and catches Knox in the side of the jaw.

24

____

Edward

"For someone who's quite controlled, you sure lost it." My wife bathes my knuckles. We're back home after that shit-show.

To say Arthur was not happy with my behavior is putting it mildly. He glared at me, then pivoted and walked out of there with Tiny on his heels.

When the Great Dane refused to leave Arthur's side, I decided to let him be. Apparently, the mutt has not only taken to my grandfather, but has also decided to adopt the old man as his current companion. Besides, the old man could do with the company. Then, there was Knox. The satisfaction on his face made me realize he'd been baiting me, and I had fallen for it. I lost my control for the first time since… Since I found out *she* was in love with my best friend.

Then, Knox left. My other half-brothers didn't bother to congratulate me. Except for the youngest, Brody. He's the only one who came up and congratulated me and my bride. Then he, too, left. Sinclair and our other friends gathered around us. He wanted to call a doctor to have my knuckles looked at, but I had refused. Instead, I told them Belle and I were leaving.

I should have apologized to them for the disaster of the evening, but all I could think of was to get out of there with her. To make sure no one else could see her in that dress. That possessiveness I always feel around her seems to have multiplied since I slipped the ring on her finger.

I need a little time and distance to understand why I reacted the way I did. I needed...to get my emotions back under control and back in the box I've sealed them in for so long. I turned away all other offers of help. I looked around for Tiny, but the pooch had decided to follow Arthur out. Apparently, I was also a shit dog-sitter; the mutt decided to cross over to my grandfather's side. I shoved the thought aside and hustled Belle out of there.

She managed to toss her bouquet to the wedding planner and then, we were out of there. I drove us home, then went to my room. She followed me and insisted on cleaning my bruises. It seemed churlish to protest, so I let her. When's the last time someone took care of me? Perhaps, after the incident, when I found myself at the hospital. And then, it was the impersonal touch of the nurse. Belle's touch, though, is gentle. She drops the blood-stained cloth, reaches for the antiseptic and glances at me from under her eyelashes. "This is going to hurt."

I don't reply.

"Do you want some whiskey to help with the pain?"

When I stay silent, she firms her lips, then pours the antiseptic over the torn skin of my knuckles. I hiss out a breath, but the pain cuts through the remnants of anger. My mind finally slows down. I look on as she holds my palm between her much smaller ones, then she bends her head and blows on it. The burning sensation fades. When she looks up at me, our gazes hold. Color flushes her cheeks. The air between us heats. Her lips part, and I can't take my gaze off her mouth. She swallows, and the pulse at the base of her throat accelerates. When I raise my free hand and dig my fingers into the thick strands of her hair and tug, she shivers. When I pull my bruised hand from her grasp and press my thumb to her lower lip, her breath hitches.

"So fucking gorgeous." I drag my thumb down her chin, the column of her neck to where her pulse flutters like a pinned butterfly. I continue down to where the neckline dips at her cleavage. She shudders. I hook my thumb in the cloth and tug. The delicate material rips.

She gasps. I expect her to cry out; instead, her pupils dilate. A low moan bleeds from her lips.

"So fucking alluring. You come across as all virginal, but you have a dark side."

She draws in a sharp breath, but doesn't contradict me.

I slide my fingers inside her wedding dress and cup her breast, and goosebumps shiver up her skin. I pinch her nipple between my finger and thumb and when I tweak it, she cries out. The sound arrows to my groin, and my cock extends.

"So fucking beautiful. You're a siren I can't resist, despite my best efforts." I urge her down to her knees. She goes willingly, then looks up at me. There's complete trust in her eyes. A submissiveness I knew she possessed, but seeing her at my mercy, waiting for me to command her, shoots a thick arrow of lust up my spine.

"Unzip me," I order.

"What?"

"You heard me."

She looks like she's going to hesitate, then reaches up and undoes the button of my waistband. When she lowers the zipper, the sound of the slider over the metal teeth is loud in the silence.

"Take it out."

She hesitates. Her cheeks are pink; a fine sheen of sweat beads her upper lip. Nervousness is writ in every curve of her body, and fuck, if that doesn't entice me more.

"Don't keep me waiting, Belle."

She reaches inside my briefs and curls her fingers about my length. The blood drains to my groin. "Fuck." I tighten my fingers in her hair.

When she inches my briefs down enough, my cock springs free.

"Oh, my god." She stares at the throbbing length. I follow her gaze to where the bulbous head of my length stares back at her, the crown an angry purple, pre-cum clinging to the slit. The contrast between the dark skin and her pale pink-tipped fingers, which don't meet around the girth, intensifies the throbbing ache at the base of my spine.

"You're so big," she whispers.

My shaft twitches in response, and her gaze widens.

"So hard." She squeezes me from crown to base and back, and I almost come.

"Open your mouth," I snap.

She glances up at me, a trace of fear in those eyes mixed with need, and it's my undoing. The pressure in my balls intensifies.

I ease her face forward until her lips graze my cock. Shockwaves spiral through me. "Bloody hell." And I haven't even slid my dick inside her mouth.

She holds my gaze, then flicks out her tongue and licks the crown.

A groan vibrates up my chest.

She blinks, then sweeps her pink tongue around the rim of the head, and my entire body shudders. A small smile curves her lips, then she opens her mouth.

25

———————

Mira

I part my lips to take him inside my mouth, but he's already pushed my head forward, and his dick slides across my tongue. My heart rams into my ribcage, and my pulse rate sprints like it's running a marathon. The throbbing between my legs accelerates in tandem. My entire body has turned into an oscillating pendulum, each swing taking it closer to breaking point. The muscles of his shoulders flex under his jacket. He's still dressed in his three-piece suit with the tie knotted around his throat. Every part of him is covered except for his cock, the crown of which is in my mouth. I guess you could say that's covered too. I curl my fingers around the base, and when I squeeze, a growl emerges from his lips. His golden-brown eyes catch fire, and a bead of sweat slides down his temple. He's affected by the blowjob I'm giving him. A flood of triumph pools between my legs.

I open my mouth wider, and he pulls me forward enough that his cock hits the back of my throat. I gag. Saliva drips down my chin, and tears squeeze out from the corners of my eyes. His chest rises and falls, and a flush steals up his cheeks. Other than that, his features are inscrutable. His shoulders could be carved from granite, the muscles of his body so coiled with tension, he could be the spring of a wound-up clock.

He pauses with his dick pushed into the back of my throat, the girth so wide he's pushing against the walls of my mouth. I swallow and he heaves out a breath. The nerve at his temple pops. He digs his fingers deeper into my hair and maneuvers me forward. And when I open my mouth wider, a flicker of satisfaction laces his features. He slides down my throat. "Good girl."

My toes curl. Moisture drips down my thighs. He releases his hold on my hair, only to wrap his fingers about my throat. He pulls me back, enough that the tip of his cock rests between my lips. "Breathe through your nose," he instructs.

I do.

"Once more."

I draw in a breath; my chest rises and falls.

When I exhale, he tugs me forward, and his cock sinks down my throat. My gag reflex kicks in. I swallow it back, and I must be doing something right, for a growl rumbles up his chest. He increases the pressure around my throat, enough that my lungs burn. I can feel his cock press against the sides of my throat. I feel the length of his cock encased in the column of my neck. And the sensation is like nothing I've experienced in my life—which is not saying much, seeing how woefully inexperienced I am at anything related to sex.

I may have read spicy romance books and managed to sneak a peek at porn videos online when I was sure I wouldn't be found out. None of that prepared me for how demeaning it feels to be on my knees servicing him. Nothing equipped me for how erotic it would feel to be used by him. *Take me. Treat me like your possession. Do to me, anything you want. Whatever will bring you pleasure. Manipulate my body. Utilize my flesh. Fill my holes the way they have never been before. I am yours to do as you please. Only yours.*

He must sense my thoughts, for his jaw hardens. A muscle flares to life below his cheekbone. His gaze is harsh, but the fire in his eyes tells me he's feeling everything right now. It's the first time he's given me a glimpse of the molten, churning miasma of conflict he carries within him.

And I should be upset with him for taking my mouth like this. No warning. Nothing to tell me he was going to use my body, and yet—

there's a strange sense of power in knowing it's *my* body causing him to lose control again. I'm the reason he lost his temper earlier. Slowly but surely, Edward is opening up—despite himself—and it's thrilling and humbling at the same time.

So much control holds him back. How will it be when he finally loses himself completely? His cock thickens further, filling my throat, pushing down on my tongue. Tension vibrates off of him. I sense his body shudder and know he's close. That's when he pulls out, only to pinch my nipple. He tweaks it, and the jolt of pain cuts through the jumble of sensations. All of my senses seem to sharpen. I glance up at him, his cock once more poised at my lips. He releases my tit, only to haul me up to my feet. Then, without releasing his hold on the nape of my neck, he hooks his fingers in the already torn front of my dress and rips it all the way to the hem. A part of me thinks I need to protest. It's a Karma West Sovrano creation, which must be worth thousands.

"I'll buy you many more." He pushes aside my panties and shoves two thick fingers inside me. I gasp, try to squirm away, but he holds me in place. He begins to weave his fingers in and out of me. I'm so soaked, there's a slurping noise as he thrusts in and out of me. It seems to please him, though, for he gives me a barely perceptible nod. It's not like I had anything to do with it. My body's a kite, and he holds the reel which controls the string.

He adds a third finger, and a whine spills from my lips. It seems to spur him on, for his movements intensify. Every time he shoves his fingers inside me, my entire body jolts, and I rise up to my toes with the force of his thrust. When he pulls it out, I settle back on my heels. In-Up-Out-Down, the rhythm echoes through my body. The next time he plunges inside me, he curves his fingers and hits a spot deep inside me. Sparks of sensations oscillate to my extremities. My knees knock together, and I sag, impaling myself further on his digits.

And when he presses his thumb into the swollen bud of my clit, I cry out. I grab hold of his shoulders, and he watches me closely as I sweat and pant and moan and plead with him. The words are garbled. I dig my fingertips into his jacket, and feel I'm poised on the verge of something big, something new, something so different and yet, so familiar. Something the primal part of me recognizes, but my mind and my body can only guess. The trembling shoots up my legs, my thighs, and squeezes down on my belly, only to zip up my spine. And I'm going to—

He pulls out his fingers. In one smooth move, he stands and turns me around so I'm forced to grab the edge of the counter. He pulls off the remnants of my dress then tears off my panties. I cry out but hold his gaze in the mirror as he fits his cock to my opening. He stays poised there, one pulse. Another. Then, he impales me.

26

———————

Edward

"Eddie," she cries out my name. The sound goes straight to my cock, and I grow bigger, harder, more insistent. I need to pause. I need to give her time to adjust. I dig my shoes into the floor, tighten my thighs, and wait. Wait. Her pupils are dilated, and there's only a circle of blue around the black. Her mascara has streaked down her cheeks, a dribble of saliva drips from her chin. The remnants of her dress are on the floor, and her left tit is out of her bra cup. Her color is high, and her hair is a cloud of spun gold with violet streaks about her shoulders. She looks used and messed up and yet, there's an innocence to how she licks her lips, a stubbornness to how she refuses to break the connection of our gazes.

She's stubborn, has a tenacity I'd have never guessed, and has the most gorgeous curves I've ever laid my eyes on. She's a goddess, a siren, a vixen—and an innocent. How could I have gotten so lucky to have found her? How could I have resisted her? How can I let her come any closer, when she's already wriggled her way under my skin?

"You're so fucking tight, so hot; your cunt is a work of beauty," I growl through gritted teeth.

She opens her mouth, but before she can speak, I pull out and thrust into her again. Her entire body jolts, and she cries out. I wait until her breathing slows again, until her eyes clear, and she, once more, holds my gaze. I pinch her clit, and she shudders. I begin to rub that hard little knob, and she wriggles and writhes, but I hold her in place. I strum her pussy lips and am rewarded with a gush of moisture between her legs. I pull back slowly, stay poised at her opening, and this time, when I plunge forward, she throws her head back, showing me the length of her neck. I begin to fuck her in earnest. In-out-in. Each time I sink into her, she shudders and cries out. Each time I pull out, she whines. Her little noises, her groans and whimpers drive me over the edge. I rub her clit, and her eyes roll back in her head. I tilt my hips, piston forward and into her, touching her deep—so deep inside, I almost come. With a growl, I manage to hold back, then lean down and press my cheek against hers. "Open your eyes."

She cracks open her eyelids, and I look into her eyes as I slowly, inch by inch, bury myself inside her one last time. I flick her clit and command, "Come," and she shatters. A high-pitched whine emerges from her lips as she shudders. Her knees give out, and I hold her up as her body twitches and jerks with her climax. When she closes her eyelids and slumps, I pull out. When I look down, I notice the blood on my cock. *What the—?*

I lift my hand, notice the stain on my fingers. *A virgin? Of course, she's a virgin. She was told she was going to have an arranged marriage.* Most likely, she was instructed to keep herself unsullied. And I sensed it. My subconscious sensed it, but I was too caught up in my own ghosts to acknowledge it. I thought I felt some resistance when I took her but put it down to my size. And she didn't tell me. *Why didn't she tell me? Maybe, because you had your cock down her throat, you bastard.* I hold her limp body close, manage to pull up my briefs and pants and zip up, then scoop up her limp body and walk over to the bath.

I lower her to her feet, balance her, and run a bath. When it's half-full, I shut off the water, divest her of her bra, then lower her into the tub. I keep her upper body upright and run a washcloth over her face, her breasts, down between her legs. My still hard cock strains against my pants. My balls are so hard, they weigh a ton. I acknowledge the need, the blinding desire that still runs through my veins, and watch it as it infiltrates every pore of my body. I'm good at punishing myself. It's the one thing I learned in my days as a priest that's stuck with me, and

I've become an expert over the years. Practice makes perfect, after all. When I raise my gaze to her face, I find her eyes are open.

"You didn't come."

I tilt my head and continue with my ministrations, trying to keep my actions as clinical as possible—like that's possible with her? Especially not with the massive column between my thighs, and my balls, which are as hard as the iron I pump in the gym. I finish up, throw the cloth aside, then reach down and lift the plunger. The water begins to drain. I rise to my feet and hold out my hand. She grips it and I pull her up, then grab a towel and drape it about her shoulders. I wipe her down quickly, trying not to glance at the column of her neck, or her plump breasts, the dip of her waist, the curve of her belly, and the alluring mound below. I wrap the towel around her, then lift her in my arms.

"I can walk," she protests.

I carry her to my bedroom, lower her to her feet, and pull back the covers. "Get in."

"This is your room," she points out.

When I don't reply, she firms her lips. "I thought you said you didn't want us to share a bed."

"We're not going to share a bed."

"But—"

"Why didn't you tell me you were a virgin?"

She glances away. "I...thought you knew."

I rub the back of my neck. "If I had been thinking straight, I might have guessed and gone slowly." I shake my head. "Get in the bed, Belle."

"First, tell me why you didn't come."

I blink. The mouth on her. The very sexy, hot hole that was my undoing. That is, until I was ensconced in her pussy. This woman isn't afraid to go toe-to-toe with me. Unlike my employees. It's refreshing and invigorating and—I will not think about how much I want her right now. I reach over and tug on the towel so it slides off of her.

"Oh!" Her cheeks turn pink. A flush creeps up her chest. Her embarrassment fuels the lust in my veins. My cock throbs, a burning sensation extending out from my groin. She glances down at my crotch and swallows. "You're still hard."

"And you're not yet in bed."

She scowls, then slides in under the cover. I pull it up until she's covered all the way to her neck, then sit down next to her on the bed. "Are you sore?"

Her flush deepens. "A little."

"I wish I'd known this was your first time. If I had—"

"You wouldn't have made love to me?"

"I wouldn't have fucked you," I agree.

Her face falls, and a hot sensation stabs at my chest. I'm too attuned to her. Too sensitive to her needs. Too responsive to her change in emotions. She glances away, and when she looks back at me, her gaze is haunted. "Is it fucking if you didn't come in me?"

I shrug.

"The only reason you made lo—penetrated me is because you needed to consummate the marriage."

I incline my head.

"And you married me because you want G-Pa to confirm your position as the CEO."

"You knew this already, Belle," I murmur.

She bites the inside of her cheek. "Knowing it and living it are two very different things."

"Are you having second thoughts?"

Why am I asking her this? It's not as if I'm going to let her go. Especially now.

My fingers tingle. I want to reach over and push back the hair from her face. I want to crawl into bed with her, turn her over and pull her into me. I want to spoon her, watch her as she falls asleep, then wake her up by crawling in between her legs and eating her out until she comes again… I want…what I can't have—the kind of intimacy that comes from having confidence in another. That emotional oneness that means you never have to second guess yourself when you're with them.

I want her sweetness to soothe my hard edges, her innocence to throw me a rope so I can climb out of the dark place I've descended into, her sunshiny nature to illuminate the blackness I've held close. I'm changing, and it's all because of her. I want to push her away, yet I find myself circling back to her, always. I want to teach her how it could be to open herself up and offer herself to me. I want her to know the satisfaction of putting her trust in me. Of allowing me to wring every last drop of desire from her body, of fulfilling every wish of her soul. The ecstasy she'd feel giving herself to me, comfortable in the belief she can stop me anytime. The exhilaration that comes with letting me push her boundaries, believing in me enough to put her faith in me.

Faith. I'm asking her for the one thing I've lost. I no longer believe in the greater good. I'm no longer sure there's a higher power. I'm no longer convinced of the purpose that guided me for most of my life. I'm a stone sinking slowly in a river of depravity. I lost my moorings and found her, and it threatens every principle I've sworn to live my life by since *her*. I cannot…will not let this woman turn my life upside down. But I also cannot bear to see her hurt.

"Belle? Do you regret marrying me?

"Would it matter?"

"I'm not going to let you walk away…"

She scoffs. "I didn't think you would."

"I'm also not sorry I took your virginity."

Her jaw drops.

"Nor for the pain I caused you."

She gasps. "Christ-on-a-bus, don't hold anything back, will ya?"

"It's best you find out what kind of a man I am."

"A hurt, broken, emotionally unavailable, sadistic dominant?" She scoffs.

I look at her with interest. "You're beginning to understand me."

"I liked you better when I merely thought of you as recovering from a broken heart."

"That's a very romantic picture of me; afraid the truth is not so black and white."

"Oh, you're nothing but shades of grey." She peers up at me, and her blue eyes are clear and bright, the gaze of someone who doesn't have to carry around the burdens of a lifetime.

"And black." I set my jaw. "There are parts of me you don't want to come in contact with."

"The very fact you're warning me off, tells me more about you."

I smooth the covers under her chin. "And what will you do when you're disappointed? What will you do when you realize you'd have been better off if you'd never met me?"

27

Mira

"And that's the last you saw of him?"

Summer pats the little boy who's fast asleep in his crib. I wrapped up work, then came to her place. She was putting her son to bed, and I stayed with her as she spun a story for him, something involving dragons and space travel and rockets, complete with hand gestures which had entranced him. He resisted sleep; they always do. A couple of times, he closed his eyes, and we were sure he'd drifted off, only for him to open his eyelids and cry out as soon as Summer started to move away. But she persisted, and he finally fell asleep. We've stayed just to be sure he doesn't move. And she strokes his back in rhythmic beats that have me curling up in the armchair and burrowing my cheek into the cushion.

"Haven't exchanged a word with him since, and it's been a week."

She gives me a strange look. "Don't you two share a room?"

"Um… Yes." I change my position, looking for a more comfortable spot in the chair. "But I fall asleep before he comes to bed, and he's gone before I wake up." It's a lie, I know. But you can't expect me to tell her

I'm not sharing a room with my new husband, can you? I love my friends but draw a line at sharing such intimate details with them.

"And you work with him, so you see him in the office?" She pushes the hair back from her baby's forehead, a soft smile on her face.

"He's been busy in meetings, and communicates with me through emails," I murmur.

"So he spent your wedding night with you, but then he was gone?" she asks slowly.

"Something like that." I don't want to go into details about what happened that night. That my husband let his control slip and fucked me, but he didn't come inside me. It still counts as consummation, though; I looked it up online. The Oxford dictionary defines the completion of a marriage by an act of sexual intercourse, which is defined for these purposes as complete penetration of the vagina by the penis, although ejaculation is not necessary. So there you have it, ladies and gents. My husband has made it clear to me he 'fucked' me and did his duty by consummating the wedding. And now, he's making it clear he doesn't want anything to do with me.

I thought I could catch him in the office, at least, but he's made sure to stay ensconced in his room in meetings.

He turned the glass wall between his office and my desk into an opaque sheet, so I can't look in. The symbolism isn't lost on me either. And when it was time for lunch, he asked the receptionist to bring it to him. She, with the long nails and false eyelashes that graze her forehead. I hated her slim figure and pixie haircut on sight. Hated her even more when she came out smirking and walked by me without a second glance. *Bitch.*

"Guess he must be busy?" Summer rises to her feet, then bends and tucks the covers around her son.

"I suppose." My voice isn't convincing.

She kisses her son on the forehead, then straightens and leads me out of his room. She pulls the door half shut, and we walk down the stairs into the kitchen. She pulls out her phone, makes sure the app linking to the baby cam is active, and places it on the island, then busies herself making us both herbal tea. I slip onto the stool and watch her pour the hot water into the cups. She slides one over to me, then sits on the stool next to me. "I know you got married in a hurry—"

"Which is putting it mildly."

"But as you know, I believe in love at first sight, so I'm not as surprised as some of the others."

More like lust at first sight on my side, and convenience at first sight on his, but I don't say that aloud.

"I know you and Sinclair, too, had a rushed courtship—" I begin to say, but she laughs.

"He thought my father was responsible for what happened to him and Edward and their friends. He wanted revenge, so he blackmailed me into marrying him."

"What?" I gape.

She shrugs. "I needed the money he promised in return. It was a logical arrangement, only—"

"You fell in love."

"He fell first." She laughs. "Then he fell harder. He'd wanted me all along, but didn't know how to express his feelings. So, he hatched this very convoluted plan to marry me. All to avoid talking about his emotions. Sound familiar?"

"It does. The only difference is, Sinclair loved you. Edward? I'm not so sure. He sees me as a convenience. I was the first eligible woman he came across, and he had to fulfill his grandfather's conditions in order to retain his role in the company, and—" I firm my lips. "Oh, shit, I just gave everything away, didn't I?"

She looks at me with soft eyes. "Nothing I hadn't already guessed."

"But I signed an NDA. Please don't say anything."

She makes the motion of zipping her lips.

"So you knew all along this was a marriage of convenience?"

"I could tell he has feelings for you—"

"He does not," I protest.

She merely smiles in that enigmatic manner women who are at peace with themselves, who've been through this merry-go-round and decided to get off, have.

"I was there when he was pissed on your behalf with his grandfather. Then, he beat up his half-brother because he dared kiss you too close to your lips, without his permission."

I wince. "That's just him being all possessive...because I'm his 'wife.'" I make air quotes. The light from above flashes off of my rings. She glances at them.

"He gave you his grandmother's engagement ring."

"Only to make sure everyone believes in this make-believe relationship."

"But it's not make-believe for you, is it?"

I begin to nod, then scowl at her. "Sneaky."

She laughs. "And you always wear your heart on your sleeve. I like that about you, Mira. I like that a lot."

"Doesn't help when you're trying to play a game with your husband and you don't know the rules."

"Make up your own."

I frown. "What do you mean?"

"He's attracted to you, Mira. He can't take his gaze off you when you're with him. He's possessive about you—"

"Which makes no sense; I'm his wife in name only."

"So test him."

"How?"

"Use his weakness."

"He's Edward, the emotionless robot who's convinced he can't be redeemed. He doesn't have one," I grumble.

She continues to look at me with a meaningful look on her face.

"What?"

When she only gives me a small smile, I sigh. I take a sip of my herbal tea, then place the mug on the coffee table.

"I suppose his one indication of fallibility is losing his temper with Knox," I admit.

And the fact he lost control and fucked me on our wedding night. He was unable to resist me. Of course, he had to do it because G-Pa made it a condition—the marriage had to be consummated. Still, he didn't have to actually do it. He could have lied to G-Pa, and everyone would have believed it. But apparently, he's not a liar. Which is good, right? It means he'll be truthful with me, as well. I draw in a breath. "You're saying I should play on what seems to be his vulnerability and use it to get a reaction from him?"

28

Edward

"I don't care how risky it is. I've decided we're going to take over the company." I glance between Knox and Sinclair. We've spent most of the morning trying to find a way to combine the forces of the Davenport empire with that of 7A—the company I co-own with Sinclair and the rest of the Seven—to launch a joint takeover. It's a deal set with minefields and egos that could send the entire acquisition into a tailspin. It took Knox and Sinclair four hours to conclude the deal's not doable.

"I don't accept no for an answer," I growl.

Sinclair leans back in his chair. "Neither do I, old chap, but sometimes, the writing is on the wall."

"And this is one of those times," Knox says in that gravelly voice of his. The sunshine streaming in through the floor-to-ceiling windows illuminates every single dip and cranny of the scars on his face. I can take credit for the newest one on his temple. Not that it takes away from his appeal. If anything, it seems to have increased his popularity with the women-folk, most of whom tittered and stared at him as we walked through the maze of cubicles earlier.

Thankfully, my wife wasn't at her desk. She went out for an early lunch. I know this because I moved things around to make sure she was out when my half-brother prowled in, along with my best friend. Now that I've shut Baron out of my circle, and because, except for Sinclair, the rest of the Seven are either traveling for work or with their family, I've found myself spending more time with him. Given the joint history of the incident which binds us, there's a level of trust I share with Sinclair that should make this joint venture successful. But of course, Knox—that douchebag—has his own interests to protect.

"If you'd bother to look at the figures, you'd see we turn a profit in twelve months," I snap.

"With losses for six of those."

"The higher the risk, the higher the return." I shrug.

"Like your marriage?"

Anger squeezes my guts, my fingers tingle, and I curl them into fists and try to rein in the burn that eats through my veins. He's trying to provoke me. I know that. I also know G-Pa is watching to see how I settle in—at work and with my new bride.

He called to say he'll be making an announcement soon, confirming my role as CEO, but he hasn't mentioned when he'll do it. Meanwhile, Knox will use every dirty trick to show I'm not fit. And it's important to me to get my grandfather's approval. My parents didn't give two shits about me, whereas my grandfather—even if it had been for his own selfish needs—decided I'm his heir. And I'm not going to fuck it up. I don't need a shrink to tell me this only highlights another issue in my psyche. In addition to the ones I already carry around, but whatever. I have a right to this company, and I'm not letting go of it.

"Something you want to tell me?" I narrow my gaze on Knox.

He leans back in his seat and shrugs. "Not really."

"I do." Sinclair scowls at me. "Don't be an arse, Ed. Don't go making choices that will endanger the company when you're not thinking clearly."

"Who said I'm not?" I lower my voice to a hush. Not that it has any impact on Sin. Motherfucker's as alpha as they come.

"The fact that you're here, instead of taking your gorgeous wife on a honeymoon, is enough of a giveaway that you're not in the right space."

"Don't fucking talk about my wife."

Knox flicks an imaginary piece of dust from his tailored jacket. "Don't get your knickers in a twist. Just stating what I see."

"What I see is a lost opportunity. I'm going to push this deal through, with or without you." I set my jaw.

Knox inclines his head. He doesn't seem disturbed by my announcement. "Well then, my work here is done." He rises to his feet and nods at Sinclair. "Sterling." Then without another glance at me, he prowls toward the exit. He heads out, and the door snicks shut behind him.

"Why do I get the feeling there's something up his sleeve?"

"Why do I get the feeling you're about to commit career suicide?" Sinclair sighs.

"Don't you trust my judgement?"

He scrutinizes my features. "Frankly, not in the state of mind you're in at the moment."

"Nothing's wrong with my state of mind."

"It will be when you find out Knox is talking to your wife." He jabs his thumb over his shoulder.

I glance toward my computer screen, showing a live feed of her desk outside my office, and stiffen. He's right; there's Knox, leaning a hip at my wife's desk. He says something, and Belle throws her head back and laughs.

He continues to talk, while she leans over to grab a paper and write on it. He says something else, and she looks up at him with a soft expression about her eyes. I gape. *What the hell is happening? I look up at the window separating us, to be certain I'm not seeing things.* That's when she reaches out to touch his arm and—"What the fuck?!" I jump up so quickly, my chair topples over. I race out the door, and before she can withdraw her hand, I grab his arm and twist it, throwing him aside. "Get away from my wife."

"You are crazy, just crazy!" She fumes at me.

After I went caveman and pulled Knox away from her, he didn't retaliate. Much to my disgust, he smirked, dusted off his jacket, and left. He didn't say a word, but the smug glitter in his eyes told me I'd allowed him to provoke me again. He turned and prowled off. Sinclair shook his head at me, told me to rethink the acquisition before I went through with it, then he asked Belle to take care of me and left. I marched back into the office, and she followed. I told her to leave; she'd planted her hands on her hips and scowled at me. I mirrored her stance and glared back. She didn't look away. Interesting. *My little Belle is finding her spine.*

"I think you need to leave." I jerk my chin toward the door.

"I think you're avoiding me," she bursts out.

"What gave you that idea?"

"The fact I haven't seen you or spoken to you since our wedding night?"

"I've been busy." I shove my hand in my pocket. Technically, not a lie, because I've thrown myself into work.

"Too busy to spend time with your new wife?"

"New fake wife."

"Not so fake after you took my virginity." She tips up her chin.

"I told you, I'm not apologizing for it."

"I'm not looking for an apology, but you're not talking to me, either."

"Did you expect me to whisper sweet nothings and tell you how gorgeous you look because"—I look her up and down, taking in the purple dress nipped in at the waist to accentuate her sumptuous figure—"you know you do."

She blushes. "I'm not looking for compliments."

"I'm making a statement."

She looks at me with confusion in her eyes. "Only you can deliver praise and look like you don't mean it."

"But I do."

"I know you do, but your face—" She shakes her head. "The expression on your face says you don't care."

"Because I don't?" *That's it, buddy, keep telling yourself that.*

Her lips tighten. "You're an asshole."

"And I can't stop thinking about your other virgin hole."

Her color deepens. "I didn't come in here to be insulted." She pivots and flounces toward the door. I slip my phone out of my pocket and swipe my finger across the screen. There's a clicking sound. When she reaches the door, she pushes at it, but it doesn't open. She turns and frowns at me. "Open this door."

I yawn.

Her eyes flash silver blue lightning at me. "Edward, open the door," she says through gritted teeth.

"That's not the name you used when I was inside you."

She swallows. "This is not funny, Ed."

"First, call me by the name only you do."

"You mean, douchewaffle?"

I almost allow myself a chuckle. Almost. My life is way more fucking entertaining when she's around. I can watch her all day—which I do, whenever I get the chance, anyway—and not be bored. Every action of hers entrances me. Every word that comes out of her mouth enchants me. Her scent bewitches me. Her curves captivate me. Everything about her has held me in thrall since the day I first saw her. Since she came into my life, it's turned into a patchwork of technicolor. I want to resist her, but my defenses are crumbling. It's pissing me off, but the more I try to put distance between us, the more thoughts of her invade my mind. As for my body? Every part of me remembers how it felt to be buried inside her. My cock thickens, and my thigh muscles harden. I widen the space between my legs, then crook my finger at her. "Come 'ere."

29

Mira

His voice is hard with that mean edge that propels a zing of sensations up my spine. When I hesitate, he lowers his arms to his sides.

"Come. Here. Belle."

I set my jaw, "And if I don't?"

"You know you want to," his tone softens. "You know you want me."

I don't. I don't.

"You do." He states the fact without malice. The expression on his face is confident, but his gaze is tortured. It's as if he senses the struggle going on inside me and recognizes it, and maybe that's what makes me place one foot in front of the other. When I come to a stop in front of him, his eyes flash.

"Say my name," he demands.

The rasp in his voice makes my insides melt. My breath stutters. My scalp itches. He's not touching me, but the way he rakes his gaze over my features, down the thrust of my breasts, to the space between my legs, he might as well be.

Then he sinks down to his knees, and I cry out. In seconds he's shoved my skirt up around my hips, leaned in, and pushed his face between my legs. My knees buckle; my head spins. He inhales a deep breath, and every pore in my body seems to breathe fire.

"What are you doing?" I say breathlessly.

"Smelling my wife's cunt," he snaps, "you have a problem with that?"

"N-noooooo!" The word is pulled from my mouth, for he's clamped his teeth around my clit and tugged. Shockwaves bolt up my spine. My fingers tremble. My heart rams into my chest and I'm sure it's going break out of my ribcage. He slides his big hands around my butt cheeks and fits me snugly over his mouth. Then he begins to lick me through the fabric of my panties. The combination of the smooth silk combined with the lapping sensation of his tongue is sheer torture. I dig my fingers into his hair and tug. "Edward, please Ed."

He makes a growling sound at the back of his throat, then slides his palm down the back of one thigh. He applies pressure and I raise my thigh. There's a ripping sound and he throws my leg over his shoulder.

"Fish on a turbocharger," I cry out.

There's a huffing sound, then he looks up at me. "Your swearing is very creative, but you don't want to use the Lord's name in front of me."

I glance down and the sight of his head between my thighs propels another burst of goosebumps over my skin. "Sorry." I swallow, trying to get my thoughts together. "I didn't realize it offended you. Especially since you're a former-priest—"

"You're mistaken."

"I am?"

"I don't believe in Him anymore."

O-k-a-y. "What do you believe in then?" The question is out before I can stop myself. His jaw hardens.

"I believe in myself."

"And love?" I know the answer, and yet I have to ask. *Stupid, stupid. Why did I have to open my big mouth?* My worst fears are confirmed when his features close further.

"It's not for me."

I try to pull away, but he holds me in place.

"Don't be angry. You knew the score before we got married. You knew I wasn't cut out for a relationship. You knew we weren't going to sleep together."

"So I'm good enough for you to penetrate me—"

"It's not going to happen again."

"—but I'm not good enough for you to make a sperm donation?"

His jaw tightens. "This what you want to be discussing now when I have my head up your skirt?"

"You started it, Buster."

"And I'm finishing it." With that, he shoves my panties aside and stabs his tongue inside me. My eyes roll back in my head. I hold onto him as he begins to thrust his tongue in and out of me. In-and-out, in imitation of how he penetrated me with his cock. It's not as thick or as long as his cock, of course… And, as if he's reading my mind, he swipes his tongue up my pussy-lips and curls it around my swollen clit, and at the same time, he stuffs three fingers inside me. I whimper, and it spurs him on. He moves his fingers in and out of me, continues to worry my clit. Then he adds a fourth finger a-n-d… I was mistaken. I love his cock, but the combination of his fingers and his tongue is so very wicked. He laps up my core, curls his fingers inside me, and the orgasm rams through me. It sweeps up my thighs, folds around my center, then zooms up my spine. It explodes somewhere at the back of my eyes, and I forget how to breathe. Then, I hear a keening sound and realize it's me crying out. The ecstasy fades away to be replaced by a glowing warmth. I'm aware of him rising to his feet. He scoops me up in his arms, walks around the desk and sits down with me in his lap. He holds me close, and I cuddle into him. I breathe in the familiar scent of woodsmoke shot through with that sharp tang, the way the air smells before a storm, which is so uniquely him. "Eddie," I whisper.

He tightens his arms around me. I push my ear into his chest and the bang-bang-bang of his heart gives away his state of arousal. That, and the length of concrete digging into the space between my naked asscheeks.

"My panties—" The word comes out as 'pahntiieesh,' and I realize I'm slurring.

"Shh, don't worry. I have some spare ones here for you."

"Hmm, okay." I cuddle closer, then snap open my eyes. "You have spare panties for me in your office."

He doesn't reply, and I interpret that correctly as an affirmative answer.

I glance up and meet those amber eyes of his. "Why do you have spare panties for me in your office?"

He tilts his head.

I sigh. "Did you know I was going to come in here, and that you were going to—"

"Make a mess in my lap?"

"What?" I wriggle this way, then that enough to catch a glimpse of the damp spot on the front of his pants. Heat flushes my cheeks. "I didn't mean to—"

"I'll wear it as a badge of pride."

I blush deeper, and the hard column underneath me extends further. "You still haven't come."

"I haven't come in two years."

30

Edward

Fuck, fuck. Fuck. Didn't mean to blurt that out. And since when do things slip past my control? Since when do I ensure there's an entire wardrobe change for a woman in the closet in my office? Since I met her. Since I got married to her. Since I feel this responsibility for her. This deep tenderness and need for her. This desire to make love to her. This compulsion to dominate her. To ensure she is always high from the pleasure only I can bring her. To mark her flesh and dig my teeth into the curve of her shoulder, to look into her eyes as I bury myself inside of her. To teach her who she belongs to. For she is mine. *My wife. My life. My love. Fuck... I can't have fallen for her in such little time.*

I wanted to keep her at arm's length. Instead, I can't stop myself from holding her in them. Close to me. Against my chest where I can smell her, feel her softness against me, assure myself she's safe and cared for. My pulse rate accelerates further. A bead of sweat trails down my spine. *I can't let myself feel so much for her. I will not break my vow. My self-control is the only thing I have left, and I will not willingly relinquish it.*

Some of my thoughts must show on my features—another first—for she cups my cheek. "Eddie, what's wrong?"

I want to tell her. I want to tell her why I can't be a better husband to her. Why I can't give her what she wants. Why I'll never be the man she deserves. Why I will not break the vow I made to myself. Why I'll never demand she submit to me, though every inch of me craves to feel her come apart, bit by bit, around my cock. I want to see her shudder as I bring her to the edge. I want to play her body like it's an instrument made for my pleasure. I want to do the most degrading, filthy things to her and watch her fight back before the inevitable capitulation.

She holds the power to destroy me; a power she's snatched from me without trying. She's more dangerous than the incident that changed me. Bit by bit, she's peeling back my layers, and revealing the man I'd hoped to become. I want to be everything for her…but can't. *I can't.*

"I can't."

"What?" She frowns.

"I can't do this."

"Do what?"

"This—you, me… It's not worth it."

She swallows. "I… I'm not sure what you mean."

I begin to lower her to the ground, but she throws her arms about my neck and clings. "Eddie, please talk to me. Don't shut down."

When I don't respond, she bites her lower lip, and of course, my dick instantly stabs against the restraint of my pants. Everything about her is designed to tempt me, to allure me and seduce me. I thought I could control myself around her— Ha, the joke's on me.

I thought I could resist her. Instead, I'm falling for her. I need to put distance between us again. I need to ensure there's no opportunity for me to be enticed by her.

Once again, she must read something in my gaze, for alarm flits across her features. She scrambles up, and pulling her skirt up further, she straddles me. "Eddie, no, don't do this." She pushes into me, so her breasts are flattened against my chest. Those hard nipples of hers dig into my jacket, and despite the layers between us, I can feel their outline against my chest, can sense the beating of her heart like it's my own. Can intuit the confusion that grips her, the appeal, the craving, the concern in her eyes. And that's my undoing.

"I don't deserve this. I don't deserve you."

"Why do you say that? Why do you beat yourself up so? The little time I've spent with you has shown me you're not the persona you project to the world. You're not hard, or emotionless; quite the contrary.

You feel so much." She slips a hand under my jacket, and my heart thuds against her palm. "You're real, and vital, and alive, and there's so much inside of you. You have so much to share with the world. You care deeply, Edward—too deeply—and that's the problem."

My pulse rate surges, and my stomach goes into a spiral, "I have no idea what you're talking about."

"Yes, you do. You feel everything. You see everything. You're so instinctive, so intuitive, so sensitive. You know exactly how I feel, which is why you stopped yourself earlier."

"I fucked you once… Without coming inside you, I might add. And only so when I tell my grandfather the deed is done, I'm not lying. And you think you know me?"

She winces, and of course, my heart stutters, but I push aside the pain.

"You're my husband."

I shrug. "We've been married for a little over a week."

"You don't have to spend time with someone to know them. I mean, you do"—she shakes her head—"but I trust my instincts, and they say you're not as mean or as ruthless as you make yourself out to be."

"Your instincts are wrong this time."

"I don't believe you. If I were wrong, you'd have fucked my ass, like you intended to, but you stopped yourself."

I stiffen. "Don't second guess me."

"Isn't that right? You wanted to do it, but you knew it would hurt. You knew I wasn't ready, so you stopped. Instead, you gave me pleasure —so much pleasure. You're a giver, Edward. But you think it's a weakness. So, you try to hide it behind all that bluster."

I yawn.

"Don't do that." She firms her lips.

"Do what?"

"Pretend you don't care, when the way your heart is racing, the way your eyes have turned bleak, the way the muscles of your shoulders bunch and your chest-planes tense, tell me the opposite."

Fucking hell, how does this woman see past the barriers I've erected against the world? How does she see into my soul every single time? How does she read me so clearly, when no one else has in the past? How can she, with a few words, destroy the remnants of my control?

"I don't know how much more plainly to tell you this, but I. Don't. Care."

She sets her jaw. "You're lying."

"I never lie." *And I did. For the very first time in my life, I lied. I. Fucking. Lied.* Something inside me splinters—the last bastion that has held back my shadow self, the partition I laid down to ensure the darkness inside me never peeked out. The last time I gave in to the darkness inside, I lost everything. And this time… This time, I'm going to lose her.

I squeeze her hips with enough force that she gasps. Whatever she sees in my face makes her gulp. "E-Eddie… You're scaring me."

"Good."

"I… I think… I need to leave." She tries to slip off, and I laugh.

Her gaze widens, and her blue eyes deepen until they're sheets of the deepest aquamarine. "You… You laughed? I've never seen you laugh. It should be reassuring but, it…it's not."

"Glad you're smarter than you look."

"That's not fair. You're saying that to hurt me."

"I haven't even started, baby."

She swallows. "You won't do it, Edward. I know you're not as heartless as you portray yourself."

"This heart might beat"—I slap one hand over hers, which is still inside my jacket—"but it's not capable of loving anyone."

Her features crumple, then she gets a hold of herself. "I know you don't mean it. I know you, Edward. I've seen you with Tiny—"

"A mutt—"

"The way a person treats a pet says everything about them. Everything. And you"—she searches my features—"you are all heart."

"What I am, is so hard that I can no longer wait to have your virgin arse."

31

———

Mira

He's being salacious in his choice of words so he can shock me. And I am shocked. And aroused. His dirty talking voice rockets a buzz of lust to my core. My thighs tremble, and my scalp tingles. He must sense the effect on me, for a look of interest comes into his eyes. "You like that, Belle?"

"Of course, not. Why would I like it if you're purposely being filthy in your speech."

"Because—" He shoves his hand between my legs and cups my bare pussy.

I gasp.

"—I can feel the moisture drip down your thighs and dampen on my crotch. I can"—he draws in a sharp breath—"smell your arousal intensify. I can—" He shoves two fingers inside me.

I whimper.

"—feel you clench down on me because you're empty. I can—" He pulls out his fingers, only to run them up the cleavage between my asscheeks.

I flinch, try to pull away, but he smears the moisture on my forbidden entrance.

"Edward," I groan. "Please. Edward."

He continues to hold my gaze, continues to tease my puckered hole. I instantly tense, and he leans in and runs his nose up my throat. "Your scent drives me crazy. You smell of sweet apple blossom and innocence, and it makes me want to mess you up."

"It's my shampoo." Goosebumps pepper my skin.

"Your shampoo?" He nuzzles my jawbone, my cheek, up to the corner of my eyes. It's almost sweet and gentle and romantic and so like the man I know he is inside. My muscles slowly unwind. A warmth steals up my limbs. I sink into him, feel my legs go lax, my thighs, my butt-cheeks… In a flash, he slides a finger inside me and past the ring of muscle in my back hole.

I gasp and bear down on him. "Edward, Ed." I dig my fingers into his hard shoulders. "Please, Ed."

"Shh, I promise, you're going to enjoy it."

"I'm not yet."

"You will." He continues to whisper kisses over one eyelid, between my eyebrows, the other eyelid, down my cheek, to the shell of my ear. When he flicks his tongue inside, I shiver. When he bites down on my earlobe, I moan. And when he continues the path down my cheek to the other side of my lips, I can't stop myself from turning to meet his lips. For a second, we stay there, gazing into each other's eyes, his lips touching mine, our breaths mingling, being shared, our eyelashes almost tangling. Something flickers deep inside. Those silver sparks I've seen before, joined, this time, by flashes of gold, sparkling, almost festive. "It's like it's already Christmas," I whisper.

His lips twitch, then he brushes his mouth over mine once, twice. The third time, I sigh, and he slides his tongue between my lips. He licks the seam, and my nipples tighten until they're pinpoints of need. He drags his tongue over my teeth and, fish in a train, those fires on my body, which are never too far from the surface, ignite again. I'm burning up, little pinpricks of need clawing at me from inside. I whine, and his body tenses. I lean in and push my tits against his chest, and a shudder grips him.

He's destroying me, but I have the power to tear him apart, too. This knowledge is an aphrodisiac that skyrockets the lust in my veins. I wrap my arms about his chest and force my muscles to relax. One-two-three,

I bite down on his tongue, and his entire body turns granite hard. The tension thrums off of him, the heat spooling off of his chest and slamming into mine. I gasp, and he absorbs the sound, then tilts his head and deepens the kiss. He drinks from me, ravages my mouth. As soft as his kisses were earlier, this is all inflexible and demanding, with a touch of meanness that is so very him. Both sides are him. The tenderness and the ruthlessness, the gentleness and the ferocity, the compassion and the brutality.

He showed me the first without wanting to, and the latter... He wants me to see it, feel it, sense it, imbibe it. Like he did when he took me to the BDSM club, he thinks if he shows me his hidden depths, I'll panic. That I'll run and hide and never want to be in his vicinity.

What he doesn't realize is I'm made of sterner stuff. I'm a survivor. I've learned to depend on myself. I persevere. I don't give up easily. I hope. And yes, I pray. And I believe. In him. In us. Most of all, I believe in myself, and it's time he saw that, too.

I slide my hand over his jacket-covered arm down to the back of his broad palm, and then his fingers.

I fit a second broad digit to my back hole and urge him on. His gaze widens, then a look of determination sweeps over his features. Without taking his eyes off of mine, he pushes his finger inside.

A slight pain threads over my nerve-endings. Nothing I can't bear, though. And the fullness... It's a little uncomfortable. Okay, very uncomfortable, but he doesn't move. He stays that way, allowing me to adjust to his size. We stay silent, communicating with our eyes, then he brings his other arm up and wraps his fingers about the nape of my neck. It's a gesture of complete confidence, of domination, of ownership, a sign that he can do what he wants, a signal to my body to turn to a melting gooey mess. It's comforting and arousing and sends a signal to every part of me that I'm ready. *I'm ready.*

"I'm ready," I whisper.

He nods. "Good girl."

Oh, my god, that's it; I'm undone. A small sound escapes my lips, and that's enough. His gaze crackles, his forearm bunches, and he begins to move his fingers in and out of me, in and out. Widening me, loosening me up, preparing me for him. And I want him. Oh, my god, I want him so very much. I want everything he can give me. Everything. And more. I want so much more. "Edward, please."

This time, when he smiles, it's a curve of his lips that has nothing to do with pleasure. It's an expression of satisfaction. Of approval. I've passed some test I didn't even know he'd set. I open my mouth to ask; but before I can say anything, he stands up, lowers my feet to the ground, spins me around, and bends me over his desk. I blink and realize my cheek is pushed into his desk, and my ass is up in the air. Then he kicks my legs apart. There's a ripping sound and my already torn skirt splits further.

"You're an animal," I gasp.

"Finally. Took you long enough to recognize it."

He shoves my skirt up as far up as it will go, so it's bunched under my armpit, then he urges my arms to my sides, curls my fingers around the edge of the desk.

"You good?"

I nod.

"Hold on tight."

"What—" A line of pain zips up my spine. It takes me a minute for my brain to catch up with my nerve cells. Then I yell, "Did you spank me?"

"Yup." His big palm connects with my left cheek, then the right, then the left, before he pauses. "I spanked you four times."

"What are you—" I yell again as he brings down his palm, alternating between my asscheeks, four more times. Four slaps, four more zings of pain that skitter to my core, curl around my clit like a lasso and pull tight. I moan and pant and curse. He laughs. The bastard laughs. I've never seen him enjoying himself so much.

"I hate you," I say through gritted teeth.

"Not yet."

He rubs his palm across my throbbing butt cheeks, and the contact sends another swish of sensations bursting up my spine. My brain cells feel like they're melting. Everything around me seems to sparkle. He seems to have brought the Christmas spirit to life without lights, a-n-d I might be a tad high on whatever reaction he's eliciting in my body. Heat covers me. The edge of his jacket chafes my backside as he bends over me. He pushes my hair away from my face and stares into my eyes. "How are you feeling?"

"I'm fine," I say in a dreamy voice.

He wraps his fingers, once more, around the nape of my neck. I sigh. I like when he does this; I like it a lot. He draws long strokes down my back over my blouse and skirt, down to the base of my spine, and up again.

Warmth seeps into my shoulders and my arms, and the muscles of my back unwind. I stretch under him, feeling like I'm a cat, feeling my lips stretch up in a smile. He bends and presses his lips to mine, and it's soft and sweet and hard and demanding, all at once. *Jeez.* "Where did you learn how to kiss like that?"

"It's you," he murmurs into my mouth. "You make me want to show you how good it can be when I make love to you."

"Hmm." I smile. *He said 'make love to you.'* My gaze widens. I open my mouth to ask him…when something fat and blunt teases my forbidden hole.

32

———————

Edward

Only when the words are out of my mouth, do I realize what I've said. And that she heard it, and that there's no turning back now. I tried to show her my true self, and I let the truth slip out— dammit—the very reason I lost my composure, the very reason I lied earlier. And now, it's all out there. And I know she's going to ask me about it, and I'm not ready to talk about it—not now, not for a while. So like the coward I am, I tilt my hips, push forward, and breach her.

"Eddie," she cries out. No one's ever called me by this nickname, and hearing it from her lips sends the blood draining to my cock. My cock thickens impossibly more, pushing up against her walls. I wait, wait, allow her to adjust to my size. Then, when the trembling in her body recedes, I propel my hips forward and bury myself inside her.

She groans.

So do I.

And because I can't stop myself, because I'm falling for her—and my heart knows it, though my brain hasn't yet caught on—and because she's so fucking gorgeous laid out in front of me, and because her lips are a better taste, better than any liquor I've ever drunk, I lower my head and press my mouth to hers again. She parts her lips willingly, and I ease my tongue over hers. The taste of her is potent and sweet and complex and innocent, all mixed into one. It goes straight to my heart and ties a lasso around it, then heads to my cock. My shaft twitches. I draw of her breath, lick into her mouth, absorb her whimper, and when I straighten, she looks at me with so much trust, that ball of sensation in my heart expands until it bleeds into my skin and covers my entire body. I hold her gaze, then lock my fingers around the nape of her neck. "Do you trust me?"

She nods.

And it undoes me, all over again.

I reach down and around her, then begin to strum her pussy. Color flushes her cheeks, and she moans. Her muscles relax even more, and I slip deeper inside her. "You're so tight... So hot... So perfect." I grit my teeth and allow her to adjust, once more, to my intrusion.

I continue to play with her pussy lips, circle her clit, and when I slide my fingers inside her cunt, she moans. "It's too much. You're filling me up. I can't take any more."

"You can," I say with complete confidence in her. "You will. You're my Belle."

"And you're a beast," she moans.

I like that name even more, though I don't say that aloud. Instead, I rub her clit with the heel of my palm. "Open up and let me in, baby."

She willingly widens her legs further. I continue to slide my fingers in and out of her, and when I add a fourth finger, she shudders.

"Ohgod, ohgod, ohgod," she chants. I don't stop her. Even if I don't want to hear His name from her lips. Whatever she wants, whatever she needs, It's hers.

Except me. I can't give her myself. Not more than what I've already shared.

But I can make her come one last time. I pull out but stay poised at the rim of her back entrance. She shivers, and when I propel myself forward, I slide all the way in. My balls slap against her slit, and the entire desk shakes. A glass crashes to the ground, but I don't stop. I pull out, once again, and still holding her gaze, push into her. I bury myself to the hilt, hitting that spot deep inside her.

"Oh—" she gasps. "Oh my—" I release my hold on her neck, squeeze her hip and position her at the right angle. This time, when I push into her, I hit that spot again. She opens her mouth, but no sound comes out.

But I know. I know she's close. She's almost there. Her back curves, her thighs clench, and she squeezes down on my cock and my fingers. I pull out and push forward, again and again, and when her pupils dilate until only a circle of blue is visible, and the skin over her knuckles is stretched white, and that tell-tale shudder spirals up her hips, I lean over, place my lips above hers and command, "Come."

"You didn't come, again."

She shoots me a sideways glance. I keep my gaze focused on the road ahead. After she shattered under me, I pulled out, then scooped her up in my arms, and took her into the ensuite. I helped her out of her clothes and, brushing aside her protests, cleaned her up. Then, I showed her the walk-in closet I had built especially so I could store clothes for her. She seemed taken aback by the range of clothes—all in her size, including the underwear.

"You bought all this?" she asked.

When I nodded, her gaze widened. "It's not easy to find plus-size clothing; it must have taken you a lot of searching to find this array of clothes."

"It was worth it. You're worth it." I helped her out of her clothes, and while she stood naked, I worshiped her with my eyes. I stored every curve of her body in my mind—her heavy breasts, the nip of her waist, the flaring of her hips, and those fleshy thighs that haunt my dreams. I wanted her to sit on my face, so I could take my time and make her come again. I wanted to crawl up her body, settle between her legs and finally, *finally* bury myself inside her. I almost lost my resolve and did just that, but at the last moment, I managed to tear myself from her. I left her to find a suitable change of clothes.

She chose a below-the-knee skirt, a blouse, and a jacket in a peach color that turned her skin to ivory.

She's so fucking beautiful, my wife. If only I could give her the kind of love she deserves. For the first time, I'm wondering if marrying her was a mistake. I didn't want anyone else to have her. I was selfish. *I am selfish.* I've spoiled her life, and I have to make up for it.

Once she was ready, I hustled her out of the office, not caring that it wasn't even five p.m. As I steered my wife toward the elevator, the receptionist shot me an alarmed look. When I didn't acknowledge it, she jumped to her feet and walked over to me. "Are you okay, Sir? You've never left office this early before."

"I wasn't married then. I am now."

Belle draws in a sharp breath.

My receptionist ignores her and takes a step in my direction. "If you need anything else — ?"

I squeeze my wife closer. "I have everything I need."

This time, Belle turns to me, a question on her features, which I pretend not to notice.

I hustle her into the elevator, then hold her close as the elevator doors close on the receptionist's crestfallen features.

"I think she has a crush on you," Belle teases.

And I'd like to crush you in my arms, is what I want to say, but I don't.

We ride in silence for a few more seconds, then she turns to me, "Is it true you've never left the office this early before?"

I nod.

"You didn't have to leave early because of me."

Yes, I do. I want to spend every second of every day with you. The first time I saw you, my heart hurt, and the throbbing in my groin has become a permanent fixture. My balls need to be drained before it gets to be too much. Too bad, I'm not going to indulge myself.

Something of my thoughts must be revealed in the stance of my body, for she stiffens, then scans my features. "Edward, have you taken a vow of abstinence?"

33

Mira

"I'm no longer a clergyman, as you're aware." He continues to focus on the road.

"But you said you haven't been with any woman for a while, and whenever we make love—"

"You mean when we fuck—"

"You used the word 'love,' earlier."

"What?" He frowns.

"You said—"

"I know what I said, and it was a slip of the tongue."

"I thought you said you don't lie?" I narrow my gaze on him.

He tightens his fingers on the wheel and continues to drive. "I don't. Except when I'm with you, apparently."

I blink. I hadn't expected to hear that. "Are you saying—"

"People say all kinds of things when they're having sex."

"We weren't having sex; you didn't come."

"I made *you* come… And hard, as I recall."

On cue, my backside smarts. I shift around, trying to find a more comfortable position. I try to be discreet about it, but he notices it, of course, the bastard.

"Does your butt hurt?"

"What do you think?"

"I think I enjoyed seeing my palm print etched into your arse."

Oh, my god, what is it about him saying arse in that British accent of his that has me all hot and bothered again? "I don't know what game you're playing—"

"Not a game."

"—but I'm not going to be put off by you demonstrating your kinky side."

He blinks. "My kinky side?" he asks slowly.

"Spanking me, then the, uh—backside entry."

"You mean anal?"

My flush deepens. I'm not a prude. I've read enough super-spicy novels and listened to even more of them, so of course, I know my way around the smutabulary, but I've never been able to say that world aloud. Never mind the fact that, an hour ago, my husband's monster cock was up my ass. Oh, shoot, I *am* a prude.

"Exactly," I say in a prim voice. "Since you took me to the BDSM club, I know you're not vanilla in your preferences."

"Not vanilla?" There's something in his voice that makes me cast a quick glance in his direction. The divot to the left of his mouth tells me he's finding this entire conversation amusing.

"It's not funny," I protest.

"It's not," he agrees.

"Then why are you smiling?"

"Because you think what I did to you was kinky."

"It was."

"You have no idea," he says in that voice that has more than a hint of darkness to it.

A ripple of heat squeezes my belly. "You mean, that was the beginner's level introduction to smutty sex?"

"I mean, that was the pre-kindergarten level introduction to my depravity."

"Oh." I know my mouth is open and that I'm staring at him, but it's the first time we've had an open conversation about something... So what, if it's about his perversions.

"So you have, uh…different tastes, but you haven't been with a woman since…"

"Since I left to go traveling, two years ago."

"You…you haven't been with a woman in two years?" I stare.

He merely stares at me.

"But you go to the BDSM club."

"And as you've experienced firsthand, I don't have to ejaculate in order to indulge my debaucheries."

Oh, my god! The heat in my stomach expands into a full-blown forest fire, which instantly spreads to my extremities. My lower belly clenches, and I squeeze my thighs together to tamp down on the yawning emptiness.

"For someone who was a virgin until a week ago, you sure relish the dirty talk," he murmurs.

"Only when it's you doing the dirty talking."

He chuckles, then seems to realize what he's done, for he wipes all expression from his face.

"It's okay to laugh and smile and cry and show emotion. You are human, after all."

"And it's because I allowed myself to be human, because I chose to give in to my emotions, that I'm here today."

A hot sensation stabs into my chest. It's as if he's plunged a burning rod into my heart. He seems to realize what he's said, for he scowls. "I didn't mean—"

"Yes, you did. You're regretting that you married me."

"Not for the reasons you think."

"So you *do* regret marrying me."

He steps on the accelerator and the car speeds up. "I never regret my actions."

"Expect the time you gave in to your emotions and lost the woman you loved."

Tell me you don't love her. Tell me you love me. You said it earlier; just say it aloud again.

But he doesn't. The muscles at his jaw line flex, but he stays silent, focuses on the driving. In another ten minutes, we drive up in front of his townhouse.

We stay in the car; the silence stretches, then he states, "I'm not the man you think I am." His voice is emotionless. "I'm not a knight in shining armor. I'm not Prince Charming."

"No, you're the beast, the villain. You're Hades, and Severus Snape, and Loki, rolled into one."

"Severus Snape?" He frowns.

"Point is, the darkness in you is what I find so attractive."

His jaw tightens. "You don't know what you're talking about."

"Sure, I do. I know that every time you look at me, you feel something, but you're so convinced you'll never own your emotions again, you won't admit it."

"It's why you should have never married me, Belle." His tone is serious.

And when I search his features, I realize he believes it, too. I swallow hard. "I married you of my own free will."

"Did you?" There's something in his features, an expression I can't interpret.

A cold sensation spirals down my spine. I shiver, then shove it aside. "I did," I say in a firm voice.

"What you got a taste of in my office is not even a starter course."

"I'm not scared, Edward. I want to be your main and your dessert. I want to be your eight-course meal."

He scoffs, "You, the newly deflowered virgin... You have no idea what you're talking about."

"No, don't do that." I cut my palm through the air. "Don't patronize me. I am not a child."

"You were one not too long ago."

I shake my head. "You don't get to diminish me. I know what I'm doing."

"Do you?"

"I do. I knew what I was taking on when I left home and moved to a new city. I knew what I was doing when I agreed to marry you."

"You didn't have a choice."

"I could have refused you and my father. I could have walked out."

"But you didn't."

"That's right." I straighten my spine. "I chose the tough route, because it was my responsibility to help my father. I don't shirk my duties."

"So that's what this is?" He looks me up and down. "You want to sacrifice yourself at the altar of my depravity because you want to live up to the duty of being my wife."

"Yes." I tip up my chin. "I won't shirk from my obligations."

"You have no obligation toward me."
"How can you say that? I am your wife."
"And I will not corrupt you further."

34

Edward

"Why are you not with your wife?" Arthur frowns.

"Because I didn't want to miss poker night." I focus on my cards, while well aware of the suspicion in his eyes.

I'm not doing a good job of playing the newly-married husband desperately in love with his bride. In fact, I'm screwing up my role so badly, even my grandfather believes something is wrong.

"For a man enjoying post marital bliss, you seem strung tightly," Knox drawls.

Asswipe is trying to get another response from me, and this time, I will not give in to him.

I accompanied Belle to the door of the townhouse, made sure she was in safely, then instructed my housekeeper to cook dinner for her. I had no interest in the poker game, but I did want to see my grandfather face-to-face. He still hasn't confirmed me as CEO, even though I'm in charge of all the key decisions of the company. I'm not going to bring it up with him, of course. I'm more strategic than that.

It's why I asked Sinclair to invite Arthur and Knox for his weekly poker night. Our mutual friends who'd normally attend are out of town.

It's the perfect opportunity to get facetime with the old man, without asking for a meeting. As for inviting Knox? It's a chance to demonstrate I don't hold a grudge.

I hoped to get a reading on my grandfather. But from what I'm seeing, he's not very happy with me.

"I'm taking my wife on our honeymoon over Christmas," I declare.

"You are?" Arthur looks up from his cards.

"I have a property in Cornwall. Very picturesque and isolated…and romantic. The perfect way to spend Christmas."

Arthur's features relax. "That sounds like the ideal getaway."

"It is."

"I'm pleased you're taking your duties as a husband seriously. If the wife's happy, everything else in your life will fall in order." He nods.

I incline my head to show I agree with him.

"I assume you'll do this properly and not work while you're away?" Knox murmurs in a casual tone. Which doesn't fool me at all. Mother-fucker will try any which way to take control of the company.

"Oh, I'll make sure I'm connected to the internet while I'm gone. Remote working and—"

"Absolutely not. You need to focus on your wife and your marriage completely while you're gone. It's very important you make it your priority."

"Oh, I can still attend meetings. The takeover we spoke about in conjunction with the 7A company—"

"Will be taken care of," Arthur declares.

I glance at Sinclair, but his expression indicates he has no idea what Arthur is talking about.

"The takeover is in a delicate phase." Sinclair looks up from his cards. "We'll probably sign the deal during the last week of December, and as the main signatory, it makes sense for Edward to be on the calls and—"

"—it's not right to disturb the man, no matter how important he is, on his honeymoon."

"But he's the key decision maker," Sinclair points out.

"Which is why I'm bringing in someone else with signing powers."

I stiffen. There it is, then. The old man never did intend to hand over the running of the company to me. He may have made me CEO, but he was never going to let me have veto power.

Knox throws down his cards. "Now, that's what I'm talkin' about."

He leans back in his seat. "You've made the right choice, Gramps. I won't let you down."

"Of course, not." Arthur's eyes gleam. He's hiding something, all right. He reaches over and scratches Tiny behind his ears. The Great Dane yawns. He welcomed me like an old friend when I walked in today, then abandoned me to take Arthur's side. There's a bond between the two of them which Arthur clearly relishes. When Tiny decided to stay with Arthur, I was worried about the mutt being shuttled around between homes, but I'm realizing Tiny has a mind of his own. He decides who's going to be his dog parent, and right now, he's adopted my grandfather as the adult in his life. He's softening up the old coot too, going by how Arthur smiles at the group.

Come to think of it, he's not the only one thawing. First, Tiny; then, Belle. Between the two of them, my life has been turned upside down.

Footsteps sound, then a man walks into the room. He's tall—as tall as me, six feet three inches, at least—broad shouldered, muscled in a way that hints at time spent doing physical work, and not just the gym kind. This man spends time working with his hands. He's wearing a black suit, which stretches over his physique and indicates its tailor made for his dimensions. His dark hair is peppered with grey at the temples.

I take in all of this, but what holds my attention are his features. They are so familiar. So like Knox's and like my grandfather's. He's... *Nope, can't be.*

"Arthur." The new guy nods in my grandad's direction.

"You don't mind, I invited Nathan here to join your poker night, Sterling?" Arthur phrases it as a question to Sinclair, but his tone makes it clear, he isn't asking for permission so much as informing.

If Sin is surprised, he hides it well.

"Of course." Sinclair rises to his feet, pulls up a chair, and slides it into the space between him and me.

"Thank you." Nathan slides into the seat, then jerks his chin at Knox, who's been glowering at him from across the table.

"You must be Knox," Nathan murmurs.

"The fuck are you?"

"I'm your oldest half-brother."

"What the fuck?" Knox throws his cards down on the table. "Is this a joke, Arthur?" He turns to our grandfather. "Because if it is—"

I scan Nathan's features and see the truth in his eyes. "It's not a joke, Knox."

"I want to hear it from Arthur," Knox says without taking his gaze off of our grandfather.

Arthur pets Tiny one more time, then turns to face Knox. "This is Nathan Davenport, my oldest grandson."

"I thought *he* was your oldest grandson." Knox jerks his chin in my direction.

"So did I." Arthur looks at me with an apologetic expression. "I found out about him at the same time as Edward. I reached out to Nathan and Edward at the same time, but Nathan never replied."

"I was traveling." Nathan shrugs.

"And now, you're conveniently here, in time to claim a part of the family fortune?" Knox growls.

"I'm independently wealthy." Nathan's lips twist, "I'm here because—"

"I asked him to come," Arthur interjects. "Turns out, before your father met Edward's mother, he had a son with his childhood sweetheart. She was sixteen when Nathan was born. Your father refused to step up to his responsibilities."

"What a surprise." Knox snorts.

"Greta paid off Nathan's mother, so she could leave with him and bring him up far away from us."

Nathan's jaw tics, but he doesn't comment.

"Apparently, your father knew if he came clean to me, I'd disinherit him. Greta didn't want that for him either. The two kept this a secret, but Greta wanted me to do right by Nathan."

"How did you find him?"

"His mother didn't keep her promise. She couldn't help but name your father on his birth-certificate." Arthur glances around the table. "Nathan grew up with the Davenport surname."

"A name I never wanted to be associated with. A name I should have gotten rid of the first chance I had," he says in a matter-of-fact voice.

"But you didn't." Arthur turns to him. "Family ties, dear grandson, can't be broken that easily."

"You trying to convince yourself or me?" Nathan drawls.

"You're here, aren't you?" Arthur puffs on his cigar.

"Grandma sure kept a lot of secrets from you." Knox lowers his chin to his chest.

Arthur's shoulders tense, then he seems to get a hold of himself. "And she wanted to make amends for it.

"By asking you to split the family fortune amongst those who don't deserve it?"

"You will apologize to your brother," Arthur booms.

"That's half-brother, and I will not," Knox shoots back.

Arthur sighs. "When you reach my age, you'll realize, family is all that matters."

"Good thing I'm not your age yet," Knox sneers.

Nathan looks like he's about to say something, then firms his lips.

"Any other long-lost relations we need to know about?" Knox tips up his chin in Arthur's direction, "Any other 'grandsons'"—he makes air-quotes—"lurking in the background with whom we'll need to split control of the company?"

"No grandsons," Arthur murmurs.

"But there are *others*?" I ask.

"My oldest son is Edward's adoptive father. And you're aware of my middle son, your biological father." He directs this statement at me and Knox before looking around the table. " The one you haven't met is my youngest," he murmurs.

"I knew it." Knox slaps his hand on the table with such force, the cards jump.

Arthur purses his lips. "We, uh…had a falling out, which caused him to leave home. It also resulted in me wiping all traces of him from my home, which is why you didn't know of his existence. I'm sorry to say, I hurt your grandmother deeply with that." The old man swallows.

"You're hurting us with these revelations," Knox points out.

"I promised Greta, on her deathbed, I'd reunite my family." He sets his jaw.

"More like, you're setting us up for a fight with all these new entrants," Knox mutters under his breath.

"And where is this long-lost uncle?" I ask slowly.

"I haven't been able to track him down. Maybe, he wants to stay hidden." Arthur pats Tiny's giant head.

"Maybe he *should* stay hidden." A nerve throbs at Knox's temple. "You expect us to accommodate yet another relation—no offense, Edward—"

"None taken." I shrug.

"— and slice up the family fortune because you've decided to make up for your sins in your old age?"

There's silence, then Arthur blows out a breath. "I understand how difficult all of this must be for you, especially when you were groomed to be my heir-apparent. Your father was a loser. The only good thing he did was sire you boys. I thought long and hard before bringing in first, Edward and now, Nathan, but it's for your own good, Knox."

Knox snorts.

"You're not made to be the CEO. Yet," Arthur declares.

Knox's jaw tics. "Don't hold back, Gramps," he growls.

Arthur holds up his hands. "I know, you're upset. But I promise you, when you look back, you'll understand it was for your own good."

"That's what they always say," Knox says in a bitter voice.

"You'll still be on the board of directors and lead on one of the smaller companies—"

"I just won't be CEO," Knox snaps.

"You'll never lack for money," Arthur points out.

"I just won't have the power." The tendons of Knox's throat bunch.

"I've given you a foothold in the company. When you prove yourself, you can climb the ladder like everyone else. There's nothing keeping you from staking a claim to be the CEO."

Knox stares at him steadily, "And he has the experience I lack? That's what you're trying to say, aren't you?"

Arthur lowers his chin to his chest. When he speaks, it's in a matter-of-fact tone, "Edward's had a few knocks in life, enough to make him worldly-wise. Nathan joined the navy and has been posted all over the world. He has experience making decisions involving the lives of people."

"Navy, huh?" Knox glares at the new guy.

Nathan tilts his head.

Arthur looks between us. "I realized it wasn't fair that I put the entire burden of leading the company on Edward, given he's just gotten married."

Motherfucker. The old man asked me to marry in order to ensure my inheritance. Now, he's using it as an excuse to hold it back from me, as well. I thought he was canny...but he's positively Machiavellian.

Arthur's features are all innocent as he turns to Knox. "I don't have much time left—"

Knox makes a rude noise, which all of us ignore.

"—and when your grandmother died, she left me information on not only how to track down Edward, but also Nathan."

"And you didn't think it important to mention it to me?" I ask mildly.

"It came as a surprise to me, too. I only found out a few days ago," Nathan offers.

Arthur pretends to be hurt. "I hope you boys are not going to gang up on me. I merely want what's best for the family, and for the empire *I* have built from scratch."

No missing the emphasis on the 'I' there.

"It was your grandmother's wish that I bring all her grandchildren together, and that they have a vested interest in working together to grow the business," Arthur continues.

"Decision-making by community never works," Knox warns.

"Oh, you don't have to worry about that." Arthur lays his cards down on the table face-up—a Royal Flush, no less. "The veto power rests with both Edward and Nathan."

Knox draws in a sharp breath.

Sinclair raises his eyebrows.

Arthur looks very pleased with himself.

This...is unexpected. It's not what I had in mind when I decided to make being the CEO of the Davenport empire my focus. This...changes things. Considerably. Anger squeezes my chest. A cold sensation percolates through my blood. I trusted Arthur—perhaps naively, I realize now. I hoped I would find in him the sense of family I hadn't had with my own parents. I miscalculated. Once more, I've allowed my emotions to rule me, and it has come to bite me in the arse. Lesson well learnt.

"This is bullshit." Knox jumps up to his feet. "You are going senile, old man." He stabs a finger at Arthur. "And you"—he turns to Nathan—"can go to hell."

He pushes away from the table, grabs his jacket off the back of his chair, and stalks out.

We sit there in silence for several moments.

"Now that that's out of the way,"—Sinclair grabs the bottle of whiskey—"who can I top up?"

"You're pissed." Sinclair half carries, half drags me up the steps of my townhouse.

"What I am is pisshhed… Pissshhed… Pishhhhhed offfffff." My words are slurred; I can hear them as if from far away. This is not being drunk. This is…medicinal. *Yep, that's all it isssshhhh. Fuck, I'm slurring in my head now, too.* I miss the next step, stumble and would fall face first if Sinclair doesn't grab my shoulders and straighten me.

"Fucking hell, Priest, what's wrong with you?"

"Whatssssh wrrrrong is that I trusssted that fucker."

"You mean Arthur?"

"Ar—fucking—thur… My fucking grandfather. I shhhhouldn't be surprised; my parents didn't give a fuck about me, eeeeither. And after the incident, if it hadn't been for B-B-Baron, I wouldn't've sssshurvived."

"Have you spoken to him at all?" His voice softens. "You guys were the best of friends and—"

"I don't need him in my life. In fact,—" I push away from him, stumble, but manage to find my footing. *Why the fuck is the door swaying in front of my eyes?* I put one foot in front of the other, reach the door, and am about to knock when it swings open. The most beautiful woman in the world, aka, my wife, stands there. She's wearing a pair of yoga pants that cling to her thick thighs, and a tiny T-shirt that outlines her gorgeous breasts. Heat tugs on my lower-belly. My cock thickens. Not that drunk, then.

"Wife, you're fucking gorgeous."

"And you're pissed." She slaps her hands on her hips, and her top tightens further. Now, I can see those sweet nipples outlined against the fabric, too. I lean in, intent on taking a bite of those gorgeous double-D tits; only, I lose my balance and stagger. She throws her arms about me. I bend and take a long sniff of her hair. Apple Blossom. Any remaining blood drains to my cock. My head spins. I begin to topple over. She yelps, sways. My knees begin to give way, when a firm hand under my bicep pulls me to my feet again.

I shake my head to clear it, pull away from Sinclair, then brush past her and step inside. I'm dimly aware of Sinclair supporting me on one side. Then, she slides her arm about my waist from the other. I lean my weight on Sinclair and tuck her closer under my arm.

"Alright, let's get you to your room." Sinclair urges me forward. One step at a time, one foot in front of the other. *Why is everything so blurry?*

I hear a voice singing from far away. Weird; it's a familiar voice, but what-fucking-ever. There will no longer be any emotions in my life. That much is clear. Then, we're climbing up the stairs, down the hallway, into my bedroom. The mattress floats up to meet me. I spin on a cloud of white and grey and blue and red. So much red. Anger, pain, suffering. I draw in a breath, and my lungs burn. It's dark, so dark.

There's a groan; someone else is there with me. I try to open my eyes, but realize I'm blindfolded. Try to move my arms, and realize my hands and legs are tied. I begin to struggle in earnest, trying to break the ropes that bind me, but they seem to tighten with my efforts. My muscles burn, my heart pounds in my chest. Sweat pours down my face. Pain screeches up my arms, and I realize the restraints are cutting into my wrists.

Let me go, I didn't do anything wrong. Let me the hell go. Oh god, oh god, why am I here? Help me, Lord. If I get out of here, I'll forever be grateful. I'll make sure I don't run away from school again. I'll be a good boy, I promise. Please, God, please. Tears squeeze out from the corners of my eyes. Wetness drips onto my lips. *Help, help me, please don't punish me like this please.*

"Edward."

I need to get out of here. I didn't do anything wrong. I didn't. Don't punish me, I beg you.

"Ed, Eddie."

There's a rustling sound as the door creaks open, followed by footsteps. I try to move my arms and legs but realize I'm tied up. The space around me lightens, enough for me to make out another figure tied up not far from me. I blink until the person's features come into focus. It's Baron. Fuck. I strain at my restraints, but they don't give. The footsteps come closer; I try to push away from it. Arms reach for me, and I strain away. "Don't touch me. Don't fucking touch me. Don't."

"Eddie, it's me!"

I snap my eyes open. Baby blues meet mine. Thick eyelashes, flushed cheeks, rosebud lips. I draw in a shuddering breath, and the scent of sweet apple blossoms coils deep in my chest.

"Ed,"—she swallows—"you were dreaming."

"And now, I'm not." In one swoop, I've flipped her on her back on the bed and slammed my palms on either side of her head.

35

Mira

"Eddie." My heart crashes into my rib cage. "Ed, are you okay?"

He doesn't answer. He's planked over me, so his weight is not on me, but his big body is so close, the heat from him crashes into me and sinks into my blood. It feels like I'm in a sauna. Sweat breaks out over my upper lip. "Edward, it was a dream."

"But *you're* not," he says in a hard voice, which is darker, meaner than how he's sounded before. My pulse rate leaps. My pussy clenches. *I should not be aroused by the viciousness in his voice, but I'm learning, I'm not the woman I thought I was. I enjoy it when he looks at me like I'm an object made for his pleasure. I adore it when he manipulates my body to bring himself satisfaction. I'm positively giddy when he touches me like it means nothing to him. What does that say about me? Is that why I was attracted to him right away, because I sensed the darkness in him? Because it touched that part deep inside of me which I'd hidden but somehow known existed? Known I was waiting for someone like him to flick a switch and let out the pleasure seeker inside of me?*

"I'm not," I say softly.

"You're *my* wife."

"I am."

"And you are *duty-bound* to do everything I ask of you."

I swallow. He's repeating my words back to me, but from his mouth, they take on a darker meaning. Goosebumps dot my skin. A jitteriness twists my lower belly. Moisture bathes my pussy, and it takes everything in me not to whine with fear and anticipation…and need. *Oh god, I'm turning into a puddle of want under him.* And the way his nostrils flare, he senses it.

"Will you, Belle?" he growls. The sound is harsh and demanding, and it rips through my defenses. That melting puddle I am turns into a seething ache. One that can only be satisfied by him.

"Yes," I croak.

He bares his teeth in response. I shiver. Another thing different about him. He's allowing his emotions to show on his face, something I've hoped for, but also… It's so unexpected. It turns him from that cold, unemotional man into someone whose control has snapped. Someone who feels everything intensely. Someone I knew existed underneath the seemingly detached front he's always presented. But there's a difference between knowing it and facing it. He's let the beast inside out to play and I…am the recipient of the consequences.

"And you'll do anything I ask."

I nod.

"Anything?"

He tilts his head, an inquiring look in his eyes. The angle of his head, the way he's watching me closely, the way those amber eyes of his gleam, he could be an apex predator, stalking his prey. Another jolt lances through me. I brace myself, and nod again, then cry out when he drops his head and drags his nose up my cheek.

"Your scent drives me crazy. It makes me want to throw you down and rut into you. It makes me want to throw you over my shoulder and carry you away where no one else can see you. It makes me crazy, and I hate it. I fucking hate how you make me want things I shouldn't."

There's a thread of desperation woven through that darkness in his tone. It gives me the courage to dig my fingers in his hair and tug. He straightens and glares at me. His gaze is so hard, so filled with lust, my heart almost stops, then starts again. It also spurs me on to declare, "Good!"

His gaze widens, then a resolute look comes into his eyes. "I'm going to use you. I'm going to do things to your body, you could have never imagined in your wildest dreams. I'm going to stuff your holes and you're going to take everything like a good girl."

My toes curl. My breath hitches. I begin to pant and can't stop myself.

"I'm going to have you begging and writhing and wanting to come, but I won't let you."

I swallow.

"Not until you've forgotten who you are and where you are, and all you know is my touch, my gaze on you, my fingers inside you, my cock throbbing in your cunt, and you're crying for release and then... Perhaps, I might consider it."

"You...you're cruel," I moan.

"And you love it."

"And you have a big ego."

"And the balls to go with it." He lowers himself and the evidence of his arousal nudges the cleft between my legs. He's so big, so heavy... And I've felt him inside of me, but somehow, he feels thicker, more swollen, more solid, more everything.

"I want you inside of me. I want you to come in me."

His gaze flickers. "And I want to see you cry. I want your tears to cleanse the burden of my past. I want your innocence to dissolve the darkness in me. Can you do that for me, Belle?"

There's a plea in his voice, which is strange. He's promising he's not going to be easy on me, and... I don't want him to be. I want him to come to me unvarnished. Show me who he really is. I want the unadulterated version of him. I want everything he can give me. I want him. HIM.

"Yes." I nod slowly. "Yes, I can do that." Then, I reach up and slap him.

36

Edward

My head snaps back. The pain slices through my head, spikes my blood stream and ignites my need. My cock is so hard, I'm sure I'm going to come any second.

She raises her hand again, and I grab it, twist it over her head, then do the same with her other. I transfer her wrists to one hand; the other, I wrap about her neck and squeeze. "You've done it now."

Her gaze widens. The blue is now a deep indigo, which is almost black.

"Do you want me to punish you again? Is that it? Do you like my handprints on your butt? Do you like pain?"

Her lips part.

"You a pain slut, Belle?" I look between her eyes. "You trying to provoke me into hurting you?"

"Why don't you find out?"

My muscles bunch. Every pore in my body seems to come alive. "You don't know what you're asking for."

"You don't know who you married." She holds my gaze, her own steady. "I don't back down. I don't frighten easily. And I never give up. I know who you are, Eddie. Deep down, I know you're not the hardened indifferent man you portray to the world. I know how much you're hurting. And I want you to share it with me. I want you to use me and pleasure me. And yes, I want you to take from me so you heal. But it's not all altruistic. I want you to show me how it can be with you. I want you to wring every last orgasm from my body. I want you to give me so much pleasure, I can't think of anything else but you, I—"

I swoop down and close my mouth over hers. I kiss her hard, I mean to punish her for her impertinence, for provoking me, for being there for me when I woke up from my nightmare, for stealing my peace of mind from the first moment I saw her. For…agreeing to become my wife. For becoming…mine. Mine. *Mine.*

I deepen the kiss, and when she moans, I swallow the sound. I release my hold on her throat, only to cup her tit and squeeze. She shudders. I pinch her nipple through her camisole, and her entire body jolts. The beat of her heart thuds faster against my chest, and I feel each thud like it's my own. I'm drowning in her. I'm losing myself. And this time I can't… I won't stop it.

I soften the kiss. I share breath with her, lick her mouth, press my lips to hers, and she melts into me. I continue to kiss her, taking my time, learning the shape of her mouth, the cupid's bow of her upper lip, the softness of her lower lip, the way she sighs and makes that little noise at the back of her throat that sends a spear of heat to my groin. And when she groans, I slide my tongue over hers, and the taste of her fills my senses. Her scent surrounds me and every pore in my body seems to open to absorb more of her. When I finally pull back, her features are flushed. Her hair a cloud of purple-streaked gold about her shoulders, and her mouth is swollen.

"Open your eyes."

She raises her heavy eyelids to reveal dilated pupils. A fresh burst of need tightens my belly. Without breaking the connection, I pull up her camisole, then bend and close my mouth around an erect nipple. I bite down and she cries out.

"Oh, my god!"

I release it with a pop, and when I suck on her other breast, she writhes under me. "

"It's too much. I can't take it. I can't."

I release my hold on her hands, only to slide down her body. When my face is level with her crotch, I slide my finger in the waistband of her lacy underwear and snap it. I pull it free, then press my face into her pussy and breathe her in.

She shudders, digs her fingers in my hair, and tugs. Pin-pricks of awareness travel to my cock. My balls harden, and the ever-present tension in my groin shoots up. I slide my hands under her hips and urge her legs over my shoulders. Then I begin to eat her out.—her slit, her pussy lips, that throbbing button of desire between them. She whimpers, tries to pull away, but I hold her in place. I continue to ravage her cunt, thrusting my tongue in and out of her sopping wet channel. She whines, shudders, squeezes her thighs around my face, smothering me with her flesh, her touch, her scent, and fucking hell, I'd die happily right now. I squeeze her ample butt cheeks and she arches into my touch. Thrusts her pelvis up so my tongue dips deeper inside her. Fat drops of her cum slide down my chin, and when I nibble on her swollen clit, she mewls. More moisture squirts from her slit and I lick it up.

A trembling sweeps up her legs. "Please Eddie, please," she cries out.

I know she's close, so I tear my mouth from her cunt, crawl up her body and kiss her. "Taste yourself."

She licks her lips and her cheeks flush further. "I'm sweet?" she whispers.

"Like honey, or nectar, an aphrodisiac that makes me want to lick your every hole."

"Oh." She pants.

I reach down, and because I fell asleep in my slacks, I lower my zipper. When the blunt head of my cock nudges her opening, a trembling grips her.

Once more, I urge her to lock her ankles around my waist, then rise up on my knees to get traction. I slide a cushion under her to elevate her hips, then in one smooth thrust, I impale her.

37

Mira

The breath squeezes out of me. He's bigger than I remember, and thicker. I'm spread around him, pinned to the bed, and he's pushing against my channel walls. I was so wet, he slipped in easily and yet, his girth is such that flickers of pain travel to my brain.

"It hurts," I gasp.

"You knew it would."

"I'm not scared."

"You should be." With that, he thrusts his tongue between my lips and drinks from me. His cock throbs inside of me, and the sensations that ping through my blood signal the pleasure that's on its way. He kisses me until all my attention is focused on where his lips meet mine and his tongue mates with mine. It's a single-minded worshipping of my mouth, which wipes all thought from my head. Then, without breaking the kiss, he pulls back until he's poised at the rim of my slit. When he breaks the kiss, I survey his features.

His cheeks are flushed. His eyes are alert. He surveys me closely, and this time, when he propels his hips forward and breaches me, the entire bed jolts. He slides inside all the way to the hilt, and I'm sure I can feel him in my throat. He stays there, watching my face, taking in every expression I'm unable to hide.

And when I part my lips, he slips his thumb inside my mouth. I suck on his digit and his eyes blaze. He drags his wet thumb down my chin, my cleavage, to the space between us. He circles the part where his cock is plugged inside me, and I can't stop the mewl that slips from my lips. He plants his hands on either side of my head and pulls out slowly enough for me to feel every throbbing inch of his length. His next plunge sends a shockwave of sensations up my body, and he doesn't stop.

In-out-in, his movements speed up. Each time he sinks inside me, he hits that secret spot in my core. Sweat breaks out on his beautiful shoulders, and the tendons of his throat stand out under his skin. His features are so stark, they seem lined with pain, and his gaze has an almost helpless quality to it. He continues to fuck me, never breaking the connection of our eyes, and it's so intimate. More intimate than anything I've ever encountered in my life.

I dig my heels into his back, feel the planes of his back give and flex with each move. I dig my elbows into his shoulders, locking my arms about his neck. Like a machine, he continues. His body is a blur of motion, a power drill that has only one goal. Taking us to the top, together.

"Come with me," he orders. His body is wound so tightly, every inch of his body seems to be carved from stone, the muscles under his skin taut, the expression on his face strained. The heat of our bodies melds and traps us in a furnace of mutual desire. Then he slides his hand under my butt, into the cleavage between my ass cheeks, and when he slides it inside my forbidden hole, the climax blazes up from my toes. It shoots up my legs, tightens around my core and zips up my spine. I arch my back, open my mouth and when I cry out, he's there. "Now," he growls.

And I shatter. The orgasm bursts behind my eyes, the white noise a roaring in my ears. The climax seems to go on and on. When I begin to float down from the high, I realize he's still inside of me.

"Open your eyes as I come inside you, wife."

I manage to prop open my eyelids and hold his searing golden gaze. He fucks into me one last time, then his gaze widens, the flames inside his eyes flare into a shower of gold and silver, and with a low roar, he pours himself inside me. His body shudders, and his shoulders quiver. I hold onto him, tightening my grip as he empties himself. When he begins to slump, I tighten my grasp about him. He buries his face against my neck, and I turn my cheek into his sweaty hair. I inhale that edgy, spicy scent of his and fill my lungs with Edward.

"I'm too heavy." He begins to move, but I refuse to let him up.

"Stay. I like your weight on me."

The aftershocks convulse through him — or that might be me. At this moment, we feel like the same person. His muscles grow heavy, and when his body twitches, I realize he's fallen asleep. I close my eyes and drift off.

Something wet licks between my legs. My nipples tighten. Sparks prickle along my skin. I moan, then gasp when a sucking sensation on my clit fans the sparks to flames. I crack open my eyes and look down long enough to glimpse his head between my thighs. Holy shit, the sight of his dark hair in contrast to my white skin, the intensity with which he's focused on eating me out, the way he squeezes the backs of my thighs as he holds them apart, create the most carnal sight I've ever seen.

"Eddie," I moan.

It seems to spur him into action. He rises up on his knees then stretches out next to me. He turns me so my back is to his chest, pulls me in snug, then urges me to bend my knees. "What're you doing?"

In response, he turns my head and kisses me. The taste of me and him intertwined together fans the flames that run through my veins. And when he nudges his cock into my slit, they become a forest fire. He slips inside me, filling me, stretching me in that pain-pleasure way. He brings his hand up to squeeze my nipple, and my pussy clenches.

"You're so fucking perfect," he whispers against my mouth. Then rocks into me, then again. He presses tiny kisses up my cheek, then to that erogenous zone behind my ear. He ravishes the column of my neck and slides his hand down my stomach.

I flinch.

"What's wrong."

"Nothing."

"Tell me," he orders.

"It's —" I swallow. "I've never had a flat stomach. I'm not exactly thin."

"You're perfect."

Tears prick my eyes. "Nice of you to say that, but a size sixteen is not everyone's idea of beauty."

"It is mine." He leans back so he can look into my eyes. "You are my idea of beauty."

His cock twitches inside me as if to punctuate his words.

"And you call yourself emotionless."

"Except when I'm with you. You get under my skin—with your sweetness, your gentleness, your gorgeous curves, and your beautiful mouth."

"And you don't like it."

"I don't." He lowers his head until his mouth hovers over mine. "I love it."

I walk into Edward's office and come to a stop. He's standing at the window, his back to the room, his phone held to his ear. It's snowing outside. A reminder that Christmas is less than a week away. It's my favorite time of the year, but in the rush of events that have swept me in their wake over the last few weeks, I haven't been able to focus on it. I have to get him a gift; but he doesn't believe in Christmas. Did he believe in it when he was a priest? Of course, he must have. Will he ever get over what had happened? I'd like to think last night is an indication that he might.

He came inside me twice, then woke me up, once again, before dawn when he slid inside me. He didn't seem to be able to get enough of me.

He was so gentle that last time, so tender. He brought me to climax and it almost felt dreamlike, suspended as I was between that half-asleep, half-awake state. He came inside me again, and I drifted off to sleep.

I woke up when he brought me breakfast in bed. He'd already showered and dressed. He kissed my forehead and told me he was leaving for the office. He said I could take the day off, but I wasn't able to stay away. I wanted to be near him.

Then, there's also the fact that he didn't take off his clothes when he made love to me. And it was making love. He could call it by another name, but he wasn't fooling me.

I take in his tall form, dressed, as always, in his three-piece suit. He was dressed in a similar one last night—when Sinclair helped him up the stairs and onto the bed, where he passed out, fully dressed.

I've never seen my husband naked. He turns and sees me. His lips curve in a smile, one that reaches his eyes. It lights up his features, making him look so much younger. Is this how he looked before her? Before he left the church? Before the incident?

He pockets his phone and stalks toward me. I'm aware of the answering smile which curves my lips.

He reaches me and takes in my features. "Sleep well?"

"Did you?"

"The best." His smile widens.

"I missed you." I curse myself as soon as the words are out. Because it's true and because I don't want to come across as clingy and because... I don't want him to sense how much in love with him I already am.

A strange expression crosses his features. "You shouldn't be so open with your feelings," he says in a guarded voice.

I scoff. "I know you missed me, too. Saying it aloud does not minimize your standing as an alpha-male."

"Thought you said I was an alphahole?" His eyes gleam.

"And you take it as a compliment?"

"Isn't it?" He smirks.

Fish on an e-scooter, this is the first time he's smirked. And it's hot. So hot, my panties just melted, and I'm wet all over again. Good thing he didn't use that particular weapon against me earlier or I'd have never been able to resist him. The sun rays glint off his hair, which is so dark, there's a blue hue around it. His tawny eyes are a brilliant gold. The sense of power that clings to him is so potent, I almost orgasm spontaneously. You'd think having slept with him would lessen his appeal, but it's only made me even more conscious of how attracted to him I am.

There's a knock on the door. It opens, and Edward glances over my head. The color fades from his cheeks. "Ava?"

38

Edward

She walks in, and I wait for my heart to jump into my throat. Wait for my pulse to speed up, for that familiar hollowness to squeeze my stomach… But I experience none of that. Of course, I'm surprised, but that's due to the unexpectedness of her visit. Seeing her does not hurt me the way I thought it would to see someone I once loved. I know then, I'm over her.

I glance down and see the shocked look on my wife's face before she composes herself.

"Ava, how lovely to meet you." She walks forward and holds out her hand.

Ava shakes it. "You must be Mira."

"I'm Edward's—"

"Wife." A smile curves her lips. "I was so happy when I heard he'd married."

"Right." There's a note of caution in Mira's tone. And something else…something like fear. It's what propels me to draw abreast with them. I look from my future to my past.

"What can I do for you, Ava?" I manage to keep my voice steady.

Her presence isn't affecting me the way it used to; doesn't mean I'm not reeling with images from my past. Images I've kept locked away in a place I haven't visited in a long time. I hadn't looked at another woman since her, not until Belle. Now, here she is, in my office, and it doesn't hurt the way it did when I last saw her with Baron. Still, I haven't forgotten the fact that she chose my friend over me. And the fact that I made love to my wife last night; the fact I allowed myself to break my vow of abstinence, my promise to never be involved with another woman—I curl my fingers into fists. Belle crumbled my defenses. And now, my past is here to confront me.

"I tried to reach you." She wrings her fingers. "I know you don't want to talk to me, but"—she looks from me to Mira then back at me—"but we need to speak."

"I'm not sure there's anything left to say."

"It's about Baron."

When I hesitate, she holds up her hand, "Please. Five minutes; that's all I ask."

"I… I'll leave you two to catch up." Mira begins to leave, but I grip her shoulder. "Mira, this isn't what you think it is."

She looks from me to Ava, then back at me. "If it were, you'd better believe I wouldn't stand for it." She nods at Ava. "I hope we can get to know one another. Maybe we could get a coffee?"

"I'd love that," Ava replies with another smile.

Mira walks out the door. I watch her leave, and when I turn to Ava, she has a knowing look in her eyes.

"What?"

"You love her."

"She's my wife."

"You. Love. Her." Her eyes gleam.

"Of course, I do."

"I'm so happy for you, Edward." She begins to reach for me, then hesitates. "I came to tell you, you need to move on, but I'm happy to see this was a wasted trip."

"It was." The words come out shorter than I intended. Enough for her to peer into my features. "You're still angry with me and Baron."

"What gave you that impression?"

"The fact that you never attend any of the gatherings with your friends? That you avoid us all?"

"I've been busy." I raise a shoulder.

"And now you're married. You should bring Mira around so she can meet us."

"I intend to take her on a honeymoon first."

Her features light up. "That's good. She seems like an amazing woman."

"She is." I glance toward where I can see her seated at her desk through the glass-wall of my office. *Why do I miss every moment apart from her?*

"I really am pleased for the both of you," Ava murmurs.

"Thank you." I incline my head.

She bites the inside of her cheek. "It's not my place but... Have you told her about the incident?"

I stiffen, then draw myself up to my full height. "You're right, it's not your place to ask that question."

She flinches. "I'm sorry. Really, I am. But I had to ask. Especially since Baron still has nightmares over what happened. And this, after years of therapy."

"Baron agreed to therapy?" I blink. The Baron I knew was as adamant as me on not relying on anyone else for help—well, other than each other. We always had the other person to talk to when things got hard.

And I cut him off. And turned my back on his friendship. I had to. It was the only way I could get through that phase of my life. Strangely it doesn't bother me now, to think of him and Ava together. Is it because I found Belle? Because she fits me in a way that makes any other relationship in my life pale in comparison?

"He did, after I pleaded with him." Her features soften. "I'm not saying it's the answer, but it has helped him find some measure of peace."

"How is he?" I ask in a cautious tone.

"He's good." She scrutinizes my features, then sighs. "I wish you'd call him; he misses you. Not that he'll admit it to me, but I know he does. You two were closer than brothers, and you both have been together through so much. He's tried to reach you so many times, Ed. I wish"—she swallows—"I wish you'd give him a chance."

Guilt seizes me. I haven't answered his calls or his emails. Sure, I wanted them to be happy, but I couldn't bring myself to witness it first-hand. But the lack of reaction to seeing Ava assures me thoughts of her no longer hold sway over me. The only woman who occupies my mind now is Belle. And it's been her from the moment I saw her. Ava and I were never meant to be. I suspected it, but meeting Belle has shown me, there's only one woman for me. Her.

"Goodbye, Ava."

"You'll call Baron?" she pleads.

I hesitate. "I'll think about it."

"That's all I ask."

I walk Ava past Belle's empty desk—*where the fuck did she go?*—and see her off at the elevator. When I return, Belle's desk is still empty. I push open the door to my office and walk inside to find Belle standing behind my desk. She's staring at my computer screen, a wrinkle between her eyebrows.

"There you are; I was worried when I didn't see you at your desk earlier."

"Is that why you have a camera trained on me?"

I stiffen, then force myself to move forward until I stand next to her. I follow her gaze to the screen, knowing what I'll see. A quadrant view. One of which shows her empty desk. I forgot to shut down the view when I took the phone call earlier.

"I can explain." I touch her shoulder, but she pulls away.

"Why would you do that?"

"There are cameras all over the floor," I murmur.

"Are you tracking anyone else?"

"Of course, not."

"So for all these days, you were watching me. While I was outside your office door and doing my work, you kept an eye on me?"

"I wanted to make sure you were safe."

"Safe?" She throws up her hands. "I'm in the office. What could happen to me?"

"Things aren't always what they seem. You think you can trust someone, but really, they're putting on a front."

A wrinkle appears between her eyebrows. "What are you talking about?"

I cut my palm through the air. "It doesn't matter."

"Of course, it does. This is about you, Edward. About your past, about your experiences that hold you back. And you promised you'd share them with me."

"And I have."

"If by that, you mean, finally consummating our marriage properly —"

"I came inside you. I haven't allowed myself that release in two years. That doesn't give you the right to plumb into my past."

"Does she know about it?"

"If you mean Ava, yes, she does. Baron told her."

She firms her lips. "So she knows things about you, which your own wife doesn't."

"You don't have to worry about her."

"I saw your face when you saw her; you were shocked." She swallows.

"Only because I wasn't expecting to see her."

"What did she want?"

"She came to tell me to move on, but I told her it was a wasted trip."

"Oh." She blinks rapidly.

"I told her she needn't have bothered to come."

"Whys that?"

"Because she's my past. I expected it to hurt to see her, but it didn't. Seeing her proved to me I'm over her."

"You are?" Her expression softens.

"Now, I realize you're the only woman for me. I knew that from the moment I saw you, but it's not something that was easy for me to accept. For too long, I've been focused on keeping my emotions to myself. I didn't want to be involved with anyone else. I didn't want anyone else in my life."

"You don't want me in your life, either."

"I confess, I didn't. I resisted it for a long time."

"And now?"

"Now, I know there is no future for me without you."

Her features soften. "Then you'll tell me about the incident?"

39

Mira

"I can't." He turns and stalks to the window again.

"Why not? Don't you trust me?"

"It's not that." He drags his fingers through his hair. "It's not something I speak about to anyone."

"But I'm your wife." I move toward him.

"Just because I came inside you does not entitle you to know everything about me."

I stop so suddenly, I stumble, then manage to right myself. "That's not fair," I whisper.

"I'm sorry," he says without turning around to face me. "I didn't mean it that way."

"But you don't think of me as your wife in the real sense, either."

"I already told you, you're the only woman for me."

"But you won't tell me about the incident?"

"I—" His shoulders rise and fall. " I can't. I don't talk to anyone about it."

"Maybe you should. Maybe you need to see a therapist about it and—"

"No. Absolutely not." His spine goes ramrod straight.

"It's not a sign of weakness to speak to a therapist."

He doesn't answer.

"Edward, I don't know what happened to you, but you're not over it. You're still dealing with the fallout of it. It's colored your life so far. It's what caused you to lose…her."

Not that I'm complaining, but I'm not going to mention that.

He turns his head so I can see him in profile. "You're psychoanalyzing me?"

"Only because you don't want to go to a professional. When she married your best friend, you swore off women. You didn't sleep with anyone for two years. You were, technically, celibate. That's… unusual."

"That didn't stop me from watching others masturbate," he says in a harsh tone.

I flinch.

"That didn't stop me from touching other women and making them come, either."

"You're saying all this to hurt me. And I know you're doing it because you're hurting inside."

He turns to face me, and his features are, once more, schooled into that mask I've named his 'Priest face.' Not that I knew him when he was a priest, but I imagine that's how he came across to his congregation. All stern and upright and erect a-n-d…

No, that did not make me think about his cock. Not at all. This is not the time to have images of how his big, fat dick felt inside me. How he squeezed my tits and slide his finger into that forbidden part of me. How he made me come, and then how he allowed himself to orgasm inside me. How it felt to receive hot streams of his cum. Fish in the street, these are not the kinds of X-rated thoughts to have when we're having a serious discussion. Not to mention, when he's all but admitted he doesn't regard me as his wife in the truest sense of the word. "And am I allowing myself to be distracted by salacious thoughts? Of course, not."

His gaze narrows. "You're distracted by salacious thoughts? About us?"

"Of course, not." I redden.

"That's what you said aloud."

"So?" I tip up my chin.

"So you were thinking about last night and how I wrung orgasms from your body?" There's a knowing glint in his eyes.

"Fine." I throw up my hands, "I was thinking about how you made me come, and yes, I said that aloud. But it doesn't change the fact that you're unable to tell me about the incident. It's what made you who you are. It changed your life forever, and you can't share it with me."

The light in his eyes banks, and his features harden. He's switched back to his hot priest persona. *How sad is it, that even though he can't share his past with me, even though he prefers to keep so many of his thoughts and emotions to himself, even though his unfeeling demeanor is back, I find it sexy? He's hurting me, and I'm no less attracted to him. Where's my survival instinct when I need it?*

"Don't ask me to do that. It's something I'd prefer to forget, to move on." He scowls.

"And have you? Either forgotten it, or moved on from it?"

His jaw tics.

I look between his eyes, "You can't bury what happened and pretend everything is fine when it's not. You can't move forward until you resolve the issues associated with what happened."

"And have you moved on from the fact that your father traded your future for his company?" He sneers.

"You know, I haven't." I glance away then back at him. "The difference is, I've talked about it and shared my feelings with you. I didn't try to keep anything a secret."

"Not all of us can be so perfect." He curls his lip. "Not all of us can go around wearing our heart on our sleeve and sharing our emotions with the world."

I stiffen. "Not all of us are unfeeling jerk-holes."

He raises a shoulder. "Never pretended otherwise."

I rub at my temple. "I know you're lashing out at me because you're hurting."

"I'm simply stating a fact. As for my hurting, you don't have to worry; I have ways to manage the fallout from it."

My heart leaps into my throat. The blood thuds at my temples. "What do you mean?"

"I have good coping mechanisms. It's how I've survived this far, after all."

"You're talking about the BDSM club?" I swallow.

He inclines his head. "You don't have a problem if I go without you, do you?"

"And if I did?" I set my jaw. "I'm your wife. We're married. And you're telling me you're going to a BDSM club without me?"

"And since I've broken my 'vow of abstinence'"—he makes air-quotes with his fingers—"there's nothing to hold me back, is there?"

Anger squeezes my guts, and the band around my chest tightens. I try to draw in a breath, but my lungs burn. *How dare he taunt me with that? How dare he treat me with such little consideration? How dare he break my heart? I will not stand for it. I allowed my family to walk all over me. I kept my father's best interests at heart, but that doesn't mean I intend to put up with his bullshit.* "Was I a dutiful daughter? Yes, I was. Did I want to be a dutiful wife? Yes, I did. But you know what? Fuck that."

His gaze widens. I realize it's the first time he's heard me swear aloud. *Well, watch out, buster, there's more where that came from. I refuse to take this insult lying down. I refuse to allow my ego to take a beating. I refuse to hand over my power to anyone else.* "So, you're going to the BDSM club, hmm?"

"That's what I said." He yawns, then pulls back the sleeve of his expensive jacket and glances at his $10,000 dollar watch. "Look at the time. I need to get going. As for you, you need to get back to your desk. You need to cancel the rest of my appointments for today. I'm going to be busy with other things." One side of his lips curls.

Fish-on-a-stick, if he thinks I am going to stand aside and let him leave, he is so wrong. I shrug out of my jacket, and it falls to the ground.

"What are you doing?" He frowns.

In answer I reach behind, unhook my skirt, then shimmy it down my thighs. I kick it aside, then look up to find his gaze is fixed on my legs. Color smears his cheeks. A nerve throbs at his temple. He seems entranced by my little strip-tease. Not the finest or most coordinated, I admit, but that hasn't stopped him from curling his fingers at his sides into fists.

"Belle," he says in that deep, hard voice of his. There's a thread of anger, a threat running through it. A shiver squeezes my legs. My nipples tighten. *Do I know what I'm doing? Of course, not. But my instinct says I'm on the right track. Am I pissed off with him for saying he'll go to the BDSM club? You betcha. And am I going to teach him not to throw that in my face again? What do ya think?* I grip the hem of my blouse, pull it over my head, and when I lower my arms, I gasp, for he's standing in front of me.

"You…sure move like your namesake."

His gaze is fixated on my chest. I'm wearing a bra, but it's see through. Which means, he can see my nipples stand to attention through the sheer fabric. He licks his lips.

"Don't you want to ask who I'm talking about? No matter, I'll tell you. It's Edward from Twilight, the vampire who glows in the sun. He moves really fast, like you did."

"Thought you were a Jacobite?" His voice is low and hard, and the promises hidden in there slingshot a trembling to my core.

"I... I think I'm converted." My fingers twitch, and the blouse slithers to the floor.

A muscle works at his jawline. His features are rock hard. I don't know what he's thinking, but when I glance at his crotch, the massive tent there gives me an idea. I've felt his cock inside me, but honest to god, the watermelon he's sporting makes me take a step back.

He slowly raises his gaze to my face. "You shouldn't have done that."

"I'm just getting started." I reach behind me, unhook my bra, then I toss it at him. He swoops up his arm and catches it. The cool air sweeps over my naked breasts. That's the only reason I'm sporting goosebumps on my chest. It has nothing to do with how his gaze is fixed on my tits. Or how my nipples are diamond hard, or how my panties are so damp, I could probably wring moisture from them, or how those sparks, which are never far from the surface when he's around, have flared to full-blown flames.

"Belle," his voice is thick. The skin over his knuckles is stretched white. He seems to be holding onto his control by a thread, and fish-in-a-kettle, it's the most erotic thing I've ever seen. That this gorgeous, handsome, emotionally-wounded man who's practiced self-control most of his adult life is so close to going into a tailspin, thanks to my strip-tease, surges a rush of power through my veins. I slide my fingers into the waistband of my panties. His chest rises and falls. I begin to slide them down, not taking my gaze off of him. I'm rewarded by his shoulders swelling, pushing at the fabric of the jacket he's wearing, so I'm sure it's going to pop at the seams. I relish the movement of his throat as he swallows. The way his chest rises and falls, how he stares at my core, waiting for it to be revealed, as I slowly slide my panties down my hips, my thighs, my legs. I step out of them, and his entire body goes still. That's when I straighten and toss them at his face.

40

Edward

Without taking my gaze off her damp, pink pussy, I catch her panties, and bring them to my nose. A deep whiff, and that apple blossom scent of hers, laced with something tart, sinks into my blood. My already thickened cock strains against my pants. One last whiff, ignoring the pulsing sensation that grips my balls, I slip her panties into one pocket, then wind her bra around my fingers. Her gaze widens. I raise my fingers and twirl it. She hesitates, then slowly turns in place. When her magnificent butt is facing me, I touch her shoulder. Goosebumps snake down her back.

I sink to my knees, dragging my stubbled chin across the curve of her butt. A whine spills from her lips, and a slash of fire sears my groin. *Fuck!* I rise to my feet and walk over to perch on edge of the desk. "Turn around."

She trembles, then complies.

"Crawl to me."

She gapes. "What?"

"Don't make me repeat myself," I warn.

She swallows, then tips up her chin, and in a graceful move, lowers herself to her hands and knees. Then, holding my gaze, she crawls forward. With each move, her gorgeous breasts swing, her butt twitches, and her thighs quiver. The color on her features deepens and extends down her chest. I widen my legs, and when she reaches the space between them, she pauses. Her face is level with my crotch. *Perfect.*

"Sit back on your heels."

She does. I'm instantly entranced by the golden triangle between her legs. I ease my foot between her knees. She shudders but obeys and slides them apart. A-n-d there it is, between those pink pussy lips, that knob of Venus, that little sugar-plum, that devil's doorbell, her clit.

"Fold your hands behind your back."

A mutinous look comes into her eyes. "If this is your way of punishing me—"

"It's my way of taking what my wife is offering."

"Oh." She blinks.

"Now, do it." I lower my voice to a hush. She pales. The muscles of her arms twitch. Then she slowly locks her fingers behind her back.

"Good girl."

A groan boils up her throat.

"You like it when I praise you?"

She nods.

"You like it when I touch you?"

She nods again.

"You like it when I fuck you?"

She frowns. "You know, I do."

"Good, because from now on, you need to earn all three."

"Excuse me?"

"You heard me."

I slip my booted foot up the valley of her thighs, and when I press into her core, she gasps, "Eddie."

I begin to rub on her clit, stroke up and down her slit, again and again. When I withdraw, the tip of my boot glistens.

"So wet. Can't wait to feel my cock inside your weeping cunt, hmm?"

She swallows, then presses her lips together. My wife likes to defy me. How sweet. It gives me more to work with. It inspires me to show her how it can be when she finally surrenders to me. Oh, I don't want to break her. I merely want her to put her trust in me. I want her to hand her body over to me willingly, secure in the knowledge that I'll always know what she wants. I'll always treat her like the queen she is. I'll always ensure she's taken care of. That she never lacks for anything. That she's always pleasured and secure, that she has the power. One word from her, and I'd stop this.

"If you want me to stop, say so."

She blinks.

"You can always leave."

"And you'd go to the BDSM club?"

I glance away, then back at her. "You were right. I said it because I wanted to get a rise out of you. I would never touch anyone but you, Belle. You should know that. You are my wife. My. Wife."

Her lips part, and her chin trembles. "Do you mean it?"

"The only lie I've ever told in my life, was to you, and it didn't feel good. I'll never tell anything but the truth, from now on. But I also need time."

"Okay," she whispers.

"Okay." I widen my stance to accommodate my throbbing arousal. "If you want to leave, now would be a good time."

"And you won't go to the BDSM club?"

"I won't."

"But if I stay, you won't let me come?"

"Not until you earn it."

"What do I have to do to earn it?"

"Stay and find out."

She nods slowly. "Okay."

Thank fuck. I release the breath I was holding. If she'd refused, would I have let her leave? Probably not. Good thing she'll never find out.

I lower the zipper on my pants, reach inside my boxers, and take out my cock.

Her lips part. Her pupils dilate. Her gaze is fixed on how I stroke my swollen shaft from base to crown, and again. Pre-cum glistens on the swollen head. I scoop it up, reach forward and smear it over her lips. She licks it up, then opens her mouth again.

"Good?"

She nods.

"Good." I cup the back of her head, then position my cock between her lips. I tug her forward, and my shaft disappears into her mouth. *Fucking hell, I've never seen a more erotic sight.* The feel of her moist tongue grazing the underside of my dick draws a groan from my lips. I grit my teeth, trying to tamp down on the rising tension in my belly, but the feel of my wife's mouth as she licks around the rim of my cock, the sensations it rockets to my extremities, surely warrant a poem dedicated to it.

I pull back, and when I push in again, I hit the back of her throat. She gags; drool drips from her chin. A trail of moisture slides down her cheek leaving a black trail in its wake. It's so perfect, I almost come in her mouth. I squeeze the base of my cock to hold back my orgasm, then pull back again. "Open wide," I order.

She complies, and this time, when I push forward, I slide down the warmth of her throat. It's tight and hot and perfect. She's perfect. And she's my wife. *Mine.* My balls draw up, and the pressure at the base of my spine curls in on itself, growing harder, higher and when she swallows, I know I can't hold back. I pull back, and the climax boils up. A roaring sound fills my ears, and I come.

41

———————

Mira

He paints his orgasm on my face, my mouth, my tits. He comes and comes, and there's so much cum, it drips down my chin and clings to my nipples. He holds me in place with his grip on the back of my head, but even if he didn't, I wouldn't move. This… He's given me power over him. He's used my body, and it brought him so much pleasure, I know for a fact, he wouldn't have been this open and he wouldn't have let himself be this vulnerable with anyone else. *So why can't he tell me about the incident? Why can't he share what happened to him? Why is he holding himself back? And why has he never taken off his clothes in front of me?*

He squeezes out the last of his cum, then reaches down and massages it into my cheeks, across my mouth, down my throat, and around my breasts. His cock twitches, and by the time he raises his gaze to mine, he's hard again.

"You're gorgeous," he murmurs, and tucks a strand of hair behind my ear. "You deserve better."

"I want you."

"I'll never be able to give you what you want."

"I don't believe that."

"Believe it." He tucks himself inside his briefs and zips himself up, then pulls me to my feet. He hauls me to him, fits his mouth over mine and kisses me. There's a desperation to how his lips close over mine, a yearning to how his tongue tangles with mine. An anguish to how he holds me close, a sea of agony to how his thighs push into mine. When I place my hand over his heart, it's galloping with all the emotions he'd never allow himself to reveal. And when he releases me and peers into my eyes, I glimpse the regret in them before he shuts me out.

"Don't do that, don't hide what you're thinking. Don't conceal whatever thoughts are going through your mind. Don't brush aside the sadness, the fears, whatever it is that feels too big for you to face alone. We'll do it together."

He doesn't respond.

"Edward…" I cup his cheek. "Talk to me."

He looks at me through that mask of the hot priest again. "I think we need to take a trip."

"A trip?" That's the last thing I expected him to say.

"I promised Arthur I'd take you on a honeymoon."

"A honeymoon?"

He rubs his thumb across my mouth. "So you can earn your orgasms."

———

I glance at the flakes of snow that float down, only to melt when they touch the car. Outside, the Christmas lights on Regent Street light up the city. The display windows of the shops show off their festive decorations. There are crowds of people on the sidewalk. Families, children, everyone is out shopping. I can make out the shop windows of Hamleys —the biggest toy store in London—and the throngs of kids with their parents milling around outside. One day, when I have kids, I'll be able to buy gifts for them, put up a Christmas tree at home, and surprise them on Christmas morning with their presents. Of course, I do need to get pregnant first. I cross my fingers. Hopefully, my time will come before too long. It has to. Meanwhile, I'll have to make do with the gift I bought for Eddie, which I have hidden in my handbag.

We left the office an hour ago. He hasn't told me where we're going. When I asked, he said it was a surprise. Before we left, he led me to the ensuite and told me to shower. When I emerged with a towel knotted between my breasts, he gestured to the walk-in closet.

I opted for a skirt and a full-sleeved blouse, teaming it with a wool-lined leather jacket. Combined with a scarf, gloves and a hat, I was ready to go. He looked at me with approval when I strode out, then wrapped up the call he was on.

When I asked about clothes for the trip, he said it was all taken care of. Then, he ushered me to his Jaguar, slid into the driver's seat, and we were off.

Now, I reach over and fiddle with the dial of the radio until I find a favorite radio station. The notes of WHAM!'s "Last Christmas," as interpreted by Ariana Grande, fill the car.

I begin to hum along to it.

"You really do like Christmas?" He shoots me a sideways glance.

"You really don't?"

One side of his lips quirk. *Hooray! That's a win.*

"When you smile, your entire face changes. You look younger and innocent."

His eyebrows draw down. "But I'm not."

I glance away. *Why did I have to go put my foot in my mouth?*

The music changes to Mariah Carey's, "All I Want for Christmas."

He winces.

When I reach over and shut off the music, he doesn't protest. We drive in silence, and once we cross the city limits, he relaxes a little.

"You must have celebrated Christmas when you were a priest?"

He hesitates, and I'm sure he's going to stay silent, but then he nods. "It was a special time of the year, when the spirit did seem to infect the congregation. It changed the tone of the prayers. There was something magical about the hymns. The one time when the veil between this world and the next seemed to thin enough to feel the presence of The Other."

He lapses into silence, and I swallow around the ball of emotion in my throat. "That was almost poetic."

"That's when I was a believer."

"What do you believe in now?" The words are out before I can stop them. Because I need to know what it is that drives this man. When he walked away from his calling, how did he cope? By his own admission, he was unmoored. *What is he holding onto now? How does he move from one day to the next when what he once put his faith in doesn't exist anymore?*

When he doesn't answer, I touch his shoulder. He flinches, and it's as if someone slapped me. I begin to retreat, but he grabs my hand, then brings it to his mouth and kisses it, before placing it on his knee. "Sorry, I'm still getting used to having someone else in my space, in my life."

"You didn't think it through when you decided to marry?"

One side of his lips lifts. Another almost-smile. *Whoo-hoo, that's a score right there for me.*

"I hadn't thought it through when I asked you to marry me. I didn't realize how you were going to turn my world upside down. How you were going to occupy space in my mind, my thoughts… My heart."

I freeze. "Did you say—"

"My heart, yes. I swore not to lie to you anymore, remember?"

"So you do have feelings for me?"

"Isn't that evident?"

"But you still don't trust me enough to take your clothes off in front of me?"

42

Edward

"Don't ask that of me... Yet." I tighten my fingers around the steering wheel. *Haven't I unbent enough? Haven't I shared more with her than with anyone else, including Ava? Except perhaps, Baron.* He knew the boy I was. She knows the man I've become. I've allowed her a peek into my thoughts, I've confessed to having feelings for her. *What more does she want?*

"I'm sorry, I shouldn't have pushed you." She begins to pull her hand back, but I hold onto it. I slide my fingers through hers and she seems to relax a little. "I never thought you'd ever come out and tell me you have feelings for me, and I know how difficult that must be for you."

"Do you?" I ask, not because I don't believe her, but because I'm genuinely curious. *Could this woman understand, when I've tried and failed at that task so many times myself?*

"Yes." She nods. "Yes, I do. You think I'm young and naive, but I am wise in the ways of the world. I saw how it tore my father apart when my mother died. How he tried to do his best when he married my step-mother. How he hoped to replace the mother-shaped hole in my life and the wife-shaped one in his with another family, despite knowing it would never work. She was gone, and nothing we did could alleviate the pain that was left behind. And when he realized he had only worsened the situation, he retreated into his business. He poured his love, his feelings, his desires into it… Which is why I couldn't say no when he asked for my help to save it."

My shoulder muscles stiffen.

"He replaced my mother with his work, with building this empire which he was going to hand over to someone else one day, anyway. Not me or my half-sisters, because we weren't interested in running it, but to a stranger. And when I realized that it would be you, it felt right."

I release my hold on her hand and place it back on the wheel. *It was wrong. I shouldn't have done it, but how can I tell her that? When we're beginning to establish the foundations of a fragile trust that we'll need if we're going to build this marriage? No, I shouldn't tell her the truth behind what happened yet. Not until I'm sure she'll never leave me.*

"I met you and knew you were the one. Okay, not me, but my subconscious knew. And I fought it because I was all set for an arranged marriage, after all. But when my father said he wanted me to marry you, I knew it was a sign. All the pieces were falling into place. Of course, it had to be you to run my father's company. It was always you, Eddie."

I'm aware of her gaze on my profile, of the yearning in her features, of the love that shines in her eyes and, like a coward, I don't turn. If I do, I'll be lost. If I do, *all* will be lost. If I do, I'll have to confess to her everything that I set in place to bring us here. And I'm not ready yet. *She's* not ready yet. I need to find a way to tie her to me, so she'll never leave. I need some kind of assurance that when I share the extent of my machinations, she won't have a choice but to look past it. I need a guarantee, but what?

The silence stretches. I'm aware when she finally turns to look forward. She places her hands in her lap. A few more miles pass, we pass a road sign, she looks at it, then turns to me. "We're going to Cornwall?"

"Penzance." I nod.

"I've always wanted to go there," she exclaims.

"It's one of my favorite places," I murmur. *Another thing I've never told anyone. See, I'm sharing more of myself.*

"The scenery is so beautiful." She gazes at the forests we're passing by. We've been driving steadily since we left London. After we cross East Devon, I turn onto a B road, and the scenery grows more wild, more untamed. There's a ruggedness and yet, a desolation, to the terrain that resonates with that darkness I'm no longer able to hide.

I glance toward her. "It is."

She turns, and our eyes meet.

"I want you to know, I'm on birth control. I decided to get a prescription when I realized we were getting married."

Something streaks across the corner of my vision. I hit the brakes, turn to face forward, and the car screeches to a halt. The impact throws me against my seatbelt. I know she's wearing her seatbelt because I checked before we left, but it doesn't stop me from throwing my arm out in front of her.

There's another flash of white as the rabbit disappears into the undergrowth.

"You okay?" I turn to find the color has leached from her features. Her shoulders tremble. I unhook my seatbelt, reach over and take her in my arms. "You're good. I'll never let anything happen to you."

She nods against my shoulder. "Wh-what happened?"

"A rabbit ran across the road. I stopped in time."

"Oh, thank god." She burrows deeper into my chest. I tuck her head under my chin and breathe in her scent. My heart thunders in my chest, echoing hers.

"I'm glad you didn't hit it," she says softly.

"You sure you're okay?"

"Yes." Her voice sounds steadier. I hold her for a few seconds more, then release her and scrutinize her features.

"I promise, I'm fine." She half smiles.

I reach for the bottle of water and hold it out. She takes it from me, screws open the top, and takes a sip. Some of the water slips down her chin, and before I can stop myself, I wipe it off.

She flushes a little, and says, "Thanks." She hands it back to me, and I take a few gulps. I put it aside, then take another deep breath.

That scared me more than I'd like to admit. If something had happened to her, if she'd been hurt—my heart crashes into my ribcage and sweat breaks out on my brow—I wouldn't have been able to live with myself. But she's fine; nothing happened to her. And I intend to make sure it stays that way.

I turn to her. "Ready to go?"

43

Mira

I hear my name and open my eyes. I yawn, then sit up and look around. Lights. The entire place is lit up. We're in queue behind a long line of cars, and the sign on the side of the road says, "Angarrack: Twelve Days of Christmas."

"I've heard of this village. It hosts one of the most famous Christmas light displays in the country."

"It does." He nods.

I sit up, take in my surroundings. Edward eases the car forward, following those in front. We make our way through the quaint village streets. The display pays homage to the Twelve Days of Christmas with the illuminations counting up from the first day of Christmas. The houses are lit across rooftops and at the sides, and there's even a display on the river over which we drive.

"It's beautiful." I can't take my gaze off the lights.

"It is," he murmurs.

I shoot him a glance, but he's focused on the driving. The sidewalks teem with tourists, families with kids, couples, all taking photographs of the lights. It's so festive. I feel like I've been dropped into the pages of a storybook Christmas. Finally, we pass the display with twelve drummers drumming, for the Twelfth Day. "Oh, I want a picture. Can I get a picture?"

Edward brings the car to a halt at the side of the road.

I grab my phone and step out, then gesture to him. "Can I take a picture with you?"

He hesitates.

"Please?"

He seems like he's going to refuse, then nods. He gets out of the car and follows me. I hold up my phone, posing for a selfie, then realize he's standing too far away.

"Come on." I hold out my arm. "I need you in the frame."

He walks over to stand next to me. I bend my head in his direction. He stands stiffly, unsmiling. I reach up on tiptoes and use my fingers to curve his lips. "There, that's better."

I look back at the screen, begin clicking, then freeze, for he's put his arm about my waist and drawn me into his side. I snuggle in, take a few pics, then show them to him. "Not bad, eh?"

He grunts.

I roll my eyes. "You are the original Grinch, aren't you?"

He says something under his breath that sounds like 'what-fucking-ever.'

"Do you want me to take your picture?" I turn to find a tiny woman, who must be at least seventy, smiling at us. She has short grey hair cut in a bob and is wearing a sparkly green dress with black wedges on her feet. "You look so cute together." Her smile increases in intensity. "Would you like me to take a picture of the two of you?"

"No, we don't—" Eddie begins, but I cut him off.

"We'd love that." I hand my phone to her, then step back. He pulls me close again. I wrap my arm about his waist, and he brings his other around the front of my shoulders, embracing me in the circle of his warmth. I draw in the crisp evening air, redolent with pine and cinnamon, and laced with his darker scent. Little goosebumps dance across my skin. I smile, placing my cheek against the steady drumming of Eddie's heart. Contentment seeps into my blood. I sigh, cuddle into his side and pose for a few seconds more.

"All done." The woman walks over and hands the phone to me. "Are you on your honeymoon?"

Next to me, Eddie tenses. "Why do you ask?"

The woman blinks.

I dig my elbow into my husband's side. "What he means is, it's so nice of you to ask. Yes, we are."

"Oh, isn't that wonderful." She claps her hands. "Young love, so amazing. Did you enjoy the lights?" She waves her hand in the air. "I head up the organizing committee for the Christmas Lights."

"They are gorgeous," I exclaim.

"This must all seem so quaint to you big city folk. Where are you from?" She beams at Eddie, who makes a snarling sound at the back of his throat.

I nudge him, then interject, "He's from London."

"And you're from the US, aren't you, dear?" She turns her smile on me.

Edward's muscles bunch further, and I rush in before he can say something else to upset her. "From New York, and I can tell you, these lights have more character than the Christmas lights on Times Square."

The woman seems taken aback, then claps her hands again. "You flatter us, dear, but I'll take the compliment."

Tension drums off of Edward. He wraps his arm tighter about me. "We have to go," he growls.

I lean forward and take the woman's hand in mine. "Thank you so much. We need to be on our way." I lower my voice. "My husband gets churlish when he's hungry."

"You mean, he's hangry." She laughs. "Please, don't let me keep you. Come again next year." She waves as we make our way back to the car.

Once we're seated, I turn to him. "You could have been a little more polite."

He sneers.

"No, really; she was just being sweet and helpful."

"She was asking too many questions." He scowls.

"She was making conversation and being nice, is all."

"She can be nice to someone else."

"Would it kill you to be a little more civil to her? She was a sweet old lady. She couldn't hurt a fly."

"Threats come in all shapes and forms, and when you least expect it." He sets his jaw. "It's my job to watch over you."

I throw up my hands. "Nothing's going to happen to me."

"You bet, it won't. I'm going to make sure it doesn't."

We set off again, and when we're clear of the village and back on the road, I turn to him. "What happened to you, Edward? What made you so suspicious of everyone and everything. Was it the incident?"

When he doesn't answer, I scrutinize his features. "It *was* the incident, wasn't it?"

"Don't." His jaw hardens. "I told you, I'm not ready to talk about it."

"When will you be ready?"

"I'm not sure."

"Will you *ever* be ready?" I know I'm pushing him, when I should be giving him space. But I wish he wouldn't shut me out. I wish I didn't have to second guess his reactions. I want to be understanding, but I'm only human. And his wife. And he's, my husband. I trust him. *Why can't he trust me? Will he ever trust me?*

Maybe I shouldn't have come. I thought spending time alone with him, away from our day-to-day cares, would help bring us close. Now, I'm not so sure.

I turn to face forward. Darkness has fallen, and the headlights illuminate the road before us. We begin to climb up a hill, the road winding its way around another village. The lights of the city below come into view, and beyond that, the darkness of the sea. Even though it's too dark to make out the scenery, something tells me the view will be spectacular in the daylight. It begins to snow again, and by the time I see the sign that says we're entering Penzance, some of my earlier anger fades away.

I'm being too hasty. We've only been married a few weeks. He's beginning to open up to me, not by much, but more than when we first met. I need to be more patient. Also, we've only just left London. We haven't even reached our destination. I can't possibly expect him to open up and spill his secrets while he's busy driving.

I need to give this... give *us*, more time. I shoot him a sideways glance, "Thank you for taking me to see the lights, anyway. Especially since, I'm sure you didn't want to be there."

He raises a shoulder.

"That's why you drove through the village," I say slowly. "You wanted me to experience the Christmas lights. You knew I'd love it. You did it for me."

He stays quiet, and anger crawls up my spine.

"Oh! You could, at least, take credit when it's due." I turn on him. *Okay, so I'm not as patient as I'd like to be.* "Why do you have to be so stubborn? Why do you have to hide behind that severe facade when you're so much more inside? Why, Edward, why?"

His biceps bulge, and his shoulders seem to swell. And when he finally speaks, his voice brooks no argument. "Because I will never be able to love you the way you should be. Nothing you tell me will convince me otherwise. I'm broken, Belle. I'm not a good man. I'm not the kind of person you want to spend the rest of your life with. I'm all wrong for you, Belle. I never should have brought you out here."

His thoughts echo my earlier thoughts, but hearing it from him sends a chill of foreboding through my veins. "Don't say that."

"You wanted to know more about me. Well, this is it. This is who I am. Cold, distant, unfeeling. Unable to appreciate the kind of woman you are. Unable to give you what you need to thrive."

"I need *you*," I insist. "I want to be with you."

He turns off the main road and onto a road that curves around the hillside and heads down toward the water. Below us, the sea stretches out, a mass of darkness, and I shiver. I wrap my arms about myself. He must notice it, for he flips a switch and the air circulating through the Jag grows warmer. He positions the vents, so they're focused on me, then presses the button for the seat warmer. That's the kind of man he is, so cued into my needs.

He won't let me get cold, will make sure I want for nothing… Except maybe, for an emotional commitment from him.

No, that's not true. Regardless of what he says, we've made so much progress. If not, I wouldn't be here. If not, he wouldn't have taken this step of bringing me with him to a place where it will only be the two of us for the next week. Another shudder rolls through me. This one is thicker, syrupy. This one is the kind that slides through my bloodstream and coils between my thighs. He reaches the level of the beach, drives down a road, that's rocky enough to make the Jag bumps as he eases it along. He finally brings the car to a stop and switches off the engine. In the silence that follows, broken only by the sound of metal cooling, he stares through the windshield. "Do you really need me, though?"

"Of course, I do."

And when he finally looks at me, the pain in his eyes shoots an arrow through my heart.

"Eddie," I whisper, "what is it? You can tell me anything."

"Are you sure?"

44

Edward

"I'm not who you think I am."

"So you keep saying."

"I can't be redeemed, Belle. There are things in my past, things I've done, things which were done to me… Things that cannot be undone."

"Tell me, Eddie, I want to know everything. I can help, Eddie."

"And if I don't want you to?"

She swallows.

"If I don't want to share them with you, what then?"

Her features pale, and her eyes take on a hurt look. And when she glances away, it's as if the sun has been hidden by an eclipse. A-n-d this is me. The bastard who cannot help but hurt her. I saw her at Angarrack, witnessed the happiness on her face, her friendliness as she spoke to that woman. Her exuberance as she skipped along to take a picture in front of the lights.

And then, I came along and spoiled it all. I was suspicious of that woman, of everyone near her. It's ingrained in me to be cautious, and she's right; it's because of the incident. *Could I come out and tell her that?*

No. Could I have been more reticent, more withdrawn through the journey? Of course, not.

I thought I'd learn to lower my walls, to give in to her wants, her needs, to share my past, the events that formed me. I want to dig out my heart and lay it at her feet. I want to shatter the last remaining barriers around my soul and give her a peek. I want to show her I can be the kind of man she'll flourish with. The kind who will compliment her, who will be her partner, her other half. Who will not hold her back. Who will be worthy of her trust. I want…a present and a future with her. The kind I could never imagine for myself. I want her. Only her. And when she finds out what I've done to bring her to me, she's going to hate me. And I have to tell her everything. It's the least I can do. If I were a better man, I'd let her leave me… But I'm not. Instead, I've brought her to the one place where it won't be easy for her to leave.

"I'm sorry," I force out the words. "Sorry I hurt you."

When she continues to stare straight ahead, I run my fingers through my hair.

"This is who I am, Belle. I'm not the kind given to romantic gestures and—"

"You took me to see one of the most famous Christmas light displays in the country when you couldn't stand being there. You gave me your grandmother's engagement ring. You picked out our wedding rings. You're wrong, Edward." She stabs a finger at me. "You are the most romantic person I know. You know, instinctively, how to please me. If you'd only let yourself be and stop hiding behind that alpha-holish, brutish, don't-give-a-damn-front."

I scoff. "I brought you to the middle of nowhere for your honeymoon. I don't think that's romantic."

"Is this place special to you or not?" She scowls.

When I don't reply, she snorts. "That's what I thought. Bet you've never brought anyone else here."

Again, I stay quiet, and she throws up her hands. "That's what I mean. Your every gesture is romantic."

"My spanking you was romantic?'

"Yes."

"My withholding orgasms was romantic?"

"You promised you'll make up for it when I earn them."

"My making you crawl was romantic?"

She swallows, then nods. "It was demeaning and derogatory and, it turned me on," she whispers.

"I didn't hear you."

"It turned me on, okay?" she yells.

Satisfaction slithers through my veins. "What else turned you on?" I ask with interest.

"Everything. Everything you did. Everything you do. How you treat my body like it's your possession. How you order me around. How your voice goes all deep and dominating when you order me around. How you eat me out like it's your favorite dessert."

"It's better than that," I admit.

"How you squeeze my tits like it's your favorite sport."

"It's more thrilling, actually."

"How you look at my butt like it's not disgusting."

"It's not."

"But I'm so big. All my life, I've been teased about it. It's why my stepmother and stepsisters didn't want anything to do with me. They acted like I was contagious. Like if they ate with me, or spent time with me, they'd become fat, too."

"And if I ever meet them, I'll set them straight. How dare they shame you like that."

"For a while, I thought I was contagious, too, you know? I'd hide in my room. I wouldn't eat in front of anyone. That old thing about a fat person caught eating..." Her eyes gleam with unshed tears.

"And your father never did anything?"

"He was never around. He was drowning his sorrows in his work," she admits.

"Just for that, I should hold back from this merger. I shouldn't transfer the funds he needs to save his company."

"No, don't do that." She reaches out and touches my shoulder, and a shot of lust zips to my groin. I move away, only because if I don't, I'm likely to unsnap her seatbelt and haul her over to me, and I don't want to ravish her here, in the front seat of a car. Also, I wouldn't be able to stick to my plan of edging her. I wouldn't be able to hold back, and I must. I need to bring her body to the brink, and then hold back, and do it over and over again, so when she finally comes, the orgasm will be the single most moving experience she's ever had. Which means, I need to hold myself back, too.

Her features crumple, and I know she thinks it's because I don't want to touch her, but that's so far from the truth it's laughable. I should set her mind at ease, but I also know if I don't, when I finally touch her, it's going to be doubly pleasurable. So, I school my features into a mask and narrow my gaze on her.

"Give me one reason I shouldn't teach that man a lesson. A man who stood by and let your life be turned into a living hell. A man who didn't hesitate to barter you."

She winces again, then sets her jaw. "Because...I would never forgive myself if his business fell apart because of me. It's his life. Besides, all of those employees depend on him for support. I will not be responsible for them losing their livelihoods."

I stare at her. And keep staring. The seconds tick by. She shifts in her seat, looks away, then back at me. Sitting here, in this enclosed space with her, her scent intensifies by the minute, and my cock extends by the second. My pants are so tight, I'm sure I won't be able to walk properly, and I need to, if I need to get her in safely.

"Fine," I snap.

"Fine?" She blinks.

"You want me to go through with the takeover of your father's company; I'll do it."

Then, I push the door open and step out. Pausing only to adjust myself, I walk around and open the door to her side. "Coming?"

45

Mira

"A lighthouse?" I gape at the structure looming above us. I was so absorbed in him I didn't notice where he'd stopped. I didn't even notice the building when I got out of the vehicle. He held out his hand to help me, and I hesitated before taking it, given his reaction earlier. But he stands there, his features unmoving, his body stiff, and I know he'll stand there for hours, days if needed, until I take his hand. So I do.

Shockwaves scatter up my arm. I feel him tense further, the muscles of his forearm flexing under the ever-present suit he wears. Then, he tugs lightly and helps me to my feet. Small dots of snow float down and only melt when they touch my cheeks. A wave crashes against the shore. The sound is wild and desolate, but also welcoming. A contradiction. Like him.

"Come on." He begins to lead me over the rocky path toward the edifice standing sentry over us. It's lit by a single spotlight from the ground. It turns the tower into something out of a painting.

"Wow." I blink. "This is your secret hideaway?"

"I come here at least once a month, to get away from it all."

How like him it is. A building that has the ability to warn sailors, to look out over the sea and surrounding land, to spot a storm before it hits. To stay tall, silent, unwavering in the face of challenges. To persevere. And cut a romantic figure. If there were ever a personification of Edward brought to life, it would be this lighthouse.

We reach the door at the bottom, and he lets go of my hand long enough to punch in a few buttons on the keypad set into the wall. Of course, he has an electronic lock, paranoid as he is about security. The door unlocks with a click; he walks in, hits a switch, and lights come on. I take in the spotless space—a surprisingly spacious hallway, with the walls painted white, a carpeted floor, and two chairs pushed up against the far wall with a window between them.

"I had the place converted after I bought it." He leads me to the spiral staircase in the center and gestures for me to go up.

I climb the stairs. By the time I reach the top, I'm out of breath, and I reckon we must be at least six stories up. I step onto the floor at the top and gasp. The entire space has been converted into a very spacious, open plan apartment. On one side is a kitchen, furnished with a cooking range, an oven, a refrigerator, and even an island. It flows into the living space with a sectional, and an armchair facing a fireplace, above which hangs a massive flat screen television. On the other side is a king-sized bed, with bedposts. And there are cleats embedded into each of them. The kind used to secure ropes. O-k-a-y? I tear my gaze away long enough to notice a door nearby. He steps over to it and pushes it open. "This is an ensuite bathroom."

I follow him and peer inside. It has everything, including a large shower space.

"And here"—he walks toward a set of sliding doors and pushes them open—"is the walk-in closet." It's a miniature of the closet in his office. On one wall are his suits; on the other, women's clothes and shoes.

"Are those—"

"Your size."

"And you had these clothes brought all the way here for me?"

"I had a team get to work to have it all done in time."

I should be used to how he thinks forward, how he makes sure I'm always taken care of. A warmth invades my skin. I glance around at the floor-to-ceiling windows that form one side of the circular area. Set in front of it is a clawfoot bathtub. Everything is sparkling. Everything smells fresh. There are even flowers in a vase in the middle of the island. And there's a bookcase between the bed and the living space. One I head toward. I run my fingers down the spines and gasp. "Spicy books?"

"It's what you love to read."

"I guess you found out from Summer?" He doesn't reply, and I know I'm right. There are more books on the shelf above: Shakespeare, Harry Potter, Sun Tzu and *The Art of War*, *Brave New World* by Aldous Huxley, Kafka, Oscar Wilde, Tennessee Williams, thrillers and murder mysteries. As eclectic as the man himself. I tear myself away from the books, walk toward the floor-to-ceiling windows and peer outside. It's dark, but the spotlight illuminates the snowflakes which seem to have picked up in intensity. I turn and take in the entire space and Edward standing in the center of it watching me. Above us, there are skylights in the domed ceiling—currently dark, but I'm sure when the lights inside are switched off, I'll be able to see the stars in the sky. "This place is gorgeous." I half smile.

He doesn't smile back. His features are set in stern lines that pinch my nerves with anticipation. He prowls toward me, his steps deliberate, his gaze filled with intent, and when he stops in front of me, my breath catches. He slides his fingers around my waist, then down to grab a handful of my butt. A shudder grips me.

"You like that?"

I nod.

Then he cups my breast with his free hand and squeezes. "And this."

"Yes," I croak. "I mean, yes, I do."

"What about this?" He drags his hand down to slide it between my legs. He cups my pussy, and my heart drops to the place of contact. I open my mouth, but all that comes out is a whine.

"I believe that's a yes?"

I manage to nod. Manage to not give into the weakness invading my knees.

He releases his hold on my core, only to draw up the fabric of the skirt I opted to wear. And all I can think of is, *thank god, I didn't wear jeans or pants. But why did I have to wear stockings?*

"Hold this up." He nods to where the skirt is bunched around my waist.

I scramble to do so, my movements so quick, it's almost embarrassing. And when he grips the nylon at my crotch and tears a hole, I cry out. He shoves the gusset of my panties aside, stuffs two fingers inside my channel, and I'm so wet, and so swollen with desire, I almost come right then. He curves his fingers inside me, watching my features closely. I know he's taking note of just how responsive I am, and it should embarrass me, but I'm beyond caring. I part my legs to give him better access, begin to ride his fingers. The climax weaves up my thighs. "I'm coming; I'm —"

He pulls out his fingers, brings them to his mouth and sucks on them. My orgasm hovers there for a second, another. *Come on, come on.* I almost cry out in disappointment when it fades away. He removes his fingers with a popping sound. "Delicious."

"Is it?"

"Here, taste." He brings them to my mouth and when I suck on them, the sweet-umami taste of my cum coats my tongue. My stomach chooses that moment to growl. He tilts his head. "Hungry?"

46

Edward

"Where did you learn to cook?"

"I taught myself." I bring some of the pasta to my mouth and chew on it. I sent her to change into more comfortable clothes, and proceeded to cook. When she returned, she wore the sleep shorts and camisole I laid out for her. *Good.* She watched me as I'd cooked, and I paused to offer her small tastes of the food. Then realized watching her little, pink tongue lick the sauce off the ladle was turning the entire experience into an erotic episode. My pants grew too tight, and my balls hardened, and that wouldn't do. I needed to ensure she was fed, so I stepped away and focused on the cooking. Soon, I plated out the food and slid it over to her, and we both dug in.

"You taught yourself?" She scoops up more pasta with her fork.

"You sound surprised."

"It's really good, is all," she offers.

"I had time on my hands when I went traveling after leaving the church. After years of not allowing myself to indulge, it felt necessary to feed all of my senses, so I took some classes in different countries."

Her brow furrows. "*All* of your senses?"

I nod.

"So you were with women?"

"You know I didn't have penetrative sex with anyone for two years," I remind her.

"But you did do, uh…kinky stuff with them?"

"I watched. And I may have touched—"

She pauses with her fork halfway to her mouth.

"I was experimenting."

"Experimenting?"

"I knew my tastes ran to the extreme. I wanted to see how much."

"And what did you find?"

"That BDSM helped me deal with the trauma from my past."

"You mean inflicting pain on another helps you release your own?"

"And inflicting it on myself." I take another mouthful of the food, then nod to her plate. "You need to eat."

She places her fork on her plate. "I think I've lost my appetite."

"Are you jealous that there were other women I used before you?"

"Maybe?"

"You don't need to be."

She tips up her chin.

"You're the only woman I've wanted to bind to me. You're the only woman I've wanted to mark. You're the only one I married—"

"Fake married."

"I think we're past that, Belle."

She purses her lips. "I want to believe you. You brought me here, and I can tell this place is special."

"So are you."

She flushes, then picks up her fork and begins to eat. *Thank fuck.* The thought of her going hungry sends a physical ache through me. I plate out more food for her. She protests, but I insist she eat it. Then, when she's done, I cut a large slice of chocolate cake.

"Did you bake that?" Her eyes widen.

I allow myself a small smile. "I could've if I'd had more time, but this is from the housekeeper."

"Housekeeper?" She looks around the place, then back at me. "You have a housekeeper?"

"A caretaker and his wife who live in the village. They take care of the place and make sure it is stocked when I'm going to visit. They shopped for fresh ingredients before we arrived."

"You sent them a list, I'm assuming?"

I shoot her a glance. "And you guessed this, how?"

"You're so particular about everything. Of course, you'd make sure your favorite haunt has groceries, which you specified."

I continue to stare at her, and she raises her gaze to meet mine. "What?"

"You're not eating the cake." She looks down at the untouched slice. "I... I'm full."

"You love chocolate cake."

"How do you know that?"

"Who doesn't like chocolate?" I ask lightly.

"You don't."

I tilt my head. "That *is* true."

"You really don't like chocolate?" She gapes.

I shake my head. "Not unless it's 100% cocoa."

She makes a face. "That's too bitter for me."

"Not a big fan of sugar."

She groans. "So you also don't like cookies and apple pie, I suppose?"

"But you like them all. Which is why—" I scoop up a piece of the chocolate cake with my finger and hold it out. "Open."

"I shouldn't," she murmurs.

"You absolutely should."

"It'll go straight to my thighs."

"Just how I like it."

"It will—"

"Open. Your. Mouth. Belle."

She instantly parts her lips. Fucking gratifying. I slide my finger between them. She closes her mouth around the digit and licks off the last bit of icing.

"That is sinful." She makes a sound that goes straight to my groin. I can feel the suction of her mouth all the way to the crown of my cock. I scoop up more of the icing with my finger and smear it over her lips.

Her breath hitches, and her cheeks pink. Then she flicks out her tongue and licks it off, and every cell in my body stands to attention.

She swallows. "I shouldn't want more, but I do."

So do I.

I pick up some more of the cake and hold it out. She leans forward and licks it from my fingertips. Our gazes meet, the air thickens, grows saturated with need. My thigh muscles grow even harder. I'm fucking torturing myself. I take another dollop of the icing, lean over and drag it down her chin, her throat, to where the dark shadow of her cleavage is visible, then over her sleep camisole. She's not wearing a bra underneath, and her nipples are outlined through the silky material.

"I just showered."

"I want to shower you with my cum."

She gasps. "Is that filthy? It is. Am I aroused by it? I am. This is soooo wrong." She shakes her head.

"All the good things in life are. A lesson I learned the hard way. Come here, Belle."

She swallows, then slides off the stool and comes to stand in between my legs. I push the hair back from her flushed cheeks, and her breathing intensifies.

"There are going to be a few rules as long as we're here."

"Rules?"

I nod. "Rules to ensure your orgasms bring you the most pleasure possible. Rules to ensure you have the greatest number of orgasms in the shortest period of time."

"Oh."

Her voice is so breathless, so excited, I almost smile. This woman makes me act out of character. It's a constant surprise. One I relish. One I'd miss if she weren't around. It's the main reason I need to ensure she never leaves me. It's why I need to gratify her, ensure she's so high on endorphins, she's addicted to the sensation only I can rouse in her.

"First rule, no clothes." I snatch a knife from the counter, slide it under her camisole straps and twist.

47

Mira

The camisole strap splits. He does the same to the other. The lacy fabric slithers down my chest and stays suspended—held up only by my nipples, which are saluting at him. They're so hard, and my breasts are so heavy, I feel weighed down. I reach up to tug off the fabric, but he clicks his tongue.

"Second rule: you'll do everything I ask."

"Like I don't already."

"Third rule, if you talk back, you'll be spanked."

I swallow. The fading palm prints on my butt twinge in response. My pussy clenches down, and I know I'm already making a mess between my legs.

"Fourth rule—" He slides the knife under the waistband of my sleep shorts. He flicks his wrist, and cuts through the fabric. Does the same on the other side. He places the knife down on the table with care. His every movement is restrained, controlled. His fingers are steady—unlike mine, which tremble with need. And when he turns to face me, there's almost a bored look on his face. *Ohmigod, do I find that hot? I do find that hot.* The fact that I'm turned on, but he seems so indifferent to the million little butterflies that take flight in my belly, only intensifies my arousal. I shuffle my feet, begin to rub my thighs together, but he shakes his head. "You can't alleviate your need."

"But I itch there."

"Good."

"Just a little chafe of my thighs," I whine.

"Nope."

"It'll only take a second." I flutter my eyelashes at him. "I'll slide in a finger and touch myself once. Just once."

"No, Belle." His voice is hard. "You cannot touch yourself. You cannot get yourself off. You definitely will not allow yourself to come."

"But why?" I pout. "What harm can it do?"

"Do you trust me on this?"

As soon as the words are out, his feature grow tense. *Trust.* That word is like a boulder between us. I want him to have enough faith in me to tell me about his past. But do I have enough confidence in him, enough to hand myself over to him? To entrust my orgasms to his expertise? Do I trust him enough to spend the next few days with him doing everything he wants? Allowing him to do what he wants with me? Not sassing him? Maybe not the last... But the rest? Yeah, I do. He may not be ready to talk about himself, but with everything he does, we come closer. The more time we spend together, the more layers I unearth. And everything I find out about him only makes me want him more.

So, his question was a rhetorical one, in all likelihood. Still, when I nod, his chest rises and falls. His shoulder muscles relax. Huh? Was he tense? Did he think I would refuse him? And if I had, what would he have done? Would he have convinced me otherwise? Would he have spanked me, then kissed me and brought me to the edge, only to hold back my orgasm again? Probably. And the specter of it is not altogether unwelcome.

"Choose a safe word."

"A safe word?"

"If you need me to stop at any time, you only have to use it."

I bite the inside of my cheek, "I don't think I'd ever want you to stop whatever it is you're doing."

His eyes flash, then he cups my cheek. "Much as I am tempted to agree, it would be in your interest to choose one."

I take in the intensity on his features then nod. And don't have to think twice when I say, "Fleabag."

"Your safe word is Fleabag?"

"The series with Andrew Scott as the Hot Priest."

"The Hot Priest?" He frowns.

I peek at him from under my eyelashes. "'Course, you're hotter, Eddie."

I must say the right thing because an expression of satisfaction crosses his face. "What, am I going to do with you?" His throat moves as he swallows.

"Anything you want."

"Anything?"

My heart beats so loudly, it drowns out all other thoughts. "Anything."

I expect him to pull off my torn clothes, then throw me to the ground and ravish me. Instead, he peels my camisole down my arms, then lowers my shorts until both pieces are in a puddle around my ankles.

He grips my hips, lifts me up, kicks the fallen clothes aside, then sets me down. He does it in one uninterrupted move. His biceps bulge, his shoulders turn into rocks of delightful muscle, and his chest swells, but he doesn't breathe heavily. Or show any sign of strain on his face. Of course, he's strong. I've seen the cut of his physique, felt it's impossible wall-like planes dig into my softer curves, but just how powerful comes home to me with this maneuver.

After the years of laughs and jeers in school, and the averted glances of my half-sisters, the graffiti on my locker calling me 'fat face,' the fact that he can handle me like I weigh nothing…is the most erotic thing I've ever encountered. And now, he's going to touch me all over. He's going to fondle my tits, and squeeze my hips, and pinch my clit, and oh god, I want him to. I want him to bite my flesh, mark my thighs, rub the throbbing space between my legs and bring me to the edge. I draw in a breath, and when his scent sinks into my blood and his heat cocoons me like the soothing steam of a sauna, I sway toward him. He steadies me with a hand on my shoulder, then steps back. He reaches for his phone and swipes the screen. The haunting strains of something classical, something deep and complex and so soul stirring, it pours liquid heat through my veins, fills the space. Another sweep and the lights dim. He places his phone down on the island and holds out his hand. "Dance with me."

As if in a dream, I place my palm in his, the other on his shoulder.

He grips my hip with his big hand, the fingers so long and thick, they seem to cover most of my back. And no, my waist isn't the slimmest, and my hips are wide. I've tried to hide my figure—or lack of one—my entire life. But he seems to revel in my softness. He guides me across to the space in front of the floor-to-ceiling windows.

Outside, the dark expanse of the water is broken by the lights of ships in the distance, snowflakes float down in a dance almost as sensuous as the one he leads me through. The music flows over me. He holds me close as we move around the room. His hold on me is sure, his every step confident, yet so light I feel like I'm floating. He holds my gaze, and his own is intense, but there's also a softness around the eyes. Something that indicates he's at peace. Like he's finally coming into himself. It's why he brought me here. He might not have said it aloud— or even admitted it to himself—but having me here is like giving me an insight into his personality without speaking. It's a very Edward move. Dominant and sure and also, so passionate. So emotional. Like this song. The notes rise in crescendo, and tears prick the backs of my eyes.

When the song fades away, he slows to a stop but doesn't release me. "You're crying." He bends and licks the tear drops that skates down my cheek. "Why are you crying?"

48

Mira

"It's... I'm not crying. Not really. It was the music. It was haunting and sad and hopeful, all at the same time."

"The dance before when someone you love becomes a memory," he murmurs.

I widen my gaze, but before I can say anything, he places a finger on my lips. "That was my past. Mired in darkness, filled with a yearning I thought was for my past, when it was me anticipating my future. Anticipating a curvy woman who would sweep into my life and turn my plans upside down. A future which is here. A future I want to see with you. A future which is you."

"Eddie." I move in closer.

He releases my hand only to wrap his arms about my waist. "Forgive me for everything I did to get you here."

"There's nothing to forgive."

He smiles a little. There's something sad in the turn of his lips, something that squeezes my heart. "What is it? Please, tell me."

He hesitates, when the next song comes over the speakers. The familiar notes fill the space, and "Ceilings" by Lizzy McAlpine, starts to play. I was not expecting that. Especially after that classical music piece that almost torn my heart out. Not that "Ceilings" isn't sad, but there's something about that first piece that was timeless. Something that forced my emotions to the surface. Something that made me feel I'd been afforded another peek into his soul.

"That's an eclectic play list," I murmur.

"I'm an eclectic man."

"You don't say." I loop my arms about his neck. "It suits you. You're not what I expected you to be, Mr. Chase."

"Neither are you, Mrs. Chase."

My heart stutters. My fingers tremble. I'm not used to being referred to as Mrs. Chase. At the office, no one dares call me that. I'm still his assistant, and no one has even alluded to our marriage. Either they haven't heard about it—which can't possibly be true, considering I've seen the women eyeing my ring—or he told them not to ask me about it. I frown. "Did you tell the people at the office not to ask me about our marriage?"

His features turn into that mask I'm beginning to recognize as his refuge when he doesn't want to speak.

"You did, didn't you?"

"I might have sent a company-wide email, one which you were not copied on." He continues to lead me in a slow dance, one in which his thighs press against mine, his hips cradle mine, his chest is like steel against mine, and his hands... His big palms are like a brand on the curve of my hips. He slides them down to cup my butt-cheeks and I shiver.

"You're d-distracting me," I stutter.

"Am I succeeding?"

"Almost." I look between his eyes. "Why did you do that?"

"I knew you wanted to work and be independent. You want a life outside the house. You want to find out who you really are and what your likes and dislikes are. You want to get to know yourself better, and I didn't want to stand in the way. And I wanted you to have it, without being embarrassed that you're my wife. I don't want you to work anywhere else, either. I want you with me, but also I want you to feel comfortable coming into work."

"You knew this, even though I never mentioned a word to you?" My steps slow. "And you were looking out for me in ways that never would have occurred to me." *When was the last time someone was so considerate toward me? So thoughtful, so attentive?* He might come across as cold and insensitive, but really, the opposite is true.

"Don't make me out to be something I'm not," he warns.

"I'm not. I'm drawing my conclusion based on facts."

We slow to a stop. The song over the speakers changes to The Weeknd's cover of "Jealous Guy." While Lennon was supreme, The Weeknd brings something darker, deeper, almost twisted to the lyrics, while losing none of the pain of the original. If any song embodies my hot priest, this is it.

"Don't believe everything you see. It may be different from what you interpret it to be."

"Not possible." I slide my palm down to place it over his heart. *Bam-bam-bam.* The thunder of the beats mirrors mine. "Your heart doesn't lie."

"Neither does my cock."

I slide my hands down to cup the bulge between his legs. I squeeze, and his shoulders seem to swell. The expression on his face doesn't change, though.

"Or my mouth." He bends and places his lips on mine. His mouth is hard, but his kiss is so sweet, he simply shares my breath and continues to brush his lips over mine, slowly, so slowly. I melt into him. He drags me up on tiptoe, and that bulge at his crotch feels like a boulder, only hotter, and alive, and throbbing with unspent desire. I moan into his mouth, and his grip tightens, but his lips stay barely touching mine. Fireflies seem to have taken flight in my belly. I seem to be lit up from inside, the need for him burning bright. "Eddie," I whine.

He cups my cheek and looks into my eyes. "Remember this moment, baby. Remember how much I want you. Remember how every part of me needs you. How every breath I take is for you. Only you. Remember."

There's something fervent in his gaze. Something vehement and fiery, and yet also, guarded. Something he wants me to recognize without coming out and telling me. Is it about himself? About me? About—

He looks over my head, then turns me around to face the glass window. "Look."

49

Edward

"A shooting star? No, there's more than one," she gasps.

"It's a meteorite shower."

"Should I make a wish? I definitely need to make a wish. " She squeezes her hands together while her gaze follows the blazing streaks of the stars in the night sky. Her lips move. She continues to watch the skies after the trails fade. "That was incredible." She sighs.

"What did you wish for?"

She shakes her head. "I can't tell you."

"Of course, you can."

"If I do, it won't come true." She turns and sees the skepticism on my features. "It's true. What did you wish for?"

"I didn't."

"You didn't?"

"Everything I want is here in my arms." I pull her close.

"Then you won't mind if I push this jacket off your shoulders?" I let her move it down my arms. She tosses it to the side, and it lands on a chair. Reaches for my tie, and I let her unknot it. When she pulls it off, I take it from her.

"I'm going to blindfold you."

"O-k-a-y?" I wrap it over her closed eyelids and secure it, then tug to make sure it's not too tight, but also taut enough that she can't peer through the gaps.

"This is unnerving," She laughs; the sound is nervous. A hint of anticipation, mixed with apprehension spools off of her body. I'm instantly hard. The blood in my veins begins to pump. I cup her breast, and she swallows. I tweak her nipple. She groans. And when I drag my fingers through her slit, she's already creaming.

"Fuck, you're so wet." I bring the moisture to my mouth and suck on my digits. My already excited cock stabs into the fabric of my pants.

"It's not fair, I can't see you."

"But you're going to experience everything so much more intensely." I scoop her up in my arms. She gasps in surprise, then holds on. I stalk toward the bed and when I throw her down on it, she bounces once. Her hair ripples out behind her. Her ample breasts, the fold of her stomach, her plump thighs—all of it calls to me. But I cannot give in to her siren call. Not yet. I prowl toward the closet, step inside, and walk out with a few coils of silk rope.

I ease her up to sitting, then urge her to fold her knees so her feet are flat on the bed. I pull her thighs apart, then can't stop myself from running my fingers up her exposed pussy. And when she groans, I curl my fingers around her swollen clit, before I suck her cum off my fingertips.

"Oh, god," she moans.

"God has nothing to do with this," I promise. I loop the rope around one thigh and tie it to her ankle. Then I repeat it with the other, before I position her wrist at her ankle and tie that, too, then repeat it at the other side.

"Do you want to use your safe word?" I look at her flushed features.

"No," she says without hesitation.

"Good girl."

Her breathing instantly grows choppy. Her chest rises and falls. She flexes her thighs, trying to squeeze them together and I click my tongue. "You're not allowed to alleviate your needs, remember?"

"That's a stupid condition."

"It's to help you orgasm harder."

"Yeah, yeah, that's what you keep saying. This mythical orgasm seems like something out of a fairytale."

"Only the dark smutty ones."

She gapes. "How do you know about them?"

"I read."

"Have you read my—" She gasps again, because I've finished securing her wrists to each ankle. I test the knots to make sure they don't bite into her skin but are tight enough to restrain her. Her muscles are tense, and I turn and kiss her. She begins to relax and when she parts her lips, I slide my tongue between them. I swipe it over the seam of her mouth and she whines, then melts into me.

"What's my name?" I murmur.

"Eddie," she groans.

"Such a good little slut, you are." I slide two fingers inside her slit, and she bears down on it. I press my thumb into her clit, and her entire body jolts. "Eddie. Oh, Eddie."

"I'm right here." I weave my fingers in and out of her, in and out. Her breath comes in little pants, sweat beads her upper lip. I lick it off, and she chases my mouth with hers. "So greedy for my cock."

"I am," she pants. "I want to feel you inside me."

I slap her pussy, and she cries out. "You asshole."

"That reminds me." I scoop up some of her cum, then smear it around her forbidden hole.

Her entire body shudders. Who'd have guessed my Belle has an erogenous zone in the unlikeliest of places.

"I want to come, please, Eddie," she whimpers.

"Not yet."

She pouts, then gasps when I loop the silk around her chest, and under her breast. I knot it at the back before crossing it over her shoulder and under the opposite breast. When the chest harness is done, I move way, and admire my artwork. "Beautiful."

A shiver grips her.

"If you could see yourself through my eyes, you'd know you're the most gorgeous woman in the world."

"Only in your eyes."

"That's all that matters. Your body was made for my ropes."

"Shibari; that's what this is." She lowers her chin to her chest. "Have you practiced it with anyone else?"

"No one who has your curves. No one who wears it like you. No one whose flesh will show off the marks of the ropes like you will. No one who I have fucked after tying them up."

I kneel between her bent thighs, then slowly ease her on her back. In the crab style I've tied her in, her wrists are linked to her ankles, which are up in the air. The result, all her beautiful bits are open and ready, and right there. All offered up to me in the most alluring of ways. All showcased and waiting to receive my ministrations.

I run my finger down the dip in her lips, to her cleavage, down to the hollow of her navel and when I trace the valley between her pussy lips, she mewls. When I follow the trail to her back hole, she whimpers.

"The sounds you make; they're driving me out of my head." I lower my zipper, then grab my throbbing cock. I pump it once, twice, then fit the angry head to her weeping slit. "I'm going to fuck you now."

50

Mira

That's all the warning I get before he kicks his hips forward and impales me. I'm so wet, he slides right in and hits that hidden heart of me deep inside. My breath whooshes out, and a groan boils up. He stays embedded in me, his cock throbbing, pushing against my inner walls. In this position, I am spread open and at his mercy. I can't see him, but I can feel the heat of his body as he looms over me. I feel the thickness of his thighs digging into mine. I feel the bones of his hips pressing into mine. I can sense his massive chest poised over my body like a bird of prey, a beast ready to break me.

"Eddie, please," I pant. Not sure what I'm asking for, only knowing I need more, so much more.

He presses his finger into my lower lip. "Open."

I do.

The next second he tears off my blindfold. I blink as he comes into focus. His golden eyes are almost silver with lust, his jaw hard, a fierceness to his features as he scans mine. "I want you to see this." He spits into my mouth, and I almost come undone. *No, this is disgusting. How could he do this?*

He notches his knuckles under my jaw and pushes up. I close my mouth.

"Swallow."

I do.

"Good girl."

Oh, shit. My pussy squeezes down on his cock; my nipples are so hard, they ache. Sparks zip down my body to knot with the tension at the base of my spine.

"You take everything I give you so beautifully," he growls.

I can't take my gaze off of him. Can't move, can't breathe. Pinned to the bed with his monster cock inside me, I can merely look into his eyes. See the silver-gold flares that light up deep inside. See his soul—scarred and broken and knitting itself back together. Because of me. A thrill of power barrels through my veins. I squeeze my inner walls again and am rewarded by the undulation of his muscles. He may have me tied down, but I have him at my mercy.

He reads the expression on my face, for a cunning look comes into his eyes. He pinches my nipple, turning it to the side with such suddenness, my breath catches. A blast of pain squeals down my body. Sweat slicks the space between my breasts, and I pant. So does he.

"Fuck!" He grits his teeth, then pulls out and stays poised at my opening. This time, when he slams into me, the entire bed jolts. He throbs inside of me, then pulls out again and thrusts into me. And again. As much as he's denied me an orgasm so far, something inside him seems to have tipped over the edge. And oh, my god, am I glad to be at the receiving end of all that intensity. That restrained violence. That passion that clings to every angle of his body.

He picks up even more speed, the sound of flesh hitting flesh filling the space. I am dripping, probably making a mess on the bedspread. The evidence is in the embarrassing sucking sound that sputters though the air every time he pulls back. It seems to urge him on, for he slaps both hands down on either side of my head, kicks his hips forward and drills into me. He stays there, still looking deep into my eyes. The world retreats. Everything stops, but for his gaze that holds me in thrall, and his cock that pegs me in place.

"Eddie, I love you."

He pulls back, and the next time he thrusts into me, the orgasm barrels up my body. "Come for me, Belle," he growls.

And I do. I ride the climax, all the way to the top, and when it breaks, I cry out. I hear him groan as he follows me over into the abyss. As the darkness subsides, and I open my eyes, I find I've been untied. He's rubbing a flowery ointment into my skin. I try to move, and my entire body protests.

"Stay still." He places his big palm between my breasts, and the weight of it is calming. I close my eyes and follow the gentle touch of his fingers over my ankles, my thighs, my wrists, and around my breasts.

Then he pulls the cover over me, turns me on my side and spoons me. I'm instantly in heaven. Am I smiling? Yes, my lips are curved. He wraps his arm about my waist, pulls me in and fits his knee into the space between mine. The heat of his body drugs me and pulls me down. I allow myself to float away.

When I wake, silvery light shines through the skylight and from the windows. The sight of the sea stretching out with the pink streaks of dawn on the horizon stops me. I take in the awe-inspiring sight, then pause. I'm in bed alone. I sit up, look around, and spy the open door to the bathroom. The sound of running water reaches me.

I slip out of bed, then wince as my muscles protest. Every step I take warns me of how sore I am in between my legs. I increase my speed, reach the bathroom and slip in. Steam fills the space, and beyond the fogged walls of the shower cubicle, I make out Edward with his back to me, head thrown back, as the water pours over him. Tall and broad, he could be carved out of stone. My belly clenches, and the honey of desire oozes through my veins.

I walk across the bathroom floor, open the cubicle of the shower and slip in. The steam wafts aside, and I spot scars crisscrossing his back. Pain squeezes my chest. I must make a noise, for he looks over his shoulder. His gaze widens, then that stony countenance drops over his features. "What are you doing here?"

51

———————

Edward

"Your poor back." She traces her fingers down the scars. I pull away, but she closes the distance to me, then kisses the puckered skin.

Goosebumps pop on my skin, despite the heat of the cascade I'm standing in.

She rubs her cheek against my back. The muscles of my shoulders turn to concrete. My heart thrashes against my ribcage. My stomach twists itself in knots, and I feel dizzy. I dig my palms into the wall, forcing myself to stay unmoving. She traces the blemishes all the way to the nape of my neck.

My cock lengthens, and my balls tighten. I came inside her again last night, and it was earth-shattering. Again. And when I pulled her body to mine, buried my nose in her hair and closed my eyes, I slept deeper and longer than any other night. The last time I slept this peacefully was before the incident. And when I woke up in the morning, I slipped my upright cock inside her and finished off in a few jerks…like a teenager. She moaned in her sleep, but I managed not to wake her. Then, I crawled out of bed. I decided to take a shower because, if I stayed in bed a second longer, I'd make love to her again, and I didn't want to disturb her sleep. And it was 'making love.' I can't kid myself any longer.

I switch off the shower, and in the silence that follows, I hear her sniffle. "Who did this to you?"

"I did."

"What?" She steps back and stares at my back in horror. "You hurt yourself?"

When I don't reply, she pushes her wet hair back from her face. "Why would you do that?"

"To punish myself."

"Is this because you couldn't have her? Is that why you did it?"

"I deserved it."

"No one deserves so much pain." She reaches out and, once more, traces one of the hardened trails of skin. "No one," she leans in, but before she can replace her fingers with her mouth, I turn and catch her wrist.

"I'm tainted, Belle."

"I don't care. Whatever happened before is in the past. I'm your future—you said it yourself."

I lower her hand, then drag my fingers through my hair. "I need to get dressed."

"No, not until you tell me why you scarred yourself."

"I lost what I thought was my one chance at happiness. I couldn't face my best friend anymore."

"You mean Baron?"

I nod. "I didn't want to see any of the Seven, either. They'd been my constant companions since our school days. We went through…a lot together. It formed a bond between us. But after Ava and Baron got together, I couldn't stay in London. I wanted them to be happy. I'm the one who told Ava to go back to Baron—"

"You did?"

"It was clear she loved him more. I had my chance and I lost it when I left her. I needed time to get my head on straight. I was a priest and I'd sinned. Everything inside me told me I was in the wrong, but I couldn't reconcile it with how I felt when I was with her. It was a mindfuck."

She reaches out for me, and I hold up my hand. "Don't touch me."

Her features fall.

Fuck. I squeeze the bridge of my nose. "I just… Let me get this out while I can Belle."

She nods, then tucks her arm into her side.

"I left her. I told Baron to watch out for her and I left. When I came back, I realized they had fallen in love. I saw them together, and I knew I couldn't be all the things she needed. I knew I wasn't in any space to hold down a relationship. How could I, when I hadn't figured out who I was and what I needed? She chose me. She even moved in with me, but seeing her face every morning, realizing how much she missed him, I told her to return to him."

"You did?"

"What Baron felt for her... It was different. He adored her. He wanted to take care of her. He needed her, and she leaned on him. They turned to each other in my absence and discovered they completed each other. I couldn't stand in their way."

"So you sacrificed your own happiness?"

"I did no such thing. I knew I couldn't be happy until I'd dealt with my own devils, so I walked away from them."

"Oh, Eddie." She wraps her arms about herself, and I notice the goosebumps on her skin. I scoop her up in my arms and walk out of the shower stall.

"What are you doing?" she squeaks.

"You're cold." I manage to grab a couple of towels on the way out, and when I reach the bed, I lower her to the ground. I dry her shoulders, her breasts, her waist, her thighs, down to her feet, then back up to her core. I pat it, then say around the ball of lust in my throat, "Spread your legs."

She does.

I slide the edge of the towel over her slit and back again.

She moans.

I do it again, and she shudders. The sweet scent of her arousal bleeds into the air, and I feel my cock stand up and salute her. *Fuck.* Can't keep my hands off of her, can't keep my gaze off of her pussy. If only I could spend days buried inside her tight cunt, I might get this insane need to rut into her every time I'm near her out of my system. A-n-d, who am I kidding? The more time I spend with her, the more I want her, the more I can't let go of her. I'll never get enough of her, and that is the truth. And when she finds out my truth, she'll hate me. And I can't let that happen. I can't. I let the towel drop to the bed, then I lift her up and throw her on it.

52

Mira

"Hold yourself open for me," he growls.

Fish in the snow, his words are hard and demanding and… I can't say no. I manage to widen the space between my legs, then reach down and hold open my pussy lips.

"Good girl."

I'm not ashamed to say, I almost climax. Just from his words. The way he says it, it makes me feel like the most special person in the entire world, and the luckiest. He stares at my glistening cunt—I can feel the moisture gathering at my slit—then reaches down and squeezes his cock from base to tip. It's the first time I've seen my husband without a stitch of clothing, and the reality far surpasses my dreams. Sculpted shoulders, corrugated chest, concave waist, not to mention, the eight pack he sports like he works out every day, and those thick powerful thighs without an inch of fat on them. He's pure muscle, all the way down to his calves and his bare feet. Something about his feet shoots my blood pressure through the roof. I have a foot fetish—correction I have an Edward fetish. He widens his stance, and my gaze is drawn up to where he massages his thick cock once more, all the way to the crown. There's a vein running up it, and moisture drips from the slit.

"Put three fingers inside yourself," he commands.

"Th-three?"

He merely arches an eyebrow.

I swallow as my heart descends to the space between my legs. The blood roars so loudly in my ears, I'm sure the sea has risen all the way to the top of the lighthouse. I slide three fingers into my opening and pause.

"All the way in."

"I… I can't."

"You took my cock inside you; your fingers are nothing."

Moisture drools from my core. I thrust my fingers inside, and sensations vibrate out from the intrusion. I'm so sensitive, flickers of heat zip through my blood.

"Hold out your fingers and show me your cum."

OMG, that dirty talking mouth of his is going to make me orgasm without him having touched me. I manage to glide my fingers out and show them to him.

"You're wet enough for what's going to come, turn on your front.

I hesitate.

He glares at me, and frissons of anticipation spark up my spine. I turn over.

"Stay there."

I hear him move around, hear the slither of the silken rope over his palm. Goosebumps splatter on my skin. *Oh god. Ohgod, ohgod. He's going to use the ropes again, and I'm going to love every second of it. What is he doing to me? To think I was a virgin less than a month ago and now I can't wait for him to tie me up and fuck every hole.*

"I can hear you thinking, and I'm going to deliver on it."

A whimper escapes me. I sound so needy, so greedy. So ready for everything he has in mind.

He lifts my foot then pushes down until my leg is fully bent at the knee, then slips the rope just below the knee and above the ankle, tying me in a frog legged shape. He does the same to the other side. Then I sense him straighten.

"What's my name, Belle?"

"Eddie," I breathe.

"Such a good little slut, you are."

A shiver of pleasure swirls through my blood like cream poured in coffee. I begin to squeeze my thighs together, but he grips my knee and holds them apart. "Remember, you can't alleviate your need."

"That's ridiculous."

"That's called a frog-tie."

"What?" I blink.

"Tying your legs the way I have."

"You mean, it helps you reach any of my orifices conveniently?" I scoff.

"Exactly." He sounds pleased. Because clearly, he got the response he wanted. Because I walked into the trap he'd set me. I firm my lips.

"Aren't you going to ask me what I'm going to do next?"

I want to. Of course, I do, but I'm not giving him the satisfaction of doing what he expects. I stay silent and hear him chuckle. The bastard chuckles, which, coming from someone who has a hard time curving his lips in a smile, is enough to make me glare at him over my shoulder.

"Next is the box-tie," he informs me.

Like I need to know the name of whatever convoluted knot he's going to drape over my body?

He places one knee on the bed, then the other on the other side of my body.

"Place your cheek on the bed." He gently urges me, then when I'm positioned to his satisfaction, he begins to knead my shoulders. He digs his fingers into the tensed muscles, and when they relax, a warmth seeps through my blood. "Draw a deep breath," he orders.

I do.

"Now let it out." He guides me through a series of breathing exercises, at the end of which my body seems to have turned into a puddle. I don't even feel the knots around my legs, except for the pleasant stretch on my hamstrings. And when he pulls me up so I'm sitting on my heels, I don't protest. Not even when he twists one arm, then the other, so they're folded over the small of my back. He passes the ropes around my upper arms and chest, then loops them around my wrists. When he tightens the ropes, I realize the position causes my breasts to thrust out. Also, my knees are spread wide enough for my clit to be bared, and because I'm balanced on my knees he can access my forbidden back hole. The position feels natural enough that I could hold it for hours. Which is the effect he was going for.

"You should see how you look, tied up, with my ropes marking your skin, with your flesh curving around my knots. It's the most erotic thing ever." He walks around to the other side of the bed, so he's facing me. Then drags his gaze down my body. "Fucking hell, you're a vision, Belle."

Color heightens his cheeks. His chest rises and falls. And when my gaze is drawn to his crotch, I find him erect and hard, with his cock standing up against his stomach. It also looks even bigger than earlier. Like seeing me tied up is lending an added stimulus to his arousal. I know the way he's watching me is definitely boosting my horniness.

Then his brow furrows. "Something's missing."

53

Mira

He moves away only to return with a bowl in his hand. He scoops up something and holds it out. "Open."

My pussy clenches at once. Only he could turn that one word into something so salacious, I feel like he's talking about other holes in my body. I part my lips, and he slides his finger over my tongue. I'm overcome by the dark taste of chocolate, the tanginess of cherries, the sweet taste of brandy, the bite of citrus, and the hint of apple. "Christmas pudding?" I frown.

"I'm going to decorate you with it."

"You're joking."

He tilts his head, a serious look on his face as he takes measure of my body.

Not joking, then.

He scoops up some more of the mixture, then draws a circle around my breast, before dabbing it on my nipple. He does the same with the other side. He continues to trace sticky lines down my stomach before filling my belly button with the gooey stuff. I wriggle, but he shoots me a glare. "Stay still."

Of course, I oblige. How can I not when the dominance in his voice brooks no argument. He smears the concoction on the skin above my pussy, then down the crease of my inner thigh. I squirm, but when he makes a warning noise at the back of his throat, I freeze. He rubs some of it over the tops of my thighs, coming close to my core, but never touching my pussy.

"Eddie," I whine.

"What do you need, Belle?" He raises his gaze to mine.

"You know what I want."

"You need to ask for it."

I scowl. He dabs some of the pudding on the tip of my nose, then across my lower lip.

"Those are not the only lips I want you to touch," I plead.

"Ask me." He brings his finger to his mouth and sucks his digit. And when he pulls it out, it makes a popping sound that kickstarts a flurry of activity in my lower belly.

"Okay, fine, can you please touch my pussy?"

"And?'

"My cunt."

"And —"

I swallow. "I don't want that stuff to stain your bed."

"I'll lick it up before that happens."

"Oh," I gulp audibly. He's going to lick this off my body. He's going to lick all the parts where he's rubbed in this icky mixture. It shouldn't turn me on further, but oh god, it does. He's going to stuff his tongue into all the nooks and crevasses of my body and I...want him to. "Put it in my pussy," I mumble.

"I didn't hear you." His lips curl a little at the edges. He's smirking. Ugh, and that only makes him hotter, and I'm tired of all this teasing.

"Fuck me with your monster dick," I yell.

"As you wish." He places the bowl on the side table, then climbs onto the bed facing me. He leans in and licks the stuff on my nose, the gesture almost affectionate, then brushes his lips over mine. Just a feather light touch. Enough to make me want more, so when he pulls away, I chase his mouth.

"Greedy girl." He weighs my breasts in both of his big hands. The calluses on his fingers chafe my tender skin. The sting combines with the tension in my stomach, and the result is a sweet pain which goes to my head.

"Eddie, please," I moan.

He bends his head, bites down on my nipple, and my eyes roll back in my head. And when he pays similar attention to the other, I almost collapse. He grips my hips and holds me up, then proceeds to lick his way down my stomach, over the fold of my belly, and when he swirls his tongue into my belly button, I cry out, "Eddie. Eddie. Eddie."

I try to pull away, but his grasp is firm. He holds me captive as he licks and sucks and bites his way down the pudding tracks, which means, he circles my pussy, coming closer and closer to my aching core. My clit is so swollen, my slit so moist, the hollow in my center seems to be growing by the moment, and I try to close my legs, but he releases his hold on my hips, only to grab my thighs and splay them wide. He lays out on his front and shoves his face into my pussy. I cry out, then whimper when he slurps his way up my pussy lips and over my clit. Sweat drips down my cleavage, and my teeth snap together. I'm shuddering so hard, it's like I've caught a fever. Not that it makes a difference to him.

He lays his head on my thigh and blows on my cunt. I cry out. He slides three fingers inside me and twists, and the climax screams up my spine. I throw my head back and wait…wait for the orgasm. Only, he pulls back. The orgasm hovers there like a wave about to crash on the shore; only, it's as if someone has pressed the rewind button. It retreats.

"No, no, no," I pant.

"Yes." He raises his head, then eases me onto my back. It should be awkward, but really, the way he's tied me up, he can move me around, and no part of my body protests. I lay there with my legs bent at the knees, splayed like a frog.

He stares at my exposed center, and a flush climbs up his chest. As turned on as I am, I realize, he is, too. As needy as I am, the thick length of his cock standing to attention seems almost painful.

Then he draws his whiskered chin across my pussy, and I cry out, "Oh my god!"

He instantly stiffens. "Told you, God has nothing to do with this."

Before I can react, he lowers his head and draws his tongue up my slit.

54

Edward

I can't get enough of her. I can't. Tied up in my knots, wearing the marks of the rope I've wrapped around her, with her flesh flushed by my ministrations, she's the most beautiful creature to grace this earth. I drag my tongue up her pussy lips, and when I bite down on the swollen knob of her clit, her entire body shudders. Her thighs quiver, and her breasts swell. She makes that telltale moan at the back of her throat, and I know she's close. Not to mention, she's so wet, I can't stop lapping at her entrance. I continue to eat her out, and when full body shudders grip her, I rise over her. I fit my cock to her opening, and plunge into her.

"Eddie," she gasps.

"You're so wet, so tight." I grit my teeth, giving her time to adjust to my size. No matter how many times I take her, it feels like the first time. "Belle," I groan and push my forehead into hers. "You feel so fucking good."

She clenches down on my shaft, and the tiny flutters of her inner-walls embracing my shaft, drain the blood to my groin. I begin to fuck her in earnest. In-out-in, and again. Every time I bury myself in her, the entire bed shudders. Every time I pull out, she moans in frustration. The heat generated from us presses down on my back. Sweat drips down my forehead. The next time I slam into her, she cries out. Her back arches, and her eyelids flutter down.

"Look at me as you come, wife."

She manages to meet my gaze, and her pupils are so dilated with lust, and something else, something soft that sends me over the edge.

"Come with me." My balls tighten. "Come right now, Belle."

Her mouth opens in a soundless cry. She topples over the edge, and I follow her. My climax seems to go on and on, as I pour myself into her. When she slumps, I begin to pull out of her. The mix of her cum and mine slides down her thigh, and I reach down and stuff it back inside her cunt.

"What are you doing?" Her voice is slurred.

"Making sure you take every last drop of what's mine."

When I'm satisfied, I sit up, pulling her up with me. Then I reach behind her and untie the knots at her back, then at her legs. I ease her back onto the bed and stretch out her arms and legs. I begin to massage them with long strokes, and she sighs, "That's so nice..." She yawns.

"Sleep." I kiss her eyelids closed. Her body twitches, and I know she's out. I walk over to the bathroom, returning with a warm wash-cloth, and run it down her body. Then I pull the covers over her before walking back to the bathroom and tossing the washcloth in the hamper. I get dressed but can't tear myself away from her. So I pull up a chair and watch her sleep.

Can I give you my confession? I've done this before—watched her sleep. Before she even knew me. There, I've told you. Now I need to confess to her, and accept whatever penance she deems fit. But not yet. Not until I know she's bound to me in a way nothing on earth can break that connection. A few more days, is all I need... I hope.

She stretches, yawns, then her gaze finds mine. "What time is it?"

"Not even noon."

"What are we doing today?"

"Not much, considering..." I nod toward the window.

She follows my gaze, and her mouth drops open. "Whoa, it's a snow-storm out there."

"It is. And it's supposed to go on for a few days."

"A few days?" She turns to me. "So we're stuck inside here?"

"Seems that way."

"Hmm." She sits up, and the sheet falls to her waist. "I wonder how we're going to fill our time?"

***

Perhaps, that was a rhetorical question. There's never been any question in my mind that I'm going to use the time to get to know every inch of her body thoroughly. And she seems perfectly amenable to my plans.

I took her in our bed, again, then made us lunch. For dessert, I had her on the island. And I told her I'm not much a dessert-eater—ha! I let her catch a nap while I worked out, needed to keep up my energy for the coming days, after all. Then, it was an early dinner, for which I reheated a casserole.

Post dinner, we curled up in the settee in front of the fire while the snowfall outside was so dense, it felt like we were marooned on an island.

She stretched out, and I read to her from one of her spicy books. She began to squirm, and when she looked at me with her dilated eyes, I knew what she wanted. I positioned her on the bed, on her knees with her behind in the air and a pillow under her chest. When I pulled her arms back and tied her wrists to her ankles, she moaned with excitement. The cum running down her inner thighs, and the gleaming pink of her pussy told me how turned on she was. Which, in turn, turned me on. There was so much wetness, I scooped it up and used it to lubricate her back channel. She shuddered. I thought she'd protest, but she pushed out her butt in invitation. I checked in with her, made sure she called me by the name only she does, then I fucked her there. I made sure she orgasmed before I allowed myself to come. Then, I made sure to clean her up before I curled around her and fell asleep.

When I wake up, the light coming in through the windows is a golden yellow. It's stopped snowing, and the sun illuminates the arches of the clouds in the sky and highlights her curves. She's standing naked at the window, with her hand pressed into the glass. The light turns her hair to a cloud of spun gold, and outlines the dip of her waist, the flare of her round bottom. My cock hardens at once. Without conscious thought, I prowl toward her, then wrap my arm about her waist and bring her against my naked body. Apparently, now that I've shown myself naked to her, I feel comfortable enough to stay that way.

"Mmm." She turns around and reaches up to touch my face. "Merry Christmas."

I tilt my head, unable to bring myself to say the words. There was a time when I looked forward to this time of year, when I threw myself into the spirit of the season. When I led Advent services, led community efforts, visited the older parishioners at home to bring them the Eucharist. I also presided over the Christmas Eve Mass, and I enjoyed it. I used the season to help families reconcile differences and learn the importance of helping others. I was good at my chosen line of work.

Now? It all seems so pointless. To have believed in something and been happy at that time… I suppose, that counts for something. It certainly helped me through some tough times, providing hope when I was bereft. Only now, I question if my faith was misplaced? I believed…and was let down. This time, I'm not leaving anything to chance. Or some nonexistent or uncaring god. This time, I'm in control. I'll make sure I get what I want… Her.

I cup her cheek, then bend and kiss her lips. "Sleep well?"

"I did." Her lips curve in a smile.

So beautiful, so open, so happy, so everything I'm not. My heart catches. I tighten my grip on her.

Her forehead furrows. "And you?"

"Never better." No nightmares, no ghosts from the past haunting my thoughts. I feel refreshed and full of energy and…my cock throbs between us. "Horny."

She glances down, then up at me, her eyes wide. "Again?"

"If you're too sore —"

She shakes her head, then pulls out of my grasp. "But you'll have to catch me."

55

Mira

I saw the play of expression on his face, knew he was thinking of things he wouldn't share with me. And I'll admit, it upsets me. I want to confront him about it, but if I do, it'll cause him to shut down, which I don't want. Especially after how he took me last night. Tying me up is how he expresses his emotions toward me. Maybe he can't say the words aloud, but how he worships me with his body tells me he's halfway—more than halfway— to falling in love with me. And I don't want to spoil the intimacy that's sprung up between us.

Marooned here in this lighthouse, miles from anywhere, it's just him and me, and I want to enjoy the feeling. I want to…make him laugh, lighten the thoughts he's having. I want to just forget about the real world for a while. Which is why I slip out of his embrace and taunt him to catch up. And he doesn't disappoint. A sly look comes into his eyes, and he prowls forward.

I take a few steps back, stumble against the settee, straighten and move around it. His lips curl as he continues to walk toward me. He knows he's going to catch me. I know he's going to catch me. But… I'm going to make him work for it.

I scramble back, cursing my boobs which flap around my chest. But then, he notices them, too. His gaze locks on my chest, and it's his turn to stumble. Holy shit, he's distracted by my body. He seems to love my figure—always tells me so, shows me how much he enjoys it in how he handles my body, but I'm self-conscious enough that I need constant reassurances. And what's more of an ego boost than to have this gorgeous, confident man lose his footing when he sees my boobs?

I bring my hand up to play with my nipple, and his body tenses. He picks up his pace. I glance around, then dart around the bed. He stalks toward me and when I play with my pussy lips, he bumps into the bed. "Shit."

I giggle.

He frowns, then his forehead smoothens out. "You know what happens to little brats?"

I shake my head.

"They get taught a lesson."

"Oh." Moisture oozes out from my slit. I scoop it up, show him my glistening fingers. "Wanna taste?"

He nods.

"Too bad, you're not getting any." I bring my fingers to my lips, making a popping sound the way he's done in the past.

His gaze narrows. "Belle," he growls.

"Is that a sushi role between your legs, or are you sashimi to see me?"

He blinks. "What was that?"

"A…a…joke."

"I'm not laughing."

"How about knock-knock joke?" I hop from foot to foot. Behind me, is the wall; to the right, a glass window; and to my left, a bed. There's only one way out. I jump up on the bed. He's at the foot of the bed, and the various parts of me that jiggle once again seem to get his attention. He sweeps his gaze from the hair on my head, which is a rat's nest, no doubt, all the way down to my toes, which I dig into the mattress, then back to my face.

"Knock-knock," he says in a hard voice.

"Who…who's there?"

"Dozer."

"Dozer, who?" I ask in a cautious tone.

"Dozer some great tits you got there." His tone is still without expression but his eyes wear a glint.

I scoff, "That the best you can do?"

He slaps his palms on his hips and scowls. "Knock-knock."

Here goes nothing. "Who's there?"

"Hop on."

"Hop on, who?"

"Hop on this dick."

I make a gagging sound and begin to edge toward to the far side of the bed, away from him. I reach it, jump down, and move toward the kitchen area.

"Knock-knock," he growls.

"Who's there?" I tip up my chin.

"Iguana."

I frown. "Iguana, who?"

"Iguana touch your tits." He races toward me. I shriek, run toward the kitchen island, and circle it.

"Knock-knock." He bares his teeth.

"Who's there?" I pant.

"The dentist." He moves to one side of the island, while I dart to the other.

"The dentist, who?"

"I heard you have some cavities that need filling." He races around the counter, and I run to the side opposite him.

"Knock-knock." He rolls his shoulders. The movement is so menacing, my stomach flips up into my throat. And when he lowers his chin and glares at me, every drop of blood I have drains to my clit. "Who's there?" I gasp.

He takes a step toward me; I sidle to the side.

"Can I come in?" He cracks his knuckles. He's doing it to intimidate me, and he's succeeding. Also, I can't wait to have those thick fingers on me, in me, pleasuring me, plucking on my nipples, playing with my clit, intruding into my forbidden hole. My heart flutters like the wings of a dragon fly. "Can I—" I swallow. "Can I come in, who?"

"You!" He throws himself over the island.

I scream, turn and run away, but he's too fast. I hear him hit the floor, then footsteps race toward me. He grabs me around my waist and throws me over his shoulder. I'm breathing so hard, and my blood is pounding so hard in my temples, I think I'm going to faint. My hair tumbles over my face. I push it aside, orient myself to realize he's reached the bed. Then, he throws me on it on my back, and covers me with his body.

He stares into my face, his chest rising and falling, his eyes slightly wild. Apparently, I did the right thing by asking him to chase me; seems it not only broken the chain of his brooding thoughts, but also turned him on even more, as evidenced by the massive thing that stabs into the curve of my belly.

"I'm going to have to punish you, Belle." His voice, by contrast, is almost casual. But I'm not fooled. I know by the way his jaw tics and his left eyelid throbs, by the way the tendons of his throat stand out under his flesh, he means it. He reaches down between us and notches his cock into my slit.

56

Edward

I kick my hips forward and in one sweet thrust I'm home. Inside her soft melting pussy which embraces me like it's missed me.

"I missed this," I confess.

"I missed you, too." She cups my cheek. "Missed you so much."

Her soft words are like balm on my wounds. Her eyes glisten with empathy, with tenderness, with love. She wears her heart in her eyes; she has nothing to hide, unlike me. I urge her to lock her ankles about my waist, then plunge into her and bury myself, again, to the hilt. She gasps; her mouth opens, and I stay there, pushing forward with my knees until I'm fitted into her. I stay there, and she flutters around me. "That's it, baby," I croon.

"Eddie," she gasps. She winds her arms about my neck, digging her fingernails into my back. I want her to mark me. I want to replace the scars of my past with blemishes she's bestowed on me.

"I'm here." I begin to pump my hips forward and fuck her in earnest. Her body moves forward with the force of impact, and the headboard cracks against the wall. Something falls to the ground behind me, but I ignore it. I'm too focused on the expressions that flit across her face; the heightened blush that climbs up her chest and neck; her whines and whimpers as I rut into her, over and over again. Looking into her eyes as I fuck her is the most intimate experience of my life.

"I love you," she whispers.

"I…" *love you.* I want to say it. I do. But the words stick in my throat. Instead, I tilt my hips, and sink into her with enough impact, my balls hit her inner thighs. I hit the space deep inside her, then push in further. That familiar shuddering sweeps up her hips, her back arches, and when she begins to cry out, I close my mouth over hers and absorb the sounds. She shatters around my cock, and I grunt as I come inside her. When she begins to slump, I lean back, taking in her freshly fucked features. Then, because I can't help myself, I press a kiss to her forehead before I pull out and throw myself on the bed next to her. She curls into my side, and I wrap my arm around her and pull her closer.

"I first saw you in Brooklyn a year ago."

"A year ago?" She doesn't react. *Maybe my idea of fucking her until she's so filled with endorphins she won't be able to react to my revelations is what's keeping her calm? Now you know how morally grey I am. And yes, I'm a bastard. But you know that already.*

"I was there for a work meeting. I was in my car, saw you walking home from the subway. I followed you to your townhouse."

"My father's townhouse," she corrects me. So, she doesn't think of it as her home, interesting.

"Over the next week, I trailed you to your part time job at the preschool, to meet your friends in Manhattan."

"O-k-a-y?"

"I also got access to your devices."

"What do you mean?" There's a thread of curiosity in her voice. But her muscles are still relaxed. I draw circles over her hip, and she shivers. And when I lean in and kiss her lips, she melts into me further. "I had an investigator break into your room and put hidden cameras and listening devices there."

"You put hidden cameras and listening devices in my room?" She asks slowly.

"Also, in your phone and on your Kindle."

"Why my Kindle?" She frowns.

"It's the device you spend most of your time on; more than your phone."

"And how did you find that out?"

"I saw you reading on your Kindle in the coffee shop, and on the subway, and even while walking to and from the subway, something which was so dangerous, I ended up following you to make sure you reached home safely."

"You followed me home from the subway to make sure I reached home safely?" Her brow furrows.

"It was either that or reveal myself to you, and I wasn't ready for that."

Something of what I'm saying seems to infiltrate through her subconscious, for her gaze widens. "You're saying you saw me before we met at Gio's wedding?"

I nod slowly.

"And you first saw me in Brooklyn?"

I stay quiet, letting her read the assent in my gaze.

She rubs at her temple. "And you bugged my room in my father's home?"

I nod.

"How did you do that?" The wrinkle between her eyebrows deepens. "My father's home has security."

"Nothing my team couldn't bypass. I also had eyes and ears on your apartment in London."

This time, she pushes away from me, and I don't want to let her go. I don't want there to be any distance between us, but I release her... For now.

"In my a-a-apartment?" she stutters.

I reach for her, but she pulls away. A hot stab of pain squeezes my chest; I rub at it. I knew it was going to hurt when I finally told her. But I had to tell her. Even though everything in me warned me if I did, I could lose her.

And what if I didn't tell her? I've managed not to, so far. But now, when I'm so close to her, when it feels like so many walls have come down between us, when I'm beginning to show her who I am, when she knows my darkest desires and hasn't run yet, I know it's now or never. And it has to be while we're here, when she can't run and leave me. While we're still snowbound. But it won't last forever. It's stopped snowing, and the sun has started to shine, and once it thaws, we'll have to return. And then... I won't be able to stop her from leaving. But for now, I can keep her here, even if she hates me.

"I had to make sure I knew where you were at all times."

"I don't understand. You had cameras on me and listening devices. You were tracking me; you knew where I always was?" Color fades from her cheeks.

"I had to make sure you were safe at all times."

"There was no threat to me," she protests.

"And this was the only way to be sure." I rub the back of my neck. "I know this is a lot for you to take in but —"

"So when you offered me a job —"

"I knew you needed it. I knew your preschool had gone out of business, and you were running out of options."

She pales further. "You used that to your advantage."

"I saw the opportunity and took it."

She shakes her head. "So, you already knew everything about me. You knew —"

"That I wanted you to be my wife? Yes."

"Fake wife." She swallows. "You wanted me to marry you to satisfy G-Pa's terms, so you could confirm your role as CEO of the company."

"And you still believe that? After everything that's happened between us the last few days, you still think that?" I look between her eyes.

She holds my gaze for a second, another, then looks away. "What other explanation is there?"

57

Mira

He had me followed. He invaded my privacy. He's known who I was for a while. He knew everything about me when he asked me to work for him. It was all preplanned, including asking me to marry him. My head swims. And yet, somehow, I'm not overly surprised. It explains why, when I met Edward I felt like I knew him. I felt like I had seen him. It's why it always felt like he was hiding something from me. I just never thought it would be something so big.

"Everything you told me was a lie." I begin to inch toward the edge of the bed.

"Do the last few days seem like a lie?" He raises his hand as if he's going to reach for me, then lowers it. "I'm not good at expressing myself through words, Belle."

"Don't call me that."

"You can't negate everything that's happened between us just because the way it started was a little unorthodox," he growls.

I rise to my feet. "You stalked me. Bugged my devices. Had cameras on me. Had me followed. You manipulated me into working for you, knowing I didn't want to work in the role of a personal assistant. You knew I worked in a preschool. If you had so much information on me, you'd have known I've always wanted to work with kids, yet you offered me the role of your PA."

"I wanted you close to me."

"I was right outside your office, and you still had a camera trained on me."

His jaw tics. "You have to understand, I'm not good at sharing what's mine. Left up to me, I'd have had you locked at home, and not allowed anyone to see you."

I glance around the space. "Is that why you brought me here? So you could hide me away? I'd question whether you also arranged for a snowstorm, but not even you could do that."

His eyes flash, then he glances away.

I raise my hands to my mouth. "Oh, my god, you knew there was a storm on the way."

"I might have heard about it on the weather forecast, yes."

"So you planned it so that we'd be here and unable to leave."

He drags his fingers through his hair. "It's not like that."

"It is exactly that. You had it all planned. You knew my every move. You knew my past, who my father was—" I lower my arms to my side. "You knew he was going to arrange my marriage. Did you also arrange for his business to go under so you could use it as leverage?"

When his left eyelid twitches, I know I'm right. He must see the realization sink in, for he slides his legs over the side of the bed and stands.

When he moves toward me, I throw my arms up. "Don't touch me."

His features twist. A haunted look comes into his eyes. He seems helpless and forlorn, and so lonely, and… I cannot let that get to me. I cannot let the devastation in his gaze soften me. I can't allow him to get close to me again. Not after everything he just revealed.

He looks away, then back at me. "When we return, you can lead on the initiative to set up childcare facilities in the office."

It's not what I expected him to say, so I stay quiet.

"I've wanted to set up childcare services in the office for a while, and you would be the perfect candidate to drive that." He lowers his chin to his chest. "You know you want to help with this project."

"I do." I put more distance between us. "But it doesn't change what you did. Things which I may never be able to come to terms with."

Color drains from his features. "Don't say that." His voice is hoarse like he's been yelling, or maybe it's all the lies he's told me.

"You did something unforgivable. You betrayed my trust."

"I didn't have a choice."

"You could have come out and told me you liked me."

"Liked you?" He pronounces the words like they are something foreign.

"And maybe, we could have gone on dates."

"Dates?" The furrow between his forehead deepens.

"You know. Dinner, a movie…? Like normal people."

"Normal people." There is a strange look in his eyes, something I can't quite place. A mix of surprise and disbelief.

"Yes, normal people. People who respect boundaries and know they can't just plant cameras and listening devices on others. People who think of more than running a company, and who don't earn billions and make more in one day than most of the planet does in a year. People like me."

"You're wrong."

"What do you mean?"

"You're not a normal person," he says through gritted teeth.

"Of course, I am."

"You're the most genuine person I've ever met. The most honest, the most generous, the most empathetic. You care about others more than yourself, and that is not normal. Not even faintly normal. People are selfish and cruel and hurt others to get what they want."

"Like you hurt me?"

He winces. "I… I didn't want to hurt you. Quite the contrary. I wanted to make sure you got everything you wanted."

"I didn't ask for all this." I wave a hand in the air. "All I wanted was a home of my own, a family, a man who loves me."

"I—" He swallows. "I…care about you, Belle."

"You have a funny way of showing it."

"It's the only way I know."

"And I'm sure you're going to use the incident to justify the way you turned out. You're going to tell me the incident is the reason you're an uncaring, unfeeling, calculating person…who I hate."

"You don't hate me."

"I do now." I pull the sheet off the bed and wrap it around my shoulders.

His features take on a dissatisfied look. He seems like he's about to say something, then draws in a sharp breath. "Everything I did…was from a place of wanting to woo you."

"Clearly, we differ on that definition," I scoff.

"Give me one chance." He shuffles his feet. "Just one chance to win your heart."

"Why should I, when all you've done is lie to me and make me believe in a relationship which doesn't exist?"

"But it does. Everything that's happened between us—all of it is true. From the first moment I saw you, I knew there was no one else for me but you. I recognized you, Belle. I knew we had a connection. I knew I had to have you in my life."

"And me? What about me? You didn't think about what I wanted, or what I needed—"

"Only every second. I knew you didn't want to marry a perfect stranger—"

"You were a perfect stranger."

"I was your boss; you'd gotten to know me. You knew there was chemistry between us."

"Oh, so that makes it all justifiable. That you gave me a job under false pretext, a job I was woefully unqualified for—"

"And which you performed well."

"—and just because we were attracted to each other doesn't mean I wanted to marry you."

"Marriages have been built on less. And you have to admit, the physical connection between us is mind-blowing."

"But I want more." I turn on him. "I understand, you express yourself through your actions. I think it's why you wanted to tie me up. It's how you showed me you care for me, in your own way. It's how you wanted to share with me what you feel for me. But if you can't give words to your sentiments… If you can't open your mouth and elaborate what it is you feel for me… Then, I'm not sure we have a future, especially after—" I tug the sheet tighter. "After everything you just told me."

"I'm sorry, I hurt you. I'm sorry, I couldn't play by the rules. I'm sorry, I wasn't open about my intentions. But if I had been, would you have given me a chance?"

I stay silent.

His throat moves as he swallows. "I know what kind of a person I am. I know I'm not good enough for you."

"What are you talking about?" I frown.

"I spied on you, yet I couldn't tell your stepmother and half-sisters were not treating you well. I'll never forgive myself for that."

I rub at my temple. "They were subtle about how they hurt me. Oftentimes, their remarks almost seemed like compliments, but I knew they were meant to be hurtful."

"I should have paid more attention."

"It's not like you could have intervened," I point out.

"I'd have found a way. If I had been a better man, not so focused only on my own needs, I'd have stepped in. It's why you should have married someone better, someone who could be more open with his emotions and give you the emotional security you deserve. Someone 'more normal.' Someone who'd give you a white picket fence and a house in the suburbs and—"

"And you're wrong. Those are external trappings. I just want someone who loves me."

His chest rises and falls. A fleet of expressions crosses his face. He opens his mouth, and I'm sure this is it. This is when he'll say those three words that will change everything. Instead, when he speaks, it's to growl, "Nothing can change the fact that we're married." He continues in a hard voice, "The ceremony was real. The paperwork around it was real."

There's a tinge of desperation in his voice. *Edward and desperate? Nope, that must be my imagination. He's a lying, conniving, bastard. That's who he is.*

"Are you hearing yourself? I'm talking about the fact you violated my personal boundaries." That's not all he violated, but the physical aspect of it… I can't bring that into the equation, because I enjoyed it. Damn him, but he took me to heights I didn't think I'd ever reach. He showed me the kind of pleasure that's imprinted on every pore in my body—his touch is stamped into my skin and his name is painted into the most secret parts of my body, thanks to the intensity with which he fucked me. And it was *fucking*. It *wasn't* lovemaking. I might have fooled myself into thinking otherwise, but it wasn't love. It can't be love. The fact he overstepped the limits of my personal space, breached my faith… It's not something I can look past.

"And you're still my wife."

That's when his phone buzzes.

58

Edward

"You shouldn't have rushed back," G-Pa says from his bed. Tiny is on his haunches near him, and G-Pa keeps reaching out to pet him. The Great Dane welcomed me and my wife when we arrived, then went back to being by my G-Pa's side. The friendship between the two of them has deepened since I last saw them.

"Of course, we should have." My wife slides into the chair next to G-Pa's bed and takes his hand in hers. "I'm glad you're okay."

"There's nothing wrong with me," he insists.

"Of course, not," she says in a soothing voice.

"Don't patronize me, young lady," he says in a half-stern voice.

"Me, patronize you?" she says in an innocent tone. "As if I'd dare."

"Oh, yes, you would." His eyes twinkle, before he darts his gaze in my direction. "Of course, you have my permission to do what's needed to keep my grandson in line."

Like I'm not pussy-whipped enough? Aside from the fact I seem to lose my voice when I want to tell her I love her, I've lost all free will. I've lost the ability to do anything except stay close to her, and look at her, and touch her to make sure she's real. Which, considering the reason I took on this role in my grandfather's company was to find focus, has turned my world upside down. I found my reason for living the day I saw her, but I didn't recognize it. It was only after marrying her and realizing there was no better sound in the world than calling her 'my wife' that my world found its axis. I found my grounding. My anchor. My re-entry back into reality. My equilibrium. She is my foundation. My life. *Mine.* So why am I not able to tell that to her?

"I'm glad you're okay." She places her other hand over his and squeezes.

"It was nothing," he huffs.

"It was a fall," Knox growls from where he's standing at one corner of G-Pa's bed.

"I was barely hurt." G-Pa sets his jaw.

"You fractured your toe," Nathan says in a mild voice. He's the one who messaged me. He was trying to make amends for the fact my grandfather decided to share my veto power of the company with him. My older half-brother leans a hip against the windowsill. It's as far away from the rest of us as possible. Clearly, I'm not the only one who has issues. Nor am I the newest member to join the family fold and meet his extended family for the first time.

"It was a hairline fracture," G-Pa protests.

"It could have been much worse if Tiny hadn't found you," Knox growls.

"Tiny found you?" I glance toward the Great Dane, who looks at me with his big melting eyes.

"I didn't have my phone with me when I fell in the bathroom. Luckily I didn't lock the door. Tiny pushed the door open and came in when he heard me groan. I gestured to him to go my nightstand and grab my phone and bring it to me. I wasn't sure if he could understand me—"

"But he did?" my wife exclaims.

"He did." G-Pa pats the big dog's head, and he places his chin on G-Pa's bed and looks up at the old man with adoring eyes.

"Aww, you're a hero." She drops to her knees and hugs the dog, who looks at me over her shoulder with a smirk... No, he really has a smirk on his face. He's in her good books, while I've been banished to the doghouse. I resist the urge to bare my teeth at the mutt. He's just a dog. So what, if my wife feels more kindly toward him at the moment.

"I'll be at my desk in the office before you know it," G-Pa declares.

"You need to rest your foot," Knox reminds him.

"My foot!" G-Pa snaps.

"That's what he said," I nod.

"I second that," Nathan rumbles.

G-Pa looks at the three of us, a considering look coming into his eyes. "So, it takes me being on my deathbed for my family to form a united front."

"You're not on your death bed," I point out.

"I have a fracture," he groans.

My wife snickers at me over her shoulder. I begin to smile back, when she must realize what she's done and that she's supposed to be pissed off with me, for she turns back to G-Pa. "You were just saying you were completely okay."

G-Pa slumps back against his pillows. "I think, I'm feeling a little weak…" He ends his sentence on a moan, which is more theatrical than pain-filled.

"We could get the doctor back in. He did say if the pain got worse he could inject you with painkillers," Knox offers.

"An injection?" G-Pa pales. "That's not needed. I just need some rest, is all." He pretends to yawn.

"We should leave you." My wife locks her fingers together.

"You take good care of her, you hear me?" G-Pa glares at me from across the room. "I don't want to hear any complaints from her."

She bites down on her lower lip, probably to stop herself from slinging a host of grievances against me. Problem is, it makes me wonder how it would feel to have those lips wrapped around my cock and her fingers digging into my thigh as I grip her jaw and —

"Edward, did you hear what I said, boy?" G-Pa booms.

"Yes, you want the family together for Sunday lunch." *Kill me already.* An entire afternoon with my half-siblings is not my idea of a relaxing weekend, or a relaxing anything. Or anything approaching relaxation. The only thing I want right now is to take my wife home and find a way to make things up to her. Perhaps, she'll allow me to hold her and sniff her hair, and if I apologize enough, she might let me bury my dick inside her tight, moist hole.

"That's right. I expect to see the both of you there."

"I'm sorry but —" I begin but my wife interrupts me.

"Of course, G-Pa, we'll be there."

"But —" I begin, but she scowls at me over her shoulder. Pathetic arse that I am, I'm so grateful for the fact that she acknowledges my presence—only the second time since we left the lighthouse earlier today—that I zip my lips and watch as she turns back to Arthur.

She leans over and kisses his cheek. "You should rest up. We'll see you for Sunday lunch."

Which means, she's not planning to leave me… Yet. Which gives me time, until Sunday, to woo her back. She wanted to be dated and courted. Well, I'm going to re-invent the meaning of those words. I walk over and hold out my hand. She looks at it, then back up at me, and I'm sure she's going to refuse, but then she places her much smaller hand in mine. The stress in my shoulders leaches out. Fucking hell, if every minute of my time is going to be spent bathed in so much tension, then I'm headed for the coronary my wife predicted when she first set eyes on me. By then, I already knew everything it was possible to know about her, but it wasn't a replacement for spending time with her. For discovering her likes and dislikes, how she wrinkles her forehead when she's thinking, how she sighs when she sips her coffee, how she makes those little moans at the back of her throat when she's aroused, how her lips thin when she's angry with me.

And yet, I can't regret the fact that I invaded her privacy. That I watched her unobserved. That I snooped around her life. That, since I set eyes on her, I've made sure to have eyes on her all the time. How can I, when a part of me worries that I won't be able to prevent bad things from happening to her? Is this how it feels to love someone? When your heart feels like it's being torn out your chest, and every time you think about how vulnerable they are, your chest tightens, your lungs burn, your pulse rate shoots through the roof and you're sure you're having a panic attack?

"Ed?" She squeezes my hand. "You okay?'

She called me Ed. Not Eddie. But also, not Edward. That's another sign there's a chance here for me to put things right… Right?

When I don't reply, she grabs my collar, pulls me down, then goes up on tiptoe and kisses my lips.

59

Mira

He doesn't kiss me back. His lips are hard, his chest unmoving. He bent enough for me to reach his mouth, but other than that, I might as well be kissing a stone. Shit, what possessed me to do this, in the first place, and when I'm so pissed off with him? I'm sure it had nothing do with that haunted look in his eyes, or the granite-hard set to his jaw, or how he looked at me like it was the last time he was seeing me. Like he expected me to run out of there and never look back.

And I was tempted, don't get me wrong. But also, the part of me that's responsible and dutiful and never gives up in the face of a challenge, the part of me that already loves his grandfather like my own, the part that is still attracted to him, so help me god, the part that hasn't forgiven him for how he got me here but cannot resist the urge to be physically close to him—that part took over. Before I could talk myself out of it, I acted on the urge to take his mind off whatever he was thinking, whatever caused that despairing look in his eyes.

And now, he's not reacting. Ugh, this is a mistake. I begin to back away, but he swoops his hand around my waist, drags me close, back on my tiptoes, and regardless of the fact his family is watching, he kisses me

—not the polite peck on the lips I attempted, but a nip on my mouth until I part my lips so he can slide his tongue over mine and suck on it, and share my breath, and sip from me until I lose my balance and sway against him. At which point, he pulls me closer, wraps his arm about my waist, and announces we're leaving.

I have just enough time to register the satisfaction on G-Pa's face, the mild surprise on Nathan's, and the smirk on Knox's before we're out of there and he's hustling me toward the car.

"What's the hurry?"

He doesn't reply. He merely walks me to the car, tears open the door on the passenger's side, all but throws me in, and proceeds to snap the seatbelt around me, before he takes the driver's seat. His door slams shut, and he grips the steering wheel, but he doesn't start the car.

"Ed?" I ask softly. "What's wrong?"

"What's wrong is that you should be hating me now. You should be telling me go take a long walk off a short pier, and never set eyes on you again."

"I'm tempted," I confess.

"And yet, you kissed me."

"I, uh... G-Pa was watching, and it seemed like a good time to convince him the marriage is genuine, and you... You looked so desolate."

"I *am* desolate...without you."

I shake my head and glance away. "Don't. Please, don't make this more difficult."

"Why *did* you kiss me?"

"Told you already, it was all an act to convince your grandfather about the veracity of our wedding."

"Didn't seem like an act."

"Just because there's chemistry between us doesn't mean anything. And just because I kiss you, doesn't mean I've forgiven you for everything you did."

His fingers tighten on the steering wheel. "I'm sorry I crossed boundaries I shouldn't have. I'm sorry I hurt you. I'm sorry I upset you. I'm so sorry it's causing you so much distress, but"—he swallows—"it helped ensure you were safe and well, and given a choice, I'd do it all over again."

I whip my face in his direction. "Are you hearing yourself? Have you crossed the line so many times that you can't tell what's right and wrong? Have you forgotten what it is to be a decent human being?"

"That, I never was." He laughs without humor.

"You were a priest and served your parish; you must have been a decent human being then."

"I was, and then I wasn't."

"What do you mean?" I frown.

"I walked away from my faith. Then I turned my back on my best friend. I couldn't face the fact the woman I thought I loved chose him over me. I was envious about their happiness. I was envious of them. That's how far I had fallen."

"You were human."

"I couldn't stand to see them together."

"Understandable."

"I hid away, hoping to get my life back together, but I flitted from one focus to another, until I saw you. I saw you and my world rightened."

"You...can't tell me all this, Edward. It doesn't make what you did right."

He blows out a breath. "Then tell me how to put it right, Mira, because I have no fucking clue how to make things up to you."

"You have to stop this entire tracking me and having eyes on me and following my every movement baloney, Ed."

He shakes his head. "I... I'm not sure I can do that."

"You have to." I set my jaw. "And you need to tell me why you feel compelled to shadow my every move. Why are you convinced I am in danger? Is it because of the incident?" I scrutinize his features. "Is that what's making you paranoid about my safety enough to have me followed? Do you have to have eyes on me because that's the only way you feel reassured?"

He squeezes his lips together. "I told you I need more time to tell you about what happened."

He must see the disappointment on my features for he blows out a breath.

"Belle, I—" He rubs the back of his neck, "I want to tell you what happened. I swear, I do. And I will, I promise. Just give me a little time okay?"

A crushing sensation squeezes my ribcage. My shoulders feel heavy. I thought...he might make up for what he did by sharing more of himself. I refused to let him down in front of his family; I wouldn't walk out on him or show my anger toward him in front of them. Did I do that because I wanted to use it as leverage against him? Maybe. I think a part of me hoped it would demonstrate goodwill and encourage him to trust me. Maybe it would put enough pressure on him to reveal the secrets from his past. But it didn't work.

I know I'm not being fair. I know how painful this must be for him. I'm sure whatever happened to him contributes to his need to watch over me at all times, but if he won't tell me anything, how can I understand his actions? Then there's the fact he's been watching me for almost a year.

All this time, I've had a stalker, and I didn't even know it. And now that I do know, every rational bit of me is telling me to run away.

But there's another part of me saying I just need to listen to his explanation, and it will make sense. Maybe, it's not as creepy as it sounds. On the other hand, maybe, that's just wishful thinking. I'm just so overwhelmed, I don't know what to think… Or feel… Or do.

It's clear he cares about me, and he would never harm me. So that means he can't be a stalker, right? And sure, he wants me enough to take me to his place where he likes to hide out from the world, and he desires me enough to tie me up and mark me and fuck me. He's protective enough to be my shadow and follow my movements. And even though he hasn't been able to say the words, it's obvious he loves me. Only, that's not enough for me.

I want to be a part of his life. I want to help him, but every time I try, he shuts me down. Perhaps, he does trust me. Maybe, he doesn't want to talk about his past because his trauma is deep, and it will reopen old wounds to do so. He says he needs more time, which is understandable. I just need to be patient. Which I can't be when I'm working in such close proximity to him, and falling more in love with him every day, and becoming impatient when he doesn't open up to me. I need to find a way to get perspective on this situation.

"I need another job." I look away from him.

"No."

"I can't work in such close proximity to you. Not when I'm trying to find a way to be patient and give you the time you need to come to terms with your past."

His jaw tics. "Your life is with me."

"Not when you can't let me help you. I'm trying to be understanding, but it's difficult for me to watch you in pain and not do anything about it. I... I think we need some space."

"No, we don't." He flattens his lips.

"You asked for more time to tell me what happened. Surely, you can extend the same courtesy to me?"

He draws in a breath as conflicting emotions flit across his features. "You don't want to be my assistant?"

"I... I *can't* be your assistant. I need to find some perspective on this situation. Surely, you understand that?"

He stays silent for a few seconds, then nods. "Okay."

"Okay?" I blink.

"Instead of working for me, you can set up and run the workplace nursery, as we discussed."

I hesitate. *That's something I'd love to do.*

"You'd be helping the others who work in the building, who need childcare so they can work without this weighing on their mind."

He knows I'm thawing and he's pushing his advantage. *Of course, he is. That's the kind of man he Is. You show him a weakness, and he makes the most of it. I even told him that's one of the things I admire about him, so how can I get angry?*

"Okay." I turn to him.

"Okay." His shoulders relax.

"And you'll stop monitoring my movements."

His chest rises and falls. "If that's what you want."

"I do." I swallow. "And one more thing..."

He turns to me, and there's a mixture of fear and resignation in his eyes. "What is it?"

60

Edward

"Didn't expect to see you at poker." Sinclair blows out a cloud of cigar smoke from the other side of the poker table. "Shouldn't you be on your honeymoon?"

"Been there; done that." I train my focus on my cards. The image blurs in front of my eyes. I reach for my twentieth—or is it my thirtieth?—cup of coffee of the day in a bid to clear my vision. This is what happens when you're running on three hours of sleep. I'm lucky I caught that. And only because I managed to snag her nightshirt from the laundry basket and buried my face in it. Y-e-a-p, I'm the pathetic sod who can't fall asleep without sniffing his wife's scent. That's what I've been reduced to since she moved into a spare bedroom down the hall. That's what she asked of me, and I couldn't say no. At least, she's still under my roof. That has to count for something.

It's been a week, and I've missed her every second of it. She also took charge of the on-site-nursery and had it up and running in five days. When that woman sets her mind to something, nothing gets in her way. To be fair, I'd already prepared the space and purchased the neces-sary supplies, but she interviewed, hired, promoted, and managed the hell out of it. I managed to watch from afar, managed not to interfere, managed to even have the cameras and bugs on her phones and Kindle de-activated, managed not to have any new ones installed in her guest room or in her new car. I can't lie to her on this again. Can't justify looking her in the eye and saying I haven't stuck to my word.

It almost killed me, but I did it. And if it means I follow her in my car to and from work, at a distance, to make sure she reaches her destination safely? Well, that's not a crime. I'm not engaging anyone else to do it. I'm doing what any good husband should do; I'm looking out for my wife.

Good thing no one around the table knows that.

"He doesn't look like he's been on his honeymoon. In fact, it doesn't look he's been on holiday at all." This, from Knox.

"Shut the fuck up," I grumble.

"It's the early days of being married, you'd be better off bonding with your other half and all that." This, from Nathan, who sounds like he doesn't give a fuck, either way.

"Who invited you here, again?" I frown.

"I did." Sinclair rolls the cigar to the other side of his mouth. "You don't mind, do you, ol' chap?"

I glare at him, but he merely shrugs. Of all the people, Sinclair should know Nathan is not on my list of favorite people, but he went ahead and invited him. Which is his way of telling me I need to build bridges with this man who's an equal decision maker in Davenport Industries. Or rather, equal decision-maker after my grandfather, considering he hasn't yet handed off full control to me. And Sinclair's right. Arthur has shown he trusts Nathan as much as me.

Given my adoptive father, Arthur's oldest son wants nothing to do with him, and my biological father who is also Nathan's father is dead, it makes Nathan his oldest grandson and the logical successor to Arthur's fortune. It also makes him my closest competitor for the position of my grandfather's heir.

Strangely, that doesn't bother me the way it might have before I met my wife.

Before I realized the most important thing in the world is taking care of her—her safety, her security, her happiness, her future. All of that takes precedence. It's disconcerting and, also, grounding, in an unexpected fashion. It's why I don't rise to the bait when Nathan nods his chin in my direction. "Trouble in paradise, I take it?"

"None of your business," I growl.

"It's affecting your performance at work, so it is my business."

I still, then glance up from my cards. "Explain?"

"You missed a crucial loophole in the takeover documentation for the Young Group. Of course, I spotted it and fixed it prior to signing the deal."

"What loophole?"

"One that would have cost us close to a million dollars, but it's been taken care of."

"I don't let loopholes slip by me."

"You did, this time." He jams his cigar between his lips. "Might have to do with the fact you leveraged this takeover for your marriage, and—"

I reach over and grab his collar, then haul him forward. "Shut the fuck up."

He smiles, the satisfaction in his eyes showing he's proven his point by getting a rise out of me.

"Let him go," Sinclair snaps.

I glare at Nathan. His smile grows wider. I tighten my hold on his collar, then release him. He sits back; so do I. But our gazes are locked.

"Thought you could control your temper better," he says in a mild voice.

"What do you want?" I square my shoulders. "Why did you accept Arthur's proposition of sharing the veto power?"

"I have enough money, thanks to my investments. What this brings me, is power...and the breadth of control that comes from being the joint CEO of the Davenport group."

"Joint CEO?" I frown. That's when my phone vibrates. I glance at the screen to find Arthur's name on the caller ID. I fix my gaze on Nathan and answer: "Arthur?"

There's silence, then, "I'm only G-Pa when your wife is around, I take it?"

It's my turn to stay quiet.

Arthur sighs. "What I'm going to tell you is going to upset you."

"You don't say?" I ask dryly.

"You're newly married, and I want you to focus on your wife, and—'

"Cut the bullshit and give it to me straight."

He blows out a breath. "I want you to share the CEO role with Nathan."

I glance up at Nathan, who's watching my reaction. He was expecting Arthur to call me, no doubt. I roll my shoulders. Somehow, I'm not as pissed off as I should be to hear this news from my grandfather. Maybe my wife is already softening me up? That must be the reason I haven't lost my temper yet. In fact, the thought of not having to shoulder the decision-making role on my own, having another ear with whom to discuss the daily challenges, is a relief. It means I'll have more time to devote to my wife. In fact, the thought of not being CEO, at all —*nope, not going there. You're not giving up the role you've been angling for because a woman, are you? Nope, no way, am I conceding defeat to Nathan already.* Not when I know Arthur's proposing this joint-CEO deal as some kind of test to ascertain who is best placed to be his successor. "Is that all?" I bark into the phone.

"Yes, I wanted to be the one to tell you—"

I hang up the phone. Yes, I hung up on my grandfather, the Chairman of the company. Yes, I should be more worried about the repercussions of my actions, but given I have him on the defensive, given he went back on his word and decided to make me *not* the CEO, but the *joint*-CEO of the Davenport group of companies, somehow, I doubt I have much to worry about. And if he's upset? I couldn't give a shit about it. Considering all I want to do is get out of here and back to my wife.

Nathan raises the cigar to his lips. "I take it, Arthur told you he's decided it's best you share the role with me?"

"I take it, you're not aware I've won this round?" I place my cards on the table, face up. It's a straight flush. Knox throws his cards down in disgust. Sinclair shakes his head and tosses his hand on the table.

Nathan slowly reveals his. I take in his Ace, King, Queen, Jack and Ten of Diamonds. "Guess it's me who wins." He smirks.

"Guess I *let* you win." I drain my coffee and rise to my feet. "I'm not giving up control of the company without a fight."

"Anything less, and it would be boring." He tilts his head.

I jerk my chin at Sinclair and Knox, then walk out of there and to my car. By the time I reach home, the anger inside me has coiled around my guts and poisoned my veins. I march up the stairs and throw open the door to her room, but she's not there. I enter, and it feels like I've stepped into a garden of apple blossoms. I'm instantly hard. My heart picks up speed. And my mind...

It begins to replay how it was to tie her up and bend her over the bed and fuck her. How it felt to fall asleep inside her and wake up and push my face in between her legs. How it felt to curve my body around hers and hold her while she snored those ladylike snores. I sit on the bed, reach for her discarded blouse and bring it to my face, and sniff. *Mistake.* My balls harden, and my pants tighten until I'm sure I'm going to come in them.

I drop her blouse and glance around the space, taking in her cosmetics on the dressing table, the half open door to her closet, the towel she's slung over the bathroom handle. Her books are on the bedside table, one of them annotated with post-it's sticking out from between the pages. The drawer below is half open. I walk around and pull it all the way, spying some very interesting gadgets.

Is this why she wanted to move to another room? So, she could pleasure herself...without my knowledge? So, she could orgasm while thinking of someone else? So, she could torture me with images of her moaning herself to sleep with some inanimate objects inside her while I'm harder than a stallion on a stud farm in the room nearby? I snatch up one of the vibrators, something thick and long and veiny, but I'm proud to say, it's not thicker or longer, or as veiny as my cock.

She could have the real thing; but instead, she's here stuffing this lifeless dildo inside her pussy... Inside *my* pussy. I bring it to my nose and sniff, and it's as if I'm back between her thighs. *Fuck.* I take another deep breath, when the hair on the back of my neck rises. I turn toward the door and find her standing there. She's wearing a pink skirt which stretches across her thick thighs, and a matching jacket with a blouse underneath that dips toward the valley of her cleavage. Color flushes the column of her throat, up her cheeks. "What are you doing here?"

61

Mira

"Give me that." My handbag falls from my grasp. I cross the floor, reach for the stupid vibrator, but he holds it out of my reach. I jump up, and he extends his arm. I leap onto the bed make a grab for it, but I'm nowhere near close to touching it. "That's mine," I protest.

In response, he lowers the vibrator, and when I try to get a hold of it, he steps away. He brings the device to his nose again and sniffs, the way I saw him from the doorway. Goosebumps pop on my skin.

"I washed it after I last used it." I tip up my chin.

"I can still smell your cunt on it."

I gasp, "You're filthy."

"I want to be filthier." He fixes me with that glare that has moisture rushing out from between my thighs. *No, no, no. I'm not going to let our mutual chemistry get the better of me.*

I walk to the other side of the bed and step down. "What are you doing here?"

"Checking to see if my wife's doing okay."

"I'm well, thank you. You can leave now."

"Not before you tell me what you're doing with these." He glances from the instrument in his hand to my open drawer.

"You're infringing on my privacy again," I cry.

He pauses. His shoulders seem to swell. I'm sure he's going to tell me off, but to my surprise, he nods. "You're right; I'm sorry."

He eyes the vibrator one last time, then slips it into the drawer with the other implements I have there. He shuts the drawer, then straightens and turns to me. "I'm sorry. I didn't mean to intrude. I came looking for you, didn't find you, then saw the open drawer and couldn't resist. I didn't mean to peek, I swear."

He apologized to me? His features are set in grim lines. His lips are flattened. He seems to mean it.

One week. I haven't seen him for a week. He's always gone when I wake up in the mornings and comes home much later than me in the evenings. At least, I think he does, because I never hear his footsteps go past the doorway of my room, no matter how late I stay up reading.

I moved out of my role as his assistant to work on setting up the childcare facilities on the second floor of the office building. I threw myself into getting it up and running. Things went smoothly, not least, because of the generous budget he allocated for the project. Turned out, he'd already organized the permits, as well as the space needed to set up the nursery.

I wanted to refuse to lead on the project, but the childcare facilities will benefit everyone, and the children deserve only the best. So, I swallowed my pride and proceeded with my plan.

Today was the first day we opened, and already, we're full, and with a waiting list. We had to turn away parents from the buildings nearby, with regret. The facilities are only for the employees of the Davenport group of companies. It's a crying shame that more companies didn't invest in such services for their staff. It only increases productivity, as many studies have proven, but big corporations still hesitate to invest in something so essential. Not Ed, apparently. I suppose I have our interactions to thank for that. If, because of me, children can benefit, then I almost didn't mind the fact that he was spying on me before we formally met. Almost.

"I think you should leave now." I cross my arms about my waist.

He nods, then stalks toward the door, pausing only to retrieve my bag from the floor and place it on the bed. He reaches the exit, when I call out, "Did you see me... take care of myself when you had cameras in my room in my father's house?"

He pauses, then nods.

Heat flushes my cheeks. That beat between my legs, which always flares to life when he's around, amplifies. "How could you do that?" I burst out.

"How could I not?" He turns to face me. "I wanted you. I knew I shouldn't; knew I was all wrong for you, but I couldn't let go of you."

"So you trapped me in this marriage?"

He curls his fingers into fists at his sides. "I wish I could say I'm sorry for influencing events so you find yourself here, but—"

"You're not?"

"How can I be, when you're more important to me than life itself."

"What you are is obsessed with me," I cry.

"I'd rather be obsessed with you than anyone else. I'd rather devote my life to taking care of you. All I want is to see you happy."

"So you'd release me from this marriage if that's what made me happy?"

He flinches, his jaw tenses, and he seems to force himself to unclench his fingers. He straightens his shoulders. "Is that what you want?"

I run my fingers through my hair. Tiredness grips me. My feet seem to wobble, and I sit down on the bed. "I don't know what I want."

He takes a step toward me, and I throw up my hand. "Actually, I do know what I want, for now. I need you to leave me alone."

"Have you eaten?"

"I don't want your sympathy. I don't want you to cook for me. I don't...want to see you, is all."

"Have you eaten yet?"

"Didn't you hear what I said," I snap.

He holds up his hands. "I heard you." He turns and leaves, his shoulders slumped. The door snicks shut behind him. And of course, I miss him. Which makes no sense. After how he treated me, how he got me to marry him under false pretexts, I shouldn't want him. I shouldn't miss him. I shouldn't go to sleep every night wanting to wake up next to him.

I'm sure it's because he's the first man I've slept with. The first man to bring me to orgasm, to show me it could be even better than my smutty books made it out to be. And for a while there, in that light-house, with the snowstorm raging around us, I was sure he was 'the one.' I thought I'd get my happily ever after. I didn't realize I'd fallen for someone whose heart is morally grey, and whose past holds secrets I'll never be privy to.

I climb into bed and curl up on my side. I should hate him. I do hate him… I think. But I also miss him. And there's nothing keeping me here. I could leave, go to one of my friend's places. But wouldn't that be running? Would that resolve anything? Staying under his roof is a constant reminder of him, of how it could be with him. But leaving… Images of him and our time together would only haunt me more. No, I need to weather this out the way I've done the storms in the past. On my own. Me, myself, and I. I smile. That's how I've always consoled myself. *I have myself.* And him. *Not him. Don't think of him.* I close my eyes and drift off until a knock on the door awakens me. I sit up and realize it's dark outside. I reach for my bag and pull out my phone. I've been asleep for an hour. I also have missed messages.

> Summer: Haven't heard from you since you got back. Are you ok?
>
> Gio: Bitch, how was the honeymoon? Why no word from you?
>
> Penny: Forgotten us already?

I haven't been in touch with any of them because… What am I going to say? I'm not used to having friends, let alone ones I confide in, and I want to tell them everything but… Not yet. How can I, when I don't know what to say? I drop my phone on the bed, head to the door and open it.

There's a tray on the floor, with a bell-shaped cover on it, the kind they use in hotels for room service. I look up the corridor, but the door to Ed's room is shut. I pick up the tray, shut the door with my hip, then walk to the bed and place it there. When I pull off the lid, my gaze widens. Vegetable lasagna, with a slice of chocolate cake on the side. There's even a small bottle of red wine and a glass.

I glance at the door, again. Ed must have cooked it for me—or his housekeeper might have. He mentioned to me he has staff, although I haven't seen anyone around. But someone's cleaning the house, and there are cooked meals in the refrigerator. So, maybe he didn't cook it, but he took the trouble to bring it up to me.

Tears prick my eyes, and I wipe them away angrily. Why should I feel moved by that? He's not doing anything out of the ordinary. He also didn't ask me where I was so late — I'd been working getting everything sorted at the nursery, and it was barely ten p.m. by the time I got home but the husband I know would have asked me where I'd been — No, he wouldn't have allowed me to come home on my own. And I know he wasn't tailing me because he was in my room when I walked in.

Unless he has cameras on me in the nursery? There are the usual security cameras there, but I haven't noticed anything else. *Not that I'd know what to look for.* I dig my heels into my eyes. *Argh, I have to stop thinking like this. He promised not to do it anymore, but I'm still not sure if I can trust hjm. And I'm tying myself up in knots. Maybe I should just go and confront him? Yes, that's it; I'll just ask him the question. Otherwise, I'm not getting any sleep tonight.* I glance at the food, and my stomach rumbles. *Let me ask him and I can come back and eat afterward.*

I march out of the room, then down the corridor. I tap on the door, but there's no answer. I knock more loudly, then wait.

When there's still no reply, I push open the door to his bedroom and enter. A bedside lamp is on, casting a golden glow over the bedroom. The sound of the water running reaches me. I walk past the bed and toward the open door of the bathroom. It doesn't even occur to me to stop. I should leave, but my legs don't heed the warning.

I slip inside the bathroom, and the heat surrounds me, embraces me, seduces me...leads me to where he's standing in the shower, fully clothed. One fist is pressed into the wall; the other arm hangs by his side. His head is bent. The water drips down his hair and plasters his clothes to his back, his butt, his thighs. I step into the shower, and he still doesn't notice me. His shoulders bunch; a shudder runs down his spine.

Is he... Nope, not possible. He's not... He can't be crying, can he? As I watch, he raises his fist and smashes it into the wall. The muffled crack splits the air.

"Ed, stop."

62

Edward

One second, the pain squeezes up my arm; the next, she's there. She slips into the space in between me and the wall of the shower cubicle, wraps her fingers around my wrist and urges me to lower my arm.

"Why did you do that?" She surveys the reddened skin over my knuckles. "Why did you hurt yourself?"

"I hurt you." I try to pull my hand from hers, but she holds on; and while I'm stronger than her physically… Emotionally, this woman is my rock. I've come to depend on her in ways I never thought were possible. I've come to need her for her sunshine, her warmth, the way she shines a light in the dark crevasses of my soul. How she illuminates the secrets of my past, treats me with compassion, and brings them to the front of my mind. She forced me to look in the mirror, to acknowledge the man I've become—bitter, unscrupulous, one without a conscience. One not above resorting to unethical means to get what he wants. A man who is the opposite of everything I ever hoped to be. A man who wants to stay true to his calling, to his vow to serve the greater good. Only, I hadn't faced the ghosts of my past.

Not until she processed all the wrong I'd done her and decided, shockingly, not to walk out on me.

Not until she reminded me—with the goodness of her nature, her generosity, her magnanimity, her kindness of spirit—to see the positive, the good in everyone and in any situation.

By being herself, she reflected back to me how in the wrong I was... I still am. How I shouldn't have let my ego get the better of me and twisted the circumstances around her to force her into this marriage with me. "I'm so sorry, Belle."

She looks up at me, and when our gazes hold, that chemistry between us heats up. The air grows thick, the heat in the air pushing down on us.

"Ed"—she swallows—"please don't punish yourself like this."

"I deserve all of this, and more, for how I changed the course of your life. You should have had the freedom to choose who you wanted to be with."

"That choice was never mine to make. Not when I was headed for an arranged marriage anyway. At least, I knew you...somewhat. I suppose, it was the lesser of evils."

I wince. "Why didn't you rebel? Why didn't you tell your father you could choose the man you were going to marry?"

"I thought about it. Perhaps, if I'd met someone else, someone I wanted to be with, I would have, but from the moment I saw you, there was this attraction, this longing, this need to be with you. And when I found out you were my arranged match, I thought all the stars were aligning. I didn't realize you'd manipulated things to look that way."

"Belle—"

She places her fingers on my lips. "And even now, after I found out just how much you engineered things so you could marry me... When I should hate you and want you out of my life, all I can think of is how much I miss you. I'm such a loser."

"You're not."

"I hate myself."

"But I love you."

Her gaze widens.

"I've wanted to tell you so many times over the past week, but I couldn't bring myself to. You...my wife, are far more courageous than I am. You're able to speak your mind, unlike me. You're able to share how you feel, while I… When it comes to the stuff that matters in life, turns out, I'm not the man I thought I was."

"But you are, Eddie. I don't know what the incident did to you, but I know it couldn't have been easy. And yet, you picked yourself up and moved on. You survived. You lost the woman you thought was meant to be your soulmate —"

"She's not; you are." I cup her cheek. "You're everything I prayed for all through those years when I was a priest."

She frowns.

"Oh, I don't mean I prayed to find a soulmate. But I prayed for peace, for a way to still the thoughts that never allowed me to sleep, the images from my past that haunt me. I asked for a way to release the hurt, the pain, the sorrow. And the only time I find any measure of stillness is when I'm with you."

The water pours down over the both of us. Her hair sticks to her forehead, long strands plastered to her cheek. I reach behind her and shut off the shower. The silence envelops us, punctuated by the drip-drip-drip of the last remaining drops of water. Then that, too, cuts out.

"Eddie, the way you twisted things around in my life —"

"Is unpardonable."

"The way you engineered the situation around me so I had to marry you —"

"Is reprehensible."

She swallows, then wraps her arms about her waist. "I should leave you."

"You should."

"But I'm not able to bring myself to."

Every muscle in my body tenses. My pulse rate shoots up further. And my heart… It stutters, then starts again.

"I hate myself for not being able to walk away from you."

"Don't." I go down on my knees. "Don't do that. I'll never be able to forgive myself if you do. You're an angel. The kind of woman I don't deserve. And I won't blame you if you hate me forever."

"I wish I could."

I take her palm in mine and kiss her knuckles. "I'm so sorry I hurt you. I truly am."

She cups my cheek. "I know what happened to you made you put up walls, so you'd come across as cold-hearted and uncaring about the consequences of your actions. It's why you pretended to be so unfeeling, when I know deep down you're anything but."

My heart booms in my ribcage; pinpricks of disgust course down my back. *Tell her, tell her.* I open my mouth, but nothing comes out. I try again, then shake my head.

Her lower lip trembles. "It's okay, Eddie. I know you'll tell me when you're ready." She half smiles, then pulling her hand from mine, she brushes past me and out of the shower cubicle.

I rise to my feet and follow her. Grabbing a towel from the shelf, I draw abreast and place it about her shoulders. "I'm sorry," I swallow. "I really am."

* * *

"Where the fuck are the sales reports? They were supposed to be on my desk an hour ago."

The woman on the other side of the desk pales. "I... I..."

I glare at her, and she takes a step back. "I... I..."

"Have you forgotten how to speak?"

"I... I..." She—whatever her name is—continues to gape at me like a dying fish. *Enough of this nonsense.* I rise to my feet. She yelps, then turns and scampers out of my office.

"Fuck!" I drag my fingers though my hair, then grab hold of whatever is nearest, which happens to be my empty coffee cup, and throw it in the direction of the doorway.

The man entering ducks—quick reflexes, I'll give you that—then straightens and smirks. "Getting your jollies by scaring your employees?"

"Get out." I point my finger at Nathan. "Out."

He prowls over to the window. "Nice view."

"I told you to leave."

"For a man who has the best office in the building, you sure don't pull your weight."

"The fuck you mean?"

"First, you almost cost us a million dollars; and now, you missed the board meeting."

"No, I didn't."

He merely stares at me over his shoulder.

Something in his gaze makes me reach for my phone and check my calendar. *What the—!*

"Exactly." He walks over and leans a hip against my desk. "You've been going to pieces."

"No I'm not."

"You also forgot poker night."

"I did?" I slump back in my seat. It's been a week since my wife walked in on me smashing my fist into the wall of the bathroom—it's intact, I didn't even scratch the surface. I did suffer some lacerations on my knuckles. Apparently, I'm not even strong enough to put my fist through a wall. Although, to be fair, it's tile. What's worse, though, is that I haven't seen her since. Her preschool is doing well; more than well. It's at full capacity, with a waitlist to get on the waitlist, or so my HR manager informed me.

I've tried to stay focused and attend my meetings and conference calls, but if you ask me what I did or said, I wouldn't have a clue.

Every evening, I get home, and after making sure she's eaten her dinner—my housekeeper has been instructed to keep meals ready and have them delivered to her room; she lets me know when she makes the delivery—I walk over to her room and stand in front of the door, hand raised and ready to knock.

But I never do. If I did, I'd be going back on the promise I made to myself to give her space. So, I stand there, knowing she's inside. Knowing she hasn't moved out—the house staff have confirmed she's there—but I never hear a sound from her room. I curl my fingers into a fist at my side to stop myself from beating down her door. I stop myself from insisting she open the door. I force myself to walk away because I'm done infringing on her personal boundaries.

Besides, what right do I have to have to talk to her or hold out hope for any kind of relationship when I haven't been able to share my past with her? She deserves to know how tainted I am. She deserves to know I'm not worth her attention, in any form. She deserves so much more, and I can't give it to her.

So, I content myself with the knowledge that she lives under my roof. She's my wife; nothing's changing that. Not even if she left me—which she hasn't. And if I still believed in a force greater than myself, I'd thank that presence. But I don't.

Instead, I bury myself in work... Or pretend to. But going by the fact I missed the meeting—which would have determined if I'm confirmed as the CEO—clearly, I'm not being successful at that, either.

Truth be told, I don't care. I curl my fingers into a fist. Enough of this pretending otherwise. *I. Don't. Care. I don't care if I'm no longer the CEO of this company. It doesn't matter if Nathan takes over my role. I no longer have to pretend to care for the things that I thought I once did.*

I loosen the tie around my collar.

"You okay?" Nathan frowns.

"Do I look like I'm okay?"

"You look like shit."

"You don't look so hot, either." I scan the hollows under his cheekbones. Not that I give a fuck, or that I want to indulge in any kind of banter, but the man's standing in my office with a furrow between his brows, and dark circles under his eyes. And clearly, spending time with my wife is rubbing off because I feel... I wouldn't say a sense of empathy, but definitely a smidgen of understanding, toward the worry in his eyes.

"What's wrong, didn't the old man confirm you as his heir yet?"

He gives me a curious stare. "As a matter of fact, he didn't."

"He didn't?"

"He's happy to keep the status quo going, with both you and me holding veto powers. He seems to think you need to be cut some slack, given you're newly married and all."

"Is that right?" I stroke my chin.

"Seems he has a heart. So much so, he insists I should be the next to marry if I want to keep my veto power."

I chuckle, then turn it into a cough.

"Something funny?" he growls.

"Funny? Of course, not."

"I was thinking..." He looks uncomfortable. "Ah—" He clears his throat. "I was thinking you might dissuade him about this notion."

"You mean, about you getting married?"

"Exactly." He nods. "Especially since, it's not like you're particularly happy after having done the deed."

"What gives you that idea?" I stiffen.

"The fact your wife is no longer your secretary—"

"We thought it best not to work in such close proximity, given we're married now. We wanted to, uh, not make things uncomfortable for those around us. Also, Belle's skills are better utilized setting up and running the childcare facilities. That job is more important than being my assistant."

"—and the fact that she takes the tube to work, while you come by car."

I stiffen. "She's an independent woman."

"And that the two of you missed Sunday lunch, despite the old man having asked you to attend."

"Fuck."

He nods. "So, it seems the two of you are struggling to figure things out."

"Early days of marriage. It's normal."

"If you say so." He doesn't sound convinced.

"In fact, the best thing the old man did was insist I get married if I wanted to stay on as the CEO."

"O-k-a-y?" He levels a disbelieving glance in my direction. "Of course, you didn't forget to send out a company-wide email letting everyone know about the child-care facilities your wife will be leading on for the company. An initiative which you should have informed me of, considering I'm joint-CEO—"

"I'm informing you now." I shrug.

"An initiative which has resulted in our employee satisfaction scores surging by fifty percent in yesterday's organization wide survey, which" —he strokes his chin— "in turn, is bound to increase productivity by at least fifteen percent. A fact which might even justify the unplanned investment behind this scheme you've already made."

My wife was right about how providing daycare services will impact productivity, after all. Apparently she's right about a lot of things. My phone buzzes. I pull it out of my pocket, glance at the screen, then jump to my feet. "I have to leave."

63

Mira

"I'm fine. It's probably because I didn't stop for lunch today." I try to sit up, the room tilts, and I find myself flat on my back again.

"You're not okay." Adela places a palm on my forehead. Demand for spaces in the preschool has spiraled so quickly, I need more help. When she volunteered, Ed signed her transfer to my department immediately.

"You're burning up," she murmurs.

"My throat did feel a little scratchy this morning," I admit.

"You need to see a doctor."

"Nothing some paracetamol won't sort out." I cough. "Just don't tell my husband."

"I called your husband," she says at the same time.

I gape at her. "Why did you do that?"

She blinks. "Uh, he's your husband? Also, he happens to be the CEO of the company, and I want to keep my job, and—"

"How is she?" Ed bursts into the reception area of the nursery, which is where my legs chose to give way from underneath me. He moves so quickly, his feet don't seem to touch the ground. He sinks to his knees next to me and rakes his gaze over my features. "Why is she so pale?"

"She has a fever…and mentioned a sore throat, and—"

"Call Dr. Weston," he orders her.

Adela looks between us, then nods and excuses herself.

He continues to stare at me, the look in his eyes so intent, that when he reaches for me, I flinch.

His throat moves as he swallows. He raises both of his hands, palms facing me. "I won't hurt you."

"I know."

"When I heard you'd fainted—"

"I was out for barely a few seconds."

All the color drains from his face. "A few seconds."

"It's probably because I'm dehydrated."

"Dehydrated?" He sways.

"Ed? Eddie?" I touch his hand, and he trembles, then seems to get a hold of himself. "I'm going to move you to the couch, Belle." He hesitates. "If that's okay with you?"

I blink. *He's asking me for permission to move me?* He didn't just scoop me up and march me over and sit down with me in his lap. And I'm grateful he queried me first, but also… I want him to do what he thinks is right for me, because I do enjoy it. I do. My head spins, and it's not just because of whatever bug I've caught. It's this constant warring inside of me where he's concerned that's tearing me up inside. I want to hold onto the independence I've fought so hard for all of my life. I want him to not give me a choice where my wellbeing is concerned. I want him to manipulate my body as he's always done because he knows what I need. And because I know when I tell him no, he'll stop.

It's because he wanted me so much, because he couldn't stand the thought of me belonging to anyone else, that he masterminded events so I ended up married to him. And while I'm not sure if I've forgiven him for that, the fact that he had such a strong yearning for me, that he desired me and longed for me enough to pull strings until I became his, is a powerful turn on.

"Belle?" His voice softens, "Please? I can't stand to see you lying on the floor."

"It's carpeted," I point out, then cough. And he seems to grow even more pale. His fingers curl into fists. "Belle, I'm begging you."

"Yes." I stop my lips from twitching. "You may carry me, but you can't place me on the couch."

"Where then?"

"Your lap would be better."

He draws in a sharp breath, then nods. "Your wish is my command." He scoops me up, then prowls over to the couch and sits down, gathering me close. I curl into his broad chest, turn my nose into his vest, and breathe deeply. That dark, spicy scent of him settles in my blood, and some of the tension drains out of my shoulders.

He balances me with one arm, then pushes the hair off my flushed forehead. His fingers tremble. Because I can't stop myself, I reach up and twine my fingers through his. "I'm fine, really."

"Really, you're not."

He places our joined fingers over my heart, as if to reassure himself that I'm here and alive.

"When I got the message that you'd collapsed, I felt like I was going to die. I felt like everything inside me had dissolved and was floating away into the ether. I felt so helpless. It's all my fault."

I stare. "How is it your fault that I'm sick?"

His lips flatten. "I should have taken care of you. I should have paid more attention to you. I should have made sure you were taking your vitamins—"

"Why would you want to make sure I'm taking my vitamins?" I shake my head. "Honestly, the last thing I want is a helicopter husband."

"A helicopter husband?" He frowns.

"Yeah, a husband who constantly hovers over you and wants to make sure you're fine."

"What's wrong with that?"

"It can be stifling?"

"It's a way of showing I care for you."

"There are other ways of showing it... Like not trying to control everything in my life."

His jaw tics. "I'm trying, Belle, I swear. I'm trying to be the kind of man you'd be proud to call your husband, but I'm a little short on practice and—"

"What seems to be the problem here?" A man bustles in. He's tall and broad-shouldered and is wearing a tux.

"Wes." Edward jerks his chin.

"You do realize I'm a heart specialist." The man stares at my husband.

"You're a doctor. I trust you. End of story." Ed sets his jaw.

"You're a heart specialist?" I blink.

"A cardiologist," he confirms.

"There's nothing wrong with my heart."

"Of course, there isn't. My friends prefer I take on the role of family doctor, when it comes to their loved ones." He gives a long-suffering sigh. "And I can't refuse. It's almost routine they call me whenever I'm at a social occasion. So much so, I never leave without carrying everything I need to attend to these house calls."

"I'm so sorry he pulled you away from whatever event you were at." I gesture to his tux.

"I don't mind, and I know the only way to put this wanker's mind at rest is if I examine you quickly." He places his bag on the floor, pulls up a chair, then reaches for my wrist and takes my pulse.

"Uh, I fainted," I offer.

Ed interjects with, "She collapsed and was out for a few seconds, and —"

The doctor glares at him. "I'm talking to my patient."

"And she's my wife," he snaps.

"And if you want to see her well and on her feet again, you'll let me have a conversation with her," the doctor says in a steely voice.

To my shock, Ed lapses into silence.

I stare at the doctor with respect. "I'm Mira."

"Dr. Weston Kincaid." He half smiles. "Let's look at your throat." He does a quick examination, then reaches for his bag and pulls out a thermometer.

He takes my temperature, then makes a *hmm* noise. *Gosh, I hate it when they do that. Like they know something you don't. Which they do. But does that make me nervous? It does.*

My nervousness must communicate itself to Eddie, for his arms around me tighten. "You're going to be okay," he whispers.

"Yes, she will. Her tonsils are enlarged, and the lining of her throat shows signs of redness. She probably has a strep infection," the doctor declares.

"A strep infection?" Eddie frowns.

"It's been going around. Some of the children had it; I probably caught it from them." I shrug.

"I need to take a throat swab to confirm it."

"Go on then, what are you waiting for?" Edward pulls me into his side.

The doc reaches for his bag, then gestures toward us, while looking pointedly at Ed. "If you can give us some space — ?"

Edward only holds me closer.

"It's okay." I pat his chest. "I'll be fine."

He hesitates, then kisses my forehead, places me on the couch gently, and backs away.

The doctor takes the throat swab. A few minutes later, he reads the test results and nods. "It's as I thought. Any allergies I need to be aware of before I issue the prescription?" he asks me.

"No allergies," I say at the same time that my husband snaps, "She's not responsive to penicillin."

I turn to him. "Oh, I forgot about that, but how did you know?"

He merely tilts his head. "I made it my business to acquaint myself with your medical history.

Of course, he did. He knows everything about me, and I should definitely be pissed, but in a roundabout way, I'm also pleased he remembered.

"Oh, that's good to know. I can prescribe something in its stead." The doctor completes his examination and sits back. "I'd like you to come to my clinic tomorrow so I can draw some blood and run some tests."

"Blood? Tests?" Ed stiffens. "What's wrong with her? What are you not telling me?"

The doc sighs. "It's routine; nothing to worry about. I want to make sure she's not anemic."

"Anemic?" Ed's gaze narrows.

"It means lack of iron in the blood," I say in a soothing voice.

"I know what it is."

"Then you'll know, it's not serious, and I am prone to it. My vitamin D levels may have dropped, as well."

"What?" Ed looks down at me, then cups my cheek. "Oh, my god, that's not good."

"It happens when you're a woman." I resist the urge to roll my eyes. "Especially due to my, uh, heavy cycles."

"When did you last have your period?" the doctor asks in a casual voice.

"Uh, three… No, four weeks ago, now." I hesitate. "Maybe longer." Now, it's my turn to gulp. "You don't think… No… I, uh, I'm on the pill."

"Best to take the guesswork out of it and take a pregnancy test."

"A pregnancy test?" My head spins.

Behind me, Edward's chest hardens. "Why don't you give her a full check-up when we see you tomorrow?" Ed growls.

I slap at his chest. "Excuse me, you could ask me if I want a full check-up done."

He squeezes his eyes shut, and when he opens them, there's remorse in them. "Would you get a full check-up done? Please?" he adds in a cajoling tone. His eyes are soft, and there's a plea in them. One I can't turn down. Especially since I can feel the tension strumming under that massive chest of his.

"Okay." I turn to the doctor. "What time do you want me there?"

"There's no way I can be pregnant." I wring my hands.

The doctor had emailed the prescription over to the pharmacy and he'd sent his team to pick it up. He'd also warned them that it had better have reached his home before we did. I exchanged glances with Adela, who merely shrugged and told me she would lock up the place before leaving for the night.

Ed called for his car, then carried me to it, placed me gently in the back seat and got in with me. I was surprised he wasn't driving but I kept quiet. Best not to add to whatever gamut of emotions he seems to be experiencing. For a man who, until a month ago, had trouble conceding he felt anything—let alone, giving voice to his feelings—he seems to have done an about-turn. I've never seen him this perturbed.

Now, he makes me lay down in the backseat with my head in his lap. Then, he proceeds to caution the driver to go slowly, until we're barely crawling along. He made sure I downed a bottle of water and some fruit before we left the office. And only because I insisted I couldn't eat anything else.

I try to sit up, but he coaxes me to lay down again. His thigh feels like a column of steel covered with the smooth fabric of his pants.

"I really can't be. I haven't missed a day of my contraceptive pills."

"Maybe you did, and you don't realize it." He strokes my hair. I swallow around the ball of emotion in my throat. He's so tender, so gentle. So everything I need.

"I'm strict about it. I need to take them to regulate my cycle and manage my cramps. But then, I've never been late, either..." My voice fades. *Which means, I might be pregnant.* The realization sinks in. *I might be carrying a child. His child. Ed's child. A family. I might have a family of my own. The family I've always wanted.*

But Ed... He wasn't very receptive when we spoke about children. But then, he also said we wouldn't be sharing a bed, and that there would be no sex—both of which haven't held true. Of course, there are other things he didn't tell me, either. All of which now seem secondary to the fact that I might be pregnant with his child.

When I look up, he's staring out the window.

"Eddie," I whisper, "how do you feel about it?"

"About what?"

"My possibly being pregnant? My—us having a baby?"

"How do *you* feel about it?" He looks down at me, and his voice is cautious. His features are back to being that bland mask I can't read.

"You know how much I want a child."

He lowers his chin, "Does that mean you'd be happy?"

"It means if I am pregnant—and that's a big if, but *if* I am—I'd be very happy." I search his features. "And you?"

64

Edward

"When I found out you'd collapsed—" I look into her eyes.

"I fainted," she insists.

"—I made a deal with God."

"With God?" She frowns. "I thought you and He weren't on speaking terms?"

"We weren't, but when I saw the text message from Adela, my heart stopped. I thought I was going to die. I knew then, I couldn't go on without you. I knew then, I'd do anything to make sure you were okay. I..." I swallow. "I promised Him I'd drop the grudge I have against Him. I promised I'd believe in Him again. All he had to do was make sure you were okay when I got to you. Those minutes it took to reach you as I ran down the steps, were the longest of my life."

"You ran down twenty floors?" She gasps.

"Of course, I did. No way, was I going to wait for the elevator to arrive."

"Eddie, you—" She shakes her head. "You're the most confusing person I've ever met."

"Look who's talking. When I look at you, I see my biggest passion, my only love, my greatest regret."

"Because of you how you got me to marry you?"

"Not only." I blow out a breath. "There...there are things I need to tell you."

"About your past."

"Also that."

Her forehead furrows. "What do you mean?"

"Let's get you inside the house and make sure you eat something, then take the medicine the doc prescribed, and—"

"And you're delaying the inevitable."

I rub at my temple. "Just give me this, Belle, please." I cup her jaw. "Just a little more time for you to look at me without hate in your eyes."

She sits up. "I would never hate you."

"No more than what you already do?"

"I'm pissed at you." She narrows her gaze. "And I don't understand you. And you confuse me a lot with your actions. And I don't want to say I'm fine with your stalking tendencies and how you're obsessively into me, enough that you didn't want me to marry anyone else, enough for you to plant devices in my room and in my Kindle, but a part of me almost understands—" she squeezes the bridge of her nose, "I can't believe I'm saying this but, it's almost flattering that you want me so much. So no, I don't hate you, but I don't agree with your methodology, either."

"And I can only agree with everything you say."

"Why are you being so agreeable?"

"Why shouldn't I be?"

She purses her lips. "I think I prefer you being your usual alternating between growling at me and being cold toward me."

"All of which has always been a cover for the depth of what I feel for you."

"I know that now. So I doubt you can tell me anything more that will make me hate you."

"We'll see." I square my shoulders.

"You sound like you want me to hate you."

"Maybe your hate is easier than any other emotions. Maybe I'm scared that one day, you'll love me, and then what am I going to do?"

"You'll accept it, Eddie. That's what you'll do. You'll accept the fact that you can be loved. That you're worthy of it. Whatever happened to you in the past does not define you. Your future doesn't define you. Power and money don't define you." She places a hand over where my heart beats in erratic thumps. "This… What is inside you, this goodness, this man who has always wanted to help others, who still helps others —"

"No, I don't."

"You signed off on the quotes for the nursery, and then for Adela to help me out, without blinking an eye."

"I had a vested interest in that."

"You give away a lot of what you make from your investments to charity."

I blink.

"Don't deny it. I found out from Summer, so I know it's true."

"Hmm, I need to have a talk with her," I scowl.

"That's what I mean. You do these things and then pretend it doesn't mean much, when it does. Most people who have money use it to make more for themselves. They don't go about donating it to charitable causes."

"I don't need the money, so I donate it. It doesn't mean anything." I raise my shoulder. "Besides, it makes a difference between life and death for so many others."

"That's what I'm talking about. You don't even realize how much of a softie you are."

I blink slowly. "You sound like you almost like me."

"I don't dislike you," she murmurs.

I suppose, that's a start. And why am I trying to talk her out of it, when all I want is for her to feel a fraction of what I feel for her?

"I just wish you'd realize, it's as important for you to learn to accept as it is to give. If you can't accept what people offer you, then it's as if you look down on the people who accept from you."

"What? No. I'd never do that."

"Then why is so difficult for you to receive the concern I have for you?"

She's right. I've shunned anybody showing understanding about how the incident affected me. I hate it when people pretend to identify with what I've been through. I turned my back on any sympathy my parents tried to show me. Not that they tried particularly hard, but I rebuffed any efforts on their part. I made it difficult for them to care for me in any way. I've even kept the Seven at arms-length, despite the fact we went through the incident together. And when Baron and Ava got together, I distanced myself from both of them. I stopped communicating with Baron—the one person who knows exactly what I went through; he was there with me. He suffered almost everything I did. *Almost.* For even he doesn't know the extent to which I was hurt... But he has a good idea. More than the rest of the Seven. More than anyone else, except her. And it's not because I've told her much, but she's looked behind my facade, she...has an inkling.

"You're right." I tuck my elbows into my sides. "It *is* difficult for me to accept help from anyone."

"Including me?" She peers up into my eyes. "Will you let me help you?"

65

Mira

He scooped me up in his arms and carried me inside our—his—okay *our* home. I was feeling better, and wanted to tell him so, but I also sensed this need inside him to take care of me, so I let him. He carried me into the living room and placed me on the couch. Then, proceeded to fluff the cushions behind my head and pull a comforter over me. Then, he handed me my Kindle, along with a large glass of water he commanded me to drink and told me to occupy myself while he got my dinner.

Yep, he did order me there, like the bossy-pants he is, but it felt right. I barely read a couple of pages before he came back with a tray of food. He'd heated up the chicken soup—which he'd called ahead and asked his housekeeper to prepare. There was also crusty bread, which he buttered for me, and he made me eat it all as he watched. Then he gave me the medicine Doc Weston had prescribed—something safe, in case I am pregnant. I told Ed I was feeling better, but he'd hear none of it. He insisted I swallow it down, then offered me a cup of herbal tea.

When I finally lean back with a sigh, he slips onto the couch and replaces the cushion under my head with his thigh. For a few seconds, I lay there, once again, enjoying the feel of his firm flesh. I rub my palm over the silky material of his pants, and he places his much bigger palm over mine.

"Don't," he murmurs.

"Why not?" I look up at him.

"Because we need to talk."

"I don't want to talk," I pout.

His features soften. He pushes my hair back from my cheek and tucks the cover under my chin. "Tomorrow then."

"Okay," I murmur.

He begins to drag his thumb over my lower lip, then catches himself. "What do you want to watch?"

"Watch?"

"On the streamers. I have all of them."

"Anything romantic, like—"

He groans, "Don't tell me *The Notebook*."

"—*The Notebook*." I nod.

He rubs the back of his neck. "Okay."

I blink. "You don't mind watching *The Notebook* with me?"

"There's a first for everything, I suppose." He raises a shoulder.

"You've never seen *The Notebook*?"

"Not my normal taste, but I've heard about it, like it's the most romantic movie ever."

"It is," I agreed with a smile.

"Also I've been… Otherwise occupied for a lot of my life."

"You took your role as a priest seriously, didn't you?"

He hesitates, then rubs at his stubbled cheek. The sound of his nails over his whiskers pulses goosebumps over my skin. Oh, my gosh, I'll never not be attracted to him. And at some point, he discarded his jacket and rolled up his shirt-sleeves so the tendons of his veiny arms flex. And everyone knows, forearm-porn is the easiest way to turn on a girl. Also, he's still wearing his vest, and the way it contours the planes of his chest should be banned.

"—Belle, you okay?"

"Yes, of course, why do you ask?" I clear my throat.

"You had a dazed look in your eyes." He touches my forehead. "Your fever hasn't increased, has it?"

"Nope, the medicine I took is making me drowsy, is all."

He runs his fingers though my hair. "You should rest."

"You evaded my question again."

He sighs. "There's nothing to evade. I tried to deliver on my responsibilities toward my congregation with the utmost sincerity. I felt I was making a difference in peoples' lives. I tried to be a spiritual guide, a counsellor for couples, and I loved teaching young minds. It was deeply satisfying and yet"—he swallows—"something was missing. I knew I wasn't addressing the real reasons I was pushing myself so hard to feel needed. And when I had a crisis of faith, I left."

"You did what felt right at that time."

"I turned my back on everything that defined me." He firms his lips.

"That took courage."

"That was cowardly of me," he says at the same time.

I begin to sit up, and he doesn't stop me. "It's all about how you look at things, isn't it? It's your mindset. You think you were running away, I think you knew it was time to leave and find yourself, so you could deal with whatever happened earlier in your life."

His lips curve. "When did you become so wise?"

"I was born wise." I smile back.

Our gazes hold; the air between us shimmers and grows heavy. My thighs clench, and my pussy feels like Niagara Falls opened up between them. *OMG, I did not just think that!*

"I can read what's on your mind," he warns.

I scoff, "You cannot."

"I did, but I'm not going to elaborate because you need your rest." He urges me to pillow my head in his lap, then reaches for the remote. Between the familiar scenes of *The Notebook* playing on the screen and the gentle touch of his fingers combing through my hair and whispering down my neck—which is both soothing and a turn on—a warmth steals over me. I close my eyes and drift off. I have a vague recollection of him carrying me to bed, me protesting, and him kissing my forehead.

He slides me into bed, pulls the covers over me ,and I'm asleep again. When I wake up, dawn is breaking through on the horizon. The silver light pours through the un-curtained windows. I turn on my side and realize, he's stretched out on the bed, on top of the covers. He's still wearing the same shirt with his sleeves rolled up, and he's folded his arms over his vest. I take in his shoulders, his chest, those lean hips, the powerful thighs, his bare feet. He must have discarded his socks at some point in the night. His toes— *Oh, my god, his toes—why do I find the sight of them so erotic?* I manage to drag my gaze back to his face, and the sight of his thick eyelashes fanned over his cheekbones, that hooked nose, the mean upper lip and that plush lower lip, now parted slightly in sleep, draws me to him.

Before I can stop myself, I throw off the covers, then inch closer. I play my mouth over his, not touching him, but drawing of his breath. That scent of woodsmoke surrounds me. That sharp tang in the air, which reminds me of an incoming storm, a sensation I always associate with him, envelops me. I lean in and touch my lips to his. That's when he opens his eyes.

66

Edward

Her blue gaze holds mine. Her breath mingles with mine. She keeps her mouth on mine, doesn't back away, and I let her kiss me. She licks my lower lip, and my groin tightens. She nips on my mouth, and it takes everything in me not to throw her over on her back and plant my hips between her thighs and grind into her to show her exactly what she's doing to me. Instead, I curl my fingers into fists, push them into the mattress, and savor the sensation of her exploring my mouth. She drags her tongue across the seam of my lips, and my blood begins to thud at my temples. She takes small bites of my chin, down the column of my throat, and nudges her nose into the hollow between my collar bones. She draws in a deep breath, and it's my head that spins. I feel the beat of her heart against mine, the flutter of her fingers as she clutches at my vest, and when she reaches for the button of my waistband, I wrap my fingers around her wrist. She looks up at me, a question in her eyes.

"We need to talk."

A flutter of fear pulses over her features, then she nods. "Okay."

I cup her cheek. "I love you." I bring her forehead to mine and draw in her familiar scent.

"I love you," she whispers against my mouth.

And I want to kiss her. Want to move her on her back and press her into the mattress and show her how much I worship that gorgeous body of hers, but I will not. Not until I've come clean with her. And if she decides she never wants to see me again, then I'll have to accept it. I'll have to walk away from her and spend the rest of my life making it up to her. I'd do everything possible to win her back. I have to. I don't have a choice because without her, I'm nothing.

She brushes her knuckles over my cheekbone. "Eddie?"

"Yeah." I open my eyes. "Let me make you some breakfast."

"That was good." She scoops up the rest of the omelet with her bread and chews on it. "I shouldn't be eating like this."

"Like what?"

"Like I have a healthy appetite."

"You do have a healthy appetite."

"And everything I eat goes straight to my thighs."

I take in the faded T-shirt and sweatpants she changed into earlier and shrug. "All the more for me to bite on."

She reddens. "I can't believe you said that."

"And I can't believe you'd put yourself down. I love your curves, love the thrust of your tits, the swell of your hips, the fleshy spread of your thighs that invites me to park my head between them and close my mouth around your juicy core."

"Oh—" she swallows.

"Not to mention, your peach of an arse which I can barely keep my hands"—I flex my fingers—"and my teeth"—I snap them—"off."

She shifts in the chair. "Okay, fine, I get the picture."

I push away my half-eaten plate. "I threw your contraceptive pills away."

She laughs. "No, you didn't. I have them in the drawer of my bedstead."

"I replaced them with multi-vitamin tablets that look exactly the same."

"Eh?" She blinks. "You replaced my oral contraceptives with multi-vitamin pills?"

I nod.

"What?" She shakes her head. "Why?" She drags her fingers through her hair. "You're not making any sense." She swallows.

"I…realized I want to have children with you, after all."

"And you couldn't have simply told me that?"

"I couldn't."

"Why not?" She jumps up to her feet and slaps her open palm onto the top of the island where we're seated. "You knew I wanted them! I would have been happy that you did, too. I"—she shakes her head—"I need time to process this." She turns and begins to walk away.

"I'm sorry. I should have been upfront with you. But I was scared…" *There, I've said it. Another confession.* And, once again, I feel lighter. It took giving up the cloth to understand the power of speaking the truth.

She stops and turns to face me. "Scared?"

"Scared that when I finally tell you what happened to me with the incident, you won't want to have my child."

She scoffs. "Nothing that happened to you would ever change my mind about having your child. Since the moment I saw you, all I wanted was to be yours and have a family with you. Do you understand?"

"I was kidnapped when I was twelve."

She freezes.

"So were the rest of the Seven: Sinclair, Saint, Weston, Damian, Arpad, Baron and me. We were in the same school, in the same class, and we were targeted by the same person. We were held for ransom. All except Sinclair, whose family wasn't as wealthy as the rest of ours. He happened to be in the wrong place at the wrong time."

"Oh my god, Eddie." She presses her knuckles into her mouth.

"We were kept blindfolded and tied up. Each of us was abused"—I swallow—"in different ways. Some of us emotionally; others physically. Baron and I—" I grip the edge of the counter. "Baron and I, we"—I squeeze my eyes shut—"we were held together. We were made to do things to each other. We—"

A soft touch on my cheek makes me snap open my eyes. "—you don't need to tell me anything more."

"I do." I curl my fingers around her wrist and tug on it. And when she lowers her hand, I weave my fingers through her much daintier ones. She doesn't resist, thank fuck. "Baron and Ava know what happened, but none of the others know exactly what went down. They suspect, of course, but they've never pushed me to open up. Not the way you have."

Her eyes fill with pain and empathy and so much love, and that's my undoing. This woman—she understands me the way no one has. I've been unfair to her; the way I've treated her is all wrong, and yet, she's here for me. "You should leave; you should walk away from me."

"That would be the easy way out."

"If you stay, it's going to be harder on you."

"Maybe,"—she squeezes my fingers—"but it'll be worth it."

"It scarred me, what happened. We were held for a month—"

"A month?" she gasps.

"By the time the cops found us, we had all suffered in different ways. It bonded us together, but it also made us feel different from everyone else. We didn't feel like we belonged. It made us emotionless, angry men who pursued wealth and power to fill that emptiness inside us."

"Were the perpetrators ever found?"

"Much later, and not by the police. Thanks to the investigators we employed over the years, we tracked down those responsible. But that's not all."

I look away then back at her. "The person who provided information about us to the kidnappers, and thanks to whom the perpetrators had enough leads to abduct the seven of us... That person walked into my church for confession when I was a priest."

She draws in a sharp breath. "What...what did you do?"

I shift my weight from foot to foot. "Turned out, he went to the same school as us, which is how he was able to spy on us. But he was repentant about what he'd done. He needed redemption. He wanted to confess his sins and be forgiven. And I... I couldn't forgive him."

"Of course, not."

I look into her eyes and all I see is understanding.

"He asked me for forgiveness, and I... I wrapped my fingers around his throat and squeezed the life out of him."

67

Mira

"You took his life?" I stare.

"I thought I had but I managed to stop in time," he swallows. "The kidnappers… They made Baron and me touch each other, and bugger each other, and… I hurt my best friend." He squeezes the bridge of his nose. "And to find the man responsible for everything that happened was in my church, confessing his sins and asking me for forgiveness, felt like a cruel twist of fate." He lowers his hand and meets my gaze. "I couldn't control the anger and the hate inside me from pouring out." He curls his fingers into fists, "I thought I wouldn't be able to spare his life."

"But you did."

An expression of anguish twists his features. "I was a priest. What I did went against everything I believed in. Everything I had spent my life in pursuit of, until that point."

"What you are is human." *And what I should be is more shocked.* I should leave. After all, I'm standing in the presence of someone who almost killed another person. Someone whose life was changed forever, through no fault of his own. Someone who was forced to do the most reprehensible things, which scarred him forever. Someone who's coming clean and sharing his deepest secrets with me. It's not easy for him to do so and yet, he's doing it anyway. *If I were in his place, would I have done the same thing? I'll never know.*

What I *do* know is, this is Eddie, my husband, and I don't hate him. Far from it, I'm finally beginning to grasp the motivations behind what he does. Why he's so aloof. Why he's put up so many walls between himself and the world. Why, he's so paranoid about my safety. Everything he's been through has taken his trust in the world and forced him to be ever-alert to the dangers around him. Finally, I understand him better. I get why he's so protective of me and fears for my safety. I square my shoulders.

"You did the right thing."

His gaze widens.

"I can't even fathom how you went through everything you did and are still a functioning member of society. If what you did helped you find some peace then, so be it."

"Belle," he whispers.

"Are you surprised I'm not freaking out more?" I half smile.

"A little." He lowers his chin.

"How can I be upset when, clearly, that man was responsible for the trauma that you and your friends had to deal with?"

He shakes his head, and his features take on a tortured look, "And I was supposed to teach and uphold the sacraments of my faith. I was supposed to help individuals navigate moral and ethical dilemmas. I was meant to counsel and support my flock and help them overcome sins and make amends. Instead, I committed the most heinous sin of all. Worse, I'm not sorry about what I did."

His shoulders shudder. All the color leaches from his face. A tear squeezes out from the corner of his eye, and I swear, I can see the child he used to be peeking out from behind his watery eyes.

I can't stop myself from throwing my arms about him. "Oh Eddie, I am so sorry for what you went through."

Another shudder rocks his big frame. His arms are tucked into his sides. He seems to be curling into himself, trying to make himself smaller and occupy less space. It's a contrast to the tall, broad, confident man who always knows what he wants and doesn't hesitate to go after what he sets his mind on, and... A part of me has always known it was a front. I've known he was hiding something inside, something that changed his life and impacted him in ways that not even years of therapy can undo, but this… What he's telling me is not something I could have imagined he went through. I knew it would be awful, whatever it was he was going to tell me—because I always hoped he would eventually tell me. But this…terrible secret of his… It's so much worse than I could have ever imagined.

I pull his head into the curve of my shoulder and hold him tightly. He feels cold, and distant, and yet, the little shiver that grips him gives away just how much he's suffering. "It's okay to hold me," I whisper.

He stiffens, and every muscle in his body seems to turn to stone. Then, he releases a breath. His body slumps a little, and he wraps an arm about my waist. I turn my face into his neck and take a long breath of Ed into my lungs. That spicy woodsmoke, the tang of electricity which ripples over my skin… All of it is so familiar, so very dear to me. "Oh, Eddie." I sniffle. "I wish you hadn't had to go through that."

"Me too." His hold tightens. "I really am so sorry for how I hurt you. I'm sorry I switched out your oral contraceptives."

"Why did you do that?"

"Because—" he swallows. "Because I was sure once you found out how I'm tainted—"

"You're not." I lean back in the circle of his arms. "You're not, Eddie. You came through the challenges thrown at you. You picked yourself up again and again. You moved on. You didn't give up."

"I don't deserve your beauty, your generosity, your love." He looks between my eyes. "I don't deserve you."

"That you don't," I murmur with a little smile teasing my lips.

That divot makes an appearance at the edge of his mouth. "But I want you. I want you so much, Belle. I love you, like I've never loved anyone else before. And at the risk of you hating me, can I say, I don't regret having eyes on you before you knew who I was."

"Ed!" I slap at his chest. "Take that back."

"I apologize, again, for infringing on your life without your permission"—he looks away, then back at me—"but it's because I knew you were there that I could carry on. It's because I knew there was a goddess who makes this world a better place that I could continue living. You gave me hope, Belle. You made me realize there was more to life than just the existence I was eking out. You gave me something to look forward to. Something to anticipate, something to aspire to. I knew then, if you were connected to me in some form, if I had you in my life, if I could have your love, in any small way, if—" He slides down to his knees and takes my hands in his. "I can't live without you Belle. And I'll do anything to make you happy. I'll do anything to make up for the grief I caused you. You mean everything to me, and I know my methods of showing it so far have been unorthodox—"

"—to say the least."

"Please give me a chance. One chance. That's all I'm asking. Let me show you I can be the kind of man you'll be proud to call a husband."

I'm already proud to call you a husband.

"Let me show you how good it can be between us, Belle."

"I already know how good it can be, but… You broke my trust, Ed. How do I know you won't do that again?"

"I won't." He brings my hands to his mouth and kisses the edges of my fingers. "I can't. Not when I know how close I came to blowing it all. You're my life, my breath, my heart, my everything. What can I do to make you believe that?"

"I'm not sure."

He peers into my features, then nods. "I deserve that." He sits back in his chair, still holding my hands in his. "I'll be here for you, Belle. Always."

"I know that. I also know you're a good man at heart. Which is why this is so difficult for me."

"Take your time." He half smiles.

"Thank you," I whisper.

He brings my fingers to his lips and kisses them again. Then he turns and pushes a paper bag in my direction.

"What's that?"

"Pregnancy tests."

"Oh," I swallow.

"I had them delivered, along with your prescription."

I make no move to touch the sack.

"It's best we find out for sure," he coaxes me.

I gulp. He's right, of course. But oh, my god, this is what I've always wanted, and if I'm not pregnant, what then? And what if I am? How does that change everything?

"It's okay; I'm here." He pushes the hair from my cheek. "Whatever the result, whatever you decide, I'm here for you."

"Okay." I rise to my feet, then snatch the bag and walk toward the bathroom at the end of the corridor. When I step in, he follows. "No." I turn to him. "Please. I need to do this on my own."

He looks like he's about to refuse, then steps back. I shut the door, lock it, then walk toward the counter and pull out the pregnancy tests. The blood drains from my face. I manage to pull out one of the pee-sticks, then place it on the counter. I look at the mirror and splash some water on my face. I can do this. I can. I pull down my yoga-pants, perch on the pot and pee on the stick. Then, I place it on tissue paper, clean myself up, flush, straighten my clothes, and walk back and forth on the bathroom floor.

"You okay?" Ed knocks on the door.

"Yes, just, ah… Waiting for the results." I wash my hands again, dry them, then sneak a look at the test. "No," I whisper. "No, no, no."

68

Edward

I hear her gasp, then the muffled thump of a body hitting the floor before the sound of crying reaches me.

"Belle!" I knock on the door. "Let me in."

She doesn't answer, just continues crying.

I try the handle, but it doesn't open. "Belle!" I rap on the door again. "Let me in, please."

The weeping seems to escalate, my heartbeat keeping pace. *Fuck… Fuck, fuck, fuck. It's my fault she doesn't trust me enough to be with her now when she took the test. And it's my fault she's not letting me in right now so I can comfort her. It's my fault I'm listening to my sweet wife cry and I'm not able to do anything about it.*

"Belle, please—" I swallow. "Please, baby, it's killing me to stand out here and listen to you weep. I'll do anything, anything to stop it; anything, Belle, please."

There's no response. The sound of her crying fades and there's silence. Dread is an anchor in my stomach, a twist in my guts, a burning sensation in my heart. I push my palm into the door and place my forehead against it. If this is how it feels to be helpless and not be able to do anything for the one person who is more important to you than anything in the world, I don't want to feel this again. I sink to my knees. Then, for only the second time since I left the priesthood, I beseech him, *Please, God, please help me. Give me one chance to set things right with her. I beg You, if You're there and if You're hearing me, allow me near her. Please, I—*

The door swings open. She stands in front of me. I look up into her features. Her nose is red, her eyes swollen.

"What is it, Belle?" I rise to my feet.

She shakes her head.

"Tell me, sweetheart." I move forward, and she takes a step back.

That anchor in my stomach drops to my feet. It feels like I'm drowning. I need to be strong. For her. "Belle, let me help you."

She locks her arms around her waist. "Okay."

"Okay?"

She nods.

"What do you want from me? Tell me, baby, please. I'll do anything. Anything to make things up to you. Anything to make you feel better."

"Anything?" She tilts her head. There's a feverish look in her eyes now. "Anything?" she asks in a shrill voice.

"Anything." I nod. "Whatever you want."

"I want you to fuck me."

"What?" I rear back.

"I want you to turn me over that countertop right now and fuck me. Can you do that?"

"Belle, no." I reach for her again, but she slaps me away.

"I'm not pregnant," she cries.

"You're not?"

Her features crumple, "I want so much to be a mother."

I close the distance to her, but she steps out of reach.

"I can't believe, despite your replacing my contraceptive pills, I didn't get pregnant." She hunches her shoulders. "What's wrong with me? How could I not have conceived? Why?" She begins to weep in earnest. This time, when I pull her to me she doesn't resist.

"I really wanted this child." Her voice breaks.

"I'm so sorry, baby." I kiss the top of her head, but she only weeps harder. And when she collapses against me, I pick her up, carry her out into the living room and sit on the couch with her in my lap. I rock her until she falls asleep, then I carry her to bed. I call the nursery at the office and arrange for Adela to cover for her absence. Then, I message Summer.

———

When she wakes up, I survey her features. "How are you feeling?"

"Not great," she groans and closes her eyes. "I have a headache."

"This will help." I hold out two Ibuprofen capsules. She takes them, along with the glass of water I offer her. Once she's swallowed the pills and chugged down most of the water, I place it on the nightstand.

She lays back against the pillows and takes in my features. "I'm sorry," she croaks.

"For what?"

"For my breakdown." Her lower lip quivers.

"You never have to apologize for sharing your sorrows with me. I want to be the one you turn to when things don't go the way you hoped they would. I want to be the one to help carry your burdens. I want to share your pain. Please, don't ever hide from me. To know you were suffering, and yet be unable to reach you... I felt like my heart was being torn out of my body." I catch her hand, then bring it to my mouth and kiss her fingers. "Besides, I'm as much to blame, Belle. I couldn't get you pregnant; I failed you."

She shakes her head. "Neither of us is to blame. It's not like everyone gets pregnant right away. Some women try for years and—" Her chin trembles.

"Shh, don't think about that. We'll tackle tomorrow together. For now, you need to rest and recover." I press my forehead to hers. "Close your eyes."

I let her sleep for a few more hours, not able to take my eyes off of her. My phone keeps pinging with messages from the office, but I ignore them. Funny how I thought the job and confirming my role as the CEO of the Davenport Group was a priority, when really, none of that matters. Life isn't about sitting at a desk, perusing spreadsheets, and signing mergers or steering acquisitions.

Life is a plus-size blonde with a heart so generous she could reform the grumpiest of souls. A woman whose smile lights up my soul. A woman whose gaze is like looking into the eyes of the divine. I swallow. A goddess who's shown me the error of my ways. Who's helped me make peace with Him. Something I didn't think would ever happen in my life. She swept into my life and turned it upside down.

She changed my mindset, turned my life inside out. She's shown me what it's like to be vulnerable. To share the parts of me I never have with anyone else. She…completes me, in a way I hadn't thought was possible. She makes me a better man. Someone who's rejoined the land of the living. Someone who can feel the range of emotions in their messiness and their predicaments. Someone who feels the highs and lows of being human. Of being here, in the now, and experiencing what it is to be alive. Someone who's able to see a future with her. And with our child.

When she told me she wasn't pregnant, a flash of disappointment gripped me. It surprised me because I never thought I'd have children. Not until she'd told me how much she wanted them.

For so long, the concept of a family was that of my parish. The people I served. Then, for a brief while, it was the hockey team when I had been their general manager. I wanted the best for all of them.

I function best when I'm looking out for others. I've never thought about what that means for me. Until she came along and began caring for me. She's the only one who looks at me like I'm her world. With her understanding and her love, she's changed who I am, until I no longer recognize myself. And all I want is for her to be happy. For her to get everything she wants. I take her hand in mine, then go down on my knees and place my forehead against our joined fingers.

69

____

Mira

The sound of a baby's crying percolates through my sleep. I must be dreaming. *Am I dreaming?*

"Oh, sorry, didn't mean to intrude," a voice says.

I fight my way up through layers of drowsiness to find Summer standing in the doorway, and in her arms, is a toddler. The baby whose crying I must have heard. Her gaze moves from my face to that of the man who's kneeling next to the bed. His fingers are twined with mine, and his forehead is pressed into the back of my palm. My fingers twitch. I want to reach out and run them through his thick hair. But before I can act on my impulse, he looks up at me. "I called Summer; I hope you don't mind?"

I shake my head.

"I thought it would be good for you to have some company—" He swallows. "—someone with whom you could talk?"

I nod, unable to speak. His features are drawn, and in the sunlight pouring in through the open window, he looks haggard. There are dark circles under his eyes, and his cheekbones are hollow. I, on the other hand, feel refreshed after having napped. Our gazes meet. There's warmth in his, and regret, and love, so much love. He catches my hand, then brings it to his mouth and kisses my fingers.

The baby yells again. Ed releases my hand, then walks over to Summer and holds out his arms. "Want to take a walk, little man?"

He blinks, then jumps into Ed's arms.

"O-k-a-y?" Summer looks stunned. "He's been stuck to my side since he woke up this morning. Which is why I brought him along."

"Can he eat blueberries?" he asks her.

"Yes, luckily, he hasn't exhibited any allergies."

He turns his attention back to the boy. "Whaddya think? Would you like some blueberries?" The kid babbles something, and Ed nods. "Blueberries, it is." He turns back to Summer. "Can I get you some coffee?"

"Yes, please," Summer says with enthusiasm.

"And tea and croissants for you, wife?" He looks at me over his shoulder.

OMG, I'll never get over how it feels when he calls me wife. Also, that's sneaky. If he continues to call me wife in that brandy-laced voice of his, I'll never be able to think straight. I'll never be able to decide what I want my future to look like. *Do I want to stay with him? How do I get past everything he's told me? How do I trust him again? And why is it, I still feel safe with him? Especially after he told me how he stalked me. How he took the life of another man.* My mind spins, and when I rub at my temples, he frowns.

"You okay, wife?"

I nod. "I'm good, just uh, still waking up, I think." I clear my throat. "And tea and croissants sounds wonderful; thank you."

He searches my features for another second, then the toddler tugs on his chin and draws his attention. "Okay, come on little man, let's get you some blueberries and milk, maybe?" He looks at Summer, who folds her fingers together in a gesture that says, *please and thank you and you are a lifesaver.* He walks out of the room, and Summer heads toward me. "He's so good with kids; he's going to make a great father someday.

Tears prick the backs of my eyes. *I know he will. Only, it's not going to be as quick as I'd hoped.*

She must notice the distress on my face, for her features soften. "Oh, Honey, how are you feeling?" She drops into the chair. "Edward messaged me. I hope you don't mind that I came over."

"It's good to see you. I suppose, I could do with someone to bounce my thoughts off of."

"Hit me, sister." She toes off her boots, then pulls up her knees and settles into the armchair.

"Did... Did Ed tell you what happened last night?"

"He just said you weren't feeling well, and it might help you to have another woman around."

I nod slowly. "I found out I wasn't pregnant."

"Okay?" She frowns. "I didn't think you two were going to try for a child right away."

"It was an accident. No, it wasn't an accident." I glance toward the doorway.

She follows my line of sight, then jumps to her feet, walks toward the door and closes it. "There, now we can talk freely." She curls up in her armchair again.

"He substituted my contraceptive pills with vitamin pills."

She freezes. "You're telling me Edward switched out your oral contraception?"

I nod.

"And you found out because—?"

"He told me. He also revealed he spied on me."

Her gaze widens. "Edward spied on you?"

"He saw me first, in Brooklyn, when I lived in my father's house, a year ago. I had graduated and was looking for jobs in New York, and I couldn't afford to live on my own. I hated having to do it but moving back home helped me save enough to buy a one-way ticket out of there and to London."

"How did he spy on you?"

"He had someone install cameras in my room and bugged my phone. And my Kindle."

"Oh, my god." Summer presses her hands to her mouth. "And he confessed all of this to you?"

"Yep."

"Okay." She runs her fingers through her hair. "How do you feel about it?"

"I don't know," I say honestly. "When I thought I might be pregnant with his child... I was willing to forgive him for everything. Having a child, the one thing I have always yearned for, seemed to make everything right. But then—"

"—you found out you weren't."

I nod.

"And now you're angry with yourself for feeling so ready to forgive him because you thought you got what you wanted, a child?"

I nod again.

"And now you're wondering what to do?"

I raise my shoulders. "What am I going to do? Do I leave him? And go where? Do what?"

"And what is Edward saying?"

"We haven't discussed anything in great detail, but he says he's sorry for what he did. No, let me rephrase it: he's sorry his actions hurt me, but he's not sorry he did it."

"What does that mean?" She places her chin on her knee.

"That watching me saved him. That if he hadn't been able to see what I was up to on an ongoing basis, he's not sure what he would have done."

She rubs at her temples. "Babe, this is a lot to take in."

"You're telling me."

"No wonder, he thought you could benefit from talking to someone else."

"You've known Edward longer than me. What do you make of all this?"

"The fact that he turned stalker on you? That he was so obsessed with you, he had to watch you via secret cameras?"

I wince. "When you put it that way, it does sound creepy."

"Question is, why aren't you freaking out more about it?"

I throw up my hands. "Don't you think I'm not asking myself that question? Where is my self-respect, my dignity, my ego? Am I such a doormat that I'll allow him to get away with what he did?"

"Or maybe, you're flattered that he was so focused on you?"

"Eh?" I narrow my gaze.

"Are you flattered by the fact he was...*is* so infatuated by you."

"Maybe?" I wriggle around, trying to find a more comfortable place in the bed. "My mother died when I was young, and my father never paid much attention to me... And my stepmother and sisters? Let's just say, they didn't care what I did, as long as it didn't affect them. And then, to find out this man took one look at me and decided I was the one for him."

"That's what he told you?"

I nod. "Only, he didn't act on it, like a normal man. He decided to get fixated on me. And then, oh, yeah… When he realized my father's business was in trouble, he stepped in and told him he'd marry me in exchange for saving his company."

She whistles.

"Exactly."

She moves around and drapes herself sideways on the chair, so her legs hang over one of the arms. "When Sinclair and I met, he came onto me in the conference room of his office, then filmed me and used the video to blackmail me into marrying him."

"He did?"

"Also, there was this whole thing of him holding my father responsible for the incident, so he wanted revenge and decided to take it by marrying me."

"Oh." I stare at her. "Was your father responsible?"

"He gave information to the people behind the incident to save me and Karma. He didn't have a choice. And Sinclair seemed to think he didn't, either, but—" She raises a shoulder.

"But—?"

"But of course, there's always another way. Was I pissed off with Sinclair? Yes. Did I want to leave him? It crossed my mind, but I was already in love with him. I couldn't see a life without him. And then he changed. Turned out, it took the love of a good woman to reform him. And of course, he apologized and said he'd do anything to make me happy, and"—she tilts her head—"I chose to believe him. Not that I'm advising you to do the same."

"You're happy, though?"

Her lips curve in a soft smile. "Very. He's the best husband ever, and as a father, he's so devoted. He's changed his entire life for us and maintains we're the best thing that's ever happened to him. He says we help him stay grounded."

"You got your happily-ever-after." I try to keep the wistfulness out of my voice but don't think I succeed, for she leans forward and takes my hand in hers.

"Oh, honey. It wasn't easy, but I persevered. I just knew it was Sinclair or nothing. I guess, I didn't hold his actions against him. He'd been through so much, and then he showed he could change. Again, I'm not saying that's what you should do—"

"So, what should I do?"

"I can't tell you that." She shakes her head. "But what I can tell you is that you'll know, when you know. And if you can hang in there until you know... Well,"—she purses her lips—"do you think you can do that? More to the point, do you want to do that?"

70

———————

Edward

I hold the door to the car open. My wife swings her legs over the side and places her feet on the ground. When I offer my hand, she hesitates, then takes it. The breath I hadn't been aware of holding rushes out of me. Each time she doesn't attempt to put distance between us, I send up a prayer. Yep, me, the man who decided he didn't want anything to do with HIM, apparently, can't go an hour without beseeching Him to give me a chance to show my wife how much I love her. How much I want her. How much I can't do without her in my life.

My wife straightens, and when I take in that gorgeous turn of her stocking-clad ankles, that familiar bolt of lust squeezes my groin. I shove it aside, continue my perusal up the flash of her legs, those thick thighs covered by a bright red coat that falls to below her knees. It brings out the color in her cheeks and the golden streaks in her hair.

Yesterday, when I arrived with a blueberry-sated kid, as well as a housekeeper in tow with breakfast for her and Summer, she wouldn't meet my eyes. But she didn't refuse my help when I plumped the pillows at her back, then placed the breakfast tray on her lap. She also didn't mind when I broke off a piece of croissant and fed her, and she took the cup of the tea I poured her. Then, I made sure to occupy the toddler while she and Summer visited.

After Summer left, I ran her a bath and waited outside while she bathed. Then, I insisted she take a nap while I dismissed the house-keeper and cooked an early dinner for her. We ate in front of the television, and when I pulled up another chick flick — *The Fault In Our Stars* — she didn't protest. And when I pulled her close and offered her my shoulder and a box of tissue when she cried, she accepted both. She fell asleep tucked into my side, and I carried her up to her room, tucked her in, and stretched out over the covers.

This morning over breakfast — which I'd cooked — I told her we were expected for dinner at G-Pa's place to bring in the New Year. I'd expected her to decline the invite, but she'd said she was happy to come. Of course, she said she loves the old man, and she wants to see Tiny. Clearly, the dog has a bigger share of affection than me. Not that I blame her.

It's a wonder she's even talking to me, after everything I told her. It's a wonder she hasn't told me to fuck off. But that's my wife. Sweetness and honey and all things nice… And I so want to taste her again. I want to bury my nose in her hair and take a long sniff — I confess, I manage a quick one when I help her out of the car. I also savor the feel of her delicate fingers in mine as I lead her up the path to Arthur's town house. And the warmth of her skin through the wool of her coat as I slide it off her shoulders. The creamy length of her throat, the nearness to her curves, the flare of her hips which pulled the dress tight across her rear… And fuck, the dress she's wearing. It clings to her in all the right places, showing off her lush figure, and when she turns to look at me over her shoulder, I have to tear my gaze away from her butt and hand the coat over to Arthur's staff. Her cheeks have gone pink. So, she noticed me ogling her, but she doesn't comment. If anything, the gleam in her eyes indicates she's pleased by my reaction. I step past her and lead her to the living room, where the rest of the family is gathered.

We step inside the room and Sinclair claps me on the shoulder. "Good to see you man." I nod.

"Glad you both made it." He looks from me to my wife, then back at me. "What are you both drinking?"

"You the bartender? Why are you here anyway?" I tighten my stare.

"Arthur's orders. Someone has to keep the peace while you Daven-ports trade scowls and looks which could tear the skin at ten paces."

"Count me out of that." I raise a shoulder.

His forehead wrinkles. "Thought you and Nathan were in competition for the CEO role."

"He can have it."

"You told him that yet?"

"I will. Also, sparkling water for me," I add.

"A glass of champagne would be nice." My wife nods.

"Coming up." Sinclair walks away.

I spot Summer across the room with her boy. She's deep in conversation with Ava. I must stiffen because my wife turns to me. "You okay she's here?"

"Are *you* okay she's here?" I scan her features.

"She's no threat to me," my wife murmurs.

"No one is a threat to you. You're it for me."

She looks between my eyes, a troubled look on her features, then she turns away. "That must be her husband. Baron, is it?"

I take in the tall man with blonde hair who has his hand around her waist and I notice the baby carrier next to Ava. I wait for the inevitable churning of my guts, that stabbing sensation in my chest, but there's nothing. Only the feel of her hand still in mine, of her presence next to me. Unable to stop myself, I wrap my arm about her shoulder; that's when she goes rigid.

At first, I think it's because of me, but then I look down at her face, to where she's eying a trio of woman gathered in a corner. The older among them has a pinched look to her features. She's wearing a dress which accentuates her too-thin figure, the kind run-way models favor and which many seem to aspire to but makes me want to offer her a thick-juicy burger. Given the lack of expression on her face and the too-smooth expanse of her forehead, she's pumped her features with botox. The two younger women, one blonde, the other brunette, sport dissatisfied frowns. Their faces are painted with an overly generous application of make-up, enough to turn them into caricatures of themselves.

When one of the staff comes by with a tray of food, the brunette waves them off with a sniff. The blonde notices my wife; her gaze widens. She leans in and whispers something to the older woman. All three of them turn to look at my wife. Tension thrums off of her, and my insides twist. I pull her close into my side, and to my surprise, she melts in, which tells me she's feeling threatened by them. And anxious. And anyone who makes my wife feel that way is not welcome here. I take a step in their direction, and she grips my arm.

"Where are you going?"

"To tell them to leave."

"You can't…you can't do that."

"I can."

"They are G-Pa's guests."

"They make you unhappy."

She looks away, then nods. "That's my father's wife and their two daughters."

"Your evil stepmother and your half-sisters?"

My poor attempt at levity must work, for she gives me a small smile.

"We don't have to be here; we can leave," I say softly.

She looks torn, then slowly shakes her head. "We came here at G-Pa's invitation. He wants us here. You want to be here."

"I want to be where you are."

She turns her gaze on mine and, again, that confused expression flits across her face.

"What is it?" I take in her features. "Tell me, wife."

"It's… " She opens her mouth then shuts it. "Nothing." She squares her shoulders. "I'd better go get this over with."

71

Mira

My heart feels like a sledgehammer. My ribcage trembles with each beat. *Am I nervous about meeting my stepmother? What do you think? And I shouldn't be, really. They can't hurt me. No, strike that. They can hurt me, but it's time I learn how to deal with it. Besides, they don't know anything about me. So what, if I grew up under the same roof as my half-sisters? They've spent their lives pretending I don't exist. That's when they weren't making fun of me. As for my stepmother… Does she hate me? Boy, does she.*

She sees me as a threat for my father's affections, and I don't know why, considering my father has found it difficult to look at my face since my mother's death. I know, I remind him of her. He's said so on a few occasions, in the days he'd make an occasional appearance in my life. But it must have been too distressing for him, given how he blocked me out of his life.

So why do I feel so duty-bound toward him? Why is it, I felt as if I were the one responsible for doing what was needed to help his business? It's what my mother would have wanted. Given she died when I was little, it's not a conversation I've ever had with her, but if she'd been alive, I know she'd have wanted me to fulfill my obligations of a daughter.

She'd have also wanted me to be happy.

Perhaps, she'd have stood up for me and convinced my father not to go through with the tradition of an arranged marriage for me. Or maybe not, considering she and my father had an arranged marriage, too, and they were very happy, by all accounts. And seeing my stepmother and half-sisters has only brought home all the insecurities I grew up with.

But I'm stronger than that now. I *have* to be. And it's best to face them now and get it over with. I begin to wipe my damp hands down my dress, then stop. The last thing I want to do is stain the fabric. When I chose it earlier, I thought—no, I knew— it looks good on me. I like how the silk clings to my curves, how it outlines my hips and stretches across my thick thighs. How it bares my neck. I knew it would capture his gaze and focus it on my figure.

I wore it because a part of me wanted to bask in his admiration. I wanted to flaunt my size sixteen figure knowing he loves it. He's told me so often enough that, for the first time in my life, I'm secure about how I look. I no longer watch what I eat. I don't berate myself for not working out every day at the gym. For the first time since I can remember, I like what I see in the mirror. And it's because of him.

The way Eddie touched me and kissed me and worshipped my body. The way he hasn't wanted to allow me out of his sight since the first day he saw me… Yes, it's obsessive, but it's also flattering. So, flattering. So, gratifying… So, pleasing that he loves me for what I am. He doesn't want me to change. He hasn't demanded anything I can't give him…

He's the first man to adore my lush figure. The first to relish my size sixteen curves. He tied me up before he fucked me. He loves how my flesh embraces the knots. He was aroused by the marks left on my hips and my thighs by the cords. He was fixated on me, but then, I'd rather he be infatuated by me and consumed by me than by anyone else. I'd rather he dominate me than any other woman.

He loves me. And I don't want any other woman to occupy this space in his life. I'd rather he focus all of his considerable attentiveness on me. That his scrutiny stops and ends with my face, my body, my soul. He's mine. I'm his. And I love him. I don't want anyone in my life, except him. He loves me. He wants me. He finds me beautiful… More than that, he thinks I am the most alluring woman in the world.

And that gives me the courage to walk up to the women who've been responsible for so much of the sadness in my life. They fall quiet as I approach. And when I reach them, all three of them stare at me. They take in my dress, Chanel, and my heels, Balenciaga. Eddie filled my closet with only the best brands, all in *my* size. And while I could have been churlish and not accepted any of it, they looked so appealing, and they looked so good on me. I may be stubborn at times, but I'm not stupid.

Maybe, he's doing it to win me over, but I'm confident it's also because he loves how I look in them. His adoring gaze when he saw me was everything. His possessive touch as he helped me with the coat, and later, helped me remove it, gives me the wherewithal to hold out my hand to my stepmother. "Matilda."

Her eyebrows rise, and she seems taken aback by my confidence. She ignores my hand and continues to study me. I place my left palm on my hip, and her gaze widens. She sees my engagement and wedding rings—good. It's the first time I'm meeting her without a trace of nervousness—because, you know what? Somewhere on the walk over, as my mind went over how much my husband cherishes me, my uncertainty faded away, leaving in its place, a quiet belief in myself.

That's what Edward has done for me. He helped me find myself. All it took was my husband showing me how much he values me, how much he wants me, how he sees me as everything he needs, for me to find my trust in myself. Seeing myself through his eyes gives me the self-assurance I thought I'd never find. He's helped me find my faith. He's changed my life. He's shown me I'm not less than anyone else. He's taught me to love myself, and as a result, I've learned how to accept love. And for that, I'm willing to give him a second chance.

"Mirabelle." My stepmother looks past me, in the direction of my husband, before turning her gaze on my features. "I suppose congratulations are in order on your nuptials?"

I lock my fingers together. *I will not be nervous. I will not allow the memories of all the way she's insulted me over the years to get to me.*

When I was a kid, and I found out she was my new stepmother, I was so excited. I threw myself into her arms when my father introduced her, and she played along. She pretended to care for me, long enough to win my father over. Enough to worm herself into his affections, enough to make him trust her to look after me while he was away on work.

It was only later, I realized, she found ways to isolate me from him. She'd worked herself into a place where most of my father's communication to me came through her, where he never had the opportunity to see me or hear from me directly. I felt so lonely. Even more so, once my half-sisters came along. I'd thought it would be wonderful to have sisters, but she shut me out.

She turned all her attention to them, and while she put me in the care of a string of nannies, she made sure none of them stuck around long enough for me to form a bond with them. In a way, it turned out to be a blessing, of sorts, for the women she chose to care for me were not exactly affectionate.

I ended up missing my mother so much, I turned to food to make up for the lack of love in my life. I was trying to fill the mom-shaped hole in my life with the rush of endorphins that came from filling my stomach. It's also when I decided I wanted a family of my own. Children I could love and make up for the lack I had in my own life.

"Uh, is that your engagement ring?" Eleanor, my older half-sister, grabs my hand. I try to pull away, but she tightens her hold on me. She peers at my finger and sniffs. "Nice stone, but why isn't it a diamond?"

"I like it." I yank at my hand again, and this time, she releases it.

She tosses her hair over her shoulder. "Of course, it was an arranged marriage, so love wasn't part of the equation." Her voice is disdainful.

Heat flushes my cheeks. My stomach twists. *My husband loves me. He does.* She doesn't know what goes on in my marriage. I open my mouth to tell her off, when a server comes by with a tray of hors-oeuvres. I reach for it, and Kate, my younger half-sister, exclaims, "Oh, honey, are you sure you want to eat that?"

Eleanor takes one of the fried mozzarella sticks from the server's tray and bites into it. "It's soo good." She smacks her lips. "But you shouldn't eat it; it has too many calories."

My guts churn. My pulse rate spikes. A crawling sensation pricks my skin, and I retract my hand. Eddie's appreciation of my curves made me so comfortable in my own skin that I forgot I hate eating in front of others.

When I hit puberty and my unhealthy eating habits meant my weight had ballooned, Matilda insisted on rationing my food. She'd serve treats to my half-sisters but tell me I couldn't have any because I was too heavy, and she was looking out for my health. She'd also serve me too-small portions, explaining she was trying to help me control my weight. All of this meant I often went to bed hungry.

Once, I'd been unable to sleep because I was starving. I sneaked down to the kitchen after everyone was asleep and stole food. She caught me in the act, and Kate teased me mercilessly about it. The result? I stopped eating with them. For years, I preferred to have my food delivered to my room and eat on my own.

Then there was the time Matilda took the three of us shopping for clothes. I was suspicious when she invited me to come along. After all, she never treated me as part of the family. But she was so sweet, and when I hesitated, Eleanor and Kate insisted I join them. I was so happy they were including me in their activities that I agreed.

We'd reached the boutique, and Matilda insisted I try on clothes that were a size too small for me. Then she looked at me with disappointment and commented that if I lost a little weight, they'd fit me better.

Eleanor and Kate tried on the prettiest dresses in the shop. They modelled them, and Matilda oohed and aahed over them. She bought them all the clothes they'd tried on, then turned to me and proclaimed, once I slimmed down, she'd buy a new wardrobe for me too. Meanwhile, she was "more than happy" to buy me my plus-size clothing, but really, wouldn't it be best if I waited? It would be an incentive for me to lose weight. With sweaty palms and a piercing pain in my heart, I agreed.

She proceeded to take us to a fast-food joint as a 'treat,' then looked at me disapprovingly when I ordered a burger. I settled for not eating, while the three of them tucked into burgers and shakes. I reached for one of the fries from Kate's plate, and she burst into tears and complained to Matilda that I was stealing her food.

Of course, she and Eleanor had looked at me with judgement. I was a fat girl; I couldn't restrain myself when it came to food. It was one of the worst days of my life—one to which I directly attribute many of my insecurities with food and my weight. Suffice it to say, I never went out with them anywhere after that.

The waitstaff moves on to serve someone else, and I heave a sigh of relief, only to stiffen when Matilda gestures to my dress. "What a lovely color, my dear." She turns to Eleanor. "Doesn't it give the illusion of taking inches off her hips?"

"It does." Eleanor beams. "In fact, it almost flattens her stomach."

"It definitely makes her look a size smaller." Kate taps her chin with a talon-like fingernail. *Too bad she hasn't stabbed herself in the eye with it.*

How many times have I heard the three of them hold a conversation about me like I wasn't there? Only I *was* there. And I was hurt. And I still carry the emotional scars from their torment. That confidence I thought I'd shored up oozes out of me.

I take a step back, only to connect with something solid. Something warm. And hard and ungiving. Something that supports my weakening knees that threaten to give out from under me. I draw in a sharp breath, and his woodsmoke scent surrounds me. That tingle of electricity, which I've always felt in his presence, loops about my shoulders. My muscles relax, and when he places his big hands on my hips, the comfort from his touch knocks away the moment of self-doubt which had crawled into my chest.

"Belle's lush figure is what I love about her. No, that's wrong." He tucks me closer. "Her big heart is what I adore about her. And her giving nature. And how she wants to take care of those around her. She is the most authentic, most unselfish, most beautiful soul I have ever met. As for her curves? They're what make her even more special. My wife is worth a hundred, no, a million of you." He turns to my stepmother. "You insulted my wife and made her unhappy today. For that and for all the times you've upset her during her growing years, I'm going to cut the salary paid to your husband by eighty percent."

Matilda laughs. "Who are you to have any say over my husband's income?"

"He's the man who owns my company," my father's voice cuts in.

Matilda looks from my husband to my father, who's walked over to join us. "What do you mean?" She scowls.

"My business needed an infusion of cash to stop it from going under. Mira's husband stepped in. As of today, he owns a majority interest in the shares. In effect, he has control over my paycheck, and hence, over our future."

Matilda's gaze widens. "You never told me."

"You didn't need to know." My father raises a shoulder.

"This doesn't change anything." She waves her hand in the air.

"Actually, it does." My father widens his stance. "Since my salary is going to be cut to a fraction of what I used to earn, we'll have to trim our monthly outgoings. No more vacations—"

"What?" Eleanor slaps her hands on her hips. "I promised my friends I'd take a trip to Barbados with them. I can't let them down,"

Our father ignores her. "No more buying new dresses," he proclaims.

"I can't do without one for my debutante ball!" Kate bursts into tears.

Matilda pulls her close then glowers at my father. "Now, look what you've done."

"As for you"—he looks my stepmother up and down— "I'm going to cut your allowance by eighty percent."

Matilda stiffens. "You're joking."

My father shakes his head. "I should have done this much earlier for how you mis-treated Mirabelle all these years. I'm seriously thinking of divorcing you."

Matilda gapes, then a sly look comes into her eyes. "We've been married long enough, that if you did, I'd be entitled to a good portion of your money."

My father smirks, and it's a look I've never seen on his features before. "Remember the pre-nup you signed?"

Matilda draws in a sharp breath.

"That's right. You don't get a penny if we divorce," my father says in satisfaction.

Matilda narrows her gaze on my father. "I am your wife; you can't treat me like this."

"And Mira is my daughter. When I married you, I told you she was the most important thing in my life. I told you I wanted you to be a mother to her. Yet you mistreated her all these years."

"I did my best," Matilda snaps.

"And it wasn't enough."

"Don't blame me for your shortcomings," Matilda says in a low voice.

"You're right, it's my fault. I was too caught up in my grief. I was so self-absorbed I didn't intervene, even though I sensed my daughter was unhappy. But thanks to Edward, I realize I can make amends." My father looks between Eleanor and Kate, "I take responsibility for how the two of you turned out. I was an absent parent. I should have inter-vened in how your mother brought the two of you up. For that reason, I won't disinherit the both of you from my will. But consider yourselves warned. I expect to see changes in your attitude and your behavior toward your older sister. You'd do well to remember, she *is* your sister. And I love all of my girls. You, on the other hand"—he turns to Matilda —"I'm contemplating changing my will, so you don't see a penny of my fortune."

"You can't do this." Matilda purses her lips.

"Oh, I can, and I will. Unless—"

"Unless?" Matilda frowns.

"Unless Mirabelle tells me not to."

Matilda stiffens. She curls her fingers at her sides, then slowly straightens them out, before she turns to face me. "I am your stepmother. I did the best I could with you, but you were a difficult child. Always sad, always overeating. What was I supposed to do?"

I look away. All of my life, I wanted a chance for things to change between me and my father's wife and their children. I hoped, one day, they'd accept me as part of the family. I hoped... I'd be accepted by them, get their love. Maybe that's why I decided to go home after graduation, while I was looking for a job. It was a last-ditch effort to get their approval. A final bid to find the belonging I'd always yearned for. But it's not the reason I turn to my father and say, "You don't need to cut her out completely."

72

Edward

"You're too forgiving." Cyril takes Belle's hand in his. "Anyone else in your position would have taken the opportunity to hit them where it hurts most, but not you."

After she made that announcement, I told her stepmother and half-sisters to leave. They marched off, similar expressions of petulance and arrogance on their features. Not one of them thanked her. Not one of them acknowledged her generosity.

Her father watched them go with a resigned expression before taking my wife's hand in his. "I am so sorry for everything you went through. I knew she wasn't doing right by you. I knew the three of them were making you unhappy. I knew it was my responsibility to stop them, but I didn't. I should have stepped in earlier. I should have told them to back down. I—" His eyes gleam with unshed tears. "I failed you. I failed your mother."

"No, you didn't." My wife goes into his arms. "You did well, Daddy. You were struggling with your grief. I know how much you miss Mama. It couldn't have been easy for you."

"I knew I wouldn't be able to take care of you. I was barely functioning, myself. Barely able to get through every day. It's why I married her. I hoped she'd be a good mother to you. Instead, I ended up hurting you."

"Don't apologize, Dad, please. You did your best."

"But it wasn't enough. I am so sorry I wasn't there for you when you needed me. So sorry, I put the interests of my company before your happiness. I am so sorry I put pressure on you to fulfill the obligation of an arranged marriage. I should have allowed you to choose your own life partner. Instead, I used you as leverage. Can you ever forgive me for it?"

"There's nothing to forgive." She sniffles.

He steps back and surveys her features. "If you're not happy"—he glares at me, then back at my wife—"if you want out of this arrangement, you only have to tell me. I'll give up everything to see you content."

"I'm… I'm…" She swallows. "I'm happy."

The tension drains out of my shoulders. I'm not sure what I was expecting her to say—that she hates her life. That she's trapped. That *I* trapped her? That *I* destroyed her life? If she wants to leave me, this is the chance. With her father's help, she could start a new life. She could file for divorce, and I wouldn't contest it, *if*…that's what she wants. I'll never go a single moment without thinking of her, but *if* she wants to be free of me… I won't stand in her way.

"You sure?" Cyril looks at her closely. "If you want to leave him—"

"I'm good, really."

He surveys her face again, then nods, before turning to look at me. "If you do anything to upset her, you'll have me to contend with."

"Understood, and I appreciate the sentiment."

"There they are." Arthur walks up, Tiny by his side.

The mutt brushes against my wife, who pats his big head. "How's my boy?" she says in a soft voice. "Did you miss me?"

Tiny makes a purring noise in his throat and leans into her touch. And damn, if I don't envy him. She loves him, that's clear. Could she still love me after everything I've done?

"I see you got rid of the three witches with a 'B,'" Arthur drawls. "No offense." He glances at Cyril.

"None taken." Cyril shrugs.

"Why did you invite them?" I lower my chin to my chest. "They're not family."

"They had a role to play." His eyes gleam, but the expression on his features does not change.

I stare at him, and he meets my gaze with an innocent look. *What the —? Did he invite them, knowing they'd prompt me to come to her rescue and help her make up with her father, thus providing more common ground between my wife and me? Nah, he can't be that strategic.* I frown. *Can he?* I tilt my head. *It'll bet that's why he invited Baron and Ava.* The canny old man wanted to prove to me I'm truly over my past. It's time to move forward, and what better way to bring that home than by having my best friend and the woman who I once thought I loved over for our family dinner? For me to able to look at them without feeling an ounce of envy or yearning. It proves to me, even more, that she is my future.

I glower at my grandfather; he beams back, a look of satisfaction on his features. The man is devious with his schemes. And of course, he'd justify it by saying he did it with our best interests at heart. In this case, sadly, I must agree.

Tiny looks between us and whines.

"I think he's hungry," my wife offers.

"He's always hungry. The dog has the appetite of a horse." Arthur clicks his tongue, and Tiny rises up and walks over to him. "Let's eat."

Arthur taps his fork against his champagne glass, and the talk around the table dies down. "I propose a toast."

"Oh, no," my wife whispers. I follow her glance to where Tiny is watching the bottle of champagne, which has been placed in a bucket next to Arthur, with an unflinching gaze.

"Shit, what was Arthur thinking?"

"Thinking about what?" Nathan asks from next to me.

"The champagne." I nod toward the bottle on ice. "The mutt likes champagne."

"You're kidding." He blinks.

"Nope." I shake my head."

"Umm, maybe we should do something?" my wife interjects.

"And steal Arthur's moment in the limelight?" Knox smirks from across the table.

"What are you'll nattering about?" Ava turns to my wife. She's seated next to her with Baron on her other side. My once-best friend, with whom I parted on good terms when he and Ava had gotten married —then failed to keep in touch with him. I've also avoided meeting his eyes all through dinner. *Loser* that I am. Because what can you say to a man who was practically your brother, in all but blood, and who you decided not to talk to because you were jealous. *Face it; you hated the fact he got the girl you thought you loved.* And I'd have continued thinking that way, but for the fact I found the one I really wanted. *And then you did everything in your power to alienate her. She should leave you. She should never forgive you. You should never forgive yourself.* How am I going to repent for what I did? I reach for the flute of champagne and raise it.

"Thank you to all of you for coming here to bring in the New Year. Congratulations to Edward—the first of my grandsons to get married."

"—but not the last." Knox coughs, and Nathan glares at him. He continues to smirk and raises his flute in Nathan's direction.

"A big welcome to the family, Mirabelle. You put up with Edward every day, and I can only thank you for that."

"Hear, hear," Sinclair calls out from across the table, and it's my turn to scowl at him.

"He doesn't deserve you, my dear, and if you ever need someone to kick his arse"—Arthur smirks, —"you only have to ask."

"And me," Sinclair adds.

"And me," Nathan calls out.

"I'll be at the head of the line," Knox growls.

I glance sideways to find Baron trying to hide a smile and failing. I scowl at Tiny, wondering when he's going to make a move. So far, he's been watching the bottle, but has seemed content to sit panting, his tongue lolling out one side of his jaw.

"Which brings me to the next point of business."

"Didn't realize this was a work thing," Nathan muses.

"With Arthur everything is work." Knox bares his teeth in what he must think is a smile; he resembles a shark who's smelled blood in the water.

"What's happening?" my wife whispers to me.

"Not sure." I place my arm about her shoulder, and she doesn't shake it off. Which is good, right? To be honest, I'm waiting for the other shoe to drop. I'm waiting for her to lose her temper with me and tell me she hates me and that she'll never forgive me. But none of that has been forthcoming. I rub the spot of tightness in my chest. Shouldn't have drunk so much coffee today. In my agitation over whether she was coming to dinner with me, I paced the floor of my home office, tried to work, kept going to the kitchen, hoping to run into her, and ended up swigging too much coffee.

"I'm confirming Nathan as the CEO of the company."

Knox stiffens. My wife turns to me. "Did you know this?"

I nod.

Nathan glances at me, a look of surprise on his feature that turns to wariness. "No," he growls.

I raise a shoulder. I had a word with the old man earlier today and told him I wasn't interested in being the CEO, not when it would mean being away for work and committing to working around the clock. I intend to spend a lot more of my time pursuing the only thing important to me—taking care of my wife's needs and making sure she wants for nothing. Arthur didn't seem surprised. If anything, he seconded me and told me I was making the right decision.

Nathan turns to fix his glare on Arthur, not that it makes a difference. The old codger wears a grin on his face. His eyes twinkle. "Which means, Nathan, you have three months to get married."

"Fuck." Nathan's fingers stiffen on the stem of his flute, which cracks. The champagne spills; the glass hits the table and rolls to the end. That's when Tiny jumps up on his hind legs and snatches the bottle of champagne and downs it.

<hr>

"That was eventful." I unlock the front door of my house and gesture to my wife to enter.

"I can't believe no one noticed us leaving."

"They were too busy trying to find Tiny," who, after emptying the bottle of champagne in one, dropped the bottle at Arthur's feet and grinned. No, he really grinned. There was a smile on his face, until he noticed the stunned look on my grandfather's features and realized he'd committed a booboo. Which is when he bounded into the house—with Nathan, Knox and Sinclair in hot pursuit.

I turned to find Baron at my elbow. "We need to talk," he said.

"Yes, we do,"—I looked away, then back at him—" but not now."

"Not now,"—Baron nodded— "but we will."

"We will." I held out my hand, but he bypassed that and hugged me. I was surprised, then hugged him back. Something settled in my chest.

I've missed my friend. But I'm not that selfish, bitter man who cut him and Ava out of my life. I am a husband in love with his wife. I'm ready to make amends and move on with my life. Baron must sense my thoughts because, when he stepped back, he's smiling. He walked back to Ava and I... I left with Belle.

On the ride home, I hoped she'd forgiven me. I prayed she'd find it within her to give me a second chance. I've made my peace with Him, thanks to her; and I'm not beyond turning to Him in the hope he'll work a miracle and have her forgive me.

Now, I slide the coat off her shoulders because it's a legitimate way to be close to her. As is the sniff I take of her hair. How else am I going to sleep if I don't store up her scent in my lungs?

"Did you sniff me?" She glances over her shoulder, a strange look on her face.

"I…did," I admit.

"Can I sniff you back?"

I nod, sure my mouth is open in surprise and not doing anything to hide it.

She goes up on tiptoe, places her nose close to my neck, and takes a deep breath. A shiver grips her, and I can't stop myself from rubbing her arm. "Are you cold?"

"Electricity." She looks up at me. "Every time I smell your scent, a frisson of something runs up my spine."

"And every time I look at you, every time I see you, every time I sniff you, I know I wouldn't be able to bear it if you left me. Don't leave me, wife, please." I go down on my knees. "I can't function without you. I can't see myself without you. I wouldn't know what to do with myself. My heart would stop beating; my body would stop functioning. I am nothing without you, wife, nothing."

73

Mira

"Oh, Eddie." Tears prick the backs of my eyes. His every word is like a balm on the jagged wound in my heart. One I hadn't even been aware of. Maybe I've been numb since he confessed to me. Not just about what he did to me…but what happened to him. I'm still digesting the details. That talk with Summer helped, of course. It put things in perspective. He's a complex person, my husband. So many layers to him. Layers I'm still unwrapping.

"I love you, wife. More than anything. You have to believe me."

"I do." I swallow.

He looks up at me and his eyes shimmer. "Then don't leave me."

"I need…some time, some space to decide what I want. You understand that?"

He nods. His fingers tighten on mine, then he kisses my knuckles. "Whatever you want."

"And you can't stalk me or put cameras or bugs on any of my devices, or even in my car."

He doesn't seem happy with it, but nods.

"And I'll need to move out of the house."

"No." His lips thin.

"If you love me, you'll let me have this time."

A tortured expression flits across his features, then he nods slowly.

"And I won't be working at the office nursery."

"What?" He rises to his feet. "Don't do this, wife. It's the fact that you're under my roof during the day that lets me breathe."

"Nothing is going to happen to me." I cup his chin. "I promise. I just need to be on my own, so I can think things through."

He doesn't respond.

"You helped me find myself; now give me a little time to figure out what's in my mind."

His expression grows more intense. "Wife, I—" He squeezes the bridge of his nose, then lowers his arm. "This is what you need to figure things out?"

I nod.

"What are you going to do? Where are you going to live?"

"I still have my flat."

"Didn't you sublet it?"

I nod. "To a friend who moved to London, but she's happy to share with me."

"And what are you going to do?"

"I've been saving the very generous salary you've been paying me. I'm going to invest it in the preschool where I used to work."

"I thought that shut down."

I nod. "The owners took out a loan and are going to re-open it. I'm putting my money in, so I'll have a share of it."

"Look at you." Pride shines in his eyes. "I am so proud you're doing this."

"Oh." I blink. I was sure he'd tell me he would buy out the preschool for me. The fact that he didn't, and that he's encouraging me in this venture, is a surprise. And it feels so good. I throw my arms around his neck. "Thank you, husband."

His entire body stiffens, then a shudder runs up his spine. When I lean back, he has a look of shock on his face.

"What's wrong?" I murmur.

"You called me husband."

"You are my husband, last I checked." I turn and begin to walk away, putting an extra twitch in my butt and an extra bounce in my step. Knowing he's following me, knowing his gaze is firmly fixed on my ass. I reach the kitchen, head to the kettle, and fill it. Then switch it on and set it to boil. I place my palm on my hip and turn to find he's standing by the doorway, watching me, a hungry look on his face.

"Would you like a cup of tea?"

"Sure." His voice is hoarse.

I pop out one hip; he swallows. And when I push my hair over one shoulder to reveal the low neckline on the back of the dress, he reaches up and loosens his tie. Stifling a smile, I turn and rise up on tiptoes to reach for the teabags, when suddenly he's behind me. His heat sears my back, and his fingers brush mine as he gets to the pack of teabags before me.

"Here." He places it on the counter, hesitates, then slowly backs away. *Whoa, he's really giving me space.*

I place a teabag in each cup, pour the water in, then hand him a cup.

"Want to watch the fireworks on the tele and usher in the New Year?" He holds out his hand, and I place mine in his.

He leads me over to the living room. I place the tea on the coffee table, sink down into the couch, then kick off my stilettos and pull my legs up under me. He sits down next to me, and switches on the television, before reaching for a blanket and placing it over me. I snuggle in, and when he places his arm over the back of the couch and behind my neck, I lean in and push my cheek into his chest.

The television screen shows New Year celebrations in progress from around the world. I snuggle into him, and he wraps his arm about me and pulls me even closer. As the New Year dawns in different countries, the TV beams images of fireworks and celebrations from their respective capital cities.

"I'd love to travel to all these places," I murmur.

"Anything you want." He runs his fingers through my hair. "I love you, wife."

I turn my nose into his chest and kiss his vest-covered abs. "I love you, too, but—"

The planes of his chest tighten, "But?"

"But I still need time to work out what I want for my future."

On screen, the ten-minute countdown to the New Year begins. Fireworks commence over the Thames, highlighting the London Eye, the Shard, Big Ben, the Houses of Parliament, St. Paul's Church, and other landmarks.

"It's gorgeous," I gasp.

"You are."

I glance up to find he's staring at me. Heat flushes my face. "I was talking about the fireworks."

"I only see you."

He presses a kiss to my forehead, then directs me back to the television. A dazzling display of pyrotechnics, lights, and music illuminates the night sky on screen. The fireworks are choreographed to a soundtrack that gets my blood racing. My heartbeat speeds up. My pulse thrums to the beat. Or maybe it's because of his nearness. How tenderly he holds me. How I know he stares at me like I'm the most important thing in his life.

I keep my gaze focused on the spectacle unfolding on the TV. London's skyline is transformed into a canvas of colors and patterns as the fireworks continue. It's spectacular and breathtaking and even more special because I'm bringing in the New Year in his arms.

When the final ten-second countdown begins, he notches his knuckles under my chin, stares into my eyes.

"Can I kiss you?"

74

Edward

She nods. *Thank fuck.* Without wasting a second, I lean in and gently fit my mouth over hers. I pour all of my feelings into the kiss. My love for her, my need for her, my apology for how I turned her world upside down. My regret for everything I did that upset her. I'm only a man—hopelessly, completely devoted to his wife, and I try to signal that through my lips on hers. I nip on her lower lip; she moans, parts her lips. I slide my tongue over hers and deepen the kiss. She melts into me. Every pore on my skin is alive, heat squeezes my chest, and my groin hardens. I pull her into my lap, slide my hand over her butt and squeeze.

She gasps, then leans back. "Eddie—" she swallows. "I... I'm not—"

I place my finger over her mouth. "I'm sorry." I squeeze my eyes shut. "I'm trying to be the kind of man you want, but I seem to be making a mess of it."

I release her, and she slides back onto the couch. "It's okay."

"It's not. I want to do everything right. I can't fuck this up, wife; not when it's my last chance to win you over."

"Is that what you're doing? Winning me over?" she asks with a laugh.

"Not doing a great job of it, obviously." I adjust myself, then rise to my feet. "Can I take you to bed?"

She blinks.

"I mean..."—I rub my fingers through my hair—"can I carry you to your bed? And only because I know your feet hurt after wearing those pumps."

When she nods, I switch off the television, then scoop her up in my arms. She cuddles into me, and I walk up the stairs, then place her on her feet next to the bed. I walk into her closet and emerge with the T-shirt—my T-shirt—she likes to wear to bed. I place it down, then bend and kiss her forehead. "Goodnight, wife."

Before I can change my mind, I head for the doorway.

"Eddie," she calls out.

I stop.

"You need to make your peace with Baron."

I don't reply.

"You need to move on from what happened, and this is the only way out."

I stay silent, and she blows out a breath. "For me, husband? Please."

She knows I'll do anything for her. *Even this.*

It's been two weeks since she moved out. Two very long, lonely weeks, during which I've been barely functional. I knew I was being insufferable at work, until Nathan barged into my office yesterday and barked at me to take the day off and not come back until I've gotten my shit together. I left and wandered the city aimlessly. I kept finding myself walking in the direction of her flat and barely managed to stop myself before I reached it.

Instead, I went home, changed into my running gear, and ran until I was too tired to think straight. Then I went back home, crawled into her bed, under her bedclothes, to try and find some shut eye. Still, I stuck to my promise. I had already removed all my hidden cameras and wiretaps from her devices and her car and had told my investigators to stop following her.

It feels like I cut off a part of myself, but I've done what she asked of me. I also managed to not text or call, and fuck, if that hasn't just about killed me. If it weren't for the fact that Summer is keeping me updated

—without my prompting—that they're hanging out with mutual friends and she's good, I don't know what I'd do.

I wake up very early, after managing to get a few hours of sleep, and decide to go for another run. Now, I gaze at the skyline of London spread out over me.

There are no tourists at Primrose Hill at this time of the morning. It's quiet, except for the footsteps of the jogger who runs by. To the side a couple works out. He holds onto her legs as she goes through a series of sit-ups. Then she does the same for him. They're equal partners, at least for the duration of this exercise session, and so in sync, it hints at their being together for a while. They finish their workout, and he helps her to her feet, then pulls her close and kisses her. She laughs and hugs him, before they jog down the hill.

That's when I see him. A tall man with broad shoulders wearing a pair of sweats. He begins to jog up the slope. His gait is familiar. The way he holds himself straight, his elbows tucked into his sides, his steps even as he approaches me—all of it is so very familiar. As he nears me, I focus on the view once more. He reaches the bench I'm sitting on and sinks down on the opposite side. For a few seconds, we stay silent. His breathing evens out. I reach for my bottle of water and offer it to him. He takes it without comment and chugs from it, before placing it in the space between us.

"Thanks, man," he murmurs.

I nod. "Sorry it took me a while to reach out to you."

Baron shakes his head. "Never too late. I'm glad you did."

"I almost didn't,"—I rub the back of my neck—"but she insisted."

"The wife always knows best," he says without any hint of sarcasm.

"No disputing that." I laugh. "And how's the kid?" I swallow. There, I said it. When I found out Ava was pregnant, it hurt. And I couldn't understand why my reaction was so extreme.

I'd already accepted Ava and Baron were meant for each other. He'd been looking for her since he'd first seen her as a girl. I was the man who abandoned her to find myself. At the time, I blamed her for being the reason I left the church, but time and perspective showed me I would have done so anyway. Meeting her and realizing I hadn't dealt with any of my issues was the trigger. But if not that, it would have been something else.

So, it was a shock when hearing they were having a child left me in despair. It took falling in love with my wife and realizing there's a chance I might lose her to put that in perspective. Because as much as it hurt to see Baron and Ava together, and to find out she was pregnant, nothing compares to how devastated I was when my wife asked me to give her space to figure things out.

The fact I can't see her every day, can't be in the same space as her, can't look into her eyes or watch as she works in the nursery—all of it is gut-wrenching. It feels like someone reached into my throat and pulled out my heart. For she has it. She has me. And when I can't be with her, it feels like everything is pointless. Like I've reached the end of my line. Like nothing I do has meaning without her being part of it.

"The kid's good." He laughs. "We're going through the entire sleepless night thing, but man, Ava is so fucking good. She's up at all hours of the night nursing, and I try to relieve her, but of course, the baby needs her right now. I try to stay up with her, and she insists I get my sleep because I have to work the next day. Like that matters. She's doing the most important thing possible—the real stuff, the stuff that's messy and genuine and bloody tough. And she's still worried about me."

"I know the feeling."

He peers closely at my features. "That's good, Ed, really good."

I finally meet his gaze. "I'm sorry I didn't stay in touch with you. I… I needed time… Or maybe, that's an excuse. To be honest, I wasn't thinking straight. I didn't want to be jealous of the two of you. I know you two were made for each other, and yet… I couldn't stop myself from wanting what you had. I felt terrible about it but couldn't stop myself. I was envious of the two of you, and I'm not proud of it."

"It takes guts to accept it, and even more courage to share that with me," he murmurs.

"Yeah, well…" I scratch at my unshaven chin. "My wife told me I needed to talk to you."

"And here you are." His lips curve in a smile.

"Indeed."

"And now, you have what Ava and I do." His smile widens.

"I do." I allow myself a small smile. "What we went through, Baron, was the kind of thing that turns men into addicts and makes them do things that destroy their lives. We're lucky we didn't end up there."

"Thanks to the women in our lives who stopped us from going off the deep end. They helped us find the humanity in ourselves. They helped us get in touch with our emotions and all that shit. Which we used to look down on." He chuckles.

I rub the back of my neck. It's true, what he's saying. When the seven of us would get together, before any of us met our women and got married, we'd look down on anything to do with sentiments and feelings. And all the stuff that makes life worth living. And when the men started getting hitched, we'd mock them for being pussy-whipped. I didn't realize there's a special kind of happiness in meeting the right woman. In coming home to her every night. In waking up next to her every morning. In sharing life's ups and downs, the good and the bad, and the stuff that makes it all so worthwhile.

There's a touch on my shoulder. I glance up to find Baron watching me with serious eyes. "She's too good for you, of course."

"Of course." I half smile.

"And you're torn about something related to her?"

I'm not surprised Baron sensed that. We've been through so much together. Amongst the seven of us, Baron and I have always shared a special bond. One I didn't value until I didn't have it in my life. Wisdom truly is based on hindsight, and... When it comes to her, I'm going to make sure I never have cause to say that.

"I may have done things which caused her unhappiness. I was selfish. I only thought about myself. Now, I see I could have done things differently. She's the most important thing to me, and now, I realize... I should have approached her in a different fashion. I should have been more open, allowed her to see my foibles, my weaknesses, my fears"—I wince—"the hurt, the pain I hold within me. I should have allowed her to feel it. I should have—" I swallow around the ball of emotions in my throat. "I should have told her how much I loved her much earlier."

"But you did tell her, so don't be too hard on yourself. You're facing your feelings. You're embracing the fall-out from the incident. You're allowing yourself to be vulnerable, Edward. You're on the right path..."

"But?" I look between his eyes.

"But"—he opens, then shuts his mouth— "it's not my place to say it."

"I want to hear it." Before I ceased all communication with him, Baron was my conscience. After the incident, when my parents turned their backs on me, when I turned to alcohol and drugs as a teenager to cope with the guilt I felt about what had happened to me, it was Baron who rescued me from myself. Also, he's a successful husband and father. If anyone knows what I should be doing to ensure I don't fuck up this chance I have been given at finding true love with Belle, then it's him. "Tell me, Baron." I squeeze his shoulder. "You'll be doing me a favor."

"You need to forgive yourself for everything that happened to you."

I lower my hand and glance away.

"You know I'm right, Edward. You need to complete this journey you're on. You need to heal yourself, so you can be whole again, for her."

75

———————

Edward

"Go on." Baron nods toward the church in front of which we're parked. I took his advice to heart. I knew what I had to do, the final step in finding absolution. When Baron realized I intended to go back to the same church where I'd served as the pastor, he immediately insisted on driving me. "I'll wait here for you," he adds.

"You're a good friend," I pause with my hand on the door handle. "I'm sorry I didn't keep in touch with you and Ava. I'm sorry I hurt the both of you."

"It's in the past." Baron cuts the air with his palm. "What you're doing is very brave, Edward, make no mistake."

I step out of the car, then head for the doorway of the church. My heart begins to hammer in my chest, and my pulse rate shoots up. My breath comes in pants, and it takes everything within me to push open the door and step inside. The scent of incense envelops me, transporting me right back to the days I spent here preaching to my flock. We hit morning rush hour traffic on the way here, but the church is still empty. And so silent, every thud of my heart feels like it's playing through a boombox. I swallow down the ball of emotion in my throat, take a step forward.

Like a tractor beam, my gaze is instantly captured by the cross on the wall at the end of the aisle. The sunlight pours in through the stained glass from above it. I step forward, and the light blinds me for an instant. I move past it, and it's as if I can see everything in relief. Dust motes dance and beckon me forward. My footsteps make a hushed thud that echoes in the space. The candles flicker in the side chapels in the distance. And when I pass the confessional where I almost took a life, the hairs on the back of my neck stand up. That's when I know, I've done the right thing by coming here. I need to face the past so I can move forward... With her.

The scent of beeswax, of wood and stone, the vibrations of all the prayers by the faithful who have passed through this church before me, embrace me and urge me on. I reach the altar and sink to my knees.

I lower my chin to my chest, press my palms together in front, and close my eyes. For a few seconds, I allow myself to flow into that space deep inside of me. The one I haven't visited since I left the priesthood behind. Oh, I prayed to Him when I found out she was unwell, and again, in the hope He'd help her forgive me. But I didn't truly face my past. I didn't ask Him for forgiveness for killing the man who facilitated the incident and everything that happened to me and the Seven.

I didn't ask Him to help me forgive myself. I didn't ask for His help to dissolve these feelings of unworthiness which have haunted me since my abuse.

I haven't allowed myself to revisit any of it since turning my back on Baron and Ava...and the Church. I left to travel.

I've spent so long running away from my past... But I'm done now. Baron's right. It's not enough to reconcile with Him, as I've barely done with my recent prayers. No, I need to ask him for absolution.

I traverse that familiar path to the deepest part of my heart, and when I think I can't go deeper, I sink even further into that nothingness I once used to be so familiar with. That emptiness where I could face myself. That sense of being here and yet, also, being in a space where all of my walls drop away. Where I, once more, stand naked before Him.

"My Lord, I am heartily sorry for having offended Thee,
    and I detest all my sins, because I dread the loss of heaven

and the pains of hell, but most of all because they offend Thee, my God,
who art all-good and deserving of all my love.
I firmly resolve, with the help of Thy grace,
to confess my sins, to do penance, and to amend my life.
Amen."

The words pour out of me. I allow the feelings of hurt, despair, of loneliness…of guilt, of fear, of hate, and revenge—all of it—to gush forward. I open myself up and allow His healing touch to embrace me. I allow that feeling of repentance to consume me. I bow my head and surrender to His grace. To that sense of oneness that has always resided in me, since I was little. That feeling of peace which has evaded me since the incident.

I see the loathing which has become a part of me since the incident. The guilt I've carried since I almost took a life. The envy which ate into me when I watched Ava and Baron.

And I feel the relief of having found my sweet Belle. The love that overwhelmed me when I saw her but which I didn't allow myself to acknowledge, until I was shocked into realizing I could lose her.

And really, all of it is His doing. It's He who led me to her. He who brought her into my life. All I am, is His instrument. I renounce myself to His will and ask for His guidance.

Show me the way, Father. Tell me what to do next.

"Edward?"

A familiar voice reaches me. I look around to find a fellow priest and friend, who was ordained with me and served with me in this very church.

"Zephyr, Brother, I have come to confess."

"You seem lighter." Baron shoots me a sideways glance as we wait for the signal to change.

I went into the confessional and allowed myself to speak without reservation. I hadn't realized how much I needed to do that until, with every word I spoke, the load I carried lifted. Oh, I'd confessed when I was a priest, but I was a different man then. Everything I've faced since leaving the Church has changed me. I've matured, and I've fallen in love. I found her, and she helped me find my faith. In a strange way, I had to lose myself completely to find the true me again. I know, I'll need more therapy to deal with the repercussions of the incident, and my later actions. But I know, coming full circle and revisiting the Church, where I found my faith and lost it, only to be united with it again, is pivotal in healing myself.

"Thank you, Baron." I turn to him. "I couldn't have done this without you."

Baron shakes his head. "The credit goes to you for having the courage to take the first step. I didn't do anything. I—"

My phone buzzes in my pocket, and Baron pauses. I pull it out, then sit upright and answer it. "Wife, are you okay?"

76

Mira

"Let me through, that's my wife in there," Eddie's angry voice reaches us.

Dr. Kincaid and I exchange glances, but before he can say anything, my husband barges into the examination room. It's a tiny room with just enough space for the exam table and the doctor—who is not a small man —and with Eddie's big body in the space, it seems to shrink even further in size. He walks over to me and rakes his gaze down my features. I'm the one on the exam table, but he's the one who looks pale, like he may be about to faint.

There are dark circles under his eyes, hollows under his cheekbones, and he's lost weight. Just enough to make him look leaner, meaner, and hungrier than when I last saw him. And god, I've missed him so much. It took everything within me not to reach for the phone and call him over the last two weeks.

I left to give myself space to think, and I knew the only way I could work through my thoughts was if I focused on myself. I threw all of my efforts into the new preschool—worked on the curriculum, the staffing requirements, health and nutrition plans for the children.

We decided to revamp everything and start from scratch, doing things a bit differently this time. I was in my element, and the fact I'm building something that is, in part, my own, makes me almost giddy with happiness. I feel fulfilled, for the first time in my life. But I also miss him.

It doesn't matter that he stalked me, was obsessed with me, and used my circumstances to steer me into marrying him. No matter what he's been through, no matter the mistakes he's made, I missed my husband. And when the motorcyclist hit me this morning and I crumpled to the road, my only thought was that if I died then, it would be without telling him how I feel about him. That I love him and want to spend every moment with him. Apparently, it took my life flashing in front of my eyes for me to realize he's in my corner. He's my ride or die. He's the man for me.

He takes my hand in his, then brings it up and kisses my knuckles. "Wife, you're, okay?"

"I'm okay, honestly. The motorcycle just brushed me."

"You were hit by a motorcycle?" He sways.

"I'm fine; nothing is hurt."

"You have scratches on your cheek." He surveys my features. And when he brings his fingers to the bandage on my forehead, his fingers tremble. "Your poor face."

"It's nothing, really."

"It's not nothing." The skin around his lips tightens. "And your legs--" He looks down at the expanse left uncovered by my skirt.

"I know, I have a few scratches there, and a wound on my knee, for which I had to receive a couple of stitches, but really, I'm fine."

"Fuck!" He drags his fingers through his hair. "Stitches? You had to have stitches?"

"Just two," the doctor says in a dry voice.

"Don't make it out to be less than what it was." He turns and points a finger at the doctor. "You're supposed to make it all better. Instead, you're standing there doing nothing."

"I'm a doctor, not a magician," Dr. Kincaid protests. "Also, she's a little shaken, but the wounds are minimal. The man who ran into her called for an ambulance right away. In fact, he's waiting outside, and —"

"He's waiting outside?" My husband pivots and stalks toward the door, but the doctor steps in his path. "Easy, Tiger. Accidents happen."

"Not with her, they don't," my husband growls.

"It would have been a lot worse if he'd gone on his way without bringing her in," the doctor says in a soothing voice.

"That's no excuse."

"That's true." He hesitates. "All I'm saying is, don't go out there and beat him up. And not in a hospital, for chrissakes."

"Alright then, I'm going to drag him out and smash his face in, and—"

"Fleabag!"

He stiffens. Is it because I used the safe word? I've never used it, but it seemed like the only way to stop him. But I didn't expect to see the shock on his face when he turns to face me.

"Wife?" He swallows. "Did you just—"

"Say fleabag?" I nod. "Didn't see any other way of stopping you. It was my fault. Honestly. I was in my own world and crossed when the pedestrian cross sign was red. It was *my* fault."

He draws in a breath, then slowly walks back to me. He takes my hand in his again and holds my gaze. "I'm sorry, I lost my temper. Seeing you hurt and helpless is more than I can bear. I've been berating myself ever since Weston called me and told me you were in hospital. It's a good thing I was with Baron when I got the call, or I might not have made it here."

I stare. "You were with Baron?"

"You were with Baron?" Dr. Kincaid asks at the same time.

"Yes, I was." My husband flushes. He releases his grip on my fingers, then stuffs his hand in the pocket of his sweatshirt.

A sweatshirt, people! Not that I don't find his three-piece-suited-and-vested look sexy, but Eddie unshaven and in a hoodie, and in grey sweatpants that outline that appendage between his legs, is drool-worthy. I squeeze my thighs together. My husband darts me a look. A gleam comes into his eyes as if he senses my reaction to his presence, but he doesn't comment. Instead, he gives me that half smile which brings out the divot in his cheek. "I took your advice."

"I'm glad you did," I murmur.

"About time the two of you made up," Dr. Kincaid growls.

"Someone talking about me?" Baron walks in. "Weston." He and the doctor bump fists, then he fixes his gaze on my husband.

"I spoke with the man outside who was responsible for the accident."

My husband begins to speak, but Baron raises his hand. "The man was digging a groove in the floor with his pacing. He was extremely sorry and apologetic. And at the risk of being beaten up, by all counts, it wasn't his fault."

"It wasn't. I was the one who ran into his path. I crossed when I shouldn't have."

"Glad you're doing okay." Baron smiles at me.

A nurse walks in, then stops when she sees all three men. And whoa, the three of them together are like a rugby defense team, with their height and broad shoulders. Lord alone knows how it is when all seven of them are in the same room. It probably results in an overload of pheromones that attracts all the women within a square mile of them.

"Oh, I'm sorry, Doctor Kincaid. I didn't realize you were still here. I wanted to check if the patient is being admitted?"

The doctor looks at me, then shakes his head. "I'm discharging you. You need to take it easy though, get some rest, lots of fluids... And stay warm."

"I'll make sure she does," my husband vows.

"Thank you, doctor" I tell him.

He smiles and nods at me, claps Baron on his shoulder, shakes Edward's hand, and leaves.

Baron looks between us. "Can I give you both a lift home?"

77

Edward

I walk toward my wife and scoop her up in my arms, leaving Baron to get her bag.

"I can walk," she murmurs.

"Not when I can carry you."

To my surprise, she doesn't protest. She snuggles in, and I take her to the car. I place her in the back seat, then walk around and slide in next to her.

"Where to, folks?" Baron looks at us in the mirror.

"Her address is —" I begin, but my wife cuts me off. "We're going to your place."

"We are?" I jerk my chin in her direction.

"We are," she confirms with a soft smile on her face.

Baron meets my gaze in the rearview mirror, nods, then eases the car forward. In the forty-five minutes it takes us to reach home through traffic, she falls asleep on my shoulder. I manage to text my housekeeper and let her know she can finish up for the day and leave. I want my wife all to myself when I get her home. She opted to come with me, probably because she feels weak and shaken, and while I never want to see anything like this happen to her again, I'm not going to waste this opportunity to hold her. We draw up at my place. I thank Baron, then hook her handbag over my shoulder and carry her inside. When I approach her bedroom, she stirs. "Are we home?"

Home. She called this home. *I hope she thinks of my home as her home, too.* She's probably out of it; that's why she called it home.

"We are." I walk into her room, but she shakes her head.

"Your room." She looks up at me with her big blue eyes. "I want you to take me to your bedroom."

I swallow. "Are you sure?"

She nods.

"I don't want you to feel beholden to me for anything. I know I rushed to the hospital, and I know I was worried about you, but I don't want this to make you feel compelled to want to be with me."

"And what if I do want it?" Her gaze intensifies. "What if I told you I've missed you and couldn't wait to be with you. And when I was run into and fell to the ground, all I could see was your face in front of my eyes. And I realized that if I can't be with you, my life will be incomplete."

"Then I have to say, He's listened to my prayers." I start toward my room.

"You've been praying?"

"Not daily, and nowhere near as much as I did in my past life as a priest. But I admit, I've been beseeching Him to give me a second chance with you." I glance down at her. "You have to know nothing is worth seeing you hurt. I'd rather you be safe and unharmed than have you here with me, having almost been run down."

"It was just a nudge, honestly." She rubs her cheek against my chest. "And the guy who was on the bike was really sorry. I was sure he was going to burst into tears when he helped me up on the sidewalk. And I told him I was okay, but he insisted on calling the ambulance. And then Dr. Kincaid happened to be at the hospital as they brought me in—"

"I'm glad he was, and that he called me."

"I'm glad he did, too. The only person I wanted to see then was you."

I place her on my bed gently, then sit down next to her. "How are you feeling? Do you want something to eat? Maybe some herbal tea?"

A buzzing sound fills the air. I pick up her bag and bring it over to her. She pulls out her phone and answers it. "Hi, Summer. No, I'm okay."

I can hear the woman's voice rise in pitch on the other side.

"No, I'm good, really. I'm here with Eddie."

The voice on the other side says something, and my wife blushes. "I'm sure, I don't want you to come and get me. Honestly, I'm good. Yeah, I'm spending the night here." She nods. "Thanks, I'll keep you updated." She switches off the phone and slides it into her bag. I place it on the nightstand.

She leans back against her pillows and yawns again. "I'm so tired."

"The shock must be wearing off." I pull the sheets up to her chin. "You should rest."

"That was Summer. She asked me if I was moving back with you."

My heart somersaults in my ribcage. Sweat pools under my arms. I'll never take what we have for granted. Never take the fact that she's my wife and in my bed as a *fait accompli*. Never stop myself from telling her how much I love her, every day, for the rest of my life. And if You're really up there and watching over me, then please, let her say yes, please. I swallow, and when I don't say anything, she lowers her chin to her chest.

"Don't you want to know what my reply was?"

78

A week later

Mira

"What made you decide you wanted to be with him?" Summer peers through the huge floor-to-ceiling windows at the snowflakes that float down to the ground. It's been snowing since the morning, enough to cover the trees with white and disrupt the trains in the city. Enough for the weather people to predict that this will be the heaviest snowfall in the last fifty years, or something like that. Truth is, I'm happy to snuggle up on the couch in the living room and watch the snow from here. I'm happy for my husband to wait hand and foot on me. He insists on carrying me everywhere in the house, and on bathing me and feeding me. He's given the housekeeper — who I finally managed to meet and say 'hi' to — the week off so he can tend to me alone.

He also hasn't gone to work; hasn't even checked his phone. So much so, Nathan finally called *me* and asked to speak to him. He must have invited himself over because, a few hours ago, he arrived at our doorstep. Summer was right behind him. I convinced Edward I'd be fine with her for company for a few hours. He told Summer to keep an eye on me and retreated to his study with Nathan to catch up on his office related matters, but only after I insisted he leave us.

She turns to me. "He does seem cray-cray about you."

"He is." I nod.

"And you're sure you want to do this?" She waves in the direction of the doorway he disappeared through.

I nod again.

"What made you decide to forgive him?"

"It wasn't just one thing." I wind a strand of hair around my fingers. "Or maybe, it was the way he knew I was resistant to Penicillin, something I tend to forget."

"But he remembered?"

"He did...when the doctor asked. If he hadn't, I'm sure he'd have recommended Penicillin for me, and that wouldn't have any impact. Frankly, that shook me a little. That he knew it and had the presence of mind to bring it up to the doctor, when"—I swallow—"when my own father doesn't know that about it."

"Oh, honey." She walks over and sits down on the couch next to me. "I'm so sorry."

"Of course, he seems to be coming around. He did stand up for me at Arthur's New Year party."

"The one where the Witches of Eastwick were kicked out of?"

I laugh. "The same. And he came to my rescue when they were horrible to me, too."

She nods.

"No one has been in my corner for so long. All those years growing up and feeling on my own, trying to win my stepmother's approval. It's only after meeting Eddie that I realized I was looking for a place to call my own. I was looking for..." I glance about the living room with its elegant, yet comfortable couch; the deep armchairs; the fireplace he lit earlier; the Christmas tree up in the corner, which he hasn't taken down yet, at my request; the windows that look out on the garden; the floor lamps lit at intervals; the lush carpeting on the floor—all of it is so Eddie and yet, also, so me. If I'd picked out the furniture for the place, I'd have probably ended up with the same look. "Home. I was looking for somewhere to belong to, but meeting Eddie made me realize home is wherever he is."

"You realized all this while you were away?"

I nod. "I know it should have taken me much longer, but for that small accident I had. It shook me, and all I wanted was Eddie by my side, holding my hand and telling me it would all be okay."

She smiles a little. "And you've forgiven everything he did?"

"Do I forgive him for spying on me without my permission and for replacing my contraceptive pills?" *And for almost taking the life of a man who was responsible for what happened to him and his friends. A man whose actions emotionally scarred a twelve-year-old boy for life?* I shake back my hair. "I do."

Besides, who's to say what's right and wrong. Aren't these rules made by man, after all?

She begins to speak, and I hold up my hand. "All I know is, good or bad, he's mine. He stalked me because he wanted me. He replaced my birth-control pills because he thought he was tainted by the incident. He was sure if I found out what he'd been through, I'd never want to be the mother of his child."

"And now?" She tilts her head.

"Now, I believe he loves me enough to never do anything to hurt me again."

She looks into my features and her smile broadens. "I'm so happy you and Ed found each other. I always worried about him. Of all the Seven, he's the one the incident affected the most. He's the one who seemed to carry the most secrets. He's also the most sensitive, though he never showed it. I always hoped he'd find a woman who'd love him as he is and you, my dear friend, are the perfect foil for him."

She throws her arms about me, and I hug her back. When the doorbell rings, she sniffs and breaks away. "I invited Gio and the girls. I hope you don't mind. It felt like the right time to celebrate."

She walks away and opens the door, and when my friends join me, I can't stop myself from smiling widely. I've found my tribe, and my man, and oh my god, it's everything I hoped for, and more.

"Is there a party in progress?" My husband walks past Gio, sprawled in one of the armchairs, and Penny, in the other. Both are holding glasses of champagne. Summer and Abby are in the kitchen, getting us all some snacks. He approaches me, leans a hip on the arm of the couch, then leans in and kisses my forehead. "How's my wife doing?"

"I'm perfect." I beam up at him.

He holds my gaze, and when that tiny divot appears in his cheek, I fall for him all over again. He leans in and kisses me. I allow myself to sink into his embrace, to draw in his scent and curl my fingers around that rock-like bicep of his, when the sound of someone clearing their throat infiltrates my subconscious. My husband softens the kiss, surveys my flushed features, and a smirk curls his lips.

"I'm off then, Ed," Nathan rumbles from his position in the doorway of the living room.

"Don't forget the site visit tomorrow," my husband says without taking his gaze from my face.

"Site visit?" Nathan frowns.

"It's one of Arthur's new pet projects. A bakery he's set on acquiring."

"A bakery?" Nathan stiffens. "The fuck does he want to do that?"

"You know the old man," Eddie manages to tear his gaze from mine and train it on Nathan. "Once has his mind set on something, he's not going to veer from it."

Nathan snorts, "More like, he's going senile."

"And his befuddled image is just that." My husband raises a shoulder." A front. He's a canny bastard who knows what he wants."

"Which is to get his grandchildren married off," Nathan says in a bitter tone.

"Not that I'm complaining." Eddie pulls me closer.

Nathan looks between us, and a strange look crosses his face. A mixture of longing and jealousy, if I'm interpreting it correctly. "You're a lucky wanker—sorry about the swearing ladies." He apologizes to my friends.

"We've heard worse." Gio waves a regal hand. "We're married to men who were all growly-faces like you at one point—"

"Then they fell for the right woman and reformed," Summer says with a sunny smile.

Nathan squares his shoulders, and his expression morphs into one of resolution, like he's making up his mind. "You mean, they're hooked to the ol' ball and chain?" He coughs.

"We heard that," Abby sings out as she and Penny enter the room with a bowl of popcorn, another of nachos, and a third one with salsa.

"A fate I intend to avoid at any cost," he growls.

My husband and I share a quiet smile. Gio and Penny, on the other hand, have no qualms, bursting into laughter.

"Poor man." I shake my head. "I feel sorry for what's coming."

"Something I'm missing?" Nathan frowns.

"No, nothing." Eddie stifles a grin. "Just as long as you make it to the bakery tomorrow."

Nathan drags his fingers through his hair. "Feels like a waste of my time. What do I know about the bakery business, anyway?"

To find out what happens next read Nathan and Skylar's story **HERE**

READ AN EXCERPT:

Skylar

"I can't do this." I lock my fingers together and narrow my gaze at my reflection. I'm in the tiny bathroom adjoining my office at the back of my bakery—my baby, my enterprise into which I've poured my lifesavings. And now, it's going to shut down. Unless I find the money for the rent next month, and for the utilities to keep the lights on so the sign on the shopfront continues to be lit up in pink and yellow neon, and for the supplies I need to continue baking. Etcetera. Etcetera. *Cutie Pie* is more than my dream; it's my whole life. What I've worked toward since I was sixteen and knew I was going to become the most phenomenal baker in the world. And now, I'm going to lose it.

"Sure, you can." My brother encourages me from the doorway. He grins. "You can do anything you set your mind to."

"That's what I used to think. It's why I started this pastry shop." That was six months ago. Followed by weeks of working eighteen-hour days and barely getting any sleep in my little apartment over the shop. Days of churning out my favorite cakes and pastries, showcasing the best ones on social media, and in short, doing everything possible to get my business off the ground. All, to no avail.

"Don't give up. You have to believe this can take off," Ben murmurs.

"Oh, trust me, I want to believe. But blind faith in yourself can only take you so far, apparently." Despite having viral posts take off on social media and having a surge of customers over the past month, I'm still not making enough to salvage my business.

"Success is what's beyond the dark night of the soul," my brother, ever the wise one between the two of us, remarks.

"Is that a saying among you Royal Marines?" I scoff.

"It's—"

The bell over the door at the front of the shop tinkles.

"—your destiny." His lips curve in a smile.

"What?" I blink.

"The bell—it's your future calling."

I roll my eyes. "If you say so."

"Go on, your customer is waiting." My brother walks over and kisses my forehead. "Good luck. Remember, when one door closes another one opens."

"If only I still believed that." I make a rude noise.

He steps back and wags a finger under my nose. "You'll see; it will work out." He turns me around and points me in the direction of the doorway leading to the shop." Go on, now."

"Whatever you say, big brother." I was ten when my father passed, and Ben became the de facto father figure in my life. I'm fifteen years younger than him, an "oops baby," born when my mother was in her early forties. I hero-worshipped Ben who, in turn, allowed me to tag along to all of the activities teenaged boys indulge in. He stepped into my father's shoes. He took care of me and never let me feel the loss of my father. "If I don't find a way to pay off my debts today, I'm shutting down," I insist.

There's no answer. I turn to find my brother has left the shop. Not that I blame him. He only has a two-week break before he has to ship out again. I suspect he's gone to meet his current squeeze. Ben never lacks female companionship.

As for me? I need to face whatever's in my destiny. Ben's right about that much. With a last tug at the neckline of the blouse which dips a little too low in the front, and which I wore to try and cheer myself—big fail there—I march out behind the counter, and all the air whooshes out of my lungs.

The man standing on the other side is so big, he seems to take up all of the space in my little bakery. He's tall enough, his head almost grazes the ceiling. And his shoulders—those shoulders I once held onto—are wider than I remember. They're broad enough to block out the view of the rest of the space.

His biceps stretch the sleeves of his suit, which must cost my entire annual rent to buy, given its tailor-made finish. He's wearing a black silk tie, and his jacket is black. A suit? I've never seen him in a suit before, but OMG, does he do it justice. I take in that lean waist, and those massive thighs, which seem ready to burst the seams of his pants, and between them, the tent that was the object of my obsession for so long.

"There was no one at the counter when I walked in. No wonder, you need a cash infusion," a familiar voice growls.

What the—? How dare he say that! I tear my gaze from the part of him that has always turned my insides to mush, and train my gaze on his face, and all remaining thoughts in my head drain away. I was prepared to give him a piece of my mind, but all of the pieces have scattered.

Those eyes. One piercing blue, the other an amber brown. Those heterochromatic eyes, which have always had the effect of reducing me to a mindless blob of need, stare into mine. My entire body hurts. My shoulder muscles turn into cement blocks. My stomach twists. It feels like I've run into a wall. Frissons of shock reverberate down my spine, and when he rakes his gaze down to my chest, his entire body seems to tense. He brings his gaze back to my face, and it feels like I've been punched in the guts. Again.

"What are you doing here?" I manage to croak around the ball of emotion in my throat.

"I might ask you the same question." His jaw tics, a muscle spasms at his jaw, and he curls his fingers into his sides. There's so much tension radiating from him, I feel faint. Apparently, he doesn't like what he sees.

That makes two of us. Nathan-fucking-Davenport. My brother's best friend. The man I've had a crush on for more than half of my life. The man who turned me down when I threw myself at him the day of my eighteenth birthday party. Not before he kissed me, though.

He hauled me to him, thrust his tongue in between my lips, and ravaged my mouth. He squeezed my ample butt and drew me against him, and I felt every inch of what he was packing. The kiss seemed to go on and on. My head spun. My knees gave way underneath me. I stumbled, and he straightened me. Only to tear his mouth from mine and stare into my face. His chest heaving, his breath coming in gusts that seemed to swell his shoulders. He raked his gaze across my features, like he was seeing me for the first time. Like he wanted to throw me down and mount me right there.

"Nate…" I breathed his name, and he released me and jumped back.

A look of confusion, then regret, then anger swept over his features.

I felt his rejection even before he blanked all expression from his face. "I'm sorry, I shouldn't have done that." He turned on his heel and walked out of my birthday celebration, and our house. And my life.

That was it; he cut off all communication with me. I never saw him again. Over the last five years, I've heard about his progress in the navy from my brother, but I never set eyes on him. Until today.

"You're the last person I want to speak to." I cross my arms over my chest, thereby pushing my breasts up higher. His eyes move down before he forces them back to my face. *It's not that I want to flaunt my double-D tits. Okay, okay, maybe I do. Maybe, I want to make him realize what he's been missing.* I'm proud of my assets. I might be a size sixteen, but I've never tried to conceal my full figure. So, what if I want to turn and hide right now?

"The feeling's mutual," he growls.

He actually growls. I draw myself up to my full height. Not that it helps, considering I'm only five feet four inches tall, and he's a good foot taller than me. Still, this is my space. "This is my shop, and you need to leave."

"Trust me, I wouldn't be here if I had any other option."

"What's that supposed to mean?"

"You're looking for a bailout."

"Excuse me?" I gape at him.

"Your business is in trouble. You need money to pay off your debts."

My flush intensifies. Heat crawls up my cheeks, all the way to the roots of hair, followed closely by anger. *How dare he walk in and throw my failure in my face? How dare he not talk to me all these years, only to reappear at the worst possible moment? And right after my brother told me it was my destiny come a-calling when the bell to the shop rang.*

"Wait, did Ben put you up this?"

"Eh?" He stares at my lips. His gaze is so intent that frisson of awareness, which has crackled up my spine since he arrived, flares into a full-blown shiver. I shake my head, ignoring the buzz of electricity that has always hummed between us. "Are you here because Ben asked you come by and help me out?"

A weird look comes into his eyes. He rubs at his temple. "I'm here because my grandfather is the chairman of the Davenport group of companies, and he thinks your bakery would make for a good investment."

"He does?"

"I'm yet to be convinced," he sneers.

So that's how it's gonna be, eh?

He glances toward the counter, taking in the various desserts on display, and his frown deepens. I follow his gaze and take in the tray of cupcakes displayed: Sp1cy Scene, Red Room, Velvet Ties, Purple Patches, Cave Wonder, The Vanilla Vajayjay, The Earth Moved. You have to admit, they're innovative names for the treats.

I named the first one in jest, but it proved to be a hot topic of discussion among fellow spicy book readers like me. Before I knew it, I ended up naming all my desserts in a similar vein.

In fact, the dessert shaped like the backside of a woman and called Spanking New keeps selling out. And then my other hit, a chocolate cake shaped like a vibrator and called C1itasaurus. Yep, they loved that one. Also, another raspberry-infused one in the shape of a fig called Moist Goodness. And finally, the doughnut-shaped treat called—you guessed it—AlphahOle, which is always a hit when I cater at book events.

"Is this a joke?" He stabs his forefinger at the display.

A-n-d that was the absolutely wrong thing to say. No one insults my baby— my bakery, my dream—and expects to get away unscathed.

"I can assure you; they are popular amongst my customers."

He turns those searing eyes on me, and it feels like I'm looking into the coldest depths of a frozen lake. The surface seems able to bear my weight, but one wrong step, and I'm going to fall right through and never find myself again. I try to breathe, but all of the oxygen in the room has been sucked out by his presence. My pulse crashes in my ears, and my nerve endings are so tightly stretched, I fear they'll snap any second. And when he stabs a hand in his pocket, pulling the fabric of his pants taut over that bulge between his legs, a slow thud flares to life between mine.

I *cannot* find him attractive. Cannot risk acknowledging this chemistry that thickens the air between us. Not when I need his help to save my business. Not when I know who he is, and he's definitely out of bounds. Forbidden. Sirens go off in my mind. *Back away. It's not worth taking on the humungous backlog of complications that're going to come with having anything to do with him.*

Then a look of boredom crosses his face. He yawns, and my pulse rate shoots up.

Strike out everything I felt earlier. It's definitely worth taking on every challenge that comes with getting him to cough up money, because by god, he needs to realize the world doesn't revolve around him. How can anyone be this full of himself? This insensitive.

Anger squeezes my chest. Adrenaline laces my blood. *And how dare he turn the most important meeting of my life into…into…something that doesn't merit even a few seconds of his attention?*

"I've seen everything I need to see. Goodbye." He turns to leave.

Think! You need to say something to stop him. You cannot afford to piss off the one guy who might be able to help save your bakery.

"Wait, don't you want to taste my wares?" I burst out.

He freezes mid-step. His shoulders seem to swell. The planes of his back rise and fall, and the jacket pulls even tighter. *Is he going to burst out of his skin and go all Hulk on me?* I swallow. And when he turns slowly and makes a growling sound at the back of his throat, I have to stop the yelp that almost spills from my mouth. Every single cell in my body has woken up and is doing the hula. *Stop that. You can't feel this drawn to this… to this arrogant beast who rejected you.*

But I also need his help. I have to save my business from going bust. And if that means swallowing my pride, then so be it. I tip up my chin and straighten my back. "I… I mean, maybe you want to taste my Honey Pot?" *Ugh. Didn't mean it to come out like that.*

His left eyelid twitches, and he seems one step closer to either having a breakdown or walking away. Neither of which is desirable.

"Oh, shoot. What I meant to say is, you'll definitely like the Purple Patches." I point to the range of cupcakes showcased under the counter. "Or of course, you could try The Clitasaurus?"

"The whatasaurus?" He tilts his head. His gaze is, once again, fixed on my mouth. My thighs clench, and moisture laces the flesh between my legs. I push away the burst of awareness which seems to have stuck its claws into my skin. No way am I going to give in to his magnetism, which has only multiplied in the years since I last saw him. Especially not when his jerkhole factor hasn't reduced either.

It's always been a mystery to me why I found his arrogance such a turn on. Now, I'm also reminded of how he always managed to get on my nerves. Not that it stopped me from throwing myself at him. A mistake I'm not going to make again. When I named that particular cupcake, it seemed like a stroke of genius. Having to pronounce it aloud in front of the Hulk, however, negates any laughs I've had about it so far.

"Uh, you know what I mean?" The color of my cheeks deepens and spreads to my chest. My entire body seems like it's on fire.

"No, I don't," he says in a low, hard voice.

I shiver. "You know that…that… pink pastry between the blue cakes that looks like…" I glance around, then slide open the glass door to the under-counter area. I pull on a pair of gloves, reach in and, instead of the Clitasaurus, slide one of the fig-shaped desserts onto a plate. I place it on the counter. "Actually, I think you should eat my Moist Goodness, and everything will be clear to you, and—"

I hear a gnashing sound, and when I dare to peek a glance at Mr. Grouchy Face, the muscles of his jaw ripple. *Oh no, at this rate he's going to crack a molar. Or two.* I blink rapidly, "Maybe we should start afresh?"

"Start afresh?" he asks in a tone that implies he'd rather have never met me.

Yeah, me too. Unfortunately, I don't have that luxury. "You know, pretend we don't know each other. Pretend the last few minutes never happened?" Pretend *that kiss* is not seared into my brain, and into other parts of my body I'm not going to think about.

I hold out my hand. "Skylar Potter." Then, because I hate my life and because, apparently, the connection between my brain and my mouth has been lost under the force of his glower, I smile. "No relation to Harry, as you're aware."

"Harry?" He looks at my slim, pink-tipped fingers, then back at my face, and makes no move to shake my hand.

I set my jaw. *Oh, my god, he's so rude, I should slap one of the pies baking in my oven into his face; only, they're too good to waste. Also, I can't risk messing up a pie when I need every sale I can get.* Every part of me wants to turn and run out of here. But I can't. *I owe it to myself, to my dream, to give this one last shot. I will not give up easily. I will not. I will stay polite, even if it kills me.* I manage to bare my teeth in the resemblance of a smile. "You know, Harry Potter? Boy wizard? *Evanesco.*" I pretend to flick my wand in his direction.

His jaw hardens further.

He looks pissed. The tips of his ears have turned white. Also, the end of his nose. Also, the vanishing spell on him didn't work. His Royal Dickness is still here, larger than life and glowering at me.

"I'm totally immersed in the Potterverse. Oh, and Taylor Swift. I love Taylor Swift." I beam at him.

His frown deepens.

"I'm guessing you're not a Swiftie?" I nod.

"What's that?" he asks in a contemptuous tone.

"Those of us who love Taylor Swift call ourselves Swifties."

"Sounds contagious," he sneers.

I ignore his cantankerous attitude because I need to charm him. And because I do need him to fork over the money I need. "I love her songs, don't you?" I chirrup.

His fingers curl into fists at his sides. Which is not a good sign. Then, because I love to go from the sublime to the surreal, I smile even wider. "Guess which Hogwarts's house Taylor Swift belongs to?" I toss my hair over my shoulder.

"Hogwhat?" He seems like he's about to have a cardiac event. Or like he went to sleep and woke up in an alternate reality. This is bad. So bad. And I have to go and put my foot in it by prompting him, "Hogwarts."

"Hogwhat?" he snaps again.

This time, the light goes on in my brain. "Oh, you haven't heard of Hogwarts." I snicker. "That's okay, I wasn't alive when man landed on the moon." *Don't say it, don't say it.* "Unlike you."

He blinks slowly.

Zip your lips. Just shut up already. "Not that I'm implying you're old or anything. The grey in your hair adds to your distinguished appearance. Besides, you're only fifteen years older than me." *Oh shoot, I don't think that makes it better.*

The veins on his throat stand out in relief. I try to swallow, but my throat is so dry, it feels like sharp knives line my gullet. I flick out a tongue to wet my lip, and his eyes gleam. He watches my mouth with a predatory gaze. Every part of his body seems to have turned to stone, watching me with such intensity, he seems to have turned into a predator who's planning every possible way to jump me.

The silence deepens. It doesn't stop me from shaking a finger at him. "You, mister, need a crash course in pop culture. Although, I suppose I shouldn't expect someone who has grey at his temples to have a sense of the zeitgeist."

"The fuck you talking about?" he bites out through gritted teeth.

"Whoa, hold on, no need to show me your horns now." *Although, I'd love to see the one between your legs.* "In fact, you look so angry, I'm expecting you to breathe fire at any moment." *You can turn into a dragon and carry me away anytime.* "And seriously, you should taste this." I push the plate with the moist, pink and purple, fig-shaped cake in his direction. It has a silver button between the lips and there's glitter around it.

"My desserts are awesome; one bite, and you'll be a convert." I nod.

He stares.

"Unless you're worried, you'll get addicted to my sweet bits." I tip up my chin.

Did I say *my* sweet bits? I did say *my* sweet bits. *Somebody kill me.* But he must see the challenge in my eyes, and alpha male that he is, of course, he doesn't back down.

Without taking his gaze off of my face, he licks the cream from the hollow in the center. A thousand little fires flare to life under my skin. I swallow; my breath grows shallow. He bites down on one of the plump lips, and a shiver grips me. I clutch at the edge of the counter. The pulse at the base of my throat speeds up. And when he pops the other lip into his mouth, I gulp. He brings his thumb and forefinger to his mouth and sucks on them, and a breathy moan leaves my lips.

"Not bad." He shrugs.

I stare. "What do you mean, 'not bad'? *That* is my bestseller."

"It was okay." He looks down his nose from his superior height, "I admit, the names you give your baked goods are creative, but I'm not sure that's enough for me to approve the takeover."

"Takeover?" I stiffen. "Who's talking about a takeover?"

"It's the only way I'd consider investing in your business."

"I only need help," I say through gritted teeth.

"That's putting it mildly. I reached out to the bank you took the loan from—"

"You reached out to my bank?" I burst out.

"You don't think I'd be here without due diligence—"

I cut in, "The terms of my deal with them are confidential." I lock my fingers together.

"Not when you're about to go bankrupt. When they realized the Davenport group was considering an acquisition—"

"An investment; a loan; that's *all* I'm looking for. Something to tide me over and buy me some time until I get back on my feet."

"Keep fooling yourself. You might be a good baker—"

"So you did like my dessert?" I declare in a triumphant voice.

"—but you're not a businessperson, by any stretch of imagination."

Oh, my god! What I wouldn't give to wipe that smug look off his face.

"There are ups and downs in any business." I lock my fingers together. "Things will bounce back."

"There are ups and downs, and then, there are downs and more downs," he drawls.

Anger thuds at my temples. *I will not lose my temper. I will not.*

He slides his hand into his pocket. "Not that I don't understand your reluctance to sell out."

"You do?"

"Of course. You've invested your sweat and blood, and likely, your entire savings into the venture. Too bad, you didn't have a financial person advising you."

Of course, he'd say that. Nate's always been a numbers whiz. I heard that from Ben. It's why, even when they were in the navy together, Nate was quickly put in charge of strategy. He was the person coming up with the game plan, while Ben was always on the front lines. And Nate's sharp brain helped him always stay ahead of the enemy. He saved Ben's life many times, or so my brother informed me over the years. Too bad, his best friend's temperament leaves much to be desired.

"I would be willing to consider a merger instead of an acquisition of your little business." His gaze flicks about the place and back at me.

"*Little* business?" I curl my fingers into fists. *Breathe, count back from ten. Do not give into the impulsive need to throw a pie in his face.*

He wipes his thumb under his lip, a considering look in his eyes. "Of course, I don't have to do anything. But given you're Ben's little sister, and he wouldn't want me to leave you in the lurch, I might have a proposition that could help both of us."

"Of course, you do."

My sarcasm is lost on him, for he looks me up and down. "Marry me."

To find out what happens next read Nathan and Skylar's story in The Unwanted Wife

Want an exclusive bonus epilogue featuring Edward and Mira? Click HERE

Read an Excerpt from Nathan & Skylar's story in The Unwanted Wife

Skylar

"I can't do this." I lock my fingers together and narrow my gaze at my reflection. I'm in the tiny bathroom adjoining my office at the back of my bakery—my baby, my enterprise into which I've poured my life savings. And now, it's going to shut down. Unless I find the money for the rent next month... And for the utilities to keep the lights on so the sign on the shopfront continues to be lit up in pink and yellow neon... And for the supplies I need to continue baking. *The Fearless Kitten* is more than my dream; it's my whole life. What I've worked toward since I was sixteen and knew I was going to become the most phenomenal baker in the world. And now, I'm going to lose it.

"Sure, you can do it." My brother encourages me from the doorway. "You can do anything you set your mind to."

"That's what I used to think. It's why I started this pastry shop." I was twelve when I discovered I was good at baking. That, combined with my love for desserts, meant I knew what I wanted to do with my life.

Two years ago, I moved to London to work at a well-known patisserie. I began scouting for a location for my place while I saved every single penny I could.

A year ago, I found the perfect place, and my little artisan bakery with coffee shop seating was born. Of course, I work eighteen-hour workdays, which means I have almost no social life. I barely manage a few hours of sleep in my little apartment over the shop. But nothing can dampen my spirits. I'm spending my days churning out cakes and pastries. It's what I've dreamed of for so long. Only issue?

I don't have the money to advertise, and despite having a social media post go viral—which is when a lot of people look at your social media feed—and result in a surge of customers, I'm not making enough to salvage my business.

"Don't give up. You have to believe this can take off." Ben's voice is confident. If only I shared his optimism.

"Oh, trust me, I want to believe. But blind faith in yourself only takes you so far." I wish I could do better at spreading the word about the place and bringing in new customers. I seem to suck at everything outside of baking. It's why my business is on the decline.

"Success is what's beyond the dark night of the soul," my brother, ever the wise one, remarks.

"Is that a saying among you Royal Marines?" I scoff.

"It's—"

The bell over the door at the front of the shop tinkles.

"—your destiny." His lips curve in a smile.

"What?" I blink.

"The bell—it's your future calling."

I roll my eyes. "If you say so."

"Go on, your customer is waiting." My brother walks over and kisses my forehead. "Good luck. Remember, when one door closes, another one opens. Or the one I prefer, she who leaves a trail of glitter is never forgotten."

"Eh?" I stare. "What does that have to do with my situation?"

"Nothing, but it did cheer you up."

I roll my eyes, then can't stop myself from chuckling.

"That's my girl." He pats my shoulder.

Yep, that's my brother. The ever-cheerful, never-surrender person. "You'll see; it will work out." He turns me around and points me in the direction of the doorway leading to the shop. "Go on now."

"Whatever you say, big bro."

I was ten when my father passed, and Ben became the de facto father figure in my life. I'm fifteen years younger than him, an "oops baby," born when my mother was in her early forties. I hero-worshipped Ben, who, in turn, took care of me and never let me feel the loss of my father. And when my mother passed away, he took a leave of absence and came home and stayed with me, until he was assured I was ready to pick myself up and move on. He's the most important person in the world, in my life, in so many ways. And the fact that he fights wars so I can be safe is a source of the utmost pride for me. It's one of the reasons I feel terrible about being on the verge of bankruptcy. I want Ben to be proud of me.

"This is my last chance to get things right. If I can't find a way to pay off my debts, I'll have no choice but to shut down." I hear my words and realize I'm being negative. The exact opposite of my brother. I expect him to tell me off, but there's no answer. I turn to find he's left the shop. Not that I blame him. He has a two-week break before he has to ship out again. I suspect he's gone to meet his current squeeze. Ben never lacks female companionship.

As for me? I need to face whatever's in my destiny. If only my every decision didn't impact Hugo. If only I weren't running out of money to keep him in the care home that provides round-the-clock attention for him. If I can't pay next month's fees—no, I'm not going there. I will not contemplate the repercussions of what would happen if I didn't come up with the money, and fast.

With a last tug at the neckline of my blouse, which dips a little too low in the front, and which I wore to try and cheer myself up—big fail, there—I march out of the kitchen and go behind the counter. And all the air whooshes out of my lungs.

The man standing in the middle of the bakery is so big, he seems to occupy all of the space in my little bakery. He's so tall, I have to tilt my head back to meet his gaze. And his shoulders—those shoulders I once held onto—are wider than I remember. They're broad enough to block out the view of the rest of the space.

His biceps stretch the sleeves of his suit, which must cost my entire annual rent to buy, given its tailor-made finish. He's wearing a black silk tie, and his jacket is black. Wait, a suit? I've never seen him in a suit before, but OMG, does he do it justice. I take in that lean waist, and those massive thighs, which seem ready to burst the seams of his pants, and between them, the tent that was the object of my obsession for so long. He prowls over to the counter and whoa, that predatory walk of his, the way he seems to glide across the floor with the gait of a barely tamed animal turns my bones to jelly.

"There was no one at the counter when I walked in. No wonder, you need a cash infusion," a familiar voice growls.

What the—? How dare he say that! I wrench my gaze up to his face. And any remaining thoughts in my head drain away. I was prepared to give him a piece of my mind, but all of the pieces have scattered.

Those eyes—one piercing blue, the other an amber brown. Those heterochromatic eyes, which have always had the effect of reducing me to a mindless blob of need, stare into mine.

My entire body hurts. My shoulder muscles turn into cement blocks. My stomach twists. It feels like I've run into a wall. Frissons of shock reverberate down my spine, and when he rakes his gaze down to my chest, his entire body seems to tense. He brings his gaze back to my face, and it feels like I've been punched in the gut. Again.

"What are you doing here?" I manage to croak around the ball of emotion in my throat.

"What do you think I'm doing here?" His jaw tics, a muscle spasms in his jaw, and he curls his fingers into his sides. There's so much tension radiating from him, I feel faint. Apparently, he doesn't like what he sees.

That makes two of us. Nathan-bloody-Davenport. My brother's best friend. The man I've had a crush on for more than half my life. The man who turned me down when I threw myself at him the day of my eighteenth birthday party. Not before he kissed me, though.

He hauled me to him, thrust his tongue between my lips, and ravaged my mouth. He squeezed my ample butt and drew me against him, and I felt every inch of what he was packing. The kiss seemed to go on and on. My head spun. My knees gave way underneath me. I stumbled, and he straightened me. Only to tear his mouth from mine and stare into my face, his chest heaving, his breath coming in gusts that seemed to swell his shoulders. He raked his gaze across my features, like he was seeing me for the first time. Like he wanted to throw me down and mount me right there.

"Nate..." I breathed his name.

"Starling," he whispered against my lips. The sound of his voice seemed to cut through his reverie, for the next second, he released me and jumped back.

A look of confusion, then regret, then anger swept over his features. I felt his rejection even before he blanked all expression from his face. "I'm sorry, I shouldn't have done that, Skye." He turned on his heel and walked out of my birthday celebration, and our house. And my life.

That was it; he cut off all communication with me. I never saw him again. Over the last five years, I've heard about his progress in the Marines from my brother, but I never set eyes on him. Until today.

"You're the last person I want to speak to." I cross my arms over my chest, thereby pushing my breasts up higher. His eyes move down before he forces them back to my face. *It's not that I want to flaunt my double-D tits. Okay, okay, maybe I do. Maybe, I want to make him realize what he's been missing.* I'm proud of my assets. I might be a size sixteen, but I've never tried to conceal my full figure. So what if I want to run and hide right now?

"The feeling's mutual," he growls.

And the sound is so freakin' hot, so caveman like, my ovaries seem to quiver. Just because my body can't control itself doesn't mean I find him attractive. Nope, it doesn't mean anything that I haven't stopped thinking of him all these years.

I draw myself up to my full height. Not that it helps, considering I'm five-feet four-inches tall, and he's a good foot taller than me. Still, this is my space. "This is my shop, and you need to leave."

"Trust me, I wouldn't be here if I had any other option," he sneers.

"What's that supposed to mean?"

"You're looking for a bailout."

"Excuse me?" I gape at him.

"Your business is in trouble. You need money to pay off your debts."

My flush intensifies. Heat crawls up my cheeks, all the way to the roots of hair, followed closely by anger. *How dare he walk in and throw my failure in my face? How dare he not talk to me all these years, only to reappear at the worst possible moment? And right after my brother told me it was my destiny come-a-calling when the bell to the shop rang.*

"Wait, did Ben put you up this?"

"Eh?" He stares at my lips. His gaze is so intent that the frisson of awareness, which has crackled up my spine since he arrived, flares into a full-blown shiver. I shake my head, ignoring the buzz of electricity that has always hummed between us. "Are you here because Ben asked you to help me out?"

A weird look comes into his eyes. He shifts his weight from foot to foot. "I'm here because my grandfather is the chairman of the Davenport Group of companies, and he thinks your bakery would make for a good investment."

"He does?"

"I'm yet to be convinced." He crosses his arms across his chest.

So that's how it's gonna be, eh?

He glances toward the counter, taking in the various desserts on display, and his frown deepens. I follow his gaze and take in the tray of cupcakes displayed: Spicy Scene, Red Room, Velvet Ties, Purple Patches, Cave Wonder, The Vanilla Vajayjay, The Earth Moved... You have to admit, they're innovative names for the treats.

I named the first one in jest, but it proved to be a hot topic of discussion among fellow spicy book readers like me. Before I knew it, I'd ended up naming many of my desserts in a similar vein.

In fact, the dessert shaped like the backside of a woman and called Spanked is one that customers seem to love. Then there's my other hit, a chocolate cake shaped like a vibrator and called Clitasaurus. Yep, they love that one. Also, another raspberry-infused one in the shape of a peach called Moist Goodness, not to forget the honey-glazed fruit cake in the form of a beehive called the Honey Pot, and the strawberry and cream-topped, fig-shaped shortbread I named Sweet Bits. Finally, the doughnut-shaped dark chocolate glazed treat called—you guessed it—Alphah0le, which readers love when I cater at book events.

You'd think business is booming, and I certainly have my share of loyal customers, but it's not enough to keep me in the black. I need to bring in new customers, and a lot more of them.

He stabs his forefinger at the display. "Is this a joke?"

Skylar

A-n-d that was the absolutely wrong thing to say. No one insults my baby—my bakery, my dream—and gets away unscathed.

"I can assure you; they are popular amongst my customers."

He turns those searing eyes on me, and it feels like I'm looking into the depths of a frozen lake. The surface seems able to bear my weight, but one wrong step, and I'm going to fall right through and find myself trapped. I try to breathe, but all of the oxygen in the room has been sucked out by his presence. My pulse crashes in my ears, and my nerve endings are so tightly stretched, I fear they'll snap any second. And when he shoves a hand in his pocket, pulling the fabric of his pants taut over that bulge between his legs, a slow thud flares to life between mine.

I *cannot* find him attractive. Cannot risk acknowledging this chemistry that thickens the air between us. Not when I need his help to save my business. Not when I know who he is, and he's definitely out-of-bounds. Forbidden. Sirens go off in my mind. *Back away. It's not worth taking on the humungous backlog of complications that are going to come with having anything to do with him.*

Then a look of boredom crosses his face. He yawns, and my pulse rate shoots up.

Strike out everything I felt earlier. It's definitely worth taking on every challenge that comes with getting him to cough up money, because by God, he needs to realize the world doesn't revolve around him. How can anyone be this full of himself? This insensitive?

Anger squeezes my chest. Adrenaline laces my blood. *And how dare he turn the most important meeting of my life into… into… something that doesn't merit even a few seconds of his attention?*

"I've seen everything I need to see. Goodbye." He turns to leave.

What the—? He's leaving? Does that mean he's decided against investing in the bakery? Think! You need to say something to stop him. You cannot afford to piss off the one guy who might be able to help save your bakery.

"Wait, don't you want to taste my wares?" I burst out.

He freezes mid-step. His shoulders seem to swell. The planes of his back rise and fall, and the jacket pulls even tighter. *Is he going to burst out of his skin and go all Hulk on me?* I swallow. And when he turns slowly and makes a growling sound at the back of his throat, I have to stop the yelp that almost spills from my mouth. Every single cell in my body has woken up and is doing the hula. *Stop that. You can't feel this drawn to this... To this arrogant beast who rejected you.*

But I also need his help. I have to save my business from going bust. And if that means swallowing my pride, then so be it. I tip up my chin and straighten my back. "I... I mean, maybe you want to taste my Honey Pot?" *Ugh. Didn't mean it to come out like that.*

His left eyelid, the one covering his blue eye, twitches, and he seems one step closer to either having a breakdown or walking away. Neither of which is desirable.

"Oh, *Fraggle Rock*. What I meant to say is, you'll definitely like the Purple Patches." I point to the range of cupcakes showcased under the counter.

"Did you use *Fraggle Rock* as a swear word?" He stares.

"I did. It's because my mother hated me swearing—being a girl, and all that." I roll my eyes. That condition had *not* applied to my brother. "So instead, I began to use names of TV series as swear words. Also, you could try the Clitasaurus?" I look at him hopefully.

"The whatasaurus?" He tilts his head. His gaze is, once again, fixed on my mouth. My thighs clench, and moisture laces the flesh between my legs. I push away the burst of awareness which seems to have stuck its claws into my skin. No way am I going to succumb to his magnetism, which has multiplied in the years since I last saw him. Especially not when his jerkhole factor hasn't reduced, either.

It's always been a mystery to me why I found his arrogance such a turn on. Now, I'm also reminded of how he always managed to get on my nerves. Not that it stopped me from throwing myself at him. A mistake I'm not going to make again. When I named that cupcake, it seemed like a stroke of genius. Having to pronounce it aloud in front of the Hulk, however, negates any laughs I've had about it so far.

"Uh, you know what I mean?" The color of my cheeks deepens and spreads to my chest. My entire body seems like it's on fire.

"No, I don't," he says in a low, hard voice.

I shiver. "You know that...that...pink pastry between the blue cakes that looks like..." I glance around, then slide open the glass door to the under-counter area. I pull on a pair of disposable gloves, reach in and, instead of the Clitasaurus, slide one of the fig-shaped desserts onto a plate. I place it on the counter. "Actually, I think you should eat my Moist Goodness, and everything will be clear to you, and—"

I hear a gnashing sound, and when I dare to peek at Mr. Grouchy Face, I see the muscles of his jaw ripple. *Oh no, at this rate, he's going to crack a molar. Or two.*

I blink rapidly. "Maybe we should start afresh?"

"Start afresh?" he asks in a tone that implies he'd rather have never met me.

Yeah, me, too. Unfortunately, I don't have that luxury. "You know, pretend we don't know each other. Pretend the last few minutes never happened?" *Pretend that kiss is not seared into my brain, and into other parts of my body I'm not going to think about.*

I pull off my gloves and hold out my hand. "Skylar Potter." Then, because I hate my life and because, apparently, the connection between my brain and my mouth has been lost under the force of his glower, I smile. "No relation to Harry, as you're aware."

"Harry?" He looks at my slim, pink-tipped fingers, then back at my face, and makes no move to shake my hand.

I set my jaw. *Oh, my god, he's so rude, I should slap one of the pies baking in my oven into his face. Only, they're too good to waste. Also, I can't risk messing up a pie when I need every sale I can get.* Every part of me wants to turn and run out of here. But I can't. I owe it to myself, to my dream, to give this one last shot. *I will not give up easily. I will not. I will stay polite, even if it kills me.* I manage to bare my teeth in the resemblance of a smile. "You know, Harry Potter? Boy wizard? *Evanesco.*" I pretend to flick my wand in his direction.

His jaw hardens further.

Ooh, he looks pissed. The tips of his ears have turned white. Also, the end of his nose. Also, the vanishing spell on him didn't work. His Royal Dickness is still here, larger than life and glowering at me.

"I'm sooo immersed in the Potterverse. Oh, and Taylor Swift. I love Taylor Swift." I beam at him.

His frown deepens.

"I'm guessing you're not a Swiftie?" I nod.

"What's that?" he asks in a contemptuous tone.

"Those of us who love Taylor Swift call ourselves Swifties."

"Sounds contagious," he sneers.

I ignore his cantankerous attitude because I need to charm him. And because I desperately need him to fork over the money I need. "I love her songs, don't you?" I chirrup.

His fingers curl into fists at his sides. Which is not a good sign. Then, because I love to go from the sublime to the surreal, I smile even wider. "Guess which Hogwarts' house Taylor Swift belongs to?" I toss my hair over my shoulder.

"Hogwhat?" He seems like he's about to have a cardiac event. Or like he went to sleep and woke up in an alternate reality. This is bad. So bad.

And I have to go and put my foot in it by prompting him, "Hogwarts."

"Hogwhat?" he snaps again.

This time, the light goes on in my brain. "Oh, you haven't heard of Hogwarts?" I titter. "That's okay. I wasn't alive when *Titanic* hit the cinemas, either..." *Don't say it, don't say it.* "Unlike you."

He blinks slowly.

"I meant the movie, not the actual event when the Titanic hit an iceberg and sank."

His jaw tics.

"Not that you were alive when the Titanic sank." I cough. "Even *I* know you're not *that* ancient."

A nerve pops at his temple. That's not a good sign, is it? *Zip your lips. Just shut up already.*

"Not that I'm implying you're old or anything." I try to contain my laughter and end up snorting—ugh, bad habit. "The grey in your hair adds to your distinguished appearance. Besides, you're only fifteen years older than me." *Oh no, I don't think that makes it better.*

The veins on his throat stand out in relief. I try to swallow, but my throat is so dry, it feels like sharp knives line my gullet. I flick out a tongue to wet my lips, and his eyes gleam. He watches my mouth with a rapacious gaze. Every part of his body seems to have turned to stone. Watching me with such intensity, he seems to have turned into a predator who's planning every possible way to jump me. If he had a tail, I think it'd be swishing from side to side.

The silence deepens. It doesn't stop me from shaking a finger at him. "You, mister, need a crash course in pop culture. Although, I suppose, I shouldn't expect someone who has grey at his temples to have a sense of the zeitgeist."

"The fuck you prattling on about?" he bites out through gritted teeth.

"Whoa, hold on, no need to show me your horns." *Although, I'd love to see the one between your legs.* "In fact, you look so angry, I'm expecting you to breathe fire at any moment." *You can turn into a dragon and carry me away anytime.* "And seriously, you should taste this." I push the plate with the moist, pink-and-white, fig-shaped shortbread in his direction. It has a button between the lips made of edible silver leaf and there's glitter around it.

"My desserts are awesome; one bite, and you'll be a convert." I nod.

He stares.

"Unless you're worried you'll get addicted to my Sweet Bits." I tip up my chin.

Did I say *my* sweet bits? I did say *my* sweet bits. "I meant the dessert that I've named Sweet Bits, not *my* sweet bits." I hear my words, and argh, didn't mean for them to sound so… provocative. But I'm not going to apologize for that. Hell no.

"Well? You going to taste it or what?" I scowl.

He must see the challenge in my eyes and, alpha male that he is, of course, he doesn't back down. Without taking his gaze off of my face, he licks the cream from the hollow in the center. A thousand little fires flare to life under my skin. I swallow; my breath grows shallow. He bites down on one of the plump lips, and a shiver grips me. I clutch at the edge of the counter. The pulse at the base of my throat speeds up. And when he pops the other lip into his mouth, I gulp. He brings his thumb and forefinger to his mouth and sucks on them, and a breathy moan leaves my lips.

"Not bad." He shrugs.

I stare. "What do you mean, *not bad?! That* is my best-seller."

"It was okay." He looks down his nose from his superior height. "I admit, the names you give your baked goods are creative, but I'm not sure that's enough for me to approve the takeover."

"Takeover?" I stiffen. "Who's talking about a takeover?"

"It's the only way I'd consider investing in your business."

"I only need help," I say through gritted teeth.

"That's putting it mildly. I reached out to the bank you took the loan from—"

"You reached out to my bank?" I burst out.

"You don't think I'd be here without due diligence—"

I cut in, "The terms of my deal with them are confidential." I lock my fingers together.

"Not when you're about to go bankrupt. When they realized the Davenport Group was considering an acquisition—"

"An investment; a loan; that's *all* I'm looking for. Something to tide me over and buy me some time until I get back on my feet."

"Keep fooling yourself. You might be a good baker—"

"So you did like my dessert," I declare in a triumphant voice.

"—but you're not a businessperson, by any stretch of the imagination."

Oh, my god! What I wouldn't give to wipe that smug look off his face.

"There are ups and downs in any business." I lock my fingers together. "Things will bounce back."

"There are ups and downs, and then, there are downs and more downs," he drawls.

Anger thuds at my temples. *I will not lose my temper. I will not.*

He slides his hand into his pocket. "Not that I don't understand your reluctance to sell out."

"You do?"

"Of course. You've invested your sweat and blood, and likely, your entire savings into the venture. Too bad you didn't have a financial person advising you."

Of course, he'd say that. Nate's always been a numbers whiz. I heard that from Ben. It's why, even when they were in the Marines together, Nate oversaw strategy. He was the person coming up with the game plan for their team. It was Nate's sharp brain which helped them both stay ahead of the enemy; or so my brother informed me over the years. Too bad his best friend's temperament leaves much to be desired.

"I would be willing to consider a merger instead of an acquisition of your little business." His gaze flicks about the place and back at me.

"*Little* business?" I curl my fingers into fists. *Breathe, count back from ten. Do not give into the impulsive need to throw a pie in his face.*

He wipes his thumb under his lip, a considering look in his eyes. "Of course, I don't have to do anything. But given you're Ben's little sister, and he wouldn't want me to leave you in the lurch, I might have a proposition that could help both of us."

"Of course you do."

My sarcasm is lost on him, for he looks me up and down. "Marry me."

To find out what happens next read Nathan & Skylar's story in The Unwanted Wife by L. Steele

Read Summer & Sinclair Sterling's story HERE in The Billionaire's Fake Wife

Read an excerpt from Summer & Sinclair's story

Summer

"Slap, slap, kiss, kiss."

"Huh?" I stare up at the bartender.

"Aka, there's a thin line between love and hate." He shakes out the crimson liquid into my glass.

"Nah." I snort. "Why would she allow him to control her, and after he insulted her?"

"It's the chemistry between them." He lowers his head. "You have to admit that, when the man is arrogant and the woman resists, it's a challenge to both of them, to see who blinks first, huh?"

"Why?" I wave my hand in the air. "Because they hate each other?"

"Because," he chuckles, "the girl in school whose braids I pulled and teased mercilessly, is the one who I—"

"Proposed to?" I huff.

His face lights up. "You get it now?"

Yeah. No. A headache begins to pound at my temples. This crash course in pop psychology is not why I came to my favorite bar in Islington, to meet my best friend, who is—I glance at the face of my phone—thirty minutes late.

I inhale the drink, and his eyebrows rise.

"What?" I glower up at the bartender. "I can barely taste the alcohol. Besides, it's free drinks at happy hour for women, right?"

"Which ends in precisely—" he holds up five fingers— "minutes."

"Oh! Yay!" I mock fist pump. "Time enough for one more, at least."

A hiccough swells my throat and I swallow it back, nod.

One has to do what one has to do… when everything else in the world is going to shit.

A hot sensation stabs behind my eyes; my chest tightens. Is this what people call growing up?

The bartender tips his mixing flask, strains out a fresh batch of the ruby red liquid onto the glass in front of me.

"Salut." I nod my thanks, then toss it back. It hits my stomach and tendrils of fire crawl up my spine, I cough.

My head spins. Warmth sears my chest, spreads to my extremities. I can't feel my fingers or toes. Good. Almost there. "Top me up."

"You sure?"

"Yes." I square my shoulders and reach for the drink.

"No. She's had enough."

"What the — ?" I pivot on the bar stool.

Indigo eyes bore into me.

Fathomless. Black at the bottom, the intensity in their depths grips me. He swoops out his arm, grabs the glass and holds it up. Thick fingers dwarf the glass. Tapered at the edges. The nails short and buff. *All the better to grab you with.* I gulp.

"Like what you see?"

I flush, peer up into his face.

Hard cheekbones, hollows under them, and a tiny scar that slashes at his left eyebrow. *How did he get that?* Not that I care. My gaze slides to his mouth. Thin upper lip, a lower lip that is full and cushioned. Pouty with a hint of bad boy. *Oh!* My toes curl. My thighs clench.

The corner of his mouth kicks up. *Asshole.*

Bet he thinks life is one big smug-fest. I glower, reach for my glass, and he holds it up and out of my reach.

I scowl. "Gimme that."

He shakes his head.

"That's my drink."

"Not anymore." He shoves my glass at the bartender. "Water for her. Get me a whiskey, neat."

I splutter, then reach for my drink again. The barstool tips in his direction. This is when I fall against him, and my breasts slam into his hard chest, sculpted planes with layers upon layers of muscle that ripple and writhe as he turns aside, flattens himself against the bar. The floor rises up to meet me.

What the actual hell?

I twist my torso at the last second and my butt connects with the surface. *Ow!*

The breath rushes out of me. My hair swirls around my face. I scramble for purchase, and my knee connects with his leg.

"Watch it." He steps around, stands in front of me.

"You stepped aside?" I splutter. "You let me fall?"

"Hmph."

I tilt my chin back, all the way back, look up the expanse of muscled thigh that stretches the silken material of his suit. *What is he wearing? Could any suit fit a man with such precision?* Hand crafted on Saville Row, no doubt. I glance at the bulge that tents the fabric between his legs. *Oh!* I blink.

Look away, look away. I hold out my arm. He'll help me up at least, won't he?

He glances at my palm, then turns away. *No, he didn't do that, no way.*

A glass of amber liquid appears in front of him. He lifts the tumbler to his sculpted mouth.

His throat moves, strong tendons flexing. He tilts his head back, and the column of his neck moves as he swallows. Dark hair covers his chin —it's a discordant chord in that clean-cut profile, I shiver. He would scrape that rough skin down my core. He'd mark my inner thighs, lick my core, thrust his tongue inside my melting channel and drink from my pussy. *Oh! God.* Goosebumps rise on my skin.

No one has the right to look this beautiful, this achingly gorgeous. Too magnificent for his own good. Anger coils in my chest.

"Arrogant wanker."

"I'll take that under advisement."

"You're a jerk, you know that?"

He presses his lips together. The grooves on either side of his mouth deepen. Clearly the man has never laughed a single day in his life. Bet that stick up his arse is uncomfortable. I chuckle.

He runs his gaze down my features, my chest, down to my toes, then yawns.

The hell! I will not let him provoke me. Will not. "Like what you see?" I jut out my chin.

"Sorry, you're not my type." He slides a hand into the pocket of those perfectly cut pants, stretching it across that heavy bulge.

Heat curls low in my belly.

Not fair, that he could afford a wardrobe that clearly shouts his status and what amounts to the economy of a small third-world country. A hot feeling stabs in my chest.

He reeks of privilege, of taking his status in life for granted.

While I've had to fight every inch of the way. Hell, I am still battling to hold onto the last of my equilibrium.

"Last chance—" I wiggle my fingers from where I am sprawled out on the floor at his feet, "—to redeem yourself..."

"You have me there." He places the glass on the counter, then bends and holds out his hand. The hint of discolored steel at his wrist catches my attention. Huh?

He wears a cheap-ass watch?

That's got to bring down the net worth of his presence by more than 1000% percent. Weird.

I reach up and he straightens.

I lurch back.

"Oops, I changed my mind." His lips curl.

A hot burning sensation claws at my stomach. I am not a violent person, honestly. But Smirky Pants here, he needs to be taught a lesson.

I swipe out my legs, kicking his out from under him.

Sinclair

My knees give way, and I hurtle toward the ground.

What the—? I twist around, thrust out my arms. My palms hit the floor. The impact jostles up my elbows. I firm my biceps and come to a halt planked above her.

A huffing sound fills my ear.

I turn to find my whippet, Max, panting with his mouth open. I scowl and he flattens his ears.

All of my businesses are dog-friendly. Before you draw conclusions about me being the caring sort or some such shit—it attracts footfall.

Max scrutinizes the girl, then glances at me. *Huh?* He hates women, but not her, apparently.

I straighten and my nose grazes hers.

My arms are on either side of her head. Her chest heaves. The fabric of her dress stretches across her gorgeous breasts. My fingers tingle; my palms ache to cup those tits, squeeze those hard nipples outlined against the—hold on, what is she wearing? A tunic shirt in a sparkly pink... and are those shoulder pads she has on?

I glance up, and a squeak escapes her lips.

Pink hair surrounds her face. *Pink? Who dyes their hair that color past the age of eighteen?*

I stare at her face. *How old is she?* Un-furrowed forehead, dark eyelashes that flutter against pale cheeks. Tiny nose, and that mouth—

luscious, tempting. A whiff of her scent, cherries and caramel, assails my senses. My mouth waters. *What the hell?*

She opens her eyes and our eyelashes brush. Her gaze widens. Green, like the leaves of the evergreens, flickers of gold sparkling in their depths. "What?" She glowers. "You're demonstrating the plank position?"

"Actually," I lower my weight onto her, the ridge of my hardness thrusting into the softness between her legs, "I was thinking of something else, altogether."

She gulps and her pupils dilate. *Ah, so she feels it, too?*

I drop my head toward her, closer, closer.

Color floods the creamy expanse of her neck. Her eyelids flutter down. She tilts her chin up.

I push up and off of her.

"That… Sweetheart, is an emphatic 'no thank you' to whatever you are offering."

Her eyelids spring open and pink stains her cheeks. Adorable. Such a range of emotions across those gorgeous features in a few seconds. What else is hidden under that exquisite exterior of hers?

She scrambles up, eyes blazing.

Ah! The little bird is trying to spread her wings? My dick twitches. My groin hardens, *Why does her anger turn me on so, huh?*

She steps forward, thrusts a finger in my chest.

My heart begins to thud.

She peers up from under those hooded eyelashes. "Wake up and taste the wasabi, asshole."

"What does that even mean?"

She makes a sound deep in her throat. My dick twitches. My pulse speeds up.

She pivots, grabs a half-full beer mug sitting on the bar counter.

I growl, "Oh, no, you don't."

She turns, swings it at me. The smell of hops envelops the space.

I stare down at the beer-splattered shirt, the lapels of my camel colored jacket deepening to a dull brown. Anger squeezes my guts.

I fist my fingers at my side, broaden my stance.

She snickers.

I tip my chin up. "You're going to regret that."

The smile fades from her face. "Umm." She places the now empty mug on the bar.

I take a step forward and she skitters back. "It's only clothes." She gulps. "They'll wash."

I glare at her and she swallows, wiggles her fingers in the air. "I should have known that you wouldn't have a sense of humor."

I thrust out my jaw. "That's a ten-thousand-pound suit you destroyed."

She blanches, then straightens her shoulders. "Must have been some hot date you were trying to impress, huh?"

"Actually," I flick some of the offending liquid from my lapels, "it's you I was after."

"Me?" She frowns.

"We need to speak."

She glances toward the bartender who's on the other side of the bar. "I don't know you." She chews on her lower lip, biting off some of the hot pink. How would she look, with that pouty mouth fastened on my cock?

The blood rushes to my groin so quickly that my head spins. My pulse rate ratchets up. Focus, focus on the task you came here for.

"This will take only a few seconds." I take a step forward.

She moves aside.

I frown. "You want to hear this, I promise."

"Go to hell." She pivots and darts forward.

I let her go, a step, another, because... I can? Besides it's fun to create the illusion of freedom first; makes the hunt so much more entertaining, huh?

I swoop forward, loop an arm around her waist, and yank her toward me.

She yelps. "Release me."

Good thing the bar is not yet full. It's too early for the usual office-goers to stop by. And the staff...? Well they are well aware of who cuts their paychecks.

I spin her around and against the bar, then release her. "You will listen to me."

She swallows; she glances left to right.

Not letting you go yet, little Bird. I move into her space, crowd her.

She tips her chin up. "Whatever you're selling, I'm not interested."

I allow my lips to curl. "You don't fool me."

A flush steals up her throat, sears her cheeks. So tiny, so innocent.

Such a good little liar. I narrow my gaze. "Every action has its consequences."

"Are you daft?" She blinks.

"This pretense of yours?" I thrust my face into hers, growling, "It's
not working."

She blinks, then color suffuses her cheeks. "You're certifiably
mad—"

"Getting tired of your insults."

"It's true, everything I said." She scrapes back the hair from her face.
Her fingernails are painted... You guessed it, pink.

"And here's something else. You are a selfish, egotistical jackass."

I smirk. "You're beginning to repeat your insults and I haven't even
kissed you yet."

"Don't you dare." She gulps.

I tilt my head. "Is that a challenge?"

"It's a..." she scans the crowded space, then turns to me. Her lips
firm, "...a warning. You're delusional, you jackass." She inhales a deep
breath before she speaks, "Your ego is bigger than the size of a black
hole." She snickers. "Bet it's to compensate for your lack of balls."

A-n-d, that's it. I've had enough of her mouth that threatens to never
stop spewing words. How many insults can one tiny woman hurl my
way? Answer: too many to count.

"You—"

I lower my chin, touch my lips to hers.

Heat, sweetness, the honey of her essence explodes on my palate.
My dick twitches. I tilt my head, deepen the kiss, reaching for that
something more... more... of whatever scent she's wearing on her skin,
infused with that breath of hers that crowds my senses, rushes down my
spine. My groin hardens; my cock lengthens. I thrust my tongue
between those infuriating lips.

She makes a sound deep in her throat and my heart begins to
pound.

So innocent, yet so crafty. Beautiful and feisty. The kind of complication I don't need in my life.

I prefer the straight and narrow. Gray and black, that's how I choose
to define my world. She, with her flashes of color—pink hair and lips
that threaten to drive me to the edge of distraction—is exactly what I
hate.

Give me a female who has her priorities set in life. To pleasure me, get me off, then walk away before her emotions engage. Yeah. That's what I prefer.

Not this… this bundle of craziness who flings her arms around my shoulders, thrusts her breasts up and into my chest, tips up her chin, opens her mouth, and invites me to take and take.

Does she have no self-preservation? Does she think I am going to fall for her wide-eyed appeal? She has another thing coming.

I tear my mouth away and she protests.

She twines her leg with mine, pushes up her hips, so that melting softness between her thighs cradles my aching hardness.

I glare into her face and she holds my gaze.

Trains her green eyes on me. Her cheeks flush a bright red. Her lips fall open and a moan bleeds into the air. The blood rushes to my dick, which instantly thickens. *Fuck.*

Time to put distance between myself and the situation.

It's how I prefer to manage things. Stay in control, always. Cut out anything that threatens to impinge on my equilibrium. Shut it down or buy them off. Reduce it to a transaction. That I understand.

The power of money, to be able to buy and sell—numbers, logic. That's what's worked for me so far.

"How much?"

Her forehead furrows.

"Whatever it is, I can afford it."

Her jaw slackens. "You think… you—"

"A million?"

"What?"

"Pounds, dollars… You name the currency, and it will be in your account."

Her jaw slackens. "You're offering me money?"

"For your time, and for you to fall in line with my plan."

She reddens. "You think I am for sale?"

"Everyone is."

"Not me."

Here we go again. "Is that a challenge?"

Color fades from her face. "Get away from me."

"Are you shy, is that what this is?" I frown. "You can write your price down on a piece of paper if you prefer." I glance up, notice the bartender watching us. I jerk my chin toward the napkins. He grabs one, then offers it to her.

She glowers at him. "Did you buy him, too?"

"What do you think?"

She glances around. "I think everyone here is ignoring us."

"It's what I'd expect."

"Why is that?"

I wave the tissue in front of her face. "Why do you think?"

"You own the place?"

"As I am going to own you."

She sets her jaw. "Let me leave and you won't regret this."

A chuckle bubbles up. I swallow it away. This is no laughing matter. I never smile during a transaction. Especially not when I am negotiating a new acquisition. And that's all she is. The final piece in the puzzle I am building.

"No one threatens me."

"You're right."

"Huh?"

"I'd rather act on my instinct."

Her lips twist, her gaze narrows. All of my senses scream a warning.

No, she wouldn't, no way—pain slices through my middle and sparks explode behind my eyes.

READ SINCLAIR AND SUMMER'S ENEMIES TO LOVERS, MARRIAGE OF CONVENIENCE ROMANCE IN THE BILLIONAIRE'S FAKE WIFE HERE

READ LIAM AND ISLA'S FAKE RELATIONSHIP ROMANCE IN THE PROPOSAL WHERE TINY FIRST MAKES AN APPEARANCE, CLICK HERE

READ AN EXCERPT FROM THE PROPOSAL

Liam

"Where is she?"

The receptionist gazes at me cow-eyed. Her lips move, but no words emerge. She clears her throat, glances sideways at the door to the side and behind her, then back at me.

"So, I take it she's in there?" I brush past her, and she jumps to her feet. "Sir, y-y-you can't go in there."

"Watch me." I glare at her.

She stammers, then gulps. Sweat beads her forehead. She shuffles back, and I stalk past her.

Really, is there no one who can stand up to me? All of this scraping of chairs and fawning over me? It's enough to drive a man to boredom. I need a challenge. So, when my ex-wife-to-be texted me to say she was calling off our wedding, I was pissed. But when she let it slip that her wedding planner was right—that she needs to marry for love, and not for some family obligation, rage gripped me. I squeezed my phone so hard the screen cracked. I almost hurled the device across the room. When I got a hold of myself, for the first time in a long time, a shiver of something like excitement passed through me. *Finally, fuck.*

That familiar pulse of adrenaline pulses through my veins. It's a sensation I was familiar with in the early days of building my business.

After my father died and I took charge of the group of companies he'd run, I was filled with a sense of purpose; a one-directional focus to prove myself and nurture his legacy. To make my group of companies the leader, in its own right. To make so much money and amass so much power, I'd be a force to be reckoned with.

I tackled each business meeting with a zeal that none of my opponents were able to withstand. But with each passing year—as I crossed the benchmarks I'd set myself, as my bottom line grew healthier, my cash reserves engorged, and the people working for me began treating me with the kind of respect normally reserved for larger-than-life icons—some of that enthusiasm waned. Oh, I still wake up ready to give my best to my job every day, but the zest that once fired me up faded, leaving a sense of purposelessness behind.

The one thing that has kept me going is to lock down my legacy. To ensure the business I've built will finally be transferred to my name. For which my father informed me I would need to marry. Which is why, after much research, I tracked down Lila Kumar, wooed her, and proposed to her. And then, her meddling wedding planner came along and turned all of my plans upside down.

Now, that same sense of purpose grips me. That laser focus I've been lacking envelops me and fills my being. All of my senses sharpen as I shove the door of her office open and stalk in.

The scent envelops me first. The lush notes of violets and peaches. Evocative and fruity. Complex, yet with a core of mystery that begs to be unraveled. Huh? I'm not the kind to be affected by the scent of a woman, but this... Her scent... It's always chafed at my nerve endings. The hair on my forearms straightens.

My guts tie themselves up in knots, and my heart pounds in my chest. It's not comfortable. The kind of feeling I got the first time I went white-water rafting. A combination of nervousness and excitement as I faced my first rapids. A sensation that had since ebbed. One I'd been chasing ever since, pushing myself to take on extreme sports. One I hadn't thought I'd find in the office of a wedding planner.

My feet thud on the wooden floor, and I get a good look at the space which is one-fourth the size of my own office. In the far corner is a bookcase packed with books. On the opposite side is a comfortable settee packed with cushions women seem to like so much. There's a colorful patchwork quilt thrown over it, and behind that, a window that looks onto the back of the adjacent office building. On the coffee table in front of the settee is a bowl with crystal-like objects that reflect the light from the floor lamps. There are paintings on the wall that depict scenes from beaches. No doubt, the kind she'd point to and sell the idea of a honeymoon to gullible brides. I suppose the entire space would appeal to women. With its mood lighting and homey feel, the space invites you to kick back, relax and pour out your problems. A ruse I'm not going to fall for.

"You!" I stab my finger in the direction of the woman seated behind the antique desk straight ahead. "Call Lila, right now, and tell her she needs to go through with the wedding. Tell her she can't back out. Tell her I'm the right choice for her."

She peers up at me from behind large, black horn-rimmed glasses perched on her nose. "No."

I blink. "Excuse me?"

She leans back in her chair. "I'm not going to do that."

"Why the hell not?"

"Are you the right choice for her?

"Of course, I am." I glare at her.

Some of the color fades from her cheeks. She taps her pen on the table, then juts out her chin. "What makes you think you're the right choice of husband for her?"

"What makes you think I'm not."

"Do you love her?"

"That's no one's problem except mine and hers."

"You don't love her."

"What does that have to do with anything?"

"Excuse me?" She pushes the glasses further up her nose. "Are you seriously asking what loving the woman you're going to marry has to do with actually marrying her?" Her voice pulses with fury.

"Yes, exactly. Why don't you explain it to me?" The sarcasm ́. tone is impossible to miss.

She stares at me from behind those large glasses that should make her look owlish and studious, but only add an edge of what I can only describe as quirky-sexiness. The few times I've met her before, she's gotten on my nerves so much, I couldn't wait to get the hell away from her. Now, giving her the full benefit of my attention, I realize, she's actually quite striking. And the addition of those spectacles? Fuck me—I never thought I had a weakness for women wearing glasses. Maybe I was wrong. Or maybe it's specifically this woman wearing glasses... Preferably only glasses and nothing else.

Hmm. Interesting. This reaction to her. It's unwarranted and not something I planned for. I widen my stance, mainly to accommodate the thickness between my legs. An inconvenience... which perhaps I can use to my benefit? I drag my thumb under my lower lip.

Her gaze drops to my mouth, and if I'm not mistaken, her breath hitches. *Very interesting.* Has she always reacted to me like that in the past? Nope, I would've noticed. We've always tried to have as little as possible to do with each other. Like I said, interesting. And unusual.

"First," —she drums her fingers on the table— "are you going to answer my question?"

I tilt my head, the makings of an idea buzzing through my synapses. I need a little time to flesh things out though. It's the only reason I deign to answer her question which, let's face it, I have no obligation to respond to. But for the moment, it's in my interest to humor her and buy myself a little time.

"Lila and I are well-matched in every way. We come from good families—"

"You mean rich families?"

"That, too. Our families move in the same circles."

"Don't you mean boring country clubs?" she says in a voice that drips with distaste.

I frown. "Among other places. We have the pedigree, the bloodline, our backgrounds are congruent, and we'd be able to fold into an arrangement of coexistence with the least amount of disruption on either side."

"Sounds like you're arranging a merger."

"A takeover, but what-fucking-ever." I raise a shoulder.

fhis is how you approached the upcoming

ɔnder why Lila left you?"

ɔiggest ring money could buy—"

ɔnake an appearance at the engagement party."

. off on all the costs related to the upcoming nuptials—"

. own engagement party. You didn't come to it. You left her

to face her family and friends." Her tone rises. Her cheeks are flushed. You'd think she was talking about her own wedding, not that of her friend. In fact, it's more entertaining to talk to her than discuss business matters with my employees. *How interesting.*

"You also didn't show up for most of the rehearsals." She glowers.

"I did show up for the last one."

"Not that it made any difference. You were either checking your watch and indicating that it was time for you to leave, or you were glowering at the plans being discussed."

"I still agreed to that god-awful wedding cake, didn't I?

"On the other hand, it's probably good you didn't come for the previous rehearsals. If you had, Lila and I might have had this conversation earlier—"

"Aha!" I straighten. "So, you confess that it's because of you Lila walked away from this wedding."

She tips her head back. "Hardly. It's because of you."

"So you say, but your guilt is written large on your face."

"Guilt?" Her features flush. The color brings out the dewy hue of her skin, and the blue of her eyes deepens until they remind me of forget-me-nots. No, more like the royal blue of the ink that spilled onto my paper the first time I attempted to write with a fountain pen.

"The only person here who should feel guilty is you, for attempting to coerce an innocent, young woman into an arrangement that would have trapped her for life."

Anger thuds at my temples. My pulse begins to race. "I never have to coerce women. And what you call being trapped is what most women call security. But clearly, you wouldn't know that, considering" —I wave my hand in the air— "you prefer to run your kitchen-table business which, no doubt, barely makes ends meet."

She loosens her grip on her pencil, and it falls to the table with a clatter. Sparks flash deep in her eyes.

You know what I said earlier about the royal blue? Strike that. There are flickers of silver hidden in the depths of her gaze. Flickers that blaze when she's upset. How would it be to push her over the edge? To be at the receiving end of all that passion, that fervor, that ardor… that absolute avidness of existence when she's one with the moment? How would it feel to rein in her spirit, absorb it, drink from it, revel in it, and use it to spark color into my life?

"Kitchen-table business?" She makes a growling sound under her breath. "You dare come into my office and insult my enterprise? The company I have grown all by myself—"

"And outside of your assistant"—I nod toward the door I came through—"you're the sole employee, I take it?"

Her color deepens. "I work with a group of vendors—"

I scoff, "None of whom you could hold accountable when they don't deliver."

"—who have been carefully vetted to ensure that they always deliver," she says at the same time. "Anyway, why do you care, since you don't have a wedding to go to?"

"That's where you're wrong." I peel back my lips. "I'm not going to be labeled as the joke of the century. After all, the media labelled it 'the wedding of the century'." I make air quotes with my fingers.

It was Isla's idea to build up the wedding with the media. She also wanted to invite influencers from all walks of life to attend, but I have no interest in turning my nuptials into a circus. So, I vetoed the idea of journalists attending in person. I have, however, agreed to the event being recorded by professionals and exclusive clips being shared with the media and the influencers. This way, we'll get the necessary PR coverage, without the media being physically present.

In all fairness, the publicity generated by the upcoming nuptials has already been beneficial. It's not like I'll ever tell her, but Isla was right to feed the public's interest in the upcoming event. Apparently, not even the most hard-nosed investors can resist the warm, fuzzy feelings that a marriage invokes. And this can only help with the IPO I have planned for the most important company in my portfolio. "I have a lot riding on this wedding."

"Too bad you don't have a bride."

"Ah,"—I smirk—"but I do."

She scowls. "No, you don't. Lila—"

"I'm not talking about her."

"Then who are you talking about?"

"You."

TO FIND OUT WHAT HAPPENS NEXT READ LIAM AND ISLA'S FAKE RELATIONSHIP ROMANCE IN THE PROPOSAL WHERE TINY FIRST MAKES AN APPEARANCE, CLICK HERE

READ MICHAEL AND KARMA'S FORCED MARRIAGE ROMANCE IN MAFIA KING HERE

READ AN EXCERPT FROM MAFIA KING

Karma

"Morn came and went—and came, and brought no day..."

Tears prick the backs of my eyes. Goddamn Byron. His words creep up on me when I am at my weakest. Not that I am a poetry addict, by any measure, but words are my jam. The one consolation I have is that, when everything else in the world is wrong, I can turn to them, and they'll be there, friendly, steady, waiting with open arms.

And this particular poem had laced my blood, crawled into my gut when I'd first read it. Darkness had folded within me like an insidious snake, that raises its head when I least expect it. Like now, when I look out on the still sleeping city of London, from the grassy slope of Waterlow Park.

Somewhere out there, the Mafia is hunting me, apparently. It's why my sister Summer and her new husband Sinclair Sterling had insisted that I have my own security detail. I had agreed... only to appease them... then given my bodyguard the slip this morning. I had decided to come running here because it's not a place I'd normally go... Not so early in the morning, anyway. They won't think to look for me here. At least, not for a while longer.

I purse my lips, close my eyes. Silence. The rustle of the wind between the leaves. The faint tinkle of the water from the nearby spring.

I could be the last person on this planet, alone, unsung, bound for the grave.

Ugh! Stop. Right there. I drag the back of my hand across my nose. Try it again, focus, get the words out, one after the other, like the steps of my sorry life.

"Morn came and went—and came, and... and..." My voice breaks. "Bloody asinine hell." I dig my fingers into the grass and grab a handful and fling it out. Again. From the top.

"Morn came and went—and came, and—"

"...brought no day."

A gravelly voice completes my sentence.

I whip my head around. His silhouette fills my line of sight. He's sitting on the same knoll as me, yet I have to crane my neck back to see his profile. The sun is at his back, so I can't make out his features. Can't see his eyes... Can only take in his dark hair, combed back by a ruthless hand that brooked no measure.

My throat dries.

Thick dark hair, shot through with grey at the temples. He wears his age like a badge. I don't know why, but I know his years have not been easy. That he's seen more, indulged in more, reveled in the consequences of his actions, however extreme they might have been. He's not a normal, everyday person, this man. Not a nine-to-fiver, not someone who lives an average life. Definitely not a man who returns home to his wife and home at the end of the day. He is...different, unique, evil... Monstrous. Yes, he is a beast, one who sports the face of a man but who harbors the kind of darkness inside that speaks to me. I gulp.

His face boasts a hooked nose, a thin upper lip, a fleshy lower lip. One that hints at hidden desires, Heat. Lust. The sensuous scrape of that whiskered jaw over my innermost places. Across my inner thigh, reaching toward that core of me that throbs, clenches, melts to feel the stab of his tongue, the thrust of his hardness as he impales me, takes me, makes me his. Goosebumps pop on my skin.

I drag my gaze away from his mouth down to the scar that slashes across his throat. A cold sensation coils in my chest. What or who had hurt him in such a cruel fashion?

"Of this their desolation; and all hearts
Were chill'd into a selfish prayer for light..."

He continues in that rasping guttural tone. Is it the wound that caused that scar that makes his voice so... gravelly... So deep... so... so, hot?

Sweat beads my palms and the hairs on my nape rise. "Who are you?"

He stares ahead as his lips move,

"Forests were set on fire — but hour by hour
They fell and faded — and the crackling trunks
Extinguish'd with a crash — and all was black."

I swallow, moisture gathers in my core. How can I be wet by the mere cadence of this stranger's voice?

I spring up to my feet.

"Sit down," he commands.

His voice is unhurried, lazy even, his spine erect. The cut of his black jacket stretches across the width of his massive shoulders. His hair... I was mistaken—there are threads of dark gold woven between the darkness that pours down to brush the nape of his neck. A strand of hair falls over his brow. As I watch, he raises his hand and brushes it away. Somehow, the gesture lends an air of vulnerability to him. Something so at odds with the rest of his persona that, surely, I am mistaken?

My scalp itches. I take in a breath and my lungs burn. This man... He's sucked up all the oxygen in this open space as if he owns it, the master of all he surveys. The master of me. My death. My life. A shiver ladders along my spine. *Get away, get away now, while you still can.*

I angle my body, ready to spring away from him.

"I won't ask again."

Ask. Command. Force me to do as he wants. He'll have me on my back, bent over, on my side, on my knees, over him, under him. He'll surround me, overwhelm me, pin me down with the force of his personality. His charisma, his larger-than-life essence will crush everything else out of me and I... I'll love it.

"No."

"Yes."

A fact. A statement of intent, spoken aloud. So true. So real. Too real. Too much. Too fast. All of my nightmares... my dreams come to life. Everything I've wanted is here in front of me. I'll die a thousand deaths before he'll be done with me... And then? Will I be reborn? For him. For me. For myself.

I live, first and foremost, to be the woman I was... am meant to be.

"You want to run?"

No.

No.

I nod my head.

He turns his, and all the breath leaves my lungs. Blue eyes— cerulean, dark like the morning skies, deep like the nighttime...hidden corners, secrets that I don't dare uncover. He'll destroy me, have my heart, and break it so casually.

My throat burns and a boiling sensation squeezes my chest.

"Go then, my beauty, fly. You have until I count to five. If I catch you, you are mine."

"If you don't?"

"Then I'll come after you, stalk your every living moment, possess your nightmares, and steal you away in the dead of night, and then..."

I draw in a shuddering breath as liquid heat drips from between my legs. "Then?" I whisper.

"Then, I'll ensure you'll never belong to anyone else, you'll never see the light of day again, for your every breath, your every waking second, your thoughts, your actions... and all your words, every single last one, will belong to me." He peels back his lips, and his teeth glint in the first rays of the morning light. "Only me." He straightens to his feet and rises, and rises.

This man... He is massive. A monster who always gets his way. My guts churn. My toes curl. Something primeval inside of me insists I hold my own. I cannot give in to him. Cannot let him win whatever this is. I need to stake my ground, in some form. *Say something. Anything. Show him you're not afraid of this.*

"Why?" I tilt my head back, all the way back. "Why are you doing this?"

He tilts his head, his ears almost canine in the way they are silhouetted against his profile.

"Is it because you can? Is it a... a," I blink, "a debt of some kind?"

He stills.

"My father, this is about how he betrayed the Mafia, right? You're one of them?"

"Lucky guess." His lips twist, "It is about your father, and how he promised you to me. He reneged on his promise, and now, I am here to collect."

"No." I swallow... *No, no, no.*

"Yes." His jaw hardens.

All expression is wiped clean of his face, and I know then, that he speaks the truth. It's always about the past. My sorry shambles of a past... Why does it always catch up with me? *You can run, but you can never hide.*

"Tick-tock, Beauty." He angles his body and his shoulders shut out the sight of the sun, the dawn skies, the horizon, the city in the distance, the rustle of the grass, the trees, the rustle of the leaves. All of it fades and leaves just me and him. Us. *Run.*

"Five." He jerks his chin, straightens the cuffs of his sleeves.

My knees wobble.

"Four."

My pulse rate spikes. I should go. Leave. But my feet are planted in this earth. This piece of land where we first met. What am I, but a speck in the larger scheme of things? To be hurt. To be forgotten. To be taken without an ounce of retribution. To be punished... by him.

"Three." He thrusts out his chest, widens his stance, every muscle in his body relaxed. "Two."

I swallow. The pulse beats at my temples. My blood thrums.

"One."

Michael

"Go."

She pivots and races down the slope. Her dark hair streams behind her. Her scent, sexy femininity and silver moonflowers, clings to my nose, then recedes. It's so familiar, that scent.

I had smelled it before, had reveled in it. Had drawn in it into my lungs as she had peeked up at me from under her thick eyelashes. Her green gaze had fixed on mine, her lips parted as she welcomed my kiss. As she had wound her arms about my neck, pushed up those sweet breasts and flattened them against my chest. As she had parted her legs when I had planted my thigh between them. I had seen her before... in my dreams. I stiffen. She can't be the same girl, though, can she?

I reach forward, thrust out my chin and sniff the air, but there's only the damp scent of dawn, mixed with the foul tang of exhaust fumes, as she races away from me.

She stumbles and I jump forward, pause when she straightens. Wait. Wait. Give her a lead. Let her think she has almost escaped, that she's gotten the better of me... As if.

I clench my fists at my sides, force myself to relax. Wait. Wait. She reaches the bottom of the incline, turns. I surge forward. One foot in front of the other. My heels dig into the grassy surface and mud flies up, clings to the hem of my £4000 Italian pants. Like I care? Plenty more where that came from. An entire walk-in closet, full of clothes made to measure, to suit every occasion, with every possible accessory needed by a man in my position to impress...

Everything... Except the one thing that I had coveted from the moment I had laid eyes on her. Sitting there on the grassy slope, unshed tears in her eyes, and reciting... Byron? For hell's sake. Of all the poets in the world, she had to choose the Lord of Darkness.

I huff. All a ploy. Clearly, she knew I was sitting next to her... No, not possible. I had walked toward her and she hadn't stirred. Hadn't been aware. Yeah, I am that good. I've been known to slit a man's throat from ear-to-ear while he was awake and in his full senses. Alive one second, dead the next. That's how it is in my world. You want it, you take it. And I... I want her.

I increase my pace, eat up the distance between myself and the girl... That's all she is. A slip of a thing, a slim blur of motion. Beauty in hiding. A diamond, waiting for me to get my hands on her, polish her, show her what it means to be...

Dead. She is dead. That's why I am here.

A flash of skin, a creamy length of thigh. My groin hardens and my legs wobble. I lurch over a bump in the ground. The hell? I right myself, leap forward, inching closer, closer. She reaches a curve in the path, disappears out of sight.

My heart hammers in my chest. I will not lose her, will not. *Here, Beauty, come to Daddy.* The wind whistles past my ears. I pump my legs, lengthen my strides, turn the corner. There's no one there. Huh?

My heart hammers and the blood pounds at my wrists, my temples; adrenaline thrums in my veins. I slow down, come to a stop. Scan the clearing.

The hairs on my forearms prickle. She's here. Not far, but where? Where is she? I prowl across to the edge of the clearing, under the tree with its spreading branches.

When I get my hands on you, Beauty, I'll spread your legs like the pages of a poem. Dip into your honeyed sweetness, like a quill pen in ink. Drag my aching shaft across that melting, weeping entrance. My balls throb. My groin tightens. The crack of a branch above shivers across my stretched nerve endings. I swoop forward, hold out my arms, and close my grasp around the trembling, squirming mass of precious humanity. I cradle her close to my chest, heart beating thud-thud-thud, overwhelming any other thought.

Mine. All mine. The hell is wrong with me? She wriggles her little body, and her curves slide across my forearms. My shoulders bunch and my fingers tingle. She kicks out with her legs and arches her back, thrusting her breasts up so her nipples are outlined against the fabric of her sports bra. She dared to come out dressed like that? In that scrap of fabric that barely covers her luscious flesh?

"Let me go." She whips her head toward me and her hair flows around her shoulders, across her face. She blows it out of the way. "You monster, get away from me."

Anger drums at the backs of my eyes and desire tugs at my groin. The scent of her is sheer torture, something I had dreamed of in the wee hours of twilight when dusk turned into night.

She's not real. She's not the woman I think she is. She is my downfall. My sweet poison. The bitter medicine I must partake of to cure the ills that plague my company.

"Fine." I lower my arms and she tumbles to the grass, hits the ground butt first.

"How dare you." She huffs out a breath, her hair messily arranged across her face.

I shove my hands into the pockets of my fitted pants, knees slightly bent, legs apart. Tip my chin down and watch her as she sprawls at my feet.

"You… dropped me?" She makes a sound deep in her throat.

So damn adorable.

"Your wish is my command." I quirk my lips.

"You don't mean it."

"You're right." I lean my weight forward on the balls of my feet and she flinches.

"What… what do you want?"

"You."

She pales. "You want to… to rob me? I have nothing of consequence.

"Oh, but you do, Beauty."

I lean in and every muscle in her body tenses. Good. She's wary. She should be. She should have been alert enough to have run as soon as she sensed my presence. But she hadn't.

I should spare her because she's the woman from my dreams… but I won't. She's a debt I intend to collect. She owes me, and I've delayed what was meant to happen long enough.

I pull the gun from my holster, point it at her.

Her gaze widens and her breath hitches. I expect her to plead with me for her life, but she doesn't. She stares back at me with her huge dilated pupils. She licks her lips and the blood drains to my groin. *Che cazzo!* Why does her lack of fear turn me on so?

"Your phone," I murmur, "take out your phone."

She draws in a breath, then reaches into her pocket and pulls out her phone.

"Call your sister."

"What?"

"Dial your sister, Beauty. Tell her you are going away on a long trip to Sicily with your new male friend."

"What?"

"You heard me." I curl my lips. "Do it, now!'

She blinks, looks like she is about to protest, then her fingers fly over the phone.

Damn, and I had been looking forward to coaxing her into doing my bidding.

She holds her phone to her ear. I can hear the phone ring on the other side, before it goes to voicemail. She glances at me and I jerk my chin. She looks away, takes a deep breath, then speaks in a cheerful voice, "Hi Summer, it's me, Karma. I, ah, have to go away for a bit. This new... ah, friend of mine... He has an extra ticket and he has invited me to Sicily to spend some time with him. I... ah, I don't know when, exactly, I'll be back, but I'll message you and let you know. Take care. Love ya sis, I—"

I snatch the phone from her, disconnect the call, then hold the gun to her temple, "Goodbye, Beauty."

To find out what happens next read Michael and Karma's forced marriage story here

Read JJ and Lena's ex-boyfriend's father, age-gap romance here

Read Knight and Penny's, best friend's brother romance in The Wrong Wife here

Read Dr. Weston Kincaid and Amelie's forced proximity, one-bed Christmas Romance in The Billionaire's Fake Wife HERE

Download your exclusive L. Steele reading order bingo card HERE

Did you know all the characters you read about have their own book? Cross off their stories as you read and share your bingo card in L. Steele's reader group here

Want to be the first to find out when L. Steele's next book is out? Sign up for her newsletter here

From the author

Hello, I'm L. Steele. I write romance stories with strong powerful men who meet their match in sassy, curvy, spitfire women.

I love to push myself with each book on both the spice and the angst so I can deliver well rounded, multidimensional characters.

I enjoy trading trivia with my filmmaker husband, watching lots and lots of movies, and walking nature trails. I live in London.

Claim your FREE book

FOLLOW ME:

On Amazon

on BookBub

on Goodreads

on Audible

On TikTok

On Threads

on Pinterest

My YouTube channel

Join my secret Facebook Reader Group

Read ALL my books

BONUS EPILOGUE WITH EDWARD & MIRA

WANT AN EXCLUSIVE BONUS EPILOGUE FEATURING EDWARD AND MIRA? CLICK HERE

THE UNWANTED LOVE

EXCLUSIVE BONUS PROLOGUE TO THE UNWANTED WIFE

For your exclusive bonus prologue of *The Unwanted Love*, the prequel to *The Unwanted Wife* click here

MARRIAGE OF CONVENIENCE BILLIONAIRE ROMANCE FROM L. STEELE

The Billionaire's Fake Wife - Sinclair and Summer's story that started this universe... with a plot twist you won't see coming!

The Billionaire's Secret - Victoria and Saint's story. Saint is maybe the most alphahole of them all!

Marrying the Billionaire Single Dad - Damian and Julia's story, watch out for the plot twist!

The Proposal - Liam and Isla's story. What's a wedding planner to do when you tell the bride not to go through with the wedding and the groom demands you take her place and give him a heir? And yes plot twist!

CHRISTMAS ROMANCE BOOKS BY L. STEELE FOR YOU

Want to find out how Dr. Weston Kincaid and Amelie met? Read The Billionaire's Christmas Bride HERE

Want even more Christmas Romance books? *Read A very Mafia Christmas, Christian and Aurora's story HERE*

Read a marriage of convenience billionaire Christmas romance, Hunter and Zara's story - *The Christmas One Night Stand HERE*

FORBIDDEN BILLIONAIRE ROMANCE BY L. STEELE FOR YOU

Read Daddy JJ's, age-gap romance in Mafia Lust HERE

Read Edward, Baron and Ava's story starting with Billionaire's Sins HERE

FREE BOOKS

Claim your *FREE copy of Mafia Heir* the prequel to *Mafia King*

Claim your FREE copy of *Vicious Billionaire* the prequel to *The Billionaire's Fake Wife* HERE

ABOUT THE AUTHOR

Hello, I'm L. Steele.

I write romance stories with strong powerful men who meet their match in sassy, curvy, spitfire women.

I love to push myself with each book on both the spice and the angst so I can deliver well rounded, multidimensional characters.

I enjoy trading trivia with my husband, watching lots and lots of movies, and walking nature trails. I live in London.

CLAIM YOUR FREE BOOK
FOLLOW ME:
ON AMAZON
ON BOOKBUB
ON GOODREADS
ON AUDIBLE
ON TIKTOK
JOIN MY SECRET FACEBOOK READER GROUP
ON PINTEREST
MY YOUTUBE CHANNEL
READ ALL MY BOOKS
SPOTIFY

ACKNOWLEDGMENTS

Edited by: Elizabeth Connor

Cover Design: Jacqueline Sweet

Huge thank you to Li Iacobacci, Danielle Vale and Rachel Kroeplin, my alpha readers.

Huge shout out to everyone in L. Steele's Team Facebook reader group, you guys are awesome!